Mercenary's Honor

Mercenary's Honor

The Wild Geese Saga, Book Two

Steven M. Silver

Dedication

For the women and men of the Armed Forces of the United States of America, people of bright honor, in grateful appreciation.

Acknowledgements

One of the delights of the Wild Geese saga for me has been the construction of a future history using past historical examples both in *Mercenary's Heart* and *Mercenary's Honor*. For the record, most of the political maneuvering, all battles and the tactics used in them, all acts of courage, cowardice, and atrocity, are taken from actual events and wars in human history. As an historian, I encourage readers to explore their history books to find the events I based these novels on.

As with *Mercenary's Heart*, *Mercenary's Honor* evolved under the assistance of several long-time science fiction fans, aka Team Banzai. My thanks to them. Once again, my thanks to Eric and his technical advisor, Ian. And I thank the other elephant watcher, that noted big game hunter and sometime outlaw, David James, for his encouragement, example, and bail.

Table of Contents

Part One

Soldiers and their generals fight for many causes, worthy and unworthy, and when it comes to the battlefield the considerations may be pretty much the same, whatever the cause. The generals study each other's tactics across the battle lines, often with admiration. They are the technicians of warfare. The soldiers of the contending armies display courage (and sometimes cowardice), and the people they fight for make heroic sacrifices (or exploit the war for gain) on both or all sides, although perhaps to different degrees and in different ways. To learn what the fighting and the courage and sacrifices meant one must look elsewhere, behind the physical contest to loyalties and emotions, thoughts and ideas, moral convictions and arguments. One must ask what moral and mental content shaped the decisions that brought these people to the battlefield.

-William Lee Miller, 1995, Virginia, United States of America, Earth

Prologue

Western Mining District
Keritang, Frontier
14 March 2818

The two snipers, clad in mottled white and gray parkas, climbed the rocky face of the cliff under a dark gray overcast that looked like it might seriously add to the snow already on the ground. It was not a tall cliff, barely more than 300 meters and there were plenty of handholds and ledges to aid their ascent. They made good time until a freezing rain fell.

The rain covered the rocks in a film of ice that became thicker as they climbed the last few meters. Using knives, they chipped at the ice, trying to improve their grips. Each experienced the heart-racing jolt of having a foot or hand suddenly slide free, leaving them clinging desperately, tight-lipped with effort. By the time they reached the top they were gasping from exertion.

The leader, lying on his stomach, slowly worked his long, white cloth-wrapped rifle off his back. The sky, still dropping its icy rain, was noticeably darker. Night would arrive soon. He rolled onto his stomach and unslung his rifle. His eye at the electronic telescopic sight, he worked his rifle back and forth looking across the cold plateau.

"I don't think we can go back that way," his partner whispered, though there was no one else visible on the snow-covered plain.

"Have to take the long way home," he agreed. His partner unslung her own rifle and checked the area.

"I've got nothing, corporal," she said after a few minutes.

"Me, neither," he replied. "All right, Jackie, we're going to move. Heading zero one five."

They walked in column as night descended. Shortly after midnight the rain stopped. An hour later it began to snow, large gently falling flakes without any wind. Their light amplification goggles were only slightly better than their unaided eyes. They moved slowly, the leader checking the navigation display of his goggles. Finally, as they came upon a large pile of rocks, he held up his hand. It took several minutes but eventually they settled into position. Both rifles pointed north, into the snow-flecked darkness.

They kept the temperature controls of their camouflaged suits turned low – the cold would help keep them awake. An hour before dawn the snow stopped. The corporal adjusted his headset and spoke softly into the wrap-around microphone.

"Echo Charley."

He waited a moment, a finger pressed against the earpiece. Then he heard a response.

"Victor Echo."

"It's on," he whispered. She nodded, saying nothing beneath of the coating of snow covering her and her rifle. Like his, hers was wrapped in white camouflaged cloth. Only the sight lenses and muzzle were exposed. From twenty meters away, both were almost invisible.

Seven hundred meters away, their target slowly became visible as the dim morning light gradually increased in intensity. The dark gray concrete and metal observation post starkly contrasted with the drifted white show around it. Perched overlooking the narrow valley below, the same valley the snipers had climbed up from, it was in a perfect position to monitor anyone coming through the valley.

The old structure was a leftover gun emplacement from a series of wars that had ended with the coming of the mining combines a generation ago. An observation deck with high-powered binoculars mounted on the railing was welded onto the emplacement. It was an old-fashioned tool incongruous next to the two bulbous, man-sized sensor turrets. The snipers focused on the deck, their sight crosshairs lying gently on the railings.

"Range, seven five seven," she said.

"Pretty much what Ho`nehe said it would be," the corporal replied. Their unit's scouts had found the post two days ago during a long-range reconnaissance patrol of the valley. They spotted a pair of observers living in the emplacement's underground bunker. During daylight hours, one or the other of them would be on the platform, scanning the valley. At all times the sensors studied the ground below them, looking for movement, heat emissions, the presence of unexpected mass, and other indications of an unwanted presence in the valley.

The valley led to a mining complex surrounded on three sides by a small town. Now the rest of the snipers' unit prepared to launch an attack against the complex. If the observers or their sensors detected them as they raced down the valley, the defenders would have time to mobilize.

Which would mean the unit would not get any bonuses. Mercenary pay was based on results, not effort. Their employer, a mining combine rival of the one controlling the complex, required there be no collateral damage, which ruled out a safer night attack and its danger of hitting the town. But their unit was small. To succeed, they would have to have surprise on their side. The snipers were to ensure they did.

"Movement," the corporal said. In his sight he saw the top of a man's head as a figure moved behind the platform. Slowly the man climbed up the icy walkway, a cup of something steaming in its free hand.

"I see one," she said. "On the deck."

"Wait for the other," he said.

A moment later the second observer appeared. This was their routine. In the morning both would go to the platform to check the sensor array. The second would then descend and would spell the first later.

The second observer was halfway up the steps when he slipped and fell. He saved himself from sliding all the way down by grabbing onto a railing support. They saw him grimace with pain and say something to the first, who carefully walked over and slowly stepped down to help him. Together, they started back down, one helping the other.

"Take number two," the lead sniper said. Almost immediately her rifle cracked. For an instant nothing happened and then the fallen man jerked and a red cloud exploded behind his head. The other man froze as the lead sniper fired. The bullet caught him as he turned his head towards the snipers and he fell away from them and off the steps out of sight. The other lay in view. Quickly the snipers removed their rifle covers enough to expose the fat tubes of small missile launchers.

"Get the closest one," he said as he settled again behind his rifle. He heard her acknowledgement as he peered through his sight and touched the side of his rifle. A green crosshair suddenly appeared. It wandered as the sight sensed the wind. He touched his sight again and the crosshairs steadied. He placed it on the furthest sensor pod. A green circle appeared around the crosshairs; the rifle understood the launcher carried self-guiding munitions and supplied the target designation to the missile. He squeezed the trigger.

The electronic circuit sent a signal to the missile. The missile read the target information and then was blown out of the launcher by a small charge. Two meters in front of the rifle it ignited its motor and was instantly gone with a violent hiss and a faint trail of gray smoke. It slammed into the sensor pod with enough energy to penetrate its thin metal covering and detonated its warhead within the delicate interior. The missile launched by the other sniper took out the second pod at almost the same instant.

As the echo of the flat explosions rolled back to them across the snow, the lead sniper touched his headset.

"Echo Charley is clear. Moving to Bravo, repeat, Bravo."

"Roger, Bravo. Victor Echo is moving."

"Good hunting."

As a pair of mike clicks acknowledged his last transmission, from the north of the valley, near its mouth, six multiple-ton Human Piloted Assault Exoskeletons, HUPAX, moved forward in a fast column. Their feet kicked up snow and clumps of earth as they ran into the valley. In a few minutes, they were past the observation post and heading towards their target twenty kilometers beyond.

The snipers lay still for several more moments, checking the area. Satisfied that it was clear, they slowly rose.

"Time to get a move on," the leader said. "We've got a good little jog in front of us before we get to Bravo."

"Aye, Gwi," she said as she stood up. Kilograms of snow slid off her and she pushed her hood back, exposing her dark skin and high cheekbones to the cold air. "Not crazy about walking around in the open."

"Once we're past where we climbed up, it's only a couple of klicks until we're in rocky terrain," he said as he walked south. "Ten kilometers more and we hit the downhill part and soon after that Ho`nehe's hovercraft will be waiting for pick-up and a hot breakfast. You'll be soaking your feet in a pan of hot water before lunch." She snorted in response but otherwise saved her breath and fell in behind him.

The snow and ice-covered terrain generally was flat as they worked their way south and they made good time until they arrived at the point where they had climbed up the previous day. Now snow came intermittently as the ground became rougher, slowing them down.

They were just entering the ridges marking the start of the rocky portion of the plateau when they heard the sound of the pursuing hovercraft. She heard it first and turned, looking back over her shoulder.

"Gwielgi," she said. "People behind us."

He turned and raised his rifle, using the telescopic sight.

"One, no, two hovercrafts coming," Gwielgi said. "About a klick away. Lead one is mounting a long barrel in an open turret. Can't tell about the one behind. They won't be able to run through these rocks." He turned away and quickly moved deeper into the ridges, his partner close behind.

They heard the hovercrafts arrive at the edge of the ridges and caught a glimpse of snow thrown into the air by their powerful fans. As the turbines died down, they could hear the sound of shouted orders.

"Infantry," Gwielgi said. "We've got to get out of here."

The ground was twisted as if it had gone through convulsions eons ago. Now rock spires and boulders, some the size of small houses, thrust up in frozen violence that not even the snow could hide. The snipers plunged into the garden of rock, risking twisted ankles or worse as they fled from the enemy infantry. Panting, they struggled through the boulders and snow. Several times they found themselves in a dead end and had to backtrack and find a new way through the maze.

They came to a relatively clear area where the stones and gullies were not much more than waist high and started to cross. Gwielgi suddenly froze, his left hand thrust upward in a fist. The woman held still, not daring

6

to breathe hard. Her eyes shot back and forth as she strained to hear anything that might be an indicator of danger.

His hand flattened and slowly lowered. She crouched and saw his hand point to their left.

Enemy to the left.

Then she heard them. Several voices, angry, ordering others. The words were lost, but they were coming closer. Somehow some of the pursuers had gotten in front of them. Jackie knelt down, all but hidden behind a large rock. Her partner crouched and looked to the right. Gwielgi held up a hand, getting her attention. Then he pointed to the right. She looked and saw a low hill, shrouded in snow. It wasn't much but it looked like it had a little cover. He turned towards her, pointed at himself, and then his rifle. He raised his palm and swept it toward the enemy. He pointed at her and then at the hill. Gwielgi repeated the sweeping gesture as he pointed at himself and the hill.

You go to the hill. I will cover you. And then you cover me as I go to the hill.

She shook her head slowly but negatively. She pointed at the enemy and then held her hands close together and then crossed them. She pointed at him and herself and then the hill.

They are too close. We go together.

Gwielgi smiled without humor and raised a finger and tapped his throat. If he had not been wearing his parka his finger would be on his emblem of rank. Then he pointed at the hill again. Jackie finally nodded. She lowered herself to the ground and crawled slowly forward.

She concentrated on her movement, blessing the snow for muffling the sound of her crawling. The ground was so broken beneath the snow it felt like she was always putting her arms and knees down on the edge of some jagged blade of stone.

Jackie was at the hill and starting to circle around it when she heard her leader's rifle fire. In the cold air it cracked so loudly that she felt it through the frozen ground beneath her. There was a second of silence then a burst from an automatic weapon replied. She kept going even as stray slugs ricocheted off rocks near her.

The rifle cracked again and the automatic weapon suddenly ceased its deadly chatter. In the distance she could hear commands shouted. Jackie was behind the small hill, barely taller than she was, and she quickly rose and made her way to the shoulder away from Gwielgi. Her heart was pounding furiously and she had the sensation she would never catch her breath.

Again her partner fired and she heard a muffled scream.

Jackie made herself pause behind a large stone and take a deep breath. Deliberately she flipped the lens covers of her rifle open and checked that the safety was off. She looked behind her and saw there was a tall rock, streaked with snow and ice. She would not be silhouetted by the sky. She looped the sling around her left arm and then eased around the corner of a large stone.

The open ground extended away from her for about 400 meters. Out of sight to her left was Gwielgi. Ahead, where the ground resumed its maze of stone, she could see figures moving, ducking in behind the rocks. She lowered her eye to her sight.

She saw three men, two with rifles, one with a smaller submachine gun. As she brought her crosshairs down, she heard Gwielgi fire again and the man jerked sideways, his fur-lined hat flying into the air in a pink spray. The two riflemen dropped to the ground and pushed themselves backward. She ignored them and swung her sights further to the right, looking for people trying to cut them off.

Jackie found a man behind a rock. He had a pair of binoculars and carried a pistol. Beyond him was another man with a large pack on his back. A meter-long flexible antenna extended from the backpack. Beyond those two were other soldiers, hiding among the rocks and moving forward.

The officer first.

Jackie remembered that her sights were set for 750 meters at the last second. She did not waste breath on a curse as she pushed the glove off her left hand and felt for the adjustment knob. Not trusting the sensor's automatic rangefinder this close to a target, she turned it, counting carefully the clicks her fingers felt. Then she extended her arm, supporting the rifle.

She squeezed the trigger and the long rifle fired. As Jackie brought the sights to their new target, her right hand touched the side of the rifle and it ejected the empty round. Her finger found the trigger as the crosshairs settled on the radio operator. The man, his legs pinned by his dead officer, was trying to push the corpse off while he looked frantically for the source of the fire. Her second bullet hit him to the left of his nose.

A soldier rose from cover and ran forward, perhaps to recover the radio, perhaps to try to aid the others. She put a bullet in his chest and he skidded to a halt, collapsing into a flopping pile. None of the other soldiers moved forward. Jackie looked further to the right.

A machine gun started up and she heard bullets smacking her hill. Slowly she continued her sweep. Then she saw them. A crew of two was working a black machine gun. Like the equipment of the other soldiers, it did not appear to be a "smart" gun – no sensors guided it. Nonetheless, they had a good position on top of a flat rock. It flanked her leader's position and permitted them to put fire down towards him. But who was firing at her?

She knew machine guns never worked alone. Jackie swept her sights further to the right and then saw three soldiers, partially hidden behind rocks. One had an automatic weapon. He was firing blind at her hill, trying to pin her down. The other two had rifles. She started to ignore them when she caught the glint of a telescopic sight on one of the rifles.

The greatest threat to a sniper is another sniper. Jackie centered on the man with the scoped rifle just as he pulled further back behind the other soldier. Now she could only see the end of the rifle barrel. It moved a little and then fired. She saw the soldier next to the sniper clearly. He leaned towards the sniper, listening. Probably being told where her leader was. The man rolled back into his firing position and sighted down his rifle.

She fired and saw a puff of material near the man's neck. He dropped his rifle, and grabbed at his throat. He tried to rise to his knees, a red streak coming down the front of his gray uniform, but fell forward and slid to the edge of the rock, almost going over. His blood streamed in thin lines down the rock's face.

With the soldier slid forward, Jackie saw the left leg of the sniper, slightly extended beyond the soldier. She put her crosshairs on his calf and fired. Fabric and tissue flipped up into the air. The leg jerked out of sight. She heard her leader's rifle fire again and the sniper's rifle slid into view and stopped, caught by an outcropping. The sniper suddenly appeared, moving forward on his knees, his mouth and eyes wide open, blood covering his face. He shook and then fell forward, sliding off the rock and taking the rifle with him.

The machine gunner laid down a steady and continuous burst of fire while the soldier with the automatic weapon snapped a quick burst at her that cut her face with rock splinters. Jackie rolled backwards as another burst ripped up the snow where she had lain. She did not hear her leader firing as she backed down the hill.

She wiped the blood off her cheek with snow and, crawling on her stomach, moved towards the automatic weapon.

Jackie went forward ten meters and paused, visualizing where the machine gun and the automatic weapon were. She brought the rifle sight to her eye and raised herself. The soldier was still putting bursts into the hill. His eye was drawn to where his bullets struck, as is often the case, and his attention focused on that spot.

She fired and saw the left side of the soldier's head explode as the high velocity bullet went through his skull. She moved her sights to the left and saw the machine gunner and the assistant. The assistant was looking over the gun directly at her and his mouth was open as he shouted a warning. His hand was coming up as he started to point towards her position.

Jackie killed the machine gunner, sending a bullet through the gunner's fur cap. As the assistant desperately tried to pull the body off the gun, she shot him in the chest. He fell away from the gun.

She paused. Jackie could hear nothing but that meant little. She crawled backwards, pausing every so often to listen, and then worked her way around the hill. She found her leader lying against a rock, his rifle in his lap. He was chewing on a candy bar and had sweat on his face.

"Nice of you to come back, private," Gwielgi said.

"I was detained, corporal," she said. She saw he had a field dressing wrapped around his right knee. "How bad?"

"Broken," he said, chewing hard on the candy. "Machine gun slug. Don't think I'll be running in intramural relays next month."

"Well, you were never very fast," Jackie said, studying the wound. She looked up. "Let me rig a brace for it and we'll get out of here."

"Forget it," Gwielgi said. He had a soft voice tinged with the tightness of pain. "You've still got about nine kilometers of this to get through and then another klick or so before you get to Bravo. Take off. I'll entertain any other of these pukes who want to follow."

"Like hell," she said. She shrugged off her pack and began to dump it out.

"Jackie, get serious," he said. "You can't carry me, not that far, not over this ground. Do and you won't get to the pick-up in time and they'll have to leave you. Or even better – some friends of these people will find you and kill your butt." He closed his eyes and bit his lower lip for several seconds. When he opened his eyes again he saw she had turned her pack inside out and removed the frame struts. "You ought to leave me," he said.

"Leave you? It will be a cold day in hell when I do that."

"Haven't you noticed, lady? That's exactly what today is."

"Gwielgi, I am not going to carry you," Jackie said. "I am going to drag you, and I guarantee you are going to hate every damned meter but we are both getting out of here."

From beyond the border of the cleared area to their south and east they heard more shouted commands. Jackie quickly pulled the frame apart and then positioned the two longest pieces on either side of Gwielgi's knee. She cut some lengths from the climbing rope in her pack and used them to secure the braces. Then she quickly went through the rest of her pack's contents, repacking only an aid bag, a spare canteen, and some food. She shrugged her shoulders into the pack's straps as she took a quick look over the top of the rocks.

"All right," she said in a whisper. "We're going back around the hill the way I came. Then we're going through the position the machine gun was in. We'll have better cover from then on."

"Tougher moving as well." Gwielgi took another bite of his candy bar. He looked up at the sky. "It's going to snow again in another hour." He looked back at her. "I appreciate the gesture, but you'll never make it. How about if I order you to go on without me, Private Peregrine? You get to Ho'nehe and our grunts, come back and pick me up."

"*You* ordering *me*? We've had enough of that for the day." She flipped open a first aid kit and then looked at Gwielgi. "Look," she said, "everything we have for pain would get in the way if we have to do some more shooting."

11

"I know," Gwielgi said. He stuffed the candy bar's wrapper into a pocked of his parka. "This has all the makings of a really fun time."

Jackie shook her head as she stood and put away the kit. Her friend had a sense of humor that announced itself at the most unlikely times. She reached around him and grabbed his pack's straps. Pulling on them, she turned him so his back was towards the direction she wanted to go. She slung her rifle across her front. Crouching, she dragged him by his straps as she walked backward.

The voices faded as they crossed behind the hill. Sweat was trickling down Jackie's brown face and she pushed her hood back. She paused, listening, as she undid the upper portion of her parka.

"How you doing, Gwi?"

"No problem," he said, but she heard the tension in his voice. Having a broken leg dragged across the ground had to be hurting him, but he gave no other indication.

Jackie unslung her rifle and quickly moved to where she could see the way ahead. She was back to Gwielgi in less than a minute and started dragging him again.

Getting across the relatively open area to where the machine gun and its support had been was not as hard as getting to the hill. Nonetheless, by the time they got to the position Jackie was breathing deeply. Cautiously she dragged Gwielgi past the machine gun position.

The dead lay with white powder slowly covering them with. The machine gunner, a blond woman about her age, lay with her eyes half opened. Her eyes seemed to follow them as they made their way past the position. The occasional flakes of snow landing on her dissolved into drops of water and ran down her face. They kept going, Jackie pulling Gwielgi as she walked backwards.

During a break Gwielgi, propped against a tall black rock, looked over at Jackie.

"Why are you doing this?"

"Why do you ask stupid questions?" Jackie shrugged as she gazed through her sight and studied the ground ahead. "I take in stray kittens. It's the right thing to do. You take care of your own. The Wild Geese do not leave people behind. You owe me money. All of the above."

During the next hour the ground became rockier and progress was very difficult. When they paused, Jackie seeking a way through the tall stones, Gwielgi reached up with his free hand and grasped his pack strap, pulling Jackie towards him.

"Hold on for a second," he said. "Look, this is impossible. You'll never get there like this."

"Not leaving you," she said, breathing deeply.

"I understand that," he said. "Help me up." He slung his rifle over a shoulder and she helped him upright. He stood precariously balanced on his good leg.

"You can't walk on that."

"All right," he replied, his voice tight. "I'll run. No, listen. If I can stay on my feet, with you on the side of my bad leg, I think I can hobble a hell of a lot faster than you can drag me through this broken ground."

"Even if you can," she said, "having a broken leg hang is going to be pretty rough. That splint only gives lateral support, not vertical."

"Yeah, life sucks. Give me a hand."

It took a minute but they finally found a position that seemed to work. His right arm was draped across her shoulders and she held onto him as firmly as she could. They practiced a few steps. Gwielgi's face was drawn with the effort of taking a couple of hops but he nodded to her and they resumed their trek.

They moved much faster than before but not nearly as fast as they had to. Jackie didn't bother to check the time. They were never going to be at the pick-up point in time. She shoved the thought out of her head and concentrated on putting one foot in front of another and trying to find the easiest way through the boulders. She could feel Gwielgi jerk in pain from time to time as his foot caught a rock

They would struggle forward for half an hour and then rest for a few quick minutes. When they paused, they would try their communication devices but heard no response. Their unit's strike force was too far south, deep in the hills the valley led to. But they would patiently transmit anyway, hoping they were being heard. Several times they came to blocks in their path and had to find a way around. When they paused for a break, Jackie would scout ahead a short distance, trying to find the fastest route.

It began to snow more heavily and the wind picked up, coming at them from the north. As they struggled forward, it soon was like looking down a tunnel formed by the snow blowing past. As they made their way around a major uplift of rock, the wind suddenly picked up, almost exploding on them and driving the snow in a stream that was horizontal. Visibility was reduced to a few meters.

"We can't move in this," Jackie said, almost shouting to be heard above the howl of the blizzard. "Got to get shelter." Gwielgi nodded. She leaned him against the uplift and walked around it, looking for a cleft or ravine where they could take cover.

She found the opening to a cave. She moved back and had a moment of panic when she could not find Gwielgi, but he was where she had left him. Visibility was now so poor that it would have been easy to walk past without seeing him. She hoisted his arm across her shoulders and they struggled to the cave.

It was larger than she had anticipated, much larger. The opening was small and they barely could fit through together and had to crouch, but it rapidly opened into a large chamber more than a dozen meters deep. The floor was covered with dirt and loose rock but was much easier to move on than the ground outside. She took him to the back of the cave and slowly lowered him. She shed her rifle and pack.

"All right," she said, pushing back her hood. "Take off your pants."

It was a measure of the pain he was experiencing that Gwielgi did not make a joke. He put his rifle aside and struggled to open his parka and unbuckle his pants. He tried to push them down but the effort was too great. She took his boots off, being as gently as she could. When the right one was removed he groaned. She untied the field dressing wrapped around his pant leg and then she dragged his pants down.

His leg was bloody. The ragged hole of the entry wound above his knee was oozing blood. She felt with her bare hands and found the exit hole, larger and likewise bleeding. She opened her aid pack. She dusted the wounds with antibiotic and a coagulant. She took a pair of nanotechnology pads and pressed them against the wounds and applied two new dressings to hold the pads in place.

"I knew we should have taken nanosuits," she said. "It would have been working all this time on your wound."

"Too much weight," he said. "That climb up the cliff would have taken forever."

She reached for his pant leg to pull it up but Gwielgi held up his hand.

"Let me rest for a moment. The cold will help the bleeding slow down anyway."

Jackie nodded. She helped him take off his pack and took both of them to the front of the cave. A glance at the entrance told her the blizzard was not abating. Occasional flakes came into the cave but the wind's angle kept almost all of it out.

Jackie took rations from the packs and broke a pair of heat sticks. They were soon hot enough to put metal cups on, into which she placed handfuls of fresh snow and soup powder. The sticks would last for a half hour or more until their chemical reaction finally wore out.

When the soup was hot she took the cups back to Gwielgi. He was asleep. She woke him up and handed him the soup. He nodded and slowly drank it. She watched and made sure he finished it and then handed him the second cup. Mechanically, his eyes half open, he took it and drank it down. She took the cup and worked his pants up and secured them. She saw as she did that the inside of the pant leg was sodden with sticky blood. She closed up his parka. He was asleep before she finished tightening his hood.

Jackie went back to the heat sticks. They were still radiating a good amount of warmth. She opened her parka and sat close to them while she heated up some soup for herself, enjoying the warmth and letting the moisture inside her parka dry. Then she took off her boots, checked her feet, and changed her socks. When the sticks went cold the storm was still blowing hard. She moved to a position near the entrance with her rifle but not so close she was catching any of the wind.

Jackie fought off a yawn. She took a heat stick and broke it, laying it beside her. The radiated warmth helped fight off the cold. The wind outside seemed to be dying down, a small piece of good news. She stepped up to the entrance and tried her transmitter. There was still no response. She shrugged and returned to her position next to the heat stick. The storm was definitely easing off. Maybe in another hour or two they could travel again.

She walked to the back of the cave and checked on Gwielgi. He was asleep. She picked up his rifle and took it back to her position. Jackie

15

unwrapped the camouflage cloth and field stripped it. She carefully cleaned it and then reassembled it. After wrapping it, she did the same to her own rifle. She looked back at Gwielgi. The corporal was almost invisible in the darkness of the cave. She put his rifle to one side and cradled her own in her lap.

She stood sentry, watching the storm slowly passing. The cold worked its way into her and she had to fight to stay awake. She cracked another heat stick. It helped her stay awake for a few more minutes but then she nodded off.

Gwielgi was having a nightmare. He dreamt that he was in a dark place being tortured by people he could not see. From somewhere someone was crying out but, chained to the torturer's table, he could not move.

It took Gwielgi a moment to realize he was awake. He blinked several times before he understood where he was. His leg was throbbing and the wound had the strange, cold itch caused by the nanotech pads, but for the moment the stabbing pain he had experienced when hobbling with Jackie was a memory. Jackie? He looked around.

He heard a voice, a man's, muffled, angry, mocking. He squinted toward the cave entrance. The storm was gone and the light of the setting sun was brilliant. It took him a moment before he could make out the huddled shape near the entrance.

The shape was two figures, one on top of the other, struggling with one another. The one on top was in enemy gray. Gwielgi reached for his rifle but could not find it. The figure on the bottom was Jackie. He started to crawl towards them. The throbbing in his leg suddenly became a piercing flame, one that radiated throughout his leg. It hurt so bad he felt himself gag but he kept pulling himself forward with his arms and pushing with his good leg.

The enemy soldier did not see him. His hands were at Jackie's throat. She held his wrists but her strength was failing as he cut off her breath. Gwielgi saw one of her hands slide aside. The soldier fumbled with the front of his snowsuit.

"Now," the soldier said. His voice was hoarse. "Now."

When he was two meters away, Gwielgi made himself stand. He tried to ignore the white-hot agony of his broken leg by concentrating on getting up on his good one as quickly as he could. As he stood, his right hand reached into his left sleeve. Then he fell forward, his hand emerging holding a thin bladed knife. He drove it into the man's back as he fell.

The enemy soldier arced his back, clawing at the steel Gwielgi buried next to his spine. Gwielgi used his other hand to grab the soldier by the jaw and, holding tight to man and knife, rolled him off of Jackie. He came to rest, panting with the effort and pain, on top of the soldier who was still struggling beneath him. He twisted the knife and jerked it free. He pulled harder on the man's jaw, exposing his neck. He reached forward and slit the man's throat.

Gwielgi rolled off the soldier and lay gasping for breath. The dead man's blood filled his vision with steam and his leg hurt so badly he was trembling. He tried to move to check on Jackie but for a moment it was as if none of his muscles worked. A roaring in his ears gradually ebbed into a drumbeat that matched his heart.

Gwielgi finally sat up and saw Jackie slowly turning toward him. She tried to speak but could not. She rolled over onto all fours, her head hanging. Gwielgi could see that her parka was open and her shirt was torn. She threw up. She paused, her head lowered onto her forearm. Then Jackie slowly rose to her knees and looked over at him.

"Are you all right?" she asked.

"I'm fine," Gwielgi said. He wiped the blade of his knife on the soldier's back. "Asshole," he said to the dead man. "How are you?" he asked Jackie as he slipped the knife back into its sheath on his forearm.

"I fell asleep," she said, getting to her feet. She swayed slightly and then steadied herself. "When I woke up he was already on me. I guess he tracked us with those." She pointed at a set of goggles near the entrance, beside a rifle. "I'd used a couple of heat sticks. He probably caught the infrared and came to investigate."

"Anyone else with him?"

Jackie moved to the entrance and squinted outside. The air was perfectly clear though the setting sun was blinding. She took her goggles from her parka's pocket and pulled them on. She carefully studied the scene before she shook her head.

"We're clear for the moment," she said and then came back to Gwielgi. She looked over at the dead man and then looked at the distance from where Gwielgi had lain.

"Thanks," she said.

"No problem," he said. The drumbeat was gone and the pain in his leg slowly eased. He looked at Jackie but her face was still, showing nothing. "Are you all right?"

"I'm fine," she said. "Let's move you up to the opening."

"All right," Gwielgi said. The steam still rose from the dead man.

Jackie helped him up and carefully helped him as Gwielgi hobbled to the cave wall near the entrance.

"You sure you...?"

"He didn't rape me. You got to him before that." She squatted and reached for their packs.

"Glad of that," Gwielgi said.

"Yes," Jackie said as she gathered up their equipment. She didn't look at him. "I've been through that before."

"Sorry to hear that. Some men are pigs."

"I was a slave," she said. She paused and looked at him, her eyes a little wide. "I guess I'm a little shook, still. I've never told anyone that before."

"It's all right," Gwielgi said. "Nothing dishonorable in being a slave. The dishonor is in being a slave *owner*."

"There are days when I almost believe that," she said as she shoved things into their packs. He could see the thin line of tears coming down her cheeks.

"It's true," Gwielgi finally said after a long pause. "I know."

"How's that?" She wiped the tears with the back of her hand and smiled as she glanced at him. "Were you a slaver?"

"No," he said. "I was a slave. Twice."

Jackie looked at him for a moment and said nothing. She walked forward and put the packs down beside him. She took the soldier's goggles, stuffed them into her pack, and put his rifle further back in the cave along with the used heat sticks. Then she dragged the dead man back into the shadows. She sat down beside Gwielgi.

"How did it happen?"

"I was a mercenary, my first unit," he shrugged. "When we were getting paid, we were seized. Sold. I guess it beat paying us. My master was a soldier. I eventually was trusted enough to accompany him, carrying his gear, that sort of thing. I saved his life. Then his unit was tapped to be a delaying force while his army mobilized to beat off invaders. He freed me before the last battle. I survived, he didn't. But his people honored my manumission. I had to leave, of course. Can't have a former slave walking around, giving people ideas."

"I tried to go home but it didn't work out. I wandered around, worked as a merc, eventually got a job teaching. Backwater world, nothing ever happened there. Raiders hit the place. Those of us who knew how to fight covered the rest. When the dust settled, I woke up to find I was their prisoner. They sold me. A man who owned a major island on another world put me to work. Maybe had a thousand slaves, working his fields, machinery, computers. There was no place to run to; he controlled everything. People trying to escape, they were usually caught in the hills by the overseers and guards, brought back and killed in front of us. Object lessons. No one got away." Gwielgi leaned back against the wall, his eyes almost closed as he remembered.

"I decided to escape anyway. Did it differently. Didn't try to break out. Went after the overseers and guards. They all lived in a real big house, guards, overseers, trusties, the owner and his family, wife, children, everyone. Used a farm tool, then a knife, and then a gun, lots of guns. And then I burned down his house, with him and his family still in it. I killed everything that moved or tried to come out. I didn't leave until the ashes were cool. Then I went back to being a mercenary." He shrugged a second time. "And now I'm here." He checked his rifle and chambered a round, flipping on the safety. "You?"

"I was born a slave on Freehold," Jackie Peregrine said. "I don't remember my parents, not much. The world I was on, the prestige thing was how many slaves you had working for you."

"The ultimate status symbol," Gwielgi said, his voice bitter. "The best way to show off your wealth and power."

"I belonged to a family," Jackie said. "At first, I was used as a companion to their children, so I picked up some education. Then I was moved over to keeping house. I was thirteen. They discovered I could sing, so they moved me from keeping house to performing for their amusement. From time to time the owner would rape me. I became pregnant. That was forbidden. So they lined me up for an abortion. I was fifteen and took off. They chased me. Caught me, took me back. Did the abortion." Jackie

19

looked around, as if seeing where she was for the first time. "Made sure I'd never have children."

"Like you, I wanted to escape. I played the game, very subservient. A few years later I was with the owner and his wife when they went to the city. While we were there the Pale Riders hit the place. You know them?"

"Mercenary unit," Gwielgi said. "We worked with them on Vonmort and I ran across them on New Sudan."

"I thought you might remember," Jackie said. "This was before then, obviously. When they hit Freehold I took off in all the confusion, made my way to the landing ship field. Big city, it took them time to look everywhere, and by that time I'd found a landing ship captain who thought I was attractive. She took me on board as crew in exchange for my favors. I guess she loved me, in her way. I learned about landing ships. When we visited Sword Point I signed off and looked to join a merc unit, one registered with the SFA. The Pale Riders were recruiting. A lot of former slaves join them because they take those liberation raid contracts from the John Brown Society. Anyway, I was with them on Vonmort when we got overrun. The Geese saved me and a bunch of my mates. The Riders went into reforming status so I transferred to the Wild Geese." She paused and looked around. "Thought having my hands on weapons would keep things like this from every happening again." Her face twisted and tears flowed.

Suddenly she buried her face in Gwielgi's shoulder and he heard her sob, the heavy, gut-wrenching cries of long suppressed grief. He put his arms around her and said nothing, just watched the darkness of night descend outside the cave entrance.

Eventually, Jackie stopped crying and fell asleep. Gwielgi sat motionless, listening to her breathing and watching the moon slowly rise above the far horizon revealing a night sky empty of clouds.

Gwielgi tried his communication device. It was well after the rendezvous time but he tried anyway.

There was no response. He sighed.

Jackie woke as the moon's pale beams crept into the cave.

"Time for us to be traveling," he said. For a moment she lay still.

"Damn," she said. "I fell asleep. Again."

"You needed it, and there's no rush."

"You called?"

"No response," he said. She didn't leave his shoulder.

"We've had it, then," she said.

"Like hell." He pushed her, gently, until she was sitting upright. "I know those people, Peregrine. One way or the other, they will come for us. Yeah, we missed the pick-up. Our job now is to be where they can find us. So, we go. Besides, I'll be damned if I'm going to die in some hole in the ground."

"Aye, corporal," Jackie said and he saw a flash of white as she smiled in the darkness. She gathered up their gear, putting most of it in her pack, and checked the splint on Gwielgi's leg. She shook her head as she applied another pair nanotechnology bandages.

"How does it feel?" she asked.

"Not too bad," Gwielgi said. She looked at him. "No, really. The bandages have really deadened it. I just hope those little 'bots know what the hell they're doing and don't decide to close down something I need."

"We get back to the ship," Jackie said, "the medics are going to have a lot of fun with you."

"Don't remind me," Gwielgi said. "I'm going to ask Kheyntamenti to keep them away from me." He looked toward the back of the cave. "Leave asshole's weapon; ours are better and it's just more weight."

She rose and pulled on her pack. "You got a lot of trust in the colonel."

"I knew him before the Wild Geese." He got to his feet, or foot, by pushing himself up the wall. She helped him put on his nearly empty pack. "Our paths have crossed a couple of times over the years."

She put his arm over her shoulder.

"And Private Tsunasdi? You guys hang out a lot together. He came in with you, right? He's a friend of yours?"

"I don't know," Gwielgi said. "But I trust him with my life." He adjusted his rifle and then nodded. They began to move forward.

"He's a Currahee, isn't he?"

"Formerly of the Aniwaya Sword Sect Regiment," Gwielgi said as they paused at the entrance. "You have a problem with that?"

"No," she said.

"I do," Gwielgi replied. They stepped out into the night.

The snow impeded their movement to some degree but it helped them where it filled in the gaps between rocks. Their light amplification goggles were almost too helpful with the light of a full moon pouring down on them and they had to adjust the gain down as the moon climbed higher. At each frequent break Jackie made sure they ate something and drank from their canteens. When the canteens emptied, she stuffed snow into them and put them inside their parkas. While the temperature kept dropping, their exertions kept them warm enough.

The sun was lighting up the eastern sky to their left as they cleared the rocky ground. Before them, the ground descended in a gentle decline into the dark shadows of the mountains. Gwielgi checked his navigation system and nodded.

"We're about a klick and a half away from Bravo," he said.

"How late are we?"

"About ten hours."

"I hate making people wait," Jackie replied. They resumed shuffling forward.

Even with the snow, the going now was a great deal easier. There were still occasional rocks and boulders, but compared to the garden of stone they had been through, the hillside was like walking down a bowling alley.

They were about a kilometer from Bravo when they heard the two hovercrafts coming at them from the east.

"Persistent bastards," Gwielgi said as they got behind a low wall of rock and snow. He looked over the wall. "They don't see us, not yet. They're just sweeping the hillside. With a little luck..."

The lead hovercraft kept moving to the right, headed slightly downhill, but the second suddenly slid sideways as it came to a stop. As it did the lead one slowed down and coasted to a halt, waiting. A side hatch opened in the second and a small group of soldiers climbed out and jumped down into the snow. They were moving slightly uphill, above the snipers, their gaze on the ground in front of them.

"They've spotted our trail," Gwielgi said. He swung his rifle around and looked to the south where the hillside flattened into the valley. "No one's at Bravo."

"Then what do we do?"

"I suppose it's useless to order you to take off while I cover you."

"You got it, corporal."

"Surrender?"

"I've already had a taste of their hospitality," Jackie said. "I'd rather not."

"Me, neither." He glanced at the group of four soldiers, still plodding across the hill towards their tracks, probably ensuring it wasn't just the trail of some animal.

"All right, here's what we do. We stay low. We take out those four. Then we move from this position. Keep this wall between that hovercraft and us. The lead one will come up here when the shooting starts but he won't see much from all the snow he will blow up. The one holding still will be the dangerous one. He's got a missile launcher on his roof. We'll go back to those rocks," he said, pointing behind him.

"Now, this is important. You absolutely *have* to get to those rocks. Do not, repeat, do not, wait on me. I'm going to be low crawling. You'll get there ahead of me and can cover me. If you wait, we will not be putting down any fire and they will have a clear shot at us. Got it?"

Jackie nodded and Gwielgi slipped his arm into his sling. "Let's get to it."

She moved beside him and propped herself up on her elbows with her rifle. "I am with you," she said quietly, using the traditional slogan of their mercenary unit.

"I am with you," he repeated. Then he killed the first soldier.

He fired on the rearmost man and the bullet hit him in the head. The others split their attention with the closest turning towards the falling soldier while the other two looking towards the sound of the rifle.

Jackie's shot hit one of them in the center of his chest. He convulsed, folding around the shot and falling backwards. Gwielgi fired again and the man closest to his first kill spun in place and dropped into the snow. The fourth man was still raising his rifle when Jackie's bullet slammed into his lower jaw and exited through the back of his head.

"Go," whispered Gwielgi, and Jackie, her rifle cradled in her arms, crawled towards the far rocks. She all but disappeared into the deep snow. Gwielgi looked towards the second hovercraft and keyed his microphone.

"Victor Echo. Anyone, this is Victor Echo."

There was no response. He saw the hovercraft's missile launcher swing in his direction. A face appeared in the hatchway and he put a bullet in it. Off to the right came the building roar of the other hovercraft as it turned on its massive fans. As predicted, the newly fallen show billowed up in a cloud all around the vehicle. The hatch of the second hovercraft showed no faces but he saw muzzle flashes from within and bullets cracked over his head.

Gwielgi brought his crosshairs to one of the flashes and aimed a little above it. It stopped for several seconds. Reloading? Then it started again. He fired and it abruptly stopped a second time but did not resume. The hovercraft's turbine engines roared to life. Its broad, black skirts bulged and a cloud of snow whirled around it. Now was his chance to get back to Jackie's position. He lay in the snow and started crawling.

He had a sudden image of a gopher as he moved through the snow. He was not so much crawling on it as burrowing through it. Well, the advantage was that he would be hard to see.

Suddenly the snow in front of Gwielgi vanished, exposing him to the bright blue sky, whipped away by something that dug into the hillside on his right. The lead hovercraft, he realized, had stopped moving and its own blinding snowstorm was gone. He heard the second hovercraft cut its engines, now much closer to him. A machine gun opened up from behind and he heard bullets smacking the stones he had hid behind moments before.

Gwielgi heard the lead hovercraft reloading what sounded like an automatic cannon. There was a pause and then another blast, this one behind him. He realized that if he moved suddenly, they would have him. He edged forward slowly into the area swept by the cannon's first shot and looked to his left.

The top turret of the hovercraft was plainly visible, as were the two gunners. He slid his rifle forward until he could put his eye to the sight. The gunners were looking at the rocks the second hovercraft still peppered. He heard shouts behind him. It was offloading its infantry. He brought the crosshairs to the gunner on the left. He was talking into a microphone and pointing.

The bullet rocked the gunner backward and he rolled to the side and lay hanging out of the open turret. Gwielgi moved the crosshairs to the right but the other gunner was gone. Because of the snow, he could see nothing of the hovercraft below the cockpit but he could hear someone yelling orders from that direction. More infantry. He eyed the cockpit and wondered if the windshield glass was armored. Reflected glare from the morning sun kept him from seeing the pilot, so he approximated where he thought the person might be.

The glass was not armored. A hole appeared in the middle of the windshield and the white spider web of the impact flashed outward. Gwielgi heard more gunfire behind him from several weapons. It sounded like they were attacking the wall. Once they were up to it, they would see him. Gwielgi shook his head and rolled over on his back and raised his rifle. The first one over the low rocks would be dead, he decided.

He heard Peregrine's rifle then. Measured but rapid shots cracked through the cold, still air. He hoped she was scoring hits but could not tell from his position in the snow. He looked over at the lead hovercraft. The other gunner was slowly raising his head and the turret was traversing towards Peregrine's position.

He swung his rifle over. The man only had the upper portion of his head exposed. Gwielgi placed the cross hairs below the dark goggles, allowing for the elevation in his sights left from the last firefight. He fired and saw a lens explode as the gunner dropped into the turret.

Gwielgi heard the second hovercraft powering up, though he did not understand why it would cut down its own visibility or move from its position. He glimpsed movement at the wall. Three soldiers were climbing over. He swung his rifle back as he touched the bolt control and heard the sound of a round sliding into the chamber. He fired and a soldier dropped back. He touched the bolt control again but nothing happened. He grabbed the manual bolt handle with his fist and pulled it to the rear and shoved it forward. When he squeezed the trigger there was a hollow click. He lowered his rifle and reached in his sleeve for his knife, wishing he had been able to carry more ammunition.

The remaining two soldiers looked back at their roaring hovercraft and then back towards him. They started to raise their rifles. He pulled his knife free, knowing it was too far to throw. Jackie's rifle fired and one dropped like a puppet with cut strings. The other rolled backwards over the wall and vanished from sight.

Then Gwielgi heard the lead hovercraft also turn on its engines. He had a vision of the hovercraft running over him and wondered if he could survive such an experience. There was a sudden explosion and he saw a ball of flame rise from the turret of the lead hovercraft. Whatever Jackie had hit must have been particularly volatile.

The remaining hovercraft was moving and he saw the trail of missiles slicing the air above him. Were they shooting at Jackie? In answer another set of missiles passed over him headed in the other direction. Then he heard a hiss in his earpiece.

"Echo Charley."

"Glad you guys could find the time to show up."

"You're late."

"It's all Jackie's fault. She read the map upside down so we headed in the wrong direction for the past couple of days."

"Roger. Stay down."

"No problem. Happy to oblige."

Gwielgi fell back into the snow, his knife still in his hand. He felt the need for a long, hot bath and then a nap lasting two or three days. He was still lying there when the sounds of the battle ceased. A minute or two later someone was standing over him.

"Do you mind moving? You're blocking the sun," Gwielgi said, squinting into the light, "and I'm working on my tan."

"Give it up," Jackie said. "I've got enough tan to make up for your pale butt. I'll loan you some." She looked up and waved at someone Gwielgi could not see.

"Damned nice of you," Gwielgi said. She crouched beside him.

"Are you all right? They'll be here in a minute."

"This," he said, grimacing, "is about as good as I get."

"That's some knife," she said. "I don't recognize the style."

He started to sit up and she helped him.

"It's called a 'Fairbairn,' after the man who designed it back in the 20th Century. Cop, as I recall, working in China. Not great for throwing but for stabbing it's beautiful."

"So I've noticed," she said. He flipped the knife and caught it by the blade. He held it out to her.

"It's yours."

She looked at him for a moment and then nodded. She took it from him gently and examined the long, thin blade.

"You want to get a fitted sheath for it," Gwielgi said. "Forearm, boot, side, or small of your back, wherever you want." She looked at him for a moment.

"Thank you, Corporal Gwielgi. I am honored by your gift."

"You are welcome, Private Peregrine." He smiled. "I am honored by you."

Chapter 1: Death in the sun

5 May 2824

The sergeant lay in the middle of the crossroads, dying. Around him were the scattered burning pieces of his hovercraft. He did not know what had destroyed it or, judging by the nearby columns of fire and smoke, the other four hovercrafts in his group.

The sun's effects seemed amplified by the farmland around him. The low, green plants looked like the soybeans that his father raised, all tidy in their rows. He hated farming. That was why he joined, first, the army of the United Commonwealth and, later, a mercenary unit. Anything to stay off the farm.

The joke was on him, he decided with a grim smile. Here he was, after all these years, about to die in the middle of somebody's farm. It seemed funnier than it was and he made a short snort of laughter. It hurt and he cut it off. He rolled over onto his stomach, which hurt as well.

He tried to crawl across the hard pavement towards some bushes at the side of the road – at least he could die in the shade. He only managed a few meters before he discovered he was too weak. He wasn't sure why but it seemed like a shame that he could not get off the road. He lay his head down on the pavement. The heat of the road soaked into his body, easing the pain of his wounds. Or maybe it was just a part of dying. It didn't matter. It was good just to have the pain slack off a little.

The ground vibrated in a steady rhythm. He knew what it was without looking up but he did anyway. Walking beside the road, soldiers on line on either side of it, a 90-ton Javelin HUPAX, camouflaged in multiple shades of green and gray and tall as a house, slowly stalked through the crops.

Some farmer's going to be pissed off.

The thought set him to laughing but he cut it off again when it brought the pain back. He saw a second HUP, a slightly smaller Long Sword, moving in echelon to the Javelin. Soldiers, well-spaced from one another, walked through the crossroads. He heard the occasional command and reply. Very professional, he decided. Not a bunch of farmers, not the half-trained planetary militia they were told defended this place. He sighed. It didn't matter, not now. He laid his head back down on the road.

Someone squatted over him, shading him from the sun. He tried to look up but a hand gently held him down.

"Stay there," the man said. "For you the war is over."

He heard the man yell for a medic. Footsteps thudded up beside him and he was turned over slowly. It hurt, though the people moved him as gently as they could. They unhooked his belts and straps and tore open his shirt. The medic, who looked to be a woman half his age, grimaced when she saw his wounds but worked quickly. He looked up at the soldier squatting over him. He tried to speak but his throat seemed sealed shut. The other man held up a canteen for the medic to see. She glanced at it and then shrugged.

"Doesn't matter," she said quietly and then went back to work.

The water was warm and had an odd taste but it was wonderful. He took a couple of short sips and the soldier gently pulled it away.

"More later," the soldier said. It was hard to see what he looked like with the sun behind him but his voice was soft, the kind of softness age brings.

"Don't think there's going to be a later," the sergeant said. "Think this is about it."

"You might be right," the soldier replied, looking at the wounds with a steady gaze. "But you can never tell with this stuff."

"Sorry to be a bother," the sergeant said, his voice hoarse and weak.

"Not a problem."

The medic slapped a bag of fluid on his arm and the nanotech needle found a vein as he watched. He heard her talking into her microphone but could not make out the words.

"How did...?" His strength failed him for a moment and he closed his eyes and gathered himself. "How did you know we were coming this way?"

"We spotted your landing ship when you entered the atmosphere. Tried to hit you on your way in to the mines but we were out of position. So we set up this ambush. We were in the woods about a klick away. Hit your hovercrafts as you entered the crossroads. Your HUPs tried to circle west. Only two are still running to the landing ship."

"Did the Saber make it?"

"I don't know," the soldier replied, "but we tried to take out the biggest ones first so maybe the Saber is still going."

"Hope she makes it." He looked up. "Girl friend. The pilot."

The soldier nodded but said nothing. The medic finished whatever she was doing and stood up. The sergeant could hear her talking into her headset, calling for a medevac. He doubted that he would be alive by the time it got here but it was gracious of them to make the effort. Them. He realized he didn't know who they were. He coughed.

"Who are you people?" He grinned. "We were told there were just some militia, no threat. Farmers, weekend warriors. What are you, mercenaries?"

"Were," the soldier said. "We live here now. Couple of years. Didn't they tell you?"

"Hell, no," he said and smiled weakly. "Would have brought some friends if we'd known the party was going to be this much fun." He started coughing and for a moment it sounded like he was not going to be able to stop. "Back when you were mercs. What was your name?"

"We were called the Wild Geese," the soldier said, tapping a black emblem on his purple beret.

"Sorry," the dying man replied. His voice was very weak. "I don't think I ever heard of you."

"That's all right," the soldier said. The dying man let out a final sigh and was still. The soldier reached down and shut the man's eyes. "No offense taken."

He slowly stood and looked around. The fires from the hovercraft were almost out. The medic closed up her bag and jogged off to join her infantry platoon. He reached down and picked up a cane and walked away. He tried not to use his cane and pushed himself to walk without limping, though with only partial success. He touched his headset.

"Grunt Six, Gwielgi. Is your sweep finished?"

"Roger, captain. We've picked up five, all wounded. Doesn't look like there will much to pull from the hovercrafts. They're totaled."

"Rog, Joe. Blame that on Gunny Tsunasdi. I think he was jacked that he didn't get to chase the HUPs."

He heard a laugh and changed channels.

"Geese Lead, Gwielgi."

"Go ahead."

"Crossroads secured, colonel. All five hovercrafts are down. Five prisoners taken. The hovercrafts are totally destroyed. I don't think we can get any gear off of them."

"Copy. We're just finishing up here. Their landing ship is lifting. Looks like the Militia Swallows are trying to get in some long-range hits."

"Roger. Did the Saber get away?"

"Negative. Six up, six down. One surrendered. We'll get some equipment off the others."

"Roger. The Saber. Did the pilot get out?"

"Negative, I don't think so. It went down with the first salvo. It was up front, working as a scout. Why'd you ask?"

"No reason, boss. No reason. Gwielgi, out."

Gwielgi stopped at the edge of the crossroads and glanced back at the dead man.

"Sorry," he said quietly.

The Kodomir Militia Combined Arms Battalion (Heavy), called the Wild Geese after the former mercenary unit it was built around, finished its sweep and moved into the area of the crossroads. Eight of its sixteen HUPAX, the war machines that gave the battalion its "Heavy" designation, formed a loose, circular perimeter more than a kilometer in diameter and were joined by a dozen tanks. Softer skinned vehicles – a half dozen hovercrafts and four missile-launcher equipped APCs – entered the perimeter and set themselves up around the crossroads. Sometime later five Tiger Moth-class attack helicopters swept in from the west, slowed, and landed on the road. Their rotors slowly came to a halt as their turbines whined down.

Captain Gwielgi, his cane held in the crook of his arm like a hunting rifle, walked over to the lead helicopter and waited for its pilot to disembark. Lieutenant Leba Chinaren pulled off her helmet and ran a gloved hand through her short, sweaty hair. As she unstrapped herself from the cockpit, she looked at Gwielgi and smiled.

"That went well," she said.

"We were fortunate," Gwielgi said. "They were not prepared for us and were in too much of a hurry." He reached over and took her helmet as she removed it. "And outnumbering them helped."

She climbed down from the helicopter and walked around it, checking for damage.

"I am always in favor of unfair odds, as long as they are on our side," Chinaren said as she looked under the helicopter's tail boom. She reached up and pulled at something and then walked back to Gwielgi, dusting her hands off on her green, sweat-stained flight suit.

"True enough," he said. He touched his earpiece for a moment and then asked, "What is your flight's fuel state?"

"We have enough to return to Coyote Bay," Chinaren said. "Not a problem if Colonel Kheyntamenti is asking." Gwielgi relayed the information.

"He says whenever you want you can take the flight back to the Bay. Landing ship Ghost is going to collect the enemy HUP parts we can recover and could stop off to refuel the choppers if needed. The rest of us will follow as soon as the wounded and prisoners are secured."

"Roger," Chinaren said. "What are our casualties?"

"So far, we've accounted for seven dead and twelve wounded among the platoon these mercs hit on their way into Mining Area Beta. Casualties at the mine complex are unknown but it looks like they hit the storage and shipping area. It's still being checked out."

"The battalion?"

"Damage to some of the HUPs," Gwielgi said. "No KIA, no WIA."

"Well," she said, smiling slightly, "at least that's good news."

"This time," the older officer said. His voice sounded tired. "This time."

Chapter 2: Thunder on the horizon

5 May 2824

The HUPAX entered the base last, swinging off the reinforced highway that joined the ocean-side city of Coyote Bay with the rest of the continent. The soldiers of the Militia base defense unit watched the big machines pass their sentry posts. The camouflaged HUPs, their armor marked by the black streaks and frozen rivulets of battle damage, did not pause, though their pilots occasionally flashed their exterior lights in response to the waves from the sentries.

They made their way in a long column to the battalion area on the west side of the base, next to the airfield and landing ship pads. The rest of the battalion vehicles, parked in armored revetments, started to take on ammunition and fuel. The infantry, formed in platoons, sat in the sun, cleaning their weapons.

There was little of the usual horseplay and bantering talk. The battalion's men and women were tired. Around the clock patrols, alerts, and six raids in five months had drawn on people's reserves.

Lieutenant Colonel Alisti Mahmud al-Kheyntamenti, the battalion commanding officer, wearily followed the raised hands of a HUP technician from the cockpit of the lead HUPAX, a 110-ton Rapier. The HUP technician guided him into a protected revetment and he sighed in relief when the soldier gave him the shut-down signal. As the visualizations provided to his brain over the mindlink flickered and vanished into darkness and the HUP's powerful engine whined down, he felt the slight jar of the service gantry nudging the Rapier. He levered open the cockpit hatch and pulled off his mindlink helmet. The HUP technician leaned in, balancing himself on the frame.

"How's she running, colonel?"

"Fine, corporal. I think the rail gun may have been damaged in the engagement. Heat readings were a little high at the end, like the rounds were starting to ablate to the rails." He unsnapped the straps holding him in the pilot's ejection seat. "But get it reloaded first – keep it cocked and locked until we're sure there isn't another raid inbound." He stepped out and looked around.

"Aye, sir." The technician reached into the cockpit as Kheyntamenti stretched on the platform and touched the instrument displays. They flashed into life and the tech's fingers danced across them. "Looks like the vacuum was partially lost, colonel," the young man said over his shoulder. "It sealed itself but there is definitely air in the tube. I think we can put a temporary patch on it."

"Good," Kheyntamenti said. "We may have more to do."

At the bottom of the gantry Kheyntamenti met the battalion HUPAX Maintenance Officer, Gunnery Sergeant Sevin. The only slightly younger man grinned as his commander stepped off the elevator.

"Happy to see you brought your team all back more or less in one piece this time, sir," he said.

"We did take some hits," Kheyntamenti replied, "but they weren't expecting us and they didn't concentrate their fire. We most damage was to armor, though check on Chi Lore's HUP. He reported that he was having some missile launcher problems. And one of my rail guns has a leak."

"We got it, sir," Sevin said, glancing down at his datapad. "One of the flaps was not opening so he could only launch from the lower tier. It fed upper tier missiles into the lower tubes but it really slowed things down." He looked up at Kheyntamenti. "I'm planning on pulling the turret off and replacing it. We can work on it better in the shop."

"Can you put a replacement GTM-TAC on in the interim?"

"We don't have an available turret in the armory, though I could pull one off one of the spare HUPs."

"As I remember, you were overhauling an SLRTT2. Is it available?"

"Aye, sir, it is. We can get it on the Gladiator faster than transferring a tactical missile turret from a spare HUP, but it's going to mean Chi's going to have a very mixed configuration on that HUP." He looked at his pad again. "A GTL2 and an SLRTT2." He looked up. "A single Class-2 laser and a twin-barreled recoilless rifle. Not really a stand-off HUP, not really a knife fighter."

"Understood," Kheyntamenti said, "but Chi's sharp enough to handle the varying ranges and reloading rates. And I want to have as many HUPs 'up and up' until that star ship clears the system."

"Aye, sir," Sevin said. "Are you expecting them to come back?"

"Not really," Kheyntamenti admitted, "but they have the *potential* to come back, so we have to allow for it." He paused and watched as the last of the HUPs entered its revetment. He turned back to Sevin.

"How's the training program coming?"

"Not too badly, colonel. We completed the handling drills just before the battalion scrambled. The new people will start weapons work on the range as soon as you tell us the spares are available."

"Good. Let's move them along as fast as possible."

"Will do, sir."

Kheyntamenti climbed into a Prowler, a bulky military groundcar often used for scouting, and directed the driver to take him to the armored vehicle lager. The battalion included a tank company consisting of two platoons of Bob Cat tanks and a platoon of tracked infantry-carrying APCs. Prime movers, heavy trucks pulling large platform trailers, had met the battalion and brought the armored vehicles back, saving their tracks and engines wear, as well as the roads. The big Bob Cat tanks and APCs were still coming off their movers as Kheyntamenti arrived. The company commander, a Kodomiri captain named John Hardin, was up on a trailer, his sleeves rolled up in the late afternoon heat, using a large sledgehammer to knock loose the tie-down chains on a tank.

Hardin freed the last tie-down and the tank slowly backed up onto a ramped platform that it followed down and over to the other tanks. The captain watched it go, the hammer resting casually on his shoulder while sweat shined on his black face and soaked through the dull green of his fire-retardant coveralls. Kheyntamenti walked up slowly.

"What's the company's status, captain?" he asked. Hardin jumped slightly and then quickly turned around, dropping the hammer beside him as he snapped a salute.

"Sir, sorry, sir," he said, holding the salute, "I didn't see you there." Kheyntamenti returned his salute. "Colonel, both tank platoons can roll but could use refueling, rearming, and scheduled maintenance. One of the APCs took some frag damage, as I reported yesterday, but it is mobile. All of them need rearming and so forth as well."

"At ease, John," Kheyntamenti said. Captain Hardin tended be a little formal. A good commander, he was new to the battalion and had trouble relaxing. Well, it might take him a while to find his feet. "Go ahead with rearming and refueling but hold on the maintenance – we are still on alert until that landing ship gets to its star ship and they clear the system. When you have them bedded down, I'd like you and your platoon commanders to join me at the headquarters. Will an hour be enough time?"

"Yes, sir," Hardin responded. Kheyntamenti suspected he could have asked if ten seconds was enough and gotten the same response.

"Your people did some good work out there," Kheyntamenti said as he swung a leg into the Prowler. "I don't think those raider HUPs were expecting to find your company at that riverbank. And the ambush of their hovercrafts at the crossroads was very well done. Good use of cover and concealment and very nice shooting."

"Yes, sir, thank you, sir, I'll pass the word to the troops" Hardin said, a smile finally brightening his face. He used a sleeve to wipe away some of the sweat on his face. "I think Gunny Tsunasdi was perturbed that the APCs didn't leave much for him and his Javelin to do at the crossroads." His face became a little serious. "At the river, I thought they were going to go right through us at first, but your HUPs stopped them."

"*Our* HUPs," Kheyntamenti said with a slight emphasis, "relied on our tanks to be the anvil for their hammer." He sat down but held up a hand to his driver. "I thought they would try to side-step you, but they had gotten separated from their infantry hovercrafts and had to clear a path through your position. Trying that slowed them down more than going around would have, since your position, once they took fire, had to be reconnoitered before they attacked. Mercenaries try to avoid a stand-up fight unless the contract requires it, and fighting was not what they were paid for. Apparently, this was just a raid on the mines."

"I was a little surprised at that," Hardin admitted. "Given where they were and where their landing ship was, I thought they would skip by us as soon as they found we had the pass covered."

"Well, their hovercraft couldn't go around and over those hills and forest."

"Yes, sir, but what I meant was, they placed their HUPs in danger for five hovercrafts. Not a great exchange, especially since we ambushed the hovercrafts anyway."

"It wasn't about hovercrafts, captain," Kheyntamenti said. "Those were their people. And you don't leave your own behind."

"Yes, sir, I understand." He paused. "The Geese never did."

"Nor does the Kodomir Militia," Kheyntamenti said.

He waved his driver forward and returned Hardin's salute as they drove away.

The next stop was the infantry area. Captain Joseph Ho`nehe and Lieutenant Maggie Muldoon were found in the heavy weapons platoon area, conferring with the platoon commander, Staff Sergeant Ivan Tendelli. Kheyntamenti saw them crouched around a missile launcher, Ho`nehe and Tendelli on their backs underneath the tri-legged affair, and joined them. He nodded to Muldoon and then squatted beside the launcher.

"What's up, Joe?"

"Boss," Ho`nehe said as he wrestled with the launcher, "this is a piece of junk. We got one bird off it and the launch split the rail so we couldn't reload. The optical guidance system worked alright but the spool jammed after launch and the missile went ballistic half a klick out." He pushed himself out from under the launcher and stood up.

"They all worked fine on the range and the other two worked during the firefight but Tendelli found hairline cracks in the rails of one of the other launchers." He looked at Kheyntamenti. "I don't know if the other battalions have run into any of these problems but we ought to give everyone a heads-up."

"Agreed," Kheyntamenti said. "All right, put together a thorough report on this and include some close-ups of the rails. I'll send it up to Colonel Jonivov to forward to Militia Headquarters and send copies to the other battalions." He paused, rubbing his unshaven jaw. "General Polrany says when the spring harvest is sold, we will replace these old ones with new antiarmor missile launchers."

"That's good news," Ho'nehe said, "but the harvest doesn't go in for three more weeks back east. Be maybe a year after that before we get the weapons." He grimaced. "Given the number of times we've been hit recently, I guess we're going to have to make do with these things."

"Afraid so," Kheyntamenti said.

"Sir," Tendelli said to Ho'nehe, "I think we can repair the rails on this and the other one and weld some reinforcing straps on all of them. It will increase their weight a lot, but we can use them. As for the guidance wires, I think we're just going to have to unstring them and then put them back on their spools and reattach them to the missiles. Otherwise, we won't be certain if they're going to snag or not."

"We've got 38 of these missiles left," Ho'nehe replied. "Each one has a wire a kilometer long." He shook his head. "Let's put together our report and see if your welding idea will do the trick. As for rewiring the spools, we will need a very clean, enclosed setting and mechanical wrappers." He looked at Kheyntamenti. "Colonel, do you think the Mikoyan-Hughes people have the gear to do the rewiring?"

Mikoyan-Hughes was one of the new Kodomir companies developing many of the Militia's indigenous weapons. Their contributions included precision Frogfire missiles and technical support for a variety of military systems.

"I don't know," Kheyntamenti said. "But if anyone on Kodomir could, they are it. I'll be talking with their tech rep about some work on our Bob Cats and cannon on the seventh. I'll bring this up. Maybe they can make some suggestions about the launchers as well. Can you get me a copy of the report by then?"

"Yes, sir," Ho'nehe said, though Tendelli suddenly looked grim – report writing was not his strength and it was generally believed that he would rather face a bayonet fight, something he had done alongside Ho'nehe, than a word processor. "Don't worry," Ho'nehe added, looking at the sergeant, "I'll give you a hand with it." Tendelli's expression turned to one of relief and Muldoon smiled.

"All right," Kheyntamenti said, hiding his own smile. "Debrief of all commanders in about 45 minutes. I'll see you there." The others saluted and Kheyntamenti climbed back into the Prowler.

Battalion headquarters was a complex of buildings hastily thrown up over the past year near the HUP maintenance area. Nearby, large pits yawned where an underground facility was taking shape. Eventually most of the battalion and its support services would be underground but for now, concrete and steel revetments were about the best they could do for cover.

He stopped by his office, glanced at the pile of paperwork in disgust, and went to get cleaned up and take a shower. As he washed off the accumulated dried sweat from continuously piloting his HUPAX for the past thirty-six hours, he recalled things had been somewhat simpler when he had commanded the Wild Geese as a mercenary unit. Now that they were a part of the Kodomir Militia, he was convinced the reports, memos, letters, and messages he waded through every week weighed more than his Rapier.

As Kheyntamenti emerged from the locker room, one of the headquarters clerks handed him the folder of message traffic. He glanced through it. Nothing pressing – they would have contacted him in the field if there had been. He walked quickly into the staff conference room and someone called everyone to attention. He motioned towards the chairs and sat down at the head of the table.

Not everyone had the chance to get cleaned up before the meeting; Ho'nehe, Muldoon, and Tendelli still had faded streaks of camouflage paint on their faces. Well, he hoped to let them go quickly.

"Our status remains 'Alert' until the landing ship clears Kodomir's system. Latest sensor information shows it headed for a star ship at the stellar navigation beacon, so they probably will not be back but we're taking no chances." He glanced to one side and spotted Gwielgi. "Ops, bring everyone up to date."

"First, battalion status. All companies report ready," Gwielgi said. "Rearming and refueling is ongoing and will probably be completed by midnight. Landing ship Ghost is scheduled to arrive tomorrow from Kiroff Airfield to transport the four spare HUPs with the students to the firing ranges down on Portaka but I am holding Ghost here with the other two

battalion landing ships until we stand down from alert status."
Kheyntamenti nodded in agreement.

"Second, combat analysis. Intel on OPFOR is still coming as we interrogate our prisoners and pull down file info from Swordpoint but a preliminary summary is posted to your datapads. Tactical analysis corroborates individual reports we have so far – they thought they were on a straight raid against the mines and did not expect to encounter serious opposition. Like several of the other merc units to hit us, they did not have independent intelligence on Kodomir and were dependent on their employer. They were also cheap." Gwielgi's voice picked up a tinge of anger. "Someone out there is sending these people in to almost certain destruction. I think we ought to file a complaint with the SFA."

"Tell the Security Forces Agency on Swordpoint that we have too much of an advantage over people attacking our planet?" Captain Hardin asked. "I understand your concern about the fate of mercenaries, Captain Gwielgi, but so far their employer's failure to supply them with accurate intelligence about our order of battle is working to our advantage." He looked at Kheyntamenti. "Do we really want to give that up?"

Kheyntamenti raised a hand as he saw Gwielgi flush.

"Under SFA contract rules, if an employer," Kheyntamenti said, "is omitting critical information to a mercenary unit, that unit may abrogate its contract. At this point, we do not know how many other mercenary raiders are coming our way. Clearly, these raids are serving some purpose for the employer – perhaps they are intelligence probes of our response capabilities, or maybe they are simply soaking-off attacks, or even a diversion of some kind. If we tell the Gray Wolves on Swordpoint what is happening here, it is quite likely the employer will be chastised." He leaned back in his chair. "Mercenary units in transit would be notified and they would probably opt out of their contracts. The SFA might even ban the employer from further contracts. In any case, such a move would disrupt the plans of whoever is behind these raids. It's a reasonable idea."

"However, it is a political decision," Kheyntamenti added. "I will forward the recommendation up the chain of command with a proposed package to be sent to Alpha Centauri." He looked back at his Operations Officer. "Captain, what else do you have?"

"Back to the tactical analysis. Initial analysis reports are also forwarded to you. No deficiencies noted. Tactics sound. Gunnery excellent, especially our armored company – greatly improved from two months ago." Hardin nodded in acknowledgement. "Infantry company performed well, though it encountered problems with the heavy antiarmor missile launchers. I'd like to get back everyone's after action reports within 48 hours. We should have the full battalion AAR back to everyone within 48 hours after that." He looked up from his datapad.

"What we've picked up from the previous five raids includes five APCs and two tanks – Western Command maintenance section reports all operational and all seven vehicles are being assigned to Eastern Command." There was a groan from several officers. Gwielgi smiled. "Now, now, laddies. Eastern is hurting for armor and we have the pick of the litter out here. Besides, the tanks and APCs are not Militia standard, so integrating them is going to be a hassle. The Armored Training Regiment at Kiroff is better equipped to deal with dissimilar armor. But some good news. Doc, you want to fill them in?"

"All right, Gwi." Sevin glanced at his datapad. "From the first five raids we recovered a number of items from the bad guys, about which I'll talk more in a minute because it overlaps with Ops. But the good news referred to is the Saber we captured from this last raid. Revenant lifted it back since it had severe leg damage. It will take about a week to fix that, I estimate. It was used as a designator. Carries a full EW suite and a pair of Class One laser turrets. And the real good news is we get to keep it." Sevin looked at Kheyntamenti. "Right, colonel?"

"Correct. General Polrany is keeping all Militia HUPs with the Western Command. We've got 29 now. Sixteen are with our battalion. The rest are held for training and to replace any casualties. He really wants to have a second heavy combined arms battalion for Eastern Command but until there is a sufficient number of HUPs and trained pilots to fully stock two combined battalions, maintain a reserve, and still meet a training commitment, we get to keep all we capture or are purchased." There were murmurs of approval from around the room. "The one continuing item we have to keep our eye on at present is that we still have the training responsibility for HUPAX. That won't be assigned to the ATR until after the second battalion is equipped and only when there are enough for the

41

job. That means we will still be training HUP pilots for some time to come." He looked at Sevin. "You said you had something to add about recovery, Doc."

"Aye, sir." He looked around the room. "One of the common weapons systems we have recovered has been a pile of very long-range missiles and launchers, mostly SSM1-equivalents, but we also have a couple of SSM2-class missiles. Since most of the attackers have come to hit stationary targets like the mines you can understand why they brought them. We didn't give those units much of a chance to use them and, once we got them, we haven't used them since, as the defenders, we expect to encounter moving targets and SSMs are basically ballistic weapons."

"Like a thrown rock," Gwielgi observed.

"Right, terminal guidance but not terribly agile. Not nearly as sophisticated as our own Frogfires but they have about the same range of fifty kilometers. Nice punch for the weight, though, with a three quarter-ton warhead in the 'Ones' and twice that in the 'Twos'. Variety of manufacturers, as you would expect, but pretty compatible with standard SSM-launchers. Anyway, we have tons of them now, and I mean literally tons. We've got over a dozen SSM1s at five tons apiece and five SSM2s, at eight tons a piece." He looked at Gwielgi. "They need C-level racks but we don't have many HUPs that can afford to drop off a large laser turret just to haul around a one or two shot long-range missile launcher."

"I'll run out and get you a couple of Battle Axes, Doc," Gwielgi said. "Those 200-ton pigs are just what you need."

"I should live so long," Doc said. He turned back to Kheyntamenti. "In any case, I'd like to use them. Maybe they can serve a role in the training syllabus or we can work up some tactical doctrine where they could be used. I'd rather use them up on a range or on some OPFOR than leave them in the ammo dump and have them blow up there. They're going to leave a very big hole."

"Interesting," Gwielgi said. "You're right about why we usually don't carry them on either our HUPs or armored fighting vehicles. Our HUPS aren't big enough to mount those kinds of weapons and still have enough room for more critically needed gear." He rubbed his chin and thought for a moment. "Let me get together with Chi and Captain Hardin and see what we can come up with."

"Don't forget the helicopters," Leba Chinaren said from the back of the room. "With the engine upgrades we are getting and the changeover to MSAT cannon, we can lift more than the short-range missiles we usually carry. I'd like to take a look at those SSMs. We might be able to handle the SSM1s."

"All right," Kheyntamenti said. "That's our committee, then. Captain Gwielgi chair it, Doc, John, Chi, and Leba join in. Come up with a plan we can send up to command and let's see what we can do with those things." He looked at Gwielgi. "Anything else, captain?"

"No, sir, that's it from ops and training."

"All right," Kheyntamenti said. He turned back to the group. "Remember, we are remaining on alert status. Revenant and Zombie are standing by and Ghost will be back tomorrow. If we get hit again, we will be combat-loading those landing ships depending on our tactical decisions, so make sure everyone is ready to move quickly. As Captain Gwielgi noted, the battalion did a good job against these people, but remember the Militia took casualties. We're not celebrating. When we come off alert, I want us to focus on deferred maintenance. When the battalion is fully up, then let's see about getting our people some time off." There were nods around the table – the tradition of the battalion, carried over from its mercenary days, was that everyone worked until the job was done.

"Captain Gwielgi, I'd like to see you for a few minutes. Everyone else, meeting adjourned."

Someone called the room to attention and Kheyntamenti left, followed closely by his operations officer.

"How's your leg?" Kheyntamenti asked as they walked to his office.

"It's coming along, but slowly," Gwielgi admitted. An old injury from the Kodomir liberation battles had been aggravated during the third raid. The medical people had not permitted Gwielgi in a HUP since. "They say it will be another month of conditioning before it will be where it should be. But no more microsurgery or clone grafting."

"One of my spies tells me you went with the grunts when they did their sweep through the kill zone." He went behind his desk and gestured to a chair for Gwielgi.

"Well, yeah, I got bored with sitting in that stifling APC." He held up a hand. "I know, I know, not supposed to do that." He dropped into the chair and rubbed his knee unconsciously. "But I got a chance to talk to one of OPFOR's sergeants before he died. Corroborated what we thought. We have a copy of an old SFA summary on them, courtesy of Mister Carmichael's people."

"What does the spy service of the Free Union Prime Minister have on them?"

"Not much. I sent the file over to your datapad. It looks to me about half of the whole unit dropped on us. The remainder is likely back on Swordpoint."

"So they don't know they've lost half their people..."

"Yeah. It's four and a half months to Alpha Centauri, assuming the star ship takes the remnants directly there and no one calls ahead using subspace."

"What's your estimation of these raids?"

"Invasion coming – these are probes, checking our defenses and capabilities." Gwielgi's voice was firm. "That's why, whoever the employer is, he's using throwaway units, like the Dragons. When he's learned what he wants to know, then his main force units will hit us. The fact that he can afford to sacrifice six merc units means he has a lot of money, so we're not talking some Frontier Raider or an individual world. This has to be someone with a bunch of planets already in his pocket."

"Polrany thinks it is von Bender."

"He may be right." Gwielgi nodded his head and paused. "We are the world that got away from him, and we are looking more and more worth the effort, what with the opening of the mines here and down on Portaka. Not just growing corn on Kodomir anymore. On top of that, Kodomir in unfriendly hands would flank the remains of the Confederacy as well as all of those resource-rich worlds between here and his original holdings."

Kheyntamenti nodded. "Yes, the 'String of Pearls.' Well, I have to go see the CO and do a debrief with him." He yawned and blinked. "Sorry. A little more tired than I thought."

"No problem, boss. I know the feeling." Gwielgi paused. "You might want to know. Colonel Jonivov is not happy with Major Fielding. He was supposed to get his battalion to the valley by helilift in order to block OPFOR from the mines. Apparently, there was some kind of screw up and the battalion never got there. The Dragons creamed the security detachment at the mines. They would have taken out all of Beta complex if they hadn't seen our HUPs coming and pulled out. Word on the base is Fielding is going to be relieved and we're going to see a new commander for the infantry battalion."

"Oh, damn," Kheyntamenti said. "I was hoping Fielding was coming along. Second did all right in the previous raid."

"After stepping on their own shoelaces in the two before that. This was make it or break it time for Fielding, so the story goes." Gwielgi shrugged. He had little patience with inept military commanders, given that someone paid in blood for their mistakes. "Anyway, Jonivov may try to steal Joe Ho'nehe from us to fill the slot, or maybe Joseph Abrande from the First."

"Abrande worked with Jonivov back when he led 3rd Recon and was one of his company commanders. Imael Garito was one as well and now he's CO of First Reconnaissance Battalion under Jonivov."

"You're saying, to avoid a charge of nepotism, he may make a run at our Joe." Gwielgi grinned.

"Well, Joe would make an excellent battalion commander. If he wants the job, I would have no trouble recommending him for it."

"Sure, but I think he wants to stay with the Geese," he said. "You know he has an excellent fashion sense and he probably appreciates the purple berets."

"Don't worry," Kheyntamenti said with a smile. "I'll ask him before I approve the transfer."

"Roger, that, boss," Gwielgi said. "I'm assuming that landing ship is going to clear the system in the next few days. I heard what you said earlier but what is the chance of an administrative stand down so we can get our backed-up maintenance finished?"

"I plan to ask the CO. I'd also like to get the troops some time off. Everyone could use a break."

"Aye." Gwielgi got to his feet. "Well, I'm going to go pound on the after-action reports and see what we can do with all those missiles that Doc's worried about." He adjusted his beret and saluted Kheyntamenti. "Have fun with the colonel, colonel."

"How did it go?" Jonivov looked up from a pile of reports on his desk. Pietr Jonivov was a little below average height and wore his dark hair so short he might have been mistaken for being bald. His dark eyes were bright and steady while the creases around his mouth suggested a man who smiled frequently. He wore no ribbons on his uniform, though he had earned many, but he did wear the silver arrow emblem of a qualified Militia Reconnaissance soldier.

"Fine – they were not expecting to encounter HUPs," Kheyntamenti said and, in response to Jonivov's gesture, sat wearily in a chair opposite his regimental commander, stuffing his rolled beret under an epaulet as he did.

"I monitored the action," Jonivov said. "Your argument to use the landing ships as part of a 'quick-reaction' force I think has been fully supported. Colonel Martin linked into our net and watched how you handled things. He's going to use the recordings when he goes to Militia Headquarters next week to help Polrany argue for building an additional heavy battalion." He leaned back in his chair and smiled. "Bobby wants the battalion added to his command, needless to say."

"He can be persuasive," Kheyntamenti said, "but even if the Assembly comes up with the funds, I suspect General Polrany wants it assigned to Eastern Command and the First Regiment, not out here to the Western Ranges."

"Maybe," Jonivov replied. "Polrany has said more than once our forces around Kiroff are a bit too light. Martin will argue that the landing ships mean we can rapidly respond to an incursion anywhere on Kodomir and it makes more sense logistically and in terms of command and control to have our heavy battalions together."

"Perhaps," Kheyntamenti said, "though even landing ships take time to load up and move to another position on a planet. If they, whoever they are, start hitting the settlements in the southern hemisphere, we may be hard pressed to get there in time from here. After all, when we drove out Storm Cloud, their forces were entirely on this continent."

"Our air command is using that argument to try to get more fighters and some kind of orbital defensive system."

"Well, they may have a point," Kheyntamenti said, "and our old Swallows need at least upgrading…"

"As does damn near every other weapon in our inventory," Jonivov said. He grimaced and shook his head. "I heard the crew-served antiarmor missile launchers had some problems." Kheyntamenti nodded. "Old equipment well beyond its life expectancy, all bought on the open market." Jonivov was no longer smiling. "When you get me the report on them, I'm taking it over to Bobby Martin personally. We've got to have a reliable antiarmor punch for our infantry – can't be totally dependent on either tanks or HUPs." He leaned back in his chair. "Well, I guess that's going to primarily be an issue for command and the politicians." He paused and his smile returned. "Weren't you the one who told Polrany that if he succeeded in freeing Kodomir that one of the consequences would be he would end up having to become a politician? He referred to that in a staff conference call he had with the regimental COs a while back."

"Yes, I did," said Kheyntamenti. "Of course, back then I thought there was little chance of it ever happening, given the disproportionate forces involved. We didn't even know that there *was* an underground when he hired the Wild Geese, nor did we know where the Militia regular cadre had been sold into slavery."

"I know, I read Gwielgi's book." Jonivov shook his head. "Good yarn, can't wait for the tri-vid. A little embarrassing to be described in such heroic terms, though. But let me get us back on track – I know you want to get back to your battalion. So…" he looked down at a report, "no major damage to any battalion equipment, and only a handful of wounded. Did you get anything from those four prisoners?"

"Six, colonel," Kheyntamenti corrected. "Two of the HUP pilots survived, which we didn't know when we sent in the first report. So the count is six now. We also recovered a damaged Saber. A full report will be coming by tomorrow."

"That's good news," Jonivov said. "It will help with getting funding for the other heavy battalion since we now have a bunch of extra HUPs." He frowned. "Damn, I'm beginning to think more and more like a politician myself. In any case, did you get anything from the *six* prisoners?"

"Pretty much what we have gotten from the others." Even though obviously tired, Kheyntamenti's voice was precise. "They are on their way to command intelligence. They were half of a mercenary unit called Dahlgren's Dragons; it hasn't operated on this side of the Settled Worlds until now. They are a mixed force of HUPs and infantry. This unit has been around awhile but was carrying a mediocre SFA rating, according to the summary. So they came cheap. The other mercs were relatively new and scrambling to build reputations and contracts, so they came cheap as well. They have no idea who hired them – they all were handled through a broker licensed by the SFA on Swordpoint. Like the others, the Dragons were misinformed as to what to expect. They all agree they were told there were no HUPs here and little aviation." He shook his head. "For throw-away units, I would expect an employer to hire through one of the 'black' or 'gray' sources rather than the Security Forces Agency. I guess they want to ensure the units will abide by their contracts."

"On the other hand," Jonivov noted, "this was the heaviest unit to attack us. Six HUPs of their own?"

"Eight," Kheyntamenti said. "They held two back, along with some armored vehicles, to protect their landing zone. They were able to evacuate successfully."

"What about their landing ship?"

"Imagery shows it belongs to another merc unit that often hires out its landing ships for transport purposes. The unit itself, the Dural Fusiliers, is on garrison duty in the Siberon Duchy of the Cygnus Eastern Alliance. It has a long-term contract so its landing ship is free for hire."

Jonivov smiled. "I understand our pilots took a few shots at it as it left."

"True," Kheyntamenti said, "though it did not use its armament in defending the Dragons. We might want to send a message to the Dragons and the Fusiliers with a copy to the SFA on Swordpoint and get some clarification on the landing ship's status. Was it contracted to fight or just transport?"

"Good idea – I hadn't thought of that. Despite working with the Wild Geese since the liberation, there's still a lot about mercenaries and their contract procedures that I don't understand."

"I think there's an opportunity here for us to take some heat off, colonel," Kheyntamenti said, leaning forward. "If the employer of these merc units deliberately supplied false or incomplete information on the objective, the mercenary units may have the right to abrogate their contracts. Letting the Dragons and Fusiliers and the others who already struck us know that would be too late to do us much good, but if we tell the SFA, they may take action against the employer. The impact of that could be that merc units on their way here or considering taking a contract might pull out."

"I see," Jonivov said slowly. "Though I would think the merc units we've fought thus far would be yelling at the employer themselves."

"Possibly not," Kheyntamenti said. "We've had six raids in five months." He held up his hand and began to count off fingers. "There were no survivors of the first raid who made it back to the landing ship, that little armor and infantry merc unit called Connors' Long Swords. Their survivors are all in our hands. The landing ship was a private contractor who left pretty quickly. The second unit, the Vindicators, came slightly less than four months ago – they would still be two or three weeks from Alpha Centauri and any chance to lodge a complaint. We haven't heard anything on subspace so their star ship probably doesn't have subspace communications capability."

"Expensive system," Jonivov said, nodding. "Most civilian star ships don't have them."

"The remaining four units, including the Dragons and the Fusiliers who brought them here, have not had time to get to Alpha Centauri. So unless they've stopped in transit and used a subspace communication station or they are using a top-notch star ship with its own subspace system, the SFA doesn't know." Kheyntamenti paused. "I think whoever hired these people may have deliberately arranged transport with ships not having subspace communication systems."

"Nothing about these units has seemed top-notch," Jonivov said. "They've been hired from the cheap end of the scale. And you think our telling the SFA about the situation might cut off other units considering coming here?"

"I think there's a good chance of it, colonel. It will help that it comes from us," Kheyntamenti said, tapping the Wild Geese emblem on his beret. "While the Geese are a part of the active Militia, we have kept our official status open as far as the Security Forces Agency on Swordpoint is concerned. General Polrany thinks it gives us access to useful intelligence information and I think the Assembly sees us as having the potential to one day, in the words of First Minister Jevon, 'become an important revenue stream.'"

"The First Minister is always alert to new sources of money," Jonivov said, his expression blank. He looked down at the report in his hands. "I'll recommend to command we have you send a message to Alpha Centauri. In the short term, however, the important issue is the simple fact of these raids, all generated by an unknown party."

"Unknown?" Kheyntamenti sent an eyebrow up.

"*Officially* unknown," Jonivov amended. He dropped the report on his desk and slid back in his chair. "You and I both know, as does anyone else with eyes, that we're being hit by Baron Karl von Bender. When he invaded the Confederacy, it was to outflank the String of Pearls lying between his little empire and us. Even though he paid off those Storm Cloud Raiders with Kodomir, I think even their leader Iriki Tykaw knew that sooner or later von Bender would want to add Kodomir to his collection."

"Greed leads to greed."

"Well, he can afford it." Jonivov gestured at his desk. "According to our latest intelligence summaries, the last of the String of Pearls just agreed to join the Benderist Holdings. With their potential wealth, he more than has the means to conquer Kodomir if it gets down to it, though I think his real concern will be securing the flank of his expanded Holdings."

"What will be the position of the Free Union if that happens?"

"I don't know," Jonivov said. "Prime Minister Carmichael is totally focused on Mariah Connor and the Protectorate and their little disagreement over who should rule this chunk of the universe. Kodomir is pretty small potatoes in that whole mess. A year ago I would have said Peter Mavis Carmichael would squash anyone trying to overrun a world that has declared officially for him, as we have, even if the attacker was an ally like Bender. But now..." He shook his head. "The word I get is he is working hard to keep everyone in line – that's why he let von Bender overrun our Confederacy. He might let von Bender take a run at us as a reward for being a big supporter."

"Meaning von Bender will continue to hire mercenaries to keep us off balance until he can either gather his own strength or hire enough to come and take over."

"That's my best guess, unless we can reach some sort of accommodation with him."

"I have not heard of anything in that direction," Kheyntamenti said.

"No, neither have I. But," Jonivov paused, "Kodomir's history is filled with examples of it. Remember, Jevon thought that's what he was negotiating with Bender about before the Storm Cloud invasion. I would presume Bender knows that we are willing to be reasonable."

"Perhaps the problem is that Bender is not willing to be reasonable."

"Baron Karl von Bender, not reasonable?" Jonivov smiled. "Colonel Kheyntamenti, I'm shocked that you can even suggest such a thing." Kheyntamenti smiled slightly in return. Jonivov turned back to his reports.

"All right, get me the report when you can and a list of any material you need to replace depleted stocks." He glanced at a sheaf of papers. "A couple of other things. I'm replacing 2nd Battalion's CO. Both Captain Ho'nehe and Captain Joseph Abrande are in line for the job and would be excellent. Unlike some of the other Geese officers, Joe is well known personally throughout the Militia. Not too many people alive wear the Kodomiri Cross with Stars. Either man could kick the 2nd into shape. I know from his most recent fitness report you would recommend him for a higher command and they need an infantry type. Do you mind if I invite him in for a discussion?"

"Not at all," Kheyntamenti said. "Joe's one of the best. He won that Cross by fast thinking and raw leadership, and that's his trademark. He would be a superb battalion commander if he wants it." Kheyntamenti knew he did not have to elaborate on the point. Jonivov was the Militia officer who recommended Ho'nehe for the award.

Jonivov nodded. "Abrande's been running the training program for the Recon school, technically 3rd Infantry Training Regiment (Reconnaissance), my old command. It's not much more than a battalion in terms of total numbers and it has him behind the desk. He's another good man and General Polrany would like to see him get a field command. He's very sharp and is coming off a training billet. That could come in very handy getting the 2nd straightened out."

"Nice to have two good choices."

Jonivov nodded and then smiled. "One other thing. Some good news." He rose from his desk and went to a wall that blinked into a map of the Western Ranges Command when he touched a small control panel.

"The First and Third Chekinov Scouts are going to run a field exercise up in the Northern Training Area in two weeks against the Second Scouts and our own First Recon. Most of the exercise will be a purely grunt affair;

no armor, no air, no arty, and no HUPs. But they want the exercise to open with a simulated HUP raid." He turned back to Kheyntamenti as he pointed to the training area.

"Major William Coltrane wants his scout battalions to become more familiar with HUPs and landing ships. He's been reading the reports of our combined arms battalion and thinks his troops would benefit from some familiarization work."

"You mentioned last month," Kheyntamenti said, "he was thinking in that direction. I'm glad to hear he wants to proceed. Those Scouts are great light infantry and excellent mountain troops, but they have not kept up with using other forces." For a moment Kheyntamenti studied the map with its overlay of the exercise. "So what would he like us to do?"

"We're going to use four HUPs and simulate a combat drop into this valley. I'd like you to bring HUPs mounting an array of firepower – missiles, rail guns, lasers – so they get to see what the different configurations can do. We'll have a range set up for that. Then we'll want to do some combined work with the scouts serving as forward observers and the HUPs providing supporting fire. A Snapfire exercise." He shut down the map.

"I'll send over an op order later today. Coltrane will be available to work up the specifics. Remember, the Chekinovs are still feeling their way through this assimilation business and they have tended to keep their soldiers in the scout battalions. That's fine as far as it goes but General Polrany feels we need to get them more into the mainstream of the Militia, integrated rather than segregated. So he's pushing to increase the number of these joint exercise opportunities."

"I understand," Kheyntamenti said. "This is good news."

"Oh, well, what I meant by 'good news,'" Jonivov said as he sat down, "is that I'm going to get out from behind this desk for the exercise. While the scouts report directly to Western command, Garito's First Recon belongs to the regiment, so I'm going to get off my out-of-shape butt and join them up in the hills for a few days."

"I see," Kheyntamenti said. He smiled. "You have my sympathy. I was reminded again today how it was in the old days, before Kodomir made the Wild Geese citizens. Things were a bit simpler then."

"Agreed," Jonivov said, and gestured at his desk. "The next time mercs or Raiders come, I think I'll just drop this paperwork on them instead of our battalions."

"Probably a violation of the rules of war, sir." Jonivov smiled and Kheyntamenti continued. "I'd like to stand the battalion down as soon as that landing ship clears to catch up on rest and maintenance."

"Good idea," Jonivov said. "When it joins its star ship and leaves, take your battalion off alert and go to condition 'Charley.' Seventy-two hour status is plenty of response time. Chase your kids into town for some R and R, and take some leave yourself."

"Aye, sir, and thank you."

Kheyntamenti was still smiling at Jonivov's joke when he returned to the battalion headquarters. He stopped by his desk to survey the battalion companies and their status. Satisfied with what he saw, he began to sketch out a series of brief proposals for the exercise with the Chekinov Scouts.

The reality, of course, was that even though the Chekinovs had fought side by side with their old adversaries, the Kodomir Militia, against a common enemy, there still were divisive issues. The Assembly had declared the Chekinov Tribal Areas off limits to developers, especially mining, but the war with the Storm Cloud Raiders, the appellation given the pirate bands that came out of the Frontier from time to time, had some unexpected negative consequences. The Militia Tribal Liaison Officer cadre was still being rebuilt after the Raider massacre that drove the tribes to join the Kodomiri in their fight. The cost of rebuilding after the war had limited funding for the development of the tribes – a large number of services, including schools and hospitals, were only slowly getting into place.

And, as always among humans, there was their history. The Chekinovs landed on Kodomir over three centuries before the people generally called Kodomiri, losing their technology in the process. Who they had been and where they came from were questions lost in time and replaced by legend and myth. The next wave of human settlement made contact with what was by now a tribal people and disaster followed. Disease was the first horror, though the Kodomiri worked feverishly to find a cure. Then came the never-ending conflict over the tribal lands, lands the Chekinov regarded as sacred. Sometimes the conflict was restricted to the floor of the Assembly, but often it had been an affair of ambush and battle.

There had been combat and even atrocities on both sides, though both struggled to find a path to some sort of assimilation and accommodation. Now the Chekinov described themselves as Kodomiri, though, like many of the groups living on Kodomir, they still maintained their cultural roots within the predominant Afro-Russian blend. And there was still a distance between the Kodomiri mainstream and the Chekinov. Old wounds, biases, and prejudices were not totally erased by the joining of both sides in a violent and valiant struggle against the Raiders.

Kheyntamenti looked over his proposals and then attached them to a message for William Coltrane. It would provide at least a starting point for planning the exercise. He leaned back in his chair and stretched, gazing at the late afternoon sun. It would be good to give the troops a chance to stand down. They needed the rest.

And they would need it, he knew. Gwielgi was right. War was coming again to Kodomir.

The question was, from where?

Chapter 3: Warriors

18 May 2824

Major William Coltrane crouched in the trees at the south end of the valley. The spring sun hardly penetrated into the deep forest but the tall trees seemed to capture and amplify the heat. Sweat slowly ran down his face and neck, smearing his camouflage paint.

He moved his eyes slowly. The other members of his command group were scattered around him and, even at close range, were difficult to see. As it should be. The Tsalagi, the formal term the Chekinov people used for themselves, were a part of the forests and mountains. Even the two who were not Tsalagi, the Wild Geese liaison, Sergeant Steven Tashan, and the Militia Liaison Officer, Captain Peter Arkady, held their positions in a fashion similar to that of his own troops.

Coltrane's earphone hissed twice. He tapped his microphone at the side of his mouth and then raised his hand and slowly clenched it. Slight movement in the bushes around him reflected the passing on of the signal. Then he opened his hand and pointed downhill.

The command group moved slowly down the slope, headed for a rocky outcrop that would give them a good view of the valley. Sergeant Tashan caught his eye and tapped his own headset and then gave him a "thumbs up" signal. Coltrane nodded in response. The Wild Geese landing ship was descending on schedule.

From the outcrop they saw the entire length of the valley. A small river ran through it, its twisting course reflecting sunlight like steel. Arkady and two Scouts busied themselves with setting up a large laser designator. In a moment they had its invisible ultraviolet beam playing on a clearing half way down the valley. That would be the landing zone. Coltrane looked at the Wild Geese sergeant, almost invisible in his nanosuit that automatically mimicked the foliage around him. For a moment the man did nothing, holding his headset firmly against his ears, listening. Then he smiled and gestured upward with his thumb. Coltrane looked into the valley. There was nothing to be seen.

Arkady touched his elbow and pointed high above them. Piercing the blue of the Kodomiri sky was what looked like an exceptionally bright star, just a pinpoint of bright light. It was moving, but very slowly. The landing ship?

Then it moved sideways, picking up speed as it sped across the sky. The light diminished in size and then blinked out of existence. Only now could they hear a faint rumble of its engines. He looked at Tashan and raised his eyebrows.

Where are the HUPAX?

The Wild Geese sergeant smiled, but said nothing, just held up a finger. Wait.

For a few seconds he maintained the gesture, and then he leveled his finger. It took Coltrane a second to realize he was pointing. He turned as Arkady touched his sleeve again.

Four small orange fireballs, at about the same altitude as Coltrane, were descending into the valley. Leaving dark gray smoke trails behind them, the HUPAX were too distant to see clearly, even to the sharp eyes of the Chekinov scouts, but they were heading for the landing zone. The faint roar of their descent rocket packs echoed up the valley.

Coltrane was impressed. The HUPAX must have stepped out of their landing ship several kilometers above and then free fell before firing their rockets. Probably had to use some sort of drogue parachutes to maintain stability in the fall, he thought. Clearly, they had sensors capable of seeing the illuminated landing zone. He wondered how they steered themselves on the way down – their landing ship captain must have been very precise at giving them the word to go.

Sergeant Tashan murmured into his microphone while studying his map. Coltrane used his binoculars in time to see the four HUPs land in the clearing in formation, each facing outward, and drop their descent rocket packs. Almost immediately they were moving, coming up the riverbank.

"Tell them we are headed for the rendezvous," he said to Tashan. "And extend my compliments to the team leader. Impressive display."

He touched his own headset and ordered everyone to move to the rendezvous. Acknowledgements came in from the battalion commanders. He put his hands to his mouth a made a birdcall. He heard it relayed across the hillside and soon the whole unit headed downhill.

The four HUPAX stood at the edge of the river on a broad gravel bar. Coltrane's people were the last to arrive and join the crowd of Chekinov and Recon soldiers gathered around them.

The four HUP pilots were talking with Colonel Jonivov as Coltrane walked up to them. The regimental commander, clad in a camouflage uniform, smiled as Coltrane saluted.

"Major Coltrane, I think you know our HUP drivers," Jonivov said as he returned the salute. "Lieutenant Chi Lore, Staff Sergeant Stephanie Elinshen, Gunnery Sergeant Sevin, and Gunnery Sergeant Charles Tsunasdi." Hands were shook and Coltrane looked up at the HUPs towering over them.

"Every time I see these machines," Coltrane said, "I remember how Storm Cloud used them to massacre our people in the valley." He looked at the pilots. "And I remember how you used them to free our people. It is a strange feeling."

"I can believe that," Elinshen said. She looked up at the HUPs. Of varying heights, the tallest was slightly higher than a two-story building. "Much of their impact on the battlefield is psychological."

"The rest is their firepower and mobility," Coltrane said. "The array of weapons is astounding."

"We are ready for the demonstration," Elinshen said. "We'll pair a HUP with each battalion. Colonel Jonivov told us there are targets scattered up the length of the valley and each battalion has its own patrol route."

"Right," Jonivov said. "The battalions will work through the woods and do Snapfire designations of targets as they encounter them. The HUPs will be about 500 meters behind and will fire on the targets as they are illuminated, using lasers, rail guns, or ion weapons. As the battalions complete their courses, they will come to a location where they will see their last target at range. The HUPs will engage those last targets with missiles." He turned to Coltrane.

"While their sensors are quite thorough, the HUPs will be visually blind in the trees unless they are standing on the target. The plan you and Colonel Kheyntamenti developed will require everyone being on their toes to avoid friendly fire incidents, so we're stressing that the HUPs will not fire until they see a solid designation for three seconds. That way if someone drops a designator the HUP won't fire on a spurious signal."

"I understand, Colonel," Coltrane said. "But I have briefed the Scout battalions that fire will be instantaneous, so they will not designate *unless* they are clear. This will model combat conditions."

Jonivov paused for a moment before answering. "All right," he finally said. "Lieutenant Chi Lore, your team's orders are changed. Fire as soon as the target is designated. First Recon will operate in the same fashion." He turned back to Coltrane. "Major, we will do it your way, but make sure everyone understands what poor visual-range visibility the HUP pilots have in the trees, so tell them to keep their heads down."

A chronic problem for HUPs was their difficulty seeing around them; a HUPAX's armored cockpit's viewing ports were deliberately small to give incoming fire less of a target and usually were covered with armor while in the field.

HUP pilots depended on the visual feed provided to the optical centers of their brains through the mindlink connecting them with the HUP's computer and sensors. Besides the normal visual range, a HUP typically could amplify or magnify its viewing or make use of infrared and ultraviolet visibility. With additional and specialized sensors, other portions of the electromagnetic spectrum, mass detection, and a wide variety of exotic active and passive signals could be converted into imagery for the pilot's brain. All of it could be overlaid with tactical symbols from the machine's datalink and IFF systems. The integration of all the information was a formidable challenge for the pilot.

Stephanie Elinshen climbed the metal rungs to her HUP's cockpit. She hated using the rungs, much preferring the use of gantries or "cherry-picker" ground support equipment. But in the field such niceties of rear echelon support were not always available. She swung into the cockpit of the Long Sword. It took a moment to secure the harness on the ejection seat. She checked that the path of the clam-shell doors that would envelop the seat if she ejected were clear and then pulled on the tight, flexible mindlink helmet.

Elinshen plugged its cord into the cockpit line and then switched the power on. The instrument displays blossomed into life as the 85-ton killing machine woke up and started its built-in test sequence. Elinshen secured the cockpit hatch and felt her ears lightly pop as the cockpit was pressurized. She closed her eyes and initiated the mindlink.

The Long Sword's computer touched her brain and then suddenly, as far as her senses were concerned, she *was* the HUP. Her vision became that of the HUP's sensors. At the moment, she saw predominantly in the visual to ultraviolet spectrum, her settings used while descending and watching the laser designator of the landing zone. Where she looked a targeting reticle appeared and she knew the turreted weapons followed her gaze. Information the computer thought significant scrolled in the periphery of her vision.

She stepped without moving her body; the Long Sword stepped instead. Capable of carrying twenty tons of weapons and gear, today the Long Sword traveled light. A missile launcher occupied the upper portion of the HUP's fuselage while a rail gun turret perched on one shoulder. A small GTL1 laser turret occupied the "head" position above her armored cockpit.

"Geese Two is up."

"Roger, Two. Second Battalion is forming up at your three o'clock. You should see their transponder."

In the right of Elinshen's vision a blue triangle appeared. She looked at it and the number *2* appeared next to it. Other triangles representing the transponders of the other battalions appeared.

"Two has the 'ponder. On the move."

"Roger, Two. Have fun."

Elinshen turned and walked towards the triangle. She felt the ground underneath the HUP's metal feet and automatically balanced her self, and therefore the HUP, as she moved forward.

On Kodomir large forest areas on the northern continent of Karin compounded the problem of seeing. HUP pilots often could not visually see their target in those environments until they walked on top of them. Exercises repeatedly showed that defending infantry units would get the first shot in before the HUP spotted its opponents unless a particular sensor, such as synthetic aperture radar, magnetic anomaly, or infrared, managed to see something.

The technique to deal with that kind of situation was called Snapfire, though some of its developers had come to use different phrases, none of them complimentary. A spotter would use a designator to illuminate a target. The HUP's complex array of sensors picked up the reflected energy. If the HUP could not see the reflection, the designator would automatically tell the HUP where the target was, using its own position and determining the position of the target by the direction and distance of the laser beam. The HUP's S-computer took the information and projected it in three dimensions into the pilot's visual field. When the pilot placed the targeting reticle on the projected point, it would respond just as if it actually had a clear line of sight. Then the pilot could fire on the illuminated point. While the name implied it happened quickly, Snapfire always took time. Not only did the spotter and the pilot have to coordinate their actions, but even the firepower of a HUPAX could not always immediately reach the target. In effect, the weapons had to carve a path to the target. In forests, for example, it took time for lasers to blow apart the intervening trees.

The Wild Geese had learned to use rail guns and their hypervelocity slugs to rip through the trees and clear the way for lasers. If the firing sequence was correct, if the rail gun knocked down enough trees, if the lasers followed close enough to catch the target before it moved, if the pilot was quick enough when the target was illuminated, if the spotter could keep the target illuminated, if... Names used instead of the official one were quite colorful. The least offensive was "Splinter Making."

For HUPs equipped only with lasers, things were more complicated. Some pilots favored a "pile driver" approach of large laser turrets sequentially fired, each clearing a path for the next, while others thought a mass firing of all lasers worked better. The issue, still debated, was yet to be settled.

It was typical of the Chekinov Scouts to insist on combat conditions for their first trials. They trained hard. While they had been involved in fighting off only one of the six recent raids, they had demonstrated emphatically that their Spartan-like training worked. The burned wreckage of a mercenary armored column still littered a pass north of the mines.

Sergeant Stephanie Elinshen knew all this as she followed the Second Scout Battalion. In fact, she knew it better than most as she was one of the pilots involved in the development of the tactic. She maneuvered her Long Sword carefully, watching that she did not run up on the Scouts. This meant being far enough back that the trees she knocked over did not land on any friendly troops. The Chekinov infantry seemed alert to the dangers and were keeping well away. She nodded to herself. They were catching on to the need to be far enough away from the HUPs to avoid being hit by enemy fire or being stepped on and far enough away from the target to be able to see it without catching any of the fire directed at it.

Her visual field suddenly showed a steady yellow box to the left, towards the valley. She looked towards it and instinctively swiveled the HUP's fuselage toward the target, invisible deep in the trees, and picked up her speed. The targeting reticle slid over the yellow box of the reflected signal and turned red. She triggered her laser.

The red beam sliced from the Long Sword's head turret. It lasted only an instant but it was bright enough to dazzle the sight of anyone standing close by. The heat of the beam was so great it literally burned away the atmosphere it encountered. When the beam stopped, it left a column of vacuum. As the column collapsed under the pressure of the atmosphere, a whip-crack snapped through the air.

The beam itself exploded the trees it touched – the moisture inside them became superheated steam and ripped the trees apart from within. It happened so fast the trees did not usually have time to burn.

The rail gun slug followed a half second later. The slug, a core of hardened tungsten alloy surrounded by a sabot of copper, sliced through the vacuum of the gun, impelled by superconducting rails. As it reached the weapon's muzzle, doors snapped open just long enough for the slug to clear and then snapped closed again as pumps worked furiously to restore the vacuum. Its path largely cleared by the laser, the slug moved at ten times the speed of sound and discarded its copper sabot almost immediately. The tungsten core, extremely aerodynamic, lost little of its energy as it shot through the last few trees and struck the target, an old armored personnel carrier, and passed through it. Molten metal flew in all directions, starting several small fires.

Elinshen increased magnification and confirmed the targeting designator was still illuminating the target. She fired. Now nothing existed to block the beam and all the energy of the laser struck the thin hull of the APC. More metal flew in glowing sheets while the remainder of the hull virtually vaporized. The laser ripped through and struck the hidden smoke bomb.

She saw a column of green smoke rising above the trees as the designator signal blinked out.

"Check fire and hold, Geese Two. We have a couple of fires to put out before we can proceed."

"Roger, Scout Two. Standing by."

The problem with live fire exercises in the forest was always the possibility of setting the forest on fire. She hoped that the cached fire extinguishers near each target were fully charged. A few minutes passed.

"Blue Two, fires out. We are moving out."

"Roger, in trail."

She slowly advanced the HUP. The Long Sword was light compared to the biggest HUPAX, only 85 tons, and getting through the tall Kodomiri trees was not simple. She steered around the biggest trees but still found her progress slowed. It did not matter much, since she was following the scouts who were all on foot.

A yellow box suddenly appeared on her sensor screen. Already? It was almost directly ahead – to get a red reticle all she had to do was lower her gaze slightly from the horizontal. Still, she hesitated a second, waiting to see if the designator remained on. It did and she fired.

She could not see what she was hitting but followed the same procedure as before, firing the rail gun quickly after the laser.

"Check fire! Check fire!"

The radio call came like a blow to the stomach. Elinshen froze in her seat, instinctively putting her weapons on safe. She waited but heard nothing. Finally, she keyed her transmitter.

"Scout Two. Say your status."

There was nothing, not even the hiss of a carrier wave.

"Scout, say your status."

Still there was nothing. She switched her transmitter.

"All units, Geese Two. We may have an accident in the exercise. Ghost, recommend you lift and return to the valley in case we need a medevac."

"Geese Two, this is Ghost. Roger. I am lifting and should arrive in eleven minutes."

"Geese Two, Recon One. Sarge, what is the nature of the injuries?"

"Unknown, colonel. I got a 'check fire' and no further response to my calls."

"Roger. Let me know when you get something."

"Aye, sir." Elinshen switched channels. "Scout Two, Geese Two. Say your status."

There was a delay, but only for a few seconds.

"Geese Two, Scout Two. We have eight casualties, two serious. Can you contact the landing ship for a medevac?"

"Already on the way, Scout Two." Elinshen paused. "What happened?"

"Tree exploded. Splinters caught some of us, falling branches a couple more. Mostly what we have are lacerations, which the medics have under control. But we have a back injury and a head from a falling branch. Medics want to move both of them out."

"Roger, Scout. Landing ship ETA ten minutes. Can the injured be moved?"

"If we have to – the medics would prefer to keep it at a minimum."

"Roger, Scout. I'm going to let Ghost know. Back in one."

She switched channels once more.

"Ghost, Geese Two. We have casualties for medevac. We need you to land as close as possible. I will be your beacon."

"Understood, Geese Two. Our medics and sickbay are standing by. Nature of the injuries?"

"We have several with lacerations but the serious ones are a head injury and a back injury."

"Roger."

"Ghost, come on over to Tac Five. Break. Recon One, did you copy?"

"Roger, Geese Two. I'll monitor Tac Five."

Elinshen switched back.

"Scout Two, Geese Two. Ghost is inbound and will home on me. Recommend you move the battalion up the hill and get them out of the way. I'll get as close to the injured as we can."

"Understood."

Elinshen walked forward and drove a path towards the wounded. She could feel the resistance of the trees against her. Just short of the injured, carefully watching what was around her, she turned her HUP down the hill. She pushed the trees apart. Where they resisted, she used her lasers to cut them down. Soon a fairly clear path led from the target area.

"Geese Two, Ghost. We're descending. We have your beacon. Position fixed. You can get out of the way."

"Roger, Ghost. The injured are just uphill. I've made a path."

"Roger, we see it."

The Long Sword moved out of the landing zone. Elinshen looked up and saw the Viper-class landing ship descending, its engines putting out bright columns of fire. Trying to avoid starting forest fires, Ghost's captain switched her engines on and off, trying to use the aerodynamic shape of the landing ship to slow it down. As it landed, tree trunks and branches flew about. Smoldering small columns of smoke were scattered around the landing zone.

The landing ship's bay doors slid back before it touched down and a loading ramp quickly reached out to the hillside. A medic team carrying stretchers ran down the ramp and disappeared into the forest, following the rough path carved by the Long Sword.

"Scout, Geese Two. Medics on the way."

"Roger."

Then there was nothing to do but wait. Elinshen watched the clock, occasionally taking a sip of water from a canteen.

"Ghost, Medic Lead. We have both injured strapped in and are coming to you now. Estimating five minutes. We will need immediate evacuation to Coyote Bay. Ask them to have a helo standing by for transport to the hospital. Sending vitals to sickbay. Two other injured are walking and will accompany us. The others will remain here."

"Ghost copies."

After a few minutes, Elinshen saw the small group emerge from the trees. They wasted no time and moved quickly up the ramp. Before the ramp was completely withdrawn the landing ship rose and moved forward, ignoring the danger of fires. In a few seconds, it was gone, disappearing behind the mountains.

"Geese Two, Scout Two. We are ready to resume the exercise."

Elinshen blinked. She knew Chekinov, had fought with them against Storm Cloud, and had received briefings on them like all members of the Militia. When it came to war or preparing for war, they were deadly serious, much like her own first people, the Currahee. Still, it was surprising to hear the call to continue right after the accident.

She grinned in her cockpit and decided she liked these people. They reminded her of her...

"Roger, Scout Two. Let's do it."

Chapter 4: The machinations of princes

18 May 2824

The woman, her hair streaked with gray, keyed the security pad and entered her office, leaving the noisy hall behind. Her rented office was not very large – any money she did not use for expenses went into her pocket. She threw her dark cape over a small table and sat behind her desk. The furnishings were thin with just a few chairs, her desk, a couple of small tables, and little else. But her computer console and communication equipment were all top of the line. Black's Gray Wolves, the rulers of Swordpoint and the administrators of the Security Forces Agency, could provide whatever you wanted for the right price and she had the best.

On top of which she had her own encryption devices. Of course, there was a good chance the Gray Wolves could penetrate her security systems. But that didn't matter. Her employer was not planning on going to war with the Gray Wolves.

She placed her hand on the dead screen of the console and it sprang to life, recognizing her fingerprints. She then entered a series of passwords, confirming that she lived and that no one was breaking into her system by the simple expedient of cutting off her hand and using it to fool the system. She shook her head. It seemed pretty melodramatic, but her employer paid her well and regularly, so she did not mind the process.

Several subspace-conveyed messages waited for her. While the subspace communication system was well capable of conveying video across star systems, her employer chose to only use text. She tapped the first message.

>Message begins: Dahlgren's Dragons evacuated Kodomir on 5/5/24. Heavy casualties. No dispute on release of contracted funds held by SFA. No bonuses earned. Remains of landing party not expected to arrive Alpha Centauri for four months. : Message ends<

Well, she thought the Dragons were a little light for the contract, but the employer seemed uninterested in the results. "No bonuses earned" meant they had not inflicted any damage to their target, the group of mines the Kodomiri called "Mining Development Area Beta." She touched part of her screen.

A list of previous contracts sprung open: six raids and all failures. The first two had been against the Militia bases at Kiroff City, the capital, and Coyote Bay. The next three targeted the biggest mining complex, Alpha. Collateral damage to the Militia had been minimal. Half the mercenary units had not had HUPAX support and none had aviation. She shook her head. Her employer seemed intent on throwing money away. Well, as long as *her* paycheck cashed.

She quickly added the latest defeat to the contract list and deleted the message. She tapped her screen for the next one.

>Message begins: Contracts seven, eight, and nine should take effect over the next three months. Advise if schedule cannot be maintained. Important. : Message ends<

She looked back at the list of contracts. Everything already was underway. The three mercenary units would be hitting Kodomir right on their contract dates. She grimaced. She had already told her employer that. Was someone getting nervous? She dictated a quick reply and then read the next message.

>Message begins: Contract 10 funding now on deposit your operational account with the Traders Exchange Database. Parameters of Contract 10 are as follows.

A. Unit must field at least twenty-four (24) HUPAX; preference will be for larger unit.

B. Unit must have a SFA rating of at least 78; 85+ is preferred.

C. Contract will be for a military raid – primary target is the Militia base at Portaka. Destruction of 50% of existing, permanent structures will constitute successful completion of the contract.

D. Secondary target is the industrial and refining complex east of the Portaka Militia Base. Full Bonus will be tied to each 10% of the complex destroyed.

E. Secondary target is the Kodomir Militia. Full Bonus will be tied to each HUPAX destroyed. 1% Bonus for each ten Militia KIA.

F. Tertiary target is the Kodomir Militia base at Coyote Bay. This target may accrue bonus payments utilizing criteria in (E) above.

G. No penalty for collateral damage.

H. As with other contracts, unit must be registered with TED/SFA.

Contract fee is raised 25% above standard used thus far. Full Bonus to be set at 5% of total contract fee. Usual parameters for unit expenses granted.

Most important. Unit must strike Kodomir no later than 1 November 2824. Advise if unable to meet deadline. : Message ends.<

Coyote Bay again? But what was the industrial complex? And where was Portaka? She waved her hand over her console and a holographic projection of Kodomir blossomed above her desk. There it was, in the southern hemisphere. She touched a corner of the projection and the view of the continent expanded. Another touch overlaid colors of population density, geographical features, cities and towns, and so forth. She studied the map for a moment, her brow furrowed as she concentrated.

Portaka was exceedingly uninviting. If the rest of Kodomir was made up of tropical islands and fertile agricultural landmasses, Portaka compensated for all the greenery by being about as desolate a piece of rock as it could be. Extending from just south of the equator down to the Antarctic zone, it was mostly desert, broken by mountain chains that kept moisture from penetrating to the interior. What little vegetation there was seemed to be clinging for its life on the coastlines, where the few towns hung on. The Militia base there was little more than an airfield with a chain-link fence around it or was when this information made its way to the Gray Wolf database. She smiled; easy kills and almost a guaranteed bonus.

If Portaka seemed an inconsequential but easy target, the industrial complex was clearly significant and she wondered why her employer had not targeted it in the past. Of course, the Militia Base at Coyote Bay would be a hell of a fight to gain any target bonuses. But making the base on Portaka a primary target made no sense. What was the point? Were her employers crazy?

She thought about the pattern of raids. Always under strength or weak units sent against hard targets. Now she would hire a relatively powerful unit, but send it against an extremely easy target with the lure of bonuses if successful. That was it, she decided. The bonus strikes on Coyote Bay were just lures, like the incomplete information on the Kodomir Militia she had supplied the previous mercenary units. Well, perhaps her employer was not crazy. Still, what purpose was served with these attacks that were programmed to accomplish nothing, other than keep the Kodomiri on edge?

Was that the point?

She deleted the message and paused, thinking. Then she touched her keyboard and dictated her ad. It would be posted in the SFA hall and in the employment database. Mercenary units would respond and she would begin the filtering process. By the end of the week she would have a contract signed.

But not today. After she finished dictating, she was going to take the rest of the day off.

Counselor-General Andrea Richelieu was anything but crazy, though she sometimes felt her job would drive her to that state. She walked down a long and well-polished hall, her heels clicking lightly. The hall was large, more than 200 meters wide, and featured tall, unobstructed windows. The view of the distant mountains was breathtaking, even for those who saw it every day. The great hall was one of three forming a massive triangle with a major branch of Stellar Alliance government at each apex. Each hall had a unique view because Totenheim, the capital world of the Stellar Alliance, deliberately kept its natural beauty as intact as possible.

Richelieu nodded to the others, mostly people working for her, who crossed her path from the desks on either side of the hall. As she approached the door to the Prime Minister's office, the sentry snapped to attention and the door opened. She entered the office quickly and stopped in front of the minister's desk.

Selena Mordieu, Prime Minister of the Stellar Alliance, was a short woman and slightly stocky. She did not bother with the stylish clothes favored by women attending her at social gatherings and especially avoided them when at work. She appeared, then, like some minor bureaucratic functionary. But a look into her sharp, intelligent eyes revealed how easy it would be to underestimate her.

"According to my Military Minister," Mordieu said without looking up from the report she was editing, "the preparation of our armed forces will be completed in 90 days, slightly ahead of schedule." She looked up and smiled slightly. "I think he was showing off a little and trying to make his ministry look good."

"If everything is ready in 90 days," Richelieu said, "then he deserves to show off. The preparations for a major expeditionary force of regimental size are extensive. Fortunately," she added slowly, "he has several very competent generals working for him."

"*Touché*," Mordieu said, sliding the report away from her, her smile larger. "And how are things on the diplomatic front?"

"Six raids are completed," Richelieu said. "Our person on Kodomir reports very little damage done."

"Good, good," Mordieu said. "And the remaining raids?"

"All are in transit by star ship and will strike within the next several months, as planned. The final raid contract is being posted and our broker will provide us with the details."

"I am not happy with the expense," Mordieu said. "It may attract the attention of the Parliament's budget committees."

"As I explained, Prime Minister," Richelieu said, "the final raid is *key*. It has to be successful enough to fully alarm the Kodomiri while not doing more than is necessary to produce that psychological state. This means discipline, and a large and well-disciplined mercenary unit is going to be more expensive than the other units we have used."

"I understand that." Mordieu got up from her desk and walked to a wall displaying a large, glowing map. She studied it for a moment, her hands behind her back. "I agree with you – my concern is with the possibility of providing our opponents in the Parliament with political ammunition to use against us."

Richelieu said nothing as Mordieu looked at the map with its dozens of star systems. The Prime Minister turned back to her.

"I would like confirmation that the Kodomiri are placing the blame for these raids on von Bender. Can our person there provide us with that information?"

"Perhaps," Richelieu said. "He is well placed for monitoring Militia activities, but not quite so for gathering information from the areas of government determining the identity of the attacker."

"Our spy can't get close to their spies, is that it?" Her smile was broad.

"I am afraid not," Richelieu said. "And we want to be careful about exposing him to scrutiny."

"Well, if he can find out anything without entailing major risks, ask him to see what he can find out." Mordieu turned back to the map. "I read your analysis of von Bender's take-over of the worlds between Kodomir's old Confederacy and his Holdings. The economists believe you are being somewhat optimistic about how quickly he can exploit them. They think the cost of garrisoning them plus maintaining his own frontiers plus digesting most of the Confederacy is going to soak off any immediate profits and that it will be at least two years before he can translate his gains into power."

"They might be right," Richelieu said. "My job is to ensure that we are prepared for the worst-case scenario. Whether he needs two years as they say or a year as I say, there is no doubt what he will do then."

"Then he will come after us," Mordieu said. "No question. Even if it means dragging the rest of the Free Union with him. And, again, under those circumstances, there is no question we would be overwhelmed."

"None," Richelieu agreed. "Therefore, we must move quickly and in self-defense."

"That is true, but it is incomplete," Mordieu said. She fell silent for a moment, her eyes fixed on the map. "The Settled Worlds is descending into chaos, thanks to the greed and paranoia of Peter Mavis Carmichael. His attack on the Protectorate was very ill advised. For some, like von Bender, that chaos offers opportunity. And I must admit I agree with him in at least that regard. This is *our* opportunity. We may be able to gain a base on Kodomir. That would checkmate von Bender's expansion in our direction and, at some point in the future, serve as our springboard to finally tear down von Bender's Holdings."

"True," Richelieu said. "Your grandfather's Alliance was once a shield protecting the Settled Worlds from the Frontier. There was great honor attached to the Mordieu name. Though it fractured, the shield can be restored. The key is von Bender, and the key to him is Kodomir."

"Kodomir was once a part of the Alliance," Mordieu said. She turned away from the map and returned to her desk. "It departed after my grandfather's death, one of the last worlds we lost as the old Stellar Alliance empire slowly collapsed. My impression was that it did so reluctantly, pressured by the Free Union. My hope is that they will return gladly. All I am attempting to do is to convince them to do that which common sense and our past relationship should lead them to."

"But they have expressed no interest in joining us," Richelieu pointed out. "After the destruction of the Confederacy, their subjugation by those Raiders left them with a bitter taste for being ruled by others."

"Hence the raids," Mordieu said. "They must be reminded of their vulnerability. They are weak and alone and in a very dangerous part of the Settled Worlds. Carmichael's Free Union allowed von Bender to invade the Confederacy, though they were supposedly proper members of the Union as well. And von Bender used Raiders, to the disgrace of his name and the Free Union. With Carmichael tied up in his war with the Protectorate, we might be able to gain our foothold without interference from the Union. And what is a *de facto* recognition of our sphere of influence might become formalized."

Richelieu said nothing, having heard the argument before. Indeed, it had been *her* argument, used repeatedly as she worked to get Mordieu to see the opportunity and to act on it.

"Positioning our forces will be critical in terms of timing. Is the Defense Minister taking into account the time needed for transporting our forces?"

"Yes," Mordieu said. "The General Staff understands the importance of a quick response. We will have the 21st Grenadiers conducting landing ship maneuvering and boarding exercises nearby, a leap away. Star ships are at the ready for transporting the landing ships. While they are currently unaware of our plans for Kodomir, the 5th Assault Regiment is likewise a single leap away and can be used for reinforcements if need be. I wish we could have led with the 5th, but their commander, Colonel Garcia Petron, is not as politically reliable as I would like." Mordieu scratched her nose as she paused and thought for a moment. "We have been reluctant to approach the Kodomiri diplomatically for fear of tipping our hand prematurely to von Bender and, through him, Carmichael. Is that still your recommendation?"

"Yes, ma'am. Though I think we may have presented such a low profile as to overdo it. I would recommend that we increase our contacts with the Kodomiri slightly. Place some bids on their spring harvest at very favorable prices, request intelligence on activities in the Frontier and offer to share some of our own, that sort of thing."

"Just being a good neighbor, eh?"

"Indeed. Nothing overtly military or suggestive of treaties, just typical diplomatic contact. Perhaps build up our consulate on Kodomir and increase the frequency of nonmilitary contacts."

"That makes sense. I want them familiar with us, seeing us as no threat and having shared interests. No sense of pressure. When we make our offer, I want them to come to us willingly."

"And they will come, Prime Minister," Richelieu said. "They will come."

"I don't think they are going to come," General Manuel Mannerheim said as he stood at parade rest and stared out the consulate window. It was late evening in the capital of Kwangdo and there was little to see. He turned back to the Special Envoy, Esteban Baer, and frowned. "Cooperation has not been very forthcoming on the part of these people," he said. "But you would expect elementary courtesy."

Baer held up a hand. "It is not a problem, general. I understand the situation here."

Ambassador Felipe Bostan nodded in agreement from behind his desk. "General, the Kwang people are very proud. If you look back out the window to the east, I think you will be able to make out the remains of their principal military base. It is nothing but rubble. They have not forgotten that we are responsible for the destruction of that base and the collateral damage to the civilians near it."

"Nonsense," Mannerheim said. "That was entirely the fault of Iriki Tykaw and those Storm Cloud pirates. Not a Benderist soldier was involved."

"That's not entirely accurate, general," Bostan replied. "First, those Raiders were hired by our Baron. Second, two of our landing ships brought air support. I grant that our pilots did not fire a shot, but we were here. And among the Kwang, it is well known that Storm Cloud was here only because the Baron used them just as he did on Kodomir."

"You're right," the general admitted. "But that was two years ago. Storm Cloud left here quickly enough."

"And turned Kwangdo over to us as they left. The association between the Raiders and Baron von Bender is quite strong." Baer shrugged. "True, they did not have the time to commit the kinds of atrocities here that they did on Kodomir, but they did enough to make our occupation a problem."

A knock at the door interrupted conversation as an aide stuck her head in. Bostan stood and glanced at the others and then nodded to the aide. The door opened and the Kwang delegation entered.

There were three of them and all were clearly uncomfortable. Ambassador Bostan stepped forward. Carefully ignoring General Mannheim, he introduced the Special Envoy.

"Please allow me to present to you Special Envoy Esteban Baer, personally sent by Baron Karl von Bender. Envoy Baer, this is Premier Ishio Sakai, Parliament Chief Speaker Edenta Yamato, and Minister for Foreign Affairs Lieutenant General Thomas Akagi."

The delegates nodded their heads but did not extend their hands. Baer ignored the slight and made a point of bowing.

"I appreciate and am honored by your consideration," he said. "This is not a pleasant evening for traveling."

"Indeed," General Akagi said, his voice a low growl. Sakai looked at him out of the corner of his eye and the general fell silent.

"The weather is most foul," Sakai said. "And our need to travel through it to return to our homes unfortunately forces me to ask what service we might be to the Baron's Special Envoy?" The temperature of the room seemed to drop.

"The Baron seeks a normalization of relations between himself and the citizens of Kwangdo," Baer said. "He appreciates that mistakes were made when necessity forced him to deal with the old Confederacy of which Kwangdo was once a part. He has asked me to convey his personal apologies." Baer bowed and held the bow for several seconds. Finally, Sakai returned it, though his own bow was shallow. "He has asked me to present this hand written apology to you." He handed over a large envelope. "This apology will be given to the Kwangdo news services so that all will know his reasons for coming here and his absolute sorrow at the conduct of those in his employ."

Baer paused for a moment, waiting to see if Sakai would open the envelope. When he did not, Baer continued.

"Baron von Bender, as you know, is a long-time supporter of Prime Minister Peter Mavis Carmichael. When the Confederacy under Viscount O'Ryan hesitated to declare for the Free Union as the war with the Worlds Protectorate escalated, Baron von Bender felt compelled to ensure the safety of his Holdings. After all, the Confederacy was only a few star ship leaps away. Believing that a quick move would avoid a prolonged and bloody war, and would work where diplomacy had not, he enlisted the assistance of a Frontier unit only to discover it was not the honorable mercenary unit it had claimed to be but Raiders. Their assaults on your world and Kodomir were brutally carried out and damaged the long-term objectives of the Baron. Besides conveying his apology, I have been sent here to see if it is possible to close the rift between Kwangdo and the rest of his Holdings." He handed over a second envelope.

"As a preliminary gesture of his desire to make amends and to integrate Kwangdo into its proper place within the Holdings, he is going to do the following. No reciprocity from the Kwang people or government is required. First, an indemnity will be paid to Kwangdo to repair all damages not yet repaired and to compensate those who were injured during the attack. Second, the Kwang armed forces are to be officially reinstated with the exact force level to be determined by negotiation. Initially, the Baron would like to see the raising of a regiment and pledges to supply equipment and weapons needed for the unit. Third, he officially invites the Kwangdo government to send a voting representative to the Holdings Assembly to occupy an equal position with all other representatives. Fourth, he officially invites the Kwangdo government to send an ambassador to his court. Fifth, and finally, he wishes to open negotiations on all issues currently facing the Benderist Holdings and Kwangdo. I am his representative and I am charged with full powers of negotiation. In the event of my absence, those negotiations may be continued by Ambassador Bostan. These negotiations may take place here, on Kwangdo; again, a gesture of the Baron's good faith."

Baer studied the impassive faces of the delegation for a moment. "Gentlemen, we are all aware that a time of confusion and chaos is descending on this area of the Settled Worlds. These conditions may prove to be dangerous. It is important that we take steps toward unity, for together we may avoid much of that danger." The delegates stared for a moment in silence.

"We will, of course," Sakai finally said, "study the Baron's proposals carefully. The process of reaching a negotiated settlement of our present difficulties may be prolonged, but the end goal of peace is a worthy one." He fell silent. Finally, he nodded to Baer and the delegation turned and left the room.

After the door closed, Mannheim let out a low whistle. "You are going to negotiate with *them*? Good luck, Mister Baer."

"They are angry," Baer said. "But we knew that already."

"On the other hand," Ambassador Bostan said, "we have to start somewhere. I think the initial gestures were good ones."

"Yes, we spent a lot of time on them," Baer said. "By not tying them to any reciprocity, we place them in a position of trying to find an honorable response. Most likely that will be expressed as a willingness to enter into negotiations."

"I'm concerned with the business of rearming the Kwang," General Mannheim said. "Only they and the Kodomiri fought when the Baron seized the five worlds of the Confederacy."

"Well, the Kodomiri fought only because the Baron hired idiots," Baer said with a grim smile. "The Kwang fought because their honor was at stake. That's their strength and weakness. But as for raising the regiment, they will have *our* weapons and equipment. If things turn sour, we control their logistics and can simply turn off the supplies they need to keep their army working. On the other hand," he paused and looked over at the general, "von Bender is right. The Settled Worlds *are* descending into trouble. This war between the Free Union and the Worlds Protectorate may destabilize half of the Settled Worlds. Unity is the key, because that will help us build an island of stability in what is turning into a war-wracked sea. Yes, the Baron likes to see his flag on other worlds, but the issues we are facing now are far more serious than the ancient and simple struggle for control the Settled Worlds. He is convinced that the dangers are greater than ever before."

Baer walked over to a sideboard and poured himself a cold glass of water from an ice-filled carafe. He took a sip and then turned to the other two men.

"I think he is right. Neither Peter Mavis Carmichael nor Mariah Connor has the skills needed to attain more than a stalemate, and as the Free Union and the Protectorate exhaust themselves in their struggle, all the other old conflicts will resurface. Some will act out of opportunity while others will act out of fear. They already have begun that process. The Settled Worlds are going to burn." He took another sip and looked at the general.

"Our goal, then, is clear. We do *not* want to simply be an occupying force here, depending on the passage of multigenerational time to get them to accept rule by us. Besides, that seldom works. What we want, what we need, is to have them as allies. That is going to be our focus." He finally smiled. "After all, general, wouldn't you like to command a division of Kwang soldiers?"

"Certainly, Mister Baer," Mannheim replied. "Though I suspect their first military objective would be to carve me a new asshole." All three men laughed. "But, yes, these people make good soldiers. If Storm Cloud didn't have surprise when they attacked, they might have won. They have scrupulously honored their formal surrender – your department's insistence on that was a good read of their character. But one thing still troubles me."

"Allow me to guess," Ambassador Bostan said, "Kodomir."

"The ambassador appreciates my obsessions," Mannheim said.

"As does the Baron," Baer said. "Kodomir is the chink in our armor. Whoever holds it flanks the entire line formed by the old Confederacy and has a straight shot to the String of Pearls. We have to secure Kodomir, there's no question of that."

"How and when?"

"I will be going there soon, hopefully after the negotiations here are well underway. Diplomatic means are preferred, of course, at the moment. We are stretched thin, though our forces are growing. As for the 'when,' well, as soon as possible. I think the Baron may make some sort of diplomatic overture to Kodomir soon, though it would be better if the other worlds of the old Confederacy, like Kwangdo, were happily allied with us. Friends influence friends, you see. In any case, the Holdings will finish the incorporation of the old Confederacy, including Kodomir, one way or the other."

"I have heard," Bostan said, "that someone has struck at Kodomir several times already."

"I read your report," Baer said. "Our intelligence service is not sure, but opinions seem to suggest two culprits. Either Frontier-based forces, probably outlaw Raiders, trying to take advantage of Kodomir's relatively weak position, or another Settled Worlds power moving against us."

"Raiders are a very real possibility," Mannheim said. "Kodomir is right on the border with the Frontier and I assume Raider groups within that area are well aware of Storm Cloud's overthrow. But your person on Kodomir suggests that the attackers have all been mercenary units. That indicates another power as I doubt Raiders would hire registered mercenaries, even through brokers. I read that the Stellar Alliance is on the move, consolidating its position. But they are barely strong enough to challenge the Holdings and certainly could not challenge the Free Union."

"They would not be strong enough at all if we were not forced to tie down much of our military force on nine newly-acquired worlds – that same statement holds for the Free Union." Baer looked at his glass. "I believe they see an opportunity. And if they choose the point of conflict, they can bring overwhelming power to bear." He took another sip of water. "In any case, gentlemen, I think these coming times are going to require us to be very nimble on our feet."

"I appreciate your candor," Bostan said. "But is conflict inevitable? With the Settled Worlds disrupted by the Free Union – Protectorate War, is not now the time for consolidation and maintaining the integrity of the Holdings, rather than embarking on an expansionist policy? Why extend ourselves onto Kodomir?"

"Ambassador," Baer said with a slight smile, "the case for consolidation and holding still is made every day in the Baron's court, and until recently those of us who have recognized that the current situation demands new thinking have been very much in the minority. However, times change. Not only do we now have opportunities that did not exist before to restore the Holdings to the breadth of their former grandeur, but also, we have an obligation to preserve them against our enemies. General Mannheim noted the Alliance is expanding, taking advantage of the same opportunities as us. If we hold still, Mordieu and her Alliance will soon be swallowing us." He shook his head and studied his glass of water.

"The 'Stasis Faction,' as the Baron calls them," Baer said, "has had its time. Besides, the economy of the Holdings is largely built upon a steady expansion. We have built a military force out of proportion for the economic power we possess. The only answer is expansion, thus providing us with the resources to maintain our forces."

"Which are then enlarged to hold onto our conquests, thus necessitating further expansion," Bostan said. "This is a course of action which requires us to conquer everything."

"And the problem with that would be precisely what?" Baer put down his glass. "That has been the dream of every dynamic ruler, from the days of the First Wave of colonists on down to the current leaders of the various political groups and independent worlds. Face it, ambassador. We have entirely too much to lose by holding still."

"But we may lose everything by expanding," Bostan said. He held up his hands. "Envoy Baer, I understand that I and the other members of the 'Stasis Faction' are out of favor and the Baron is giving you and the generals free rein. I appreciate you hearing me out, though I doubt I have expressed a viewpoint you did not encounter repeatedly in the Baron's court."

"And still do," Baer said, nodding. "Our invasion of the Confederacy is seen by the Baron as a test case of the expansionist philosophy. If we can consolidate – to use your phrase – our grasp on this area and successfully begin the exploitation of its resources, then the Baron may finally unleash us in earnest. If we fail, well, my faction will again become the minority."

And you will be looking for a new job, Bostan thought, though his face betrayed nothing. Maybe you will end up ambassador on a backwater, hostile planet like Kwangdo while I take a position at the Baron's court as a Special Envoy.

"Time is the issue," Mannheim said. "Can we consolidate our alliances with the new worlds under our dominion, build up our military forces, and checkmate whoever is coming at us through Kodomir, all before the roof caves in? Time," the general said, "time is against us. We need time."

Chapter 5: Ice

18 May 2824

"I need a little more time."

The scout lay on her stomach, her heated, white-camouflaged suit barely protecting her from the howling cold of the Farnham wind and repeated her transmission. Her goggles and facemask protected her, but icy fingers still worked their way into her clothing. Her nanotechnology suit, snug against her skin, could have provided her with warmth and camouflage but she needed to preserve its power and this had been a very long mission. It was far from over.

Though she ignored the discomfort, she was tired – she had walked twenty kilometers across the frozen waste in the dark to get to this position. Now the sun was just above the horizon behind her. Her long-range binoculars were pressed firmly against her goggles and she studied the view carefully.

Like an iceberg of rock, the hill, a kilometer and a half away from the scout, jutted above the surrounding snowfield. Off to one side a tall mound of dirt and debris, half the size of the hill and steadily eroded by the winds of Farnham, testified to work taking place underground. Closer to her by half were the processing plants receiving ores from the mine under the hill. As she watched, a cargo train emerged from behind the hill, riding the single line monorail leading to the processing plants, only 500 meters from her. Near the plants were the living quarter domes of the mine operators.

The Wild Geese shut down the mines when they liberated the enslaved Militia personnel Storm Cloud sold to the operators. And when they freed the Militia, they freed all the others working and dying underground. The slaves mostly were from the Settled Worlds, like the Militia. Some were from the Frontier. And a handful of women and children were...

The scout focused her binoculars and flipped through the electromagnetic spectrum. There they were. Two patrolling HUPAX came around the far side of the hill. She noted their size and visible armament. The scout touched her headset.

"I see two HUPs in the open. Javelins. Recoilless rifle cannon, laser turrets, missile launchers. The HUP hangar is still in the location described by the Wild Geese and matches what our sensors revealed on the way in. There are now additional ground-based laser turrets and towers. One perimeter around the mine, one around the processing plant and living quarters and a scattering the length of the monorail line. Transmitting imagery now – cross-check with our passive scans to update objectives."

"Good to be back, Marjessa?"

The scout snorted a short laugh. Actually, there was tightness in her stomach as she looked at the mine. Nonetheless, few others had the familiarity with the area she did. Beyond tactical utility, she had another reason for being there.

Vengeance.

"I wish we could have come here sooner."

"Aye. This time *we* will liberate whoever is held below."

"The debt will not be paid, true-word?"

"Aye. This is not about the debt."

No, not the debt they owed their liberators, those Wild Geese mercenaries. This mission was what they owed themselves and the others who had died in the mines. That was why she lay on the ice instead of in the cockpit of a HUPAX – for reasons some might describe as primitive, she needed this particular part of the mission.

She watched the patrolling HUPs. They walked in a circular path, swinging around the processing plant and heading back towards the mine. She waited until they went behind the hill.

"Now."

Hell descended on Farnham. She knew where to look to see it coming but for a moment there was nothing. Then she saw them. Five HUPAX coming from the south, racing toward the mine. Somewhere behind them, hidden by the low cloud of ice crystals blown across the flat snowfield, were a half dozen armored personnel carriers. She glanced upward. There were the three landing ships, their triangular formation perfect, descending towards a point to her north. For a moment the scene was silent with only the low howl of the wind.

She got to her feet, freed her automatic weapon and ran towards the living quarters and administration domes. The thunder of the landing ships came as she ran. Out of the south long-range missiles arced across the sky, hungrily seeking their targets. From somewhere in the complex a distant klaxon sounded and the bay doors of the HUPAX hangar began sliding back. She ignored all of it and concentrated on getting to the mine headquarters.

By the time she got to the dome she could hear the lightning snap of ion pulse weapon fire. The HUPAX hangar was completely engulfed in flame. Laser fire cracked around her, some of it outgoing from the defense turrets. She looked over her shoulder as she got to the main entrance hatch. The landing ships were down and almost casually blowing away the laser turrets and towers.

She turned back to the hatch. It was unlocked. She threw it open and stepped inside.

The room was crowded, which pleased her. The people, mostly men but some women, stood frozen. She kept her weapon leveled on them and reached up and pushed her hood back. She lowered her goggles below her chin. She looked around the room.

She looked at each carefully. For a moment, she recognized no one but then she saw a familiar face.

"Calhoun," she said. The man looked at her nervously. "I am Marjessa Boyington." She paused, staring at him with dark eyes. "You do not recognize me, do you, weak-heart?" He slowly shook his head negatively. Then he paused and his eyes widened. "Or perhaps you do? Do you remember the Currahee? Do you remember those you buried alive? Do you remember the children?"

Boyington fired, the first rounds knocking Calhoun down. People screamed, scrambled to get out of the room, to get to weapons. She cut them down in short bursts, her face devoid of expression. Someone got to a gun and fired at her – a streak of red ripped across her cheek. Still Boyington continued firing. She dropped to the floor and shoved a fresh tubular magazine into her four-barreled submachine gun and resumed firing as she stood.

She emptied her third magazine into the dead, blowing pieces of clothes and flesh into the air. She stopped, with the only sound the faint fall of blood drops. For a moment she stood still, looking at the dead. Robot-like, Boyington reloaded.

She went from room to room in the dome, looking for other mine personnel, and what she did in those rooms Boyington never talked about later. When she was done, she stepped outside and leaned against the dome, waiting for her people. APCs appeared and soldiers jumped out. She held up a hand.

"This one is clear, sergeant," Boyington said. "After you clear the others, rig it to blow when they do." The soldier sketched a salute and led his squad towards another dome. She sighed and reached inside her suit. She pulled out a canteen and took a long drink.

She heard explosions and glanced up. The processor plants, one after the other, blew apart. After the engineers were done with them, all the domes would be leveled. Nothing would be left standing. The mission of Task Force Iroquois was one of annihilation.

An APC swung up to her accompanied by a HUPAX. The earpiece of her commo unit came to life.

"You got here before me."

Boyington looked up at the snow-white HUPAX, its pilot hidden from sight behind the armor of the cockpit. Only the red arrow and feather emblem on the HUP's shins broke the camouflage.

"Aye," she said, "but I did not have to deal with their HUPAX."

"They were not much to deal with. The mine is secured. Do you wish to go there?"

"Immediately."

"It is strange to be here again."

"It is, but it is *good* to be here."

Boyington climbed into the APC and it shifted into gear. Glancing out the window she saw her friend Charlene Tanner guiding her Rapier HUPAX, staying alongside the APC, covering it.

They stopped in front of the mine dome. The great sliding doors were wide open and soldiers clustered within. She leapt from the APC and walked inside. Slaves were slowly emerging into the dome from the mine itself. A soldier walked up to her.

"There are only thirty slaves here, Captain Boyington," he began.

"They are no longer slaves," Boyington said with more emphasis than she intended. "Don't call them that."

"Understood, Captain," the soldier said, barely pausing. "They were still working on the central shaft, digging it out. They had just gotten to the first lateral galleries, some of which were intact. Your friends did a good job for the time they had in collapsing this complex. They took a real interest in their work."

"Looks as if we nipped it in the bud," Boyington replied. "Well, rig it to come down, this time totally."

The soldier saluted and went back to his men. Boyington watched the slaves, the *former* slaves, she corrected herself. She hated that word. Had she looked like that when the Wild Geese freed her? Medics were moving them quickly into APCs and transporting them to the landing ships. She touched her headset.

"All squads, report. Any mine guards or operators still alive?"

"Captain Boyington, we are bringing them to the main warehouse. We are downloading their computers, seeking data on the owners, and should be done within the next half hour. An engineering team is at the power plant and dome complex. Estimating twenty minutes to complete their task. Nothing else to report."

"Understood. I will go to the warehouse. Let me know when the teams are secured from their tasks." She turned to leave when the soldier came back.

"We have seven mine guards and four operators in custody." He gestured to a small group of people near the entrance of the mine. They had their arms folded against the cold – though the temperature was still well above freezing inside the dome, it was falling rapidly.

And it is going to become much colder, she thought.

85

"Take them to the warehouse. Tell them it is warmer there."

The sergeant nodded, a smile holding no humor on his face. He walked over to the group while Boyington climbed into the APC.

A few minutes later Boyington was at the warehouse. There were over twenty mine guards and operators gathered in the center of the large room, covered by soldiers. She waited by the door. The group of guards and operators from the mine were hustled in after a few minutes. As she listened to the radio calls, other prisoners arrived. It took longer than expected but finally the last team reported. She stood on a small crate.

"Do you know who we are?" She looked around the room that was as silent as death. Not even the wind disturbed the silence. "You may know us as Currahee. Now, do you know who we are? We are the people you kidnapped and made slaves. You murdered over three hundred of us. We are the people whose children you killed. Do you know who we are?" She made herself pause, feeling the flush of anger. The temptation to level her weapon and kill them all was almost overwhelming.

"When I worked in your mine I met a man, one of the people who brought our liberators. I told him we would survive. I told him we would live to bury you people. Do you know who we are?" A series of flat explosions, muffled by the rising wind, came from outside the warehouse. "When the Wild Geese came, they let you live and told you to run. You disregarded what they said. Now *we* are here. The explosions you hear are the other buildings. All of them are to be destroyed. The mine is gone. Your power plant is gone. This building will be a block of ice in a matter of hours. You have three choices." She took her automatic weapon and tossed it to a soldier.

"You can remain in here and freeze to death slowly. You can go outside and freeze to death quickly. Or you can become our *Dedeloquasgi*. That means you can leave with us. To do that you must prove worthy." She opened her suit and pulled out a large fighting knife. With a flick of her arm, she threw it into a nearby crate. Then she pulled out a second one and held it casually in her hand.

"It's what we call *Atsilvquodi*, a chance to live. All you have to do is take that knife and prove your worth, your courage. Against me." Boyington paused and let herself smile. "Any takers?" She looked at the crowd. A few glanced nervously at the soldiers and at each other. Most avoided looking at anything other than the floor. But no one stepped near the knife.

"Suit yourselves," she said. She walked pulled the knife free from the crate and put both away. The soldier tossed the submachine gun back to her. They filed from the room. She paused at the door and looked back. Then she spat on the floor. Vapor steamed from it; the warehouse already was freezing.

"Slavers," she said, and her contempt was colder than the rising wind.

Chapter 6: Scramble

17 June 2824

First Minister Alexis Jevon moaned without realizing it as he awakened to the insistent buzzer. His hand reached out in the darkness and fumbled for the communication unit before he found the button.

"Jevon here," he said, his voice slurred with exhaustion.

"General Polrany, sir," the low voice of the Kodomir Militia's only general filled the room. "I am sorry to have to awaken you, First Minister. A star ship has just appeared in close orbit over Kodomir. Our orbital sensors show two landing ships have detached from it and are inbound." Jevon sat up in the darkness and the bedroom lights came on.

"Another raid," he said. It was not a question. "What about the landing ship coming in from the star ship at the navigation beacon? Is it still coming?"

"Yes, sir. Our nav beacon sensors are still tracking it. It has not responded to any calls and is classified hostile."

Jevon got up and began dressing. "When will the other two land?"

"They could land within twelve hours, though that would mean landing on the south pole and there's not much there. Allowing for planetary rotation and their current approach path, it looks like they will be in position to drop on the Kiroff city area in thirteen hours. If they do no other maneuvering, they will be in position to drop on Coyote Bay or Volgagorsk about 90 minutes after that. Another 60 minutes will give them a good position for Portaka."

Jevon sat on the edge of his bed, pulling on his shoes, thinking. "What about the other landing ship, the first one? How long now before it gets here?"

"Still giving it an ETA for the day after tomorrow. It has not altered course or changed acceleration in response to the appearance of the others."

"They're not working in cooperation?"

"If they are more merc units, it's highly likely they don't even know of one another – the others did not. I imagine they are to figure out who else is coming." Polrany was silent for a moment. "I've mobilized the Second Regiment and they are getting the Combined Arms Battalion onboard their landing ships. The Armored Training Regiment here is moving out, as is the First Regiment. The Militia Air Force has its ready squadrons on alert status now and will have two more up within the next two hours. So, the two primary targets are covered."

"What about Portaka?"

"The garrison has been notified but without reinforcements there is little they can do. As per our operational orders, I have instructed their commander to notify the local civilian authorities to begin evacuation away from possible industrial targets and he is ready to pull his troops out if it looks like they are really the target."

"Good. We can rebuild buildings but I don't want to lose people unnecessarily. If they do come for Portaka, how quickly can you respond?" For a moment Polrany said nothing.

"Sir, if the two landing ships land on Portaka, we might want to consider leaving them alone and wait for the third one. We have little to lose on Portaka that we cannot replace. On the other hand, if we commit to its defense, that may leave us open to an attack somewhere else."

"And if the two land here, then the third might go to Portaka since we will be committed." Jevon ran a brush through his hair. "All right, I'm going to join you at Militia Headquarters."

"Yes, sir," Polrany said.

The Swallows, variable-geometry atmospheric fighters, looked like ghosts perched on the edge of the Kiroff Airfield runway, their gray sky camouflage serving to hide them in the slow-moving mist that even the sun did not penetrate as more than a dull, dispirited light. From time-to-time rain would walk through the taxiway and visibility would become even worse.

Major Blaine Toland yawned so hard his jaws cracked. He hated sitting on "strip alert," waiting for the word to go. It was now almost twelve hours since the unknown star ship blinked into existence close over Kodomir and released its pair of landing ships. For the past two he and his squadron had been poised to go.

Of course, the ground crews had it worse, trying to find shelter underneath the fighters. He had radioed for replacement crews but none of the people huddled under his Swallow's wings wanted to leave their posts with the raid still inbound. At least an airfield canteen vehicle was parked nearby and the crews were getting something hot to drink.

"Sundance Lead, Militia Six Actual. How do you copy, over?"

Six Actual? That was General Polrany.

"Militia Six, Sundance. Loud and clear."

"Roger, Blaine. Just wanted to update you. The landing ships are maneuvering. It looks like the Kiroff area is the target. First Regiment has a combat team loaded on our Vipers and they are holding in Depford Valley. The rest of the regiment is ready to roll. ATR is deployed to your northwest, below the Dnieper Marshes. Second Regiment has the Combined Arms Battalion loaded on its landing ships and they are standing by. The 3rd and 4th Fighter-Attack Squadrons are on alert, as are both helo squadrons."

"Well, we'll try to leave all those people something to shoot at." It was reassuring to hear what was backing up Toland's small group.

"Roger that. Good luck and good hunting. Polrany, out."

Blaine flipped on his tactical display. Landing ships could land almost anywhere around Kiroff. The land, except for the marsh and mountains to the northeast, tended to be fairly flat. Someone carrying out a planetary assault with a large number of landing ships might land far enough away that the forces could all come down at once and deploy, a process that would take time to get to their objective.

And the only objectives of consequence were Kiroff City and the airfield south of it.

On the other hand, two landing ships could only carry a quicker deploying small raiding force. Whether piratical Raiders or another mercenary force, they would want to be close to their target so they could hit it and get out.

Kiroff offered a variety of targets – the Militia base at Kiroff Airfield, some light industry bordering the airfield and extending up to the southern suburbs of Kodomir's capital city, and various political and command facilities in the city itself. His eyes drifted down the map to the airfield.

The first six merc units did not know the nature of Kodomir's defenses. These people probably did not either, since two landing ships could not carry enough to be a severe danger to the Militia. But certainly they would be scanning the area as they approached, which meant they would know that there were at least some forces located on Kodomir. But those forces were spread out.

So, if I was a mercenary trying to fulfill my contract, and my target was somewhere around Kiroff...?

They would land near Kiroff Airfield, he decided. If they carried HUPAX, they would drop them as they came down. Risky, using rocket descent packs, but it saved time. The HUPs would run towards their target, either the airfield itself or the surrounding industry, maybe both. The landing ships would provide long-range fire support.

They wouldn't deploy the HUPs to the north, not in the suburbs. Whatever force they had would get tangled up in the streets and buildings. Hard to maneuver and it would slow them down. So, east, west, or south of the field. Could he narrow it further?

West and south were open farmland, out to well past the horizon. No concealment or cover. If they landed out there, they would give the base defenses, and they would anticipate at least some defenses, a clear, unobstructed shot at them as they came in.

But to the east... Beyond the base and the scattered warehouses and light industrial buildings, there was little. The ground became slightly broken and punctuated by low, rippling hills. All that was out there was a couple of gravel pits and a rock quarry. Further away was a national park.

The rock quarry. For a moment his eyes remained locked on the map. The quarry was where his father and almost twenty others were taken and executed by Iriki Tykaw, leader of the Storm Cloud Raiders. Tykaw himself had personally shot almost every person, starting with his father, demanding to know where Polrany was, demanding to know where

Kodomir's off-world funds had been placed. But his father, First Minister Brevar Toland, had said nothing, nor had the others.

Blaine had never been to the quarry. The recovery of the bodies had taken place secretly at night while he was helping Polrany escape and eventually recruit the Wild Geese. When he finally came home, he was shown where the underground had buried his father, near the banks of South Fork River. They asked if he wanted to move the remains to the family site at their church. He had stood on the bluff overlooking the river, thinking, and then finally decided to let his father lay where the underground had placed him. It was not a formal graveyard, but those who died with him at the quarry surrounded his father's body. Blaine decided that was good company and so did the families of the others.

Naturally the Assembly built a memorial there, but it was not ostentatious and the view of the river and the rolling ground beyond remained undisturbed.

He pulled his thoughts back. The quarry and the gravel pits were little more than a kilometer away. For someone looking for cover it would be a good place. He keyed his transmitter.

"CIC, Sundance Lead. Update on the landing ships?"

"Sundance, they are entering the atmosphere. Trajectory looks good for us, though Coyote Bay is still possible. We are about to launch you to clear the airfield."

"Roger. Break. Sundance squadron, we're going to launch in a moment. Flight leaders, stay close to Kiroff. I suspect we are the target and I think they may land to our east."

The other flight leaders acknowledged. Blaine slid back his canopy. The ground crew already was moving. He drew a circle in the air over his head and got an exaggerated nod from one of the crew. He opened the throttle of the Swallow and pressed the ignition switch. Instantly the engine began a low, rising whine followed by a growl. The various cables attached to his fighter were pulled free and stowed on the auxiliary power unit. The ground crewman stood in front of the fighter, his arms crossed over his head, holding Blaine in place while his canopy slid forward and locked into position.

"Sundance, CIC. Scramble. Repeat, scramble."

"Roger."

He looked at the crewman and raised a hand and brought it down like an axe. Immediately the crewman motioned him forward and then pointed down the taxiway leading to the runway, only meters away. Then he came to attention, snapped a salute, and as the fighter swung in its turn, its wingtip close to his face, raised his hand in a clenched fist. Blaine knew the signal and returned it.

Good luck. Good hunting.

The captain of Gladiator, the lead Alligator-class landing ship of the two entering Kodomir's atmosphere, swore quietly to himself. It was bad enough that a weather front obscured their target and had done so for the hours of their approach. Now his sensors were worthless, blinded by the ionization of atmospheric entry. Communication, even with the other landing ship, a Union-class ship named Paratus, was impossible as well.

He glanced again at the electronic warfare screen, its last images before entry still displayed. There were the routine emissions from Kiroff and the cities and towns scattered across the continent, including some fairly powerful ones from Coyote Bay. They had all been more or less constant during their approach from the star ship.

But near Kiroff, near the south edge of the city around the airfield, there had been an unexpected spike. He studied it again – there was little else to do as Gladiator continued to burn a hole through the atmosphere. He finally punched his intercom control for the HUP bay several levels below him.

"Jaeger Lead, Captain Thatch. Take a look at this EW indicator we got just before ionization. What does it look like to you?"

"Got it, Jim. Let me study it for a second."

Thatch looked at the countdown clock. Almost out of the burn. He flexed his fingers; he always personally conned Gladiator during a combat drop.

"Jim, this looks a little like a HUP transmission. Did we get any data?"

"Negative. It's all encrypted. It was mobile and our snap view suggests it was moving, west to east, outside the perimeter of the base."

"Odd. Our employer did not mention any HUPs down there. None since they hired that merc unit to drive off some Raiders."

"Well, keep your head up. They may still be in the area or the local farmers may have salvaged a couple from the Raiders."

"Understood. Let's play it safe. Change in landing zone. Landing ship LZ remains the hilly terrain two point five klicks east of the Militia base center point. New HUP landing zone is now one point seven five klicks east. Advise Paratus that we will not drop our HUPs on the base and we will hold on the new LZ until joined by AFVs. Copy?"

"Roger, copy." Captain Thatch felt some small relief at Jaeger Lead's decision – better to be cautious until they were sure of what was going on down there. "Stand by for end of burn. Good luck, Jaeger Lead, and good hunting."

Jaeger Lead, Ken Walsh, tightened his seat straps again, an old nervous habit, just as the first high G load kicked in. The roar of Gladiator's engine caused his HUPAX, a fast Short Sword, to vibrate in its bay clamps. One of his data screens flashed and then a count-down clock, recalibrated for the new landing zone, ran down the seconds.

Walsh switched over to his mindlink. The instrument screens dimmed and he saw imagery directed to the visual centers of his brain. The countdown clock appeared while the HUP computer performed the last checks of his rocket descent pack.

Walsh favored medium altitude drops, high enough to see what was happening below but low enough tracking fire control systems had as little time as possible to hit anyone. Not that there would be such sophisticated systems on Kodomir. This backwater world, according to the intelligence supplied by their employer, had little more than an infantry-based militia. Very few were full-time, professional soldiers. He had seen news items in the past about Kodomir – the Storm Cloud Raiders, little more than a mob of bandits, overran its defenses in a single morning and it took outside mercenaries to finally drive them away. They would not have much to oppose their landing.

"Stand by. Clamps free."

Thatcher's voice was punctuated by the clang of the clamps snapping back into the bulkhead. Across from Walsh, his second in command moved her HUP, another Short Sword, toward the opening hatch. He walked his HUP forward until he was alongside her.

Visibility from inside a HUP was poor – the small ports were usually covered by armor except when a maintenance worker needed to move one of the machines. Walsh used the mindlink to see through the Short Sword's sensors but, even with them, there was not much below to see. It looked like they were just entering the undercast. Walsh glanced down and saw a map of the terrain below, complete with contour lines and various symbols of structures. At least the landing ship's radar and other sensors could punch through the clouds. His and the other HUPs would fall with their active sensors off to avoid giving their positions away. Maybe those farmers would think the landing ships were just traders coming to call. In any case, no sense giving the show away early.

"Jaeger Squad, go, go, go!"

Walsh walked his HUP forward, stepped into the gray, and fired his descent rockets. A tunnel graphic opened in his visual field and the glowing crosshairs showed him perfectly centered in it and on the right trajectory for the new landing zone. He did not have to modify the burn at all. The computer agreed with him. Perfect.

There was a flash of light to his left, dimly seen through the cloud.

"Lead, Two. I'm taking fire! Missiles!"

He looked at his scope and saw nothing. They were too high for ground-based defenses to be hitting them without any launch warning. What was going on?

"Sundance, CIC. We have two landing ships inbound; apparent trajectory will take them east of the base. You are weapons free."

"Sundance, roger, weapons free." Blaine deliberately tried to sound calm in his response; some of his pilots were new.

Blaine brought his Swallow around in a gentle turn out of the racetrack pattern south of the airfield the squadron had been flying. His data screen, using relayed information from CIC, showed two landing ships descending rapidly. Still in the ionization, probably. He keyed his microphone.

"Sundance, set speed point nine Mach."

The variable geometry wings of the fighter swept backwards, blocking his view down to the left and right. No matter. He wanted to hit these people while they were still in the air and that meant he wouldn't have to look down for them.

"Sundance, CIC. Heads up. They are firing their engines and dropping HUPs."

"Lead copies."

On the inside of his visor the relayed information showed a cluster of small red dots appearing around the large ones of the landing ships as he looked in their direction. They were in the thick of the clouds. Fine. They wouldn't see it coming if they kept looking down.

"Sundance Alpha, target closest HUP. Slash fire and turn away. Bravo Flight, take the second one. Don't hang around and get smacked by their landing ships." Blaine's orders were the same ones he had given in the squadron ready room and again while they all waited in their aircraft; he hoped it was enough for the new pilots.

Hell, almost everyone flying today is new.

The thought was chilling but factual; Kodomir had lost almost all of its Swallow pilots during the first hours of the Storm Cloud invasion.

Blain used the computer projection of the CIC datalink to align his fighter, even though his own sensors did not have a target yet. He suspected, based on his own experience in a HUPAX, the raiders would drop with their active sensors off to avoid detection and rely on their landing ships to let them know what was going on. But the ground-based sensors of the Militia were much more powerful than those carried by HUPs, and a HUP seen from below provided a very large and unstealthy target for even conventional radar.

The HUPs were less than a kilometer from the ground when his HUD showed a lock for his missiles. He squeezed the trigger. As the first two antiarmor missiles disappeared into the mist of the cloud, he rolled and pulled the Swallow in a tight left-hand turn.

The rest of his flight, formed in right echelon, fired and did the same thing. He eased out of his turn and throttled back, giving the rest of the flight a chance to catch up. Then Blaine continued the left turn as the other three fighters joined.

Each Swallow carried four heavy antiarmor missiles and fired a pair on their first pass. Because of the manner of the attack, the missiles were not all targeted on the same portion of the enemy HUP. However, Blaine's flight, coming at the HUPs from the side, scored most of their hits on the HUP's left weapons pylon and leg. One pair, fired by the last fighter, slammed into the HUP's descent pack, igniting the chemical rocket fuel stored within.

Walsh saw a bright, sustained glare in the gray to his left. The glow paced him for a second and then dropped rapidly, leaving him behind. He heard a quick yell.

"Ejecting!"

Then the glow was gone. Before he had a chance to think of what had happened, Bravo Flight's missiles arrived. Walsh had been hit by fire before but it was still a shock to have four missiles slam into the left side of his HUP. There was a thud of an internal explosion near the shoulder connection of the weapon pylon, thankfully contained, and his damage indicator showed the pylon and its weapons as useless. He keyed his transmitter.

"All Black Cats, we are under attack! Dash Two is down, I am hit. Missile fire. Cut your rockets and drop. Flare landings."

Walsh shut down his descent rocket. Immediately the HUPAX accelerated, stabilized by a small parachute that did nothing to slow him. He watched the altimeter and prayed there were no unexpected hills below him. A warning tone began beeping in his headset but he ignored it. When the altimeter indicated 300 meters, he punched the descent rocket. It fired full bore, slamming him into his reclined seat at four times his body weight as it desperately fought to stabilize the HUP and break its fall.

Walsh hit the ground hard enough to bounce his head on the seat's headrest. He dropped the smoldering descent pack and looked around. It was raining. He was between two small hills and his passive sensors showed the rest of the Black Cat HUPs landing near him. At the western edge of his visual field he could see various red dots, the defenses of the Militia base. Their target, the grain processing and storage facilities, would be slightly north of the base. It was time to get moving.

"Black Cats, form on me. Formation Victor. Sensors on. Keep your heads up. I'm not sure what was firing on us but I don't want any more surprises. I'm taking us north and using these hills to block fire from the base. Remember, we want to just knock down some buildings and then get the hell out of here. If anyone gets Dash Two's beeper, mark it for retrieval."

"Jaeger Lead, Dash Three. I have the impact site of Two's HUP, about 250 south of me. No beacon."

"Roger, mark it as navigation point Delta." Walsh took a breath but did not let himself think about what might have happened to Two. "Break.

Gladiator, tell the AFVs to swing through Delta and see if they can find Two's beacon. If they take fire, drop back as per plan and set up a perimeter around the landing ships."

"Gladiator, roger."

Walsh walked forward and the Black Cats formed an inverted V with his HUP in the lead. Despite the loss of Dash Two's HUP, they would be able to reach their target and there was little anyone on the base could do about it. Fixed defenses were useless against HUPs.

Captain Joseph Abrande, lying among the weeds and brush of the hills the Black Cat HUPs moved through, touched his headset and listened to his recon teams' reports. The teams formed a broad band around Kiroff, especially in the hills to the east of the base. They were in their third hour of waiting in their camouflaged positions. The light weapons of the Third Reconnaissance Battalion would have little effect on seven HUPs, but that was not why 3rd Recon was out here.

They were the Militia's eyes. Not subject to electronic warfare countermeasures, they used the oldest sensors known, human eyes and ears, and fed what they learned back to Militia CIC.

3rd Recon was not entirely without teeth. Each team of two carried a designator, a sighting system capable of viewing throughout the electromagnetic spectrum and placing an invisible ultraviolet laser light on a target. The Militia had weapons that could see the light and use it to guide on. One weapon was the Diamondback guidance package for artillery of 105 millimeters and larger. Even moving HUPAX could be struck by a Diamondback-equipped artillery round and if the round was large enough the HUP could be in serious trouble.

Another weapon was the Frogfire missile. Longer ranged than the standard missiles carried by most battlefield weapons systems, these programmable missiles could fly in low under sensors or go for range by traveling high parabolas. But the keys to their power were their warheads. They had two types. One was a 1200-kilogram shaped charge. It could kill any HUP it hit and seriously damage even a large landing ship. Because more of its weight was explosive than casing, it was more powerful than the largest artillery cannon round and had much greater range.

But the other warhead was the one of choice. It contained 110 shaped charge cluster bombs. What made it so dangerous was the fact that the descending warhead, guiding the reflected light of the designator, could be programmed at launch as to when to drop its cluster of bombs, thus varying its impact zone size. Thus, it could be concentrated to chew up a fixed position, spread slightly to score multiple hits on a group of moving AFVs or HUPAX, or spread widely to take out infantry. Worse for those on the receiving end, the cluster bombs had their own guidance systems and computer brains.

Abrande listened as his teams tracked the HUPs moving north, towards him. He looked through his designator, scanning the southern horizon, but saw nothing yet. His partner touched his arm. Corporal Jennie Dema Nimeroff, her eye still fixed behind the electronic sight of her sniper rifle, held up one finger, then another. Abrande swung the designator a little further to the west and saw the dark silhouettes of a pair of HUPs moving between two low hills. He touched his headset.

"Charlie Three has them," he whispered. "Still coming north. I count five, no, seven, repeat seven, HUPs."

"CIC copies. Blackheart Lead, are you ready?"

"Affirmative. Dragons are still circling. Charlie Three, it looks like the low ground to your south is going to be the kill zone."

"Roger that, Blackheart," Abrande replied; Blackheart and Dragon were the two teams of Militia HUPs moving to encircle the mercenaries. "We're hunkered down and ready to light them up. If it comes to that…"

"Sundance, CIC. Shift your target to Landing Ship One."

"Roger, CIC. Good luck."

"Thanks, Sundance. All right, Blackheart Lead. It's all yours."

Abrande heard the distant roar of the fighters fading away as they changed course. He did not know if a fighter squadron could kill a landing ship but they could certainly keep it entertained. In the meantime, he and the others would try to keep things interesting for these merc HUPs.

Kheyntamenti, Blackheart Lead, listened to the other section of HUPs, Dragon, report in. All were keeping their sensors off to keep the mercenaries from knowing they were walking into a trap. He had feared they would drop directly onto the Militia base, thinking they could disable its defenses quickly and then proceed at their leisure to whatever their primary target was, if not the base. But the mercs had elected to drop away from the base. Moving through the low hills as they swung north was a good idea – he would have done the same thing. What the mercs did not know was the area was seeded with recon teams.

Nor did they know that another fighter squadron, an attack helicopter squadron, and an entire regiment prepared to attack them. They did not know a battalion of long-range missile APCs was now in range, ready to join their fire to six batteries of self-propelled artillery and a Frogfire battery. And they did not know there were twenty Wild Geese HUPAX forming a noose around them.

But they were about to find out.

The Militia's electronic warfare section had been working, trying to identify what frequency the mercenaries used. They flashed the information to Kheyntamenti and he switched over to it. He took a breath and keyed his transmitter.

"This is Colonel Alisti Mahmud al-Kheyntamenti, Kodomir Militia. I advise you to hold your position. You are surrounded by overwhelming force."

For a moment there was nothing. Kheyntamenti keyed his microphone again.

"I repeat, you are surrounded by overwhelming force. We are prepared to accept your surrender. You will not be harmed. We will abide by the Articles of War of the Organization of Settled Worlds."

"Overwhelming force? Sorry, colonel, but a planetary militia is not enough to keep us from our target."

"Whom am I addressing and what unit are you?" At least the mercenary was talking.

"This is Major Kenneth Walsh of the Black Cats. We're a mercenary unit under contract."

"Are you registered with the SFA?" Kheyntamenti's question was designed to find out what kind of unit he was dealing with. If the Black Cats weren't registered, then there was a good chance they were a "gray" mercenary unit, which meant their reliability might be dubious.

"Of course – we're not Raiders, colonel."

Abrande saw the HUPs slow. He spoke softly in his microphone as he leaned forward and put his eye to the designator sight. He touched a button and a purple dot appeared, letting him know where the laser was touching. A kilometer away a battery of self-propelled guns swung their guns towards the HUPs, taking their initial point of aim from the HUPs' coordinates. The laser measured their location to within a centimeter and the designator transmitted the information through an active datalink that allowed the guns to align themselves initially very accurately. The same lasers would guide the shells once they were in flight.

"Major Walsh," Kheyntamenti said, "be advised your contract is fraudulent. Your employer has provided you with inaccurate intelligence on the military forces deployed here on Kodomir. The same was done to the other six mercenary units that preceded you. They were all virtually annihilated."

The HUPs stopped. Abrande watched as they pivoted their fuselages back and forth, searching for targets.

"Colonel Kheyntamenti, what are you talking about? What other six mercenary units? What withheld information?"

Kheyntamenti's lips were tight; Walsh sounded agitated. Things could be about to go very wrong.

"The other six units were," he said, "Avignon's Avengers, the Second Red Horse Infantry, Donaldson's Light Panzers, Stone's Saber Cats, the Skua Scouts, and the last unit was Dahlgren's Dragons."

"The Saber Cats were here? When?"

Almost three months ago," Kheyntamenti said slowly; there seemed to be genuine concern in Walsh's voice. "They were commanded by Major Jill Cartwright. They were a mixed force of APCs, light tanks, and hovercraft."

"I know what their force composition is, colonel. What happened to them?"

"They conducted a raid against a mining complex near the city of Coyote Bay. They were told they would be up against a planetary militia armed only with a handful of medium armored fighting vehicles, probably exactly what you've been told."

"What happened to them, colonel?"

Kheyntamenti decided there was nothing to be gained by lying. "One column was ambushed in a valley. The other was hit trying to come to the rescue of the first. Their landing ship was disabled; no one escaped off planet."

"What about Jill, what about their CO?"

"She didn't make it," he said. "She was part of the blocking force that enabled the others to get out of the valley."

There was silence for a moment.

"Yeah, that sounds like Jill. The Sabers were once a part of our unit. We split up a year ago."

"Major, it's time to stand down," Kheyntamenti said. "Shut down your HUPs and tell your landing ships to cease-fire. We will hold our fire. You will be treated honorably. The Kodomir government is willing to release you, without your weapons, and permit you to board your landing ships and leave. If you abrogate your contract, which I believe you have a right to do, the government would be interested in discussing a replacement contract with you."

"Colonel, you may have handled the Saber Cats, but you're facing seven HUPAX now, not a dozen or so light armor vehicles. Maybe I should be accepting your surrender instead."

"Major. the force you are facing includes three infantry battalions, an armored regiment, reinforced, air support in the form of attack helos and Swallow fighters, more artillery and missile support than you can imagine, and over 20 HUPAX. If it makes any difference to you, the HUPs are crewed by very combat experienced pilots, most of them veterans of the Wild Geese mercenary unit."

"You're shitting me. I know the Wild Geese. They were a scout unit like us on the drop on Blair Atoll. You guys were them? How did you end up part of a militia?"

"It's a long story, which I would be happy to tell you over a tall cold one, but first you have to stand down, major."

"Colonel, with all respect, we have a contract. And the Black Cats have never failed a contract. I think we're going to have to turn down your offer and call your bluff."

"Major, you haven't failed your contract, your employer has. You were deliberately lied to, all part of a plan to test our defenses."

"You will have to prove to me that we cannot win, that there is more here than some fixed laser turrets and old tanks, colonel."

"I can do that, major," Kheyntamenti said. It was time to show some cards and get this game over. "Here's what we're going to do. I'm going to let you see some of what we have. We're going to do it slowly. I'm going to have one group come into your view. Take a long look at them. Tell your people to keep their weapons pointed down. If any of your HUPs raise a turret, we will open fire."

Abrande watched the Black Cat HUPs and licked his lips. This was a hell of a gamble. True, the Militia could annihilate them, but if they decided to fight when they saw the HUPs, they would get some hits in of their own. Abrande understood the reasoning behind the attempt at negotiating surrender rather than fighting it out, but... He double-checked his designator and made sure it was still lasing the lead HUP. If it hit the fan, that bastard was going to be the first to die.

"All right, colonel, let's see what you have."

"Major, check your nine o'clock. The first HUP you see is me, in a Rapier. Now coming up slowly beside me is a Trebuchet. To its right is a Javelin. Now, at your three o'clock. Two Gladius. There are two more at your six. Up ahead, just coming over the hill, that's a Scorpion. And a Scimitar. And another Gladius. Now, that's all I'm going to let you see but if you will check your sensors, you'll see another nine HUPs spread out behind the hills on all sides. Out beyond them to the west you'll see the indicators for the lead elements of an armored regiment. Your landing ships can probably confirm the air assets. Take your time and tell me what you want to do. I remind you, don't move. After six raids, we are a little trigger-happy."

Abrande watched through his sight. He upped the magnification and looked at the cockpit. He wondered what the pilot inside was thinking.

"The deal is, we shut our HUPs down and you let us board our landing ships and leave? You keep them? What about our armored vehicles?"

"If you choose to leave, we keep the HUPs. You keep the vehicles. If you decide to accept a contract with us, you keep your HUPs. In either case, we will supply the SFA with information supporting you in abrogating your old contract and collecting the rest of the funds held by the SFA."

"All right, colonel. We surrender. What do you want us to do?"

"Do I have your word not to take any aggressive action?" Kheyntamenti fought to keep the relief out of his voice.

"Yes, sir." There was no mistaking the disappointment in Walsh's.

"Then you can remain in your HUPs. Follow me back to our base. We have service gantries there that we can use for you to dismount. Much easier than climbing down. The armored vehicles that have moved to your drop zone area, have them return to the landing ships. We have landing ship facilities at the airfield. Have your ships join us there. We'll have our air units stand back. Then we'll sit down and see where you want to go from there."

"Sir, I'd like to have our vehicles stay in the area of the landing zone. We have a HUP down in the area and we haven't located the pilot yet."

"Understood, major, but we have her. One of our recon teams picked her up. She's injured, pretty badly, but we're going to get a helo over to them and get her to the base hospital." It had never occurred to Kheyntamenti to use the captured Black Cat as a hostage to force Walsh's compliance.

"Thank you, sir. I'll send the vehicles back. We're ready to follow you." Now Walsh sounded relieved.

Abrande let out a long sigh as the Black Cat HUPs turned and followed the Rapier. When he first heard Kheyntamenti's proposal he had thought it was the damnedest idea anyone had ever come up with, but Kheyntamenti insisted that the mercs would honor their contract unless the force facing them was overwhelming or they felt the contract was invalid. It looked like they had bought both approaches.

Raid seven was history. Raid eight was still coming.

Chapter 7: Enter the Cats

18 June 2824

Walsh leaned against the wall and shook his head, looking down at the hallway floor. Gwielgi stood to one side, a holstered pistol hanging casually by its belt over his shoulder, and waited while the mercenary commander settled down. They were outside the room of the injured Black Cat pilot, who Gwielgi had just learned was Anna Parr.

"After our unit split," Walsh said, not looking up, "everyone got to choose whether they went with Jill and the Sabers or with me. Anna elected to go with me. Turned out she had taken a liking to me. Well, you know, small unit, wasn't too long before I took a liking to her. Not supposed to, military protocol and all that, but that's how it goes in small units." He fell silent.

"Small units aren't like regular military," Gwielgi said. "Especially if they are integrated. Men and women together, people get close."

"Yeah." He paused and then looked up. "The docs here any good?"

"Several things the Kodomiri do really well, and one of them is medicine. If the docs say they can give her face back to her, then they can."

"Yeah." He stood up and took a breath. "What are the other things they do well?"

"Their food is excellent, their hospitality is superb, their homegrown weapons industry is outstanding, but I have to tell you what they call ale here, well, I've drunk HUP wash that tasted better."

Walsh laughed. "Well, the food so far has been pretty good. What I've seen around the base suggests they know a thing or two about shooting irons. And not being dead is a good argument for their hospitality. Haven't had a chance to try their ale as yet."

"Well, we get you over to Coyote Bay, there's a bar I'll take you to. It's owned by the lady that used to work on my HUP and she's stocked it with damned near everything with alcohol in it from the Settled Worlds, Frontier, and, I suspect, the Currahee Encampment."

They walked down the hall, headed for the exit, Gwielgi buckling on his gun around his hips as they walked.

"By the way," the Black Cat leader asked, "Is that for me?"

"This?" Gwielgi looked startled for a second. "Oh, no, not at all. I got in the habit of carrying weapons years ago. Doesn't mean anything. I'm your 'liaison slash escort,' not guard. 'Liaison' if you take the contract, 'escort' if you don't and leave. Technically, you're a prisoner under the Articles of War and Kodomir Militia Military Law, but since you and your people are free to go, I'm not too concerned about you running off. Mostly, you're saving me from a desk full of paperwork."

"I did a little reading last night," Walsh said. "Got filled in a little bit about how the Wild Geese ended up here. You mind if I ask you a question?"

"No, go ahead. But let's get outside – I get a little nervous in here. The medics have it in for me, I think." Gwielgi pulled on his beret and fastened the belt around his waist. Walsh noticed that he wore his pistol low with the holster tied down, gunfighter fashion.

Old habit, eh?

The weather had improved and the clear blue sky was only occasionally broken by high white cirrus. The air was cool and refreshing, especially after the interior of the small hospital. The two men walked down the sidewalk. The base was active with construction projects.

"Colonel Kheyntamenti told me that General Polrany would do the negotiating if we opted to go for a contract."

"Yes, he's the CO of the Militia," Gwielgi said. "The contract would have to be approved by the Assembly, but I figure that whatever he negotiates the First Minister will support and the Assembly will probably fall in line with both of them."

"Yeah, that's what the colonel said." Walsh looked at Gwielgi from the corner of his eye. "So, my question is, what kind of guy is Polrany?"

"Hmm, interesting question," Gwielgi said. He thought for a moment. "When he hired us, he didn't like mercenaries. Figured they were too unreliable when things got tough."

"Well, some units are like that," Walsh said.

"True enough. But he changed his view, at least about us. More importantly, the man is an old-fashioned patriot. Loves Kodomir and the people here and what the place stands for. He can be counted on to always choose what is best, or at least what he thinks is best, for Kodomir."

"According to what I read, he kind of backed into being in charge of the Militia."

"Yes, that's true. At the time of Storm Cloud's invasion, he was the senior officer in Kiroff – just happened to be in town to testify before some committee. Just a light colonel. But the more senior people were all out west, out of the action. He took charge and almost held the Raiders off. Anyway, the First Minister promoted him to brigadier general, the only real one they had. He's been OIC Militia since."

They stopped as an armored convoy rolled passed, headed for the tank facility south of the runways. Walsh shook his head.

"Man, I had no idea as to the firepower here."

"The Militia traditionally was an armor-and-artillery outfit. So they've always had a lot of rolling stock. Storm Cloud mauled their old Armored Training Regiment, which was based here, but didn't touch the rest of their tanks and APCs, other than to make a handful operational. Over the past year they've tried to replace their losses."

"You've got about 30 HUPs, 37 if you count the Black Cat HUPs. Coupled with all the armor and air I've seen, it would take a pretty serious attack to take Kodomir."

"I hope it gives people second thoughts. Remember, though," Gwielgi said as he stepped off the curb, the last of the APCs whining past, "those HUPs are still yours if you elect to take the contract Polrany is offering."

"We're over a barrel," Walsh said. "We can leave, but without our HUPs. If we want our HUPs back, we have to take the contract."

"You would rather Kheyntamenti had pulled the trigger?"

"No, don't get me wrong." Walsh shook his head. "I will always be in his debt for doing such an honorable thing. I could have lost everything, everyone, in a heartbeat, including the landing ships. I suspect that if I had been in his position, I would have shot first and discussed options later." He shook his head again. "I don't quite understand why he didn't and then picked up the pieces of our HUPs later." Gwielgi held up a hand and stopped.

They were on a street, very much like all the others crisscrossing the northern half of the base. In the distance new buildings were going up, but the burned-out shells of others still remained.

At their feet the sidewalk was bordered by a shallow trench and old concrete pipes, each as round as a man's thigh. All were holed and damaged, clearly from bullets and shrapnel. Walsh looked down. Empty shell casings were everywhere; it was impossible to walk without stepping on one. He followed Gwielgi's gesture and saw a waist-high marker and bronze plaque. At its base were small bundles of flowers, some fresh, some faded. He read the inscription:

"Hold until relieved."
Wild Geese Infantry Platoons
14 May 2822
Semper Fideles

"Lieutenant Joseph Thuan Ho`nehe held this position with our infantry, about 40 people. Over there," Gwielgi pointed, "where all the construction is going on, Storm Cloud had somewhere around 800 troops in barracks." He squinted and looked in that direction. His voice was quiet. "The Militia hit them from the north and a couple of attack helos struck – so the Stormies figured they had to get out of there, that, and take out the people blocking their HUP pilots from scrambling. All of them came right at Joe and our people." Gwielgi pointed at the trench.

"The Geese dug in behind these pipes. Their orders were to hold until relieved, that's what the quote is all about. It became hand-to-hand. When it was over, the Geese had 75% casualties, killed or wounded. But the Stormies fell back. Afterward, you could walk from here to where their barracks were and never touch the ground." He went silent for a moment.

"Well, Joe got the Kodomir Cross with Stars, the highest award the Militia has, and the University of Kiroff began setting up these markers all over the place. Historical society thing, won't change anything, including sweeping up the casings. When people come by, I think they take a couple as souvenirs." He shrugged. "There's one at the subway station where the Militia recon snuck in under the enemy's defenses, and there's another over by the HUP facility where the Cheks pinned down the Stormie HUP drivers, one up by the northern perimeter. Hell, they put one just about everywhere. Each one has got a little Latin or Greek quote on it – academics love that stuff." Gwielgi smiled.

"You see tourists and classes of school kids being bused around the base and other places, following the markers." Gwielgi shook his head. "Makes me feel like all this is ancient history."

"The kids leave the flowers?"

"Sometimes. Mostly it's the adults. These people, they are big on gratitude, responsibility, and all that kind of thing. Anyway, if you are looking for reasons why Kheyntamenti didn't kill you all, this is one. Not the only one, but this is one. Enough people have died on Kodomir."

Walsh looked around and finally nodded. "All right," he said. "I get it." He looked at Gwielgi. "If Polrany comes through with even a minimum contract, you people have the Black Cats."

"Major Walsh," Stevar Polrany said from across the conference table at Militia Headquarters in Kiroff, "you will have to excuse my abruptness but we have another raid inbound that we have to prepare for, so I am somewhat limited on time."

"I understand, sir." Walsh sat as the only Black Cat, though Polrany had several staffers with him, including a representative from the First Minister's office, a thin black man named Philip Deal. Polrany studied a bound booklet for a moment.

"I understand," Polrany said, rubbing at his thick moustache as he read, "that you have sent a message to the Security Forces Agency via our subspace communication system formally requesting abrogation of your contract with your current employer on grounds that the employer deliberately withheld information concerning your target that would have led to the destruction of your unit." Polrany looked at Walsh, who suddenly had the feeling of being a student in front of his first drill instructor.

"Yes, sir."

"Colonel Kheyntamenti, who cannot be here, informs me that, at the request of the First Minister's office," he nodded at Deal, "documentation has been independently sent to the SFA substantiating your claim." He looked over at Gwielgi. "I would think the Gray Wolves would have sufficient intel on the Militia to provide that corroboration themselves?"

"Yes, sir," Gwielgi said. "Their files on us are probably pretty up to date. Even the old numbers of the Wild Geese available in past files would have shown that the units hired to raid here, including the Black Cats, were insufficient for the task. However, given that abrogating a contract is such a serious thing, and given that Kodomir is offering a new contract to the Cats, the colonel felt, and I agreed, that all supportive evidence available should be provided to the SFA."

"I see." Polrany's eyes darted back to Walsh and considered him for a moment. "Major, why did you not check the information the Gray Wolves had on us?"

"I understand why you are asking, sir. Only an incompetent commander would take his unit against a target without checking with all available intelligence. I wish I could have, sir," Walsh said. "But we lacked the funds to purchase even an abstract on the Wild Geese, much less get a copy of the Kodomir Order of Battle. We were pretty broke and relied on what our employer told us." He paused for a moment.

"If you've studied my unit's history, you will see that we split into two units. The reason for the split was financial. We were too big or too small for most contracts. We were running out of money. So, the Saber Cats were born. They got approached shortly after they listed themselves with the SFA and, in turn, let us know their employer was looking for other small units. What she was looking for were small, cheap, expendable units. We fit the bill." His voice was touched with anger for a second. "Most of our advance for this contract went to pay for repairs on Gladiator, our lead landing ship. No one has pulled a full paycheck in eight months."

Polrany looked at his booklet. "Major, it appears that another reason both units were selected was because of your low Gray Wolf ratings. The Saber Cats were, of course, on their first assignment. The Black Cats, according to our sources, had a rating of 60 on the standard hundred-point scale." He fell silent. Then he looked at Walsh.

"I am authorized to offer you a contract to provide a garrison here on Kodomir. It takes into account your unit's size and SFA rating. The duration would be for a year with an option to extend under the current terms of up to another year without renegotiation of the contract."

Walsh sat back in his chair, his eyes narrowing. Garrison contracts typically ran for a year and were considered good duty for mercenaries, unless attacks were in the offing. But extensions most commonly were in six-month increments. Polrany slid a paper across the table.

"Here is a draft of our proposed contract. We will pay for half of your usual maintenance expenses and will absorb the costs of housing your personnel and equipment, including the construction of maintenance facilities for your vehicles and HUPs. We used your SFA file for computing our offer, which is based on equivalent ranks from the Militia pay scale."

"Not on the proposal are medical expenses – we will pay for those and supply medical services to supplement your own, which I understand to be minimal. We will also absorb any weapon upgrade costs. Part of the contract will be a review of all your weapons and, where we wish a system changed, we will supply it. We keep the old one to swap back to you if you wish to trade back at the conclusion of the contract; otherwise, you keep the upgrade."

"Anything captured from attackers belongs to the Militia. Given that we will, in effect, be upgrading your weapons anyway, I think that is fair. We will pay for repairs due to battle damage. That payment may be in supplied parts, equipment, vehicles, or HUPAX, using customary values." He slid a second sheet of paper across the table, which Walsh picked up and studied.

"This is the contract fee. We will supply half initially – we understand your financial difficulties and will help you clear your debts. The rest will be on deposit with the SFA and will be released in monthly allotments to your accounts. At the bottom of the page, you will see several bonus entries and the conditions of command. Bonuses cover actual combat and fees for the use of your landing ships for deploying Militia units. Under command, you will be under the tactical command of the senior Militia officer present, regardless of rank."

Walsh looked at both pages for several minutes and then at Gwielgi. Walsh winked and smiled.

"General," Walsh said, folding his hands on the table, "I would like a training stipulation. That is, I would like as part of the contract a commitment from the Militia to train the Black Cats in a regular and ongoing fashion to improve our combat efficiency. I would include in this our landing ship crews."

Polrany nodded. "That makes sense and is agreeable." He looked at Gwielgi. "I know the ATR could bring in their AFV people. Can your battalion's HUP training program accommodate involving their pilots?"

"I don't see a problem with that," Gwielgi said. "The syllabus is pretty well worked out at this point. The Cats could begin running their people through the basic portion almost immediately. I would guess they would get through it faster than the current students. The tactical portion could be provided at their duty station." Polrany nodded.

"That takes me to the one item not a part of the contract," Polrany said. "Our intention is to have the Black Cats garrison the Militia base on Portaka, our major southern continent, but it is not ready to receive your unit. In the meantime, you will be attached to Colonel Jonivov's regiment, as it has our Combined Arms Battalion, which you were introduced to yesterday. Do you have any other questions or changes for the proposal?"

"No, sir." Walsh hesitated. "Sir, under the circumstances, the proposed contract is generous. Like most mercs, we consider garrison duty a good contract, especially when it may include improving the quality of our unit in terms of training and equipment while we serve. For a unit of our size and rating, under any circumstances it would be a good contract. I have one concern." Polrany remained silent and Walsh took a breath.

"Sir, it's about the Saber Cats. We were more than close to them. We were literally a family unit in that we were started by several former military families who banded together. They, the Sabers, were named in honor of Major Chung-liang Stone, one of our founders. Many of us have family members with the Sabers and all of us have friends with them. I understand the nature of war. Still, I am concerned about the reaction of my people towards yours and, of course, the reverse."

The room was silent. Finally, Polrany looked at Gwielgi.

"You did not supply him with the details?"

"No, sir," Gwielgi said. "I thought it best to wait."

"It would have been premature," Polrany agreed. He sighed and turned back to Walsh. "Colonel Kheyntamenti's summary to you was correct. Their target was a mining complex north of the city of Coyote Bay. They moved in two columns down parallel valleys from their landing zone. Just north of the complex two battalions of Chekinov Scouts ambushed one column. All the vehicles were destroyed and all troops were killed or captured. The second column attempted to force its way to relieve the first but encountered our HUPs. A blocking detachment tried to cover the other vehicles as they retreated to the landing ship. However, the landing ship was heavily damaged and could not lift. Major Cartwright led the blocking force. When it was over, we took 73 prisoners, not counting landing ship crew. A large number of the 73 were wounded. A few of those are still hospitalized at Coyote Bay undergoing rehab. We counted 39 killed."

"Where are the prisoners?"

"We place prisoners from the raids at a Militia base on an island in what we call the Western Peridees, which are a chain of islands west of the port of Volgagorsk. They are housed under minimum restraint and in full compliance with the OSW's Articles of War. I will have a complete list of captured and dead provided to you."

"Sir, why didn't you make the same offer to them that you did to us?"

"Good question, major." Polrany frowned. "We tried to make it to one of the other merc units that hit us, but the Avengers thought we were bluffing. The Saber Cats never gave us a chance. They dropped close by the mines and moved very quickly down the valleys. Even knowing what the target probably was only just let us get the Scouts into position. We did not have anyone near the second column when the ambush was sprung. We did manage to get some folks to lay down their arms and the landing ship captain to stand down, but, no, it happened too fast."

"I understand, general." Walsh shook his head. "And now they are in a prison?"

"Petite Peridees is a resort island," Gwielgi said, smiling slightly. "The Militia took over a hotel and we've been housing the prisoners from the raids in it. Only way on or off the island is through the Militia base, which is basically not much more than an airfield and a small garrison. All the prisoners have given their bond not to attempt to escape or to commit any acts of violence. We have not been able to come up with a way to transport them off Kodomir, since we've been so damned busy just dealing with the raids."

"How many prisoners do you have?"

"Counting the Saber Cats and people still in hospital or rehabilitation," Polrany said, touching his datapad, "234." He looked at the pad. "Four are still in hospital and six are in a physical rehab center, all at Coyote Bay."

"Seems like a hell of waste of soldiers," Walsh said. "Sir, I have a proposal for you. Right now, you've got 224 people sucking up air and food in that hotel. What if I were to see how many I could recruit to join the Black Cats? That would reduce the prisoners you had to watch and make my unit potentially stronger."

"Major, might I point out that you do not even have a contract yet?" Polrany smiled slightly. "Nor is there any provision in the proposed contract for expanding your unit." He shot a look at Gwielgi. "However, I will consider your proposal. Our current plan is to return them all to Swordpoint at Alpha Centauri. I think some will want to do that to rejoin their units while others will be seeking new units to join. Hopefully, the star ship that brought you here will be available for transporting them – we plan on offering it a contract to take them. Maybe you can get some recruits from the rest, I don't know."

"Yes, sir. I think the Sabers will be interested in joining us at least. As for the others," he shrugged. "We'll see."

"In the meantime, I take it you will accept the offered contract." Polrany continued as Walsh nodded. "I think we will go ahead and let the SFA catch up to us on this one. It may take them awhile for them to reach a decision. There's a lot happening in the Settled Worlds, now with open war taking place between the Free Union and the Protectorate. I suspect you may find you earn that combat bonus."

Chapter 8: Snake killers

20 June 2824

In the jet-black night, the Tsalagi scouts – they preferred to call themselves that rather than the more formal and somewhat sacred term Chekinov – rolled out of the Militia helicopter as it skimmed over the ridgeline just above walking speed. The helicopter immediately banked and disappeared into the darkness. The four, two women and two men, gathered together and waited until the hum of the helicopter faded in the distance. Then there was only the sound of the wind moving through the night. The leader communicated by touch and near silent clicks of his commo unit.

He led them down the ridge into the valley. He stopped the team at the crest of a low hill and set two in position. They scanned the southern end of the valley and one nodded to him. He took the remaining scout across the valley and up another hill. Like the first pair, they found a position where they could look down the length of the valley. While his partner began scanning, he opened his pack and brought out a large roll of camouflage netting. In a matter of minutes the netting was strung over them. When daylight came it would help hide them from visual scans and in the meantime its special qualities broke up their electromagnetic and heat signatures.

The scouts huddled in the dark, intently scanning the south. For almost an hour they saw nothing. Then the first pair heard a whisper in their ears.

"We have them. Just as the Aegis drone saw. Six HUPAX, eight AFVs. Column formation."

"Roger. We have movement but no definition."

"Stay low – contacting Militia now."

"Roger. Hope those people in the machines can shoot straight."

"Aye. We are about to find out."

Gunnery Sergeant Doc Sevin lay strapped in his HUPAX, a brown and green Javelin, and watched the negative reports from the scout teams scroll onto his commo screen. The enemy could come up towards Coyote Bay through one of two valleys but no one was certain which one. The three HUPs in his team were the covering force for both of those valleys while three others remained in reserve.

He looked at time glowing in his visual field. The Wild Geese battalion was still returning from Kiroff and dealing with the Black Cats. The enemy somewhere to the south of him was supposed to be near Kiroff, like the Black Cats. Their landing ship's trajectory suggested their target was Kiroff. But a last minute, high-G burn made it clear their target was not the planet's capital. It was a raid against Coyote Bay, on the other side of the continent. That meant either the mines or the militia base. When the landing ship touched down twenty kilometers south of the city and base, it was clear the northern mines were not the target.

The plan was simple, one born out of necessity. The scouts would spot the raiders. The HUPs and Swallow fighters would, first, slow them down and then, second, kill them. It looked good on paper and had a nice ring to it, Sevin thought, but the odds were against it working.

What they needed was time for the Wild Geese Combined Arms Battalion to reinforce them. The problem was the battalion was coming from Kiroff, on the other side of the continent. That left the reserve HUPs at Coyote Bay Militia Base the job of carrying out the plan.

The rest of the Second Regiment, a battalion each of infantry and recon troops, lay in the hills immediately adjacent to the base. They did not have the firepower to take on HUPs in a face-to-face fight, but they hoped to slow them down if the enemy got past Sevin and his small group.

There were plenty of HUPAX fighting machines at Coyote Bay. Ten were operational and four were in various stages of maintenance. The problem was a lack of pilots. Lieutenant Chi Lore, Staff Sergeant Stephanie Elinshen, and Sevin were the only active pilots in Coyote Bay. The other three HUPs were crewed by Sergeant Steve Tashan, the battalion assistant HUP maintenance officer, and two of the most promising HUP students.

Tashan summed it up succinctly when he heard the idea: "You guys want to go ahead and paint a bull's-eye my HUP now or later?"

The two students, young Militia lieutenants whose previous training and experiences were in Bob Cat tanks, were clearly both eager and scared.

Chi Lore had put his forward team in HUPs heavy enough to carry a real punch but light enough to run. He was in a Long Bow, while Sevin lay in a Javelin and Elinshen was in a Rapier.

Tashan and the students were in HUPs selected to provide long-range supporting fire. Tashan had a four-legged Morning Star carrying a vertical launch system of anti-HUPAX missiles, a rail gun, and a massive GTL5 turreted laser. The students were in the two largest HUPs available on the base, a tall Trebuchet carrying multiple rail gun turrets and a four-legged War Lance carrying two bays of vertical launching missiles and a GTL2.

The Militia edge was in air power and armored vehicles. A squadron of Swallows sat on strip alert at edge of the runway. A flight of Tiger Moth attack helicopters was armed and ready nearby, topping off their fuel from portable bags lifted in by transport helicopters. A tank battalion was hurrying south from the base, having to take a longer way around the mountains the HUPs had walked over. The key was to use the edge before the attackers got out of the valley and into the open ground at the base – keep them in the valley and they couldn't maneuver well and would be easier to hit. Hold them long enough and the full battalion hurrying from Kiroff Airfield would drop on them and the ball game was over.

"Red Team, here we go. Blue Team, stay in trail by 700 meters."

Chi Lore's voice came in Sevin's ear. He did a quick scan of the instrument displays in his visual field, flipped his light amplification on, and walked forward.

Red, sensors off. We'll use the scout data until we engage. Blue, remain sensors on.

Somewhere behind them the Swallows launched, clawing their way into the air and swinging south. Sevin saw a Tiger Moth lifting nearby, the ugly barrel of its 37mm autocannon briefly silhouetted by groundcrew lights.

Well, the more the merrier.

The valley they entered was relatively straight at its northern end but twisted like a snake to the south, a fitting metaphor, since the creek running down the valley length was called Snake Creek. Farther to the south it curved towards the sea and became broader as it joined with the Brandywine River. The enemy landing ship was down there close to the juncture.

Ideally, they wanted to hit the attackers – no one was sure if they were Raiders or another mercenary unit like the Black Cats but Sevin was betting they were mercs – as they emerged into the narrow northern area so only a few of the enemy could engage at a time. However, it looked to Sevin they would not be in position in time to do this. Covering two valleys was the problem. On the other hand, the opening to the valley the enemy used was closer to the armored battalion than the other one. Maybe the air support could tangle them up before they emerged.

Red Team's HUPs went into a wedge formation while Blue Team remained in column. A line abreast formation would have been better for Blue Team but the students would have trouble maintaining formation in the rolling foothills of the valley. Tashan planned to spread them out as soon as making contact.

The valley floor was narrow, less than a kilometer at its widest, with scattered small hills and groves of trees. Chi Lore kept them to the center, frequently splashing into Snake Creek. Sevin flipped back and forth with his light amplification since its range was limited.

He saw the first strikes in the darkness ahead. Out of the black over his head, small yellow dots suddenly appeared and raced towards the far end of the valley. They disappeared and for a second there was nothing else. Then a series of flashes of reflected light illuminated the distant hills.

Other yellow dots climbed into the sky, seeking the fighters attacking the enemy. Sevin saw clusters of missiles climbing and falling at the same time. An orange glow flared behind the hills and then gradually faded. Then the Tiger Moths struck. Running parallel to the valley, they popped over the ridge on the right, firing their autocannon. Then they ducked back down. Sevin could not tell if they were hitting anything but it looked like the first burst of fire came from all eight helicopters at once and sending great sheet of flame sweeping into the valley. Returning missile fire impacted the crest of the ridge as the Tiger Moths dropped. Beams of laser fire sliced through the darkness, joining the missiles as the enemy tried to swat away the attacking helicopters and fighters.

A sudden smear of red and orange overhead marked the death of a Swallow. Burning pieces of debris fell around Red Team. Sevin flipped on light amplification in time to see a helicopter flying towards the team, dodging in and out of the trees, a small bright glow coming from its underside. The damaged Tiger Moth raced past the HUPs and disappeared behind them.

"Red Team, Scout Alpha. Multiple very large HUPAX with APCs inbound. Lead OPFOR HUPAX at your twelve, 700 meters, behind a hill. Speed 50, heading 360."

"Roger, Scout. Thank you."

Sevin saw the distant hill and took spacing to the right. At the side of the hill two tall trees suddenly whipped to the ground and a dark HUP appeared.

"Target the Scorpion. Blue Team, set up online where you are. Red, stay sensors off. Doc swing right, Elinshen stay with me."

Chi Lore's voice was calm, as if the 120-ton HUPAX coming around the hill ahead was nothing more than a target on a firing range. It was a flat, angular HUP, with two arm-like wings that extended forward. Coupled with the turret behind and above its two-person cockpit, it looked a little like the insect of the same name, though, like many HUPAX, its chassis was named after an ancient weapon. Its turrets looked up into the sky, seeking aerial targets. Three APCs clustered around its feet.

Sevin threw his Javelin into a hard right turn and swiveled his upper torso to bring all of his weapons to bear. He had a missile launcher and two GTL4 laser turrets and a 57mm chain-gun in a chin turret. With sensors off he would rely on the lasers. He looked at the Scorpion and the turrets followed his gaze. He placed the targeting reticle on the Scorpion and fired.

The flash of light from the lasers was almost blinding with the light amplification turned on. He saw the lasers hit the left arm of the two-man HUP. Chi Lore's Long Bow scored hits with a pair of laser shots as well. Just before Sevin's lasers cycled into ready status, Elinshen's own lasers split the night.

Taken by surprise, the Scorpion staggered under the fire of three HUPAX. Its pilot reversed course, backing the big HUP up while he tried to find his opponents. The APCs around him were quicker and raced towards Red Team, swiveling their missile launchers forward.

Two more enemy HUPs emerged from behind the hill, a Mace and a Trebuchet. For a heartbeat the retreating Scorpion blocked their fire. Sevin fired his lasers again just as the fire from Blue Team slammed into the Scorpion.

A flash of light marked the separation of the enemy HUP right leg from its hip connection. The Scorpion fell on its side, narrowly missing a racing APC, and throwing up a spray of earth and trees.

The Mace and Trebuchet now had a clear line of fire at Sevin. He cursed under his breath as the first ion pulse bolt of energy slammed into his HUP from the Mace and turned his visual field into electronic gibberish. Twin rail gun slugs from the Trebuchet impacted the center of his fuselage, throwing the HUP half way around. As he turned back the Mace fired again.

Suddenly Sevin's HUP was dead and out of the fight. The Mace's ion pulse weapon had sliced into the Javelin through an opening caused by the rail gun rounds and his mindlink and control systems burned away. The Javelin stood still, immobilized. In frustration, Sevin watched the two enemy HUPs walk through his targeting reticle but he could not fire. They turned their attention to the other two HUPs of Red Team.

Chi Lore and Elinshen were now on the other side of the narrow valley, using the small hills for cover as they blew apart the Scorpion's APC escorts. Blue Team continued to pour fire onto the two lumbering HUPs as they advanced, but the students were missing as often as they were hitting. Only Tashan repeatedly scored.

But four more enemy HUPs were coming into view. A pair of 125-ton, four-legged War Lances, one with its left arm gone from air strikes, led the latecomers. Close behind was another a 135-ton Trebuchet, and a second Scorpion.

"Don't these bastards have any small HUPs?"

"Doesn't look like it. Doc, what's your status?"

"I'm immobilized – controls shot away. Mindlink severed and manual controls are not responding."

"Roger. Get out of there in case one of them decides to settle on a cheap kill. Blue Team, Tashan, start backing up. Target the Trebuchet as you go."

"Blue, roger. They are ignoring you two – coming towards us. I don't think they see you."

"Roger, we're still sensors off so we're not on their detectors and they don't have line of sight. We're pulling into a ravine and we're going to try something. Keep going."

"Roger, we're leaving."

Sevin thought for a moment. None of the enemy HUPs was shooting in his direction. They probably expected to pick up his HUP as a prize and their fire was directed further up the valley, towards the retreating Blue Team. He might as well lean back and...

Then he saw the last Scorpion turn its flat fuselage towards him, uncovering its weapons in both side pylons. Someone wanted a cheap kill, as predicted – apparently, they had decided against capturing his Javelin. Maybe they didn't like smaller HUPs.

While his HUP was equipped with ladder rungs, there was only one way to get out quickly. Sevin sighed. He made sure his portable commo unit was on the active channel and checked his straps were tight. Then he pulled the ejection lever.

Metal clamshells snapped shut up around him, encasing Sevin in a cocoon of alloyed titanium. Before he could notice it, the cockpit ejection hatch blew clear and the cocoon ignited its rocket engine, slamming him into the night sky. He had a sensation of tumbling and then felt a violent shock. The ejection capsule, detecting atmosphere, deployed a parachute for stabilization, supplementing the small guidance rockets built into the capsule. Then, just before impact, it fired its rocket engine once again, braking the capsule meters short of impacting the ground at a speed capable of injuring its occupant.

As it was, when the capsule finally came to an abrupt halt, Sevin was not entirely sure he had not been killed. He clawed himself free of the restraining straps and opened the capsule.

He stumbled over a tree limb as he got out. The darkness was almost total and made more so by the occasional flashes of light in the distance from the advancing enemy HUPs. He could not see them due to brush and trees but it sounded like they were abreast of him, still driving north into the valley. The enemy Scorpion was gone, perhaps ignoring his HUP after seeing his ejection.

Sevin realized he could not hear any fighters or helicopters. Where were they? He pulled his commo unit from his survival pack and turned it on. The first burst of static almost made him jump and he plugged his headset into it, silencing the speaker. He heard Tashan reporting.

"Chi, we're almost at the entrance of the valley. OPFOR is making their way through a narrow area, so we're only seeing two of them. They've slowed down but we are running out of missiles."

"Copy. Tanks are fifteen minutes behind you. Can you hold them until then?"

"Negative. They are still coming forward."

"Roger. They went past us. I was hoping to hit them when the tanks did. All right, we do it the hard way. Red Two, get ready to go sensors on when we are in behind them. Follow me."

"Two, roger."

What was Chi up to? Sevin made his way slowly through the brush, looking for the stream that would lead him out of the valley. He smelled burned metal and flesh – there was no mistaking that unforgettable odor, one that all HUP combat pilots encountered sooner or later. It became stronger as he got closer to the stream. He paused when he heard voices. It sounded like two men and he realized that he could just hear the sound of the stream. He pulled a large handgun from its holster and moved forward slowly, wishing that he had a pair of light amplification goggles or Kodomir had a moon.

He almost stumbled on them. Two soldiers were by the stream. One was on the ground and the other crouched beside him. Sevin heard the metallic click of a safety going off as he leveled his sights on the crouching figure.

"You guys want to put down your weapons?"

"I don't think so," said the figure. Sevin saw he had a pistol. "Why don't you put yours down?"

The second figure, lying flat next to the stream, groaned.

"What's wrong with your friend?"

"Legs and arm are burned. We lost our aid packs when our APC went up."

Sevin thought for a moment.

"How about a cease-fire among the three of us? I got an aid pack and some pain killers."

"I'm not in a real hurry to put my gun down. I've dealt with militia before. You guys don't always play by the rules."

"Yeah, I know what you mean. But this is a different militia. You're up against full time soldiers. And a bunch of us are mercs. Or were mercs. SFA registered. Articles of War are in effect." He fumbled at his gear and pulled an aid pack free. "Here, use this for your buddy." He gently tossed the pack on the ground in front of the first soldier. The man made no effort to pick it up and the pistol remained steady.

"What do you mean, 'full time soldiers,' and what mercs are on this rock?"

"The Kodomir Militia has a full-time cadre as well as a bunch of reservists. They got air, as you may have noticed, arty, armor, and HUPs. I'm guessing no one told you about all that."

"We were told planetary militia, but we got some intel that you all had a few HUPs from driving off some Raiders. The old order of battle data said you had some arty and air."

"All right if I sit down?" Sevin asked. He slowly lowered his weapon. "I hurt my back ejecting." The soldier hesitated and then motioned downward with his pistol. "Yeah, the Kodomiri have a big Slavic cultural thing," Sevin said as he eased himself to the ground. "They love artillery. Some of their gunners even have priests come and bless their guns. The HUPs are from the Raiders and from my old merc unit." He slowly put his gun away.

"Yeah, what about that? What merc unit is here?" The man kept his pistol pointed at Sevin.

"Wild Geese. You got any water for your buddy?"

"Been using the creek, but don't have a container." Sevin threw over his canteen. The soldier moved slightly and picked it up with one hand. He frowned. "Wild Geese? Never heard of you."

"I have," the soldier on the ground said through clenched teeth. "Who's your CO?"

"Alisti Mahmud al-Kheyntamenti. You know him?"

"Know *of* him. Jake, this guy is legitimate."

The first soldier thought for a moment and then clicked his pistol to safe and put it in his holster. "All right, you got your cease-fire. I figure my people will stop here and pick us up on the way back from the raid. We're not here to snatch anyone, so you'll go your way, we'll go ours."

"Fair enough. Can I give you a hand with that aid pack?"

Using a small light, the two men worked on the third. A few minutes later the burned soldier was sleeping, knocked out by painkillers, his wounds covered in nanotechnology bandages. The first soldier held out his hand to Doc.

"Thanks for the assist. I'm Squad Sergeant Jake Ellington." They shook hands. "This is Guidon Sergeant Takan Nguyen. We're with Vermeil's Victors."

"You guys have some big HUPs," Doc said as he took a drink from his canteen.

"We were a security force for a combine. The CEO and Board of Directors believed in doing everything in a big way. Top money." He spat into to the darkness. "Turned out they were stealing the company blind and planned on using us to cover their escape. Major Vermeil wouldn't go along – hell, they were going to trash our pension fund. Anyway, they were all thrown in jail and the new people started spinning off chunks of the business, trying to improve their bottom line. We got spun off. We're 40% owned by the combine but otherwise independent. Do our own contracts, all that. They help underwrite our expenses and get some of the profits."

"How's that working for you?"

"Not too bad. We had two contracts before Kodomir, both pretty small. This was our biggest, a raid on the base at Coyote Bay. We're going to get a bonus for each major structure we knock down at your base."

"I see." Doc paused and touched his headset, listening.

"Steph, stay wide left. See the tail-end War Lance?"

"Roger."

"He's like a cork in the bottle. Everyone is in front of him. Sensors on. Hit him."

"Chi, Blue Lead, they are turning around."

"Roger, they know we're here. Scratch one War Lance. Back armor was pretty thin. Probably damaged from air strikes. Sensors off. Target the Scorpion."

"Chi, Blue. We just crippled a Trebuchet. It's down. We're out of rail gun and missile ammo but they don't seem to realize that. They have turned and are chasing you."

"Outstanding. We're pulling deeper into the valley."

"Heavy armor, Ajax Lead. How do you copy?"

"Ajax, Red Lead. Loud and clear."

"Roger, we are in bound with seven Swallows. Say bandit position."

"Bandits are point seven five south of Nav Bravo. Read Blue's datalink."

"Rog, three quarters klick south of Bravo. Got the link. We will be running north to south with a left-hand pull."

"Roger. Be advised we have three friendly HUPs at Nav Bravo."

"Understood. And you are on the other side of the OPFOR HUPs?"

"Roger, but don't worry about us. We are pulling back, deeper into the valley. We should be well away from your targets."

"I copy. Lead is in hot."

Sevin looked at Ellington. "The lead Trebuchet is down, legged, and that boom you heard was the War Lance. Our air guys are back. I don't think you will get to the base tonight."

Ellington shrugged. He said, "Well, it ain't over yet."

They heard the scream of the fighters as they made their runs and flashes of light erupted in the distance, followed by dull booms. They knew when the Victor HUPs emerged from the pass by the sudden bright red and purple lasers slashing into the dark sky. Sevin could feel the ground vibrate beneath him as the big HUPs came closer.

He watched as Nguyen faded in and out of consciousness. The man was in very bad shape. At least he wasn't feeling any pain at the moment, but unless real medical aid was provided, he did not have long to live.

"Well, maybe you ought to be going," Ellington said after studying the movement of the Victor HUPs. "I gather the major's pulling us out of here so I'm going to pop a flare and see if an APC can pick us up and get us back to our landing ship."

Before Sevin could reply there was a sharp crack of an explosion and the sky lit up with a flash that faded into a pulsing yellow glow just on the other side of a nearby hill.

"Critical hit on the Mace. It's burning. Nice shooting, Ajax. I think it is down."

"Thanks, Red Lead. Our choppers are inbound. I'm going to move Ajax flight against their landing ship and see if we can't cripple it or drive it off before they make it back. You guys are getting a little close together down there."

"Roger."

"Listen," Sevin said. "I think it might be better if I stay here with you two. I got a beacon. If I activate it, my people will come here as soon as possible. Your APCs might not be able to swing over here or they may not see your flare and your Guidon Sergeant needs medical aid right now. If your guys get here, fine, you both go if you want and I'll wave bye-bye. But if they don't, my guys can guide on the beacon and a helicopter will medevac him to the base hospital." He held up the beacon, little more than the size of a thick pen. "Deal?" Ellington thought for a moment.

"All right, deal," he said. Sevin nodded and thumped the beacon and then spoke into his headset.

"Red Lead, Red Three. Beacon on. Be advised, I have two OPFOR with me, one WIA and needing medevac if his people can't pick him up."

Roger, Doc. Good to hear from you. I don't think they can. Their last APC just got nailed by Red Two. Do you want us to try to get a medevac in?

"Stand by one."

"Here's the latest," Doc said to Ellington. "Your APCs are gone and a HUP can't pick up your man. We are willing to try to get a medevac chopper in. Is that acceptable?"

Ellington sighed. "Oh, hell," he finally said. "Yeah, send in the medevac. Tell your people to let Major Vermeil know its Ellington and Nguyen and he'll let the dust-off through, probably."

"Red Lead, the CO of the mercs is a Major Vermeil. The unit is Vermeil's Victors. Sergeants Ellington and Nguyen are with me. Nguyen is very badly burned and needs immediate medevac. See if he will let the medevac bird in or will we have to wait until he clears the area?"

Roger, Doc. Switching channels. Be right back.

Sevin sat in the dark and listened to Nguyen's harsh breathing. The sounds of battle seemed to ebb for a moment and then flare back up. Then quiet descended.

"Doc, Red Lead. Medevac is inbound. I think Vermeil is going to ask for permission to withdraw without further fighting but he has no way of picking up his stragglers and wounded from the APCs."

"Roger, keep me apprised of that."

"Medevac is inbound," Sevin said and Ellington looked relieved. "Your CO may request permission to withdraw. Your landing ship is under attack and our choppers are coming back any time now. So we may get a general cease fire."

"All right," Ellington said and hobbled to his feet. Sevin could see in the dim glow of the light that the back of a trouser leg was dark with blood and his eyebrows went up. Ellington grimaced. "Ah, I caught something when we bailed out of the APC. Not a big deal. Tell your people I'm sending up a flare."

As the flare popped into dancing life above them, Sevin communicated with Chi Lore. He listened for a moment.

"Everyone sees the flare," he said. "Medevac is about five minutes out. Your CO is requesting the cease-fire to extend so negotiations for withdrawal can take place. My CO is checking with command."

"Got it." Ellington looked at Sevin and appeared slightly embarrassed. "Listen, while I'm up, could you help me bandage this thing? I can't reach around behind me very well."

Sevin was finishing the bandage when they heard the throbbing beat of the helicopter. Ellington fired another flare and Doc guided the pilot with his commo unit. The small helicopter settled into a clearing twenty meters downstream and a medic jumped out and ran over to them. The three of them lifted Nguyen and carried him to the helicopter. Within a few minutes they were airborne, speeding towards Coyote Bay Militia Base.

"Doc, how's it going?"

"We're in the chopper. What's happening?" Sevin's eyes were on the medic who was working quickly but the vital signs on the med scanner were not good.

"They still have four HUPs and most of our stuff is damaged. The battalion won't be here for a while. The tanks have the valley blocked if they try to continue but Vermeil wants just to leave. All we can really hit him with are the helicopters and fighters. Command wants to offer him the same deal as the Cats but if he doesn't take it, we don't have the force to stop him from leaving, though the air guys think they can clobber the landing ship.

"Roger. By the way, the guy we're medevacing knows us. His name is Nguyen. Takan Nguyen."

Ellington held up his hand. Sevin leaned forward.

"Sarge was in the Ninth Light Lancers a few years ago. That's where he would have heard about your CO." Sevin nodded and relayed the information.

"Thanks, Doc. I'll pass it on when I hear from the colonel. The battalion is in landing ships and on their way, but they're too far away for me to raise."

In the red-lit interior of the helicopter, the medic continued working on Nguyen. Soon two intravenous bags were pumping fluids into the man. The wounds looked worse than they had on the ground, mostly because the extent of them could be seen more clearly now. Sevin watched as the medic spoke into his headset and the helicopter lunged forward but he sensed that time was moving faster.

"Chi Lore looked at the four stationary HUPs. Vermeil had asked for time to consult with his landing ship captain. Chi was willing to grant it, for each minute brought the Wild Geese battalion with its sixteen HUPAX closer. The Tiger Moths were north of the valley, clustered around their fuel bags having finished topping off. The Swallows impatiently circled overhead, eager to take on the landing ship. But Chi knew Blue Team was out of long-range ammunition and damaged besides. His own HUP had lost a pylon and the weapon attached to it. Only Elinshen's HUP was still healthy. She was eager to get back into the fight.

Stephanie Elinshen was always eager to fight, though.

"Chi, Kheyntamenti. How do you copy?"

"Loud and clear, boss," Chi said, relief obvious in his voice. "Glad to hear from you. You must be close."

"About 40 minutes from landing. We're set with sixteen HUPs plus the tank company. Infantry and artillery are about ten minutes behind us. How are the negotiations going?"

"Not sure," Chi said, shaking his head in the darkness of his cockpit. "I'm relaying from General Polrany. He's made the same offer the Black Cats got. Take a contract or get out and walk, but I don't think we have the force to press the issue. He really doesn't want these guys to get off-world."

"Roger that. We don't know if they will come back and try and fulfill their current contract. Polrany wants them destroyed if they won't surrender or take a contract with us."

"One other thing, colonel. We medevaced one of their wounded, a guy from a unit called the Ninth Light Lancers, name of Takan Nguyen. Ring a bell?"

"Not the man. The Lancers were a merc unit garrisoning an automated mining installation. Raiders overran them. Killed almost everyone, didn't take prisoners. The survivors fled into the hills. They were hunting them down for sport. We were hired to recon and assess damage. We found them and got them out on our landing ship."

"That was it?"

"There wasn't room on the landing ship for everyone, so we sent away our grunts and the surviving Lancers. Our HUPs played tag with the Raiders until the landing ship returned. Gwielgi can fill you in on the details. It happened the year before you joined us."

"Got it," Chi said. "Let me see if I can get Nguyen to talk to his CO. Maybe it will help."

"Roger. Thirty-five minutes from landing."

Chi switched channels – if Vermeil had any sense of gratitude, it might work to end the fighting.

"Doc, you still up?"

"Affirmative."

"Listen, do you think Nguyen would talk to his CO? I just got the story of how the Geese helped him and his mates. Maybe Vermeil will listen to him. We're trying like hell to convince him to take the easy way out, but I think he's going to try to fight his way clear."

"Sorry. Sergeant Nguyen died two minutes ago."

"Oh, hell. Well, we tried. Out."

Chi stared at the four HUPs. He shook his head and took a breath.

"Major Vermeil, Lieutenant Chi Lore. I have some bad news for you, sir."

"Go ahead, lieutenant."

"Sir, I regret to report Sergeant Takan Nguyen died. He was still on the chopper."

"Roger, stand by. I want to relay this."

"Roger, standing by."

Chi checked his weapons. He had started the fight with two GTL5 turrets. One of them was gone, ripped apart by that Trebuchet that seemed to be staring right at him from the middle of the valley. God, that was a big monster!

To his right, Elinshen's Rapier was virtually invisible. He knew she was more than willing, perhaps too willing, to mix it up with the remaining Victors. He would just as soon see the whole situation be settled peacefully.

"Lieutenant Chi Lore, Major Vermeil. I want to extend my unit's thanks for trying to do the right thing for Guidon Sergeant Nguyen. He was a good man and we appreciate your people trying to help him."

"No problem, sir. Sir, maybe enough good people have died today."

"Roger that, lieutenant. My landing ship tells me that they see three landing ships inbound, followed by two more. I take it we're about to have the hammer dropped on us?"

"Not necessarily, sir. General Polrany's offer is still on the table. You can stand down and evacuate, leaving your weapons behind, or you can abrogate your contract and take one from us. We've explained that you're the latest of a series of merc units who have been set-up. We are supporting one of their complaints filed with the SFA. You've been had, major."

"Yeah, I got that impression when your team slammed the door in our face coming through the valley. A lot more is here than some obsolete planetary militia. I plan on having a long conversation with that contract broker when we get back to Alpha Centauri."

Centauri? He was still thinking about making a run for it. Chi shook his head as he transmitted. "Sir, we have sixteen more HUPs coming, there's a battalion of tanks at the north end of the valley, and the rest of a reinforced regiment is on the way. I don't think you'll make your landing ship before everyone else arrives."

"Well, lieutenant, here's what we are going to do."

Chi saw the Victor HUPs move, all but the Trebuchet. It stood its ground, looking at Chi and Elinshen. His heart sank.

"I'm sending my remaining HUPs to the landing ship – they'll pick up our APCs holding the landing zone perimeter. I think they'll make it before your reinforcements arrive. Now I'm going to offer you and your wingman a deal. We mauled those other three HUPs to the north pretty good. I figure they are out of the fight. Your HUP is damaged. That Rapier looks in good shape. But so is this Trebuchet. I think the four of us could take you two out pretty quickly but I appreciate what you tried to do for Nguyen. So, here's the deal. Stand down and let us go. Otherwise, fight on."

Before Chi could respond, Elinshen's voice came up.

"Major, I have a deal for *you*. How about this? You and me, one on one. You win, all your people leave with all your gear. I win, you stand down and either walk out or take a contract."

"Who the hell is this?"

"Staff Sergeant Stephanie Elinshen. I am in the Rapier you have been watching."

"Steph, stand down."

"Sergeant, you really think you're that good?"

"Lieutenant, let me play this out. Major, yes, I am that good. I have been kicking your unit's butt all night long and I figure I can take down that pig you are in. Come on, major. No one else has to get hurt. Just us. You want Atsilvquodi, you have to earn it."

The major's laughter echoed over the commo.

"Sergeant, I like your style, whatever the hell 'Atsilvquodi' is. All right. We'll do it. Tell your people to hold off. I'll do the same. Back off a little way. So will I. Call fight on when you're ready."

The Trebuchet turned and walked away. The other Victor HUPs stopped and turned. Chi wondered what they were thinking. He keyed his microphone.

"Major, you don't have to do this. The offer still stands."

"I like your sergeant's offer better, lieutenant. When I win, we get to leave with more than you're offering. Besides, we don't like surrendering."

Chi bit off a curse and started to call Elinshen when Kheyntamenti's voice came over the unit primary frequency.

"I heard. We're twenty-five minutes out."

"I was about to call Elinshen back. I think she's gone crazy."

"Elinshen's a gunfighter, but she's not crazy. She's had a chance to observe Vermeil's skill. If she thinks she can do it, let her take a run at it. It could save some lives."

"Roger, sir. I have not seen anything like this before."

"I have, Chi. Remember, she's Currahee."

Chi moved his HUP onto a small hill. Elinshen's Rapier had disappeared in the dark and was somewhere on the slope of the mountain forming the western boundary of the valley. The Trebuchet was on the other side of the stream, just on the edge of light amplified sight.

"You ready, sergeant?"

"Go ahead, major."

"Fight's on, sergeant."

The big HUP spun to one side and accelerated, though slowly, towards the shelter of a hill. Its vaguely human-like torso swung back towards the Rapier's position. Chi flipped his sensors on and had a glimpse of the Rapier before its own sensors turned off and the blue bracket vanished from his visual field. He triggered infrared but it was too late. Elinshen was gone into the darkness of the forest.

But it wasn't dark long. Both HUPs fired at almost the same moment. The Trebuchet fired two rail guns, their hypervelocity rounds cracking like invisible thunderbolts, and a pair of GTL5 turrets stabbed into the dark. But three laser lances, lighting up the ground in all direction, impacted the big HUP, striking sparks and throwing glowing bits of armor around. A pair of flashes marked the arrival of two recoilless rifle rounds. The Trebuchet staggered but Chi could not tell what had happened to the Rapier.

Then the Trebuchet was behind the hill. Chi understood Vermeil's tactic. By staying behind the hill the Rapier would have to close with it, and that would mean coming into the open and becoming a target for the pair of large rail guns that had scored hits earlier on Chi's Rapier.

The Trebuchet slowed and finally halted. Chi had no idea where Elinshen was. If Elinshen came down the mountainside and went over the hill, the Trebuchet would chew her up. Her best bet…

The Trebuchet flinched, hit by two more recoilless rifle rounds, this time from the side. Elinshen had swung around the hill, keeping well distant. Vermeil turned his HUP, trying to acquire the Rapier. But there were more hills in the valley than the one the Trebuchet chose. By staying at a distance and keeping her sensors off, Elinshen forced Vermeil to find her visually or by her heat emissions, but as she ran among the forests and hills in the dark his chance to do that was limited. On the other hand, as long as the Trebuchet stayed where it was, it would be much easier to find.

Vermeil saw the problem and moved, anticipating where Elinshen headed. Chi saw the lasers stab into the darkness again and this time there was a flash of light in the distance. Something got hit.

"Just a little closer, sergeant."

Elinshen made no reply for a moment. Chi scanned ahead of the lumbering Trebuchet, using his light amplification to search for the Rapier, but saw nothing. Suddenly two laser beams cut through the night, momentarily dazzling him. Almost at the same instant as the large lasers flashed glowing globs of armor from the front of the Trebuchet, more armor went flying from recoilless rifle hits.

"How close do you want me, major? Keep coming, weak-heart."

Chi had a glimpse of the Rapier, running through the trees in the distance. Elinshen was using a firebreak trail and, not hampered by hitting trees, ran at almost full speed. The Trebuchet fired its lasers again, but the only thing it hit were some trees, blowing them to splinters. Then the Rapier was gone. The Trebuchet, still searching, plunged forward and away from Chi. Then it was gone as well, hidden by the forested hills.

Chi resisted the temptation to move up to see. Another moving HUP in the middle of the duel could lead to friendly fire or a general battle. He sat still and watched the remaining Victor HUPs, trying to figure out where the duelers were by where the Victor HUPs were looking.

"Red Lead, Red Two, on unit primary."

"Roger, Two. Where the hell are you?"

"About a klick down the valley. I can see you on the hill. The Trebuchet is damaged but still coming."

"How are you?"

133

"He chewed up my left side fairly well. Tends to acquire his target late. Lost one laser. Not much ammunition left for the rifles. I am leading him towards the springs that feed into the creek."

Chi glanced down at his map and found the area.

"Roger, copy. Be careful. That ground is very marshy. You don't want to get slowed down in there."

Elinshen did not reply as red lines cut through the night in her area. Chi could not tell if it was her or Vermeil doing the shooting. Then darkness returned. He watched his scope and strained to see anything in the night.

"Chi, we are fifteen minutes out."

"Roger, sir. Duel is still on."

More minutes passed. Chi could see no signs of battle, no firing. From the way the remaining Victor HUPs were moving their torsos back and forth they did not know where the fight was either.

"Oh, hell."

The major's voice was resigned. Then Elinshen spoke.

"Major, I can sit back here all day and take you apart with my remaining lasers. Do you wish to stand down?"

"Sergeant, standing is damned near out of the question, given that I am stuck in this swamp up to my butt. I appreciate your holding fire. Yes, reluctantly, I agree to stand down. Give me a moment to tell my unit and landing ship. Lieutenant Chi Lore, are you still on this channel?"

"Affirmative, sir."

"Convey my respects to General Polrany. Tell him I would be delighted to discuss a possible contract for the Victors with the Kodomir Militia. And I request a tow to get the hell out of this swamp your sergeant led me into."

The major's dry tone conveyed that delight was not what he was experiencing.

"Roger that, sir."

Chapter 9: Distant thunder

21 June 2824

Captain Gwielgi paused outside his commander's office, tugged at his gray utility jacket, and picked a piece of nonexistent lint off the Wild Geese emblem on the breast pocket. He glanced at Sergeant Elinshen. Clad in the same uniform, she stood in the hall a few paces away, her face impassive, though her eyes showed some tension. He nodded to her and then rapped on the door.

"Come," said a voice from within. Gwielgi opened the door and strode in alone, closing it behind him. Alisti Mahmud al-Kheyntamenti sat behind his desk, his hands folded in front of him. Like Elinshen, his face was devoid of emotion.

"I have the review, sir," Gwielgi said, extending a folder. Kheyntamenti reached up and put it to one side.

"Summarize it, captain," Kheyntamenti said. His voice was formal.

"Sir, the action is well known to you. Sergeant Elinshen's offer for a duel did not go through her superior officer prior to its being made. My analysis suggests that she and Red Lead could have delayed OPFOR's arrival at their landing ship by long-range harassing fire long enough for the battalion to drop and intercept. However, to do that the battalion would have had to drop within range of the Victor landing ship. We would have taken casualties."

"Has Lieutenant Chi Lore changed his recommendation?"

"No, sir, he hasn't."

"What is her statement?"

"She continues to refuse to make one, stating that she wishes to speak directly to you. Sir," Gwielgi hesitated, "I think she is looking for council. She means in the Currahee usage of the word."

"We are not a Currahee unit, captain," Kheyntamenti said. He paused. "Did she really call him a weak-heart?"

"Yes, sir, she did." Gwielgi smiled slightly. "It was the worst thing she could think of to call him. And she offered Atsilvquodi , honor, if he would fight her. Vermeil had no idea what those words meant, but he got the drift quickly enough."

Kheyntamenti nodded, not returning the smile. "Very well. Bring her in. We will make this quick – I have a meeting with Major Vermeil and Captain Walsh in fifteen minutes." Gwielgi nodded and went to the door. He motioned to Elinshen who marched in and stopped at attention in front of the colonel's desk.

"Sergeant Elinshen, Captain Gwielgi says you wish to report to me. Go ahead."

"Sir," Elinshen said, her eyes burning a hole through the bulkhead a meter above Kheyntamenti's head, "I am aware that I violated the chain of command by initiating my challenge to Major Vermeil. I am also aware that my actions could be perceived as undermining Lieutenant Chi Lore's authority and therefore dishonoring him. I offer no defense and am prepared to take whatever punishment you deem appropriate."

Standing slightly behind her, Gwielgi nodded as he looked at Kheyntamenti. Council. There were several Currahee among the Wild Geese and over time they had removed some of the mystery and myth of that hidden people. Council was a public expression of responsibility offered to ensure no others were blamed for errors.

"Sergeant Elinshen, your awareness of the situation is not the issue. This is not a court-martial, so no defense is needed. I am attempting to understand not simply the situation but your decision. Why did you make the offer?"

"Colonel, I did not believe our five HUPs, even with air support, could hold the Victors long enough to prevent their escape. In any case, the attempt would have cost us several HUPs, perhaps more, as well as additional aircraft."

"Sergeant, if you had been explicitly ordered to withdraw your offer and to return to your position beside Lieutenant Chi Lore, what would you have done?"

"Sir, I would have complied."

Kheyntamenti pulled the folder over to him and read through it. After a moment he looked up, his dark eyes boring into Elinshen.

"And what if you had lost, sergeant? What of your promise to Vermeil? The battalion was under orders not to allow them to escape. How could Atsilvquodi, honor, been granted to Vermeil so that he could have withdrawn if you had lost?"

Elinshen looked genuinely puzzled for a moment.

"Sir, there was little chance of my losing." Kheyntamenti raised an eyebrow. "Sir, I had seen Major Vermeil and the others fight. Their HUPAX were, are, very large and well-armed but they are not very good with them. Major Vermeil was having trouble quickly acquiring his targets. With my superior knowledge of the terrain, I could not lose." She paused and then continued. "Nonetheless, if I had, the battalion would have followed whatever orders you gave it."

"Nicely put, sergeant," Kheyntamenti said dryly. He glanced back down at the report. "Lieutenant Chi Lore recommended an action to be taken and that recommendation was endorsed by Captain Gwielgi. For some time I have observed your conduct and have been leaning in the direction of the recommendation. This latest incident has convinced me of its appropriateness. Do you have anything else to add?"

"No, sir." Elinshen still stood at attention, her eyes fixed and steady.

"Very well then," Kheyntamenti said. "As a unit, we are governed by Kodomir Militia Military Law and procedures, though we are allowed some relatively broad flexibility in their application. Nonetheless, there are protocols we have to abide by." He flipped the pages to the last one and looked up at Gwielgi.

"It will start on the first?"

"Yes, sir. General Polrany said that your proposal is not unprecedented and it is within Militia procedures."

"Good." He turned back to the last page of the report and signed it. Kheyntamenti flipped the report closed and handed it to Gwielgi before getting to his feet.

"Stephanie Elinshen, you are hereby promoted to the rank of Second Lieutenant in the Kodomir Militia. Your recent conduct, personal courage, and intelligent initiative indicate to me that you deserve the opportunity to function at a higher level of responsibility and authority. That was the recommendation of Lieutenant Chi Lore and it was endorsed by Captain Gwielgi." He looked at Gwielgi. "You have them?"

"Aye, sir." Gwielgi handed a small box to Kheyntamenti who stepped in front of Elinshen. He removed the small, black sergeant's pins from her epaulets and replaced them with the dull brown pins of a second lieutenant.

"Welcome aboard, lieutenant," he said and held out his hand. Elinshen, her face still impassive, shook it.

"Thank you, sir," she said. Gwielgi repeated the gesture.

"That will be all, lieutenant," Kheyntamenti said. Elinshen turned to go. "Oh, one other thing. I mentioned that we are following Militia procedures. Therefore, on 1 July you will report to the Militia Officer Training School at Kiroff Airfield to join your class. For the next three months you will be trained in everything the Militia believes a new officer needs to know. Gwielgi will fill you in on the details. That is all." Kheyntamenti was smiling as Elinshen, followed closely by Gwielgi who looked at him and cracked a grin, left the room.

"Well, lieutenant, what do you think?" Gwielgi asked as they walked down the hallway.

"Sir," Elinshen spoke slowly, shaking her head, "I thought the Old Man was going to kick me out of HUPAX, maybe out of the battalion."

"Other COs might have, and they would have been within their rights. However, he knows you and knows what you could mean to the battalion, if..." He let his voice trail off as he paused at the exit.

"Understood, captain," Elinshen said. "I still struggle with control." She pulled her beret out from under her epaulet and examined the Wild Geese emblem on it. "Do you think Colonel Kheyntamenti understands the honor he has given me?"

"I think he does," Gwielgi said. He put on his own beret and stepped outside, followed closely by Elinshen.

"So, I am to go to school?" They both returned the salute of a passing soldier.

"Yep," Gwielgi said as they walked down the sidewalk. "The Militia sends all of its newly commissioned officers to MOTS. Most of the other students will be people right out of officer candidate school, though there may be one or two people like you with actual field experience. A lot of it will be classroom work, from how to fill out someone's fitness report to the basics of Militia Law. Some tactical and weapons training, field exercises, that kind of thing."

"And then?"

"Then you come back here, though you may elect to take one of their advanced courses. You're a qualified HUP pilot. We are the Militia HUP unit."

"I suppose they will have me wear Militia issue."

"Right, their regular field uniform. But you keep your beanie. Officers going to MOTS whose units have distinctive uniform items maintain those at MOTS. So, you'll wear your purple beret."

"Good," she said. She touched the brown badge of rank on her shoulder. "Whose were these?"

"Last wearer was Lieutenant Chi Lore. Before that, they were mine." He paused and she turned to face him. "The Militia pips will go on as soon as you can get a pair but the colonel has made it a unit tradition that when anyone is promoted, their first badge of their new rank is one of our old ones. Down the road, you can pass them on." Gwielgi paused again.

"We don't have many sets of old Wild Geese second lieutenant's pips in the files, so I hope you don't mind wearing a pair that started with someone who was not Aniwaya." She came to attention and raised her hand to the brim of her beret in a salute and held it.

"Sir, I am honored to wear these badges of rank."

"The honor, lieutenant, is mine." Gwielgi raised his own hand and held it. Their hands snapped down and for an instant Gwielgi thought he saw Elinshen's eyes water. He looked away, as if gazing across the base as a pair of Swallows took off in formation, and said nothing. Currahee could be a little funny about others noticing signs of emotion.

"Oh, one thing I meant to tell you," Gwielgi said. "There's going to be a small gathering of the battalion officers at the Landing Ship Tavern tonight, 2100. Bring your chit – you're buying. It's your 'wetting down' party."

Elinshen grimaced as they continued walking. "There is not a great deal of difference in the paycheck of a staff sergeant and a second lieutenant; I hope no one comes thirsty."

"Don't worry. Jackie Peregrine said she would sell us the booze at wholesale." He grinned. "And she knows who she is dealing with." He glanced at his watch. "I have to go back." He paused and looked at his feet for a moment.

"I know it can be hard for someone raised in the Currahee traditions to function in a non-Currahee unit like ours." He looked up at her. "The discipline is not as tight, hierarchy not as strong. But beyond all that, trying to come to grip with different concepts of honor is something often very difficult, whether Currahee Aniwaya or not. If there is anything I can do to help, let me know."

"Understood, sir." She smiled slightly. "Though referring to the Wild Geese as 'non-Currahee' may not be as correct a phrase as it might appear. There is much about the unit that reminds me of some of the better parts of the Aniwaya."

"Well, honor," Gwielgi said, "real honor, is not bound by space, time, or circumstances of birth."

"Aye, sir," Elinshen said. "I am coming to understand that."

Kheyntamenti entered the staff conference room followed by Gwielgi and Sevin. The two mercenary leaders, Walsh and Vermeil, stood. Kheyntamenti waved them to their seats.

"Good morning, gentlemen," he said as he took a seat. He waited until Gwielgi and Sevin joined him. "We have several of items on our agenda and I know you both are busy settling in your units so I won't detain you any longer than necessary. You both know Captain Gwielgi, our operations officer. This is Gunnery Sergeant Sevin. He heads our HUPAX maintenance section." There were nods back and forth.

"Before we begin, Major Vermeil, have you had a chance to check on your pilot?"

"Yes, colonel," Vermeil said. He was a tall, slender man with dark hair and very expressive hands that often moved as he talked. "Lieutenant Simpson ejected from her War Lance without any problem, but her back was hurt on landing. The medics finished surgery this morning and her spinal cord is fully restored. She'll be rejoining us next week, if we can tear her away from all that good food."

"I am glad to hear that," Kheyntamenti said. "Both Captain Gwielgi and Gunny Sevin have survived ejections and been subject to the assistance of our medical services, so we have some appreciation of Lieutenant Simpson's situation."

"The food promotes healing," Sevin said, "because it encourages you to leave the hospital."

"They feed you at the hospital?" Gwielgi asked. "Since when did they start doing that? Why does no one tell me these things?"

"I have asked," Kheyntamenti said, shaking his head, "Captain Gwielgi and Gunny Sevin, if they can tear themselves away from their comedy act, to see what assistance, if any, you need in bringing your HUPs and other gear up on line. I know you both have facilities within your landing ships, but our maintenance yards both here and at Kiroff are much less cramped than anything onboard a ship. We have a fairly large maintenance crew. We also have HUP and armor weapons and ammunition to complement your own stocks and these can be drawn from as per your contracts."

"Thank you, colonel," Walsh said. "General Polrany asked me to prepare a list of needs and I can give that to Sergeant Sevin now." Kheyntamenti nodded and Walsh slid some papers over to Doc who read through them.

"We have damage to our remaining operational HUPs," Vermeil said, "plus some exterior damage to our landing ship. They only freed my Trebuchet last night, so it isn't here yet, but it is going to need work as well. I would like to give priority to repairs to our landing ship since we will need it for deployment."

"We have lift capability to move you, major," Kheyntamenti said, "but work on your landing ship can begin immediately."

"Good," Vermeil said. He turned to Sevin. "Gunny, I think we can handle most of what we need done on most of our HUPs, but two suffered leg damage and are immobile and my Trebuchet is in shambles. One of my maintenance people is bringing it out of the valley and down to the highway but they are going to bring it the rest of the way on a prime mover. I don't think it could make it the whole distance. I'd like to have it worked on with your facility rather than try to wrestle it onboard once we get our ship up here."

"No problem, sir," Doc said, making a note on his datapad. "As for the 'legged' HUPs, we can take a repair section down there by landing ship and get them fixed enough to board. Then we'll haul them up here to the main HUP repair facility."

"While you are working on your HUPs," Kheyntamenti said, "you might want to swap out weapons to configure for your garrison assignment. Captain, fill them in on the situation in Portaka."

Gwielgi walked to the wall and touched some controls. A map of Kodomir flashed into life. He adjusted the display and it centered on a large continent in the southern hemisphere.

"This is Portaka and where you will be garrisoned, hopefully soon. There is a very small Militia facility near the east coast, not far from the primary town. But the important part is the growing industrial and mining facilities, mostly northwest of the base. The town I mentioned is called Portaka City. At present, the base is not equipped for HUPs. It has few facilities. There's little more down there right now than a runway, a couple of small hangars, and a detachment that runs the Militia ranges to the west."

Gwielgi returned to the table. "Most of the environment is essentially desert, punctuated by mountains and salt flats. In the south, you get worse terrain – it's called the Badlands – but it gets some real winter weather. Volcanic, ancient lava flows, it's a real charmer. The interior, except where mining is underway, is uninhabited. There is almost no surface water, but plenty if you can drill down twenty or thirty meters. It is desolate, with extreme heat in the northern three quarters and the potential for nasty winters in the south. Most of Kodomir is prime farming land, so Portaka's interior has remained undeveloped, even unexplored except for aerial surveys."

"Until recently," Gwielgi said, "most of the significant mining on Kodomir was done in the mountains near here at Coyote Bay. Those mines were targets for some of the raids, as a matter of fact. In the past year, major deposits of minerals and strategic ores were found in Portaka, some not too far from the Militia base. We think it is only a question of time until whoever hired the units that hit us begins directing units against those assets."

"Hell, colonel," Vermeil said, turning to Kheyntamenti with a sardonic smile, "I'm glad we pulled down one of the scenic contracts. That place sounds like a hole."

"It is," Kheyntamenti said. "Nonetheless, it has to be protected. And that need will increase with time as the area is developed. The Militia is building up the base and eventually will have it in decent shape. But you'll be living out of your landing ships when you first get there." He nodded at Gwielgi.

"Until the mercenary attacks began," Gwielgi said, "Kodomir was pretty much out of the line of fire of most of the wars of the Settled Worlds. The Kodomiri were willing to go along with whoever was the biggest kid on the block at the time. 'Accommodation' was the foundation of their foreign policy. As long as they were allowed to run things domestically, they didn't care whose flag was on the pole. However, Raiders from the Frontier did strike with some regularity in the past, either here or at Kodomir's neighbors. Just for Kodomir, it averaged out to slightly less than once a year, hence the development of the Militia. We've got a detailed briefing ready for you and your people on Raiders in general, but the short line is they vary in the extreme, from simple thieves to fairly heavy and competent military units well able to seize and hold a significant portion of a planet. Kodomir has mostly been hit historically by what might be termed 'typical' Raider units: light to medium sized with occasional HUP-support intent on taking something of value."

"I heard some have seized slaves," Walsh said.

"True," Gwielgi replied. "There are markets for slaves, as you know, in both the Frontier and in the Settled Worlds." He paused. "Historically, until the arrival of Storm Cloud three years ago, the Raiders that hit Kodomir were intent on looting. In any case, for more than a year before the arrival of Storm Cloud, and in all the time since, there have been no attacks by Raiders. No one knows why. On the other hand, as you are aware, we have had a steady series of attacks by mercenary units. We do not know if they are over or if something bigger is coming or what. Colonel?"

Kheyntamenti nodded and passed papers to both men.

"Here is the order of deployment. Rather than have you sitting down there full time, General Polrany is going to use a rotation schedule. We will preposition your HUPs and AFVs as they are repaired on the base.

143

However, only about half your units' total personnel will be down there at any one time. The rest will be up here at Coyote Bay. If we get another raid inbound, it will be fairly simple to move your people down there. The air wing will be rotating Swallows and attack helos in the same pattern. And so will we, which is why the general has me briefing you."

"Polrany is a great believer in training," Gwielgi said. "So your people up here will be working out on exercises, simulators, and so forth, keeping their skills up. While in Portaka, we will have field exercises. Our battalion is ordered to oversee all that with you. The general thinks we speak the same language."

"Once a merc, always a merc, eh?" Vermeil smiled.

"We do have insight as to the needs of a mercenary unit," Kheyntamenti said, "and using training to stay sharp is always a challenge. The benefit to your units is obvious; even if no attacks take place, you will leave here with people more highly skilled than when they came."

"Colonel, the part that I am unclear about is the raids," Walsh said, leaning forward in his chair. "I think you can understand my interest. Do you have any additional intelligence as to what is actually going on?"

"At this point, the best guess is that your broker is working for Baron Karl von Bender. He hired the Storm Cloud Raiders who overran Kodomir and owns four of the five worlds that made up the Confederacy Kodomir belonged to. We think it is only a question of time..."

"Sir, excuse me, but it isn't von Bender," Vermeil said. He raised his eyebrows. "I thought you knew that."

"We have not had hard intelligence yet from any source," Kheyntamenti said. "How did you learn who it was?"

"We didn't," Vermeil said. "That is, we learned who it was *not*. When we learned of the contracts and made application, we figured, based on the public information on Kodomir, that it was von Bender who was hiring us. But our partners checked it out for us. They have some pretty solid contacts in his Holdings. They all came back negative. In fact, von Bender had only just learned of the first raid. His people don't know what is going on, either."

"Wonderful," Gwielgi said, shaking his head. "There's another player in the game."

"Aye," said Kheyntamenti, scratching his chin. "And we don't know who it is."

"The icing on this cake is a question," Gwielgi said. "What will von Bender do about someone moving in?"

First Minister Alexis Jevon shut down the communications unit on his desk. General Polrany's image flickered and then disappeared from over it. Jevon paused, his fingers idly drumming on the edge of his desk. He turned to Philip Deal.

"Do we have any way of independently ascertaining the accuracy of this information?"

The young black man shook his head negatively. "No, sir. We have no intelligence assets within von Bender's Holdings that are at all relevant to this situation. While we have maintained contact with people in the rest of the old Confederacy, I don't think any of them would be able to shed any light on this." He leaned back in his chair and picked up his large cup of tea. "Nonetheless we will make an enquiry."

"Any chance of your Free Union intelligence contacts coming through?"

"Highly doubtful, sir." He put his cup down. "With open war between the Free Union and the Protectorate, Prime Minister Carmichael's intelligence service is primarily oriented towards finding out what Mariah Connor and her people are up to. That, and hunting down traitors within the Union. Our contact with them has mostly been about the Union's need to keep an eye on the Stellar Alliance. The Benderists are thorough members of the Free Union, so even if the Free Union people knew von Bender was at the bottom of these raids, I doubt they would tell us. At least, they haven't provided us with anything useful up until now."

Jevon carefully placed his fingertips together and studied them for a moment. "So, if it is not von Bender, how is Carmichael going to react to someone starting a war in his backyard, close by the other major power, the Stellar Alliance? I would think he would be afraid the Alliance might move out of its position of neutrality and throw in with the Protectorate. They are both democracies, both strong supporters of the OSW's Traders Exchange Database and TED's push for free trade throughout the OSW."

"There is no doubt the Stellar Alliance would like to see the Free Union's protection of the Benderist Holdings withdrawn so they could move in and restore the Alliance to at least some of its former size and glory." Dean smiled. "Needless to say, we would be gobbled up in passing."

"We have several possibilities, then," Jevon said. "First, it really *is* von Bender. If Carmichael knows, then the fact he has not stopped him means the attacks have the Free Union's approval. On the other hand, if von Bender's behind the raids and the Free Union *doesn't* know, which strikes me as unlikely given our discussions with them, then von Bender is much more capable than anyone has credited him with until now and we have had it."

"I agree," Deal replied. "If he can shut out the Free Union's intelligence service after several years of working in support of Carmichael, then you're right. But I find it unlikely he can do that. This gives us a second set of possibilities based on the idea it is *not* von Bender. If Carmichael knows who it is but is not telling us, one of his ostensible supporters, then a deal has been made to secure the allegiance of someone more important. Maybe bring someone into the Free Union. And we have had it."

"But if it isn't von Bender and Carmichael really does not know?"

"Then it has to be someone very big," Deal said. "And close by. Powerful enough to keep the Free Union intelligence service from penetrating them and rich enough to hire these mercenary units to keep raiding us."

Jevon touched his desk. A map of the area around Kodomir appeared above his desk. He studied it thoughtfully for a moment.

"I always thought the raids were from von Bender, part of an effort to keep us off balance until he could take us over, either through military means or by diplomacy. Given his support of Carmichael, the silence of the Free Union intelligence service made sense. They already showed a willingness to let von Bender do pretty much whatever he wanted. But if it is not the Baron, then whom?"

"The Frontier?" Deal gestured towards the top of the map. "When von Bender recruited Storm Cloud, I have no doubt that his activities attracted the attention of the powers in there."

"I don't think so. There are groups of worlds, significant powers, in the Frontier, but we have heard very little to suggest any such group was near us and, in any case, trying to invade the Settled Worlds would be beyond their capabilities as far as we know. I think it more likely this is a visit from history."

"The Alliance?" Deal shook his head. "Selena Mordieu has been cautious about approaching us since von Bender overran the Confederacy. She's been going out of her way to not do anything to suggest to von Bender that she was trying to use us as a springboard. All her contacts with us have been very formal and very open."

"I know, but her grandfather once led an empire larger than the Holdings and the current Alliance combined. As you suggested, Kodomir, the whole Confederacy, was a part of that."

"On the other hand, she has been very successful at expanding her influence towards the Frontier. Diverting away from there towards us and provoking von Bender does not seem logical."

"Not if we are just talking about empire building." Jevon stood and circled an area of the map. "Here is the present-day Alliance. Fair sized and far bigger than von Bender's Holdings even after he took the Confederacy and the 'String of Pearls.' But the old Alliance had all of those worlds plus what became the Confederacy and us, and several others, over here, up near the Frontier, this small cluster down here, and chunks of what is now the Union and the Worlds Protectorate."

"And then it all fell apart," Deal said. "They were overextended."

"Right. So, the Duchess has been rebuilding, almost entirely by diplomatic means. With all the fighting going on between the Free Union and the Protectorate and the threat it might spread, the Alliance is strong enough to protect its members. She makes a good case: lots of individual world freedom, minimal taxes, and so on." He stepped back and studied the map. "That's been her selling point, that the Alliance is strong enough to protect its members. Carmichael permits it to exist because it declared its neutrality and because, frankly, he saw the Worlds Protectorate as the greater threat and an opportunity for expansion."

"Mordieu was probably very unhappy with von Bender's move against the Confederacy."

"That's the history part. The old Alliance fell apart when the previous occupiers of the Holdings challenged them in our area. Now, von Bender controls the Holdings – his family led the revolt, his father was the great liberator, but it was from the direction of the Holdings that the threat to the Alliance came."

"So," Deal said, looking at the map, "if Mordieu is anticipating von Bender coming against the Alliance, she is looking for a way to..."

"To come against him first." Jevon looked at the map. "I think she's sponsoring the raids. But not to gather military intelligence. Her trade delegation here could walk out to the airfield and count HUPAX. She's interested in keeping us alarmed, so when her offer to provide us with protection is made, we will accept with gratitude. Then she will use us as a base to go after von Bender. And we will happily assist her because we will think all the raids were from him." He nodded to himself. "She's waging psychological war."

"Terrorism." Deal looked at the map. "You may be right, sir, but we have nothing solid to support your scenario. If you are right, though, then Kodomir is between two enemies moving against each other, a rock and a hard place."

"Exactly." Jevon shut down the map. "Traditionally, our foreign policy has been governed by a desire to maintain our world by accommodation. We have never been strong enough to fight off any power as great as the Holdings or the Alliance. So the goal has been to keep the wars off Kodomir. Show up with enough force, we salute your flag, pay your taxes, and that's it."

"We will be unable to do that this time," Deal said, nodding his head in understanding. "Whether it is von Bender or Mordieu coming, they both need to occupy Kodomir. Mordieu needs us to outflank von Bender's forces and von Bender needs us to shore up his defensive perimeter around the String of Pearls."

"Right, and that means military occupation and Kodomir becomes a battlefield when the other side attacks." Jevon shook his head. "That 'rock and a hard place' are about to slam together..."

Chapter 10: Sharpening the blade

17 July 2824

"The ranges are cleared," Kheyntamenti said as he walked down the hallway with Major Vermeil. "They have set up a schedule for both your Victors and the Black Cats so you can zero in your weapons."

"Good," Vermeil said, fastening his HUP harness. "I know the maintenance people use all kinds of computers and laser collimators, but I like to double-check by firing live rounds."

"Always a good idea, major," Kheyntamenti said as they stepped out of the battalion headquarters. "And I meant to mention that Gunny Sevin just reported that they believe they will have the Scorpion's hip joint repaired in the next 24 hours."

"That's good news," Vermeil said. "Tell him 'thanks' for me. That's sooner than we all expected."

They stepped into a Prowler and the driver took them towards the landing ship pads. The Victors' landing ship, Vengeance, soon towered over them.

"Four of the 'Cats landed with Paratus an hour ago. Captain Walsh plans on having Gladiator go down to Portaka the day after tomorrow with his remaining three. I think we will ask him to take your Scorpion with them. If it isn't ready by then, the battalion will be sending down the students and a pair of HUPs a few days later and we'll get it onboard that landing ship for sure."

"That sounds good, sir." Vermeil smiled. "I'll probably owe him a round for hauling my HUP."

"I hope you have that round on your landing ship," Kheyntamenti said. "The CO of Red Horse Four, the construction battalion down there, says they have the living quarters up and are giving the maintenance facilities priority. I'm afraid it will be a while before there is anywhere on base you can buy something to drink."

"Damn, colonel, I don't mind being shot at by Raiders, but some sacrifices are above and beyond the call of duty."

"War is hell, major, war is hell. But Red Horse Three will be there beginning next week, and if I know engineers, I think you can count on something being available before too much longer."

Vermeil laughed and, after tossing off a casual salute, walked up the ramp of Vengeance. Kheyntamenti returned to the Prowler and headed back to battalion headquarters. All around the base forces were on partial alert.

Ordinarily, a star ship carrying landing ships would arrive at a star's navigation beacon. The beacon monitored the area around it, checking for dust and debris. If the system was inhabited, the locals would work to keep the area clear for arriving star ships. Even if there was no one to "sweep up," as the expression went, the beacon could let incoming star ships know what it saw so they could leap in to a position away from hazards. Most beacons were far enough from the planet they served that it would take a landing ship at least several days to reach, usually more.

Star ship Navigators, mind-linked to C-computers running their ships' Hawking Drives, focused the drive on the beacons to avoid emerging from folded space into something solid. Beacons had sensors capable of detecting the ripples in space caused by an emerging star ship and relaying that information to the world. And to the world's military.

A star ship could leap to a point offset from the navigation beacon, arriving closer to the world. This cut down on landing ship travel time to the world but at greater risk to the star ship, since it was difficult for a leaping star ship to know what was at the offset point. Forces attacking a planet favored offset points to decrease the amount of time the defenders had to react. The Black Cats had used one, gambling it would provide them with surprise and a faster extraction.

Despite the thrillers of tri-vid entertainment, not much combat took place in space between star ships. While transiting the space-time fold generated by the Hawking Drive, they were alone. When they emerged, star ships in or near war zones and suspecting the possibility of being fired upon deliberately kept their leaps shorter than usual so as to have sufficient charge for a short leap away. Over and above that, the relative velocities of ships in space made combat almost impossible except when holding at beacons or in orbit.

Finally, because of their precious Navigators, by custom and law civilian star ships were not fired upon. These extremely rare individuals were so difficult to replace the Navigators Guild had succeeded in making civilian star ships, even ones carrying military units, neutral in combat situations. Usually, a star ship would fulfill its contract by detaching the military landing ships and then, if threatened, announcing loudly that it was not a military ship and neutral. This policy was rarely violated, though star ships carrying Raiders and official military star ships were considered exceptions. Still, even these ships seldom found themselves attacked, regular militaries preferring to seize them.

On the other hand, landing ships could be engaged by other landing ships or planetary defenders if the enemy had enough time to react and get forces in place – one more reason for offset leap points being favored by visitors with violence on their minds.

Kheyntamenti's first order of business was the same as every other Kodomir Militia officer. He checked the latest information from the space approach control facility at Kiroff Airfield for any sign of unexpected star ship arrivals; as usual, the STC, Space Traffic Control, had nothing to report but commercial arrivals and departures. Then he turned to battalion business.

The Wild Geese occupied a unique position in the Kodomir Militia. All of its members were citizens of Kodomir, whatever their varied origins. This had happened as the first act of the Kodomir Assembly following the planet's liberation from Storm Cloud. The Geese maintained their status as a registered mercenary unit, fully recognized by the Security Forces Agency on Swordpoint. The unit was officially the Combined Arms Battalion (Heavy) of the Militia's Second Regiment, currently stationed at Coyote Bay Militia Base of Western Command. The Geese legally owned three landing ships, including one liberated from Storm Cloud, and used them to move the battalion. Four other Viper-class landing ships, also courtesy of Storm Cloud, belonged to the Militia.

In effect, the Kodomir government lawyers considered the Wild Geese a regular Militia unit that, when other duty requirements allowed, could operate as a corporate entity for off world mercenary assignment. If it ever did, the Geese would shift to reserve status. The trick was the phrase, "duty requirements." The lawyers developed an elaborate structure that included the First Minister, the Commanding General of the Militia, the CO of the Wild Geese, and a long list of other interested parties.

Financially, the unit was paid like any other Militia unit, with one added twist. In addition to the financial support all units received, including regular paychecks generally above average mercenary pay, a token monthly payment was made to the Wild Geese bank account with the SFA. These funds were available only if the unit was off Kodomir working as a mercenary unit. Almost half of all mercenary units failed within a year of starting most often to undercapitalization (or military destruction, though bankruptcy was far more common). If the Wild Geese were to go seeking contracts, they would need the funds.

Seeking contracts was not on Kheyntamenti's mind as he poured over the papers and computer screens on his desk. Kodomir had been attacked eight times by mercenaries and there was no reason to believe the raids were over. A report from regimental headquarters described growing suspicion that the source of the raids was not Baron Karl von Bender but a distant neighbor, a parliamentary democracy called the Stellar Alliance.

Kheyntamenti tabbed through the analysis of the Alliance and paused as he examined its order of battle. He slowly shook his head. They were more numerous than von Bender's military and did not have the thinning effect of having to garrison newly conquered worlds. He scanned down the list of regiments, landing ships, and star ships. The list was impressive. He tabbed to the force composition listings.

Their weapons were also impressive. The core of the Alliance military was made of HUPAX, but they had not neglected space and air weapons. Even their armored forces were formidable. Of course, quantity did not guarantee quality. He tabbed to the military history section.

He frowned. The Alliance military was *good*. Some of their units had fought border skirmishes with the Free Union before Carmichael moved on to the richer prey of the Protectorate and recognized their neutrality. Others had participated in punitive assaults against Raider forces within the Frontier. They were blooded, experienced, and competently led.

Kheyntamenti sat back in his chair, rubbing his chin. A review of the numbers indicated the Alliance could send overwhelming power against Kodomir. There was a knock at his door.

"Come," he said. Captain Gwielgi walked in and laid a folder on his desk.

"Here is the finalized syllabus for the Cats and Victors staying here and the one for their detachments operating in Portaka." Kheyntamenti nodded absently. "What's up, boss?"

Kheyntamenti said nothing, just rotated the screen with the Alliance data on it. Gwielgi studied it for several minutes and then looked up.

"Well," Gwielgi said, raising an eyebrow, "I think it's time for us to leave. I'm going to go pack."

"Can't," Kheyntamenti said. "I have a wager on the rugby play-offs."

"As near as I can tell," Gwielgi said, his voice now serious, "they could come at us with three or four times our capability initially and without breaking a logistical sweat. In a prolonged war, they would be overwhelming."

"That would be my guess," Kheyntamenti agreed.

"We're going to need a bigger gun. If it comes down to a fight, I mean."

"'If' is the operative term," Kheyntamenti said. "I imagine Jevon is going to be scrambling on the diplomatic front trying to find some kind of accommodation with these people."

"And if he doesn't? If the Alliance decides to take over all those neat corn fields the Kodomiri seem to be so talented at growing?"

"Then it will be our job," Kheyntamenti said, "to show them that the price of corn has gone up."

The Landing Ship Tavern had several advantages over the other bars located along the street, sometimes referred to by the local church leaders as the "Road of Sin," that ran parallel to the perimeter fence of Coyote Bay

Militia Base. The most obvious was its proximity to the main gate, but there were others.

Proximity was the motivator for the man coming in the front door. He just wanted a drink and did not want to walk far from the landing ship facility of the base. He noticed the sign posted next to the entrance and raised an eyebrow:

Check All Weapons At The Bar.
Only The Owner Is Allowed To Be Armed.

He shrugged. As a crewman for a landing ship loading processed Kodomir metals, he had visited dozens of worlds and was used to encountering quaint social customs. But a bar was a bar, and bars had their own customs that seemed to be constant across space.

He stepped inside and looked around. The large room was filled with tables and booths, about half of which were occupied. A pair of waitresses scurried about, delivering drinks and food. A long bar occupied the end of the room, behind which a tall, thin man served drinks. A handful of people sat at the bar and he walked over to it.

There was an open seat next to a man reading a book – a real, hardbound one – and he sat down. The bartender walked over and he asked for ale.

"What brand? We have around twenty of them."

"Well, let me try any local you have," he said. A moment later a tall mug of dark, foaming liquid sat in front of him. He sipped it and nodded. Not bad. He looked at his neighbor. The man wore his hair in a severe ponytail, but looked a little old for the style. Though clad in civilian garb, he wore an old, frayed, olive drab jacket of vaguely military design. There were faded dark areas on the jacket suggesting unit emblems and badges of rank removed some time in the past. The crewman shrugged. Another washed up soldier drinking himself into oblivion, maybe. He took a quick look at the book but could make nothing out. Bored, he looked around the bar.

The walls were covered with military memorabilia. Unit emblems, still and holographic pictures, and even some weapons, firmly secured to plaques, served as decorations. Probably good for business, he decided. Get the part-time soldiers of the planet's militia in here, make some money.

A woman appeared behind the bar. She was slightly above average height, a little on the skinny side, with bright white eyes set off by her dark skin. Her hair was cut very short, like what you might expect from a soldier. Still, she was attractive. What the hell, might as well give it a run. He motioned for a refill.

When she came back with his mug, he turned on his best smile.

"Thank you, little lady. How late are you working tonight?"

She cocked her head to one side, glanced at the older man next to him, and looked back with a smile.

"I'm here until the place closes, mister." She leaned back against the wall and folded her arms.

"Well, I'm a little new in town and I've got a couple of month's pay chits in my pants. You want to get into them?"

Beside him the older man shook his head, grinned, took a sip from his mug, and turned a page.

"That's really tempting, partner, but I'm kind of funny – I only date men."

He felt his face flush. "Hey, lady," he said, "Who the hell do you think you are, besides a barmaid?"

Her smile slowly faded. The older man closed his book, looked at the crewman and shook his head. He picked up his book and mug and moved to a stool further away.

"Laddie," she said. "First, there's not a damned thing wrong with being a barmaid. Second, I happen to be the owner. Third, you have about five seconds to make a decision – are you going to be polite and enjoy yourself or are you going to leave?"

"Look, bitch," he said, rising from his stool, "no one tells me where to go or what to do."

"Buddy," the older man said, looking up from his book, a small smile on his face, "you might want to slow down a bit. This lady can more than take care of herself, but looking around the room I think I see maybe a dozen friends of hers. Now, I don't know, you might be able to take care of a dozen trained, combat experienced soldiers, but you would still have to try to handle her and I have to tell you, she's taken down tougher men than you. You might pay attention to the fact she does not bother to employ a bouncer."

"Yeah? What is she, some kind of commando?"

"Well, funny you should mention it, but, yep, she was."

"That's a load of crap, old man."

"Mister, look at her eyes and tell me if you see anything there that looks like she's afraid." The older man looked down at his book and resumed reading.

The crewman looked at the woman. Her gaze was level and unblinking. He tried not to look away but he finally did. He muttered something and sat back down. He directed his gaze at his mug of ale as if it had suddenly become very interesting.

The older man looked at the woman who smiled, winked, and went to other customers down the bar. He took another sip from his mug and turned the page of his book.

After a while, the crewman drained his mug and put it down on the bar. He got up and started to leave but stopped. He looked at the older man and then leaned close.

"So, what *is* the deal with her?"

Gwielgi closed his book and studied the crewman for a second with cool brown eyes flecked with yellow.

"Boy, I have a feeling you are not going to leave it alone until you really get your fingers burned." Before the man could reply, Gwielgi raised his hand and got the woman's attention.

"Jackie, you still got your Fairbairn?"

The woman looked up from running a customer's chit, a puzzled expression on her face. She nodded as she walked up to the two men.

"Never without it, you know that." She cocked her head to one side. "What's up?" Gwielgi looked to one side and then pointed at a dartboard.

"Can you manage to hit the wall that thing is hanging on?"

Jackie grinned. She dipped down and sprang up. Her arm was a blur, whipping back and forward. Something glinted in the air and suddenly a thin knife appeared in the board. Gwielgi shook his head.

"I know that a Fairbairn is not designed for throwing, but that's at least five centimeters from the center ring. You've gotten really awful in your old age."

"And you could do better?" She shook her head. "A pitcher of Highlander Red if you can put it inside my knife."

Gwielgi's right hand dipped inside his left sleeve and whipped towards the dartboard. A sudden *thunk* announced the arrival of a second blade in the board.

"I'll take the pitcher, chilled, if you please," he said, not bothering to look at the target. "Tsunasdi and Elinshen are joining me later and they'll be happy to help me work through it."

Jackie stood with her arms crossed and shook her head.

"That's just showing off. All right, the pitcher's yours, but best of three to see who buys a new board."

Gwielgi laughed. He handed over his chit.

"It's on me." Gwielgi looked over at the man. "This is Jackie Peregrine. Owns the place. She was infantry in two different units, including the Pale Riders and the Wild Geese. I figure you've heard of the Riders, if not the Geese. We were grunts together until I started driving HUPs, and then she became a HUP captain just to keep me out of trouble. She's all right with a sniper rifle," he said while Jackie snorted, "and not bad with a knife." She made a mock curtsey. "But she is pure unadorned evil in hand-to-hand combat." He took another sip from his mug. "I ought to know, I taught her everything she knows." Jackie laughed.

The crewman stared for a moment. Then, saying nothing, he turned and left.

"I'll hold the pitcher until Tsunasdi and Stephanie get here," Jackie said. "You can keep working on your iced tea." She ducked under the bar and pulled the knives free from the board, shaking her head as she looked at the damage to it. She slipped one under her pant leg and handed the other to Gwielgi.

"You've been practicing," she said.

"A little," Gwielgi admitted, "but that was mostly luck. A Fairbairn really isn't a throwing knife."

"Glad you're man enough to admit it," she smiled. Jackie paused and leaned against the bar. "So, how are things? They letting you back in HUPs yet?"

"Finally, yeah, the medics said the leg was all right. Khey is going to let me go down to Portaka to work out with the training cadre down there. He says if I'm good they'll take the training wheels off in a few weeks and let me practice in traffic."

"That'll be the day," she said. "Have the intel people figured out who is behind the raids?"

"Still nothing definite. Hell, they probably wouldn't tell me even if they did know." He drained the last of his tea and slid the mug over to Peregrine.

"Well, at my reserve meeting last week they suggested that von Bender was behind it all," Jackie said. She picked up the mug and filled it with iced tea from a pitcher under the bar.

"That's my guess, but with a big chunk of the Settled Worlds going up in flames, it could be anyone. Maybe friends of Mariah Connor trying to tear up Peter Mavis Carmichael's rear area, maybe someone trying to take advantage of the confusion, who knows?"

"Well, whatever's going on, you keep your head down – remember, you don't have me around to fix up any HUPs you break."

"Ouch," he said. "That's cruel." Gwielgi grinned sardonically. "So how are things going on the home front?"

"Pretty good," Jackie said. "Mortgage on this place is just about paid off, thanks to the expansion of the Militia base. Well, that, and the fact that the guy I bought it from is now the mayor of Coyote Bay."

"It helps to know people in high places," Gwielgi said, still grinning. "But I was referring to your young man."

"Oh, things are fine," she smiled. Then her smile broadened. "I mean, they are *real* fine."

"I've been trying to tell you to stay away from these fly-boy types. Love'm and leave'm, that's how they are."

"Oh, hush," she said. "Connor is a sweet boy. Now that his squadron is assigned here, we get to spend a lot more time together."

"I don't need the sordid details," Gwielgi said. "But if Chi comes by, you might talk with him. Lieutenant Illuyshin was in one of the helicopters that flew in support of his team against the Victors. They did some good work."

"Is it true Sergeant Elinshen challenged their leader to a '1 V 1'?"

"Yep. And it's *Lieutenant* Elinshen now. Khey wasn't sure whether to court-martial her or promote her so he decided to take the easy way out and send her off to Militia 'charm school."

"She's a hell of a HUP pilot. I think she would be an excellent leader. Khey's doing the right thing, putting her in a position where the responsibility will force her to be a leader."

"I agree." Gwielgi looked over his shoulder. "There's our new lieutenant and Tsunasdi. Can you have one of the girls come over? We'll probably get something to eat."

"Sure," Jackie said. "Use that booth in the far corner. Oh, and put your knife away. I think you're beginning to spook the civilians."

"Sorry." He slipped the knife into its sheath strapped to his wrist. "I guess we won't need it."

"You haven't tried our steaks."

Chapter 11: Approaching storm

15 October 2824

General Stevar Polrany studied the wall projection and idly rubbed his moustache. The display of the Kodomir system still showed nothing from the navigation beacon sensors. He sighed. He almost wished there was something there. He stood up from his central console and raised a hand to attract his communication officer. He was not the kind of officer who led by yelling.

"Sir?" The young woman had learned that he preferred people not stand from their consoles when responding to him, but if someone could sit at attention, she was doing it. Among the Militia, especially the newer members, Polrany was a hero, elevated to almost mythical status. It was to his credit that he felt uncomfortable with that perception, just seeing himself as a soldier trying to handle things the best way he could.

"Lieutenant, get the regimental commanders linked up and online – pipe it into the conference room. And the Air CO, Major Toland."

"Yes, sir."

Polrany walked through the darkened room with its dimly glowing displays and personnel, pausing only to tap his G-2 officer on the shoulder. The two men entered the room and the intelligence officer, Major John Leppla, set up the displays while Polrany poured them both large glasses of hot tea. They had engaged in this morning routine frequently in the past and were getting pretty efficient at it, Polrany thought.

By the time he had the glasses on the table – unsweetened black tea for Leppla, very sweetened orange pekoe with a piece of lemon rind for himself – faces were appearing above the conference table.

"Good morning," Polrany said as he sat down. There was a flurry of voices acknowledging his greeting. "Major Leppla has something for you today and I have a couple of items. We'll start with status reports. ATR?"

"Good morning, sir," Lieutenant Colonel Mariah Konivov said. "The Armored Training Regiment continues in its current training cycle for reservists. Two battalions are up in the Northern Training Area while the third is here at Kiroff Airfield. No changes since our last report."

"I saw class 2-24's 'shoot for record' scores. Excellent gunnery, colonel. Please extend my congratulations."

"Yes, sir, will do."

"ITR?"

"Good morning, general," Major Paul Douglass said. "Pretty much the same as our last report with the exception that we have the recon training program now cycling down to Portaka for the desert and arctic portions of their syllabus. Should have them back in three months."

"How many are still in the class, Paul?" Polrany knew from the daily reports he received, but he liked to touch base with each of his commanders and used his questions as a way of informing his people as to what he regarded as important."

"As of this morning, 32 of the original 60, sir." He glanced at a paper in front of him. "Slightly below average at this stage, but we had several injured in the live fire exercise last week, as you know. So they will probably be recycled into the next class."

"Understood." He looked at another face, one very familiar to him. "Major Toland, status of the wing?"

"Sir, our Swallow fighters remained deployed with two squadrons each here at Kiroff and Coyote Bay. Our Tiger Moth squadrons have finished the evaluation of the SSM1s. We can lift them but not much else, so the plan to carry them is scrapped. On the other hand, we have completed a series of medium-range missile upgrades. Airgroup Two with three squadrons remains here at Kiroff. Airgroup One has one squadron attached to Western Command, one attached to the Combined Arms Battalion, and

161

one on deployment to Portaka. Our two airlift squadrons are still with Militia Command."

"Thank you, major. First Regiment remains under Militia Command, which is to say, me. The First Minister informed me yesterday that the bill to expand the Militia Officer ranks to include another Colonel and two Lieutenant Colonel designations is stuck in committee and I will be asked to testify next week." He shrugged his shoulders and several of the officers unsuccessfully hid smiles. Polrany's dread of testifying before Assembly committees was well known and, considering his demonstrated courage in combat, an irony that seemed to endear him to his troops.

"In the meantime, I have named Major Velikiyi T'sombe as XO of the regiment. Major T'sombe is known to most of you, having been Ops officer for both the ATR and Second Regiment." Polrany looked at Jonivov's face and grinned. "Stealing Major T'sombe was accomplished under extremely hazardous conditions and with much gnashing of teeth by his former CO. Colonel Jonivov, update us on the Second Regiment and Western Command."

"Yes, sir," Jonivov said, his smile looking somewhat forced. "I'm standing in for Colonel Martin who is on leave this week." His smile became relaxed. "His oldest plays rugby for U of K and he asked me to offer the wager of a bottle of Modena '32 for anyone foolish enough to believe Kiroff will not take the tournament for the second time in a row."

There were a few laughs and both Polrany and Douglass took the wager. "No way is the University of Kiroff going to do it again," Douglass said with a grin. "My alma mater, the legendary St. George University Knights, is going to walk all over those Kiroff kids." A second round of laughs came from the officers. The Knights had never advanced beyond the first round while the University of Kiroff had been in the final four teams every year for the past six. Polrany occasionally allowed these light moments in what was often a very dull meeting.

"Moving on," Jonivov said, "T'sombe is a good officer. Excellent battalion commander and one of the best Ops officers we've had. I hate to lose him, particularly as I am breaking in a new battalion CO." He glanced down at some papers. "First and Second Battalions finished a joint exercise with the First and Second Chekinov Scouts, and the Second Scouts will deploy to Portaka for desert and arctic training next week. Third Scouts and

First Recon have been practicing rapid mountain insertion via helo and landing ship. I'll have more to say about that in a moment."

"The Combined Arms Battalion (Heavy) has moved its Advanced HUPAX Training Unit to Portaka. AHTU has six HUPs, though they rotate types to match the training syllabus. They are including our contracted mercenary units in that training. The Black Cats, by the way, had all the former Saber Cats elect to join them and they have been running combined arms training with good results. The Victors have had a hell of a time getting that Scorpion I told you about fully operational again but Colonel Kheyntamenti reports that it appears to be over its problems. The Basic HTU remains here at Coyote Bay." He flipped open a folder. "Our 'houseguests' are now on their way to Swordpoint at Alpha Centauri with the exception of the Sabers and approximately 20 who elected to join either the Cats or the Victors – both units offered them employment. Colonel Kheyntamenti monitored the recruitment and tells me both units picked up some good people, particularly in the technical and logistics areas."

"I mentioned that Third Scouts and First Recon are practicing rapid mountain insertion. This air assault tactic is old hat to CAB-H, of course. You all remember their raid on Storm Cloud when it held Coyote Bay Militia Base." There were nods – the violent assault by the Wild Geese had been the opening battle in the war. "Well, what we are doing is working up that tactic to be useable in a full-fledged assault of combined arms: mobile infantry, armor, artillery, HUPs, and air. This brings a degree of complexity the Militia has not had to deal with before. However, since we have the landing ship capability and since we have a very large area to cover, it makes sense to work up that tactic. After we 'guinea pig' ourselves in the Second, then the First at Kiroff will take it on to maximize flexibility." He paused and smiled. "At least, that's what General Polrany told me."

"Pete's right," Polrany said. "When he and Colonel Kheyntamenti explained their idea to me, it seemed to be a natural extension of our current tactics emphasizing mobility and surprise. Our simulations showed, however, that as you double the force, you quadruple the command, control, and logistical complexity. Given the small support base of the Militia, it remains to be seen if we can really do this on a large scale. Nonetheless, I've ordered two CAB-H landing ships, *Ghost* and *Zombie*, down to Portaka to begin the work-up. Those crews are among our most

experienced at this kind of thing so I want to use them work the kinks out."
He looked up at Jonivov.

"How are the Scouts doing?" This was the question almost every Militia officer had. Many still had difficulty believing in their loyalty and the sight of seeing Chekinov – or Tsalagi, as they preferred to call themselves – units listed on the Militia Order of Battle still made some uncomfortable.

"Militarily, they are exceptional," Jonivov said. "I think most of us here at one time or another fought the Cheks and we all appreciate they are excellent light infantry. To be frank, I expected the 'honeymoon period' to have worn off by now. After all, the common Storm Cloud enemy is gone. But these continued raids have kept them close on a military level. It has also helped that the Militia Liaison Officer cadre is back in business. Being a MLO carries a great deal of weight in Chek eyes." Jonivov did not have to elaborate. The liaison officers over the years became advocates for the Chekinov tribes. Then, when Storm Cloud tried to seize the tribal leaders, MLOs fought and died beside their Chekinov counterparts. Polrany had heard there were numerous Chekinov babies named after those officers.

"But," Jonivov said, "the real problem remains – the Assembly has been dragging its feet building the infrastructure the Chekinovs were promised. Things are happening, but by now we expected to have many more clinics, schools, even roads finished."

"I know," Polrany said. "I've tried to partially compensate by using Militia reserve engineering units to work on various projects as their active duty assignments. Same with the medical people and so on. But we can't pick up all of the slack. I have to do some testifying in front of the Militia committee of the Assembly later and I'm going to try to work in a plug to get them to release the funds for the Chekinov tribes. This is a problem we don't need and can do something about." There were nods from the others. No one wanted deterioration in relations with the tribes.

"Now," Polrany continued, "from everything we've covered you can see our training shift to Portaka is well underway." Imagery from Portaka appeared to one side. "The base upgrade there is coming along, though slowly. It's still pretty Spartan but the training cycles are intense enough no one has a lot of free time to complain about the lack of nightlife. Since it is clear that Portaka is going to be the industrial heart of Kodomir, we need to be thinking more about defending the resources there. I'm going to want to get a regular cycle for both commands and all regiments. Eventually we will have a Southern Command stationed there, but that's years down the road." The imagery vanished as Polrany touched his desktop control panel and a three-dimensional chart of the Kodomir solar system flashed onto everyone's screens.

"Our sensors at the nav beacon are clear. We haven't had a raid in a while now. Maybe they are over. Maybe not. But we are not going to drop our guard. Impress on your reservists as they cycle into your units that we need to keep our level of alertness and proficiency high." Polrany smiled slightly. "Though given our recent history, I doubt that you will have much of a selling job." There were nods from the others as the map vanished and their faces returned.

"Does anyone have anything else we need to cover?" Polrany waited a moment and then nodded. "All right, then. I'll be getting out of the office after that testimony this week and will happily be getting out into the field to Coyote Bay and Portaka. I'll keep you all appraised." There were more nods and the faces vanished.

Polrany rose and left the conference room. Two staff officers joined him as he left the room and in low voices they quickly briefed him on his next meeting. The information was familiar, but since so much of his job was administrative, much to his disgust, Polrany had found it useful to be continuously reminded and updated on his meetings, conferences, presentations, and all the other activities he generally classified as "paper shuffling."

His next meeting took place in a smaller conference room, though one with decidedly luxurious accommodations. This room was for discussions with civilians. Today's guests were representatives from Kodomir's small but technologically advanced armaments industry. Every two weeks he met liaison personnel from Mikoyan-Hughes, Orion Aerospace, Gurivetch Advanced Technologies, and a number of other companies. Kodomir had learned a bitter lesson about depending on others for the development and supply of the weapons needed for defense and over the past year these regular meetings had evolved as a method for the Militia and Kodomir's arms industry to exchange information.

On top of that, the tea in this conference room was excellent.

After a round of greetings, Polrany gave an abbreviated briefing on the military situation, though there was little to pass on since their last meeting. Then he opened the floor for discussion. The Mikoyan-Hughes representative, a young woman who never seemed to need to refer to her notes named Sara Pleitrotsky, went first.

"General, we have completed the rewiring of the antiarmor missiles. We found almost one in eight was fouled. We also have developed a launching rail replacement system and our field technicians are currently going through the entire Militia inventory and performing inspections. So far, we've identified seven launchers as flawed."

"The fractures in the rails are not visible to inspection until they begin to fail – how are you spotting them?"

"We took a technique from our friends at Orion," she said, nodding towards another representative, who smiled. "When they overhaul one of our Swallows, they bathe structure and frame members with a fluid that fluoresces under ultraviolet light. After you wash the fluid off the surface, it tends to remain in microscopic fractures. Hit it with the light and you can see what the inspectors call 'spider webs,' fine lines of fractures. We also do high energy x-ray and other emissions scans, but the dip and wash system works well for the kind of problem the launchers are giving us."

"I'm happy to hear that. When do you expect to have all the launchers checked?"

"The big problem is just moving our inspection team around. We will finish the units at Coyote Bay next week. Then we will come to Kiroff. Portaka is last. Give us another month for inspections and two months for the installation of the replacement rails."

"Understood. By the way, I have some feedback for you. The Dragunov trials are going very well. The T and E team is just back to Portaka Militia base from their little walk in the snow in southern Portaka. They are very happy, very, very happy. The electronic igniter cold weather problem appears totally cured. They will be taking their rifles to the interior of Portaka for some hot weather follow-up, but I've given them a week to stand down." Polrany smiled. "The Dragunovs handled the well-below freezing temperatures a lot better than the team."

"Delighted to hear that," Pleitrotsky said. Polrany knew she meant it – she was in the Militia reserves and would one day be carrying a Dragunov

166

if it was finally accepted for use. "I don't have anything else, general."
Polrany nodded and turned to the Orion representative.

"Sir," the Orion officer, Ronald Murphy said, barely restraining his
enthusiasm, "we had first flight this week." This was a stir around the table
and the officer waited, enjoying it. "Project Foxtrot Four flew as per
schedule. In fact, she completed three flights. Our engineers report she is
on profile. Small items, nothing major. She will begin supersonic trials in
one week."

"That will please our air command. But I wish you would think about
changing the name. The first Phantom was little more than a lead sled and
was not an auspicious beginning for the new Kodomir aerospace fighter
industry."

"Sir," Murphy said, his voice suddenly formal, "Orion totally
appreciates the importance of Kodomir developing its own aircraft and we
know our first effort was, well, not very successful. But we are keeping the
name Phantom II because it serves as a spur. Development of the first
Phantom damn near bankrupted us, as well as letting down our people."
His voice picked up energy. "This new bird, general, she is going to be one
nasty piece of work. So advanced she will have a two-person crew, capable
of air to space, air to ground, air to air, and able to kick the hell out of
virtually every other fighter in anyone's inventory. And..." He stopped
when he saw Polrany's hand come up.

"Robert, you don't have to sell me on the concept. I'm the man who sent
a squadron of obsolete Swallows against Storm Cloud in the Depford
Valley." He was silent for a moment. "Von Bender's Firerays cut them to
shreds. I *want* the Phantom II to be everything you say. I'd just like a name
with a less checkered history."

"Sir, I appreciate your point of view, but Phantom II received over 68
percent of the vote from Orion employees. So that's what we are staying
with." He looked firm for a moment but then became nervous under
Polrany's steady gaze.

"Robert, you folks at Orion can call it *Alice in Wonderland* if you want,
just as long as Kodomir doesn't have to go looking any more for the leftover dregs of the Settled Worlds." He leaned back in his chair.

"Be it infantry weapons like the Dragunov, aerospace fighters like the
Phantom II, our Frogfire long-range precision missile, whatever we need,

I do not want us scrabbling on the open market for used cast-offs ever again. If Kodomir is to remain free and independent, then we must be able to arm ourselves." He paused and then smiled. "Forgive the speech. I have to testify before the Assembly Militia Committee again and I have been rehearsing a bit too much."

"But on that note, let me turn to Mr. Johnson. How are things at GAT?"

"We are on schedule, general," Vladimir Johnson said. "The tank plant at Coyote Bay is two months from completion. We should have our own home-grown Zhukov heavy tanks rolling off the assembly line this fall. The Militia is continuing field work-ups in the meantime. So far, the reports on those down on Portaka continue to be very positive."

"Indeed. We already have our first class of armor techs training in Zhukovs. They will meet their tanks as they come out of the factory and go with them to their units, along with their crews, who are entering the Zhukov simulators next month."

The details of coordinating the rapidly growing arms industry of the Kodomiri filled the rest of the meeting. Later, as he walked back to the Combat Information Center, Polrany thought about the confluence of history and culture that nourished that industry.

True, recent history in the form of the invasion and conquest of Kodomir by the Raiders called Storm Cloud had taught an ugly lesson about not having the most advanced weapons possible. The Militia's Swallows had been no match for von Bender's Firerays, and the old Bob Cat tanks had been hard pressed to hold back the HUPAX of the invader. An entire regiment of them had died on the ground north of Kiroff.

But Kodomiri culture traced one important line back to its Russian roots, and that included a respect bordering on love for heavy artillery. The domination of Settled Worlds tactics by the HUPAX had led to the neglect, in Polrany's opinion, of other weapon systems, and artillery was a prime example of that neglect. It was almost impossible to purchase good artillery or, for that matter, missile systems that were not designed for HUP use.

So, the Kodomiri built their own, a process they began before Storm Cloud arrived. Among the first were Frogfire missiles, which could use their own computer-based intelligence or laser designators to home in on even moving targets with either shaped-charge cluster munitions capable of damaging multiple armored weapons – including HUPAX – or single large warheads bringing an explosive impact larger than any conventional weapon in any inventory. Self-propelled heavy artillery, originally crude howitzers strapped on to decrepit APCs no longer suitable for carrying infantry, now consisted of specially designed machines easily able to keep up with tanks and lofting a Diamondback round that could follow laser designators or, though not as sophisticated at the Frogfire, use their own artificial intelligence. Using armor-piercing sheathing and following the invisible illumination of ultraviolet lasers, Diamondback rounds came in a variety of sizes.

And there was one of the problems. There was a lack of consistency and standardization in the Militia artillery. Old guns seemed to never be decommissioned. Now they had a motley collection that ranged from 105-millimeter rotary-breech howitzers capable of firing a round a second to a massive 300-millimeter gun system. That damned thing had been in the Militia inventory for close to a century and was destined, if Polrany had anything to do with it, to be replaced by more mobile weapons.

Artillery could not do the job alone, of course. Combined arms were the key. Upgrading the infantry led to the development of the Dragunov rifle system. Built around the same 8-millimeter electrically ignited cartridge, variations would serve as automatic weapons, standard rifles, light machine guns, and even sniper rifles. For the air branch there would be the Foxtrot Four, or Phantom II, as the Orion people insisted on calling it.

The prototype was a nasty looking thing, with a large shark-like stabilizer, angled wings and elevators, and a low-slung nose that looked like the front of a predator. Rather than simply varying its primary wing geometry, such as the swing-wing Swallows, the Phantoms would be able to alter the entire shape of the aircraft and literally bend and twist their fuselages. Carrying an advanced sensor package largely of Kodomiri design, Orion claimed the array of weapons it could carry would include the Frogfire, SSM1 and SSM2 series missiles, meaning that even a landing ship could be threatened by one of these fighters.

Tankers were looking forward to crewing the Zhukov, 87 tons of fast armor and mounting either a rail gun able to reach more than ten kilometers, very large lasers, or the 120mm autoloading cannon. Like most tanks, it would be a far more stable weapon platform than any HUPAX, which translated into greater accuracy at long range. Coupled with more of its weight serving as armor and a low profile, a Zhukov might give even the largest HUPs a problem.

But time was the key. As he sat down in his chair overlooking the softly glowing consoles of the CIC, Polrany was well aware that the new weapons and the capability of researching, designing, and manufacturing them were still very young. For them to have any real impact on the battlefield, for them to be the shield Kodomir needed as the Settled Worlds plunged yet again into the chaos of another major war, time was needed.

As he sipped his tea and studied the screens, Polrany understood time was the one variable he could not control.

The contract broker glanced at her computer console and bit off a curse – it was time for her to be gone and here she was still in her office in the Security Forces Agency, waiting for a call. She looked at the papers on her desk. Individuals representing a potential new employer had visited her several times in the past two weeks. They were secretive, of course. No one who was not would bother with a broker for hiring mercenaries and the extra fees a broker entailed. Yesterday they dropped off a short report, making a major issue of its confidential nature and demanding she review her security systems in her office. They had insisted she thoroughly study the papers so that she would be thoroughly familiar with their needs.

The needs were clear and not particularly unusual. They needed a unit to serve as a garrison force. The papers, of course, were careful not to provide specifics that could be traced to any particular employer. Nonetheless, they had called her three times to ensure that she was studying the report, even going over portions of it with her. She had become very tired of handling the papers.

Tired was the correct word. For the past several hours she had felt a growing sense of fatigue accompanied by a steadily increasing headache that felt like a slowly expanding hot balloon. Despite the fact they had ordered her to wait for their next call, if they did not contact her in the next ten minutes she would leave for her quarters and get a good night's sleep.

After all, it was not like she needed another assignment at the moment. The money she had received from the Alliance representative for the attacks on Kodomir and the money she had received for selling the information about the Alliance – she correctly guessed to representatives of von Bender – was more than enough for a long vacation, and anywhere would do as long as it was off Swordpoint.

Like her time, information was a commodity, something for sale. When she understood that the money from the Alliance was about to dry up, she had been very willing to sell information about her work for them to anyone who had enough cash. Most brokers, especially those working on Swordpoint, would not have dared to do what she had done, over and above any ethical qualms – the penalty for betrayal could be quite severe. After all, besides mercenaries, the SFA also provided assassins. But the money was too good to pass up and would make her leaving Swordpoint for good quite easy. She smiled as she thought of her new life.

The pain stabbed into her like a knife, so sudden and savage that she gasped. She started to rise but then every nerve in her body seemed to catch fire at the same time. She tried to draw in a breath to scream and died. She slumped forward, bouncing off her desk and falling to the floor.

An hour later her communication unit chimed. It did so repeatedly for two minutes and then ceased. A minute later her office door slid open. Two men, the two she thought were prospective employers, walked into the office. While one of them disabled the security systems she had so cooperatively shown to them during their earlier visit, the other quickly donned thin gloves. He carefully put the papers into a pouch that he sealed. He put the pouch on the console. His partner held out a bag and he carefully peeled off the gloves and dropped them in. The bag went on the console and his partner took a small medical scanner and examined the pouch, bag, and desk carefully.

His partner nodded and put away the scanner. Though the scanner claimed the items were clear of the poison that had saturated the papers, he still felt a small touch of anxiety as he folded the pouch and slipped it into his jacket pocket. His partner picked up the bag which looked like nothing more lethal than the small bags carried by the fashionable elite when shopping, down to the jewelry store logo that was large enough to let people know the owner was wealthy. Both the pouch and the bag would be in an incinerator within thirty minutes.

They glanced around them one more time and then the two contract assassins left the office.

On the floor behind them the broker lay, her dead eyes staring up at the ceiling, all time stopped forever.

Chapter 12: Crack of lightning

18 October 2824

Captain Gwielgi finished his early breakfast and stepped out of the messhall to enjoy the cool morning breeze. The sun was well below the mountains to the east of Coyote Bay Militia Base and so it was still fairly dark, but he was still on Portaka time, which meant it felt later than it was. Well, it was a small price to pay for pulling an instructor rotation on Portaka. Down there you spent most of your time running around in HUPs and in classes studying them. Up here... He frowned at the thought of the paperwork waiting for him.

But that would be later today. Right now, he was unassigned with no particular duties or responsibilities until he met with Colonel Kheyntamenti in two hours. He decided to stretch his legs and take in the morning.

The battalion area, lit by a few road and building lights, was in the western portion of the Militia base, just a little south of the main gate facing the suburbs of Coyote Bay. Though it was hard to see the rest of the base with the glow in the eastern sky providing dim illumination, he could tell that a number of new buildings had gone up.

To the east of the battalion, the runway, punctuated by a spray of red, blue, and green lights, stirred to life as aircraft engines woke up with steadily climbing whines. A little early for the jet jockeys to be firing things up, Gwielgi thought. The Militia tried not to disturb the nearby citizens' sleep if it could be avoided.

Now a distant but deep roar of Swallow fighters steadily increased. It sounded like more than one or two. He paused, trying to make out what was happening. Then he heard a distant klaxon. For a heartbeat he froze.

Not again!

The sirens in the battalion area went off. Gwielgi turned south towards the HUPAX lager, more than half a kilometer away, and ran while a public address system echoed through the dark base.

"Battle stations, battle stations. This is not a drill. We have multiple landing ships inbound."

The roar of the Swallows was now a waterfall of thunder as fighter after fighter came alive. Two flashed overhead and banked toward the north. Automatic laser and missile turrets around the base perimeter stirred to life and raised themselves as if sniffing the air, looking for scent. They rotated, looking toward the northern mountains.

Gwielgi was running when the first enemy fighters appeared overhead.

An explosion erupted near the runways; the shockwave raised dust around Gwielgi as he ran. Something burst into flame but he stayed focused on keeping his feet moving.

Thin, brilliant lines of defense lasers stabbed into the air, sounding like the cracks of immense bullwhips. There was another explosion, this one from the south near the tanks and APCs. Gwielgi heard more but distant explosions as missiles slammed into other parts of the base.

Ahead, the first HUPAX were moving. Though it was hard to see details, they immediately turned and headed south, not north, not in the direction of the first wave of the attack. Two Militia trucks carrying soldiers sped past him, and then a third, all heading south. A pair of black Tiger Moths, easier to hear than to see, swept by running fast and low. Something exploded in a flash of flame in the sky and burning pieces fell in slow arcs near the perimeter.

Gwielgi found himself crossing paths with a group of Militia soldiers, some not fully dressed, running towards the center of the base. These were reservists, at the base doing their yearly active-duty cycle. He could see the HUP area ahead and started to sprint, separating himself from the double-timing platoon.

The decision to increase his speed, he would realize later, probably saved his life, for as he turned away from the platoon, missiles came down in a shallow arc from an enemy fighter and blew the platoon apart.

Gwielgi saw a flash of light to his left, a streak of yellow, and then he was feeling concrete beneath his cheek. It was a moment before he realized he was down on the road. He could hear nothing. His ears felt stuffed with cotton but were ringing violently. He could smell blood – it was his own, a nosebleed.

Gwielgi tried sitting up but his muscles would not cooperate at first. Finally, he got to all fours. A deep, painful throbbing inhabited his head and his right leg ached. Trying to stand was impossible. Gwielgi sat back down, slightly swaying. He was dizzy and his right eye would not focus.

You're in shock.

There was some place he had to be, Gwielgi was sure of that. He tried standing again and this time made it. He looked around but could not make much sense out of the darkness and confusion as a vague wave of nausea swept through him and then vanished. His hearing was a thick roaring, like a monstrous waterfall heard through a heavy curtain. Nothing else came through. His mind cleared a little.

We're under attack.

With the thought came a surge of adrenalin. Gwielgi moved toward the HUP area. A Short Sword pounded out of one of the bays and spun south. He recognized a HUP technician but when the man ran up to him Gwielgi could not understand what he was saying. The technician pulled a field bandage out of his belt pouch and made Gwielgi hold still while he wrapped it around his head. Gwielgi waited, not sure of what else to do. Then the technician shouted something – it looked like he was shouting – and ran off.

Gwielgi looked around. The HUPAX area was empty. No HUPs, no people. The whole place was deserted. Where had everyone gone? Then he remembered the air strike. He had been unconscious. How long? The sky was lighter.

He heard a truck pull up behind him. Could he hear again? Someone leapt off and grabbed him by the arm. It was Joseph Thuan Ho`nehe. He was yelling, but Gwielgi could only understand a few words.

"South perimeter...we have...all right?"

Gwielgi let Ho'nehe take him to the truck. Multiple hands pulled him into it. He looked around as the truck rolled. There were a half dozen Wild Geese infantry around him in various stages of dress, though all were armed. He looked back at the HUP area in time to see the impact of a handful of long-range missiles.

The truck sped through the increasing morning light. Gwielgi had no idea where they were going but he could feel the dizziness lessening. The vision in his eye suddenly cleared and he blinked several times. He discovered he could hear low frequency sounds only with difficulty – the truck was almost silent. But he could make out the sound of voices. And the crack of explosions.

Suddenly the truck skidded to a halt.

Someone screamed, "Get out!" Gwielgi tumbled out the back of the truck, knocking the wind out of himself when he slammed into the road. The others kept moving, running out of sight. Gwielgi looked up and saw the truck was on fire.

He rolled away from it as its fuel cell detonated and a wave of heat flashed over him. Someone was screaming and Gwielgi realized he could hear normally. Laser fire cracked in the distance while guns hammered away much closer. Explosions slammed through the air and shook the ground beneath him. The air was filled with smoke and dust and the acrid smell of fires.

In the flickering light of the burning truck, he saw a small group of Militia soldiers moving past the wreckage of a destroyed tank and, crouching low, he ran towards them. Two of them fell, one spinning, and he dropped to the ground while the others opened fire towards targets he could not see. He crawled forward.

The first Militia soldier was dead, a head wound still draining into her short blond hair. Gwielgi looked around. The others were gone. He took her rifle, a standard issue semiautomatic weapon. His hands seemed to move of their own accord and freed the magazine. A glance showed it to be full – she never got a shot off. Gwielgi slapped the magazine back in and chambered a round while missiles howled overhead. He glanced north and saw a landing ship rising from its pad on a column of yellow-white fire, though he could not tell which one it was.

The woman had been carrying a sling of extra magazines and Gwielgi took it, slipping it over his own head and arm. He moved forward, getting to the shelter of the tank. It was not a Militia tank, he realized, and the smell of burning fuel and bodies came from its shattered hull. The southern edge of the base, marked by mangled chain-link fencing, was only a hundred or so meters away. He could easily see the main east-west highway and monorail line beyond it. The light was getting better, though the smoke and dust still limited visibility. An artillery battery began pounding at a target deep in the base.

Somewhere beyond the southern horizon the sky suddenly lit up, a glare that seemed to flood the scattered clouds forever and was far brighter than the approaching sunrise. Several seconds later, a long, low rumble came rolling. It was a few more seconds before the light faded away. A landing ship just died, part of his mind told him.

Gwielgi forced himself to stop and think. Some of the enemy landing ships were, or had been, to the north – that was why the fighters went in that direction – but their ground attack had come from the south. That meant at least one ship was there. From the looks of things, the enemy was inside the base now. He could hear gunfire that seemed to corroborate his thinking. Gwielgi looked about but could see no one else.

A glance to the south showed people coming. Whose? He lay down beside the tank and watched the running figures. It was hard to make out details in the dim light and smoke.

There were more than a dozen figures, all heavily armed. They were not Militia. Some wore full nanotechnology suits that rippled gray across black as they approached the base and its fires. Others only had nanotech vests. He lay still as they came through the opening in the fence, apparently intent on joining their people deeper in the base. They paused, the nearest less than twenty meters away, and waited. Two light, eight-wheeled armored vehicles followed them, heavy caliber cannon mounted in turrets pointing forward. The vehicles accelerated and passed the squad of soldiers and sped off into the haze of battle. The squad moved after them, their eyes looking towards the center of the base.

Gwielgi followed, staying low, and using the debris of the battlefield for cover. He had no real plan in mind. Part of himself seemed to be watching his movements.

You're still in shock.

The thought was correct, but it did not seem to make any difference. Gwielgi glanced behind him. No one else was coming. Ahead, the enemy squad slowed. Some moved forward and took cover behind the wreckages of a vehicle and a destroyed structure. The others waited behind their own cover and fired brief bursts at targets he could not see. Then they moved in turn, one group covering the other.

Fire and maneuver. They've been trained.

It was light enough to see dimly several hundred meters. Gwielgi looped the rifle sling around his left arm as he lay beside some rubble. He laid his cheek on the stock and peered through the sight. He centered it on the head of the closest enemy soldier, less than 80 meters away and slowly let out his breath as he squeezed the trigger.

The rifle cracked and Gwielgi turned it to his next target, not bothering to see if he had hit the first man – he knew he had. The second was turning, trying to locate the source of the fire, his head filling the sight. The rifle fired again, jerking back into Gwielgi's shoulder and sending an empty casing bouncing across the ground.

Gwielgi swung the sights slightly to his left, towards a man starting to run forward, unaware of what had happened to the two behind him. Gwielgi hit him in the small of the back, just below the cover of his nanotechnology vest, sending him forward on his face, bumping into the man in front of him. That man, a communication or sensor unit of large size strapped to his back, tried to bring his own gun around but it tangled in the body of the dead man. Gwielgi shot him in the face and swung his rifle to the right, attracted by the movement of another soldier running forward.

Gwielgi fired and the man dropped to his knees and then pitched forward. He swung the rifle further to the right and saw a soldier slowly standing, his arms raised over his head. He fired again, knocking the man's helmet into the air as his body convulsed from the destruction of his brain. He swung the rifle slowly back and forth, looking for more targets but could not see any. He stood slowly and wiped the blood coming down his forehead with the palm of his hand.

Gwielgi walked forward and found a small cluster of enemy soldiers with Militia covering them. In the far distance pillars of fire and smoke showed where the enemy armored vehicles died. He heard but could not see HUPs moving in the distance. Ho`nehe and several Wild Geese infantry came up from the right.

"They've been stopped," Ho`nehe said. His voice was a little tinny and distant. "Their tanks and AFVs are dead and their infantry are surrendering." He touched his head set, listening. "We're just getting word. A lot of damage in... Oh, hell." He fell silent for a moment. When he spoke again it was so quietly that Gwielgi had difficulty hearing him and had to lean forward. "It's Kheyntamenti. He says some missiles hit near the base. The Landing Ship Tavern took a hit, including Peregrine's house behind it. It doesn't look good."

Gwielgi felt his heart beating in a cadence so strong he felt it in his hands. Ho`nehe, his fingertips on his headset and looking down as he concentrated, shook his head. He did not see Gwielgi's eyes; the usual brown and yellow now seemed to glow, almost like a feral animal caught in the light at night. "Command doesn't know if this was the main attack or if they are hitting someplace else as well. Their landing ships have pulled out but we don't know if they are actually leaving or reforming to continue the assault."

Gwielgi looked at the prisoners. One was badly wounded and a Militia medic was tending to him. The other three sat with their backs to a shot-up wall. The one on the left had several small black circles on his collar while the others had inverted chevrons. He walked to them, ignoring Ho`nehe, and put a new magazine into the rifle.

"You are an officer?" Gwielgi looked at the man with the circles. His soft voice was flat.

"Yes," the man said. His voice was heavily accented. "I am Jaeger-Oberst Meiner Gehlen of the Second Grenadier Battalion. We are a mercenary unit that..."

"Shut up," Gwielgi said quietly. There was something very dangerous in his tone and Ho`nehe stepped up behind him. "Are your landing ships coming back here or are they going to hit someplace else?"

"I cannot divulge that information," Gehlen said, a slight tone of contempt in his voice. He folded his arms and stared at Gwielgi.

"Joe, take these kids and go away for a while." Ho`nehe looked at him for a second.

"Gwi, think for a minute," Ho`nehe said.

179

"I have. Take these troops and reinforce the south perimeter. I have these people. That's an order, lieutenant." Gwielgi's eyes never left Gehlen.

"Yes, sir," Ho'nehe said. He turned to the other soldiers. "All right, you're with me. Let's go." He led the others away.

Gwielgi waited a moment. The dizziness was gone but blood kept seeping into his left eye. He wiped it away absently with the back of his hand and squatted slowly beside the enemy officer.

"You said you couldn't divulge the information, which suggests you know what it is," Gwielgi said, his voice still flat. "You will tell me what I want to know or I will put a bullet through your right ankle. This rifle uses 7.62-millimeter rounds, which means you will be a long time healing when they replace your ankle. If you don't tell me then, I'll put a bullet in your right knee. I know your nanosuit will keep the round from penetrating, but your kneecap will be shattered anyway. We will keep doing that until you tell me what I want to know. I've got six full magazines, that's a hundred and twenty rounds. You are going to have a long morning unless you tell me what I want to know." He pointed the rifle at the man's boot.

"You can't be serious and expect that I would..." Gehlen's words terminated in a scream as the rifle fired.

Gwielgi tossed the officer a field bandage. "Go ahead; I don't want you to bleed to death." He waited while the moaning man recovered and finally wrapped the bandage around his ankle after a minute of agony as he removed the boot. The other two prisoners stared, their eyes wide. Then Gwielgi pressed the muzzle of the rifle against the man's kneecap.

"Now, where are your landing ships going?"

The man stared at Gwielgi, his eyes burning with hate and fear. Finally, the fear won. "Portaka, they are going to Portaka. This was a feint. We expected a quick raid here and then a pick-up and then go to Portaka."

Gwielgi stood up. "If what you told me is a lie, I will kill you." His voice was flat. He looked at all of them. "Your landing ship is dead; you've got no place to go. If you leave this spot you will be killed. I will not be far away." The expressions on the faces of the soldiers suggested none considered disobeying his orders.

Gwielgi walked towards the perimeter and saw one of the Geese infantry. He whistled and the woman jogged over. Her face was carefully neutral as she came up to Gwielgi.

"Corporal Strehl, tell Lieutenant Ho`nehe that he can take the prisoners in now." He pulled the magazine free and slid the rifle's bolt to the rear. A round clinked on the ground. He handed the rifle to the corporal and the bandoleer of magazines. "Tell him the enemy officer says the landing ships are headed for Portaka. He ought to relay the information. Tell him that I am placing myself under arrest. I'll wait here until he can arrange to have me escorted back to the battalion area."

"Yes, sir," she said. Strehl looked like she wanted to say something but Gwielgi's eyes silenced her. She turned with her load and jogged away.

Gwielgi looked around. The morning light, now flooding over the mountains to the east, illuminated a scene of destruction. Burning vehicles were everywhere and bodies lay in scattered clumps. He wiped the blood out of his eye and waited to feel something but nothing came.

The Gladius, its nanotechnology skin camouflaging the HUP in flat, drab hues of tan and light orange, crouched in the gorge, its powerful engine shut down. Beneath an oppressive sun an intermittent breeze blew dust off the plateau above it and swirled it down around the HUPAX. From half a kilometer away it was almost invisible.

And there were eyes looking for it. Twelve HUPs slowly moved across the plain the gorge faced. They were patient, holding careful formation. The light HUPs formed a loose skirmish line, constantly shifting their positions, darting about as they maintained a screen in front of the main body.

The other HUPs moved in an arrowhead formation. Several of them weighed in at more than a hundred tons and walked at the point of the arrow while the flanks were made of slightly smaller HUPs.

They were being careful. This was an exercise they had run before, one of many. The last time they ran it their opponents had embarrassed them. But that had been five weeks ago and they had practiced hard since then. They were determined to win the exercise this time.

The Gladius waited while its pilot sweltered in its cockpit. He knew they were studying the gorge and the hills that formed it. But there were many gorges and ravines, many hills. They would need a little luck to see him and they were almost abreast of him.

Then he saw it. A Saber, one of the Black Cats, paused, its swiveled fuselage pointed at him. It moved forward, its fuselage swinging away, but the Gladius pilot knew he was spotted. As his sweat rolled down his face and burned the corners of his eyes, he had only one thought.

Good.

His left hand moved across console buttons and the powerful fusion-ion engine of the HUP came to life. He knew he was suddenly appearing in twelve visual field sensor displays of his opponents but that was what he intended.

He was moving as the first reduced power laser beams lanced at him. The sensors on his HUP recorded the hits and a computer program translated them into varying degrees of damage. He swiveled his fuselage towards the other HUPs, ensuring all of his weapon turrets had clear shots and giving the appearance of getting ready to fight. His lips moved as he counted the seconds and watched his speed climb.

At seven seconds and almost 90 KPH he fired his descent pack. His forward momentum carried him out of the gorge and dropped him on top of a neighboring hill as he cut the pack and then released it. He heard a computer voice call out a warning message about simulated damage. He shook his head. *Should have used eight seconds.* Then he would have landed on the far slope of the hill, not up here in plain sight.

Nonetheless he gained the cover of the hill. At the bottom of his visual field a diagram showed the enemy team coming on quickly in a crescent formation. Close enough to each other to provide mutual support, far enough apart that they had his hill thoroughly covered. Whatever direction he ran, he was dead meat.

Very good. Now, had they forgotten about their back door?

Literally out of the plain, three HUPs rose, sand and dirt pouring off them like water. Powered down like their Gladius teammate, they had waited in a shallow trench, covered in loose sand, just another series of small hills scattered about.

But the back door was closed. The skirmish line had held its position and continued to watch for anyone coming at the main body's rear. They immediately attacked the rising HUPs, relying on their speed to make them difficult targets while they slowly retreated towards the main body.

Very, very good. Now, fingers or fist?

It would be fist. Instead of allowing his force to split, their leader was rolling all his HUPs toward the ambush force. He would take three kills and suffer little damage rather than continue his pursuit to get four but take the risk of having the skirmishers mauled. The Gladius pilot keyed his microphone.

"Gunnery Sergeant Sevin here. All right, let's knock it off and go take a shower. Nice job, 'Charley Victor.' We'll debrief back in the barn. First round tonight is on me."

Sevin heard a series of cheers and friendly insults from the "Charley Victor" – the Black Cat and Victor – HUP pilots. As he swung the Gladius around and joined the others headed back to the Militia facility, Sevin pulled a canteen from beneath his reclined seat. The water was warm and did little to immediately quench his thirst. He drained half of it nonetheless and poured the rest down the front of his chest. The air-cooling system on this HUP was acting up again and the cockpit felt like a stone oven.

He swung his HUP up alongside the Charley Victor leader, Ken Walsh. The big Scorpion towered over the low-slung Gladius. With its nanoskin repaired and displaying desert camouflage, it looked as fresh as the day it left the factory and showed little of the battle damage it had sustained when it first came to Kodomir.

"Training rules apply. Charley Victor, take your HUPs into the lager first. Instructor team, hold off until they clear. After you, gentlemen and ladies."

There were more friendly insults. Well, the instructors had been first in line to the gantries and showers enough times in the past. Let the meres enjoy their victory. The team surged forward while the instructor HUPs slowed down. The good news was that, at least for a moment, the air conditioning system kicked back on. Sevin looked over at the Long Bow piloted by Sergeant Tsunasdi and smiled to himself.

"Hot enough for you, Tsunasdi?"

"Hot? Really? I thought we were enduring yet another cold snap."

Currahee humor. A real joker. Sevin looked to the other side and saw the Rapier of Lieutenant Stephanie Elinshen. Currahee wherever I look –

neighborhood is going to hell. Her time in the Militia school had not slowed down her reflexes that Sevin could tell. He thumbed his rear view. Captain Gregor Piotrowski completed the diamond formation in a Short Sword. He was the best of the Kodomiri students, one of the first to graduate from the HUPAX training syllabus. Tapping him to do a tour as an instructor was a good decision, though Sevin preferred to have someone he knew on his wing in combat. Of course, this was not combat, just training, and having him on board as part of the HUP instructor cadre was a good way to get to know him.

An hour later, thoroughly showered and in a clean gray-camouflaged uniform with his purple beret rolled inside one of his epaulets, Sevin walked into the amphitheater they used for debriefing field exercises. He carried an insulated cup holding iced tea. Like a number of the Wild Geese, he had picked up the Kodomiri taste for the beverage. On the other hand, he had not become a purist; many of the Kodomiri still raised an eyebrow when they saw him dump ice into the brew they regarded with almost religious significance.

Everyone stood as he entered the room, including the mercenaries, and he waved them back into their seats. As a Gunnery Sergeant, Sevin was not used to having officers, even officers of mercenaries, rise at his arrival. The amphitheater was comfortable, one of close to twenty brand new buildings added to the Militia facility on Portaka in the past several months. Now that the facility was becoming a training center for the Militia, as well as increasing its importance in guarding the mines and industry of Portaka, the place was growing very rapidly. Two construction battalions plus a number of civilian contractors added to the base buildings on a daily basis.

Sevin put his cup down on the podium and began the debriefing. Though not the senior in rank, for this exercise he had been the lead instructor. The Wild Geese tradition had carried over easily into the Militia.

The desert and hills stretching west of the facility were seeded thoroughly with sensors, enabling observers to watch practice sessions in real time and record activities from a variety of angles. Re-creation of the exercise using holographic imagery was an excellent teaching tool. As he talked, displays flashed into life on the stage. It did not take long but he was gratified to see everyone was attentive and most took notes.

"So, in summary, the Charley Victor team leader made the correct decisions at each stage of the exercise. The skirmish team showed good discipline and kept focused on their area of responsibility. Once engaged, they used excellent fire and maneuver in moving back to the main force. All hands had good overall hit percentages. Weapon selection was very good. Commo procedures were tight. All in all, well done." He took a sip, grimaced, and said, "Any questions?"

There were few; this had been the sixth exercise in four days and most of the pilots were tired. When the last question was answered, Doc dismissed everyone and joined the other instructors and walked with them out of the building. The heat was great but not as bad as a HUP's cockpit while sitting powered down in the desert. After a few weeks most people adapted, though at first it was like being hit by a wall.

Around them construction was underway as usual, with heavy equipment moving prefabricated building sections around like they were a child's toys. As they watched, a single-story building was assembled on a prepared slab, already outfitted with conduits and connections for water, power, and communications. Engineers were using exoskeletons, forerunners of the HUPAX, to pick up and carefully place wall sections.

"What is that going to be?" Piotrowski wondered aloud. Beside him, Tsunasdi squinted in the heat and light as he watched the construction.

"Unfortunately, not a bar," Sevin replied. He unfolded a newly printed map from his pocket – he had gotten into the habit of getting an updated copy each morning since the sudden emergence of new buildings required continuous relearning of the base layout. "That will be," he said, pausing as he studied the map, "the new medical complex. It will eventually be four stories tall and they'll have a wing added, over towards the west." He folded the map and put it away. "Let's get back to the office and see what is on tap." He led the way to a nearby building.

"What's the weather forecast?" Elinshen asked the duty corporal as they walked into the small building.

"We have a high moving in, lieutenant," the corporal said, pushing her hair back as she stood. Elinshen waved her back into her seat. "From the southwest – it may be pushing some good winds in front of it."

"Dust storm?" Tsunasdi asked. No one liked Portaka dust storms; the worst could last for a day, some rare ones longer, and no matter how well sealed a building might be, the dust would get into everything, including beds.

"Possibly, sarge," the young woman said. "If so, it shouldn't last too long."

"Typical Portaka weather," Sevin said, leading the small group down the hall. "If it's not hot, it's windy and hot." He turned into the instructors' office and touched the controls of a console. One of the displays on the wall glowed. "Here we go."

They were studying the glowing training schedule when the young corporal stepped into the room.

"Lieutenant Elinshen?" Her voice was hesitant and anxious. "Lieutenant, Colonel Jonathan needs you in Operations. Ma'am," she paused, "Lieutenant, you better come quickly." Elinshen looked at the others and followed the nervous woman at a half-jog.

"What the hell?" Piotrowski asked and Sevin shrugged as Elinshen disappeared.

Colonel Jonathan was leaning over the communication console with several Militia officers standing close to him. Someone had put the audio through the external speakers. For a moment Elinshen could not understand what the overlapping and shouting voices were saying.

"It's another raid," Jonathan said. "Air strike on Coyote Bay." Then the voices became clear.

"Two o'clock, Yuri, two o'clock!"

"I see him! In hot."

"Missiles, nine o'clock."

"That damned landing ship!"

"Missiles, eight o'clock."

"Yuri, check six."

"Keep him off me! I'm on the leader."

"Missiles, seven o'clock. Incoming."

"Scratch one!"

"Fox two, fox two!"

"Yuri, pull left. I'm on him."

"Roger, coming…"

"Yuri's down."

"Fox three."

"Missiles, eight o'clock."

"Heads up – Zombie is lifting. Sweet Jesu, look at her!"

"Roger; go Big Z, get some!"

"Scratch one."

"I've got three over the bay, turning inbound."

"Roger, two more at their high nine."

"This is Toland. Everyone, pile on the five coming in from the bay."

"Roger, lead."

"This is Captain Peg Cochran of Zombie. Get the hell out of my way; we're taking on the southern landing ship!"

"I'm on your port, major."

"Roger, in hot. Take the high one, I'm on the leader."

"Burn, you dog-licker!"

Jonathan's voice was hushed as he leaned towards the lieutenant. "Multiple landing ships appeared in close orbit all of a sudden. No warning, no alarms from the navigation beacon sensors, no indication of a star ship anywhere." The colonel shook his head. "I think the sensors were messed with when another star ship came through ten days ago. Anyway, several landing ships came down close to Coyote Bay and launched fighters and landing troops. At least one is still there, maybe more."

"Where are the others?"

"No one is sure. I'm taking us to full alert. Right now." Jonathan pointed at an officer who spoke into a microphone. He turned to Elinshen. "You are senior tactical officer after me. Scramble all the HUPs and get them away from here. If we're hit, you may have to take tactical control of whatever can get off the base. Understood?"

"Aye, sir." Elinshen ran from the room. As she did. he heard a voice over the public address system.

"All hands, Kodomir is under attack. All hands, Kodomir is under attack. Stand clear of the base. Defense condition Alpha is in effect. Go to condition Alpha. All weapons are free."

As Elinshen emerged from the building, she saw the other instructors in a car, waiting for her. She dove into the back as they pulled away from the curb.

"What the hell is happening?" Piotrowski asked as Sevin steered the car; its computer would not allow the car to do what the gunnery sergeant was doing to get to the HUPAX lager so Sevin was running on manuals.

"Air strike, Coyote Bay Base." Elinshen's voice was clear and precise. "Multiple landing ships, but only one is engaged now. They don't know where the others went or where their star ship is. Nav beacon sensors are down."

"Orders?"

"Just what you heard. Jonathan wants us to get everything away from the base. If command here gets knocked out, I will take control of all forces." She looked towards the airfield as two Tiger Moth helicopters lifted off. "I do not think there is much here for them to shoot at but the colonel is taking no chances."

As the car slid to a stop in the HUP lager, they piled out and ran to the service gantries next to their HUPs. Her Rapier was close by and she pulled on her mindlink helmet as she ran. A HUP technician, what the Wild Geese called a HUP Captain, stood on the elevator platform next to the HUP and quickly lifted them to the cockpit.

Elinshen stepped into the cockpit and dropped into the semi-reclined ejection seat. The technician leaned in and helped her strap in. Then he tapped the top of Elinshen's helmet.

"Sir, she's up three ways. Weapons are set hot. Good hunting. I'm with you," he said as he flashed a thumb's up and gave the traditional Geese phrase. Elinshen nodded.

"With you," she replied as the cockpit hatch hissed shut. Her fingers danced across the control console and the HUP came to life. As the tech had said, the HUP was ready – propulsion systems, sensors, and weapons all flashed to life. Out of the corner of her eye through the narrow viewing port she saw the maintenance stand slide away. Her vision tumbled for a second as the mindlink connection was made and then suddenly she saw everything around her as if the HUP was not there or, more exactly, as if she was the HUP. She slid the armored covers of the viewing ports up and looked with her HUP's "eyes."

In front of her the captain stood, his crossed arms over his head, holding the Rapier in place as another HUP, a Gladius with Sevin inside, stomped past. Then the technician began to guide her forward. He pointed to the right and then snapped a salute. Elinshen turned the powerful HUP and accelerated.

"All units, this is Lieutenant Elinshen on Militia common. APCs and tanks, head for Nav Bravo. Repeat, Bravo. Pass the word as other units get rolling and make contact. Have whoever is senior contact me on frequency Blue. All helicopters get to Gamma, repeat Gamma. Pass the word and have your leader meet me on Blue. Swallows, go down to Foxtrot and set up a low orbit. All HUPs follow me to Alpha. Pass the word. Switching to Blue."

Elinshen guided the Rapier around a cluster of construction vehicles and a tall engineering exoskeleton and their startled drivers as she headed for the western edge of the base. By now the HUP was moving at over 50 kilometers an hour. The old perimeter fencing was long since torn down as the base expanded and she was soon kicking up dust in the late afternoon sun.

"Lieutenant Elinshen, fighter lead. Do you copy?"

"Aye, lead. Who are you?"

"Captain Aleksandr Pokryshkin, Lieutenant. We are orbiting over Nav Foxtrot, angels thirty with five Swallows."

"Roger, copy. Hold your position. Break. Helos, are you up?"

"Affirmative, leader. We have four Tiger Moths at Gamma, holding in the gully behind Hill 193."

"Roger. Who is leading you?"

"Lieutenant Jack N'krombe speaking."

"You are in a good position, Jack. Hold there for now. Break. Any Cats or Victors up?"

"Walsh here with six Black Cats in transit. We are just clearing the HUP area."

"Lieutenant Elinshen, this is Peterson of the Victors. We have four HUPs starting up or moving."

"Roger. I and the four HUPAX with me are Team Blue. Major Walsh, you are Team Black. I want you to form a skirmish line about a kilometer from Alpha facing the base. Mister Peterson, your people are Team Victor. Join me at Alpha."

"Team Black, roger."

"Ah, Team Victor rogers."

189

Elinshen shook her head. Peterson was a good pilot, but he was not used to leading. Nonetheless, most of the senior pilots of Vermeil's Victors were up at Coyote Bay attending staff training and Peterson would have to do.

Lieutenant Elinshen, armor lead is at Nav Bravo.

"Roger, armor. Who is in command and what do you have with you?"

"Lieutenant Michael I. Koshkin, in command, leader. I have the Bob Cat instructor cadre of six tanks. We also have two Zhukovs from the I and E team. In support, two 152, two 122, and one 107 Sierra Papas, and three missile APCs. I also have four APCs mounting infantry and two APCs empty."

"Roger, Koshkin. We will need the self-propelled artillery if they land." She shook her head; it was a typical mixed bag – would the Militia ever standardize their artillery? "Who are your infantry?"

"Two sources, leader. Some of Second Recon, some Chek Scouts, people going through the desert school."

"Roger. Hold tight. Break. Team Blue, taking it to 85."

There was a brief flurry of acknowledgements from the other pilots. She checked her sensors and navigation display. They were only a few minutes from navigation point Alpha, which was nothing more than an arbitrarily identified position in the baking hills and ravines of the land west of the base.

"Lieutenant Elinshen, this is base command. How do you copy?"

"Loud and clear."

"Roger. Stand by. Command Six Actual coming online."

"Elinshen, Jonathan. What's your status?"

She quickly briefed the commander on how she had placed the available forces.

"Good. We just got flash traffic from Kiroff. Two, possibly three, landing ships are headed this way. Another is dead."

"Casualties?"

"Unclear, but it sounds like there's been some damage to the base and parts of the city close by."

"Roger."

Elinshen spun the HUP around, facing back towards the base, now more than two kilometers away. On the edge of her sensor display she could see the Black Cats forming a weaving line. The five heavy HUPs of the Victors were just coming through the Black Cats.

Now they waited. It would not be long.

"Colonel Jonathan, we have tracking data being relayed to us by Militia CIC. Satellite infrared shows three landing ships headed this way, ETA one-seven minutes." The officer pointed at the wall display. "There are several Militia landing ships following and some fighters are trying to leg it here from Kiroff but…" The young officer's voice was tense but calm. Jonathan nodded, showing the same outward calmness. He studied the display as the lieutenant spoke.

"Very well, lieutenant." Jonathan keyed his microphone.

"Lieutenant Elinshen, we have three landing ships confirmed inbound. Seventeen minutes. They are on a direct course for us. We have some Militia ships coming in pursuit and Kiroff is trying to stage fighters to us but it is going to be an hour before any help arrives. I will use what we have here to try to defend the base but I suspect we will not do much. However, I hope we can hold their attention long enough for you to get some hits."

"Roger, sir. Break. Cats, fall back to my position. Armor, stay where you are. Shut everything down except for your commo. Helos, land at your current position and shut down. Monitor this frequency. Alek, take your flight further south by another 20 kilometers. Everyone, listen up."

Elinshen thought quickly, a plan forming in her mind.

"They are going to hit the base, probably land right on top of it. We will let them since we cannot prevent it. They will disembark their ground force and commence their raid. We will hold most of our force in position, shut down so they cannot see it. Then we will move the HUPAX up while they are busy. Our HUPAX will attack first, focusing their attention. Then the armor, on my command. Then air, also on my command. Now, this is important. No one moves until I say – the longer we wait, the better. Reinforcements are coming. If we go too soon, their landing ships will have time to wipe us out. If we time it right, they will be tangled up with us when our people get here and kill these dog-licking weak-hearts. Any questions?"

191

There were none. In the cockpits of aircraft and HUPs, and in tank turrets and armored vehicles, eyes turned towards clocks as hands shut down engines. They sat as the heat rose in a hot wind and checked that their weapons had live rounds in chambers, but mostly they watched the minutes and seconds tick off.

"Elinshen, Jonathan. We are under attack. Ion pulse weapons and missiles are impacting the northwest area of the base. Missiles are hitting where the perimeter used to be, so they are using old data. Sensors show three landing ships in a V formation. Lead landing ship appears to be an Alligator-class. I think one of the others is a Viper. I have engaged our base laser turrets and missile launchers. They are picking them off about as fast as they open fire. We're getting fire deeper into the base now. It's getting closer to us. I'll try to transmit as long as I can. I've sent the CIC crew down into the bunker. They are landing; one is less than 400 meters away. Ramp is coming down. It is a Viper. Alligator to the left. I see tanks and APCs and at least two HUPs from that ship. They just hit the admin building next door. I think we're next. Tell..."

The voice ceased. Elinshen keyed her microphone.

"All HUPAX, follow me. Keep your speed down. No dust cloud. Keep all sensors off."

Elinshen studied the map in her vision as she steered her Rapier towards the base. There was a convenient ridge that would shelter them until they were within a kilometer of the base perimeter and she guided the line of HUPs towards it. At the same time, she monitored her clock.

She guessed at how long it would take for the landing ships to disembark their ground forces. They would spread out, heading for whatever buildings and facilities on the base their leaders had picked out. Then they would destroy their targets, probably by using demolition charges rather than their ammunition. All that would take time, time she would use to get the HUPs in close so she could hit them while they were dispersed. And soon after that the Militia landing ships would arrive, and maybe some fighters. They might not be expecting much of a force here. It was a long shot, but it was the best plan she could come up with.

Elinshen followed the ridge as it took them west of the base. The mid-afternoon sun would be slightly at their backs, a small advantage. She glanced to the right and saw that her HUP's shadow was not as dark as it had been moments before. Some trick of the light? She looked towards the sun, now not far above the horizon.

The sun was a pale orange disk behind a dull brown wall. Not clouds; Elinshen had seen a Portaka dust storm before. It was hard to estimate how far away it was. Distances in a desert were always deceptive. But if the timing was right... She keyed her microphone again, risking interception of the message.

"All units stand by. We have a dust storm coming in from the west. I think it will be here in ten minutes. It looks to be a big one. So a change in plan. Your signal to go will be the dust storm getting to you. Use it for cover. Attack choppers, use your sensors and do pop up attacks. Do not close with the landing ships. Fixed wing, long-range fire only as long as those landing ships are present. Run in, shoot, and peel away. Armor, creep in under the cover of the storm. You know the layout of the base. Use cover as much as possible. Missile APCs and self-propelled artillery get coordinates from the datalink. Fire and move."

The ridge took them to a position almost directly west of the base. Elinshen watched the approaching storm. The sun was becoming noticeably dimmer but she was still having trouble estimating when it would arrive.

Suddenly it was racing down from the western hills and swallowing them in its howling wind. She could hear the hiss of sand against her HUP's armor while the far ends of the HUPAX line vanished from sight.

"All HUPAX, maintain sensors off. Stay on line. Heading zero nine zero. Forward, now. Set speed 65."

The HUPs surged up the ridge, shrouded in the blowing sand. They crested the ridge but there was nothing to see. It was like moving in a submarine at the bottom of a brown, swirling sea. Only the ground immediately around them was clear and the HUP pilots guided on each other. With sensors off to avoid detection, they were walking forward blind.

Elinshen looked at her map. Now they were less than half a kilometer from the base and still she saw nothing. Well, that worked both ways. She scanned with her passive sensors and picked up an infrared signature. The computer compared the heat pattern to its database and identified the target as an armored vehicle. For a second the target was gone, probably behind a building. Then it reappeared. The computer displayed it in her visual field with a graphic of the vehicle. She looked at it and the targeting reticle appeared over it. She fired a pair of lasers. The crack of the red spears of coherent energy could barely be heard above the wind. The target vanished, killed. Another appeared.

"I have multiple armor targets, twelve o'clock, six hundred meters. Maintain formation. Do not converge. Call your targets as you encounter them. Stay together – they will call for help and we will have more targets."

"Black lead has multiple APCs near the north end of our line. They look like hovercraft and are grounded. Probably problems with the wind."

"Roger, Black. Kill them if there is not a better target."

"Roger."

"This is Doc. I have your tanks, leader. And I think I got a strobe on a HUP beyond them."

"Roger, no joy."

She fired her turreted twin recoilless rifles at a tank and then used the lasers on another one. Immediately the periphery of her vision lit up with electronic warfare warnings. Someone was trying to get a lock on her.

"This is Victor Lead. I have two, no, three HUPs to my front. They are moving north. Having trouble tracking them. This sand is screwing up our passive sensors. Range in excess of 800 meters."

"Roger, hold your fire. Let us get closer before introducing ourselves to them."

"Yes, ma'am."

Elinshen smiled. The Victor pilot sounded very young. Odd that she had faced him across the battlefield not so long ago.

"Tankers on the roll. This storm is *thick*."

"Roger. Koshkin, our HUP line is about 400 meters inside the western perimeter of the base. We are moving east at about 30 KPH. We have seen indications of HUPAX about 800 meters to our front, moving away from your entry point. We have encountered mostly armored vehicles so far. Stay cool, keep your tanks together, and kill anything you meet. If you need help, yell."

"Roger, lieutenant. Don't worry, I am a *frontovik tankerist.*"

Elinshen had no idea what Koshkin meant, but did not have the time to ask. Her HUP had just walked into a half dozen armored vehicles, including some missile equipped APCs and at least two tanks.

She fired her three turrets of lasers directly into the turret of the closest tank, looked to the right, and punched through the thin armor of an APC with a recoilless rifle slug. Black smoke erupted from it as it jerked to a halt, severely damaged. She glanced back at the first tank and saw it was decapitated, its turret gone with fire roaring up from its hull. As she looked towards a second tank her passive sensor picked up a pair of HUPs, and then more.

"This is Elinshen. I have multiple armored vehicles and HUPAX in front of me. All HUPs converge on me and feel free to join the party. Make sure of your targets."

Something slammed into her HUP's upper structure, throwing off her aim. She pulled her sight back to the tank. Its turret was rapidly turning towards her. Elinshen fired her four recoilless rifles and the turret sheared off the hull, spinning away into the blowing sand.

"HUPAX, when you engage blink your sensors to ID your target. Do not leave them on."

An APC pulled in behind the dead tank, using it for cover. Elinshen did not hesitate. Her fire blocked by the dead tank, she walked the Rapier forward and stepped up on the tank hull. It sagged on its tracks but the hull did not buckle. One more step and she was on top of the APC.

The APC's armor was comparatively thin and it folded inward as 110-tons of HUPAX placed all of its weight on the upper surface. Something exploded internally and Elinshen kept walking forward.

"Elinshen, it looks like the base is totally covered by the storm. I'm leading our fighters in."

"Roger. See if you can hit the landing ships. Go sensors on."

"Roger, we have them. In hot."

"Leader, helo flight is lifting. We can't see anything."

"Roger, go sensors on. Hit anything you can."

Delighted to do so – flight, weapons free. Time to wash the spears.

It was another Kodomiri phrase Elinshen did not understand; didn't any of these people speak Standard? She looked around. The six armored vehicles were dead or dying but the two HUPs to her front were still coming, angling to her right. That would put them in front of the Victor heavy HUPs.

"Victors, you have two HUPs bearing zero six five from you, estimating 600 meters."

"Roger. We have them." The young man's voice was calmer now. "There are two more to their left and multiple armored targets closing rapidly, bearing zero nine five. We are remaining sensors off and engaging.

"Roger. Break. Cats, Geese, follow me, heading one two zero. My speed 45, stay on line."

"Cats, roger. It will take us a second to reform the line."

"Roger."

A group of soldiers coming out of a construction shed suddenly appeared in front of her. Elinshen fired a single laser into the middle of the group and they and the shed vanished. The wind was slowing down a little and visibility was now out to about a hundred meters. She could hear the sound of firing on either side of her.

Elinshen, fighter lead. We're hitting the landing ships. I'm passing our datalink info to all hands. They bear zero four five from you, about a klick away, in the northern part of the base.

She looked at her maps across the bottom of her visual field and saw the three red dots. Then they were displayed by red symbols in her visual field.

"Roger, got it. Nice work, Alek."

"We're in. Not all of us have missiles, lead. Let me see if I can warm things up for them with my laser."

"Negative, fighter lead. Landing ships are too heavily armed to engage with a fighter laser. Stand back."

"Sorry, leader. Having commo problems."

Elinshen cursed under her breath. Typical aviator, just like Jackie's boyfriend. An idiot. There was no longer time to worry about him, however. The mercenary HUPs were turning toward her flanking maneuver. That meant they saw her and the others, and that meant the landing ships could fire in support.

Things were about to become interesting.

Captain Aleksandr Pokryshkin was many things, but an idiot was not one of them. When the alarms went off, he had grabbed the first Swallow that he came to that could launch. Unfortunately, its missile launcher had not been rearmed since it had been on the target range, so he had been able to make only one run against the enemy landing ships before it was empty.

The Kodomiri had upgraded their Swallows, swapping out the original older single emitter Class Ones to double emitter Class Twos. Since they did not need the encompassing turrets the HUPs used, the increase in weight was not prohibitive. Though two emitters ran hotter, this was not much of a problem for an aircraft as it was relatively easy to provide airflow to assist in cooling. What it meant was the Swallows that attacked the landing ships had twice the laser punch of those that had fought against the Storm Cloud invasion of almost three years ago.

When Pokryshkin's single antiarmor missile left its launcher towards the landing ship hidden in the sand storm, he noticed that there was no return fire coming up at his flight. His electronic warfare display showed that the landing ships had all their sensors on – they were strobing multicolor spikes like insane Christmas trees.

Pokryshkin pulled around and accompanied another Swallow as it made its run. When the fighter launched a pair of missiles and rolled away, Pokryshkin kept going in. When he was within range, he fired his laser and turned away. It was a blind shot using his instruments and the blowing sand probably dispersed some of the energy, but he must have hit something. There was no return fire.

But why didn't the landing ships fire? Could the storm be interfering with their sensors or weapons? As Pokryshkin turned his fighter he glanced down and saw a flash of light in the dull brown of the sand storm. Something was firing or had just been hit. He rolled back in and took another shot. Again he received no return fire.

"Flight, something odd here. I'm not getting return fire from the landing ships."

"Lead, Dash Three copies. I don't think they can see very far. It's the storm."

"We're looking through the same storm, Three. How can that be?"

"They are *in* it, captain. That much blowing sand, besides whatever physical damage it might do to exposed sensor panels and antennas, had got to be kicking up a hell of a static electric charge on their hulls. That is probably reducing their effective range."

"Roger. All right, after your missiles are gone and as long as the wind is blowing, you can press your attacks. Go no closer than 600 meters – that's as close as I got in the last run."

"Roger, lead."

Lieutenant Koshkin heard the fighters talking overhead and nodded. He had blinked his own sensors on and off and had not gotten anything useable; the storm was making everyone blind. That was fine with him. His six tanks were moving onto the base like a massive fist, carefully keeping together. He glanced to his right through his cupola periscope. The new Zhukovs had come to Portaka to get a field test; the two to the right, low slung and dark Militia green, were about to get the test of a lifetime.

Using the datalink, Koshkin saw the plots of the landing ships. The closest one was his target. If they could get within range, they would not need sensors to hit something that big. A simple bearing would be enough.

"Support, unless we give you a priority target, you can fire on whichever landing ships you can reach."

"Tanker lead, we copy. We have Diamondback rounds. If you can laze a target, we would be happy to hit it."

"Roger. We'll see what we can do, though I don't think much reflected targeting energy will get through this storm."

The tanks, barely ten meters between them, moved through the howling wind. Visibility fluctuated. Sometimes they could barely see each other and then there would be a gap and they would be able to see a hundred or more meters.

Koshkin heard the HUPs engaging and looked at his map display. He was closer to the landing ships than to the firefight, and if he could distract the landing ships, maybe he could keep their supportive fire off the HUPs. They were the real killing power in this engagement. He nodded to himself and pulled a small amulet from inside his shirt. It was a small, silver figure of Saint George slaying a dragon. He kissed it and dropped it back inside his shirt.

Saint George, pray for me. Time for the dragon to die.

The first attackers the tankers saw were a group of infantry directly in front of them, climbing into three APCs. For an instant they could see each other clearly and then the sand obscured all sight. It did not matter.

"Gunner, fire!" Koshkin yelled as he pushed open the turret hatch and climbed up to the heavy machine gun mounted above him. As he reached it the tank's main gun fired, its smoke immediately swept away by the storm. He pulled the operating rod handle of the machine gun to the rear twice and thumbed down on the paddles, sending a long line of tracers ahead.

"Gunner, independent, fire!"

Even as his hands shook from the machine gun fire, he felt the vibration through the turret as the Bob Cat's cannon reloaded.

The cannon firing again smothered the gunner's response. Then they were among the APCs.

The one directly ahead had a track shattered. Pieces lay about and several soldiers were down. One to his right was totally engulfed in flames that were blowing almost perfectly horizontal, a victim of the Zhukovs. The one on the left was leaving, its rear ramp still down, soldiers trying to climb aboard. He swung the machine gun over and walked tracers onto the ramp and into the APC's hull. People, caught by the large caliber slugs, spun and fell to the ground, parts of their bodies thrown into the air.

Koshkin's tank fired again and the APC ahead burst into flame. The Bob Cats to his left fired and the remaining APC was blown completely apart, like a child's model. The tanks lunged forward in a shallow arrowhead formation, Koshkin's tank in the lead, and they fired on anything not Kodomiri. Enemy troops, scattered in small squads on foot or with APCs, could not hear them coming over the wind and their first glimpse of the tanks often came as machine gun tracers ripped through their ranks.

Enemy tanks fared no better. The few they encountered were upgraded mediums, similar in basic design to the Militia's own. But they were spread out and encountered in small teams and were no match for the group of Militia armor tracking through the howling sand. They were especially no match for the Zhukovs. Koshkin saw an enemy tank erupt in a flash of flame, throwing its turret over the side of the hull. Another one for the Zhukovs. Some field test, he thought.

The Militia crews, all frontovik tankerists, combat experienced tankers, did not hesitate and did not swerve. They pressed on through the storm, tearing up enemy soldiers and vehicles as they encountered them and, if sometimes the enemy was slow to get out of the way, the steel tracks of the grimly driven Bob Cats and Zhukovs brought another piece of horror to the battlefield.

"All tanks, range 640. Target: landing ship. Support force, concentrate your fire. Our fighters are already hitting it. Datalink says it is an Alligator. Keep your rounds low and hit the engines. Burn this dog-licker son of a bitch."

The crack of the long-barreled tanks, looking like armored predators from prehistory, were heard even above the wind. Koshkin, still exposed half out of the turret, looked up. It was a little brighter overhead. Somewhere up there, long-range missiles and artillery rounds were screaming in from the support armor behind him, and the Swallows were still making their runs. His tank recoiled with every round and he grimaced. It was all dead reckoning firing but they had to be hitting something. As long as the storm kept up, they had a chance.

He saw movement to the right. Figures were moving through the storm. They were not Militia. Koshkin swung the heavy machine gun and squeezed the firing paddles. Rounds as thick as a big man's thumb and as long whipped through the air. Men died in front of him, torn apart, some dead before they hit the ground. Then they were nothing more than scattered dark piles on the dirt.

We did not ask you to come here.

Lieutenant Jack N'krombe popped up over the ridge he had hid behind with his Tiger Moth flight and saw...

Nothing. His sensors had nothing and the storm obscured all sight more than a hundred meters away, sometimes less. He dropped his helicopter back down.

"Lead, Two. I saw nothing."

"Three. Me, neither."

"All right, folks. Everyone else is firing blind unless they walk into something. I didn't see anything either. We have medium-range missiles on board but I don't think we can get away with firing them at max range – this damned wind will scatter them to hell and gone."

N'krombe thought for a moment, studying his map with the datalink overlays.

"Here's the deal. They brought their landing ships down just north of the CIC. One is in the admin parking lot, looks like, and the other two are back on the rugby field. What we are going to do is lift, go over this ridge, and take up a heading of zero three zero, speed 50, altitude at about a meter. We'll hold that for about a kilometer, and then we will turn in on a heading of three one zero. That will run us right into the landing ship at this end of the rugby field. We will take cover behind the new gymnasium. Then we will close and go for the landing ship bridge. Take that out and those people are not going anywhere. Questions?"

There were none in spite of the fact N'krombe was proposing suicide as a tactic. If they were seen by a landing ship, it had the firepower to evaporate them kilometers away. He planned on taking them into rock-throwing range, but if they wanted hits, they would have to get close.

Flying the Tiger Moths close to the ground was a skill all the pilots practiced, but they seldom had to do it buffeted by a sand storm. N'krombe wondered how good their intake filters were and how much warning they would have if their engines started to seize. Well, this close to the ground they would not have far to fall.

They were so low that they occasionally had to rise to get over a piece of construction equipment like a bulldozer. N'krombe recognized where they were, seeing buildings he knew. Bodies lay scattered around, Militia caught before they could evacuate. He said nothing and kept flying.

They made their inbound turn without encountering anything. Where was the enemy? It took a moment before N'krombe realized that at this point the attackers were probably shoving everything they had at the HUPs to the west or the tanks to the south. He had relief at the thought and then guilt. While others were fighting, and maybe dying, he was still making his way to a target. He pushed the thoughts aside and concentrated on flying his helicopter.

The storm was a little lighter when they got to the gymnasium. Their target was maybe a hundred or two hundred meters beyond it. The datalink suggested it was a Viper-class landing ship. Its bridge would be over the nose of the aerodynamic fuselage. But the datalink was not precise enough to show them how the ship lay. It could be pointed right at them or they could be facing its rear.

Well, one way to find out.

"I don't know where this thing's bridge is going to be, but one of us has to get to it and, when you do, put everything you have into it. Three and four, you go around the gym to the right. Two, you stay with me and we will go left."

The others acknowledged. N'krombe took a breath and then swung to the left. For a moment there was nothing to see, just the yellow-brown of the blowing sand. Suddenly the wind fell off and he could see almost 200 hundred meters ahead.

The Viper was side-on to the helicopters and blocking the wind. N'krombe saw the bridge complex, higher up. He let the helicopter rise and kicked it sideways.

"Follow me, Two." N'krombe's voice was barely more than a whisper.

His helmet visor gave him a display of the half-hidden world around him as seen by his sensors. With a touch of his thumb on his control stick, his weapon sights appeared in the display in front of his eyes. Where he looked with the targeting crosshairs his cannon would put rounds as the computer calculated and compensated for wind speed, the relative movement of target and Tiger Moth, and all the other variables needed to be accounted for before killing things. The medium-range missiles had a simpler system since their internal guidance systems would take them wherever he looked.

None of the electronic computer guidance was necessary. He kept his helicopter so close to the landing ship that the tip of the rotor blades was less than a meter from its hull. As he rose he could see in the occasional port. Sometimes there was a startled face. Just a few more seconds.

N'krombe pivoted in front of the bridge and let himself take a second to look in as he backed away. There were people there. One was pointing at him, his mouth moving. Others were yelling, running. N'krombe squeezed the trigger of the cannon.

The rounds ripped through the fifty meters of space between the muzzle and the bridge and impacted the armored glass. Tiger Moth cannon rounds were caseless two-stage rounds. The first stage was a conventional high velocity explosive designed to propel the round out the barrel, while the second stage, a slower burning fuel inside the round itself, ignited a meter beyond the muzzle, giving the round increased velocity. "Slower burning" was relative, of course. To an outside observer a Tiger Moth cannon erupted a thin column of flame as the 37mm rounds fired in a stream. Half were solid slugs of jacketed metal, designed to punch through their target using the terrible kinetic energy generated by their almost hypervelocity. The other half, designed to kill armor, carried small, shaped explosive charges.

The bridge's armored glass shook under the pounding of the Tiger Moths' fire and held for all of a second. It never had a chance. The glass imploded before panicking hands could hit the controls that would have dropped metal armor over it and the rest of the rounds ripped through the bridge, tearing into control consoles and people. There was an almost continuous series of explosions inside the bridge.

Then the two Tiger Moths launched their missiles. Carrying warheads more than twice the weight of the cannons' explosive rounds, almost all of the medium-range missiles went into the bridge before exploding in the interior of the ship. What had been a landing ship bridge suddenly exploded into a volcano of fire in less than two seconds.

N'krombe was surprised at the violence of the explosions and fire and at the fact he was still alive.

"Take it back down to the ground, Two. Three and Four, say your position."

"This is Four. Three's down. Something hit his rotor and he veered off. I didn't hear a call but he crashed near the north bleachers."

"Roger, join on me. Let's see if we can get another of these bastards before they can see."

Elinshen watched the enemy HUP die in front of the lead Victor, a 120-ton Scorpion. It and the Trebuchet on its wing outweighed the enemy HUPs they were encountering almost two to one. She had not seen an attacker weighing more than 85-tons. With four enemy HUPs were burning, she realized they were winning the battle and the enemy was falling back. If there were any others, they were closer to the landing ships.

"Lieutenant Elinshen, N'krombe. We just took out the bridge of a landing ship, a Viper. It is burning and I do not think they are going anywhere. All emissions from it have ceased – sensor probes, commo, even power plant. I think their control systems are gone."

"Very good, Mister N'krombe. See if you can support the tankers – they are going after the southern landing ship, another Viper."

"Roger. We do not have it in sight but are moving towards it with three."

"Understood."

"Elinshen, Walsh. Completing the sweep to the north. No opposition. I think the wind is dying down."

He was right. The wind, which had been so strong it had actually buffeted the 110-ton Rapier, was noticeably lighter. Visibility was improving, even with the late afternoon light. Any second the landing ship sensors would find them and it would be all over. Multiple lasers, ion pulse weapons, and missile racks would put down an enormous amount of firepower.

An explosion so brilliant that not even the sandstorm could totally hide it flashed in front of her, followed a second later by a shock wave that actually pushed debris back into the face of the wind. Her HUP staggered.

"What was that?"

"Koshkin here. I believe you can scratch the southern landing ship. Most of us are having trouble seeing, but I think her reactor went."

"This is Warrant Officer Roy Peterson, second Tiger Moth. I can confirm the southern landing ship is history. Lieutenant N'krombe's helo was knocked down by the blast. I see him, he's all right. I'm headed towards the remaining landing ship."

"Roger. Stay alert. The storm is lifting and the enemy is pulling back in the direction of their landing ships. You can expect contact. And your *Viper* may not be able to lift, but it can still fight, so use cover as you move."

"Roger."

Visibility was improving, which meant the sensor shroud of sand was fading away. The enemy was pulling back, heading for the undamaged landing ship. Clearly, they were going to evacuate. Should she pursue? Every part of Elinshen's Currahee-bred heart wanted to close with the landing ship and destroy it and the last of the attackers. Did not a warrior's honor demand the destruction of the enemy?

She took a breath. They had won – to continue the battle would invite the destruction of many of the people under her command, even if they were able to keep the remaining landing ship from leaving. On the other hand, if the raiders elected to stay, perhaps to repair the damaged ship, then the full weight of the Militia would fall on them, not just a small group of instructors, students, and mercenaries. She decided.

"Everyone, pull back. The storm is lifting and they will be able to see us soon. Return to your original Nav points. I think they are withdrawing. Alek, get some distance but monitor that last landing ship and tell me when it lifts and where it goes."

"Fighter Lead rogers."

"Koshkin here, lieutenant. The last landing ship is out of support missile range but we can move our launchers to within range in ten minutes. Artillery can already reach it. I think we can still take this bastard."

"Negative, lieutenant," Elinshen said, smiling – Koshkin reminded her of her. "We do not have ten minutes. The storm is fading rapidly. Get your tanks out of there now. Let the artillery pound on it for however long it stays."

"Very well, lieutenant."

"All HUPAX, pull back. Maximum speed. Get as much distance between you and that landing ship as possible. Everyone, sensors off. Do not make it easy for them to track you."

As the acknowledgements came in, she spun her HUP, facing it into the wind and pushed herself forward. Even looking into the wind she could see much further than before. Had she waited too long to give the order to withdraw? Elinshen chewed on her lower lip, watching her map display with the datalink location of the landing ships slowly slide away.

"This is Captain Cochran of Zombie, inbound to Portaka Militia base. Any commander on this frequency, please respond."

"Captain, this is Lieutenant Elinshen, tactical commander. How far out are you?"

"Just completing our jump, lieutenant, and coming down from high altitude now. Should be within shooting range in fifteen, one-five, minutes. What is the situation?"

"The enemy may be withdrawing. One landing ship is destroyed, another damaged and possibly unable to lift. Their AFVs and HUPAX are headed in the direction of the remaining ship. We have a dust storm here that is beginning to pass and all Militia units are pulling back."

"Very well. I am assuming tactical command. Your orders to pull back are corroborated. Which landing ship is left?"

Elinshen bit on her lip harder. That was stupid; she should have known but she did not.

"We have a confirmed kill on a *Union*; a *Viper* is badly damaged. I do not know the class of the last landing ship."

"It's another Viper, partially outfitted to carry fighters as well as ground forces. It and another hit us with fighters; the other stayed around to land a raiding team."

"Roger. Is it coming here?"

"Negative. It's dead."

"Lieutenant, Fighter Lead. My scopes just lit up. I think that Viper is lifting."

"Zombie confirms. Keep an eye on it and let's see if it tries to take me on or leaves atmosphere."

"Roger. I've always wanted to watch landing ships fight."

"Hang around, laddie. I'm in the mood to kill another one."

The wind was still blowing but the dust and sand were noticeably less. Elinshen could see a half a kilometer without great difficulty.

"All right, she's heading for space. Revenant, Ghost, and Gladiator are in low orbit and will monitor her movement. I'm bringing Zombie in to the base. Hold your fire, people. I'm friendly."

"All units, this is Elinshen." She paused. She was no longer in command. This had been her first command as an officer. What should she say? Perhaps just the truth.

"Well done. You honored me."

Chapter 13: Costs

20 October 2824

Colonel Alisti Mahmud al-Kheyntamenti stood with his arms folded and looked out the window of his office. Outside in the morning light he could see the construction crews busy in the crisp fall air. Little of the damage inflicted by the raid two days ago was seen in the direction he faced but he was not really looking. Finally, he sighed and turned. Lieutenant Joseph Thuan Ho'nehe stood on the other side of his desk.

"Lieutenant, you're not helping the situation," Kheyntamenti said.

"Colonel, I'm sorry, but I did not see anything." The lieutenant's voice was firm.

"'See anything?' You were less than a hundred meters away from Gwielgi and the prisoners. He had just ordered you to leave them. You *had* to be looking at him."

"Sir, for the record, I was involved in securing the southern perimeter and ensuring our wounded were cared for. I did not see Captain Gwielgi do anything to any prisoner."

Kheyntamenti shook his head and sat down. He stared at Ho'nehe for a moment.

"All right, Joe. Off the record. What the hell happened? I read you Gwielgi's report."

"Khey, it happened just as he says." It was Ho'nehe's turn to shake his head. "He was with us in the truck. Just as we got to the perimeter one of the raiders' AFVs fired on us and we all jumped out. He was pretty shocky at that point. In the confusion we got separated." Kheyntamenti gestured to a chair and Ho`nehe sat down.

"I gathered up everyone I could see and we moved north, maybe a quarter of a klick, maybe a little more, and set up a defensive position around a couple of construction vehicles." Ho`nehe folded his arms and frowned slightly as he remembered the battle.

"I heard Maggie over commo" Ho`nehe said. "She was north of us in a firefight. I sent most of the Geese troopers in her direction to lend a hand while I used the people with me to try and set up some kind of blocking force facing south. We had a few infantry. The rest were construction workers, civilians some of them, techs, stragglers. All of a sudden more AFVs and some troops came through the perimeter. The AFVs went right through us, headed towards their troops near the airfield. I guess the troops were going to mop us up and then move north as well." He paused.

"They began closing with us, fire and maneuver. Total chaos. I could hear our HUPs up at the airfield but couldn't see any. You heard me on the commo yelling for help." Kheyntamenti nodded. "Some of the people with me were unarmed, just shovels and rocks. We had a few rifles, sidearms, nothing heavy. I was sweating those AFVs – if they turned around, we would buy the farm. The troops coming from the perimeter were a reinforced squad. As they closed, I heard Gwielgi. He was behind them – I have no idea how he got there or how he got a rifle, but it was like he was at a range. You could have used a stopwatch to time his shots, like he was firing for qualification record. And each time one of them would drop."

Ho`nehe fell silent and Kheyntamenti said nothing as he waited. Finally, the younger man spoke again.

"My people were firing away and then Tsunasdi and you came up – nothing like a couple of HUPs to settle the discussion." He smiled slightly but it faded. "They surrendered and you two headed east." He stopped. Ho`nehe leaned forward, his elbows on his knees and looked at the floor. "Yes, I saw the guy who surrendered. It was Gwielgi's last shot. Same rifle-range rhythm. The man had just put his arms in the air. Blam. He was down. Maybe Gwi didn't see his arms in time." He sighed and sat back in the chair, his eyes still on the floor. "One hundred and fifteen meters. Head shot. With a concussion, the medics say."

"I had the only active commo unit and got the word from you about Peregrine." Again Ho`nehe paused. "Gwi had no reaction to it, none. For a moment I wasn't sure he heard me. I told him we didn't know where the other landing ships were or were headed. Their officer, Jaeger-Oberst Meiner Gehlen, refused to say and that's when he ordered the others and me away. About a minute later I heard a shot." Ho`nehe rubbed his chin, remembering.

"Khey, I thought he had killed one of them. I finished getting my people in place and headed on back and then I saw him talking with Corporal Strehl. The rest you know."

"What did you think he intended when he ordered you away?"

"I thought he was going to rough them up." Ho`nehe looked up. "Sure, it's against the rules, but there were a lot of our people scattered around dead and those other landing ships were going to kill a lot more unless..." His voice trailed off. "I should have stayed with him. I knew he was going to do something and I let him do it." He leaned back in his chair and grimaced.

"Khey, I cannot count the number of times that man saved my life. And I let him down by leaving him with those mercs." Ho`nehe shook his head. "So, no, I did not see anything, no matter who is asking. The man was in shock, wounded, and had just heard that someone he thought of as a sister was killed. Hell, someone we *all* thought of as a sister."

"Joe," Kheyntamenti's voice was soft, "I understand. But I know Gwielgi. I've known him for many years, long before either of us came to the Wild Geese. The man you saw that morning, that was not shock, or wounds, or grief, that was *the man*." He shook his head. "Yes, he's saved your life, and you his. The same is true for everyone in the unit."

"So what are you going to do, Khey?"

"I spent a lot of yesterday putting off calls from the regiment." Kheyntamenti held up a hand as Ho`nehe's expression became alarmed. "I was told Jonivov already heard unofficially but I haven't met with him yet. If we still were just a mercenary unit, I can think of a couple of ways I might handle it. But we are subject to Militia law now. Under the Kodomir Militia Code of Military Law, crimes of this type require two witnesses for charges to be filed, and one has to be a Kodomiri, Militia or civilian. There's no question Gehlen wants charges filed, but no Kodomiri is willing to testify. Not you, nor any of the people who were with you, including the civilian construction workers." He smiled, though his eyes showed little amusement.

"I talked with a wounded engineer who was there off to one side, man name Kiesling. He said," Kheyntamenti pulled a paper towards him, "and I quote, 'I'm just sorry he didn't kill that dog-licking son of a bitch when he tried to escape instead of shooting him in the foot.' When I tried to question him further, he referred me to his union lawyer." He slid the paper to one side. "His union lawyer." Kheyntamenti shook he head. "Everyone else has said pretty much the same thing, though in less colorful terms."

"No testimony, no crime, no court-martial?"

"Except that we have Gwielgi's own statement. With Gehlen's, that's enough."

"Won't he withdraw it? A court-martial…"

"Will find him guilty. Sentencing is mandatory. He's looking at a minimum of three years in prison."

"Oh, hell," Ho`nehe said. "I should have stayed."

"You didn't, but you can still do something to save our friend. And it has to be done today."

The funeral of Jackie Peregrine was well attended. Her fiancé, Connor Illuyshin, accompanied by a small group of friends, received her ashes. The young man, his left hand still bandaged from a burn received during the raid, got up to say a few words to the gathering. He broke down and someone in a Kodomir Militia Air Force uniform led him to one side.

Gwielgi sat alone in the back of the church. He had slipped in after the service began and avoided eye contact with any of the Wild Geese sitting near the front. The person with Illuyshin listened to him for a moment and then stepped over to the Orthodox priest and whispered in her ear. The priest nodded and stepped forward.

"It is the wish of Connor that one of Jackie's old friends steps up and say a few words. Is Captain Gwielgi present?"

The church was so still Gwielgi thought he could hear its stones creak. A few people turned and looked back towards him. The air suddenly became thick, almost hard to breathe, and it had nothing to do with the incense of the service.

Gwielgi rose slowly and walked forward. The priest smiled and motioned to the podium. Gwielgi walked up to it and gripped the edges hard. His throat felt constricted but for a moment he had nothing to say. Finally, he swallowed.

"Jackie came to the Wild Geese shortly after I did." Gwielgi paused. Someone put a glass of water on the podium and he took a drink. As he put the glass down, he saw that his hand was trembling. "We both were in the infantry company. We were both snipers. She loved long-range shooting and she and I ended up spending a lot of time on the range practicing. As happens in small units, we got close. I mean," he added quickly, deliberately not looking at Illuyshin, "we became tight friends. She was like a sister – I hope I was like a brother." He took another sip.

"Like many, she had a history." Gwielgi paused and then he resumed talking, now steadily, as if with confidence. "It had been a rough road for her before she became a soldier. But she dealt with her past and did not allow it to cripple her present or her future. For a time, she never told anyone she had been born a slave. She told me about it one night when, well, we were in trouble and I was thinking maybe we would not see dawn. So, we waited and hid and tried to keep each other awake. We were alive, I guess that's obvious, when the sun came up and we made our way to the unit. It was a little rough getting there, but we did what we had to do. She didn't flinch. Not at getting through the snow and patrols we had to get past. And she didn't flinch at life. After that she never tried to hide what she had been or what she had been through."

"Eventually I volunteered to go back to HUPs. I asked her to think about becoming a technician and she maxed out on the aptitude exam. I thought she would. She went through the training and discovered she really liked working on them, on HUPs. She took on the job and I asked for her to be my HUP Captain." He looked over at Illuyshin. "That's a lot like a plane captain. She was in charge of any HUP I piloted. If we scrambled, I took her word that it was ready to go. She had my life in her hands. She never let go." The young pilot nodded his understanding.

Gwielgi paused again. "When we fought for Kodomir in the War of Liberation, I got hurt. The Geese were going in for the last time and I was too banged up to go, the medics said. She helped me convince our CO that I could handle a HUP. I leaned on Jackie getting into the cockpit, but what she really helped me with was afterwards, when we got back, and when I told her what I had done. She talked to me, mostly listened, and it helped."

"That's our history together. Two people in a small mercenary unit who had a good friendship, one in which trust was absolute. She never intended to be a soldier all her life and when you Kodomiri adopted us, made us citizens, Jackie saw a chance to build a home for herself, and she took it. I kidded her about buying the tavern and about her boyfriend, her fiancé, but I envied her. She was finding a life, a place that was more than just being a soldier." He looked at Illuyshin and the priest.

"Two other things and then I'll sit down. Jackie was made to sing as a slave and when she was freed, she vowed she would never sing again. But after that incident I told you about, she started singing again. She never said why, but I always figured she decided she would do what she liked and it didn't matter what anyone else had tried to do with it. One song she sang a lot was Thomas Moore's 'The Minstrel Boy.' It's maybe a thousand years old. The last traditional verse, well, it had something to say about living free. Most of you here have heard it more than once." He looked at Illuyshin. "I know the colonel has a recording of her performance if you ever want to hear it. Anyway, there was a third verse added many years later by some soldiers. I never heard Jackie sing it. Maybe she didn't know about it." He closed his eyes and recited the lines.

"The Minstrel Boy will return we pray
When we hear the news we all will cheer it,
The minstrel boy will return one day,
Torn perhaps in body, not in spirit.
Then may he play on his harp in peace,
In a world such as Heaven intended,
For all the bitterness of man must cease,
And ev'ry battle must be ended."

"The last thing." He turned so he was facing Illyushin. "We have a custom in the Wild Geese, and I need to put on my beret. I hope that's all right, I don't know much about your religion." The priest nodded, a slight smile coming through his beard, and Gwielgi took his purple beret out from under an epaulet and carefully placed it on his head. If it hurt his stitches, he gave no sign. He faced the urn of Peregrine's ashes and came to attention.

The Wild Geese in the pews stood and the others followed their lead. As Gwielgi's hand came up to the edge of his beret in a very slow salute, the others did the same. He held his hand there.

"I am with you," he said. And all the Wild Geese repeated the phrase. He snapped his hand down and then removed his beret. He looked at the urn for a moment, nodded to the priest, and held out his hand to Illuyshin.

The young pilot ignored the hand and embraced him in the traditional Kodomiri bear hug, which Gwielgi tried to return. He whispered in Gwielgi's ear.

"You were her brother, she told me. And you will always have the pleasure of my family's house."

"I am honored by your grace," Gwielgi whispered back, using the formal Kodomiri phrase. They separated and Gwielgi walked slowly to the back of the church. For him the rest of the service was a blur.

Later, Gwielgi found himself outside the church as people milled around, not quite sure how he came to be there. Someone in a Kodomir Militia Air Force uniform came by and handed him something and whispered in his ear but he didn't understand what was said. Then the person was gone and Joseph Thuan Ho`nehe came up to him.

"Got a minute?"

Gwielgi nodded and followed the lieutenant away from the crowd in front of the church. They stopped underneath a small group of trees and Ho`nehe looked around. Satisfied that no one was close by, he turned to Gwielgi.

"Kheyntamenti wants you to withdraw your report." Gwielgi said nothing and Ho`nehe continued.

"Under Kodomir Militia law, your statement and that of the merc are enough to court-martial you."

Gwielgi sighed and shook his head. "I know that, Joe. I'm the Ops Officer, remember?"

"Then you know it means at least three years in prison if convicted." Gwielgi shrugged and said nothing. His face was without expression.

"What the hell is the matter with you?" Ho`nehe's voice, though barely more than a whisper, was hoarse with anger. "You screwed up. All right. We both did. It's as much as my fault as it was yours. I should have never left you alone with them. You were wounded, you'd just heard about

213

Jackie, and I know she meant a lot to you. Damn it, she meant a lot to all of us." He paused and he calmed. "And you were worried about everyone else and what might happen when those landing ships came back down. I've read the docs' report. You had, you still have, a concussion. You weren't thinking straight."

For a moment Gwielgi said nothing, his eyes on the front of the church. Ho`nehe looked at his face and waited.

"Well?" Ho`nehe asked, his voice low. Gwielgi looked at him.

"I don't owe you an explanation, lieutenant," Gwielgi said, his yellow-brown eyes boring into Ho`nehe's. "But I will tell you anyway, one time. I don't know how much of that was a factor, maybe a lot, maybe nothing. What I *do* know is that man had information I wanted. I would have put a bullet through every joint in his body to get it and then one in his brain afterwards." His voice was cold, emotionless, and Ho`nehe looked at Gwielgi like he had never seen him before. "There were no extenuating circumstances, no rules of mitigation."

For a moment Ho`nehe said nothing, remembering Kheyntamenti's comments of the day before. Finally, he shook his head. "What will a court martial accomplish?"

"I don't know," Gwielgi's voice became softer. He sighed. "I don't really know. It's just, I feel like I have to straighten things out." He looked down at the ground. "This was not the first time something like this has happened," he said slowly. He shook his head and looked up. "I have to do something."

"You have to do something about *what*?"

"Me, I guess." He looked around the church grounds and passed the pack back and forth in his hands. "Yes, me."

"There's an alternative, one that doesn't involve prison. Why not hang it up and take off?"

"What do you mean?"

"Take a leave of absence. Resign. Look, if you have to straighten things out with yourself, all right. But it might be easier to do that out of prison than in."

"Leave the Geese?" Gwielgi looked down at his boots. "Well, yes, that's part of what I should do. Always been a 'clean' unit. Not right to have someone like me around."

"Look, Gwi, you and I go back a way. No one wants to sit on a tribunal handing you a court martial. I think Kheyntamenti would resign his commission and take up knitting rather than follow through on this, even if you force him. Why not take off the uniform and go do something else?" Ho`nehe made a small smile. "You got that book, everybody's buying it, and you could go sit on the beaches of the Western Peridees, stuff your toes into hot sand and stuff your gut with cold Highlander Red."

"Do you think Khey would really resign?"

"No question," Ho`nehe said firmly.

Gwielgi studied the ground again. "You might be right. A court martial would be embarrassing for the Militia and maybe make some people wonder about these crazy mercs they made citizens. Lot of stuff would get talked about; more people would get hurt." He paused and watched as the ground cars with Jackie's fiancé left. "Too many more." He sighed. "All right, I'll do it on one condition." He looked up at Ho`nehe, a smile on his lips though his eyes were devoid of expression. "You answer a question for me and tell me the absolute truth. Agreed?"

"All right, yes, I agree."

"Khey told you to tell me he would resign, right?"

"Yes," Ho`nehe said. "He said you would destroy yourself but no other member of the Wild Geese. He said that was how your honor worked."

Gwielgi shrugged. "I'll send in my resignation and clear the base immediately." He turned and walked away.

Chapter 14: The end of the beginning

29 October 2824

Kheyntamenti took a sip of tea as Colonel Jonivov read the report. He was getting used to drinking it Kodomiri-style from a glass held in a silver holder. Jonivov closed the folder, tapped its cover for a moment, and then pushed the report back to Kheyntamenti. He picked up his own tea and took a sip.

"Well, I see," he said. "This is the official statement, then, is it?"

"Yes, sir," Kheyntamenti said. "It is."

"Interesting." Jonivov got up and walked over to the low table that had his tea brewing gear. He added some sugar to his cup and then walked back. "So let me get this straight." He sat down and took a sip.

"One of the most highly decorated officers in the Militia, the Unit Historian of the Wild Geese, the Operations Officer of your battalion, has submitted his resignation and you have accepted it. This is a person with HUPAX skills, tactical training expertise, especially in our hot topic area of combined arms, and a variety of other positive attributes. He submits a one-line resignation. No discussion, you sign off on it within," he flipped open the folder, "ten minutes of its submission." It was not a question and Kheyntamenti remained silent.

"You know, I heard a funny story a couple of days back. The story was that one of our prisoners from the last raid wanted to file charges against a

Militia officer who tortured him but there was no corroboration, even though the officer in question had admitted to the act." Jonivov took another sip.

"And then I heard another funny story. Something about blowing the head off a surrendering merc. This has been an interesting week, because then I heard yet another story. Seems this officer has an unusual past. Well, a number of our soldiers nowadays have 'unusual pasts,' and I think everyone just overlooks that. Kodomiri tradition – we don't care who you were, just who you *are*. But this story says this officer may have done some things, more than once, like this in the past." Jonivov took a sip. "That maybe he got to Iriki Tykaw before anyone else and when he was done it was months before Tykaw could speak intelligibly." He stared at Kheyntamenti over his mug of tea but the Wild Geese leader said nothing.

"All right, it's handled," Jonivov finally said. "Probably for the best. Where's he going?"

"I don't know," Kheyntamenti said. "He didn't say, but I think he will stay on Kodomir."

"Why?"

"Because, to him, it is home." He hesitated for a second and then continued. "And it has been a very long time since he has had a place he called home."

Gunnery Sergeant Tsunasdi found the hand-written note on his desk and picked it up. Behind him Elinshen, studying a datapad, walked up. She glanced at Tsunasdi as he read the note.

"Is that the maintenance report, sergeant?" she asked. She studied his usually calm face. "You look like its bad news."

"It is," Tsunasdi said. He handed her the note.

She read it twice and then handed it back. The despair in Tsunasdi's eyes was easy to see. She hesitated for a moment; she knew Tsunasdi was exiled from the Currahee Encampment for cowardice. Currahee herself, she long ago had learned the man was not a coward. But the branding of him as weak-heart, the worst possible label a Currahee could bear, had, nonetheless, led to a certain distance in her interactions with him. Her upbringing, she knew, led her to only address him formally and only on unit business.

Yet now Tsunasdi appeared badly hurt. She knew some of his history with Gwielgi and also knew that Gwielgi was one of the few friends he had. Part of the wall separating her from Tsunasdi crumbled. She reached out and silently squeezed his arm.

"He will find his way back," Elinshen said. Tsunasdi said nothing but nodded.

The mining engineer walked with the quiet man across the open area from the shuttle bay to the main office building. The engineer had been here four months but still had not gotten used to the heat of Portaka, especially here in the continent's interior, though the man he walked with seemed to ignore it. The building was cooled, though, and he led the way to his office.

"Fine, fine," the engineer said about nothing as he motioned to a chair. The man sat down and waited patiently. "I have your paperwork but I want to check some things with you before we send you out. This is no place to take anything for granted." The man nodded in response.

"Fine," the engineer said. "Now, you have a hard copy of all maps. There's a copy in your vehicle's computer but computers break. Don't lose the hard copy. It's got every water hole any mining company has ever dug. We're all rivals about finding good ores but everywhere we dig, we drop a pipe to water first and we let everyone know where to find those wells when we leave. You never know, and dying of thirst is bad, real bad. So don't lose it. You have two copies, one in the field pack, one in your camping gear. Don't lose either of them." The man nodded again.

"Preventative maintenance on your portable pump, right from the manual, have to do it. Some wellheads have pumps, but they will still need to hook up to power. Most don't, have to use your pump. No sense having maps if you can't get the water up, right? Fine."

"You'll be the only person from our outfit working in your tract. Whole continent is divided into these tracts. Squares, a hundred by a hundred kilometers. Ten thousand square kilometers." He seemed to enjoy the numbers. "All yours. Don't think you'll see any visitors. Tracts are let on bids to the government. Only a few companies do exploration like we do. We find something, we claim it and either mine it ourselves or contract it to one of the other companies. That's what keeps most of them in business.

We do it all." He was proud and it showed. "Satellite exploration, over-flight imagery by drones, ground sampling, mining, even some processing and fabricating. That's you, ground sampling. Critical part. Very important."

"The papers they sent said you have desert experience and have worked as a surveyor. Well, fine, that's fine." The engineer nodded. "But every desert is different, and this one is a big one, filling up almost all of Portaka except along the coasts. Way to the south, they got ice and snow but you won't be there. So be careful. You got hard copy and computer copy of all the plant and animal stuff. They walked you through the class on that stuff. Fine. But be careful. Watch out for Hoare Cats. Bastards are smarter than a lot of people working for me."

"Your vehicle is fully ready but you'll go over it with one of our techs. Complete checklist. It uses fuel cells, solar hook-up, fine, you know all this stuff. Just want to be sure you know what is happening. We will helilift it and you to your area. You have a map of places the geologists want you to check out – surface tests, soundings, sampling analyses, whatever. Upload your info each night. You can link to satellite communications any time. Get in trouble, call for help. Run short of something, call us. Start to go crazy, call us." He blinked.

"It happens. Desert, by yourself, no one to talk to except over the link. Lot of people find it's a problem. The night is filled with stars. People get disoriented, seems to go on forever. They get distracted, drive off a cliff. Lot of paperwork." The man realized the engineer was telling a joke and smiled. "Fine, fine, but be careful."

"Pay and bonuses. You got the schedule. Anything you find, you get a bonus. Find something not on your list, you get a piece of the action as long as you don't neglect the places we want you to check. That's the big money, but it's rare."

"Did they talk to you about weapons?" The engineer leaned forward. "You ought to have something for the 'Cats, but if you want to carry one, you ought to let one of our people check you out on them. Hurt yourself, take a long time to get help even if you get a signal out. We can supply you with a couple, unless you have your own. Know about weapons?"

"I have my own," the man said, the first words he spoke since arriving at the base.

"Good, that's fine." The engineer consulted a list on his desk and nodded to himself. "Well, that's about it. The maintenance people are with your vehicle, take you through it. If everything is fine, we'll lift you out tomorrow. Any questions?"

The man shook his head.

"Fine, fine," the engineer said. He held out his hand. "Good luck out there, Mister..."

The man stood and briefly shook the engineer's hand.

"Gwielgi," he said. "Just Gwielgi."

Part Two

The Cost of Honor

If you want to play big boys' games, then you have to play by big boys' rules.
-Unofficial Slogan, Special Air Service, 20th-21st Century, Earth

Chapter 15: Devils' bargains

10 November 2824

Philip Deal, once, and possibly still, a member of the Kodomir Militia Intelligence Service, was one of the brightest people on First Minister Jevon's staff. Certainly, he worked with a sense of responsibility, but he did not have the level of responsibility the First Minister carried and there were times when Jevon envied him.

This was one of those times.

Two messages, relayed over the subspace stellar communication system, lay on his desk. Equal in size and weight, materially there was little between them. The same number of pages in the printouts, the same weight of data cubes waiting to be inserted in his console.

Deal had brought them in and carefully laid them in front of him. Now they were precise islands of information on the dark brown and polished sea of the First Minister's desk. Deal stood to one side, patient, ready to answer any questions he could and ready to seek out the answers of those he could not.

But it would be up to Jevon to take in the information and make decisions. If Deal were wrong, well, yes, there would be consequences. If Jevon was wrong, a world could die. Both men understood their different roles and burdens.

"Simultaneous arrivals?"

"Close enough, sir. Within fifteen minutes of each other," Deal said. "The message from Prime Minister Mordieu arrived first. Baron von

Bender's immediately followed." Deal's very slight emphasis on the titles conveyed his contempt of both senders.

"Well, let's see them." Jevon dropped into his chair while Deal picked up the data cubes and fit them into the projector. There was a flash of light as the holographic device adjusted itself to the information stream and suddenly the image of Selena Mordieu, Prime Minister of the Stellar Alliance, appeared. The imagery smoothed some details and she looked slightly younger than Jevon knew she was.

She was seated at a desk, hands folded in front of her, looking directly at the viewer. For a moment she said nothing, apparently waiting for a cue. She nodded slightly and began to speak.

"First Minister Alexis Jevon, I extend the greetings of the peoples of the Stellar Alliance to you and the people of Kodomir. For some time we have been aware of the difficulties Kodomir is facing. Yet we have avoided intervening. After all, many worlds around us are troubled in these times of turmoil and war and we cannot assist them all. And, of course, we have not been asked to assist. Given our history, back to a time when Kodomir was a part of the Alliance, we nonetheless have kept an eye on Kodomir."

"We did this not entirely because of old associations. Kodomir and the Alliance went their separate ways generations ago. But beyond Kodomir there are the Benderist Holdings. As long as the Confederacy existed and the Free Union exercised some restraint on its member states, we felt secure against the von Bender drive for power." She frowned and shook her head.

"But the Confederacy was conquered by von Bender. The restraint of the Free Union, of Peter Mavis Carmichael, is gone as he panders to the power blocs making up his Union to keep their allegiance in his war. Only Kodomir, gallant as always, retained its freedom, though it remains an ostensible member of the Free Union. I was urged to immediately offer Kodomir support, treaties, and all the things one friendly nation might provide to another. I did not do that. The time, I felt, was not right. I thought you would believe we simply wanted Kodomir as a springboard for our own imperialist designs on the String of Pearls and the Holdings. And I did not want to provoke von Bender or give him a pretext for moving against you." Again, Mordieu shook her head.

"Then we began to hear of mercenary units striking Kodomir. Quick, small raids, perhaps probing your defenses, perhaps trying to deplete your ability to defend yourself. I asked my intelligence agency to see what they could find out. Counselor-General Andrea Richelieu will deliver all that we learned to you personally. I have sent her to you and I expect her to arrive in three weeks. She will have full negotiation power on behalf of the Alliance." She paused.

"I want you to know, well before she arrives, that she is traveling accompanied by one of our regiments. Please be assured not one Alliance soldier will set foot on Kodomir except by your invitation. This includes the Counselor-General's personal military staff. They will remain onboard her shuttle until you or your representative give them permission to disembark."

"Why the regiment? Well, one of our proposals concerns mutual defense. If Kodomir agrees to that kind of arrangement, then I want to have Alliance forces close by to immediately fulfill any obligations those proposals might entail. After all, Kodomir has enemies who might move preemptively if any of our proposals are accepted. Certainly, the Free Union, even distracted by its war of aggression against the Worlds Protectorate, will not look kindly on one of its member worlds opting to go its own way. I genuinely believe, and I think you probably do as well, that those enemies are even now preparing to act, regardless of what Kodomir decides to do. Time is not on our side."

"The last time von Bender struck at Kodomir it was with a Raider band. His forces alone could not attack all the worlds of the Confederacy. Your heroic battle against the Raiders won you the admiration of all of us who have lived with their threat. But the reality is, if von Bender comes again, and I think he will, he will come in overwhelming force. Nothing on Kodomir, nothing on any single world, can withstand the power of the Holdings. Only the Alliance is a counterweight to his designs."

"Our proposals are layered. Of course, you and the Counselor-General will discuss them in detail. The degree of involvement and commitment is open. On a personal level I would like to see Kodomir become a full member state of the Stellar Alliance, a powerful group in its own right, restoring a point of history." She held up a hand. "I understand that Kodomir might not be ready for such an arrangement. You might favor something less, perhaps far less, that might support your security needs. I think you will find we will be very accommodating."

"But time, First Minister Jevon, time is against us. What the Benderists have taken by conquest and coercion gives them not simply additional power but position, a position that threatens Kodomir and, then, the Alliance. I believe it is only a question of time before von Bender's war machine moves against you and then us. It is in both our interests to help one another, and do so soon." Mordieu leaned back.

"There are those who will say you will be running a tremendous risk of Free Union retaliation in joining with the Alliance on any level, but I say, again, the Free Union, Peter Mavis Carmichael, has already allowed to be set in motion the forces destined to destroy Kodomir. Now is the time for you to gain your world's freedom from the Union, while it is tied down by its war. We are willing to be your shield, as we were in the past."

"I thank you for your consideration and the courtesies you will show my Counselor-General. I hope together we can guarantee the peace and freedom of our nations."

The image wavered and then vanished. Jevon stared across his desk for a moment. Then he stood and reached to a carafe of water and poured himself a glass. He motioned with it to Deal and raised an eyebrow. The staffer shook his head negatively. Jevon took a swallow and then sat back down.

"Her negotiator will be here in three weeks. If I remember my charts correctly, that means she had her standing close by. Same with the regiment."

"Yes, sir. They have been planning this for some time."

"She's counting on our history a great deal."

"Yes, sir, that's how I read it," Deal said. "Kodomir has always tried to accommodate whoever came through with the power."

"Yes. Small world, militarily weak. Just try to stay alive and not share in the fate of dozens of other similar worlds." He took a sip of water. "We used to joke about it at the Foreign Policy Institute: 'Show us your guns, hoist your flag, happy to salute it, and be on your way.' After all, who wanted to occupy a backwater farming planet?"

"Times change, sir." Deal chewed on a thumb. "She was right about our strategic position, a door that swings both ways as far as the Alliance and the Holdings are concerned. But beyond that, we don't just grow food on Kodomir anymore."

"No, indeed. The mines, the industry. We must look worth the effort."

"If her intelligence is any good and she's thinking about the long term, then it's our industry as much as our position. We are rapidly becoming weapon innovators. There will be many people interested in that ability."

"Happy to sell them anything they want as long as their money is good," Jevon said. "The other message, let's take a look at that."

Deal nodded and inserted the remaining data cube. Again, the holographic area above the projectors flashed and then a figure appeared.

"First Minister Alexis Jevon, allow me to present myself," a slim figure said. He bowed slightly. "I am Special Envoy Esteban Baer, representative of Baron Karl von Bender. I have a piece of critical information for you and I hope you will consider it with an open mind. But first things first."

"Baron Karl von Bender wishes me to convey personally his apologies for the transgressions committed by the Raiders called Storm Cloud. Their piratical actions were not representative of his beliefs and values. Indeed, I appreciate you will find it difficult to believe, but he was so appalled by their behavior he was preparing to intervene militarily to drive them off Kodomir when you liberated your selves. In all candor, his discomfort was contributed to by the expressed displeasure of Prime Minister Peter Mavis Carmichael. He found the presence of Raiders in the Free Union, even a band claiming legitimization as mercenaries, distasteful. Your successful uprising made that intervention unnecessary."

"Since then, the Baron has tried to avoid doing anything that might be interpreted as coercive towards Kodomir. I am sure your own diplomats on Kwangdo and the other member states of the former Confederacy have told you of his efforts to repair wherever possible the damage inflicted during the unfortunate but, at least from the position of the Holdings, necessary intervention against the unreasonable Viscount O'Ryan and his leadership of the Confederacy. All the former states of the Confederacy are now official members of the Holdings, not simply occupied territories."

"But a recounting of our efforts to smooth the bumps of history is not why I send this message to you. I mentioned I have critical information for you. When the Baron learned Kodomir was being subjected to a series of military raids by mercenary units, he immediately understood that the Kodomiri would assume he is behind it."

"He is not. To the contrary, he views these attacks with alarm, for they are taking place on the flank of the outermost worlds of the Holdings. If someone is preparing Kodomir for an invasion, then they are, by definition, a threat to the Holdings."

"Over the past several months he had his intelligence service and friends of the Holdings throughout the Free Union attempt to identify the employers of these mercenaries. These efforts have borne fruit. We have unquestionable proof that the ultimate employer of the mercenaries is the Stellar Alliance, once the occupiers of Kodomir. Apparently, they are trying to rebuild their empire. The Baron is determined to prevent this."

"The proof I will personally hand to you, for I am coming to Kodomir. Our mutual enemy has already acted once to cover her tracks and has killed the source of our information. This suggests to the Baron, and I agree, that the Alliance is probably already moving against Kodomir. Therefore, our 173rd Armored Brigade will accompany me. Please do not be alarmed by that statement. After all, if we meant you harm, we would not tell you of our military movements in advance. In any case, I will arrive in 23 days."

"In fact, the brigade has as its mission, should you accept it, to defend Kodomir against the invasion we believe is coming. If you accept it, we will be willing to place it under the strategic command of your Militia. I will say this again, for you may have doubted your ears. The entire 173rd Armored Brigade is being offered to you by the Baron for the defense of Kodomir and, if you accept the offer, it will be under your control." He bowed slightly.

"I think you might see how sincere the Baron is about trying to heal the wounds of Kodomir. The danger you are in is the danger that will eventually threaten us. While neither of us can change the past, together we can protect our nations' futures." The image flashed and vanished.

"What is the size of the Benderist 173rd Brigade?" Jevon appeared grim.

Deal consulted his datapad. "About the size of a standard regiment. Which is to say, about twice the size of a Militia regiment in total numbers of people and equipment and about the same size of an Alliance regiment, though it has more HUPs and less supporting arms."

"Why don't both of these bastards just stay home?" Jevon picked up the printed copies of the presentations. "That rock and a hard place you and I talked about are about to meet." He looked at the papers and then glanced at Deal.

"All right, Philip, I have some homework for you. I have several questions. Run them through your simulators and do some digging. I need options. First, what is the likely outcome of us telling both sides to just go away? Will one or both preemptively seize Kodomir? Second, what will be the outcome of accepting either side and allowing one of them to station forces on Kodomir? Will the other attack? Third, if accepting one side or the other is the best course of action, which side, short run, long run, offers us the best opportunity in terms of independence of action and existence?"

"Understood, sir," Deal said. "You don't want us to run up a scenario of armed resistance?"

"What's the point? If a shooting war breaks out between Kodomir and either of these powers, we lose. We might hold off a regiment or brigade, but if Mordieu or von Bender is serious, they will eventually send a great deal more. Saving Kodomir by turning it into a cinder is not an option."

"Yes, sir," Deal said. He chewed his thumb again, thinking. "I'll get together with the foreign relations bureau and some of the people in intelligence sections and game out some possibilities."

Jevon nodded and Deal left the room. He walked down the hall, still thinking. The First Minister was asking the right questions, he thought. But maybe he wasn't asking enough of them...

Chapter 16: Check

3 December 2824

Standing in the middle of the Residence ballroom used for diplomatic receptions, General Polrany, clad in the heavy formal Militia uniform, wondered where First Minister Jevon found the strength to keep smiling as he moved through the crowd – wouldn't you expect to see it fade just from muscle fatigue? Maybe he had the nerve endings in his face permanently altered.

Polrany put down his drink on a passing tray. Besides the crowd, the problem with having to attend these diplomatic rituals is that someone was always handing you something to drink. While he considered a glass of good vodka at the end of a hard day a compelling argument for the existence of saints if not a more exalted Being, what was served at diplomatic functions usually had too many bubbles. Everywhere they went they drank bubbles. If they weren't at the Benderist Legation, they were at the hotel virtually taken over by the Alliance representatives, or here at the First Minister's dwelling.

On top of that were all the alcohol-free meetings with the two delegations and separate meetings with their military people.

The thrust of it all, of course, was both sides wanted Kodomir to commit to them, and Kodomir, in the form of First Minister Jevon, wanted nothing to do with either. This made for some very interesting conversations between Polrany and his Alliance and Benderist counterparts. Both parties were happy to provide him with information on the other, with the information slanted so as to make the other side look particularly threatening.

Not that much slanting was necessary. The Kodomir navigation beacon area was filled with star ships that had brought each side's military landing ships. Most of those landing ships now were circling Kodomir, ready to begin landing their forces to "protect" Kodomir. How much longer Jevon could keep them from preemptively landing to settle the issue was a real question, for Polrany had noticed that the military staffs of both delegations were becoming impatient. Impatient people made mistakes. In this case, the mistake might be invading Kodomir for there was a very good chance the other side would immediately counter the move.

And that could mean war between the two sides, with Kodomir their battleground.

This crowded gathering was ostensibly a reception for all the diplomats on Kodomir, though Polrany suspected Jevon was responding to requests of the various ambassadors and their staffs to see the Alliance and Benderist people in the same room at the same time. They probably thought it was amusing as hell to watch the various delegates keep to their respective corners.

Of course, it meant people like Polrany had to shuttle back and forth between the corners of the ballroom, carefully ensuring he spent equal amounts of time with both groups. Probably their intelligence operatives were carefully timing him, trying to develop an analysis of Kodomir's probable direction based on seconds spent in inane small talk with each group. He pulled at his high collar. He seldom wore his dress uniform and the collar chaffed.

"General," Special Envoy Esteban Baer of the Benderists said, suddenly appearing beside him, "my military people tell me that medal around your neck is the Kodomir Cross with Stars, the highest award your government can bestow."

Polrany nodded.

"They told me that you personally gathered intelligence on Storm Cloud by infiltrating their base at Coyote Bay posing as a janitor, a mentally retarded janitor." Baer smiled, but his eyes examined Polrany closely.

"That is not correct, Envoy," Polrany replied. "It was not *their* base, but ours. They just happened to be occupying it at the time."

230

"Well said, general," Baer said, his smile broader. "I was misspoken. But is it true that you did that, and then led the attack on Storm Cloud armed only with a sidearm?"

"In general terms, yes, Mister Baer. I did portray a mentally retarded janitor – being just a general, I thought anything more elaborate would be beyond my reach. As for the sidearm, I should point out that my personal armament was supplemented by several hundred of our own Militia, another several hundred Chekinovs, a pair of attack helicopters, and the landing ships, infantry, and HUPAX of a crack mercenary unit."

Baer laughed while Polrany decided he would not drink anything else with alcohol in it through the rest of the reception.

"I admire your sense of self-deprecation, general," Baer finally said, raising his glass in a toast. He took a diplomat's sip – the glass touched his lips but the liquid within did not. "Those mercenaries, did you have any problems with them? To be quite frank, Baron von Bender has seldom used them and our lack of familiarity with them contributed to the terrible mistake of hiring Iriki Tykaw and Storm Cloud."

Polrany felt a wave of heat at the mention of the Raider leader and his unit. He knew it was not an accident Baer mentioned them. Nothing these diplomatic bastards said was ever an accident. It did take some guts to bring up the subject, he would grant the envoy that.

"Problems?" Polrany smiled. "An interesting question, wouldn't you say, Colonel Kheyntamenti?"

A thin officer with deeply tanned but pale skin, a hooked nose, and falcon's eyes turned toward Polrany. Baer studied him quickly. He wore the Militia officer dress uniform but had few medals or ribbons on it, though his breast pocket carried an enameled gold pin that looked like a sword. Also on the pocket was a circular emblem with a pair of birds flying across it. Over the pocket was the gold insignia of a Militia HUPAX soldier, what the Kodomir Militia called a "HUP pilot."

"Special Envoy Baer, please allow me to present Colonel Alisti Mahmud al-Kheyntamenti, Commanding Officer of the Combined Arms Battalion of the Militia Second Regiment, otherwise known as the Wild Geese."

"Ah, Colonel Kheyntamenti," Baer said, bowing slightly and then extending his hand. "Of course, of course. We were just discussing Kodomir's victory over Storm Cloud."

"Specifically," Polrany said, "the Envoy asked if we had any problems with our mercenaries."

Kheyntamenti smiled slightly, exposing very white teeth that contrasted with his face. "As I recall, general, we did have moments of disagreement, but on the whole the Geese and the Militia worked well together."

"Yes, colonel," Baer said. "I was fascinated by the story. In fact, I read the book that one of your officers wrote on the subject. I'm afraid I cannot recall the title but I remember the author's name. Gwielgi, Captain Gwielgi. By any chance is he here tonight?"

"No," Kheyntamenti said.

If the diplomat noticed the temperature suddenly drop, he acted as if he had not. Polrany glanced at Kheyntamenti and wondered if Baer knew of recent events and if this was another subtle move of some sort by Baer.

"Ah, too bad. Interesting name, Gwielgi. I was wondering if he was Welsh or Celtic perhaps. On my mother's side there are some Welsh and the name is somewhat similar to the word for…"

The conversation was interrupted when an aide leaned in and whispered something into Polrany's ear. It was almost with relief that Polrany turned back to Baer.

"Special Envoy Baer, please forgive me but I am called away momentarily."

"Of course, general, it is no problem. I hope to see you again later tonight, your duties permitting." Baer bowed slightly. Polrany returned the gesture and disappeared into the crowd.

"Colonel Kheyntamenti," Baer said, "allow me to change the subject. Do you follow the Kodomir rugby leagues?"

Polrany stepped out into a high hallway and walked with the aide toward the living quarters and offices of the residency. The aide guided him through several doors and past sentries. Eventually they came to a communication office. It was staffed continuously and the Militia here wore their field uniforms, not the formal attire of the reception. Polrany felt a flash of envy as he sat in front of a screen covering a wall.

"What do we have?" he asked the watch officer.

"Approximately twenty minutes ago," the young woman began, pointing at the screen, "an Alliance landing ship moved towards Kodomir, shuttling in from their group of star ships. While both the Alliance and the Benderists have carefully kept their formations in geosynch orbits well away from one another, this landing ship continued to close with Kodomir. Traffic Control at Kiroff received their call. They claimed their hull had been breached by something a few minutes previously and declared an emergency. They requested permission to land." The screen lit up and displayed the positions of the various landing ships. Polrany saw the Alliance landing ship was passing the area of the Benderist ships.

"Before Space TC could respond to the request," she said, "the Benderists demanded that the ship stop in place. It refused. Almost immediately two Benderist landing ships closed on it. We think both carry space-capable fighters but thus far they have not launched them. The commander of the Alliance landing ships protested, but the rest of his group is too far away to intervene. So right now, the situation is the Alliance ship is continuing to approach us and the two Benderist ships are in pursuit and closing the range. We estimate they will be in ion pulse weapon range of one another in five minutes." She paused, touching her ear piece.

"Sir, Space TC has responded to the Alliance ship and, as per protocol, has given them permission to land."

"Very well." He thought for a moment. Scenario one: if Kodomir allowed the Alliance ship to land, the Benderists might take this as a sign Kodomir was going over to the Alliance. Scenario two: if Kodomir refused permission, the Alliance might take it as a signal the Kodomiri were lining up with the Benderists. This whole thing might be a ploy on the part of the Alliance to force the issue. After all, if Kodomir responded in a humanitarian fashion and allowed its ship to land, then the Alliance might succeed in maneuvering the Kodomiri into provoking the Benderists. Then the Alliance could step in to the rescue.

Polrany shook his head. As long as Kodomir played by the rules, then these two powers would continue to try to back it into a corner. Time to change the rules...

"Can I broadcast to both groups from here?"

"Yes, sir," she said. "We're on approach control channel and they've been talking on it continuously." Polrany nodded and reached for a microphone while the woman touched the communication controls. She nodded and he keyed the microphone.

"Alliance landing ship, this is General Stevar Ivanovich Polrany, Commander, Kodomir Militia. You are cleared to land on Kodomir." He clicked off the microphone for a second and then clicked it back on before anyone could reply.

"The conditions of your landing are in keeping with the agreement entered into with your Prime Minister – you will land at a place designated by us, no one is allowed off your ship, all weapons will remain unarmed and unmanned, and you will be boarded and searched to ensure your compliance with that agreement. If you deviate from the flight path cleared by our Space Traffic Control, you will be fired upon." He clicked off and then immediately clicked back on.

"Benderist landing ships in apparent pursuit of the Alliance landing ship, be advised you are not cleared to enter Kodomir's atmosphere. In keeping with the agreement entered into with your Special Envoy, you will return to your position and stand by. Entry into our atmosphere without clearance, even in pursuit, will result in you being fired on." He clicked off and leaned back in his chair.

The young officer looked at him for a moment and then smiled.

"Sir, was the reception getting a little boring?"

"I imagine it will be much more interesting when I go back in there, captain," Polrany said. "About a hundred communication units just lit up in the ballroom. I give everyone about two minutes to make a decision." He shrugged and grinned. "We'll see it on the screen first."

It took less than two minutes. All three landing ships decelerated. The Alliance landing ship reported that its emergency was contained, its captain appreciated the Kodomiri support, and he thought he could make his way back to the rest of the fleet without further difficulty. The Benderists regretted that their gesture of support of the territorial integrity of Kodomir had been misunderstood but they were delighted that the Kodomiri had dealt with the Alliance provocation so readily and were even now moving back to their formation.

Polrany stood and handed the microphone to the watch officer. "The trick is to look for another option," he said, "when the enemy thinks you've been limited to the ones *he* chose."

As Polrany entered the ballroom the buzz of conversations momentarily ceased and then picked up again. First Minister Jevon intercepted him first and leaned forward as his aides formed an obstruction around them.

"I think they were trying to force the issue," Jevon whispered after Polrany gave him a hurried account.

"Yes, sir," Polrany said. "Though I'm not sure which 'they' it was."

Jevon leaned back and nodded and then said, loud enough for the people beyond the aides to hear, "I am happy to hear they were so cooperative. That's the kind of thing we need to see." He patted Polrany on the arm and turned toward a small group of diplomats as if the near-ignition of an interstellar war over his head was something that occurred on a routine basis.

Polrany looked around. Oh, yes, it was the turn of the Alliance people to be massaged. He signaled to a passing waiter and got a glass of water to have something in his hands. He started forward and felt fingertips on his elbow. He turned and saw an older man with Oriental features.

"Stevar?"

For a moment Polrany did not recognize him, for he had seldom seen the man in civilian clothes before.

"Saburo!" He bowed, as was the formal Kwangdo custom, and then he wrapped his arms around his friend in the custom of Kodomir. The two men embraced for a moment and then Polrany stepped back.

"I had not heard from you since the invasion. With the occupation, little word was getting in or out of Kwangdo. I thought you were dead."

"Indeed, I am." He leaned forward, his voice low, barely a whisper. "Continue to call me 'Saburo,' please, but as far as the Benderists are concerned I am of the family 'Riley,' and one of the trade delegates Baer brought with him. You met me several years ago when you visited Kwangdo and taught that course at our military academy – you stayed at my home."

"And how are things at your home?" Polrany asked in a normal tone.

"Unfortunately, my wife died some time ago," Saburo said. "I regret I could not inform you due to unfortunate circumstances."

"I am very sorry to hear that," Polrany said, feigning sorrow. His friend had never been married. "Her grace did much to make me feel at home."

"She would be pleased to hear you say so," Saburo said. He looked around the ballroom, still quite crowded. Many people were making quick glances at Polrany. "This is my first visit to Kodomir. Special Envoy Baer graciously asked my government to provide delegates to come with him."

"Ah," Polrany said, "how fortunate for me you are a part of that delegation."

"Well, as someone familiar with the previous trade agreements we had with Kodomir, they thought I might be useful. Envoy Baer says that his Baron fully supports my people opening up normal trade relations with some of our former partners. I will be spending time talking with your agricultural people and perhaps even placing bids on your spring harvests."

Polrany was sure that several people standing near them were taking in the conversation. Whose people were they?

"I would very much like to have dinner with you and remember old times. I have a bottle of an exceptional wine that I recently acquired. Do you have plans for this evening?"

"Why, no, I do not. The hotel we are using as a legation has excellent food, but I remember your descriptions of Kodomiri dishes and I would very much like to try them."

"It's settled, then," Polrany said. "The reception is scheduled to end in an hour. Let me take you to my quarters and then we can have dinner."

"I look forward to it, Stevar." The two men bowed and Polrany walked away, trying to look casual, as if nothing more had happened than he had bumped into an old friend. That was partially true.

Saburo Yamashita was an old friend, but what he knew about trade negotiations was open to question, for he had spent his life learning the trade of soldier. Polrany had stayed at his home as part of an exchange program among the military units of the Confederacy.

When he had last seen Yamashita, the officer was standing proudly on the parade ground at Kiroff Airfield, having completed the Militia's Reconnaissance Course, with honors, and receiving the Arrow emblem from the hands of First Minister Brevan Toland. Much had happened to both worlds since then, including the murder of Toland and Polrany's leaping to the position of Command General of the Kodomir Militia.

Like Kodomir, Kwangdo had fought the invasion and, like Kodomir, had been defeated in a single day. The Kwang possessed HUPs, weapons the Kodomiri did not have at the time, but had never managed used them. The opening Storm Cloud barrage collapsed their HUP hangars, trapping the war machines inside.

Polrany assumed his friend was dead, for what he had heard of Storm Cloud's behavior on Kwangdo paralleled what they had done on Kodomir, though they were on the sister world a far shorter time. But it was long enough – stories of massacres of surrendered Kwang soldiers had gotten out.

In spite of all that, here was Yamashita, decked out in a civilian suit as if he had worn one all his life, looking very much like the middle-level bureaucrat one would expect to encounter at a gathering like this. Smiling and bowing like some kind of tri-vid stereotype, Yamashita was putting on an act. He was warm with his friends – most Kwangdo were the same, but they could also quickly put up a mask with strangers. Polrany wondered what face the Kwang had shown the Benderists up to now.

Andrea Richelieu was a tall woman and a decade earlier was described as "handsome." Now she was "stately," which meant she had an air of distance about her, as if she represented some higher power. The briefing the foreign affairs officers gave Polrany stressed she was very sharp, humorless, and the real brains in the Mordieu government. In and out of political office with the changing tides of Alliance power shifts, she still tended to present herself as if a professor lecturing a graduate class. That made sense because whenever out of office she worked as a professor in the most prestigious university in the Alliance.

Polrany was a bit surprised to find himself with her. Up to now most of his contact with the Alliance people was with his military counterparts, but the colonel he had been exchanging pleasantries had deftly steered him into the small circle of people standing around her.

"General Polrany," Richelieu said, motioning toward another person in the circle, "my dear friend Colonel Marcel Petain was explaining to me the pattern of settlement on Kodomir and was describing those interesting people called the 'Chekinovs.' Did they really arrive here centuries before the people I have always thought of as Kodomiri?"

"Yes, Counselor-General," Polrany said. "There is some debate about the exact time of their arrival on Kodomir, but the general consensus is they arrived three centuries ago."

"Some time after, then, the closure of the Currahee Encampment?"

"Yes, all evidence points to that, but not long after. There are no records surviving on any Settled Worlds world which have lent themselves to identifying their home world."

"And they reverted to a tribal culture when they came here?"

"Not exactly, Counselor-General." Polrany felt himself becoming uncomfortable but he could not say why. "They crashed on Kodomir. Their landing ship, or ships, was destroyed. According to their history, a woman named Sarah Chekinov took charge and led them out of the mountains in the face of winter, led them down to the sea to the area they named Coyote Bay. She then took groups of them to different areas up and down the coast to establish their own communities to avoid overpopulating the Bay area. They lost almost all their technology. They call themselves 'tribes,' these different communities, but," he shook his head, "they were not true tribes. They choose their leaders, have settled communities, maintain agriculture, and, before the Kodomiri arrival, kept in contact with one another."

"I see." Richelieu leaned her head to one side and her expression softened. "My son's dissertation is on the first settlers of this area of the Settled Worlds and he had a chapter on the Chekinov people. I will finally be able to intelligently discuss them with him." She smiled and Polrany felt himself suddenly at ease, though part of him recognized she was trying to manipulate him. "Do you have a theory of your own, general, about their origins?"

"No, ma'am, I don't. There were so many scattered settlements in those years. Colonists would land and often vanish on distant worlds with no word of their landing ever getting out. At the time, this area was part of the Frontier, not the Settled Worlds. They might be related to the Currahee though some believe they were one of the Settled Worlds colonial efforts. Records from that time are fragmentary as the Settled Worlds went through the Arcturan War. I suspect we will never know."

"I was told their people are now full Kodomiri citizens."

"They were recognized as citizens of Kodomir by law more than a decade ago, Counselor-General, and by birthright long before that."

"And now they are in your army."

"Now they are in *our* army, ma'am. Militia officers died defending them when the Raiders tried to take their leaders hostage, and they fought alongside other Kodomiri in our liberation. It was they who declared we were *all* Kodomiri."

"But has it really been as smooth as all that, general? After all, you and they fought in battles for several centuries as they resisted Kodomiri expansion."

"That is not," a woman said, "entirely correct, Counselor-General." A woman with black hair streaked with a few gray strands gently pressed into the circle, a polite smile on her face. Her eyes, a shade of gray-blue, were steady.

"Counselor-General," Polrany said, feeling relieved, "may I introduce Anastasia Coltrane, Assembly Member? I think she might be regarded as something of an authority on Chekinov history." The woman bowed her head at the compliment and Polrany thought she winked at him, her eyes now amused.

"Ah, good," Richelieu said. "How do you become an expert on a people whose history is lost in the depths of time?"

"It helps," Coltrane said, "if you are one of the people in question."

Richelieu bowed her head. "Assembly Member Coltrane, please enlighten me."

"We did indeed resist expansion, but only in certain areas, those we regarded as near sacred. This was balanced in large measure by the fact that our history had told us to expect to be found one day. We saw the Kodomiri, to use a term to simplify the story, as the fulfillment of our history, and a confirmation of one of our Precepts."

"Yes, the Precepts. I remember my son mentioning them. Which Precept did the Kodomiri fulfill?"

"'We shall leave none of our own behind.' Thus, even when fighting did break out over the land, we understood that this was a conflict with one element of Kodomiri society and, given time, the conflict would be overcome and we would join with them."

"In spite of the fighting?" There was clear doubt in Richelieu's voice.

"In part, *because* of the fighting. We saw the Kodomiri were much like us. They lived by our Precepts, though none could speak them." She smiled slightly and glanced at the general. "When I was tracking then-Captain Polrany, our respective units clashed near a river crossing. On that day he won the engagement. I thought we had withdrawn all our people but discovered that several wounded still lay near the crossing. We returned to find them. As I watched, I saw Polrany's people tend to our wounded as if they were their own. That was not the first time I saw with my own eyes that the Kodomiri lived by the Precepts."

"Showing mercy to an enemy is unusual on modern battlefields," Richelieu said. "What was the Chekinov Precept that gesture confirmed?"

"'The first duty of the strong is to protect the weak'," Polrany said before Coltrane could answer. He held up his hand and pushed his uniform sleeve down. A thin, multicolored woven cord was around his wrist. "I was presented with this after our War of Liberation."

"The colors are of the Cold Hills Tribe, and the pattern is that of a warrior, a soldier," Coltrane said. "All Chekinov, or Tsalagi as we prefer to say, wear one." She held up her own wrist and showed the same black and green bracelet; gold and red threads were twined within it. Then she opened her blouse at her throat. A metal identification tag, its edges coated in black plastic, hung from a gold chain. "This is the identity tag of one of the nine Militia officers who died defending Chekinov during the massacre. My brother took it from her body and, after I was liberated from the Raiders, he gave it to me. Nine of us wear these, for those nine officers." She slipped the disk back. "You might think it strange, Madam Counselor-General, but over the years the strongest advocates for the Tsalagi people were the Militia. I thought it was because warriors recognize each other as such and, through that recognition, find a common bond. Beyond that, of course, they lived among us and I think they found much about us they admired, and we of them."

"Yes, we still have some frictions. Arguments over funding, political issues, all that, but we are *all* Kodomiri." She smiled. "I think we have demonstrated during the War of Liberation and the recent mercenary raids that anyone who sets foot on Kodomir with hostile intent will find the Kodomiri people are united."

"Indeed," Richelieu said. She turned back to Polrany. "I understand one of our landing ships had some difficulty earlier."

"Yes," Polrany said. "I am informed by her captain that the difficulty has been overcome and it is joining the rest of your formation."

"Ah, good, then." She seemed distracted and turned slightly away and began to address others. Polrany and Coltrane took the hint and drifted from the circle.

"You have been studying the Precepts?"

"Not really studying," Polrany said. "But I am interested and, like many and as you said, find much to admire in Tsalagi culture." Coltrane nodded.

"Of late we have become something of a campus fad," she said, smiling. "'Noble savage' sort of thing."

"Might be a little irritating," Polrany said as they walked slowly through the crowd.

"Better than being ignored," said Coltrane. "By the way, this is the third time Richelieu has made a run at identifying Tsalagi splits from the Kodomir mainstream." She stopped and took a sip from her drink. "She initiated a similar discussion yesterday with Kai Pearson, Assembly delegate from Modena. And this morning she did a quick reconnaissance on the subject with a group of academics."

"You think she has something in mind?"

"I think she's just checking her options. If the Kodomir government does not prove cooperative, then she might want to work on boring from within."

"Wonderful," Polrany said.

"The word in the room is you faced down both the Alliance and Benderist fleets when you disappeared earlier."

"Hardly," Polrany said. "We're really not sure what happened but they both did not press the issue."

"I see First Minister Jevon is trying to catch your eye," Coltrane said, glancing into the crowd. "Before you go, let me ask you something personal." She hesitated. "Have you heard from my brother?"

"Directly?" He shook his head. "No, but then I wouldn't in the normal course of Militia business. I saw William after the raid of the Saber Cats and I think that was the last time."

"How did he seem?"

Polrany thought. "Well, like a lot of the Scouts, he was tired. I got there just after the fight. He and Jonivov showed me the canyon where he ambushed their column. We talked, but it was pretty brief."

She nodded. "Thank you. I have been a little worried. I have not heard from him since then."

"If you like, I could have Colonel Jonivov talk to you."

"No, thank you, no. And, please, do not mention this to William. I do not want him thinking his older sister is checking up on him."

"Well, he will be rotating down to Portaka for the desert school next week. The course is about all we are running until the damage is repaired. I know the Militia Committee is scheduling an inspection trip to check out the damage from the raid. Given the lack of amenities there, I suspect there will be room if an Assembly representative wanted to go along."

"General, are you suggesting that I use governmental transportation for personal reasons?"

"No, ma'am," Polrany said. The thing about the Chekinovs was that half the time you could never tell when they were serious or joking and Coltrane was no exception. "Frankly, in my opinion, the committee lacks people with actual combat experience and I would favor your going just on those grounds. Also, this is the only the second group of Chekinov Scouts to go to Portaka. You ought to see how they're doing. Two birds with one stone, and if it happens that there is a third bird, I have no objection."

"Thank you, general, I will think about your idea. In the meantime, Mister Jevon is still trying to attract your attention."

Polrany nodded and walked over to the First Minister. The crowd was still dense; protocol required the most significant guest to leave first and neither Richelieu nor Baer had budged, preventing anyone else from leaving. Diplomats. Polrany shook his head.

"Did you see that an old friend of yours is in the Kwangdo trade delegation?"

"Yes, sir," Polrany said. "We are having dinner together later."

"Excellent," Jevon said, though his eyes did not look happy. "The Kwang were steady customers and it would be good to reopen our trading relationship."

"Yes, sir." Polrany stood by while Jevon smiled and exchanged a few words with a passing ambassador. Jevon leaned over to him.

"We may be in very big trouble," Jevon whispered while smiling. "Wait a few minutes and then return to the communication office. My aide Philip Deal is there and will fill you in."

Polrany nodded. He stood still while Jevon drifted away, circulating through the reception. Idly sipping at his glass of water, he waited a moment and then casually glanced at his watch. He placed his glass on the tray of a passing waiter and left the room.

Philip Deal, perhaps copying the relaxed fit of the field uniforms of the Militia officers on watch, had taken off his coat and tie and partially rolled his sleeves up. He started to stand as Polrany entered the room but the general motioned him to remain sitting. Polrany first glanced at the wall screen and then checked with the duty officer. Satisfied that things were quiet, he joined Deal at the small conference table in the back of the room.

"General," Deal said, "do you know a woman named Anna Cincinnatus?"

Polrany blinked. "Who?"

"Captain Anna Cincinnatus," he said, glancing at a paper on the table. "She is a member of Black's Gray Wolves."

"Yes, of course, it took me a moment." Polrany rubbed his moustache. "She assisted us when we went to Swordpoint and hired the Wild Geese." He frowned. "What does she have to do with anything?"

"She sent a message to Major Blaine Toland, which he forwarded to my office. The message describes the murder of a woman on Swordpoint, in the Security Forces Agency itself. The woman is a contract broker of mercenary units. In the course of the investigation, they discovered some information that Captain Cincinnatus forwarded to Major Toland. We have no way of evaluating its accuracy."

"If she had information important to Kodomir, why did she send it to Major Toland and not me?"

"Well, sir, apparently she thought you might not be the most open audience. She said in the message that she was concerned your anti-mercenary attitude might affect your judgment."

"And Blaine was a better choice?"

"Ah, well, sir, that's where it gets a little interesting and somewhat personal." Deal lowered his voice. "Apparently Major Toland had enough free time while the two of you were on Swordpoint to invite Captain Cincinnatus out to dinner and events went on from there."

Polrany was speechless for a moment and then his face was split by a huge smile.

"I'll be damned," he finally said. "I thought he was just taking in the sights."

"Apparently so," Deal said dryly. "So she sent him the information. It turns out the murdered woman was the person hiring the mercenary units raiding us. She kept double records – whoever killed her stole the first set but did not know of the second. She also kept two parallel security systems. The second one recorded the murder and the Gray Wolves caught the perpetrators as they were trying to leave. So far, they appear to be little more than contract assassins but the Wolves aren't finished with them yet."

"First, about the raids," Deal said holding up one finger. "Bought and paid for by the Alliance." Polrany raised his eyebrows in surprise. "I agree, general. I thought for some time it was von Bender keeping us off balance until he could make a more overt move. However, these records are very clear and precise. It *is* the Alliance. What Baer has told us is true, though Cincinnatus sent us much more detailed information than he chose to provide."

"Second, a key figure in all this is Esteban Baer. His operatives bribed the woman to feed them information about the raids and the Alliance plans for Kodomir. She was getting money from the Alliance and the Holdings. He naturally passed that information on to von Bender. When he was finished with her, we suspect *he* had her killed so she would never be able to tell the Alliance what she had done."

"I've never heard of him before he contacted us."

Deal nodded. "Most people have not, but they will. He's been a subject of interest to every intelligence service in the area. Von Bender's Special Envoy is a very ambitious man. He has large plans for the Holdings and has been arguing for a more aggressive, more imperialist foreign policy. He was the one who persuaded Karl von Bender to invade the Confederacy and pick up the String of Pearls." Deal shook his head. "O'Ryan's Confederacy made the fatal mistake of not declaring for either side in the growing escalation between Peter Mavis Carmichael and Mariah Connor.

As a result, we had no support when the invasion came and we provided Baer and von Bender an excuse for the attack."

"Neutrality is not always the best course of action," Polrany said. "But we've declared for Carmichael and the Free Union – would Baer still try to move against us?"

"First Minister Jevon does not think von Bender would, nor do any of our analysts. But Baer is a different question, and von Bender has given him a lot of freedom of action. We think he is hoping to stir things up between the Holdings and the Alliance so that he can drive the Baron into finally accepting his position."

"Does that force us to choose between the Holdings or the Alliance? We've been a relatively free nation for a very short period of time."

"General, the problem is that the choice between either the Holdings or the Alliance may be taken out of our hands." Deal leaned back in his chair. "Hell, we probably would have joined one side or the other eventually just to get a measure of stability in the area. And weird as it sounds, we probably would have joined the Holdings. Sure, the Alliance is more democratic on the surface, but Mordieu is somewhere to the right of Attila the Hun personally and would love to bring back the tyranny of her grandfather. In these turbulent days, don't think there isn't a lot of support among the people of her Alliance for that. On the other hand, von Bender is a feudal baron out of a child's tri-vid play; clumsy, intemperate, even violent, but he really buys into the concept of the obligations of nobility, knightly honor, the value of your word, and all the other trappings of chivalry. If we swore fealty to him, he wouldn't give a damn how we ran Kodomir. So there were pluses and minuses on both sides of the ledger." He leaned forward.

"But Esteban Baer is something else in the equation. He really is Attila. That which he cannot conquer he will destroy." He leaned back in his chair. "We think he has a connection to Farnham, which is one of two very indirect links you have to him." Polrany looked up in surprise. "Our friendly envoy is on the board of directors of over a dozen major industrial organizations. One of these groups is very shadowy. It's a mining combine and it does a lot in the Frontier. We think it bought ore from whoever owned Farnham."

"I was aware," Polrany said, "that the Wild Geese were unable to determine who owned that slave mine before they pulled out. I take it you've been able to pick up some additional information since then."

"Yes," Deal said, nodding. "When we were doing background on Baer, we saw involvement in that mining combine which had already been a focus for us just because it was doing work in the Frontier. Going through its trade records, we saw a big drop after your Geese hit the place. Then we saw another drop right after the Currahee went back a little while ago and finished the job. The freed slaves provided some bits of information that corroborate the trade record analysis. By the way, it seems the Currahee killed every bastard in the place by freezing them to death."

"I had read a briefing on that." He shook his head. "Bobby Martin said Marjessa Boyington told him when they were in the mines that the Currahee would live to bury the mine operators. I see she was not speaking metaphorically."

"Currahee are not much on metaphors, I gather," Deal said. "In any case, you have one other link to Esteban Baer, also indirect. Baer was the driving force behind von Bender's decision to seize the Confederacy. He's the one who recommended hiring Storm Cloud." He paused. "Apparently he has had a long relationship with Iriki Tykaw."

"The Special Envoy of the Benderist Holdings has a relationship with a Frontier criminal, with a Raider?"

"Exactly," Deal said. "After we overthrew Storm Cloud, we rounded up the survivors and did a perfunctory interrogation, mostly just to get their people individually identified. Those who had outstanding warrants we shipped off to whoever wanted them. Some were tried for war crimes and imprisoned here on Kodomir." He smiled.

"Most of their interrogations were conducted by state prosecutors seeking information for the trials. Getting historical background on Storm Cloud was not important. However, after the legal dust settled, some academics, always interested in such things, began to talk to the Stormies about the unit's history and they uncovered a piece of information that is now very important."

"It appears Storm Cloud's leader, Iriki Tykaw, served as liaison between Baer and other elements within the Frontier. A lot of it is very cloudy. Most of those people didn't know the details and Tykaw was not the kind of man to share information about his business with underlings. Tykaw, it turns out, may know of Baer's private business in a way that no one else does, and probably not even Karl von Bender."

"I think I know where you are going with this," Polrany said. "If von Bender realized he was being manipulated, he might pull in his horns and leave us alone."

"Well, that's a possibility," Deal said, "but not one I regard as realistic, not at the moment. The context isn't right. Both Baer and von Bender are still locked onto Kodomir as the solution to their problem with the Alliance." He took a sip of tea. "In any case, it would be to our benefit to know more about Baer and his activities. It would be very much to our benefit to know where any hard proof could be found."

"You said Tykaw knows about Baer's business. Why not get him to tell you?"

"We tried," Deal said. "He won't talk to us. However, he said he would talk to *you*."

"Me?" Polrany did not know whether to laugh or to become angry.

"In his mind, you are the only person to have ever defeated him, therefore the only person worthy of asking him questions." Deal shrugged and took another sip of his tea. He looked at Polrany intently. "General, remember, this guy had a total breakdown after he was defeated." Deal glanced at the other officers. "The word is, he was pinned in his HUP, on the verge of hysteria, and one of those Wild Geese got to him and really messed up his mind. In any case, it was four months before the docs got him talking even vaguely coherently."

"What about Jack Krager? I thought he and Tykaw had worked together before his Black Jacks were brought to Kodomir. Doesn't he know about Baer?"

"Only enough to know he didn't want to have anything to do with him. But he is the source that let us know that Tykaw did know Baer." Deal sighed. "General, a lot of what I'm telling you is not carved in stone. I admit it's guesswork. Right now, we're pretty focused on dealing with the immediate threat of the Alliance and the Holdings, but we need to know a lot more about the puppet master. That means, unfortunately, you have to talk to Iriki Tykaw."

"I think I would rather take out my right eye," Polrany said. He looked at Deal for a moment. "All right, I'll do it."

"Great," Deal said, his voice completely devoid of surprise. "What I'd like to do is give you a little time with Krager first. It might help when talking to Tykaw. Now, here's the deal with Krager. There have been none of the atrocity or war crimes charges filed against he and his people, though there is still an investigation to see if his agreement to join Tykaw falls into the category of aiding and abetting a war criminal. He's looking to make a deal and has been very cooperative. In return, we have released nearly all of his people." Deal smiled. "There are no requests for extradition of him by anyone in the Settled Worlds. He ran the Black Jacks as an unregistered mercenary unit, kind of in the gray area of the law, at least in the Settled Worlds. He actually was hired from time to time, though was never registered with the Trader's Exchange Database's Security Forces Agency. He's trying to portray himself as an ordinary mercenary, not a thief."

"Just another citizen, eh?" Polrany glanced at his watch. The reception should be breaking up. It was time to find Yamashita. "I'll see Krager tomorrow morning, Tykaw in the afternoon."

"Thanks, general. I'll catch up with you then."

Saburo Yamashita was with the other Kwang when Polrany entered the ballroom. As he had expected, the crowd was greatly reduced and people were slowly making their exits. He made eye contact with Yamashita who whispered into the ear of one of the members of his party and then walked over to Polrany.

"I'm starved," Yamashita said. "When do we eat in this place?"

"Follow me if you are not too weak with hunger." Polrany led the way, pausing to nod to Jevon.

One of the advantages of being the Militia Commanding General was the continuous availability of staff cars. His living quarters were in the Militia Headquarters near the First Minister's Residency and they were at the Headquarters in a few minutes.

Only the sentries took notice of Polrany and his guest; over the past year Polrany had ordered that no one other than the sentries should interrupt their work because of his arrival. As they entered the central hall of the

Headquarters, the Duty Officer, a tall man wearing a communication headset, was waiting for them.

"Sir, the Militia remains on Alert status. Other than that, nothing to report."

"Thank you, captain," Polrany said as he led the way to a bank of elevators. "I will be in my quarters if needed."

"Yes, sir." The officer stepped back as the doors opened. Polrany and Yamashita entered and Polrany hit the top button.

"I keep meaning to buy a house," Polrany said, "but these quarters are free and give you one of the best views of the city you can find. And the morning commute is very brief."

A chime sounded and the elevator doors opened. Polrany stepped out into a short hallway. "Those doors over there go to a staff briefing room and a tactical display room. This one," he motioned to a door opposite, "is mine." He opened it. "At least, until they fire me."

His quarters resembled little more than an upscale apartment, though their location near the top of the building meant he had a balcony area large enough to accommodate a helicopter pad. Yamashita looked through the tall sliding windows and realized it *was* a helicopter pad. Complete with a helicopter.

The apartment had a good-sized kitchen that Polrany immediately went to as he removed his uniform blouse and draped it on a chair. As they entered, they could smell a spicy, delicious aroma.

"I cheated," Polrany admitted. "I called ahead and asked Mrs. Covington, my housekeeper, to put some things on for me. But I prepared it, just had it frozen. I always prepare more than I can eat, when I get the chance to eat here and not in the mess hall down stairs. So, I freeze a lot."

He lifted the lid to a pot and looked inside. "Almost ready. Got to get the rolls." He opened the refrigerator. "By the way, my quarters are completely secured and swept daily – no bugs. Would you like wine or Kodomiri ale?"

"I have tried Kodomiri ale – I'll take the wine, thank you."

"So much for Oriental politeness," Polrany said. "Our friends in the Wild Geese have disparaging things to say about our ale, something you have in common. They do like the kind brewed by the Cheks, though." He brought out a cold bottle of wine and eased out the cork. He poured two glasses and raised his own in a toast.

"I offer the pleasure of the house," he said.

"I am honored by your grace," Yamashita replied. They sipped and Yamashita sighted. "Very good. Modena?"

"Yes, the '22." Polrany put his glass down and busied himself preparing the food. "So, how are things on Kwangdo?"

"Seething," Yamashita said. "The decision to surrender after we lost our HUPs in the first strike was very hard on our leadership. The Director for Defense resigned and has entered a monastery. The Benderists disbanded our military, though now they are offering to raise a regiment. Baer is trying to patch things up with various offers of money, membership in the Holdings, and so on. But, in the meantime, he's trying to finance his occupation of the Confederacy by a heavy load of taxes." Yamashita downed his wine in a single gulp and then grimaced.

"That was a disrespectful thing to do to that wine," he said. Polrany poured him some more. "We are paying for our own occupation and he gives us the magnanimous gift of offering to repair the damages incurred during the invasion, all the time talking to us like we were cartoon characters." He shook his head. "Stevar, he actually thinks he can manipulate us around issues of face and honor."

"Those are not insignificant facets to the Kwang character," Polrany said as he spread the roll dough out on a cloth. "I can see how someone with only a surface acquaintance with you might think those issues were useable for influence, maybe even manipulation."

"True," Yamashita agreed. He watched as Polrany ladled the thick contents of the pot onto the rolls. "Our roots can be traced back to traditional Asian perspectives. But this is not the Sixteenth Century. Our honor is in what we *do*; it comes from within, and is *not* dependent upon the recognition of others. Treat us with disrespect and the dishonor is on the perpetrator, not us." He smiled but there was little humor in it. "Of course, treat us with disrespect and we are likely to remember it." He watched Polrany work for a moment. "When these are served at dinner," he said, "they are always accompanied by a pepper and onion salad."

"Good memory," Polrany replied. "Everything is in the refrigerator, just waiting to be mixed."

Yamashita opened the refrigerator and removed bowls of salad materials. He took them to one side and added them to a larger bowl, carefully mixing them as he added each one.

"I have always admired Kodomiri food," Yamashita said. "It has an exceptional range."

"That is probably reflective of our culture."

"Somewhat like us, you do have a dominant historical culture. The influence of the Russo-Slav heritage is clear, and I should point out, with all respect, Russian cuisine is not generally highly regarded."

"No offence taken," Polrany said. "I tend to agree and suspect that is why there was a merger of Russian, African, and Celtic lines here on Kodomir – we needed somebody who could cook. Of course, unlike the tri-vid novels, none of those lines were as narrow as they might have been back on Earth a millennium or two ago."

"As is true of us," Yamashita said. "We can easily trace our cultural roots to Japan, but those of Asian genetic heritage only make up about a third of our population. But you also have another cultural line, the Chekinovs."

"Yes. Despite their name, they are not Slavic per se. Genetically, they appear to be the usual spread that you would encounter in the Settled Worlds."

"Tell me," Yamashita said, "in the genetic work-ups you have done with the Chekinovs, has anyone ever seen any indications of Currahee?"

Polrany paused. "Well," he said, "we don't have a lot of samples of Currahee bloodlines. The origins of the Chekinovs have been lost. While there are dozens of theories of where they came from, including that they were a part of the Currahee Encampment and for some reason left that region, no one has been able to prove anything one way or the other. Their own stories do not have much to say about who they were before Kodomir."

"I have read of their crash and the leadership of Sarah Chekinov," Yamashita said. "It is an epic story. How are they as Militia soldiers?"

"I am very happy to have them on my side instead of shooting at me," Polrany said. "They are excellent light infantry, very well disciplined, and their small unit tactics are very good. Only our reconnaissance units can keep up with them physically. They remind me of your own Wakizashi companies. Very light, fast, think well on their feet. Very dangerous."

"I am afraid our Wakizashi companies do not exist," Yamashita said. "At the moment."

"So, what are your plans?" Polrany folded the rolls, trapping the lumpy sauce within.

"We will fight for our freedom," Yamashita said. "The only question is when."

"You are not going to accept Baer's offers?" Polrany slid the rolls onto a large metal pan and then put it in an oven.

"You know, the offers of membership in the Holdings, under the right circumstances, might have been considered a reasonable basis for negotiations. There was a great deal of sympathy among the Kwang for Prime Minister Carmichael and the strong defense he built for the Free Union. Unlike Kodomir, on Kwangdo O'Ryan's neutrality was not greatly supported. However, under the current situation, with Benderist troops on our soil, we will do what we have to do until the time is correct."

"I wish," Polrany said, leaning against a wall and fingering his moustache, "there was something we could do."

"Things are a little complicated for Kodomir at the moment," Yamashita said. "Still, I was asked by our Prime Minister to convey several points to your government. First, our main enemy is still von Bender; Mordieu is an illusion, a slight of hand that can be lost with a whisper."

"Are you trying to be inscrutable?"

"Well, sort of," Yamashita chuckled. "But pay attention to von Bender's Special Envoy. He has some information for your government which may help you deal with Mordieu and Richelieu and do it without firing a shot."

"That would be very, very helpful," Polrany said.

"Second thing, we have learned von Bender has been stretched very thin. He has not yet translated his seizures into military power. In his desperation he is now talking about rearming us. But the piece of information we have learned concerns the machinations of his government. The Baron is, in many ways, an old-fashioned imperialist, a warlord. He will seize and hold whatever he can, but he is not stupid. If the prize is beyond reach then he will withdraw his hand."

"I see," said Polrany as he checked the rolls.

"Baer represents a faction within the Benderists which is much more aggressive in terms of acquisition. Where von Bender wanted the String of Pearls and the Confederacy as a strategic buffer, Baer's people believe they can have it all."

"'All?'"

"The whole Settled Worlds, eventually. Their plan is long term in its orientation but the ongoing war between the Free Union and the Protectorate is seen as an opportunity which may not repeat itself."

"They need to read more Settled Worlds history," Polrany said. "This kind of stupidity is ongoing among these idiots."

"I tend to agree. Nonetheless, that is how they see the future. Their goal is not Kodomir, but the Alliance. They think that will take three, perhaps five years. A decade after that they expect to control the Free Union and the Protectorate both."

"Either Carmichael or Connor would string them up by their entrails. Are they insane?"

"No, very calculating. Every world they control is one their opponents do not. Their economy is being shifted to a fascist model – continual expansion through the gains of war."

"They get more to get more."

"Exactly. Baer and his faction want to turn the Holdings into a perpetual motion machine, an economic engine driven by conquest. Similar to the Mongols and Nazis of old Earth." Yamashita looked around and spotted the spice rack. He carefully selected spices and added them to the salad.

"This plan of conquest begins with their assault on the Alliance. Karl von Bender's personal interest in Kodomir is simply to protect what he has. He does not think there is much reason to expand and certainly nothing worth the effort at this point, especially with the Free Union at war with the Protectorate and the commitments that means for the Holdings. But Baer's faction sees Kodomir as an opportunity to bleed the Alliance tactically, engage it in a war of attrition in a place where whatever damage is done will not hurt the Holdings. Right now, Mordieu, with her desire to recreate her grandfather's empire, is playing into their game without realizing it. Her desire to expand the Alliance into this area gives Baer a chance to chop off her hand. If they can destroy the Alliance regiment, they not only safeguard what they now hold, they weaken the Alliance. The

Holdings, despite their stretching of their military, has the population and now the resources, to replace losses faster than the Alliance even without calling on the Free Union."

"What would be best for Baer would be for us to do the dirty work."

"Can you defeat an Alliance or Benderist regiment?"

"Not in open combat, not by ourselves," Polrany admitted as he slid the tray from the oven. The kitchen was flooded with the delicious odor of the rolls. He placed them on a serving plate and took them over to the already set dining table.

"My government's best guess," Yamashita said, "is that Baer will give proof to Jevon that the Alliance has been behind the raids on Kodomir. He is counting on that to bring you over to the Benderist camp. Then you and the Benderists will chew up that Alliance regiment if it lands or otherwise scare them off. Either way the Alliance will be weakened."

"So," Polrany said as they sat down, "do you have any *bad* news?"

"Just one other item. Baer's faction is generating a lot of opposition within the Benderist government. The Baron has not committed himself to them totally though his son supports them. His daughter doesn't. But von Bender is giving them some room to try. His closest advisors see Baer as a danger to the Holdings and would love to take him off at the knees but he has never been wrong yet. If his plan were to be derailed, if the Holdings were to suffer a real defeat, Baer might find himself washing dishes in the Baron's kitchen instead of controlling his foreign policy."

"Interesting point," Polrany said. "The phrase everyone is using here is we are between a rock and a hard place. Maybe what you have told me will provide us with some leverage."

"My friend," Yamashita said. "It is in the interest of Kwangdo that Kodomir remain free. Some time, I do not know when, you may be able help us throw off von Bender's heavy hand." Polrany nodded but said nothing.

The two men became silent as they ate. Yamashita seemed to be totally absorbed in eating his food, carefully taking a forkful of salad between each bite of meat roll. He would put down his fork, close his eyes, and chew for a moment.

"And there are people," Yamashita finally said, "who argue there are no gods."

"I'm sure the Prelate of the Reform Orthodox Church would enjoy hearing your epiphany," Polrany said as he walked over to the refrigerator. He returned with two bottles of cold beer, placing one in front of Yamashita. "Wine is not robust enough to stand up to these spicy rolls," he said. The two men raised their bottles in a mutual toast.

As the meal ended, Polrany hesitated. There was much he wanted to share with Yamashita, but it would serve little useful purpose and might present dangers down the road. He shoved the thought of telling his friend about the information linking Baer with Storm Cloud to the back of his mind for a better time.

Later they walked down the steps of the Militia Headquarters to a waiting groundcar. Yamashita paused and then looked at his friend, holding up his hand to stop them short of the car.

"Remember what I said about your help. But the best garden flowers under the hands of the one who lives with it."

"Agreed," said Polrany, not quite sure what Yamashita meant but understanding someone might be monitoring their conversation now that they were in the open.

"Nonetheless," Yamashita said, "Once the ground is prepared, even the most dedicated gardener may need to borrow tools."

They shook hands. Yamashita backed up and ritually bowed for anyone watching to see. Polrany returned the gesture and watched as the groundcar drove away.

Once the ground is prepared... Yamashita was not saying that Kodomir would fight the Holdings to liberate Kwangdo but some day, in some way, Kodomir might lend a hand to their friends. If it was possible, Polrany knew, Kodomir would do it.

Chapter 17: Dancing with the devil

4 December 2824

Jack Krager had changed little during his months of imprisonment. He still had a cocky smile and amusement shone in his eyes. His Black Jacks had joined Tykaw's Storm Cloud shortly before the final battle. Had they arrived earlier and been deployed properly, they could have made all the difference.

The man rocked back in his chair as he considered Polrany for a moment, and then he let the chair come forward.

"You want to know about Tykaw and Baer?" He nodded his head and his smile became broader. "What's in it for me?"

"Not much," Polrany said. "I have no influence over the courts." Krager snorted and tilted his chair back. "However, since you were not a direct participant in any of the war crimes of Tykaw's group, and since you made the correct decision at the end, a decision which may have saved lives, I would be willing to express my desire that you be treated with leniency."

"War crimes, huh?" Krager slowly lowered his chair and folded his hands on the table between him and the general. "For what it's worth, general, I did not know of what Tykaw was letting his people do in Coyote Bay. I do what I have to do to survive and keep my people alive and some of it violates a lot of other peoples' laws. I don't apologize for that. But the Black Jacks never did anything like that. A brothel with children…" Krager fell silent.

"Be that as it may," Polrany said, his gaze stony, "the fact remains you are here in our custody. My question is, will you provide me with what I want to know?"

"All right, general. Do what you can with the Kodomir High Court. Who knows, maybe they'll let me walk, even give me a vacation on the Peridees. I hear they're beautiful. Now, about Tykaw…" Krager thought for a moment.

"Your people know Iriki Tykaw got court-martialed for being a thief. Two things about that deal you want to pay attention to. First, what he stole were weapons. He was an ordnance officer for a garrison near the Frontier and he would mark stuff as broken and irreparable when it wasn't. Then he'd move it out and sell it, mostly to criminals, Raiders, people like that. So that's how he knew people to start with. Second thing was, when he escaped, he killed two of his guards. Didn't have to. He had them down and out. Did it because he knew that would impress certain other people. See, he was planning on moving over to the Raiders in the Frontier from the start." Krager took a sip of coffee and grimaced. "No matter what they tell you, general, crime does not pay if you end up drinking this crap."

"Anyway," Krager continued, "he made his way out to the Frontier. He joined up with some of his former customers. He knew HUPs, was military trained, they would have bid big money for his services. But he took on Thunder Storm, as it was then called, because he thought he could work his way to the top. And he did." Krager put down his cup.

"Along the way we met up and sometimes worked together. His unit grew, while I kept mine small. You know what's going on better in a small unit; safer that way. Anyway, we were in a couple of raids together. He knew his people weren't frontline soldiers, so he always kept the tactics simple." Krager grinned. "I read that book on your War of Liberation and when I heard that he had sixteen of his HUPs come right at your capital in a straight line, I said, 'Yep, that's Tykaw!' You guys almost stopped that detachment, even without HUPs. Not bad, general." He took another sip of coffee, grimaced again, and put it down.

"But let me back up. This guy Baer had some kind of deal going and was hiring different Frontier units for special operations and security. I talked to a representative of his once. He wanted to hire us to defend some place. I turned him down. Caught a whiff of something not quite right about

257

the deal. Tykaw told me it was a slave world a little while later and I was glad I didn't. Sooner or later slavers pay with their lives and I don't mess with stuff like that. I got the hell away from Baer's people and tried to go legitimate as a mercenary unit." He shrugged. "That didn't work out. Too many warrants out for me. Anyway, Tykaw ran into Baer right after that and for a time Storm Cloud, which he called it now that he was in charge, worked for him."

"A year passes, maybe two. I'm providing security for a combine up near the Currahee Encampment area and I get this message from Tykaw. I don't know how he found me but Storm Cloud is in the area, scrounging weapons, HUPs, whatever they could find on some of the old battlegrounds, where those people tried to invade the Encampment and some of the skirmish sites from Settled World flare-ups. By the way, that's real dangerous stuff, because you never know who's going to come back and neither side was real big on taking prisoners of looters. Anyway, he comes on down and we meet up."

"Now I'm a little suspicious and thinking maybe he's getting ready to raid *me*, but he's just resting his unit. We start talking and I ask about Baer. He tells me a little about Farnham. But the one thing I remember is that Tykaw said Baer used him to do special missions. Raiding competitors, sure, that's what a lot of mercs do, but Storm Cloud was doing stuff to assist the Holdings expansion. Assassinations, raids to destabilize governments, and so on."

"That, by the way, is why Tykaw took the contract to come here. Old buddy of Baer, he was probably at the top of the list when the Holdings made its move and needed some hired guns. And Baer knew Tykaw wanted a world to call his own and so would work cheap."

"I see," Polrany said. He thought for a moment. "What if I told you Baer was trying to set the Alliance and Kodomir at each other's throats?"

"Well, that may be his style, I don't know, but if he is coming after Kodomir, then I'd like very much to be sent on my way, general, sir. Because if he takes this place, then he'll give people like me two choices: join him or die. And neither is attractive."

"He's that bad?"

"Talk to Tykaw," Krager said. "I only know what I've heard. All I can say is, Iriki Tykaw was in charge of operations for him. Does that give you a clue?" Krager slowly sipped his now cold coffee while Polrany sat in silence.

A half hour later Polrany sat in the interrogation room alone. They were bringing Tykaw and Polrany was trying to focus his thoughts. No, not his thoughts; his emotions. Tykaw was responsible for the horror that had descended upon Kodomir, a horror that resembled something out of the Dark Ages rather than the first part of the 29th Century. Slaves in mines, brothels that included children, churches looted, religious and political leaders murdered... The list was a long one.

And you beat him. Beat him so bad he went insane.

Well, *something* drove Tykaw insane. He was found psychotic when they pulled him from his damaged Javelin. Polrany had heard, very unofficially, that one of the Wild Geese had gotten to him, but there had never been anything to confirm that story.

You didn't want to know.

Of course not. The Wild Geese became Kodomiri in the first act of the Assembly after the Liberation, and most of them came into the Militia. If one of them had done something to Tykaw, though he could not think of what it might have been, something powerful enough to drive him crazy but leave no marks, then it was a story best left untold.

He heard bolts slide back in the door to the prisoners' cells. He stood automatically as the door opened and Iriki Tykaw, self-styled Duke of what he called Mercenary Unit Storm Cloud, walked in. He was manacled, wrists and ankles joined, a chain linking both sets connected to a locked belt around his waist. Guards stood on either side as he shuffled forward.

He was slightly shorter than average. His round face was lined more than it had been and his black hair, now cut prison-short, showed strands of gray. He was heavier as well, his once hard body now not getting the exercise it had in the past and his limp was a little more pronounced.

But his eyes were the same. Black, expressionless, they studied everything around them like computer-controlled scanners. He slowly moved to the chair opposite Polrany, his chains clinking in rhythm to his shuffle.

"General Polrany, I see." Tykaw nodded to himself. "I thought you would come." He managed to get into his chair. The guards did not help him and kept their expressions neutral. Polrany continued to stand and stare at him. "Sit, sit, general, please. We have a lot to talk about. And I do not get many opportunities to talk. They keep me away from the other prisoners, even the former members of my command. They seem to think someone would kill me if they got the chance." Polrany remained standing. He studied Tykaw for a moment.

The psychiatric people had told him Tykaw had largely recovered, though he occasionally had moments when he did not seem to be tracking very well. As far as Polrany could tell, there was little difference between the man across the table from him and the man he had fought.

"They told you why I came?"

"You want information." Tykaw tried to wave his hands but the chains kept them close to his waist. "Everyone wants information. Including me."

Polrany paused and then sat down. He looked up at the guards. "You can unhook his hands from his belt. Then leave us. Ask the attendant to bring in coffee for him and tea for me, please."

The guards paused. Then the senior, a tall, dark-skinned man, gestured and they released the belt chain. Tykaw sighed and put his still manacled hands on the table and smiled. As the other guard left, the senior guard leaned forward.

"Sir, we will be just outside the door. If you need us, just call. It would be our pleasure to be of assistance." He looked at Tykaw, his brown face twisted in contempt, and he left.

They waited in silence until the coffee and tea arrived. The attendant, his face carefully neutral, nodded to Polrany and left.

"I am impressed, general," Tykaw said as he took a sip. "You know enough about me to know I dislike tea and prefer coffee." Polrany said nothing for a moment.

"A variety of Kodomiri intelligence people have been in to see me from time to time," Tykaw went on, as if not willing to wait for Polrany's response. "Once I was no longer hospitalized, I mean." He made a flicking gesture on the table with his fingers, as if casting something aside. His chains clinked briefly. "I told them little. I was not being impolite," he said. "They had all the information on my unit they needed. We never evacuated our headquarters, never destroyed any documents." He smiled and Polrany felt ice. "You did not give us the chance to do any of that."

"We had few options," Polrany said slowly. "We had to move quickly. Your forces were much larger than ours."

"Not really," Tykaw said, still smiling. "After all, you had an entire world on your side. Your underground was never successfully penetrated by my people and your First Minister totally misled me."

"Misled you?"

"I thought he was a craven coward," Tykaw said. He shrugged. "One of the few times I have ever underestimated a potential threat. Nonetheless, had you waited even six months, I doubt you would have succeeded."

"Why is that?"

"Terror and time, general," Tykaw said. "Given enough terror over a long enough period of time, I do not think your underground would have been nearly as effective as it was, at least in terms of supplying you with information. And, of course, I would have had more weapons by then." Tykaw's voice was calm, as if discussing the need for rain for a good crop of wheat.

"I think," Polrany said, "our options were limited by our resources. Certainly, time was one of them. We were already aware of the initial use of terror by your unit. Naturally we wanted to strike quickly."

"Exactly what I thought," Tykaw said and seemed pleased. Polrany realized he was looking at a sociopath, someone with no empathetic bond to any other human being. Someone governed solely by his own desire for power and control. The psychiatric people had told him all that, but it was chilling to actually be facing such a person across a table.

"You understand, then, general," Tykaw said with a satisfied look on his face. "Everything I did was simply an operational necessity. It was necessary for my troops to be placated. I was low on cash and so we had to loot the churches. The population had to be cowed and I needed a way to provide my people with some release in a controlled fashion and so we instituted the brothel and seized the Chekinov leadership and all the other things." Again his fingers made the dismissive gesture. "I see you understand. I have been unable to make any of my interrogators see the point."

"You relied on your experience from the past, then," Polrany said.

"Of course. Book learning can take you only so far." He smiled. "Your tactics went well beyond anything you learned in a Militia classroom. Mine were learned on battlefields as well."

"You commanded Storm Cloud on missions with some political complexity, I was told. That experience must have prepared you for what to expect in dealing with the population of an entire world."

"To be sure," Tykaw nodded.

"I read an analysis that stated Baer's efforts to expand the Holdings owed much of his success to your skills," Polrany paused, and then added, "though of course he would disagree."

"Of course, he would disagree," Tykaw said. "The man is military trained, yes, but he was always far too reliant on subtle diplomacy, negotiating and maneuvering like a worm in the dirt." He took a sip of coffee and put the cup down carefully. "He has a rudimentary grasp of strategy and tactics at the operational level but I think I might say without contradiction that he spent much of the time I was affiliated with his organization learning from me."

"Well, that speaks well for him, I would think, that he has a willingness to learn."

"I suppose so." Tykaw took another sip of coffee and then tilted his head to one side and stared at Polrany. "Esteban Baer. That is why you came. You have learned something about him."

"We learned he is trying to play off Kodomir against the Alliance."

"Indeed?" Tykaw sighed. "He is moving against the Alliance? I did not think he was going to invade the rest of the Settled Worlds quite so soon. He must know I am here. He hates me, you know."

"Hates you? Why? Without you he would have been unable to neutralize Kodomir and take Kwangdo."

Tykaw nodded. "Well, I believe he saw me as a rival to his power. I knew of his dealings in the Frontier and his special operations in the Settled Worlds. I think he feared that I would use that information to blackmail him or even supplant him in the Holdings. In all fairness, I was about to do something like that when he made the offer to attack the Confederacy." He smiled. "I wanted a world of my own, perhaps my greatest weakness. I dropped my plans for him. But I think he still fears me."

"You were moving against him because…"

"He would inevitably move against me." Tykaw shrugged. "I was his confidant and did things for him that would be politically embarrassing if they ever got out. His Baron would be very unhappy with him. And he will inevitably move against you, and not just because Kodomir is a stepping stone to the Alliance."

"You mean he has a personal reason?" Polrany shook his head. "Nonsense. Until a few weeks ago he was no more than a name we heard in briefings. We've never dealt with the man before."

"But you have already dealt with him, general." Tykaw leaned back in his chair and smiled.

Polrany cocked his head. "What are you talking about?"

"Who do you think owned Farnham?"

"'Owned'? No, he's just on the board of directors of some mining combine that was buying ore from whoever did own the place."

"Not quite, general," Tykaw said. He smiled. "Baer is much cleverer than that. He is on the board of the combine. He also controls Farnham, personally. I know, I conquered it for him. I doubt the other members of the combine's board know one of their number runs a slave world."

"*Jesu Christos*! Are you serious?"

"Indeed, general. And that means a couple of things, not the least of which is he has reason to be unhappy with Kodomir. Your Wild Geese smashed his mine there and freed his slaves." Tykaw leaned forward. "That is the kind of personal insult he cannot live with. But above that he does not know what you may have learned on Farnham. I imagine he is walking around you people like a cat in a room full of rocking chairs. He *has* to destroy Kodomir, if not today, then tomorrow. Watch and mark my words. As Prime Minister Carmichael strips this area of its Free Union forces to fight the Protectorate and as more worlds become entangled in that little war, he will move, and now he has a direction, a place to begin."

"More immediately I understand you have problems," Tykaw said. "How are you going to deal with both the Alliance and the Holdings?"

"How would you handle the situation?"

"Thank you for asking, general," Tykaw said. "I would think that your clever First Minister Alexis Jevon is even now maneuvering for a diplomatic solution to one of the parties, most likely the Alliance.

Diplomacy, after all, is the waging of war by other means. As for the Benderists, you will fight them."

"Why?"

"Well, for one reason, they brought *me* here, and I doubt it is in the Kodomiri heart to forgive them for that." He paused but Polrany made no comment. "Second, you know that von Bender will expand until the cost is too high and then he will hold onto whatever he has seized. Until now the cost has been negligible, which has probably encouraged the expansionists in his court. Bloody him, discredit Baer, and von Bender may back off."

"Your assessment may prove to be correct."

"I think it will," Tykaw said. He paused and looked around the room. Then his eyes fixed on Polrany. "I am never leaving here, am I, general?" Polrany shook his head negatively. "Perhaps not. Time will tell." Tykaw leaned back in his chair, his chains making small clinking sounds. "But still, it is better than death and, on the whole, with one or two exceptions, the Kodomiri have treated me well enough. Better than I would have had the roles been reversed." Again, Tykaw smiled and Polrany felt cold fingers stroke his back. Tykaw was silent for a moment and then nodded.

"Very well, general, I will tell you something. Something you can use. My former second-in-command, Lieutenant General Tokovan Bedoreh, had recorded data, copies of documents concerning the actions of Esteban Baer. Proof of his involvement in Farnham, for example, as well as records of his hiring Storm Cloud for various tasks." Tykaw shifted in his chair, pulling himself closer to the table.

"This information included contracts for raids on mining competitors, of course – that kind of thing is a commonplace in the Settled Worlds. But what *you* might find interesting are the assignments to eliminate his political rivals, damage foreign governments, and all the other things he had Storm Cloud do for him. You see, it is the claim of the Benderists that they never knew what Storm Cloud was and, therefore, they were not responsible for what happened on Kodomir. They now say they thought we were just another mercenary unit. No one knew we were a Frontier Raider organization." He widened his eyes in mock horror. "'Oh, no, our hands are clean,' they now say. 'We would never have anything to do with such evil people.'" His features relaxed and he grimaced. "And it is true that Baron Karl von Bender knew nothing of us." Tykaw leaned forward.

"But *Baer* knew. He had used us for years. Now, if you have those documents and records, which include video of several meetings he had with me personally, you could discredit him. The Baron has very old-fashioned ideas and he would not tolerate in his court someone who did some of the things Baer did."

"Bedoreh is dead," Polrany said. "You killed him."

"Yes. He was disloyal. They *all* proved to be disloyal." Tykaw's eyes lost their focus for a second and then returned. "He was replaced by Kidowsky. I was told he, in turn, was killed on the streets of Coyote Bay." Polrany nodded.

"Just as well, really," Tykaw continued. "He had no sense of humor and his briefings were boring. In any case, he had all of Bedoreh's records. Find them and you have your lever to use on Baer."

Polrany remained quiet for a moment. Tokovan Bedoreh had led the invasion of Kodomir. Kidowsky was a sadist who ran Storm Cloud's secret police before his promotion to second in command of the Raiders. Memories of the desperate times of the occupation came back and he had to force them out of the way.

"This information you describe," Polrany said slowly, "could prove to be quite valuable. Why are you telling me about this without any conditions, without any deal?"

"Survival," Tykaw said, slightly surprised. "If Baer succeeds in taking over Kodomir, I am too great a political liability to be allowed to remain alive. It is also in my best interest to have you favorably disposed towards me."

"I have little influence over the Kodomir judicial system," Polrany said. "I do not think there is much..."

"I am not concerned with the courts or my jailers," Tykaw interrupted. "I simply want you to keep one of your officers away from me. Several months ago he came by, gathering material for a book he was writing. I did not know who he was until I came into the room." Tykaw fell silent and looked away. Polrany said nothing and waited. Finally, Tykaw looked back at him and for the first time he saw emotion in the Raider's eyes.

Fear.

"My memories of the last battle are fragmentary, but I remember him, his voice." Tykaw's forehead was dotted with beads of sweat and he licked his lips nervously. "I just want... I want him kept away from me, that is all I want."

Polrany watched him, slightly startled by the change. From the cold, emotionless man he had always known Tykaw to be, to this almost trembling, nervous figure, was a surprising change. He slowly nodded.

"I will leave orders that he is not to be permitted to see you," Polrany said.

"I would be very grateful, general," Tykaw said, and began to pull himself back together. "I appreciate your courtesy, one professional to another. Perhaps," he swallowed and smiled, though it was weaker than before, "we might talk again sometime."

"Perhaps," Polrany replied. When hell freezes over.

Several minutes later, after Tykaw had been taken back to his solitary cell, Polrany sat in his chair thinking. His tea, now cold, remained untouched – he did not want to drink anything that had been in Tykaw's presence. The senior guard stepped in.

"Sir, is there anything else we can do for you?"

"No, thank you." He paused and looked at the man. "I know you, don't I?"

"Yes, sir," the guard said with pride. He stood a little more erect. "Thomas Ivanovich Ivanov. I was a sergeant in 3rd Recon back when you were a captain there. I was in one of the companies and you and I worked on the scout training syllabus for a couple of months together."

"Of course, now I remember." Polrany smiled. "I was in admin. You were the one who suggested we add more hours to the land navigation course. It was a good idea."

"Thank you, sir," Ivanov said with pride. "I'm glad you remember. It's been a long time." He grinned ruefully. "After you transferred out west, I tore up my knee. Eric's Syndrome, so they couldn't clone me a new one quickly. They were willing to keep me in the Militia, working behind a desk, but I felt like, you know, after recon, everything else would be boring. Besides, my lady got used to me having regular hours." He chuckled. "So I took this job. Got my new knee a few years back and play ball with my kids every week."

"Well, I'm glad to see you are still in government service." Polrany paused and looked at the door Tykaw had left through and stood up. "Tell me, sarge. About Tykaw. What has he been like while he's been in here?"

"Not much to say, sir," Ivanov said. "The dog-licker, begging your pardon, the *prisoner*, doesn't talk much to the guards and we keep him away from the other prisoners. He reads, watches the 'vid, he's allowed to do that. Does exercises. The psych people spent a lot of time with him in the beginning, but they only come around once a month now, mostly just doing a medication check." Ivanov walked with Polrany to the exit and held the door open for the general.

"About the only thing worth noting is how he sleeps," the guard said as Polrany stepped through.

"How is that?" Polrany stopped in the doorway.

"Well, pretty much every night, he has nightmares."

Polrany nodded slowly. "Good," he said, and walked down the hallway.

Yamashita sat in Polrany's apartment, enjoying the view of the sunset. Once again, his friend fussed in the kitchen. He shook his head. Here was the commanding general of an entire planetary Militia, facing possible invasion by two stellar powers, puttering around a kitchen as if this was the most important task confronting him.

"It seems to me," Yamashita said, "Baer is becoming increasingly frustrated with his lack of progress in 'converting' Kodomir to the Benderist cause. He is also very worried about Richelieu's presence. He was not expecting to have the Alliance Counselor-General in the area when a senior diplomat would have been sufficient. He thinks this means the Alliance will act if Kodomir does not bow down before it."

"So he would force us into aligning with them by a preemptive move against us?" Polrany emerged from the kitchen holding two bottles of beer and handed one to his friend. They raised the bottles in an informal toast. Polrany watched the sunset for a moment.

"A piece of information for you," Polrany said and took another sip of beer. "The source of von Bender's information about the Alliance hiring those merc units to hit Kodomir was Baer's operative."

"There is some irony in *Baer* catching the Alliance doing something underhanded," Yamashita said.

"It takes one to catch one," Polrany said. "Baer has been engaged in some fairly nasty stuff over the years." He looked at Yamashita. "Iriki Tykaw worked for him for a period of time before the invasion of the Confederacy."

Yamashita slowly put down his bottle and stared at Polrany. He finally looked away and watched the sun dip beneath the western hills.

"I was unhappy to learn that the Kodomir judicial system does not possess capital punishment." He looked at his friend. "If we ever regain control of our foreign policy, I think you can expect a request for extradition of Tykaw."

"I will leave that one to the diplomats," Polrany said as the last of the sun disappeared. "He is the source for much of our information on Baer and his past actions. Baer's plan seems to be to get the Holdings into a war with the Alliance eventually, and then use that for a springboard for further conquest. Tykaw thinks he will hit Kodomir because we have damaged some of his property."

"The mines on Farnham?"

Polrany nodded. "Tykaw said they were his. And if he is angry with us because we damaged them, he is going to be totally pissed when he discovers what the Currahee Aniwaya did to them."

Yamashita laughed and extended his bottle. The two friends clinked them together and took a drink. As the bottles touched the table, a chime came from an intercom unit in the kitchen. Polrany touched its face.

"Sir," a voice said, "the Alliance landing ships are moving towards Kodomir. It looks like they intend to land."

"All of them?"

"Yes, sir. Wait one, sir." The speaker paused. "The Benderists are moving as well, toward Kodomir."

"Probable landing site based on their trajectories?"

"Looks like southern hemisphere, probably Portaka, sir. We cannot tell exactly where on the continent yet."

"Very well. Take the Militia to full alert. Have the Second Regiment load its Combine Arms Battalion into landing ships and prepare for orders. I am coming down to CIC."

"Yes, sir."

Polrany came back to his friend. "I'm afraid our dinner is interrupted," he said. Yamashita stood, but Polrany motioned him down. "Please, stay and eat. This time Mrs. Covington prepared it. Trust me, she's a better cook then I will ever be. I will have a car standing by to take you to your delegation later."

"Very well," Yamashita said, sitting back down. He smiled, though there was no humor in his eyes. "It sounds like the rock and the hard place are coming together."

Chapter 18: Flash traffic

6 December 2824

Colonel Kheyntamenti had to work at it, but he appeared calm as he walked down the hall from his office to the exit. The battalion was "cocked and locked," loaded on landing ships, ready to launch whenever the word was given. The question was, what word and when? Both the Holdings and the Stellar Alliance now had troops on Kodomir's soil and the Benderists had seized the torn-up Militia facility outside of Portaka City. Technically, these were acts of war but the diplomats were working nonstop to keep a full-scale battle from breaking out on Kodomir.

Kheyntamenti thought of what it would mean to have two major powers fighting each other across the surface of the planet and his expression became grim. He had seen such things in the past and he did not want that kind of devastation experienced by his new home. He paused outside the battalion headquarters and looked around.

Home.

Decades of wandering were over, *might* be over. Why couldn't these bastards leave them alone? Kheyntamenti sighed. Such questions had been asked throughout human history and he was aware of no satisfactory answers. It was his job to be ready and that was all he could do. He stepped down the walk, heading for his ground car.

As he walked from the battalion headquarters, he heard the Swallows on strip alert running up their engines, making sure everything was ready.

That was the state of the whole Militia, he thought. Sevin met him as he approached the parking area.

"Doc," he said returning the gunnery sergeant's salute, "what's the word on the last HUPs from Portaka?"

"They're fine, sir," Sevin replied as he fell in beside his commander. "Fortunately, the healthiest gear had already been moved up from the Militia facility. These last few HUPs had been damaged in the fight but nothing we can't take care of." He consulted his datapad. "Two belonged to the 'Cats, one to the Victors – that damned Scorpion got dinged again. The maintenance folks have started calling it Bull's Eye, it gets shot up so often. And a couple from the training cadre."

"I'm glad for that, at least. The Benderists seized only a handful of people when they landed on the base, just the engineers and survey teams checking out the damage and a few others. Some of the instructor cadre are unaccounted for. The list is still not complete – command thinks a few may have made it to town."

"At least the Alliance people landed in an uninhabited area."

"So far," Kheyntamenti said. "They might decide to move against the Benderists and that means our people down there are in the line of fire."

"Any word from the politicians?"

"No, not really," Kheyntamenti said, pausing beside the car. "The Benderists still aren't admitting they've taken hostages, the Alliance is claiming they landed to prevent the Benderists from 'undue influence over the Kodomir government,' and the Benderists are still claiming they landed 'only to prevent Alliance aggression.'" He shook his head and stepped into the car.

"Well, sir," Sevin said, "don't worry about the battalion. It's ready to go."

"Roger that, Gunny," Kheyntamenti said and smiled grimly. "Let's just hope it doesn't have to."

"They have to go," Jevon said. He sat down and glanced at the papers on his desk and then up at the holographic display of eastern Portaka. The Alliance and Benderist forces were two clusters of angry red symbols, one centered over the Militia Facility, the other fifty kilometers to the west and spread around a small, abandoned ore-processing plant. "We need to have those dog-lickers off Kodomir."

"The information is on its way," Deal said. "Every bit of it is in the message."

"I suspect Special Envoy Baer is going to be somewhat surprised with how we used his information. He doesn't know about the documentation supplied by Captain Cincinnatus; bless her and the Gray Wolves' collective hearts."

"Most likely he will be disappointed it did not result in us throwing ourselves into his arms," Deal replied.

"But he will be happy if the Alliance forces withdraw."

"Indeed. But will he understand what that means for him?"

Deal was silent. There was no answer to that.

"The hostages," Jevon said. "That's his trump card."

"He *believes* it is his trump card," Deal said. "He has alluded to them several times, always in the context of his wish that a peaceful resolution of the current difficulties can be found and that no accidents occur which might endanger his guests."

"In other words, 'Hold still or I will kill them.'"

"Pretty much," Deal agreed.

"The only good news is we evacuated the facility after those damned mercenaries tore it up. Otherwise, I shudder to think of what would have happened. A battle could have brought in the Alliance and we would be facing a three-way war."

"Yes, sir," Deal said. "We were lucky in that regard."

"Yes, lucky," Jevon said. He sighed. "But our throw of the dice is still in the air. And if it is successful, those hostages…" His voice trailed off, pain on his face. Again Deal remained silent.

The small group of Stellar Alliance parliamentarians, all extremely powerful politicians, walked down the well-polished hallway. Petty functionaries, mostly staff of Counselor-General Andrea Richelieu, scattered from their path. The look on their faces showed they understood a crisis was coming.

Selena Mordieu looked up from her desk as the delegation entered her office. She frowned; she had agreed to the meeting with the opposition leader, the blond-haired man in the front of the group named Rammon, but he had said nothing about bringing others from his and the other minority parties.

"Madam First Minister," Rammon began without waiting for her to speak, "information has come to our attention which requires an immediate response from you. It concerns certain military matters."

"My Military Minister," Mordieu said, frowning slightly, "is always available to respond to enquiries of that nature. Why don't you direct your questions to him?"

"The nature of the information goes beyond his area of competence," Rammon said. Mordieu saw his eyes were cold and hard, and so were those of the others. She started to speak again but Rammon held up his hand. Surprised by the effrontery, she remained silent.

"First, we are informed that a regiment of our armed forces has landed on Kodomir without invitation. In effect, an invasion force."

"That's not precisely true," Mordieu began. "The threat from von Bender…"

"There is no threat from von Bender, not to us yet. An Alliance move against Kodomir, a move without invitation, at present is meaningful only as a springboard for future operations against the Holdings, and we are aware of no decision on the part of the Alliance Assembly to start such a war. Indeed," Rammon said, leaning forward and putting his hands on her desk, "your party came to power with a platform explicitly stating that you were going to find a negotiated settlement with the Free Union and its member state, the Benderist Holdings." He straightened back up.

"Second, we are informed that for the past year you have ordered the Military Minister to slowly and surreptitiously transfer forces in the direction of the Holdings and Kodomir and other preparations needed for war." Again, Rammon held up a hand. "This is a violation of the Alliance Charter in that no military activities of this kind are to be taken without due notification and compliance of representatives of the Assembly and the worlds it represents."

"Third, we have information that for the past year you have used Alliance funds to hire mercenary units to conduct a series of attacks against Kodomir, a world at peace with the Alliance. Again, this is a violation of the Charter." Rammon fell silent for a moment. "These attacks could have served as a justification for the Free Union to counterattack and we would have found ourselves in a war."

For a moment no one moved. Mordieu's mind raced but she found it almost impossible to focus on one thought. She started to stand and then sagged back in her chair.

"You should be aware," Rammon went on, "that leaders of your party have disowned your activities. They are going to introduce a bill of impeachment, though it will not be the first one. We," he said gesturing to the others, "are introducing our own bill as we speak."

He nodded to one of the representatives who walked back to the doors of the office and threw them open. Two general officers and a small group of soldiers were waiting.

"Your impeachment is the least of your concerns," Rammon said. "Your actions are, under the Charter, criminal and, given the use of the mercenaries, constitute war crimes. Therefore, you are going to be placed under arrest pending trial." He motioned to the soldiers and they marched in. "You will accompany these people and await the pleasure of the Assembly."

For a moment Mordieu sat still, unmoving, barely breathing. After a pause, a general motioned to the soldiers and two stepped forward and, half lifting her from her chair, began to lead her away. She looked back, her face anguished, but still could not find words.

Rammon sighed and turned to the generals.

"Gentlemen, I recommend that our regiment on Kodomir leave there and return to our space immediately. I remind you that the investigation into Mordieu's actions will include the military's involvement. I don't think I have to say anything else." The generals glanced at one another, clicked their heels and half bowed to Rammon and the others, and quickly left the room with the other soldiers.

Rammon turned to the other representatives and shook his head.

"The whole Settled Worlds is plunging into chaos as a result of the Free Union – Protectorate War and she wanted us to join it." He looked at the wall map. "If Carmichael and von Bender are looking for a pretext to attack the Alliance, she has given it to them." Rammon turned to the others. "Well, let us be off. There is much we must do." He shook his head again. "Starting with a diplomatic apology to the Kodomiri."

The wind had blown steadily for two days. Fortunately, it was not one of the savage winds that periodically lashed Portaka. The dust, when it came, remained low to the ground. For the man lying in the twisted desert bushes on the hill overlooking the Militia facility, visibility was not impaired. He could clearly see the facility, what was left of it, and the Benderist troops and HUPAX patrolling its perimeter.

Gwielgi noted the time displayed in his binoculars as he saw a convoy forming up. Water-laden tanker trucks and a pair of light Saber HUPs as escorts left the base heading west. He guessed one of the Benderist battalions was out there somewhere. Another was south of the base; he had evaded it when he came up from his exploration sector swinging around it and the base as he made his way to his current position in the hills just north of the facility. He could see a third battalion was squatting on the base, along with what was probably the brigade's command and support HUPs. There would be another battalion around somewhere, probably behind him to the north. And a fifth around Portaka City, covering their rear and the bay. Over a hundred HUPAX. Just one brigade and it outnumbered the all of the Militia's HUP force at better than three to one odds.

Gwielgi moved his binoculars a little. There they were again. Three times a day a column of people in Militia uniforms were led from the gymnasium, one of the few still intact buildings, to a new, Benderist-built prefabricated single-story building. Given the proximity of the other structures the brigade had thrown up in neat rows near it, it was probably a messhall.

His earlier observations of the dozen hostages had not permitted him to see their faces. This new position, slightly higher, gave him a better view. Gwielgi carefully examined each face. A few looked familiar, perhaps people he had seen around a Militia base, but most were strangers. There was one, though, that he kept bringing his binoculars to.

William Coltrane.

What was the Chekinov leader doing down here? He studied the group again. They were all in Militia uniforms, most in the general field uniform of olive drab. But not Coltrane. He was wearing desert camouflage. Well, yes, that made sense. As the OIC of the Chekinov Scout battalions, he was a major in the Militia. Maybe he had been down here for one of the desert training schools. Looks like he was a little slow to get out of town when the Benderists landed.

Gwielgi looked around the facility. He saw few troops. Portaka was hot, entering the middle of its summer, and the Benderists were staying under cover. Roving HUPs, mostly light ones, guarded the perimeter. Gwielgi shook his head. This was typical. People got their hands on HUPAX and they began to believe they could do everything.

He reached up and adjusted his sand-colored shemagh scarf, pulling it up over his nose. The last of the Benderist landing ships was launching and the flare of light from its engines rivaled the sun. Gwielgi felt a brief vibration in the ground beneath him as the thunder of its lift-off rumbled across him. Very quickly it was high enough to leave a brief contrail and then it was gone, like all the others that he had watched that morning. Now none remained. They probably did not want them to be caught on the ground in a surprise attack.

The question was, an attack by whom? The flash warning from the mining company was brief and he found it hard to believe. Both the Alliance *and* the Benderists were landing on Portaka? Well, for two days he had watched the Benderists and still didn't know if they getting ready to go to war with Kodomir or the Alliance or both. Gwielgi sighed. He saw movement on the base and brought the binoculars back to his face.

The prisoners were trooping back to the gymnasium, guards flanking them. Short lunch, apparently. He dialed the binoculars to a higher magnification. Ah, that was it. They were carrying their food back with them.

He lowered the binoculars. Watching the facility, going back to his hidden vehicle at irregular intervals for food and water and to snatch a few brief hours of sleep, had provided him with little understanding of what was really going on.

Gwielgi slowly moved back, careful not to kick up any dust. Once behind the low hill he continued to back away, obscuring his tracks as he went. It was probably an unnecessary precaution – the Benderist HUPs never came this far out while doing their circuit patrols.

Gwielgi dropped down onto a rock-strewn wadi. He moved north, staying on the rocks as much as possible. Only a trained tracker would have been able to tell he had been there and he had seen no one from the Benderists even bothering to patrol on foot, much less track.

A kilometer up the wadi Gwielgi walked into a side ravine. His vehicle, covered with several desert shrubs, rested behind a tight turn. The plants were not simply lying there. He had made mounds of earth on the vehicle and replanted them. They were doing better than when they were growing wild, he decided.

He checked his condensers. Using solar power, they sucked water from the air. It wasn't a lot, but it was a good supplement to his supplies.

Which were running low. The company was supposed to bring him in a resupply of food and equipment, but they were not flying their helicopters under these circumstances. Well, he could live off what he caught or scrabbled from the desert. Water, though, that was a major issue. Even with the condensers, he had to get a resupply.

He could always get out of here. Four kilometers north, beyond the likely location of the northern Benderist battalion, there was an abandoned exploratory mine with a wellhead. All he had to do was get there and attach his vehicle's pump and he could bring up all the crystal clear, ice-cold water he wanted. He looked south. Sure, there was water south, in the Militia facility, and it was a lot closer, but he had no desire to try to sneak into there; it would definitely be a major risk, real trouble, and even start the war everyone thought might be about to break out.

Gwielgi broke out his satellite communication unit. There was the expected message from the company. They still did not have permission to fly their resupply helicopters. Looked like the Benderists had a fifth battalion sitting on top of their old refining complex to the west. Well, there was still the water to the north.

Gwielgi took a long drink and chewed some food without tasting it. He leaned against the vehicle. It would be dark in six hours. Good opportunity to pull out of here and head north to that ice cold water.

Yes, it would be a good chance to get away. Gwielgi began packing gear. It was time for him to be traveling.

Chapter 19: Ultimatum

10 December 2824

It was almost nine in the morning at Coyote Bay. Colonel Kheyntamenti paused and looked at his senior officers sitting in the briefing room. His presentation was broadcast to the rest of the battalion.

"So that is what we know. The Alliance regiment is deployed around an old, shut down refining complex about fifty kilometers west of the Portaka Militia facility, probably because it has water. The Benderist brigade is using our facility and has a group of our people as hostages. As I speak diplomatic efforts are underway to get both sides to withdraw. We don't know if any of those efforts are going to be effective. If they are not, then it will be up to the Militia to persuade them to leave."

"The Alliance, as you can see from the order of battle, has a combined arms regiment, the 21st Grenadiers, built around seventy HUPs. It also has a mobile infantry force with armor support and some self-propelled artillery. The Benderist Brigade, the 173rd, is almost entirely HUPAX. One hundred and five of them, to be exact, of varying weights." Someone made a low whistle. "Indeed, in raw firepower the 173rd Armored Brigade is the stronger of the two, though I would put my money on the 21st with its greater tactical flexibility and combat experience. They were blooded in Frontier clashes with Raiders, as were the Benderists, but they also fought in skirmishes here in the Settled Worlds. Both sides are actively patrolling the area between them but have so far been very careful not to engage."

"General Polrany's staff has developed military contingency plans." He smiled. "You know the general. He believes in very fast, very flexible fighting, which is exactly the business we are in. I think we can all count on some very interesting experiences if we have to fight."

"In the meantime, while the diplomats make their move, I want to ensure everything is ready and razor sharp. All company commanders will report to me as to their units' status hourly. We remain on alert, ready to launch, so let's make sure we have topped off on supplies, especially water, and ammunition. Whatever comes our way, we will take care of it." Kheyntamenti paused. "I am with you."

All those in the room stood and repeated the Wild Geese phrase back and the briefing ended. As Kheyntamenti stepped away from the podium, Lieutenant Elinshen met him.

"Sir, flash traffic from regiment," she said, handing him a single sheet of paper. He glanced at it and raised his eyebrows.

"I take it they have authenticated this."

"Yes, sir. They sent a message back through the mining company with a query only he would know the answer to." She nodded. "This is from Captain Gwielgi."

"*Mister* Gwielgi is no longer a member of the Militia," Kheyntamenti said. He read the note a second time. "Though that may be about to change."

First Minister Alexis Jevon sat behind his desk and attempted to look calm, though his heart was racing. To one side stood Philip Deal and both men were watching the main door to the First Minister's office. Perhaps the fate of Kodomir was about to walk through it.

The doors swung wide, silently, and in walked Counselor-General Serena Richelieu. As always, she appeared supremely confident. Today she was dressed in the semi-military style of the Alliance Foreign Services Department.

Come to deliver the final ultimatum. Jevon knew the sparring was over. Now would come the killing blow, and he knew what it would be. Declare for the Alliance or be occupied. As she walked towards Jevon, he knew the last of a large convoy of Alliance landing ships was departing from newly arrived star ships. The first group was already over Kodomir and he also knew a shuttle from the flagship had landed a minute earlier at Kiroff Airfield.

True, all appropriate space traffic protocols were observed. Each landing ship captain was careful to announce his or her intentions and cargo, but that only served to emphasize how many of them they were and how powerful a card the Alliance was playing.

Their cargo, after all, was the Alliance elite 5th Assault Regiment, just the sort of people you would want for a planetary conquest. Jevon frowned slightly. Now the Alliance had two regiments to play with. Deal told him that the 5th was the Alliance "fire brigade," tapped for emergency situations. They had their own dedicated landing ships and generally were found on the Alliance border closest to any perceived threat.

Well, I guess that's us. Or, at least, the Benderist Holdings.

Jevon wasn't surprised to see their arrival. There had been no response to the message sent to the Alliance Parliament through the subspace communication system. But a friendly diplomat had passed the word through his Kodomiri trade delegation that there was some kind of political firestorm racing through the Alliance capital on Totenheim. Probably mobilizing for war. Probably the message had served to speed up the Alliance plans rather than derail them.

Congratulations, Alexis. For the second time you are responsible for the conquest of Kodomir by her enemies.

Richelieu stopped in front of his desk. She nodded to Deal but kept her eyes on Jevon, who remained sitting.

"First Minister Jevon," she began, "the political situation on and around Kodomir has reached a crisis stage, I regret to say." There was no tone of regret in her voice, Jevon noticed. "Therefore, the Alliance, in order to stabilize the situation, must beg your indulgence as we ask you to finally declare for the Alliance and secede from the Free Union which has betrayed you. Together, I have no doubt we can expel these Benderist invaders, the same people who sold Kodomir to the Raider unit commanded by Iriki Tykaw and permitted the unleashing of a series of horrors on Kodomir."

Jevon held up his hand, cutting her off. Enough.

"I do not need," Jevon said, "to be reminded of the horrors – I was on Kodomir. I also do not need to be reminded that the Benderists landed on

Kodomir *after* the Alliance forces did, and both forces did so without consultation with the government of Kodomir." He slowly stood.

"I would call your attention to that Raider unit you referred to. I invite you to visit where we buried them, and count their dead. Storm Cloud no longer exists. It took us a while, but eventually we sent those invaders to hell." He leaned forward, his hands on the top of his desk. "You might think about that and remember that we did all that when we were small, weak, with little military force of our own. Times change, Counselor General, and Kodomir is ready, if need be, to fight to preserve its integrity."

He folded his arms. "We know about the 5th Regiment. Well, if we have to fight them as well we will and..." His voice trailed off as he watched a confused look come over Richelieu's face. He glanced at Deal. She doesn't know about the 5th's arrival?

His desk speaker buzzed. He punched the intercom button and a staffer's voice emerged.

"Sir, Senior Colonel Alfredo Garcia Petron, the commanding officer of the Alliance 5th Assault Regiment, offers his compliments and begs permission to address you." The staffer seemed startled. Jevon, now confused himself, mumbled his assent and again the tall, polished doors of his office swung open.

Senior Colonel Garcia Petron was tall, well-tanned, and very thin. He was also clad in a field uniform. Jevon noticed that his holster was empty, probably a requirement of the Kodomir security force. He marched forward as if he was on parade. He ignored Richelieu and came to attention in front of Jevon and brought his fingertips to the bill of his soft cap in a salute.

"First Minister Jevon, I bring the greetings of the Alliance Assembly, and the personal greetings of Prime Minister Joaquin Rammon." Jevon saw Richelieu's face drain of blood and for a moment he thought the woman was going to faint. The soldier snapped his arm down to his side. Then he removed an envelope from a large pouch on his belt and handed it to Jevon. "I was told to personally hand this to you, sir."

Jevon took the large envelope and noted the various Alliance seals on it without comprehension. He pulled the tab and extracted a single page of paper and began reading. He looked up at the colonel and then sat down and read it again. Finally, he handed the letter to Deal. He carefully folded his hands and placed them on his desk. He took a deep breath.

"The other regiment will leave when?"

"As soon as you grant permission for its landing ships to land. I have told them to form up to evacuate. If you give the word now, sir, the 21st will be entirely off Kodomir within ten days. We will have to do some shuttling with their landing ships to get them all onboard the waiting star ships, but it will not take more than ten days."

"Consider permission granted," Jevon said. He turned his head to Deal. "Tell General Polrany to let them land and let traffic control know as well." Deal nodded and began speaking quietly into his small communication unit.

"Sir," Petron said, "while you are tending to that issue, may I have two of my officers join us for a moment?"

Jevon nodded and spoke into his intercom. Almost immediately two younger Alliance officers strode in. Like their commander, their sidearms were missing. Garcia Petron turned to Richelieu.

"You are under arrest," he said. "Your involvement in acts of war against Kodomir and other activities are known to Parliament. You are stripped of all rank and diplomatic status." He looked at Jevon. "I am instructed that the Alliance will waive all rights and protections of this person if the government of Kodomir wishes to pursue any charges of its own. Otherwise, she will be returned to Totenheim for trial and punishment." Jevon shook his head. Even as he struggled with the shock of sudden changes, part of him knew it would be far better to get Richelieu as far from Kodomir as possible.

"Very well, sir." Garcia Petron said. "If at some point in the future your government wishes to extradite her or Mordieu, I am further instructed to inform you that the request will be looked on with favor." He turned back to Richelieu.

"These officers will escort you off Kodomir and return you to Totenheim." He turned away from her while the officers took her by the arms and led her away. He said nothing until the doors closed.

"I am told she and Mordieu hired mercenaries to strike at Kodomir. Is that true?"

Jevon nodded, still taking in the sudden change in events.

"I think she is going to find prison a very unhappy place for a woman of her abilities," the colonel said.

"I am a little surprised, Senior Colonel," Jevon said carefully, "that the Alliance elected to send the whole 5th just to arrest her and deliver this message."

"Sir," Garcia Petron said, clearly uncomfortable, "the 5th is here for two reasons. The first is to ensure the 21st Grenadiers Regiment does not, ah, misunderstand its orders. After speaking with its commanding officer, I am sure there will be no such misunderstandings. The second reason," he continued, now not at all uncomfortable, "is to ensure the Benderist brigade does not interfere with our evacuation."

"I understand," Jevon said. For the first time he smiled. "Are you familiar with the contents of the message from Prime Minister Rammon?"

"Yes, sir."

"And the part about, 'all assistance short of armed conflict?'"

"Yes, sir. I regret we cannot do more about the Benderists, but the present political situation in the Alliance..."

"I understand. But let me run an idea past you and see if it is acceptable. You might be able to do more than you guess..."

Chapter 20: Intervention

11 December 2824

Lieutenant General Mannheim ordinarily passed on breakfast, but today he found himself in the prefab building the 173rd Armored Brigade used for its officers' messhall. The food was nondescript, but he was nonetheless delighted. The 173rd's commanding officer, an ambitious colonel named Halleck, sat across from him and it seemed that he was hardly able to take a bite without another interruption from his communications unit. And each interruption was good news.

Mannheim took a nibble of very dry toast and reached for his coffee to wash it down when Halleck smiled again. More good news.

"Another one is landing now, general. Our scouts report their battalions are continuing to fall back to the area around the abandoned processing plant."

"Outstanding," Mannheim said. "They really are going to leave. Baer has pulled another rabbit out of his hat."

"Yes, sir, it looks that way." Halleck took a sip of his coffee. "Frankly, I was a little worried when the other Alliance fleet arrived. I thought we were going to have a fight of it."

"I don't think those parliamentarians have the stomach for a real war," Mannheim said. "It is one thing to face down a planetary militia, or hold off Frontier bandits, or even engage in some border firefights, but to face an opponent who would take the war to their precious Alliance, that would be another thing entirely."

"You're right, general," Halleck said. "Now all we have to deal with is this local militia."

"I don't think they will fight us now, colonel," Mannheim said. "Before, they might have relied on one side to help them fight the other. But now they stand alone. They have, what did your intelligence officer say, somewhere around 30 HUPs? And some of those belong to two different *mercenary* units?" The general shook his head. "We outnumber them better than three to one and we are already on their only base on this continent, close to their primary mining and industrial complexes. What are they going to do, *attack* us?"

Colonel Halleck smiled. "I wish they would, sir, so we could settle this and get out of this place." He stood and glanced out the window as a dark blue and green Benderist HUP strode past.

"Prefer a cooler clime, eh?" Mannheim smiled. "Well, we do what duty and honor require, colonel, what duty and honor require."

"It is about honor," Marjessa Boyington said quietly. The four other Aniwaya and the senior ship officers, sitting behind the long table in the star ship ready room, looked at her with serious expressions. They understood honor. She stood in Currahee uniform, her legs slightly spread, her hands clasped behind her.

"I wish to show you the recording of my meeting with our Council, when I made the request for the journey we are on, so you might better understand why we are here. Though I doubt any of you need additional understanding." Boyington stepped to one side and the tri-vid projectors flashed into life as the room darkened.

The imagery solidified and they saw Captain Boyington standing before another long table with the Council, the senior military leadership, of the Currahee armed forces seated behind it.

"It is about honor," they heard her say. Several at the table nodded in response.

General James Younger was one of those nodding. Born on Foundland, one of the original nine worlds of the group that became the Currahee Encampment, he commanded the Aniwaya, the armed forces. His personal combat record in fighting Raiders and Settled World invaders was well known. He would understand the clarity of focus provided by the word "honor."

It was rumored that Younger favored renewed contact with the Settled Worlds, but if he did, he kept it to himself. Among the Currahee, the military did not dictate policy but carried it out.

"Captain, your determination to rise to the obligation incurred by the liberation of our people on Farnham does you honor. You and the other three warriors fought for the liberation of Kodomir against the Raiders who held them in bondage. I am gratified to see you do not have a simplistic view."

"Thank you, General. What they did for us, what they did for our children, there can never be a simple balancing of the scales. I realized this after our own punitive expedition to Farnham and some time with our Elders. I spent many hours in meditation." She looked at the officers behind the table. "I consulted with several of you, trying to gain clarity, understanding."

"I believe our debt to them has made us Blood to the Wild Geese, in the traditional and formal sense of the word. If that is true, we no longer have a debt to be paid but siblings to serve. Thus, our path seems clear to me."

Younger leaned back in his chair, his sharp eyes shaded by his furrowed brows.

"When we learned of your enslavement, many felt the universe was extracting retribution against our people. As you recall, the Elders' Council discussed the issue for weeks. It was the most watched broadcast of any tri-vid program ever offered in the Encampment. The testimony of the children gave us much to think about, and much to remember from our past. Slavery…" He paused and then carefully folded his hands on the table.

"I believe there are few among the Currahee who would dispute your judgment, which comes at a time when the information we receive from Kodomir is grim. Two powerful forces have converged upon it. Our political leaders have pointed out that Kodomir, if it were supported by us, might provide us with an ally in the Settled Worlds flanking the Free Union. On the other hand, such intervention might provoke the Free Union into turning on us. Kodomir is well distant from us, to be sure, but our intended new colony, which your convoy was to begin, is not too far beyond it in the Frontier. As it is, the attempt to resurrect the old colonization plan of three centuries ago, to develop a sanctuary outside the Encampment, is in stasis again." He shook his head. "Balancing the political variables is difficult and the job of others. But your request is not about politics, but honor. Nonetheless, the simple reality is that the Aniwaya is not strong enough to fulfill our current obligations of protecting the Encampment and intervene significantly on Kodomir. And no political decision for intervention has been made or is likely to be made."

"I understand that, General. I seek permission only for a single platoon. Three pilots are immediately available, including me. We are the three who were the surviving HUPAX warriors and we have fought alongside the Wild Geese. The fourth and fifth position I would open to whoever would challenge for it." She paused. "A small group to both assist the Wild Geese and to seek clarification of the question of Blood."

"I see." He smiled. Knowing our warriors and our newest HUP pilots, the competition for those two positions could be very fierce. How do you propose to handle the applicants?

"A competition would be most appropriate, though I am concerned with the time that would be involved. I would think dozens, perhaps scores, of warriors would participate."

"I agree, Captain Boyington. Including time to arrange transportation by star ship, as well as the time of travel itself, it could be six weeks before you and your platoon arrive at Kodomir." He looked left and right and saw the silent nods of the others. So let it begin. The Aniwaya will provide a star ship and a single landing ship. He looked to his left. Colonel, we will use the Academy's simulators for the competition. Convey my respect to the commandant and ask her to ensure the simulator schedule is cleared. At the conclusion of this meeting, I will address our political leadership." He paused. "The competition will begin tomorrow. And honor will be served."

The imagery vanished and the lights came back on. Boyington stepped forward and addressed the other members of the platoon as well as the ship crew watching through the intercom system.

"The eyes of the Currahee are on us," Boyington said. "Over three hundred went as slaves into the mine at Farnham, after seventy died trying to protect the rest. You know what the slavers did, once they realized they had people of the Currahee. They became afraid. They should have been. They sent a small number of adults with all our children as a work team

287

away from the others. Separated from their children, three hundred rose up with their bare hands. They were murdered, sealed within a tunnel, suffocated. A half dozen adults, three of us Aniwaya, and over thirty children were put to work following the small seams of gems. They let the children live because their small bodies could follow the narrow seams so much more cheaply and precisely than any machines. They let us live because we took care of the children."

"We swore we would live to bury the slavers, and we did that." There were nods from the others. "But that was just simple justice. And, it is true, honor must be based on justice or it runs the risk of being a tool for tyrants and manipulators. Our honor has led the Currahee on a road that none could have foreseen and now it leads us to Kodomir." Boyington shook her head.

"These people we go to assist, who are they? They never claimed to be more than a unit of Settled Worlds mercenaries. Some were born among those worlds, as we expected, and a handful came from the Encampment, though none speak much of their pasts." She shrugged. "One thing the Currahee have learned is that honor is not in the birth but in the life. And these are honorable people. At first, I saw them simply as mercenaries. I was grateful for our liberation and would have sought some way to reward them, to balance the scales and pay our debt."

"But when Kodomir fought for its freedom and there was no more money to pay them, they picked up their weapons and fought for those people, despite the odds they faced. They fought for justice, they fought intelligently, and they fought ferociously. They fought, in other words, like Currahee. I realized there was much more to these people than I had thought. I recognized a bond with them, one that transcended origins. Puzzled, I studied and contemplated and sought, as you heard in my meeting with the Council, guidance from our Elders and others. I withdrew to a cloister until I could come to an understanding of what was the nature of the link I felt to them."

"The essence of a warrior, we have always been taught, is to be found in honor. But what is the essence of honor?" Boyington smiled. "You remember the classes, the instruction before our Elders when you sat as a child. We recited the answers to those questions with a child's comprehension. Only battle brought the true answers to our hearts and minds. The essence of a warrior's honor is not in killing – anyone can kill."

She paused, her mind going back to a bloody morning on an ice-locked world. "No, that is not where honor is. You and I know the essence of a warrior's honor is in enduring for one's people. This is what I saw in those strange people called the Wild Geese."

"When I struggled with the question of how to pay the debt we owed, I finally realized it was not simply a debt of lives, but one of *honor*. And that is a debt we owe to ourselves and can never be finally paid. When I talked with my Dideyohvsgi he gently guided me to understand that what I saw in them is what I see in us. A warrior's honor. In the ancient and first sense of the word, what I saw is that they were our Blood. Not of genetics, but of the spirit."

"This is why I go to aid them now." Boyington paused, nodded, and then sat down. For a moment no one moved. Then Rhiannon Dwyer stood. She looked at the others seated around her.

"Captain Boyington speaks from the heart," Dwyer said. "When she secluded herself in contemplation, I understood she was grappling with an important question. I do not dispute her conclusions. We have all learned that there are those of the Settled Worlds whose qualities are the equal of any Currahee warriors." She lowered her head for a moment.

"I see our journey as fulfillment of a debt of honor. We were made slaves, our people murdered, our children captive. They freed us and avenged our losses; they restored us to freedom. My honor holds that is a debt that can never be fully repaid. Are they Blood? I do not know. But our relationship to them is real and cannot be severed. Thus," she smiled slightly and bowed her head towards her friend, "you may regard both of us as responding to honor, though mine is a shade darker than our Captain." She sat back down.

Slowly Charlene Tanner rose. "When Marjessa told me she was going to have this final convocation before we made our last leap to Kodomir, my first reaction was that no meeting to explain the why of the journey was necessary. We are Aniwaya of the Currahee, and I will fight beside any Currahee, any time, against any odds." There were several nods from around the table. "I was present when she spoke to the Council, but it is only today that I think I truly grasp their significance. I am a simpler person than she and I do not have her words. But what I think is, these people, these strangers named after birds, these people became *our* people by what they were willing to do for us. Whether they know it or not, desire it or not, they are of us. Now they are facing terrible odds, again. And as before, Currahee do not leave their own behind. For me, that is how it is." She sat down and folded her hands in front of her.

A tall, young man stood at the end of the table. His name was Kyle and his rank showed him to be a lieutenant. He glanced at another man sitting next to him, who nodded encouragingly. He cleared his throat.

"Vissack and I were not with you on Farnham." Kyle paused. "I believe that we see this journey as most of the Currahee do. Are these people Blood? I do not know – that is such a powerful question that I understand quite easily Captain Boyington's need for withdrawal and contemplation. Before the Currahee were Currahee, our history tells us, our people gathered on the basis of survival but found we shared values, beliefs, and honor. They were Blood to one another, and I understand that is the use of the word she means when referring to the Wild Geese." Boyington nodded in agreement.

"For me, then, this journey is indeed about honor, the honor of a warrior in defending another warrior. Those who freed my people are facing difficulties. They have not asked for assistance, which I find in keeping with a warrior's ethic. This would be enough of a reason to go to Kodomir, I think." Kyle smiled. "There is also, I admit, the personal – I am Aniwaya and I look to do battle in a warrior's cause. This cause, defending those who saved our children, is the right cause." He sat back down. He looked at the other man, who smiled and stood.

Vissack was much shorter than the first man and a bandage could be seen protruding slightly from beneath his collar.

"Well, when Kyle and I entered the competition," he said while pulling gently at his collar, "my thinking was very simple. This was a chance to excel as a warrior. Garrison duty was boring me, and if I had to walk one more student through the basic syllabus, I think I would have gone insane." There were smiles from the others and several chuckles. "So, I placed my name into the competition. And that was *not* boring." Again, he fingered his collar and several people laughed. He waited a moment and then his expression turned serious.

"I read the account of what happened to our people on Farnham. I saw how Boyington, Dwyer, and Tanner kept the survivors alive. A debt of honor to the people on Kodomir or the Wild Geese? I do not dispute that. Clearly, there is. But there *is* a debt to the three warriors who brought their people home. That is why I am here, to pay that debt of honor. If you three decided to drop into Hell, the Currahee, I, would follow you." Vissack sat down abruptly, looking slightly embarrassed.

After a moment Boyington stood. "I called this council so that I might explain, if any explanation was needed, why I asked for the opportunity to go to Kodomir. I invited you all to speak, one to the rest, openly and forthrightly, as is our custom. We are not all the same, not exactly, but we all live, and die, by honor. I do not see any honor described in this council as darker than any other." Dwyer bowed her head briefly and Boyington returned the gesture.

"I am honored by your presence," she said. Boyington turned to the star ship captain. "Please tell your crew we are ready for the leap to Kodomir." She smiled. "Remind them we are simple wanderers, vagrant cargo haulers, nothing more than stray dogs looking for a small meal." Her smile grew larger. "Once on Kodomir we will let them see they have let a wolf into the fold."

Chapter 21: Pieces in play

12 December 2824

"Kodomir STC, star ship Long March. Do you copy?"

"Long March, this is Kodomir Space Traffic Control. How may we help you?"

"STC, the first thing you can do is tell me what the hell are all these other star ships doing here? Is there some kind of war going on?"

"Negative, Long March, not yet. Those are star ships hauling Alliance and Holdings forces. Their landing ships are in geosynchronic orbit. Keep your transponder on – no one has gone crazy enough to shoot at a star ship."

"Roger, STC. I have a free trader landing ship requesting permission to proceed to your facility at Coyote Bay to bid on processed ores."

"Copy, Long March. Put her captain on and we'll get the paperwork completed."

"STC, this is the captain of landing ship Stray Dog, Arden McCormick. We're an Alligator-class landing ship specializing in ore shipments but we'd be interested in hauling any cargo you need moved."

"Roger, Captain McCormick. My board shows two ore shipments at Coyote Bay open for bids plus a number of small cargos. You are cleared for entry to our airspace and touchdown at Coyote Bay."

"Thank you, Kodomir. I copy Coyote Bay. Projecting touchdown in four days. I have a message from a passenger for a Kodomiri citizen in Coyote Bay. Can you link us up?"

"Negative, Captain, sorry. We don't have the waveband link for private communications but I can relay. Who is sending it and to whom?"

"Roger, STC. The message is from Marjessa Boyington and it is to Alisti Mahmud al-Kheyntamenti, Coyote Bay. She says to say she and four friends are looking forward to seeing him again. That's it, nothing else. Please pass along her arrival date with the message. Many thanks."

"No problem, captain. Pleasure of the house, Stray Dog."

"Roger, that."

"Colonel, may I have a moment?"

Kheyntamenti looked up from his paperwork and saw Gunnery Sergeant Charles Tsunasdi standing in the doorway. As usual, the former Currahee had appeared silently, moving with a cat's grace. Kheyntamenti leaned back in his chair and motioned to the NCO to enter. Tsunasdi walked forward and positioned himself opposite Kheyntamenti, his hands clasped behind his back. He was silent for a moment, waiting. Kheyntamenti pushed his papers aside.

"What can I do for you, sergeant?"

"Sir, there is a rumor going around that Captain Gwielgi is in contact with the battalion." Kheyntamenti leaned back in his chair.

"Sergeant, I seem to be reminding every other person I meet that it is Mister Gwielgi." He suppressed a smile. "As for the rumor, I can say he has made contact, intermittently, with me."

"I thought that might be the case, sir. I have another question, then, if I may?"

Kheyntamenti had never gotten use to the formality that Currahee tended to fall into, especially when talking about some subject considered particularly important.

"Of course, sergeant," he said.

"Sir, Captain, ah, *Mister* Gwielgi left somewhat abruptly. Did he leave a forwarding address?"

Kheyntamenti tapped his fingertips on his desk. "No, he did not. Sergeant, it would be best if there were no speculation on the whereabouts of your friend or his current activities. It is public knowledge that he took a position with the Southern Resource Development Corporation and I think that is where matters ought to lie."

The sergeant stood for a moment, clearly uncomfortable. Finally, he nodded to Kheyntamenti and started to turn away.

"Hold a minute, sergeant," Kheyntamenti said. He paused. "What is going on?"

Tsunasdi said nothing for a moment and for the first time since joining the Wild Geese he did not meet Kheyntamenti's eye. The colonel, surprised, took it to mean something serious was at issue. He motioned to a chair and the sergeant sat down slowly.

"Sir," Tsunasdi said, "I do not know how much you know of the Currahee. But you remember my interview with you when I joined the Wild Geese. I told you I had been declared weak-heart, coward, and that I came to the unit on the recommendation of Gwielgi."

"I remember all that, sergeant, and I remember telling you your status with the Currahee was immaterial."

"Yes, sir. Do you remember, sir, when I told you about how I met Gwielgi?"

"I think I do," Kheyntamenti said, nodding. "You were in two different mercenary units, and yours was raiding a planet his was defending. You were wounded and he saved your life."

"A little more than that, sir, but close enough. He kept the local militia from killing me on the spot and he prevented me from killing myself. Twice." He grimaced. "I wanted him to make me his Dedeloquasgi, so that I might earn my honor and freedom, but he would have nothing to do with the concept. Gwielgi saw it as slavery." Tsunasdi's voice trailed off.

"He has an aversion to slavery that is very long standing," Kheyntamenti said. "If he could make a living at it, I think he would devote his life to hunting slavers down." And killing them.

"Yes, sir. And he knew of the Currahee before we were Currahee."

"What do you mean?"

"Sir," Tsunasdi said, shifting his weight, "this is not easy to talk about." He paused. "After the Third Interstellar War, when the area of the Settled Worlds contracted, you know about the original nine worlds that found themselves in the Frontier."

"Yes," Kheyntamenti replied. "The collapse of the Arcturan Empire, about 300 years ago. Whole colonial worlds were abandoned. The nine you referred to had been on different sides of the war, as I recall."

"Yes, sir," Tsunasdi replied. "Cut off, basically abandoned, they overcame their differences and united for self-protection. Raiders, various powers in the Frontier, it was a dangerous time."

"And didn't the Currahee have to give up two of the nine worlds?"

"Yes, sir. They had become unviable as settlements during the war. But we weren't called Currahee then. Do you know where the name came from?"

"It was the name of one of the nine worlds. I always assumed it took a leadership position in some way."

"It did, but not in the way you think, sir," Tsunasdi said. "During the evacuation of the two worlds, we call it the Black Trail, the people on Greenhome were moved to Foundland. They were guarded by soldiers from Currahee. The idea was that each world would guard another world's people. It would promote confidence. But as the last convoy landed on Foundland, Raiders hit and in overwhelming strength." He paused. "The soldiers from Currahee stood their ground. They refused to surrender, though it was offered to them, twice. They knew the Raiders wanted to take slaves and the people of Currahee hated slavery. So they fought for the people of another world. When it was over the Raiders were driven off but the detachment was virtually annihilated before reinforcements arrived. Only one soldier survived and was very badly wounded."

"All our people took the name 'Currahee' in honor of those soldiers," Tsunasdi said, "but there was more to it than that. As they tried to find, to build, a common ground for the people of what had been nine different worlds, they adopted more and more of the culture of the Currahee people as their foundation. Onto that was grafted much from the other worlds. The problem was, you see, and this is something we do not like to speak of, some of the worlds among the surviving seven had slaves. We finally abolished the practice when the Currahee Elders pointed out that we were doing to others what we would not have done to ourselves. It was not an easy process but our need for unity in the face of the dangers of the Frontier encouraged us. Few know of this dark part of our history. The Currahee, who to the inhabitants of the Settled Worlds appear as almost mythical knights in shining armor, reclusive in their monastery-like Encampment, had slaves." He fell silent for a moment. "We don't speak directly to this, not with outsiders, not with people who are not Blood."

"Gwielgi knows of this past," Tsunasdi said slowly. "When I asked to be his Dedeloquasgi, he saw it as just another word for 'slave.' And a Dede does surrender much control to his Dideyohvsgi, and the relationship can be rigid, student to teacher, recruit to instructor, but it is not slavery. It is voluntary, it is honorable, it brings honor to both." He sighed. "I think he understands now the difference between slaves and Dedeloquasgi, but he would never let me wear the mark of one. Nonetheless, I consider myself Dede to him and joined him in his unit and then here, with the Wild Geese." He raised his arm and pushed his sleeve back. A knotted bracelet made of a white cloth was around his wrist. "I should be wearing this all the time, but I have to hide it from Gwielgi. Usually, I only wear it in combat."

"Wait, sergeant," Kheyntamenti said, his brow furrowing. "From what I understand from the other Currahee I've known in the Geese, a Dedeloquasgi, a student, is released from that status and allowed to participate in Currahee life only by a Dideyohvsgi, the Dede's absolute teacher or mentor. The Dede 'graduates,'" he said as Tsunasdi nodded, "and begins to walk her or his own path. But if Gwielgi never knew that you considered yourself Dedeloquasgi...?"

"He doesn't know, sir." Tsunasdi shook his head as he lowered his arm. "I never told him that I interpreted his permitting me to live and taking me off the battlefield as making me his Dedeloquasgi, whether he accepted the idea or not."

"And why not?"

"Because he would have rejected it by sending me away," Tsunasdi said. "He saw the Dede's role of that of a bound servant and that concept touched his bones. He would have sent me away and my honor would have been vacated, dispersed." Tsunasdi fell silent for a moment. "I needed to be a Dede, *his* Dede."

"I think I see," Kheyntamenti said, nodding. "And, having been declared weak-heart, you need a way to regain your honor."

"Yes, sir," Tsunasdi said. He looked miserable. "Gwielgi left but I need..." Again, he fell silent.

"You need his acknowledgement that you have regained your honor? Am I being too simple?" Kheyntamenti's voice was soft.

"That is about it, sir, but there is a little more. You see, I knew a little about *why* he left and I should have helped him with the problem." He shook his head. "I did not. A Dede does not fail his Dedi, but I did.*"*

"Why did he leave, do you think?"

"Sir, he did something he regarded as dishonorable." Tsunasdi shrugged. "I would disagree with him about that, but my perspective is different."

Kheyntamenti tapped his desktop and thought for a moment.

"Sergeant, Gwielgi left because of what he did, but his concern was not about honor." He rubbed his cheek. "Your first encounter with him, when he took you prisoner and kept you from being killed. Why do you think he did that? Why did he show mercy to an enemy?"

"I did not understand it at the time, colonel," Tsunasdi said. "But I eventually came to understand that some Settled Worlds codes of conduct emphasize, to a greater degree than the Aniwaya, mercy." He shrugged. "An Aniwaya encountering Raiders on the battlefield would not accept their surrender, would not take them prisoner."

"Gwielgi showed you mercy *because* he is very cruel." Kheyntamenti leaned back in his chair and studied Tsunasdi's surprised expression. "This is between you and I, sergeant, and I will take your word that you will never repeat it to anyone else, including, if you happen to meet him again, Gwielgi."

"You have it, sir."

"I knew Gwielgi a long time ago, a very long time ago. We were both soldiers at the time and our paths crossed on several occasions and with greater frequency over the years. When I first met him, he was a 'free lance,' a mercenary, with no regard for the cause he fought for and almost as little for the pay." He shrugged. "Some get like that. He sought battle, killing, and all that followed. He was a survivor of slavery twice. The first time his master released him for his conduct on the battlefield. The second time, years later, he freed himself by killing his master and most of his master's family and many of his retainers."

"The experience left him with little in the way of a moral compass. Honor, if you had asked him, was for idiots and irrelevant. And so he was a soldier killing for no other reason than he was good at it and discovered he liked it. If he did anything good or worthwhile or honorable, it was accidental." Kheyntamenti stood up, remembering, and walked over to a small table to pour two mugs of Kodomiri tea. He handed one to Tsunasdi.

"We met well after he had been a slave the first time. He came across me when I had been left out to die by my enemies. He saved me simply because it amused him to do so. Then he left, looking for work as a mercenary." Kheyntamenti blew gently on his tea and took a sip. "He was ferocious in battle, sometimes foolishly so but usually cunning, and terrible afterwards. He tried other things. Did you know he was raised a farmer and worked as a schoolteacher? It was while a teacher he was taken as a slave for the second time. I told you how he freed himself. The killing of prisoners was the least of his actions, though there were a few lines he did not cross. He never took slaves or fought for slavers and, if he found them, he almost always found a way to kill them."

"That hatred of slavery eventually gave him the opportunity to find a moral focus for himself." Kheyntamenti sat down. "He finally saw a link between the cruelty of his behavior and the cruelty of slavery. He decided he would not be like a slaver. His problem, though, is that the impulse towards cruelty is always with him. His solution has been to be merciful, to compensate for the impulse. When he saved you, it was his effort to save himself." Kheyntamenti took another sip and put his mug down on his desk.

"As I said, he has tried other trades," Kheyntamenti said, "trying to get himself away from the battlefield and temptation. He has been a teacher, a miner, a writer, and a number of other things, but what he is best at is war. And so he has tried to harness that talent while controlling the danger it places him in and use it for something positive."

"I understand," Tsunasdi said. "There is a seduction in violence and if a person does not have a strong moral system, honor, then they can be taken away by it."

"That is his demon," Kheyntamenti agreed, nodding. "In that last mercenary raid, he found the chains he bound the demon with were slipping away. Perhaps his injuries, perhaps hearing of the death of Peregrine, perhaps it was just seeing his adopted home attacked again and again, perhaps all those things played a role, but the real issue for him was as it has always been, the darkness."

"And now?" Tsunasdi stared intently at his commanding officer.

"Now he is in a difficult position, one where he may be asked to struggle with the demon again." Kheyntamenti sipped his tea and looked out the window. They could see the ready landing ships on their pads.

"Sir, does he have to go into that struggle alone?"

"Ultimately, sergeant, we all do."

The Benderist patrol of three light HUPs of the northernmost battalion scanned the wind-ravaged metal shacks of the abandoned installation – they did not know what it had been used for – and for a moment saw nothing. Then the leader caught a glimpse of a ground vehicle moving away from it.

"Dash Two has a visual on what could be a Prowler, zero two zero at 800 meters."

"Lead copies. I have him, too."

"Want me to nail him?"

"Negative. We were told there were a couple of these prospectors around. They're harmless. Besides, if they find anything, it will be ours after we take this rock."

"Two, roger."

"And remember, we also don't want to be advertising our position if we don't have to until those Alliance clowns are gone. Looks like they're all leaving, but the colonel wants us to play it tight until they are out of sight."

"No witnesses, huh?"

"Yeah, Three, it may come to something like that. All right, he's gone into that canyon. Now let's go, we have another leg to run before we can get back to our prefabs and have a cold one. Heading three four zero, speed 60. Steer for that notch in the hills, that's our turnaround."

The three blue and green HUPAX were out of sight in less than a minute, leaving behind only their footprints in the hard ground of the Portaka desert. A slight breeze began to fill them in while the converted Prowler slowly edged out of the canyon.

Gwielgi scanned the horizon with his binoculars but could only see a little dust. The HUPs were gone. He stuffed the binoculars into a pouch and took a sip from a canteen. The mining company message had said the Benderists were allowing the surveyors to go on about their business, though everyone anywhere near their forces had elected to pull out.

Everyone except him.

Gwielgi checked his computer display. The Militia facility, now the headquarters of the 173rd, was more than twenty kilometers south of him. He had found the northern battalion's scouts and, through them, the headquarters of their battalion. He shook his head. All their patrols ran in fan-patterns. To find the point of origin, you only had to cut the tracks of two legs to be able to figure where they were, and he had cut five. He drove slowly forward until he came to the path of the HUPs. He aimed a compass down their route and took a bearing, which he fed into the computer.

Six thin red lines converged on a position about five kilometers south of him. They were using a shallow canyon that had once had a pit mine pulling borax out of the ground. According to his database, there were several buildings and structures there and, being in the canyon, they were probably in better shape than their age and the Portaka wind might suggest. Certainly, they had to be in better shape than the installation in front of him.

Gwielgi drove up to the abandoned buildings. It had been a surveyor base, back before they used helicopters and VTOL aircraft to lift surveyors into the back areas. Now only three buildings still stood, though their walls were marked by pitted metal sheeting and sand piled against them in drifts. He shut down his vehicle and got out.

Inside the first building, near a corner next to a big chunk of dust-covered machinery, a waist-high metal tube jutted up out of the ground. It was almost a meter across and capped with a flanged plate. Gwielgi attached a gripping wrench to a flange and then, making sure it was locked tight, leaned against it. Sometimes it took a lot of effort to remove a wellhead cover, but this one, after just a little hesitation, suddenly turned. Gwielgi turned the plate with the wrench until it was loose enough to use his hands.

Inside the tube was the much smaller well pipe. He attached the wrench to the cap of the pipe and was surprised to find that it, too, came relatively easy. As he removed the cap, water slowly oozed out of the pipe's mouth. He thought the water would be close to the surface, since the local aquifer was fed into by the hills surrounding the well. Gwielgi quickly spun the cap back on. No sense in wasting it.

Gwielgi went back to his vehicle and gathered up his water containers and a small pump with an attached hose. With the pump attached to the pipe, he let it slowly feed into the first container. His practiced eye estimated it would be about five minutes per container. That was fine, he was in no hurry.

While the first container slowly filled, Gwielgi broke out some food and turned on the satcom unit. He watched the unit's antenna begin its search while he heated some soup. It first talked to the vehicle's positioning system and decided where it was. Then it consulted a database of communication satellite trajectories, compared that with the current time, and then aimed the antenna up into the brilliant blue sky. The whole process took less than a few seconds.

A red light on the unit turned green. Contact. A yellow light flashed twice. Two messages. He took his soup and a piece of bread and sat in the driver's seat. The computer display had both messages ready.

12/12/24/1347L

To: G6

From: Surveyor Coordinator Office

Subj: Status

We have evacuated most staff from this office. Benderists continue to assure us there is no danger.

Alliance forces have agreed to depart Kodomir. Current estimate all ground units will be gone 12/20. Their units are pulling back to their central position, designated navigation point Tango. This is our old processing plant, closed about fifteen years ago.

Negotiations with Special Envoy Baer concerning overflights by resupply aircraft have thus far resulted in permission for one (1) flight to take place on 12/13/24/1200L. Request you update us on your position. If possible, try to get at least five (5) kilometers outside of their patrol zone. Enclosed you will find an update to your map database which shows their zone.

Be advised Militia is telling us that after the Alliance force leaves, the situation in Portaka will be highly volatile. After you are supplied, strongly recommend you consider lying low until things calm down.

<Signed> Bob Tallman

Director, Survey Operations

Southern Resource Development Corp.

<Enclosure>

Gwielgi flipped on his map display and saw the corporation overlay. The "patrol zone" the Benderists were claiming was far greater than they were actually patrolling, at least up here in the northern area. He tapped the keyboard and brought up the second message. He was surprised when the ENCRYPTED designation flashed on the screen. He accessed the encryption program and put it to work. After a few seconds, the second message flashed onto his screen.

12/12/24/1440L

To: G6

From: Surveyor Coordinator Office

Subj: Ore sample analysis 12/06/24B

Initial analysis of ore sample #12/06/24B extremely promising. Congratulations. Bonus already deposited your account.

Lab requests second sample if possible. Additional extraction tools to be included in resupply – see message 12/12/24/1347L.

Understand movement under current conditions problematical; if risk involved, use best judgment.

Be advised a great deal of concern was expressed about the possible loss of the claim site if we do not establish our precedence before competitors move in. Need second sample for final legal registration of claim. Exploitation of claim will commence as soon as practical, though details are on hold pending resolution of political situation.

<Signed> Bob Tallman

Director, Survey Operations

Southern Resource Development Corp.

Gwielgi walked back into the shed and changed containers. He placed the full one in its receptacle and locked it in place. Then he sat in the driver's chair again and stared at the message. The fact that it was encrypted didn't mean anything – ore reports always were in case competitors were listening in.

But he had submitted no ore sample on 12/06/24. He had no samples to submit, for one thing, and for another no helicopters were picking up samples and hadn't been since the Alliance and Benderists landed.

What he had done on 12/06/24 is send a message about the hostages.

"A second sample?" They wanted him to go back. And that meant this message wasn't really from the corporation. The encryption probably wasn't a major problem for Benderist military code breakers, hence the double-talk. What they meant about "Additional extraction tools" wasn't completely clear, but it read as if they wanted him to do something about getting them out.

Which was moderately insane. The hostages were merely in the middle of the Militia facility, which was only the headquarters of the Benderist 173rd Armored Brigade, otherwise known as the Red Cocks. He had seen the red rooster's head on the sides of the HUP fuselages as they stomped past.

If it was insane, then it meant that the message actually came from Alisti Mahmud al-Kheyntamenti. This was the kind of thing he would do. Hell, it was the kind of thing they had done together.

Gwielgi reread the fourth paragraph and nodded his head.

Yeah, I'll bet they're concerned about the loss of the claim. Von Bender's people will blow those hostages away when the first Militia soldier drops in. And they'll load all their HUPs into their landing ships and then they'll go downtown and obliterate Kiroff City or Coyote Bay or wherever the hell they want to go.

Gwielgi pulled himself out of the seat and walked back into the shed. The second container was full. He put the third under the hose and carried the full one back. He secured it, his movements rough.

As he slapped the final snap into place, Gwielgi spun around and walked away, his teeth clenched. He kicked a piece of rock across the ground and watched it bounce, kicking up little puffs of dust as it went. He looked up into the sky for a moment and then slowly closed his eyes.

Gwielgi sat back in the seat and checked the satcom antenna's alignment. Then he typed in a message.

To: Surveyor Coordinator Office
From:G6
Subj: Ore sample analysis 12/06/24B
Glad you are pleased. It may be extremely difficult to obtain second sample, given current situation. Nonetheless, when the opportunity presents itself, I will see if it is possible.

My position for resupply will be three kilometers NE of navigation point Lima. Will monitor SOP frequency for contact. Ask pilot to bring along some Highlander Red, if available.

<Signed> Gwielgi

He encrypted it – if anyone was intercepting their messages, they would expect that – and then sent it. Gwielgi sat in the vehicle for another moment and then roused himself to go get the last water container.

After he secured it, Gwielgi took a small bag from the vehicle and went back to the wellhead and stripped. He turned the pump on to a higher setting and wet himself down. Untying his ponytail, he washed himself, even his hair, and then carefully rinsed all the soap off. A small hand towel was enough to get dry in the Portaka desert.

After dressing, he carefully recapped the pipe. He inspected the flanged cover and then lined its threads with graphite compound. He spun it into place. Then he carefully erased his footprints, casting dust onto the pipe. The water soaked in the ground around the wellhead would be gone soon and there would be little trace of his being here or what the pipe was about.

Back in his vehicle, Gwielgi brought up his map. He was at navigation point Lima. All the old wellheads had a letter designation. His rendezvous was in a narrow canyon, well away from the Benderist patrol routes. He looked at the screen for a moment and finally sighed.

Gwielgi reached into the back. The semiautomatic rifle was secured in a rack. He pulled it free and levered the bolt, chambering a round. He clicked the safety on and put it back. Then he moved the holstered pistol from where it hung by its belt on the back of the passenger seat and placed it next to him. He looked at it for a moment. Then he got out of the Prowler and reached in and pulled out the belt and holster.

He strapped it around his waist and tied down the end of the holster. He reached behind him and adjusted the second pistol nestled in the small of his back. He moved the sheathed fighting knife hanging on the left back a little bit.

Gwielgi stood for a moment, his arms folded. Time was running out. Everything he had fled by escaping into the desert was gaining on him. He shook his head. No, not gaining on him – it had always been with him. He was going to have to make a decision, and soon. Gwielgi glanced up at the sky and then spat into the dirt. Nothing was clear, not about himself or what he would do.

He got back into the Prowler and drove away, heading for his rendezvous.

Chapter 22: Ultimatum repeated

13 December 2824

First Minister Alexis Jevon never considered himself a brave man; he had known fear so ferocious that he had wanted to throw up. Maneuvering with the Raider leader Iriki Tykaw had convinced him he was not of heroic stuff, whatever that was. He could not remember a time when he dealt with that sociopath that he did not leave with his hands trembling. The Assembly had voted him several accolades in response to his conduct during the War of Liberation. Being hailed as a hero had left him shaking his head. Could no one else see how afraid he had been throughout those terrible months? When he described, in all the speeches he had made in the aftermath of the war, how he felt that others were the true heroes of Kodomir's liberation, his remarks were always taken as a sign of his personal modesty, the kind of self-deprecation one would expect of, well, a hero.

I'm a politician – they assume everything I say is a lie, even when I say I wasn't a hero.

He was afraid again, afraid of the man standing in his office. Special Envoy Esteban Baer was a man worth being afraid of, according to the briefing Philip Deal had given him. Baer, after all, apparently scared Iriki Tykaw.

Baer held his cup of tea and gently blew on it, casual and relaxed as he sat next to an eternally smiling General Mannheim. He was wearing almost informal attire and smiling a great deal, as if the death of thousands, perhaps millions, was not what he was promising.

"My military people, then," Baer continued, "estimate the last Alliance soldiers will be gone from Kodomir within a week. In all modesty, I believe the Holdings can claim a small part of the credit for their departure." He took a sip of tea and nodded appreciatively. "Very good," he said as he put it down on the small table in front of him and pushed it to the furthest edge away. He looked up at Jevon.

"To return to my main point, First Minister," Baer said, his eyes ice, "I believe it appropriate for Kodomir to finalize its relationship with the Holdings once the Alliance forces are gone. I think our position is clear that Kodomir's vulnerability to the Alliance invaders is a threat to the Holdings. And the Holdings cannot tolerate such a threat." He paused, letting the words soak in.

"We are," Baer said in a friendly tone, "after all, both members of the Free Union. Nonetheless, while the Union has its concerns, the Holdings and Baron von Bender have their own. You understand, I think, that Prime Minister Carmichael does not object to the Holdings position in this matter – clearly, he sees the need for stability within the Union, and the threat of the Alliance would be greatly reduced if Kodomir was an integral part of the Holdings."

"If Kodomir does not declare for the Holdings, then I think it is clear that you will place us in a very difficult situation, one requiring the most extreme measures. I regret things have come to this point," he said, while his eyes showed no regret. "Our conditions are relatively straightforward and logical. Baron Karl von Bender will assume the responsibility for the defense of Kodomir, which will necessitate, of course, the conduct of Kodomir's foreign policy. In return, we will require a permanent base on Kodomir – Portaka will be a perfect position for our garrison. It will be well out of the way of most of Kodomir society. Of course, we expect reasonable support for our taking on the defense of your world. I think the resources of Portaka will accomplish this. Given their relatively undeveloped nature, this will not have a major impact on Kodomir." He sat back in his chair and brushed an imaginary piece of lint off his pants leg as he crossed his legs.

"Of course, too, military defense requires careful coordination of all related activities, hence our need to assume a major role in Kodomir's foreign policy. But more directly, your Militia will have to be integrated into the Benderist Armed Forces. The two mercenary units in your employ will be discharged, of course, as no longer needed. We will gladly assume the costs of terminating their contracts as a sign of our friendship for Kodomir." Baer smiled. "And we will provide them with funds for transporting themselves back to Swordpoint at Alpha Centauri."

"As you discuss this with the appropriate members of your Assembly, I think it important to convey to them that the Holdings are not a democracy in the traditional sense. Our military, as I said, is concerned with the degree of discipline that is used with your Militia. Planetary militias, as you know, are often regarded by professional military as, well, not terribly well controlled." He shrugged. "I think if Kodomir delays acting on my proposals, or fails to accede to them, our brigade command is going to come to the conclusion that Kodomir is a clear and present danger to the Holdings and respond accordingly. And that would mean, of course, seizing the elements of power here in the city of Kiroff. The consequences of that for the civilian population would be quite unfortunate."

"My military people also tell me they have concerns that some members of your Militia, and this reflects on the problem of discipline among such forces, may try to do something preemptively against the brigade. If that were to happen, I do not believe it would be possible to guarantee further the safety of the individuals who are our guests in Portaka." Baer let the words lay between them. Then he motioned to General Mannheim and stood up.

"I appreciate Kodomir's traditional stance in foreign policy has always been to seek a reasonable relationship with the various powers it has encountered. This is an excellent tradition and I strongly urge you to emphasize that point in your dealings with your Assembly." He paused, waiting for Jevon's response.

"Special Envoy Baer," Jevon said as he slowly stood, "I understand completely the position of the Benderist Holdings. Needless to say, for some time now I have been working with the members of the Kodomir Assembly. At the moment, I believe it safe to say that most Kodomiri are delighted to have the Alliance leaving our soil and that turn of events has occupied most Assembly representative's attention. The role of von Bender in getting the Alliance to leave will not be quickly forgotten and could be the basis for a positive relationship between Kodomir and the Holdings."

Baer bowed his head, a smirk on his face. Jevon felt a flush but held his control.

Let them think we are helpless kittens. They are about to learn they have grabbed the tail of a Hoare Cat.

"Your military need not be terribly concerned with security issues, though I appreciate," he nodded towards Mannheim, "your duty requires such considerations. We are indeed traditionally an accommodating nation and I believe we will find a method of reaching a working relationship with you in short order." He held out his hand to Baer. "Again, my thanks for your assistance in dealing with the Alliance forces."

Baer took it, his face struggling to hide the contempt he felt. Then he and his general left. Jevon sat back down and leaned his head back and stared at the ceiling. He closed his eyes.

He thought about Hoare Cats.

Gwielgi was thinking about Hoare Cats, primarily because one was tracking him with lunch on its mind. He had had only a glimpse of the feline monster out of the corner of his eye but there was no mistaking that tawny blur for anything else.

He grimaced. He was supposed to be putting up the beacons for the helicopter bringing his supplies. Instead, he was laying in the sun on a high, broad rock, two of the beacons still strapped to his back and a long rifle cradled in his arms.

The information the company gave him about Hoare Cats had been accurate but brief. They did not convey the size of the cats, for one thing. Twin-tailed with fangs resembling those of a prehistoric saber tooth tiger, their coats blended in well with the rocks and desert of Portaka, though a white-furred version was found further south. Their eyes were small and black, shielding themselves from the sun. Day hunters, he thought one could bring down a medium-sized HUPAX before breakfast and serious eating.

They were unique in a number of ways, the most significant being they were semi-sapient. The engineer had not been joking when he referred to them being smarter than some of the people who worked for him. Hoare Cats were more intelligent than almost all other animals humanity had encountered. They were named after the first settler to ever hunt them and the first to be killed by them. The joke from the mining company's class on local flora and fauna came into his mind.

Question: What do you do if you are tracked by a Hoare Cat?

Answer: Put your head between your legs and kiss your butt good-bye.

He had seen the cat crossing his trail near the Prowler and knew immediately the danger he was in. Gwielgi climbed up the rocks, hoping that he would have a clear field of view. There was no place he could go that a Hoare Cat could not, so there was no point in running.

He heard a stone rattle down to the right, below a rock outcropping fifty meters away that was slightly higher than his perch. Gwielgi started to move towards the sound but froze. On top of the outcropping was the Hoare Cat, crouched and head-on to him. It was almost invisible, especially with the sun just above it.

Did you push that stone over the edge to attract my attention? To get me to go down there, below you?

Gwielgi tried not to look at it directly. He knew its eyesight was good enough to see where his own eyes were looking. Gwielgi slowly swung the rifle towards where the rock had fallen. The cat did not move. Could he snap it the rest of the way and get a shot off?

He whipped the rifle towards the cat. It was gone. He clamped down on his emotions and made himself listen. There was no wind. The helicopter was due in an hour but he shoved the thought out of his mind. If its attempt to come at him from the right had failed…

Behind him was a sheer cliff that a cat couldn't get up unless it carried pitons, but to the left was the path he used getting here. He swung the rifle in that direction.

He heard a stone rattle again, down to the right. He looked over his shoulder. The Hoare Cat was back on its perch, crouched, looking at him.

You're playing with me.

Gwielgi knew he could not get a shot off. He paused, thinking. Then he let go of the rifle and slowly stood up. The Hoare Cat could not make the leap to where he was but for the moment it did not seem interested in finding another way to him. It just continued to watch. He faced it and then looked around his feet. He reached down and picked up several smooth rocks while keeping his eyes on those of the large animal. It did not stir, just continued to watch him, though he could see the twitch of its tails from time to time.

He judged the distance. Fifty meters. Gwielgi discarded a stone and hefted another. It felt right. He wound up and threw it at the cat.

It was on its feet before the stone went two meters. It stood as the rock hit below it. Gwielgi picked a second one. He cocked his arm and threw it. It sailed past the cat to the right. The cat followed its flight and then looked back at him.

Right. I'm playing with *you*.

Gwielgi's third rock was high by about two meters. The Hoare Cat reared up on its hind legs and extended a paw and slapped the stone out of the air. Then the cat sat down and stared at him. Gwielgi noticed that it was no longer crouched.

He had heard stories that the cats were curious about humans, though most of the stories ended with the human becoming a meal. It undoubtedly had not encountered this kind of behavior from a man before.

That is to say, it had not encountered a lunatic before.

Gwielgi grinned and shook his head. The Hoare Cat did nothing and just continued to watch him.

As he felt around for another stone of the right size and weight, Gwielgi tried to think of what he could do next. The Prowler, sufficiently armored that a Hoare Cat could not get in, was two hundred meters away. The cat could jump him from any of a dozen directions before he got back to it. He trusted his reflexes and thought there was a good chance he would kill it if it attacked, but the odds were not absolute. He saw something in the corner of his vision.

It was a vitabeast, a gazelle-like animal. Inadvertently introduced to Portaka a century before by a surface ship from one of the equatorial islands of Kodomir, they were a danger to the local habitat by their overgrazing and tendency to empty the few waterholes found in the mountains. About half the weight of a man, they were very quick. Relocation plans had floundered when traps caught everything except vitabeasts. The Kodomir Environmental Service, nagged at by the planet's environment monitoring C-computer and Planetary Planning Commission, was paying prospectors and surveyors a small bounty for eradicating them, though it was acknowledged only a sterilization program would end their invasion of Portaka. Unfortunately, the recent war had put that program on hold.

Gwielgi flicked his eyes back and forth between the Hoare Cat and the vitabeast. Upwind of both, the vitabeast had taken no notice of either the cat or human. The cat's ears were twitching toward the vitabeast, though it would not be able to get to the fast, smaller animal from its position before it would vanish. Gwielgi thought for a moment.

Hell, it's worth a try.

He slowly squatted and reached over to his rifle. Gwielgi could see the muscles on the cat bunch and both its ears switch to him. Very slowly he stood, carefully keeping the rifle pointed away from the Hoare Cat. He raised the rifle slowly to his shoulder, watching the cat and the vitabeast. The Hoare Cat went down into a crouch, getting ready to spring away.

Gwielgi's eye looked through the sight, corrected his point of aim, and the rifle cracked. He looked back at the Hoare Cat. It was gone. He looked where he had shot. The vitabeast was sprawled on the ground, dead. He wasn't sure, exactly, what he had intended, but at least the cat was gone for the moment and he couldn't stay up here forever. He flipped the selector switch to fully automatic and carefully made his way down toward the Prowler.

Gwielgi walked a few feet and then paused and listened, but he heard nothing. He was halfway back to the Prowler when he saw the Hoare Cat, standing over the dead vitabeast. It watched him. Gwielgi kept moving, walking sideways, never letting the cat out of his sight until he was in the Prowler.

Gwielgi closed and locked the door behind him and stowed the rifle. Then he took a long drink of water and shook his head and smiled. He would plant the two remaining beacons from the vehicle. It was a little crowded out there today for pedestrian traffic.

He was getting ready to put down the last beacon when he came up on the vitabeast. The Hoare Cat was gone. And so was the most of the dead animal. A back leg and portion of the hip lay in the dirt. He looked around carefully. The nearest cover was back among the rocks where he and the cat had been. He pulled the rifle free, flipped the safety off and stepped outside.

Gwielgi glanced at the remains of the kill. The rear portion was cleanly severed. The cat had even taken the entrails. He kept looking around. Then he heard a stone clicking down the rocks.

The Hoare Cat was in his old position, the rest of the vitabeast in its jaws. He looked at the remains at his feet.

Left me the butt end, eh?

Gwielgi shrugged while the cat watched him. Was the cat expecting him to take his share of the kill? One way to find out. He pulled a length of rope from the vehicle and used it to secure the haunch to the back of the Prowler. It was awkward doing it while holding on the rifle but he was not going to put the gun down. The leg would dry quickly out in the sun and, though he was not a big meat eater, he could cook some of it in the evening.

He looked up, expecting to see the cat gone, but it was still there watching him. Gwielgi started to get in the Prowler, but paused and impulsively waved. He immediately felt a small surge of foolishness and he grimaced. Perhaps he had been out in the desert too long.

The Hoare Cat did not move for a second. Then it flicked a paw forward, kicking another stone down the side of the hill. Gwielgi watched it fall as its dry clicks came through the hot air. The Hoare Cat stood up, still clutching the dead vitabeast in its jaws, turned, and walked out of sight. He had a clear shot at it for several seconds with its back turned but he did not raise the rifle. Then he got into the Prowler and drove to the rendezvous position.

Gwielgi sat in his vehicle, sipping water and occasionally glancing at the time while he listened to the communication unit. The helicopter was a few minutes late. Swinging wide of the Benderists, the pilot said.

It came down on his position, swirling dust in all directions. The side hatch slid back and a crewman jumped out, clad in desert gear with a face cover and goggles for the dust. By the time Gwielgi had gotten out of the Prowler, the crewman had dragged off three good-sized cargo boxes holding supplies. As Gwielgi came up, the crewman closed the hatch from the outside, slapped it twice, and the helicopter lifted off, its twin engines roaring as they powered the rotors.

As the helicopter sped away, the crewman turned to a puzzled Gwielgi. He pulled his face cover free and pushed back his goggles.

"How is the food around here?" Charles Tsunasdi asked.

Gwielgi did not say anything for a moment. Then he gestured to the supplies.

"It sucks. Help me get this stuff loaded," he said. They worked in silence until everything was put away and secured. The sun was just grazing the tops of the surrounding hills. Tsunasdi stood by the Prowler, patiently waiting. Gwielgi gestured and they both climbed in.

Neither man said anything during the short drive. Gwielgi halted the vehicle in front of a shallow cave. By now it was becoming dark. They off loaded some of the gear from the Prowler, working quickly but with few words.

Later they reclined around a small campfire, roasting strips of vitabeast. Gwielgi finally looked over at his friend.

"All right," he said, "what's going on?"

"You know Jevon finessed the Alliance into pulling out its regiment?"

"Yes. From time to time you could see one of their landing ships lift and the company flashed me the news."

"The Benderists are not leaving."

"There's a surprise." Gwielgi stuck another piece of cargo box into the fire.

"They have put down an ultimatum – join the Holdings, fire the Black Cats and Victors, put our military under their command, and surrender Portaka to them. If we try to do anything about it, they threaten to kill the hostages and take their brigade into Kiroff City."

"Sounds like a checkmate."

"There are pieces still in play," Tsunasdi said. "The key is to bloody the brigade. If we can do that, von Bender might pull the rug on Baer."

"How do you propose keeping the brigade from setting up shop on top of the First Minister's Residency? A bunch of HUPs would really tear up Jevon's gardens."

"We may have a way of keeping that from happening."

"And the hostages?"

"They may have to be sacrificed."

Gwielgi shoved another strip of box into the fire and a small spray of sparks lifted into the night. "That sucks," he said. He thought for a moment. "You said 'may.'"

"Correct. Colonel Kheyntamenti has asked me to see about breaking them out."

"Just like that?" Gwielgi shook his head. "Tsunasdi, stop playing me for an idiot. The next thing you are going to say is that the Militia wants to hire me to get you close to the facility. Then Kheyntamenti figures I will be unable to let you go in alone and the two of us will go out in a blaze of glory, just like in the tri-vid novels." His voice became angry. "If he really wanted to pull a commando raid, he would send Ho`nehe and some of his troops. You finally get yourself dead in pursuit of some screwed-up concept of Currahee honor and I get myself dead, period. And, oh, yeah, all the hostages get themselves dead, but some Kodomiri history professor will get a brass monument set up marking the spot where we had our heads handed to us."

"Are you done?" Tsunasdi asked, his voice low. When Gwielgi said nothing, Tsunasdi nodded. "Kheyntamenti read your report and has studied the satellite imagery. You were right – they do not have many people on guard, it is all HUPAX. One, or two, might get in and free the hostages. Our infantry already have an assignment, so he asked for volunteers. That is why I came. One of the hostages is William Coltrane, and General Polrany said it is important that the Chekinovs know that all that could be done, was done. Everyone else feels the same way about all of them."

"I am not here to die, Gwi," Tsunasdi said. "If it cannot be done, Kheyntamenti wants me to back away. I will. As for you," he shrugged and fell silent for a moment. "There is no offer to hire you as a back-handed way of easing you back into the Militia and the Wild Geese. If you want it, your commission can be reinstated, but Kheyntamenti says that is up to you, as it has always been. All he wants you to do is get me close to the facility, early on the morning of the 21st."

Gwielgi said nothing, idly poking a stick in the fire. Finally, he sighed and looked at Tsunasdi.

"I should not have made the remark about Currahee honor," he said. "I apologize."

"I have heard you on the subject before," Tsunasdi replied. "It has nothing to do with me."

"You're right, I'm just an ass."

"At times." Tsunasdi smiled. "But no harm was done."

"Good." Gwielgi pulled the stick out of the fire and studied the glowing end. "It will take two of us. They have four guards on duty at the gym at night, two inside, two outside walking around the building. Now, getting in is not a big problem. Their perimeter HUP patrols are small to medium-sized HUPs moving too fast to see much, though we will have to time it right to avoid being picked up on sensors. But once the hostages are free, it is going to hit the fan."

"Actually, we are counting on that," Tsunasdi said.

"Tell me more," Gwielgi said.

"In a moment," Tsunasdi said. "But you said it would take two of us. You are coming, then?"

"If you did not know I would go with you, I would be very disappointed," Gwielgi said and smiled.

"And the business of the commission?"

"I had an interesting experience this afternoon before you dropped by," Gwielgi said. He paused for a second, remembering the Hoare Cat. "Learned a little about honor, and about self-control." He looked back at Tsunasdi and looked a little embarrassed. "Well, anyway, yeah, I'm picking up the commission."

Tsunasdi said nothing and walked over to the Prowler. He rummaged around in the storage compartment for a moment and then came back to the campfire.

"You will need this," he said, tossing something into Gwielgi's lap. "Otherwise, you will be unable to return my salute."

Gwielgi picked it up. It was a purple beret, his beret. He looked at it for a moment. He smiled at his friend.

"Damned naked savage."

"Pirate and criminal."

"I am with you."

"Of course, you are – I always know that."

Later, after Tsunasdi fell asleep, Gwielgi got up slowly. For an old man, and he always felt like an old man by the end of the day, he moved very quietly when he wanted. He walked over to the Prowler. He reached into the back and pulled out a small pouch.

It held two Fairbairn knives, one in a forearm sheath and the other in a boot sheath. Gwielgi slipped on the forearm sheath automatically, his fingers accustomed to its feel. He paused with the other, holding it in both his hands for a moment. Then he put a foot up on the vehicle and pulled his pant leg up. He loosened his boot and inserted the knife. He then snuggled up the boot and secured the sheath's straps. When he stood up, his pant leg did not reveal the knife's presence.

But Gwielgi could feel it, holding onto him, moving with him. Even though it had been crafted for another's leg, it felt right.

Gwielgi walked back to his sleeping bag and curled up in it. Hidden in the dark, Charles Tsunasdi's eyes opened and he looked at the figure of his friend, shrouded in the darkness. He watched him for a few moments, waiting until the regular breathing of sleep came. He did not know what the coming days would bring but he felt a strange feeling, one that took him a moment to identify.

It was contentment, a feeling that he had not experienced greatly in his life. Puzzled by its appearance in this place, Tsunasdi probed it with his mind, trying to identify its source. There, he had it. Of course. A slight smile touched his lips in the darkness and as he fell asleep the source gently soothed him.

Honor is being served.

It was very late at the Holdings legation rooms in the Kiroff City Central Hotel. Dawn was not more than three hours away, but there had been much business to attend to between the Benderists and the ambassadors of a dozen worlds, all sniffing a Benderist victory in the air as the Alliance forces left Kodomir. And, of course, there was the small celebration afterwards. General Mannheim lifted his glass of sherry in toast to Esteban Baer, who smiled and bowed his head in humble thanks.

"Envoy, I am more than impressed," the general said. He downed the sherry in a single, quick swallow. "I thought the most we would get from these farmers was an agreement to allow us to use Portaka as a base, but you have taken them well beyond that."

"Don't forget, general," Baer said as he poured himself a glass of the general's sherry, "they have agreed to nothing. I expect them to come back with a counterproposal, probably along the lines of some profit sharing of

Portaka, perhaps a greater degree of independence for their military, that sort of thing." He put the decanter down on the table and dropped its glass topper into place. "Nothing major and we may want to give them a little wiggle room."

"Sir," Colonel Halleck said, his sherry untouched, "what if they decide to resist after all? Remember, my brigade is in the middle of nowhere. I dislike surrendering the initiative to the enemy and allowing them the first move. They do have over thirty HUPAX."

"Colonel, colonel, colonel," Baer said in mock exasperation. "The Kodomiri are not our enemies. We are endeavoring to make them our allies." He smiled, though his eyes remained cold. He put his class down and folded his arms.

"Colonel, your Red Cocks are going to see plenty of fighting." He looked at Mannheim, whose expression was confused. "General, these people *will* fight, no matter how much groveling Jevon did in front of us this morning. Study their history, their recent history. They are not going to surrender their freedom as long as they think there is any way they can keep it. Don't be fooled by Jevon's act," he warned.

"I expect them to do something like an attempt at decapitating the leadership of the brigade, perhaps by a HUP raid. They did that against Storm Cloud. But we are not going to allow that, so we will strike first. Besides," he said with a smile, "defeating them militarily will make the negotiations go so much easier." Mannheim smiled in response, seeing Baer's point.

"As soon as the Alliance fleet clears the system, we will bring in our own landing ships and lift the brigade to Kiroff City and strike directly into their military and political leadership." Baer said it as casually as sending someone to the store for groceries. "They will either agree, and quickly, to all of our demands, or we will burn the city down."

"Why don't we move before then, sir?" Halleck asked.

"Because I do not want to give the Alliance a reason for changing its mind, a justification for armed intervention. The political situation within the Alliance is confused, which for us is a two-edged sword. While their focus is inward towards their internal political crisis, we have maneuvering room, but too overt a move on our part might provoke a heavy response from them." Baer picked up his glass and studied the contents, enjoying the play of light through the sherry and the cut crystal. "I don't want you to even move your battalions in preparation of loading. Keep everything very normal, very low profile." He sipped the sherry and smiled.

"We have them paralyzed with the hostages. Even if they anticipate that we might move off of Portaka, what can they do? Split their forces between their two biggest cities? That will just make your strike that much easier." He took another sip. "I will join you and the general at your headquarters in Portaka in two or three days. No sense leaving *them* a hostage."

"In the meantime, keep everything calm," he repeated. "I will have the Kwang delegation continuing its discussions on trade and we will let Jevon run in circles and scheme. Then we will, once more, deliver our ultimatums. Only this time they will be delivered by your HUPAX." Baer finished his glass and put it down.

"We will see if that is not a convincing argument."

Chapter 23: Unsheathed saber

16 December 2824

Colonel Jonivov walked around the table, on which a three-dimensional map of Portaka glowed. He studied it for a moment and then motioned with his finger. A staff lieutenant increased the magnification of the eastern portion. The Militia facility suddenly filled the table. The sidescan radars and phased array sensors of the Kodomir satellites provided sufficient detail that he could count the treads on abandoned construction machines' tracks, still lying in place from the last mercenary raid.

"How many HUPs?"

"Thirty," Kheyntamenti said. "A battalion plus the five of their headquarters support unit."

"Other systems?"

"Some mobile antiair assets, mostly located on the higher ground to the west and south, eight APCs for command and control, a company of infantry with their own APCs, and some long-range missile APCs. A platoon of five wheeled armored vehicles. Some of that is used to escort their water and supply vehicles that go to their western battalion."

"The hostages are being kept in the gym," Jonivov said, "according to your captain." He rubbed his jaw. "How does he and that sergeant plan to get to them?"

"Cautiously, sir," Kheyntamenti said. "The night perimeter patrols are all conducted by their HUPs and HUP sensors generally line of sight, so with careful timing it is possible to get past them."

"You would know more about that than I, colonel," Jonivov said, getting close to the table, "but speaking as someone who has earned his living wiggling on his belly like a snake, they will have an awfully long distance to go from these foothills to the hostages."

"Yes, sir," Kheyntamenti agreed. "From the perspective of the Benderists, these HUP patrols are their *inner* perimeter. The four battalions they have further out are the outer perimeter. If any large force were to try to penetrate to their headquarters area, it would have to fight through a battalion of HUPs and then the counterattacking main body."

"Couldn't be done," Jonivov said. He squatted down and studied the terrain.

"Not by us," Kheyntamenti agreed.

"All right, I've got it," Jonivov said. "For the record, here's my prediction. Your people will come down from the hills following one of these ravines. Probably hide the vehicle well out of earshot and away from the perimeter patrols. Then they will make their way to *here*," he jabbed into the display with a finger and touched a brown, low hill. He looked up at Kheyntamenti whose face remained impassive. He looked back down at the map.

"Then they will follow this shallow wash south. They'll stick to the east side, their left, since the HUP patrol is always counterclockwise. Once past the patrol route, they will move to these buildings, what's left of them. Then they will move to the gym." He stood back and smiled. "That's what I have my money on."

"I will pass your route to Ho`nehe. He thinks they are going to be further to the west." Jonivov looked across the map and shook his head negatively.

"Now, about their getaway." Jonivov motioned and the map scale shrunk. The base suddenly was the size of a thumbprint. Kheyntamenti walked up and pointed to the southwest.

"Tight valley," Jonivov said, rubbing his chin again. "Who's driving?"

"Patricia Nguyen, Captain of Revenant."

"She ever do anything like this before?"

"No, sir."

Jonivov looked up, his eyes slightly wide. He grimaced. "All right. So Revenant says good morning. What about the water boys?"

Kheyntamenti touched the controls and the map panned further west. "They will be in this broad valley about then. About ten kilometers short of the 173rd's second battalion."

"Another twenty-five HUPs," Jonivov said.

"Good sized ones," Kheyntamenti agreed. "This was the battalion facing the Alliance force."

"All right, good place for the water boys, but what about any quick reaction force from that second battalion? They'll be coming fast and hard."

"Hopefully," Kheyntamenti said. He touched a point on the map further west. "Here, where the pass widens into a canyon. It starts here with the Chekinov Scouts and my battalion's armor and a couple of HUPs. If the force that comes is small and alone, we'll take them in the White Snake. If others follow them, we'll try to draw them down here and deal with the others in the pass."

"How long will that last?"

"As long as any of them live, until they surrender, or until the sun comes up," Kheyntamenti said.

"Who gets to do the taxi service there and back?"

"Captain Cochran has the lead of the landing ships, but we will not be coming back. We will shift to *here*," he pointed at a place further east. "Just long enough to provide morning greetings."

"That route leads to a large boxed canyon," Jonivov said, pointing back to the position Kheyntamenti had indicated earlier. "If they can get a battalion in the mouth of it, your ambushers can't climb up those sheer cliffs."

"Hopefully not," Kheyntamenti agreed. "Second Recon will be here," he pointed to the opening of the canyon. "Along with a company of combat engineers and the Black Cats and the Victors."

"And then?"

"We will choose among hopefully several opportunities."

"You know, you use that word 'hopefully' a lot, colonel." Jonivov eyed the display, frowning.

"Yes, sir."

"This all depends on some superb flying by our landing ships." It was not a question. "I did some reading, colonel. This armored cavalry raid

322

business has been a dream of armies for a couple of millennia. Sometimes it has actually worked. But no one ever did it after horses stopped being used."

"That's generally true, sir," Kheyntamenti said. "Horses could be supplied by grazing as they went and so were independent of logistical trains. Armor meant engines, which mean fuel. Deep raiding by machines became impractical until the introduction of HUPAX and fusion-ion engines. You could still raid with people, inserting them by parachute, rocketed canister, helicopter, whatever. But they went without armor."

"Next to an amphibious landing on a contested shore," Jonivov said, "the most dangerous operation in war is an airborne assault. In my humble opinion, after that comes the deep penetration cavalry raid. Second Regiment is about to perform an airborne armored cavalry raid behind enemy lines." He shook his head. "Sometimes I wish I never read history books."

Kheyntamenti smiled, flashing white teeth. He knew Jonivov was eager to go and his talk was just talk. This was the fifth time they had gone over the plan, but both officers knew plans seldom survived intact first contact with the enemy. Still, you had to start some place.

"The key to all this," Jonivov said, his eyes still on the map, "is not here. Victory will be determined on the other front." He waved and the map vanished in a blink of light. He walked to his desk and sat down. "But nothing is going to happen on that other front unless we tear these people up. My biggest concern is that they may succeed in consolidating that brigade. Right now, it is scattered and they are going to find it difficult to support one another. But once they come together, it will be very hard for us to proceed."

"Yes, sir," Kheyntamenti said. He paused. "Several of our plans have historical parallels. If they do consolidate, there is another parallel we might make use of." Jonivov looked up. Their planning had not extended much beyond the initial maneuvers and battles.

"If they do, what do you have in mind?"

"Sir, in your historical readings, did you ever encounter someone named 'Popè'?"

323

Yamashita and the Kwangdo trade delegation stood sipping tea and eating pastries, taking a break from the morning's formal negotiations with their Kodomiri counterparts. He gathered the negotiations were going well, though he could barely follow them.

He raised his cup and scanned the crowd, looking for someone. He spotted Philip Deal, talking to the Kwang delegation leader. Their eyes met for a second and Yamashita nodded. He put down his cup and looked back at Deal. The nod was returned. A moment later Deal left the break room.

A few minutes later Deal was in the office of the First Minister. Jevon and Polrany were looking at a map of Portaka as he entered. They looked up, their expressions hopeful.

"We have it," Deal said. "Subspace communication systems on a clear channel to the Kwang consul. It's on the outskirts of the capital, but it's the best we can get."

"That will be good enough," Jevon said, "if what we think we know of von Bender is accurate."

"Two keys to that lock," Polrany said. "Don't forget that. We need corroboration. It won't be enough that we fight."

"Our people are on it," Deal replied. "We found some material in Tokovan Bedoreh's records, but most is in Liban Kidowsky's, as Tykaw said. Unfortunately, the academics have gotten to Kidowsky's files and some of his records and materials are scattered among several universities."

"We only have days," Jevon pointed out. His voice was tense.

"We're pushing them, sir," Deal said. "Part of all that material was logged in by the academics, which is making some of the searching easier. But there is a fair amount that no one had gotten to. Literally, our people have to read every file. These guys were pack rats; they kept everything. We're hampered by the fact we have to keep all this secret."

"Then tell them, tell the professors what it is precisely we are looking for. Let them help the search. Ask them to keep it to themselves, as Kodomiri. Even if they leak the information, by the time Baer learns of what we are looking for, it will be too late for him to do anything about it."

You hope. Deal nodded. "Yes, sir, we'll get right on it." He turned and left the room.

Polrany turned to Jevon. "You figure a bunch of academics can keep their mouths shut?"

"They're Kodomiri, Stevar." He smiled without humor. "They can write papers and books about being involved with the Second War of Liberation and get tenure after all this is over."

The landing ship settled onto its Coyote Bay pad. For a moment it did not stir as groundcrew scurried around its base, turning on auxiliary power units and arranging gantries. A klaxon sounded and a ramp slowly extended from an amidships cargo bay as a large hatch slid to one side.

A bored customs official stood on the pad, watching the ramp. Stray Dog was not on his list of scheduled landing ships, but that meant little; free traders regularly sought profit from delivering Kodomir's products. He eyed the Alligator-class ship. For a cargo carrier, it seemed to have more laser turret and missile launcher positions than the usual. Well, maybe this close to the Frontier her captain worried a little about Raiders.

The ramp touched down on the pad. A figure clad in a midnight blue military uniform, a belted sidearm at her waist, walked down the ramp. Her boots struck the ramp with a muffled, measured clang. When she was half way down the ramp, something stirred in the shadows of the bay.

Slowly, as if adjusting to the morning light after days of being in the dark, a single Javelin HUPAX in black and gold tiger-striped camouflage emerged. It paused at the top of the ramp, slowly swiveling its fuselage back and forth, like a predator stretching its muscles after a long rest. Then it stepped out onto the ramp and the sound of its metal foot slapping down echoed across the base.

"I am Captain Marjessa Boyington," the woman said to the no longer bored customs official. "Go tell the Wild Geese the Aniwaya are here."

At that moment, it was just past noon near the Militia facility on Portaka as Gwielgi and Tsunasdi, sweating beneath their sand-colored camouflage netting, studied the base to the south. They were very close to the route Jonivov had predicted. Tsunasdi had a laser designator pressed to his face while Gwielgi supplied whispered narration as he gazed through the telescopic sight of his rifle.

"The far prefabs are their communications, the ones in the green camouflage. The brown ones to the left are command. Closer to us is the gym. To the left of the gym, those are the barracks and messhall structures. The ones to the right are some vehicle maintenance and supply."

"I only see one HUPAX repair gantry there."

"There are two others further to the south, slightly to the left. That's where they're parking their armor and support vehicles. Just beyond the command buildings."

"Got them. The ammunition dump is in those revetments next to the runway?"

"Right. They took advantage of the aircraft revetments and added to them. Near this end of the runway, you can see the four fighters they keep on alert, along with their support vehicles."

"One of them has its maintenance hatches open," Tsunasdi reported.

"Tough doing maintenance out in the open," Gwielgi replied. "I imagine they will bring in their landing ships for support as soon as the Alliance finishes leaving. By the way, those four Firerays are from their 4th Strike Fighter Squadron, according to their tail markings. Those are the same fighters that flew in support of Storm Cloud's invasion. These guys have been to Kodomir before and they pretty well wiped out the Militia's Swallows at Kiroff in their last engagement."

"Everything is a circle," Tsunasdi said. He moved the designator around the base. He would touch on a target and key the rangefinder. The exact location, measured to a millimeter, was stored in the designator for later transmission. "I do not see the hostage sentries."

"Two are always inside with them," Gwielgi said. "The other two stay in the gym during the day. At night they do periodic 'walk-arounds' of the building but tend to stay in the building then as well. It can get cold out here."

"Where does the convoy depart from?"

"Go back to the command buildings. Now, to the right, see that circular cluster of seven broad buildings, all painted gray? That's their primary supply depot. The convoy will form up just to the right of them, in about," Gwielgi paused while checking his watch, "one or two hours. They also do a run south to the battalion down there. Even days to the west, odd days to the south. A water tanker, sometimes two or three supply trucks, two wheeled tanks, an APC, and two light HUPs, usually Cutlasses or Scimitars."

"Well, they will not be our problem."

"No, just the other thirty. No big deal."

"Fifteen each. Seems fair. I think I see the dry wash you described. It looks very shallow. Not much cover."

"Not at the far end. The gully flattens out just short of where the old perimeter fence was. It's about three hundred meters from the last of its cover to that messed up building, and then another hundred to the gym itself. But all that is inside the HUP perimeter patrol route."

"Understood." Tsunasdi slowly lowered the designator. "Counting their infantry, support personnel, and command staff, they have about 200 people down there."

"Yes," said Gwielgi.

"I think we can get in without much of a problem," Tsunasdi said. "I hope Captain Nguyen is a very, very good landing ship captain."

"And I hope her clock is very, very good."

Chapter 24: Maneuvers

20 December 2824

They had done their best to make their accommodations appropriate for a Special Envoy of the Benderist Holdings, but the brigade staff still felt the field conditions of the headquarters unit were not what a high ranking Benderist official would find acceptable. It was with relief when they discovered Baer seemed indifferent to his surroundings, focusing almost entirely on watching the withdrawal of the Alliance forces.

Methodically the Alliance battalions fell back on their headquarters. Like clockwork, their landing ships arrived one at a time and were loaded and departed Kodomir. But they did not go far.

The Benderist landing ships, hanging in geosynchronous orbit, spotted what was happening first and sent the information down to the brigade headquarters. The Alliance regiments were not going to their star ships near the stellar navigation beacon. For reasons unknown, they were holding at the point their landing ships had been poised throughout their confrontation on and with Kodomir. Mannheim finally voiced the fear they all felt.

"All right," he said in the conference with Halleck and Baer, "they are hanging around, waiting. Their last units will pull out today. Maybe they just want to go in formation back to their star ships, but I don't think so. I think they are waiting to see what we do and hope they can find a way to put both of their regiments down our throat. They've taken their damned time pulling out."

"Our intelligence people say there has been an overthrow of the Mordieu government," Baer pointed out. "Engaging in a war with us is not something they would want to do during this time of confusion in their ranks."

"I don't think it matters who is in charge of the Alliance," Mannheim growled, leaning back in his chair. "All of them must recognize that we are their greatest single threat. Besides, there's nothing like a war, an outside enemy, to galvanize unity."

"So what are they waiting for?" Halleck asked. "Why didn't they fight when both regiments were here and outnumbered us?"

"Don't focus just on Kodomir, colonel," Baer said, thinking about Mannheim's words. "Remember, the Alliance is run by a parliamentary democracy. It can be hard to sell a democracy on the idea of initiating a war. They need us to provide a context which would allow them to make a claim of justification." He looked at Mannheim. "Then they could still win the fight for Kodomir."

"I didn't think they sent that assault regiment just to carry the message there had been a change in government."

"Yes," Baer nodded in agreement. "That makes sense. The question is, what would they regard as a pretext and how do we avoid it?"

A polite knock on the door of the small conference room interrupted Mannheim's answer. Halleck stood and opened the door and spoke briefly with the junior officer standing there. He turned to the other two.

"I think we are about to find out, gentlemen, what the pretext is. The commander of the Alliance force is calling me."

They moved to the center of the command building. In the dark room, punctuated by the glowing lights of consoles and screens, Halleck touched the controls of a communication unit. In front of them the image of Senior Colonel Alfredo Garcia Petron, commanding officer of the Alliance 5th Assault Regiment, blinked into existence.

"Colonel Garcia Petron," Halleck said, "to what do I owe this unexpected contact?"

"Colonel Halleck," the Alliance officer said, bowing his head slightly. "I simply wished to notify you that our last landing ship will be leaving Portaka in the next few hours, as per our previous announcement."

"Understood, colonel. But I see that your landing ships are still close by Kodomir. Is there something else you wish to tell me?"

"A simple matter of transportation, colonel. Your naval officers can confirm that we do not have sufficient star ships present to allow both regiments to leave at the same time. Until additional star ships arrive, I have elected to keep both regiments together for mutual protection."

"Protection, colonel? From what? The Kodomiri are not likely to challenge your flotilla with their handful of landing ships."

"I would hope not, colonel. My government is working very hard to arrive at an understanding with the Kodomiri." Garcia Petron's face showed little expression, as if he were indifferent to the issue.

Halleck saw Baer, standing to one side, raise an eyebrow. Was this a clue? Halleck decided to press on.

"As you know, colonel," Halleck said, "the Holdings are in negotiation with the Kodomir government ourselves. We are very concerned about their response. These people can be headstrong."

"True enough," Garcia Petron said. "That is why my landing ships remain on alert. We are very concerned about any action which might signal an assault on our force is imminent."

"We would not wish to contribute to your concern," Halleck said as he got an encouraging smile from Baer. "In the coming days we may find our relationship with the Kodomiri deteriorating…" He let his voice trail off.

"That would be very unfortunate, colonel," Garcia Petron said. "Any disputes between the Holdings and Kodomir are not our immediate concern." The Senior Colonel leaned forward and smiled. "On the other hand, if anyone were to take actions which could be interpreted as a threat to my ships, I am empowered to use all available force to protect them. For example, if a number of landing ships currently in orbit over Kodomir were to suddenly begin to move, I think such movement could legitimately be viewed as a potential threat."

Halleck looked over at Baer who nodded emphatically.

"I understand, colonel," Halleck said. "We have, at present, no plans for any major landing ship deployment and will be careful to inform you of any."

"I appreciate your consideration, colonel," Garcia Petron leaned back in his chair, his smile fading. He raised his hand to break contact but Halleck held up his own.

"Just one other thing, colonel. How long until your other star ships arrive?"

"My latest information is," Garcia Petron said, looking irritated, "the others will arrive in five days."

"Thank you, Senior Colonel. Have a safe trip back to the Alliance."

Halleck motioned with his hand and an officer cut the communication link. The last image was of an angry Garcia Petron.

"Nicely played, colonel," Baer said. "Have you ever considered being a diplomat?"

Halleck permitted himself a soft laugh. "No, sir. I find it exhausting. Much easier to fight battles with real weapons than with words."

"That bastard was hoping we would give him an excuse to intervene," Mannheim said. "'A threat to my ships,' my butt. He was *daring* us to call in our landing ships, which is exactly what we were planning to do tomorrow."

"He seemed very disappointed when I said we would not move," Halleck noted.

"I think he said more than he intended," Baer said. "When he heard you say we would not move he realized his mistake. He would *not* make a diplomat, I'm afraid."

"What does this do to our plans?"

"We are the *de facto* rulers of Kodomir right now, which is what we want from the Kodomiri," Baer said. He paced as he spoke, frowning in concentration. "We want their formal agreement to this arrangement so that we may proceed with development. Have you had a chance to review the resource estimates for this region? These simple farmers have no idea of the wealth they are sitting on." Baer shook his head. "I will make a call to Jevon, rattle him a little, and then magnanimously grant him more time, unless he is prepared to grant us everything."

"What if they elect to fight?"

"That was my prediction," Baer said. "They may still do so. On the other hand, Colonel, I think they realize that the Alliance's departure means the counterweight holding us back is now removed and they are losing their only potential ally. It is possible they will put up some sort of resistance but, as I have thought about it more, initiating a war with the Holdings would be futile, whatever happened on Kodomir." He nodded as he thought for a moment. "It will be a bitter thing for them to swallow but I am beginning to believe they will be seeking an accommodation."

"Thank you, Senior Colonel Garcia Petron," Jevon said. "The government of Kodomir greatly appreciates your assistance."

"I am afraid my assistance is mostly smoke and mirrors, sir," the colonel's face said from the viewing screen. "Sooner or later, they will call my bluff. We do need several more star ships but I imagine their operatives in the Alliance are going to discover what my real orders are."

"I understand, colonel," Jevon said. "All we ask for is a chance and you have given that to us."

"I wish," Garcia Petron said, "the situation was different. I would thoroughly enjoy sweeping this trash off your planet. As it is, I am afraid, sir, you are in an impossible position. They outnumber you in HUPAX more than three to one, their aerospace fighters, while fewer, are superior, and their landing ships outnumber yours two to one. If they attack," he paused. "Well, I regret the actions of the previous Alliance government which contributed to your current predicament."

"Thank you for your sentiments and assistance, colonel. When the current difficulties are resolved, perhaps the Alliance and Kodomir can reopen discussions."

"Yes, sir," Garcia Petron replied, his expression depressed. After signing off, Jevon turned to Philip Deal and Stevar Polrany.

"Garcia Petron may be a skilled soldier," Jevon said, "but he wouldn't make a diplomat, I'm afraid."

"Well, he's given us what he can," Polrany said. "And so have the Kwang. Now it's up to us."

"I expect to get a call from Baer in the next few minutes," Jevon said. "He will be looking to see if we have capitulated. He will offer us more time. I will appreciate his gesture and accept. I will smile sweetly and kiss his butt while you two drop a hammer on it." He paused. "We are going to drop hammers, right?"

"As we speak, it is in motion," Polrany said. "Second Regiment is reinforced, along with our mercenaries and the token Currahee force."

"Mercenaries, Currahee, and a plan taken from the 19th Century," Jevon said, shaking his head.

"Actually, just part of it is from the 19th," Polrany said, a smile creeping out from under his moustache. "Another chunk is from the 17th."

"Don't tell me any more, general," Jevon said, his voice serious. "I haven't been able to hold any food down all day." He looked at Deal. "What word on the document front?"

"We have some of what we need and leads on the rest," Deal said. "Within 72 hours we may have all of it."

"That's too long," Jevon said. "If Polrany's plan works, they will be off Portaka in 48 and coming here."

"Maybe in 48," Polrany said. "Intel estimates 48 hours is the earliest they would decide to run the bluff and bring in their landing ships. I think we have 72 hours."

"Cutting it very fine, gentlemen. I think it is going to take von Bender a while to digest whatever we give him on Baer, and if it looks like his regiment is winning, well, he may just shrug off any questions about dishonorable behavior on the part of his Special Envoy and take the win."

The communication unit in Jevon's office chimed. He looked at it and grimaced.

"I think the good Special Envoy of the Benderist Holdings has a few words for me, gentlemen." He smiled, though his eyes showed no humor. "Time to go back to work."

At the Coyote Bay Militia Base Colonel Alisti Mahmud al-Kheyntamenti stood on the bridge of landing ship Zombie and watched Ghost lift. The Viper-class landing ship turned as it rose, swinging its nose toward the southeast. It accelerated, its engines thundering across the base.

He turned to the captain of Zombie, a massive Crocodile-class landing ship, as the last echoes faded in the distance.

"Captain Cochran, please signal to the rest of the task force to raise ships and commence operations."

"Aye, sir," she said. She touched her headset. "All ships, Task Force Pueblo, stand by to rise on my mark" She watched a clock for several seconds. "Mark and raise ships. Hunting season is open."

Kwangdo Minister for Foreign Affairs Lieutenant General Thomas Akagi did not enjoy meeting with the Benderist Ambassador Felipe Bostan. He disliked meeting anyone representing Karl von Bender. But fulfillment of duty was a measure of honor, and Akagi was an honorable man. As the Ambassador entered his office, he gestured towards over-stuffed chairs to one side.

"Please join me, Ambassador Bostan," he said, bowing slightly. Bostan paused and returned the bow and then took a seat. Akagi offered tea that Bostan, who Akagi knew not to be a tea drinker, accepted.

Idiot.

"Mr. Ambassador, our conversations of the past several weeks have led me to the conclusion that there are several differences of opinions among Baron von Bender's advisors, even his family."

"Ah, well, sir," Bostan stammered, wondering if he had been indiscrete, "of course the Baron always seeks the widest possible range of opinions in an effort to select the best course of action."

"Indeed, a wise course to steer. Still," Akagi said, "it may be that some of the advisors to the Baron are not as wise as others. For example, I have been impressed by your insights and understandings in our discussions."

"I thank you for the compliment, sir," Bostan said, still on guard.

"Thus it is that when I came across certain information, my first thought was to share it with you." Akagi rose and went back to his desk. He picked up a folder and returned to his seat. Then he passed it over to Bostan.

Bostan took the folder and opened it. He read the small number of pages within it. After a few minutes he went back to the beginning and read it again.

"This information is alarming," he said, carefully laying the folder on the coffee table in front of him. "If it is true," Bostan added.

"The testimony of a Frontier Raider leader, even one recently in the employ of the Holdings, is significant but not absolute," Akagi replied. "I have it on very good authority that the corroboration will arrive in the next few days."

"I would very much like to see that material," Bostan said.

"It is my intention to share it with you," Akagi said. "I should point out that there will be a point when it will become public. However, there will be a period of a few days where you will have the opportunity to make whatever use of it you may wish."

"I see," Bostan said, glancing at the folder.

"There is one other thing I wished to inform you of, Ambassador Bostan." He rose again and touched the near wall. A screen slid down. For a moment it was blank, but then it flickered and suddenly they could see the bridge of a landing ship.

"What you are seeing is from Kodomir," Akagi said. "They have gone to some trouble to provide us with a virtually live feed through a subspace link. Quite expensive."

Bostan leaned forward and studied the imagery for a moment. "What am I seeing?"

"I believe this comes to us from the bridge of the Kodomir Militia landing ship Zombie, but they tell me they have numerous hook-ups and we will be sent information from a variety of sources."

"I don't understand," Bostan said, watching the screen.

"Oh, well, it's relatively simple, Ambassador," Akagi said. "They are going to demonstrate the fallacy of Special Envoy Baer's advocacy of conquest. You might consider making use of their imagery, by the way. After all," he paused, relishing the words he was about to say, "they plan to destroy your Baron's brigade on Kodomir."

The sun was going down in eastern Portaka and long shadows filled the areas between the hills like dark ponds.

Gwielgi sat in the dark of the shadows in the Prowler while Tsunasdi stood on the roof and scanned the surrounding hills. Gwielgi keyed up the satcom unit and waited while it sought out the closest communication satellite. As soon as the connection was made, the data from the designator was transmitted in encrypted form, this time using a Militia encryption. Gwielgi watched the communication screen and finally leaned back.

"They have it," he said and climbed out of the Prowler. Tsunasdi nodded and climbed down.

"I hope they can shoot straight," he said. Gwielgi smiled at his friend.

"If they can't, you'll be the first to know."

Together, the two men changed their clothes, donning nanotechnology uniforms. Powered down, their default color was black. The equipment bags Tsunasdi had brought with the helicopter were opened and weapons and communication gear were gathered up. Gwielgi noticed that there was two of everything but remained silent; Tsunasdi had planned on Gwielgi joining him.

He knows me better than I do. Gwielgi smiled. At least some of the time.

As they attached their gear, they would hop up and down a few times, listening for the clink of unsecured equipment. Each man took a silenced submachine gun and a pistol with extra loaded magazines along with two grenades. Tsunasdi added a satchel charge with timer and a long-range radio while Gwielgi slung a large aid pack across his shoulders. They check the camouflage of the vehicle as the last of the sun dipped below the hills.

Gwielgi checked his suit and then powered it up. For a moment he felt the itchy sensation of the nanosuit waking up. When it faded, he slipped his gloved hand underneath a large rock and lifted. The suit immediately aided his lift and the rock rose. He put it back down and glanced at his watch. Tsunasdi flipped the radio on for a second and then turned it off.

"Too soon?" Gwielgi asked, pulling the hood of the suit over his head.

"Still out of range."

Gwielgi looked south, towards the Militia base and the hostages. Then he looked at his friend.

"Same deal as always – everyone comes home."

"I am with you," Tsunasdi said quietly.

"And I with you," Gwielgi replied. He tightened a strap and nodded. "Let's get it done."

The two men stepped into the darkness and were gone.

Chapter 25: First blood

21 December 2824

The Red Cocks brigade duty officer, Lieutenant Jasul Rather, was bored. Canceling the scheduled operation against Kiroff City meant a few more days in this barren, hot place, and he was quite tired of it. The latest rumor had it that the farmers, as everyone called the Kodomiri, were demobilizing their militia and getting ready to grant Baer everything he demanded. Of course, yesterday there had been a rumor the farmers were hiring more mercenaries to come and fight for them.

Rather yawned and idly scratched his neck. There wasn't enough water coming into the facility for everyone to shower every day. The damned Alliance mercenaries who had hit this place had managed to blow up two of the three wellheads, so Rather had itches where he usually did not. He tapped the screen of his datapad and turned the page of the manual he was studying. Forcing himself to work his way through the dry book helped make the hours go past.

He glanced at his watch. He had been on Portaka long enough that he had gotten used to local time, which made it, what? He did a brief calculation. 0200. In two more hours, he would oversee the changing of the hostages' guards. The perimeter patrol had changed in the proceeding hour. Out of boredom, he reached up and unhooked a microphone and pulled it to him. He was supposed to be wearing a headset but his ears were irritated from the dust that seemed to cling to everything, including headphones.

"Patrol One, Base, do you copy?"

"Loud and clear, Base."

"How's it going out there?"

"Pretty much the same as always, Jass. We flushed some kind of animal a little while ago but there's nothing else out here."

"Roger. My logbook says your HUP had a left hip joint rotation problem they were working on. How is it?"

"Yeah, I've been checking on it. So far, so good. I think sand got past a seal this morning but they seem to have fixed it."

"Roger. If it acts up, give a yell. The maintenance section called a little while ago and they have people standing watch. You have any problems, we'll have you bring it in and wake up Patrol Two."

"Oh, they'll love that. I think I'd rather limp than put up with how ticked off they'll be."

"Roger. Next check at oh-two-one-five."

"Roger."

Rather hung the microphone up, took a sip of coffee, and focused on his reading. The middle hours of night watch always were the longest.

Captain Patricia Nguyen was working the flight controls of Ghost herself. Most of her bridge crew were happy to have her do it, for it involved the kind of flying landing ships ordinarily did not engage in.

Landing ships, as their name implied, dropped to a planet from space, serving as extremely large shuttles between planets and the fragile star ships. Even the aerodynamic landing ships, such as the Viper-class Ghost, relied on the brute power of their engines to break their falls. Their high trajectory entries and landings were the bread and butter of landing ship crews.

What Nguyen was doing was more than a little different. Soon after departing Coyote Bay, she had taken Ghost low, so low that when the landing ship crossed the beach of the northern continent at several times the speed of sound, it threw up a rooster's tail of shockwave-generated spray and flash-heated steam.

As Ghost crossed the rocky coast of Portaka, Nguyen continued to keep the ship low, using the mountain ranges to shield the ship from Benderist long-range radars and other sensors. Several of the bridge crew avoided looking out their viewports, for the gray blur of rock as they thundered down narrow valleys seemed to come dangerously close.

Nguyen did not alter her flying as darkness descended. Relying on the ship's light amplification screens, she kept Ghost low over the desert, so low that some of the crew would later claim she had had to climb to get over scattered small shrubs. She turned Ghost south at one point, swinging wide around the westernmost Benderist battalion before turning back east. Climbing out of the desert, Ghost climbed up the slopes of foothills and then raced across a broad plateau.

Nguyen matched what she saw visually with her navigation system and steered towards a canyon whose far end pointed northeast. Beside her the ship's navigator softly called off checkpoints and time.

A chime sounded through Ghost and the navigator's voice echoed through the long ship.

"All hands, prepare for braking, in five, four, three, two, one..."

Nguyen chopped forward thrust and slammed on the reverse thrusters while at the same time pitching the nose up to gain aerodynamic breaking. As the nose began to fall back, she bled off altitude and yawed right.

"All bay hatches open," she commanded, and before Ghost touched down in the darkness of the canyon the massive side hatches rolled back. As she cut power and slumped back into her seat, her flight suit soaked with sweat, she touched her headset.

"Land the landing party."

Tsunasdi adjusted his light amplification goggles as the two Wild Geese carefully lowered themselves into the dry wash and made their way across it to the east side. At their point of entry, it was a three-meter drop to the featureless sand below but the walls of the gully rapidly lowered as the wash descended from the hills toward the Militia base. They soon would be crawling on their stomachs to stay below the tops. The HUP patrol route was close to where the wash finally flattened out and merged with the earth of the Militia base. He could see the patrols' path clearly as he looked around Gwielgi – the HUPs had left footprints in their endless circling around the base and the tracks looked black through his goggles.

Gwielgi moved quickly forward, pausing every few steps, listening as well as looking. As the edge of the wash dropped, the two had to crouch to stay beneath it. Eventually they were on their hands and knees. Gwielgi held up a hand that he clenched as he looked over the top of the wash and then ducked back down. Tsunasdi froze in place, his left arm pressed against the dirt wall of the wash.

Tsunasdi felt it before he saw it, a thudding in the ground. He knew what it was. As he watched, an 85-ton Long Sword, its dark blue and green coloring making it merge with the dark, walked across the mouth of the wash, its fuselage slowly pivoting back and forth. A powerful spotlight flashed on and probed the darkness. For a second Tsunasdi was blinded, his goggles flooding with a white glare. He pushed them up on his forehead. Though his night vision was almost obliterated, he could make out the dark shape of the HUP as it paused. Its running lights glowed like jewels on the shoulder connections of the weapon pylons on either side. The spotlight blinked off and the HUPAX surged forward and again Tsunasdi felt the slight vibration in the ground as it walked away.

The use of the spotlight told Tsunasdi that the HUP pilot was not comfortable with using the array of sensors HUPAX carried, preferring to rely on visual light for close-in observation. Some people, even those who could handle the mindlink connection to the machine's S-computer, found that the insertion into their visual field of all the sensor data a HUP could provide confusing, even disorienting. Tsunasdi watched the Long Sword walk away and wondered at the Benderist HUPAX training program.

He waited but still Gwielgi did not give the signal to move forward. Then Tsunasdi saw why. A second HUP, a smaller Cutlass, came rapidly along from the same direction. It passed them without slowing down, apparently intent on catching up with the first HUP. It jogged past, displaying the bouncing movement characteristic of smaller HUPAX.

Gwielgi raised his hand and motioned forward. Tsunasdi followed him as they sprinted across the footprints of the HUPs. They rolled into the remains of a building that lay near the northern perimeter of the base. Gwielgi immediately took a position where he could see past the broken walls towards the gymnasium. Tsunasdi turned on his radio. He waited a moment, giving the radio a chance to locate itself and to find a communication satellite. He heard a click in his headset and keyed his microphone.

"Sidewinder," he whispered.

"Hammer."

On hearing the response, Tsunasdi touched Gwielgi's shoulder and raised a thumb when Gwielgi turned to look. Gwielgi nodded and looked back at the gym and the area around it. He leaned over to Tsunasdi and whispered in his ear.

"No foot patrol outside, no movement anywhere. Give Hammer the 'Go.'" Tsunasdi nodded.

"Sidewinder is go."

"Hammer is go and counting."

Tsunasdi tapped a button on his watch and nodded to Gwielgi, who made one more scan of the area and then climbed out of the rubble. Tsunasdi followed immediately behind him, keeping within arm's reach.

In the moonless night of Kodomir, the two were invisible in their black suits. They worked their way around a twisted set of grandstands and ran quietly across a rugby field, rutted from the movement of vehicles, the landing struts of landing ships, and the damage of weapons. While Gwielgi kept his focus ahead towards the gym, Tsunasdi tried to watch in every other direction.

They were at the wall of the gym quickly, though it felt like it took hours. Crouching low, Tsunasdi's hand on his back for signaling, Gwielgi led the way around the corner of the building, keeping it between them and the center of the base, and past several still upright basketball stands. Around the next corner was the entrance to the gym. Gwielgi paused. He started to lean forward and then froze. He didn't bother with a signal.

Tsunasdi could hear a voice, muffled, but getting louder. Very slowly he swung the muzzle of his silenced submachine gun towards the building corner. He heard the voice one more time. For a moment there was nothing, but then he heard the slow tread of footsteps. It sounded like one person, but it was hard to tell.

Crouched low and looking up, he had a glimpse of a figure suddenly at the corner. Then Gwielgi filled his goggles, rising and grabbing the sentry. He twisted and they both fell back, narrowly missing Tsunasdi. He had a glimpse of the man, his eyes wide, Gwielgi's hand over his mouth, and then he saw a blur of metal, amplified starlight reflecting on knife blade. He heard a faint, hissing, bubbling sound. The knife rose and fell one more time and something black spread from beneath the sentry and across the dirt. Gwielgi held the man down until all life was gone.

Tsunasdi saw Gwielgi wipe the blade quickly on the sentry's arm and then reach out to him. Gwielgi leaned close.

"Time?" he whispered.

Tsunasdi looked at his watch, the dim numbers changing.

"Twelve minutes, twenty seconds."

Gwielgi said nothing, just squeezed his arm. The knife disappeared as he looked around the corner. He raised his hand and then motioned forward with two fingers. Tsunasdi put his hand on his friend's back and they moved around the corner.

"TOT eleven minutes, mark," Nguyen said into her microphone.

"Copy, captain," the Militia officer, Captain Jan Skeller, said. "Our clock is running. Coordinates are feeding into systems. Battery, stand by for designations."

"Captain Skeller," Nguyen said, eyeing the clock, "Frogfire status?" Nguyen knew she was interrupting, but so much depended on the Frogfire missiles.

"Straight and red," Skeller replied, letting a little impatience creep into her voice. "Hot in one."

"Roger," Nguyen said and slumped back in her seat and took another long pull on her iced water. "Straight," all internal systems ready, "red," the missiles were plugged into the targeting computers. "Hot" would mean they were ready to launch. She willed herself not to say anything else.

Let the cannon cockers do what they do. You need to get ready for the next move.

Tsunasdi glanced at his watch as he and Gwielgi took up positions on either side of the gym door. *Ten minutes, ten seconds.* A dim light glowed from within. He could hear nothing but he could smell a cigar. He looked at Gwielgi.

The captain pointed at himself, then his eyes. Then Gwielgi pointed into the building. He pointed at Tsunasdi and held his hand palm up. His hand went into a fist and then uncoiled into a knife-edge that pointed away from the building.

I will go in and see. You stay here and cover us.

Tsunasdi nodded in an exaggerated fashion and Gwielgi was through the doorway.

Tsunasdi crouched, his back against the wall, and looked across the base. There was nothing to see, but he kept looking.

Captain Skeller, squeezed into the tiny control room of the Frogfire battery command armored vehicle, looked over the target list. There were no surprises and the coordinates were almost identical to the ones the satellites had measured. She keyed her microphone.

"All guns, stand by. Assignments on the datalink. Voice confirmation follows. All guns, Time on Target is a go. Frog One, targets Able, Baker One, Baker Two, Charley. Narrow spread, one-fifty by one-fifty. Frog Two, targets Foxtrot, Golf, Hotel, India. Narrow spread, one-fifty by one-fifty. Gun One and Two, target Delta, three rounds, HE; target Echo, three rounds, HE. Guns Three and Four target Juliet, one round, CBU; target Kilo, one round, HE. Transmit confirmation to me."

Skeller watched as each crew checked the information in their fire control computers and sent confirmations back to her. Quickly her screen showed all guns and missiles laid in. She looked at the clock.

Nine minutes.

Nine minutes. Tsunasdi thought he heard something behind him, something in the building, but he kept his gaze outward. A slight hiss came into his earpiece.

"Come on in, we're clear."

Tsunasdi turned and entered the door. It opened into a large room. The glow came from a hallway on the other side of the room. He quickly ran down it as he pushed his goggles up.

Where the hallway turned the body of a dead man lay, a still burning cigar to one side. The light came from a portable lamp at the corner. There was another one further down the hall, opposite a set of double doors. He stepped through.

A woman in a Benderist uniform and with the left side of her face missing lay against a set of blood-smeared wall lockers. She looked dead but Tsunasdi took a second to check. Then he walked past rows of lockers and benches, moving toward another light.

At the far end of the locker room there was a large open area. It was a second before Tsunasdi recognized it as the shower room. At the entrance to the room lay another dead soldier. This one looked very young. His unblinking eyes were open and his blood was slowly making its way to a drain.

The hostages clustered at the far end. Gwielgi was squatting with them and Tsunasdi moved alongside his friend.

"Seven plus thirty," he said. Gwielgi, blood smearing his camouflaged face and only his yellow-brown eyes showing anything, silently nodded.

Lieutenant Rather glanced at his clock. The sentries with the hostages were not due to make another report for ten minutes. He thought about calling them, just to see if they were awake but decided against it. It seemed like too much effort. He stood and stretched and checked his coffee. It was cold. Rather swallowed it in one large gulp and shivered.

He walked over to the urn and poured himself a fresh cup. Rather stretched again and glanced at the clock. No, there wasn't any purpose served in calling them early. He felt a need to urinate and stepped into the hall. The single-hole latrine was just a few steps away but when he opened its door the heavy smell of the chemicals caused him to step back.

To hell with it.

He reached back into the office and turned up the volume of his communication system. Then he walked down the hall and opened the door to the outside. He stepped out into the night.

This was better. The cool desert air was refreshing and revived him up a lot better than army coffee. Cool? It was *cold*. Weird thing about deserts, cold at night and hot during the day. Rather rubbed his hands together. The stars overhead were brilliant and he tried to pick out the formation of the Holdings. Which one was home?

"We've got to go," Gwielgi said, for the third time. The dozen hostages were still looking at him numbly, as if they all thought they were still asleep and dreaming. He reached out and shook one man by the shoulder. "We've got to go *now*."

"The others are dead," William Coltrane said, his eyes blank. "If you were injured, wounded, they killed you. There are just us. Twelve."

"I understand," Gwielgi said. "Help me get everyone on their feet."

Coltrane blinked. The request to provide help seemed to touch him in some way and he slowly stood, pulling at the woman next to him. Then he turned. Slowly the hostages assisted one another. Tsunasdi saw they were weak, probably dehydrated.

As the hostages began to move out of the shower room, Tsunasdi keyed his radio; the response was immediate.

"Sidewinder is green."

"Hammer is at six."

Rather was getting used to the cold. It was hard to see anything around him because he had to leave the door open in case there was a call. The light from the headquarters pretty well ruined his night vision, though Rather could still make out the stars. No danger of falling asleep out here, he thought. He walked back in to get his coffee and check the time.

Tsunasdi brought up the rear of the column. The hostages were more responsive, perhaps finally absorbing what was happening. He saw several glance at the dead Benderist soldiers as they made their way through the locker room and down the hall. Tsunasdi turned off the lamp in the hallway as he passed it.

They stopped at the entrance. The hostages were holding onto each other like a human chain. Tsunasdi pulled down his goggles. Then he saw they were all barefoot. He touched his headset and whispered.

"Gwi, they have no boots."

"Roger. Nothing to be done about it. Time?"

"Four plus forty-five."

"Take point to the building. I have not seen the HUP patrol."

"Roger."

Tsunasdi walked forward. As he came abreast of Gwielgi, Tsunasdi felt him unhook his satchel charge. Tsunasdi stepped out of the gymnasium and looked around. Through his goggles, the open door to the headquarters building was like a distant flare and he made out someone silhouetted by

345

the light. He reached back to the lead person of the hostages and held the man's elbow. He whispered as loud as he dared.

"Everyone, hold onto the person in front of you. We are not going to be moving very quickly, but we are going to be moving. Captain Gwielgi will bring up the rear. We do not have far to go. Stay together and help one another." Tsunasdi slid his hand down the man's arm and grasped his hand and guided it to the back of his belt. "Hold on to me," he said, and then he slowly started walking.

The hostages were like an accordion for a moment but Tsunasdi kept his speed slow, though a glance at his watch made him want to run. He took a breath and his discipline asserted itself. One step at a time.

As the hostages slowly shuffled past, Gwielgi opened the flap of the satchel charge and he looked at his watch. Four minutes. As the last hostage stepped outside, he propped the charge against the wall to one side of the door. Gwielgi pulled the fuse, arming it. It was set for fifteen minutes but there was no time to change it. He glanced over his shoulder into the darkness of the gym and then was gone.

Rather stepped out of the light and walked around the prefabricated building. He still had the need to urinate but he wasn't going to do it out front. The colonel would probably see it in the morning. His vision was adjusting to the darkness slowly but he really couldn't see much on the ground. He kicked at the earth, making a shallow trench with his boot. He could just make it out. He urinated into the trench, hoping it was all going into the hole. When Rather was done, he pushed dirt over it.

He walked towards the front of the building. In the far distance, well beyond the gym where the hostages were kept, Rather thought he saw some lights. It was a moment before he recognized them as the running lights of the HUP patrol. He heard the radio hiss and ran back into the office.

"Base, Patrol One, you copy?"

"Roger, One. Go ahead."

"Yeah, this joint is acting up again. The maintenance crew still up?"

"Affirmative. You bringing it in?"

"Roger, Base. Dash Two will remain on patrol, so you don't need to wake both of Patrol Two, just one. I'm inbound at this time but I'm taking it slow. Dash Two is continuing the circuit."

"Roger, One. I'll pass the word."

Rather hung up the microphone and pulled a handset across the small desk and touched one of the glowing buttons of the brigade intercom system. A sleepy voice from the maintenance section immediately answered. Rather explained the situation and heard an acknowledgement. He smiled to himself. Poor bastards were probably asleep. He touched another button and the First Battalion duty officer immediately responded.

"Good morning, lieutenant," Rather said, trying to sound alert. "Patrol One's Long Sword has a problem and is inbound to the maintenance area. Hip joint. The Cutlass is still making the circuit. We'll need one of the HUPs of Patrol Two to join it."

"Yes, sir," the young voice said. "One of them is awake anyway. I'll send him out. Be a few minutes."

"No rush. Give me a call when he moves."

"Yes, sir."

Lieutenant Rather hung up. A wave of sleepiness swept over him. He blinked hard and stood up. The office was too warm. He picked up his coffee cup. Time to go back outside.

Every so often one of the hostages would step on something or strike a rock with their toes. To Tsunasdi's ears the sharp intakes of breath sounded like bugle calls in the night. Still, they were still moving. He was trying to steer the column around obvious debris and thorny bushes, but his goggles did not provide very fine detail.

They were half way to the destroyed building when he saw the HUPs approaching. He stopped and slowly lay down, pulling the man behind him with him. The whole column followed in sequence, each person pulled down by the one in front.

The lead HUPAX, a Long Sword, was moving slowly, much slower than it had earlier. The Cutlass trailed behind, its floodlight on and focused on the bigger machine's legs.

Finally, the dark pair stopped, directly in front of the opening to the dry wash. Tsunasdi looked at his watch. Two minutes. The seconds slowly ticked away. Then the Long Sword turned towards them and walked, still slowly. The Saber, acting as if it was happy to be freed of its crippled companion, bounced away at easily twice the larger HUPAX's speed.

347

The Long Sword turned slightly, towards the column's right. Tsunasdi tried to remember the placement of the brigade's facilities. Was it going to park for the night, perhaps go to one of the maintenance areas?

The Long Sword passed them, less than a hundred meters away. Tsunasdi gambled and rose as it walked by, trusting that the pilot would be watching where he put the HUPAX's feet, now that he was within the brigade area, and would not be looking for escaping prisoners.

Tsunasdi reached the wall of the building. One minute. The original plan had been to pause here and let the prisoners rest but there was no time. He kept moving.

A TOT, Time On Target, is designed to have the first rounds of all involved indirect fire weapons, guns or missiles, arrive at the same instant, achieving surprise and maximizing casualties. Since different weapons, even when located in the same position, have different times of flight, they have to fire separately. The same weapons can fire multiple times and have all of their shells hit at the same time by adjusting the time of flight of each round, usually accomplished by changing charges and trajectories.

The slowest shells of the landing party self-propelled guns came from two 210mm howitzers. Their massive shells, each weighing up to half a ton, would take the longest to reach their targets. They fired first and simultaneously. The huge flashes filled the canyon as the guns recoiled on their mounts. As they slid forward their computers were already aligning them on their next targets.

The Frogfire batteries each had four missiles, each targeted separately. The launchers could only fire a pair simultaneously but the pause between launches was less than two seconds. Because the missiles carried their own guidance systems, the crews did not have to worry much about realigning the launchers. As the missiles left they were like glowing balls, lighting up the canyon walls and rims.

A pair of 122mm self-propelled guns fired the fastest shells. Using a preloaded rotary system, they were also capable of pumping out a round every second and a half, with most of the delay caused by the recoil mechanism. Each gun fired three rounds at each of its assigned targets.

As the Frogfires and 122s finished, their crews spun their vehicles around and raced to Ghost's loading ramp while the guns and launchers were still swiveling into travel alignment.

As they did, the 210s fired their last rounds. Like the others, their crews soon had the big machines rumbling towards Ghost.

Captain Nguyen watched from the bridge as the guns and missiles fired. Even through the armored hull of her ship she could hear the cannons. All she hoped was that the enemy had no one close enough to see the flash of the weapons. She turned to her bridge crew.

"Stand by to lift. Tell me when the last vehicle is onboard."

Nguyen sat at the flight controls and flexed her fingers. Now things were about to become interesting.

Tsunasdi looked at his watch, something he was trying not to do. It did not make any difference what time it was, they had to keep moving. He stepped into the dry wash and glanced behind him. He could still see the glow from the open door of the headquarters building but the HUPs were gone.

Thirty seconds.

Rather waved at the Long Sword as it passed and the pilot blinked his spotlight off and on. The HUP was noticeably limping but otherwise sounded normal. No, wait, there was a sound...

Rather heard a moan, almost a wail, and then a sound like something large, like a monorail car, was falling through the sky. He instinctively looked up just in time to see the 210mm cluster bomb unit shells pop open with quick, bright flashes. For a second, he did not understand what he was seeing; Jesul Rather's combat experience was limited, until this moment, to some minor patrol work on Benderist-controlled worlds. He had never been taken under fire by large artillery and never been fired on in the open without the armor of a HUPAX surrounding him. He paused, still looking up into the night. Then the world exploded.

The 210s had, as their first targets, the supply and fuel dumps of the brigade. Each shell released over fifty antiarmor shaped-charge finned bomblets and an additional hundred antipersonnel round bomblets. The antiarmor rounds struck like a wave of brilliant strobe lights, their explosions overlapping and sounding like the tearing of some giant sheet of canvas. The antipersonnel bomblets landed and bounced in all directions. A few went off immediately, sympathetically triggered by the antiarmor weapons or by impact with the ground. The rest armed themselves as they hit and their timers began counting down. They would go off at various intervals over the next fifteen minutes.

The Frogfire warheads also carried antiarmor cluster bombs, though they were much larger than the ones in the 210s. The Frogfires were supersonic as they came down and announced themselves with sharp cracks that echoed across the base. Their bombs lost little speed as the warheads opened and dove on their targets, the HUPAX repair bays and the First Battalion HUP area. They punctuated the ripping giant canvas of the 210s with what sounded like Hell's jackhammer. Patrol One's Long Sword caught two of the shaped charges, and one burst through the cockpit, killing the pilot. For a moment the HUP kept walking forward through the carnage until it collapsed in a pile.

The 122s had as their first targets the antiaircraft systems around the base. Their impact on the hills was almost unnoticed as laser batteries were ripped apart and missile launchers exploded and burned.

Each battery had more than one target. The 122s with their faster firing mechanisms had an advantage, needing only seconds for their computers to target their second targets. Each gun had fired an additional three rounds before they sped away.

The communication complex next to the brigade headquarters received three 122mm rounds. One was a little long – its blast knocked Rather down as he started to run back into his building. The other two were solid hits, with one taking out the power system and the other obliterating the brigade's primary transceivers.

The other 122mm self-propelled gun had aimed its last three rounds at the headquarters building. All three sliced through the building's roof and detonated just as they reached the floor. The building blew apart.

Rather, lying flat on the ground, was only aware of a flash of light. He could hear nothing, since both of his eardrums were blown out by the pressure waves. It took him a moment but he eventually sat up, pushing a piece of prefabricated wall off of himself as he did. His nose was bleeding, as were his ears, but he did not notice.

While he had been down the remaining four Frogfires arrived. Two worked over the HUP areas again. One came down on the barracks buildings. The fourth spread its bombs along the length of the runway revetments, where the brigade had set up its ammunition dump.

Almost immediately fires and secondary explosions erupted in the dump. Missile ammunition was particularly vulnerable and soon long glowing tendrils of burning missiles arced through the night.

The last rounds to arrive were the last two shells of the 210s. This time each 1500-kilogram round was simply high explosive inside a steel shell. The slow firing 210s were more accurate than the 122s and they proved it this night. They landed among the Firerays parked at the end of the runway and from each one a thousand kilograms of explosive pushed five hundred of steel casing into a thousand fragments. Blast, flash heat, and shrapnel ripped the fighters apart, setting them on fire and detonating their stored ammunition.

From the impact of the first rounds until the last 210s arrived was less than five seconds.

"Captain, last SPA onboard. Retracting ramp and closing bay door."

"Roger, lifting. Hold tight, everyone. We've got to pick up our prom dates."

A Ghost ion pulse gunner looked at her assistant, puzzled. "What the hell is a 'Prom date?'"

"Sidewinder, Hammer is lifting."

"Sidewinder, roger."

The impacting rounds momentarily paralyzed the hostages, first knocking them off their feet with the concussion of the 210s, and then hypnotizing them with the wave of explosions and fires engulfing the base. Tsunasdi and Gwielgi pulled them to their feet.

"No time to be tourists, folks," Gwielgi said. He did not bother to lower his voice. "We've got a ride to catch."

"Very nice," someone said. It was Coltrane. He was staring at the fires and the occasional secondary explosions that rumbled across the base. He turned to Tsunasdi. "I suppose we ought to get out of here."

"Yes, sir," Tsunasdi said. "We have a kilometer to go."

"Let us do it, then," Coltrane said. He took another look back. "Very nice." Then he helped get the others to their feet.

Jesul Rather, deafened by the hit on the headquarters building, stood and tried to make sense of what he was seeing. Fires burned all around him, some fed by fuel, and explosions continued to occur in the ammunition dump. Though more than half a kilometer away, the explosions were violent enough he finally noticed debris impacting the earth around him.

Rather wanted to run and get help but was confused as to which way to go. After all, he was at headquarters. Or what was left of it. The burning and exploding ammunition dump to the west looked like a wall of tortured fire, punctuated at one end by what had been the brigade's fighter flight detachment. Further south the vehicle park and HUP maintenance areas burned, though not as ferociously. But small explosions began to occur in the shadows near those installations. Was someone still shooting at them? To the east, many of the prefabricated barracks burned a strange orange as their synthetic materials went up. By the light of the fires, he saw other barracks were destroyed or damaged, though people were moving through the glare.

North there seemed to be nothing. Remarkably, the biggest surviving building on the base, the Militia gym, still stood, apparently untouched. He seized on the idea of going there – brigade sentries were there, armed. They would protect him. And they would have a working radio so he could communicate with the rest of the brigade. Half stumbling, he trotted towards the building.

The Cutlass pilot, a woman named Keera Jennings, saw the attack on the base just as she turned the corner of her perimeter sweep. Unlike Rather, Jennings knew exactly what she was seeing: a coordinated indirect fire attack. As she saw the rippling, brilliant explosions of the cluster munitions, she guessed the attack was preparation for an assault on the brigade headquarters by a ground force and immediately called for help.

"Patrol One Bravo, does anyone copy? Repeat, does anyone copy?"

"Patrol One, this is duty officer, Fourth Battalion. You are very weak, over."

"Fourth, brigade headquarters is under attack, repeat, under attack. We've just been struck by artillery. Major hits to ammunition and fuel storage sites, and it looks like our commo complex was hit. I can't see everything. I'm in a Cutlass on the west side of the base. Can you send us some help?"

"Patrol One, I'm taking us to full alert and getting the CO. We are the closest battalion to you. Are you getting any response from the other battalions?"

"Negative, Fourth. They are too far away. I think this was prep fire for a ground assault. Our fighters are gone and I can see that our armor lager was hit. Several vehicles burning. I think our barracks was hit as well."

"Roger, Patrol One. Stand by one. Stand by... Patrol One, be advised we are bringing our battalion to full alert. One company is going to be detached to you. Advise your troops to look for our HUPs in approximately twenty minutes."

"Roger, Fourth." Jennings nodded. She hadn't seen any movement in her own battalion's HUP area but reinforcements were coming.

"Patrol One, Diamond Six Actual. Do you copy?"

She felt a wave of relief. Diamond Six was her own battalion commander. Someone was in charge.

"Roger, Diamond Six. Good to hear you, sir."

"We are getting some of our HUPs moving. Patrol Two should be joining you on battalion primary. Four other HUPs are being crewed right now and will join you. Take up a tactical position on the hills to the southwest of the base – that's the most likely avenue of attack."

"Roger, Six. Be advised that Fourth Battalion has been notified and is sending us a company. Switching to primary."

Jennings spotted the two HUPs of Patrol Two coming fast in her direction. She turned southwest and ran the Cutlass through the darkness. Patrol Two was not as fast but they joined her on the back slope of the hill in only a few minutes.

"Patrol Two, go sensors off. I'll be our eyes."

"Roger, lead."

"Two, did you see One Alpha?"

"His HUP was down, Bravo, near the maintenance area. No fire, but it looked like it fell when it ran into some junk."

"Roger. He had a bad hip. Maybe it just gave out."

"Roger."

She flipped through her sensors and bit her lower lip. If an attack was coming, now was the time. Jennings saw nothing on her screens. But if they were coming, whoever "they" were, then it meant they were coming sensors off or she was in the wrong place.

At the bottom of her visual field she saw a cluster of green dots on the map display as the IFF of the reinforcing HUPs responded to her sensors. She keyed her microphone and advised them to turn their sensors off – her Cutlass was very well equipped and would spot anything closing with them.

"Patrol One, Diamond Six. I've got six more HUPs crewed and moving. I'm sending them south. They will be to your east. We'll have more soon after that. We have a lot of damage in the area but only three HUPs destroyed. Our problem is getting to them. A bunch of timed CBUs were dropped and they keep popping off. We've had several people wounded by them already. They're making it difficult for our people to get into their HUPs. We're getting an APC to shuttle them."

"Roger, Six."

Jennings felt her sense of relief grow. If the battalion only lost three HUPs, then they could hold their own against anything that might be coming at them, though she was beginning to doubt a ground attack was likely or it would have arrived by now.

Then her sensors picked up the approaching landing ship.

Patricia Nguyen brought Ghost in fast and low, just skimming the hills close enough that the landing ship raised dust swirls with its passing. She and her crew saw the fires of the enemy position before their fire control sensors picked up any targets.

She was not interested in targets unless they posed a threat to Ghost's passage as it hurried to get to the rendezvous site to pick up the hostages. Her flight path was to the west of the base, never closer than two kilometers.

Sensors showed little threat activity. Sporadic radio communications spiked here and there, probably from HUPAX, but no active sensors, radars, or jammers were identified.

Fine. You leave us alone and we will leave you alone. For now.

Jennings saw the landing ship as a rapidly approaching red rectangle in her visual field. Her data screen was flooded with information as it approached and her sensors read it more clearly. She nearly yelled her warning to the others.

"Alert! Viper-class landing ship approaching from two zero five, heading northeast. Get behind the hill! Take cover!"

Jennings saw the other HUPs in her group move forward and turn, trying to put the hill between them and the speeding landing ship. But it would be abreast of their position before they gained cover, and if it fired...

Jennings never thought of herself as brave, and she barely knew the people in the other HUPAX, but they were *her* people and she would do what she could to protect them. And there was only one thing to do.

She went into a sprint, turning west, toward the landing ship's path.

"Captain, Guns. Active strobe, fire control sensor, HUPAX."
"Roger, Guns. Kill it."

Ghost was a Viper-class landing ship and, compared to others in the Militia's small fleet, not heavily armed. Had the Cutlass remained partially hidden on the slope of the hill, only her missile launchers could have reached it and Nguyen was not interested in killing a HUPAX. But Jennings raced towards Ghost, coming out into the open.

The Cutlass, small and moving at close to 80 KPH , was a tough target, almost invisible to human eyes with its dark blue and green coloring shrouding it in the night. But the eyes hunting it were not just human. A streak of lightning from an ion pulse turret whipped in front of the HUP, momentarily dazzling Jennings. A laser bit into the ground, fusing the sand into splattered beads of molten glass. Two misses; Jennings felt hope surge.

But Ghost was descending as Nguyen guided it down to the flat plain. This simplified the gunners' firing solutions and the ship's fire control system, designed to kill nimble space fighters, keyed on the Cutlass and the next rounds did not miss.

An ion pulse weapon scored the first hit and the electrical discharge threw the Cutlass*'s* visual displays into unintelligible confusion and disrupted the mindlink. The hit was close enough to the cockpit Jennings felt a wave of heat sweep over her as the HUP, deprived of her control and relying on its on controls, stumbled and almost fell.

The lasers caught the Cutlass low, and Jennings felt the HUP lurch as armor flew off a leg in a spray of glowing metal just as the mindlink kicked back in. Something went wrong with her left leg and suddenly her speed was halved.

The starboard missile launcher had fired as Nguyen leveled Ghost twenty meters above the desert floor. As the Cutlass slowed, the missile, looking like a burning meteor, slammed into the Cutlass.

Jennings was pitched forward in her ejection seat and only the restraint straps kept her from being thrown into her displays. Smoke poured into the cockpit and her control of the HUP became mushy. A computer voice began chanting all the things that were wrong but she ignored it. The mindlink blinked off for a moment and then came back online.

All her weapons were dead except her small missile launcher. She looked at the now outlined shape of the oncoming landing ship but received no lock indicator. The Cutlass staggered to a halt, its left leg ruined, and she struggled through the mindlink to keep the HUP upright.

"Go to hell."

Jennings did not realize she said it aloud and that her voice activated microphone picked it up. She looked up almost directly overhead, the targeting reticle following her eyes, and fired the missile launcher in a salvo. The ten missiles rose into the air, into the flight path of Ghost. She saw stars vanish, covered by the bulk of the landing ship. Then there was a light beyond seeing as multiple beams of coherent energy ripped through the Cutlass.

She was dead before the missiles reached Ghost's altitude and did not see them miss.

"Captain, Guns. Scratch one. Ballistic missiles to starboard, no guidance. We're clear."

"Roger. Stay alert for fighters."

"Roger, ma'am. Scope is clear."

It was a classic nightmare. Something dark and scary is coming in the night and the only hope is to escape, but feet and legs fail, thrashing uselessly, immobilized so that steps smaller than those a baby were all that was possible. The sand in the gully seemed to be alive, sliding out from beneath their feet as they struggled away from the base.

The line of hostages had become broken as they entered the ravine and several people fell. When they moved again, Gwielgi was in front and Tsunasdi was in back.

Gwielgi had a prisoner's arm across his shoulders and was half carrying the limping man whose ankle had twisted just as they got to the mouth of the gully. The man had tried to stand and walk on it, spurred by the continuing explosions coming from the base, but could barely move.

Gwielgi looked back. Coltrane was doing the same with another prisoner. The others, their feet clearly suffering from making their way across the thorn bushes and sharp rocks imbedded in the gully, leaned on one another and were still moving.

Bringing up the rear, Sergeant Tsunasdi seemed utterly unconcerned. He was helping two people, holding onto their arms, whispering words of encouragement to the people in front of him. Did nothing rattle that man? Gwielgi shook his head and looked ahead.

They had decided that the prisoners would be unable to climb out of the gully where they had entered. It was not the most direct route, but a little way up the gully there was a branching portion that might be easier for them.

"Couple of a hundred meters, and then we're out of this," Gwielgi said over his shoulder in a harsh whisper. He did not bother to add that then it would be three quarters of a kilometer across rough ground to the pick-up point. What he said would serve as a spur for this leg. For the next leg, he would simply tell them that they were late for the rendezvous. He hoped that would be enough encouragement to compensate for their weakened conditions.

He did not see Ghost from within the gully, but they all heard it roar by, somewhere to their west. The sound energized the column and the pace picked up. Gwielgi glanced at his watch and remembered his comment to Tsunasdi, hoping Nguyen had a very, very good watch.

Now Gwielgi hoped it sucked and was running an hour or two late.

357

"All stations, this is Brigade Six. We are restoring communications and sensors. Be careful. Some areas have delayed action cluster bombs, though the worst of them seem past. First Battalion, get some HUPs to our northern perimeter. That landing ship went in that direction and it may be deploying a force there."

"Roger, Six. Diamond Six is up. We have a skirmish line of eight HUPs headed in that direction now. I'm going to push them into that first set of foothills."

"Roger, good. Let me know if you pick up anything."

Nguyen settled the landing ship onto the broad, flat area north of the base, slightly less than two kilometers from the perimeter. She touched her headset as the engines whined down.

"Snake, Hammer is green."

"Sidewinder copies. We are coming."

She eyed the clock. Fifteen minutes. Nguyen nodded to herself and leaned back in her chair and stretched. It had been a long night and it was not over yet.

Someone handed her a cold drink. She took a swallow and grimaced. It was the crap the infantry drank, good for replacing electrolytes and salts and good for killing weeds. Well, she probably needed it. Nguyen made herself take another swallow and watched her screens. The imagery suggested they had killed all four Firerays. That would make life a little easier, but she was more worried about HUPAX. On the ground, with hills pressing close, Ghost was vulnerable.

She looked at the bridge clock again. It seemed to be moving very slowly.

The line of Red Cock HUPAX swept past the gymnasium but Rather did not hear them. Feeling his way in the dark inside the building, he had found the first dead body in the hallway and shortly after that a portable lamp. He fumbled it on. The sight of the dead sentry meant little and it was not until he went down to the locker room that he realized that the prisoners were gone. He did not connect the barrage with the vanished prisoners and assumed they had taken advantage of an opportunity to escape.

He went back down the hall to where the first dead man lay. The portable field radio was there and he picked it up. It looked intact. He pushed the power switch and a small green light came on. He put his arm through one of its straps and headed towards the entrance. As he did, he brought the microphone to his lips but before he keyed it, he saw something to one side of the doorway in the edge of the lamp's light.

A HUP pilot, he had never served in any other branch. As Rather brought his light over to the object, what he saw appeared to be a small backpack, though not of a design that he usually saw in the brigade. That it could be anything other than a backpack did not occur to him. Well, he would check it out after he made his call.

Rather stepped outside for better transmission and keyed the microphone. It was hard to talk when you could not hear yourself.

"Brigade, is anyone on this frequency? This is Lieutenant Rather. I can't hear anything and I'm broadcasting in the blind. Can anyone hear me?"

He put the radio down in the dirt and knelt beside it. He keyed the mike again and noticed that a small red light came on. It went out when he released it. All right, that's the transmission indicator. He brought the microphone to his lips and repeated his broadcast.

As soon as the red light went out, he realized a third light was blinking. Partially covered by the radio's cover, the green light seemed to vibrate. Receiving? He watched until it went black and then spoke again.

"This is Lieutenant Rather. I am at the prisoners' compound, repeat, the prisoners' compound and..."

He felt a flash of heat and then a giant's hand slapped him from behind, throwing him half a dozen meters. The radio vanished before he stopped rolling, though he still clutched the microphone in his hand. It felt like someone had scraped his back with a knife, maybe several knives.

Rather lay motionless as debris landed around him. A couple of small pieces of concrete bounced off his legs and back. Then, except for the swirling dust, everything was still.

The lamp was back where he had been kneeling beside the radio, miraculously untouched by the blast.

The blast. Was the attack resuming? Rather got up, first on all fours, and then to his feet. No, no new attack. Fires still burned in the base, though a couple were out. Maybe there was nothing left to burn. Rather turned towards the gym.

Even in the dark he could see the gaping hole. The backpack. It had been a satchel charge. That meant the prisoners had help; there were commandos on the base, or had been.

Rather looked around, trying to see in the dark, but he saw nothing other than that he was alone. He turned towards the center of the base. Its fires were out, but he knew where the headquarters was. He picked up the lamp and started running.

Major Felden Pierce, Diamond Six Actual, First Battalion Commanding Officer, got to the first available HUPAX, a Saber, while the timed CBUs were still detonating. Something from one of them had hit him in his right calf, but, other than tying on a field dressing, he ignored the wound, struggling to get the small HUP out of the HUPAX lager and away from the fires.

As the battalion recovered from the shock of the attack, more HUPs joined him. Initially, he had sent HUPs to the south and west, thinking any ground attack would be coming from the hills in that direction. But *Ghost's* run past the base raised the possibility that the attack could come from the north.

Pierce took seven HUPs with him and swept north, towards the foothills beyond the gymnasium. His initial plan was to simply set up within the hills in a skirmish line while the rest of the battalion organized under its company commanders.

The Saber, like the other small HUPs of the battalion, was primarily used for scouting. Relatively low to the ground, the 40-ton offered excellent sensors. Taking the central position in the skirmish line, he walked the HUP up a gully.

The skirmish line relied primarily on light amplification as it worked its way forward. Pierce flipped through a variety of passive sensors and his infrared revealed a dully glowing trail on the ground. He flipped over to light amplification and saw a dark line through the lighter sand. For a moment he did not understand what the black strip was. He blinked on his spotlight for a moment and saw enough to tell him a column of people had been in the gully.

"Head's up, people. I've got a heat trail of a bunch of people heading north. Looks like we have troops on the ground here. Hold your current positions. Captain Maintz, you are with me. We're going to follow this trail for about a klick and see what is up. Captain Veederman, you are in charge here until I get back."

He heard the two captains acknowledge and Maintz' Rapier followed him as he moved up the gully. He spoke to Maintz as they traveled.

"I think this may have been a recon unit, calling in the fire we took. If they are heading for their pick-up, we may catch some ground vehicles, maybe a shuttle."

"Roger, sir. You figure the Alliance did this?"

"Well, it probably wasn't the locals. They don't have enough to take on the 173rd and the Alliance has two regiments in landing ships in nearby orbit, or they were. We need to know more, so if we catch these people, kill their vehicles and we'll try and round them up."

"Understood. Sir, a landing ship headed in this direction. Is that their pick-up?"

"I don't think so, captain," Pierce said. "It won't be close by, too dangerous for it. It's probably pretty far north, well beyond our other battalion up there. But it will probably send shuttles or vehicles to pick them up."

"Yes, sir."

"What's your armament, captain?"

"Two twin recoilless rifles and lasers."

"Glad to hear it. This little guy doesn't have anything except one GTL1. Apparently, it just came off the maintenance line."

"You point them out, sir. I'll knock them down."

"Roger, captain," Pierce replied in the dark of his cockpit. He smiled; whatever was going on, Maintz had a Red Cocks' heart and he was glad the man was with him.

The climb out of the gully was a small trip through hell for the prisoners. The sand was gone and jagged stones chewed up their feet; all were limping and leaving a trail of blood behind them. The path they took was so narrow Tsunasdi could not help both prisoners at the same time. He would help one forward while the other hobbled as best she could, and then he would help her while the other hobbled. At the head of the column, Gwielgi was no longer carrying his man as much as dragging him. He glanced over his shoulder and saw that the column was very strung out, well over twenty meters.

Finally, Gwielgi stepped onto the relatively flat ground above the gully. He lowered the man he was assisting and quickly moved back down the small ravine and pulled and dragged the others to the top. On his second trip to the top, he dropped his first aid bag in front of an exhausted Coltrane.

"There are some field dressings in there. Use them on the feet in the worst shape. We still have a way to go." Coltrane nodded and opened the pack. Gwielgi unhooked one of his two canteens. "Pass this around as people come up here." He handed it to Coltrane and went back for more prisoners.

As Gwielgi got to each one he would take them by the arm and whisper that there was water waiting. It seemed to help most, though there were several who appeared to be totally exhausted. They staggered with their movements mechanical and almost ineffective. On his last trip he helped one of the two people Tsunasdi was aiding.

"Time?" He whispered.

"We are late," Tsunasdi said without bothering to look at his watch. "We passed check-in two minutes ago."

Gwielgi said nothing, saving his breath as he half-carried the woman upward. Things, he decided, could not possibly get worse.

Then they heard the HUPAX.

Pierce almost missed the place where the trail turned out of the gully. It had hugged the western wall and he took a few steps before he realized that he was no longer seeing it. He swiveled his HUPs upper torso and flipped up the infrared overlay.

There it was, turning into a small ravine feeding into the gully. The trail was glowing much more brightly now. He followed it into the opening of the ravine. The larger Rapier followed close behind, looking up at the edges of the ravine.

The ground was clogged with loose rock and Pierce slipped as he started forward. He dropped the infrared and went to light amplification. The Saber slipped again and he swore quietly to himself. He turned off the amplification and turned on a pair of spotlights in the HUP's upper fuselage. He could see much more clearly now and it was easier to place his feet.

The spotlights were not stabilized and bounced as the HUP walked forward. For a moment Pierce had trouble finding the trail since the ground was mostly rock. He moved the Saber slowly, looking for the trail. It took a moment before he realized he could see something. He stopped and bent the Saber forward. There was something on the rocks.

Blood.

"Captain, Guns. Passive infrared is picking up people on the other side of the plateau, a little more than a dozen."

"Roger. Range?"

"Slightly more than 700 meters."

"Roger, stay alert. Active sensors remain off. Those could be our people."

"Aye, ma'am."

Gwielgi looked north across the relatively flat ground of the plateau. If Nguyen was still there, Ghost was less than a kilometer away. His goggles were fading on him and weren't much better than his bare eyes. He pulled them off and pulled the old cell out and shoved in a new one.

Now he could see clearly. Behind some low rocks, he could make out the upper half of Ghost. He looked back down the ravine.

His goggles dazzled him for a second before the filters kicked in as they amplified the light of the lead HUP's spotlights. The dark Saber was stopped near the bottom of the ravine, about a hundred meters away. Behind it was a taller HUP. He looked back at the landing ship. Too damned far. He grabbed Tsunasdi by the shoulder.

"Tell Nguyen our situation. Tell her we are heading *west*, not north. Got it? West. Tell her to go sensors on when we yell."

Tsunasdi nodded and spoke into his headset while Gwielgi pulled the prisoners to their feet. He did not bother to keep his voice down.

"All right, people, let's go. We've got a pair of HUPs following us and we have to get out of here *now*. Come on, get up!"

The others had heard the HUPAX and most were already on their feet. He grabbed Coltrane and pointed west.

"Take them that way, major. Do not stop, do not look back, keep them going."

"Understood, captain. Good fortune." Coltrane pulled the arm of the weakest prisoner over his shoulder and turned to the others.

"We go *now*. Help one another." The prisoners, most holding onto one another, began moving in a shambling gait that was almost military double-time. Coltrane chanted the rhythm as they moved away.

"She got the message," Tsunasdi said as he stood up. He glanced down the ravine. The HUPs slowly climbed it, carefully watching for an ambush. "She recommends we move away from this position. Some of her weapons can reach it and she will try to lay down covering fire for us."

"They'll be up here in a minute, maybe sooner. As soon as she lights up her sensors those bastards will see her," Gwielgi said. "I don't know what else they have on the base but they'll call for all the help they can get."

"She said she has a plan." He touched his earpiece. "She says she would appreciate it if we would move our butts. Apparently, this is going to be a very busy intersection in a few minutes."

Pierce did not like the narrow confines of the ravine. It would be very easy for someone to stand on the edge above them and get a free shot. Most HUPs had some difficulty shooting all their weapons directly overhead, though the Saber was better off than the Rapier. He led the way cautiously. He knew they were close to whomever they were tracking. The blood trail suggested they had wounded, which would slow them down. If they abandoned their wounded, then he would have his prisoners.

As he got near to the top of the long ramp of the ravine, Pierce looked over its edge. The blood trail went straight ahead. He turned off his spotlight and turned on his light amplification. As the Saber walked forward, he immediately saw people in the distance.

"Troops in the open, bearing two seven five, range two fifty. I don't see weapons. Hell, these are our prisoners! They must have escaped during the attack." So much for capturing an enemy recon team.

"Roger, sir. What do you want to do?"

"Well, we might as well round them up. Contact brigade and ask them to send a truck and a security detachment for them. The way they are limping, I don't think they could walk back."

"Roger, sir. Making the call."

"Very well. Come on up here out of the ravine. I'll get in front of them, you get behind them. If they try to run, put a laser shot in front of them. Brigade needs them to keep the locals in check."

"Yes, sir."

The superior sensors of Pierce's Saber saved him. In the corner of his visual field, he saw a flash overlaid with the symbols for active scanning and missiles. He turned his attention and saw a waterfall of missiles arcing towards him. Instinctively he ran forward, jerking the HUP into motion and out of the kill zone.

Ghost's most powerful weapons were designed for fights against other landing ships; for small terrestrial targets she used her smaller, secondary weapons. These were a small number of laser and ion pulse weapon turrets and anti-armor missile launchers. The ship's gunnery officer knew a single shot from the main battery would kill any HUPAX ever made and incidentally incinerate the hostages. He only freed the secondary weapons to deal with the HUPs coming up out of the ravine.

Ghost's gunners could not all fire due to the position of the landing ship. Only two of the three secondary missile launchers could be brought to bear. But the small ion pulse weapons and laser turrets had a clear angle at the tall Rapier. Spears of ruby red light stabbed in the darkness while the blue-white streaks of ion pulse energy momentarily lit up the area like strokes of lightning.

All the energy weapons struck the moving Rapier and the HUP staggered forward, directly into the path of an incoming pair of missiles that slammed into its side.

"Sensors on," Nguyen commanded. She held the flight controls in a firm grip. "Rising. Take them down, Guns."

The remaining missile launcher located on the other side of Ghost was unmasked as the ship rose and it fired. The Rapier, recovering from the impact of the combined fire, swung its turrets towards the landing ship while its pilot screamed for help over his radio. He fired his four laser turrets, scoring hits on the armored hull of Ghost, leaving two red, glowing streaks that slowly faded.

Ghost continued to use its smallest lasers but they were more powerful than any carried by a HUPAX. They fired again at almost the same instant. It was not an equal contest. The Rapier lost its right weapon pylon and a recoilless rifle turret at the end of the other pylon as a red beam sliced through it. The other lasers ripped into the middle of the HUP, sending armor spraying in glowing globs of molten metal. Another missile slammed into the same area, compounding the damage, and shaking the HUP. The pilot heard warning alarms sounding in his cockpit as he tried to turn the Rapier.

The ion pulse weapons struck the HUP virtually dead center. The mindlink and visual field became totally disrupted but the klaxon of a damaged fusion power unit had the pilot's attention. He did not need a detailed read-out to tell him his HUP was dead. He initiated the ejection system.

Immediately his ejection seat was enveloped in a steel box slamming up from the floor. An overhead hatch blew away as a rocket motor accelerated the box through the hatch and into the air. The Rapier took a step and then erupted in an explosion of white light and burning yellow tentacles from its recoilless rifle ammunition.

Pierce saw the ground around him light up like sunrise and knew the Rapier was gone. Running a zigzag course and looking for cover, he saw the landing ship closing on his sensor screen. He glanced towards the escaped prisoners but ignored them. He had more pressing business, like staying alive.

He spun the small HUP to his left, just as a red beam sliced through where he would have been. A warning chime told Pierce that a missile tracked him. He kept turning and dashed behind a tall rock outcrop. The missile slammed into the rocks, showering him with harmless fragments. He looked ahead. The entrance to the ravine was a hundred meters away. He came out from behind the outcropping and dodged left. The warning chime resumed. An ion pulse weapon, partially thrown off by his electronic counter measures, burned into the ground beside him, throwing up glowing rock fragments violently enough that his damage display showed his left weapons pylon was hurt.

Pierce twisted his fuselage right, trying to see if there was any other incoming fire and protect the arm. Through his heads-up display he saw the shape of the landing ship coming after him like some giant prey animal. For a second, he froze in shock. *Ghost*, not a large landing ship, was still larger than many ocean surface ships and Pierce had never had one coming after him. It blotted out the stars and flooded his visual field with the flare of its engines.

God, that thing's a monster!

Fifty meters to the ravine. The *Saber's* electronic countermeasures were trying to block all the active fire control sensors grabbing at the small HUP but were overwhelmed by the sheer power the landing ship generated. He cut right and a laser beam sliced into the HUP beside the cockpit, close enough for him to feel the heat come through the bulkhead. His damaged pylon took a direct hit from another laser and died, but he was willing to accept it rather than take another hit in the HUP's body.

Pierce pivoted left and leapt the HUP off a rock outcropping. Leaping into the air made the job of the missile tracking him much easier. Arcing through the air, his HUP was in the missile's element and moving at a fraction of its speed. It detonated against his back armor, hammering the dark-colored Saber as it descended. Pierce's eyes flicked down to the damage display and what he saw was death waiting to happen. One more hit...

The HUP slammed into the bottom of the ravine, stumbled, and fell. Pierce waited to die but nothing happened. He fought to get up. There was something wrong with the mindlink system and it took all of his effort to get the HUP to respond. The Saber finally stood upright. He walked forward, down the ravine, picking up speed and disregarding the danger of sliding on the rocks. He called for the rearward sensors but got nothing in response. They were probably dead, he realized. He decided against swiveling the HUP's fuselage – facing straight ahead made balancing the Saber easier. A crawling feeling made its way up his spine as he waited for a shot into his HUP's back but nothing happened.

Ghost settled three hundred meters from the top of the ravine and threw open her main hatch. Even as her loading ramp was extended, a vehicle and a half dozen crew came running down it, heading for the prisoners.

Tsunasdi stood, watching the approaching figures. Gwielgi was not to be seen, though the prisoners could be made out not far away. He started towards them when he saw a pulsing light to his left.

It was the strobe on the Rapier pilot's ejection capsule. Tsunasdi picked up his pace but slowed down when he saw a figure squatting beside the capsule. It was Gwielgi.

The Rapier pilot was injured but awake. Gwielgi stood as Tsunasdi walked up but he kept his submachine gun loosely pointed at the pilot.

"I think his spine is fractured," Gwielgi said. Tsunasdi nodded. Gwielgi looked back at the man, whose face periodically contorted in pain. Then he looked over at the fast-approaching landing ship crew, their flashlights bouncing as they ran, and the utility vehicle. He looked back at the pilot. Then he nodded. He raised his weapon.

"All right, here's what we're going to do. If we leave you here, you'll probably be dead in an hour. And it won't be easy. So, we're going to take you to our landing ship. It will not be a pleasant trip for you. Hang in there and you'll live. And leave your pistol alone."

Gwielgi turned back towards the running crew and whistled. A couple skidded to a halt and turned in his direction.

"We need a hand with a wounded prisoner," Gwielgi called out. "Send the vehicle over here as soon as our people are loaded." One of them yelled back an acknowledgment and the two ran after the others.

Gwielgi reached into the capsule and removed the pilot's handgun, checked its safety, and stuffed it into his belt. Tsunasdi opened a small first aid pouch on his belt and took out a small syringe. He flipped off the cover and jabbed it into the pilot's thigh. Almost immediately the man's face relaxed.

"Well, what do you think of the war so far?" Tsunasdi asked Gwielgi.

"Up to now it has been quite interesting." The vehicle was coming towards them while some former prisoners, assisted by crew, were hobbling towards Ghost.

"Hang around," Tsunasdi said in a rare attempt at humor. "The evening has just begun."

Chapter 26: Lure

21 December 2824

Halfway through White Snake Pass, the most direct way through the Black Mountains for anyone going west from the Benderist brigade headquarters, the pass widened into a broad canyon nearly a kilometer in width. Captain John Hardin and his armored company were staged behind the low hills on the southern side of the canyon. All power off, the tanks and APCs sat in the cool night air and waited. The only thing on was a field radio strapped to the back of the recon soldier sitting beside Hardin on the armored turret of his Bob Cat tank.

Hardin cracked his knuckles and looked around. To his left were the ten Bob Cats of his two tank platoons. The APC-equipped infantry platoon had their vulnerable vehicles further behind, but the infantry, equipped with antiarmor missiles, lay in a line close to the trail used by the Benderist supply convoys.

Somewhere off to his left, near the western exit from the canyon, were the two HUPs that formed the base of the L-shaped ambush. He had not seen them since they had offloaded from their landing ships. Hardin had never been so happy to get off a landing ship; the ride down from Coyote Bay had been conducted at such a low altitude that he had finally feigned being asleep so the people of his company would not see how afraid he was.

Hardin glanced at his watch. The enemy brigade headquarters was being hit about now if everything was going as planned but there was no way to

369

tell from here. If the attack failed to take out the brigade's communication system, his own small role would be fatally compromised. It was another way of saying, he realized, that he would be dead meat.

The recon soldier, her face blackened beneath her dark beret, touched his elbow and nodded, holding up one finger as she listened intently to her earphones.

"Enemy sighted by Team One."

Somewhere to his right, to the east, members of Second Regiment's Reconnaissance battalion, hidden in the darkness, saw the expected water convoy. Their Chekinov Scout counterparts were off to the west, watching the track as it entered the narrower portion of the pass, the twisting course of white sand that gave the pass its name. The soldier touched his arm again and held up two fingers.

"Team Two." Hardin nodded back to the soldier and dropped into his turret. He tapped the shoulder of his gunner and then climbed back up. Taking his night vision binoculars, he stood on the hatch ring of the tank commander's cupola and looked at the eastern mouth of the canyon. For a moment he saw nothing. But then came the glow of low intensity driving lights. He lowered his binoculars and saw the dim, reflected light on the canyon walls. The convoy was just short of the open area.

Hardin turned towards the next tank in line, knowing its crew watched him with their light amplification devices. He waved and received one in return. Again he dropped into the turret.

Hardin switched on his radio. This part was risky, for an inadvertent transmission with the convoy so close might give away their location, but he had to have communications ready to go. He plugged in his headset and played out enough line to allow him to climb back up on the turret.

There was definitely no need for the light amplifying binoculars. The vehicles of the convoy were emerging from narrow part of the pass and all had at least some lights on. Even their escorting HUPs were using spotlights. Perhaps they were helping the wheeled and tracked vehicles to find their way. Well, they weren't in combat conditions.

Not yet.

He watched the lead vehicle, which he estimated to be an eight-wheeled armored fighting vehicle, grind its way down the track. It was followed by a similar AFV that hung back by about a hundred meters. Behind it was the rest of the convoy. Several heavy trucks, including at least two tankers, two tracked APCs, and an AFV bringing up the rear made up the column. Seven vehicles in all. On either side of the column walked a HUPAX. The column's lights occasionally silhouetted the closest one and he guessed it to be a Long Sword. He could not tell what the other HUP was.

Hardin focused on the last AFV. That one was the key. The column continued forward, the track less than five hundred meters away from the armored company. He waited until the last AFV was almost directly in front of his tank. He turned to the recon radio operator.

"Give them the word," Hardin said to her in what he hoped was a calm voice. As the radio operator talked into her headset, she slid off the smooth back of the turret and then jumped to the ground. Hardin dropped onto the commander's seat and keyed his microphone.

"Armor Six, turn them on. Anvil, we're rolling."

"Anvil copies."

Almost immediately he heard the whine of tanks powering up; the drivers must have had their thumbs poised above the start buttons. Hardin glanced at his small instrument display and switched it to tactical. A map presentation flashed onto the screen with the enemy column represented as red dots. Blue dots were in a line to his left.

"Armor, go. Target the Long Sword."

He flipped his communication switch over to intercom as his tank lurched forward.

"Gunner, target. AFV, 12 o'clock, 500."

His tank climbed up the small hill it had hidden behind, its long gun barrel already seeking its target.

"On the way." The tank rocked as the gun roared. The armor-piercing slug of the newly installed cannon discarded its sabots into the darkness and streaked the 500 meters to the AFV. The AFV was not designed to fight tanks and its armor was no match for the hypervelocity slug.

The tank round struck the left side of the AFV, passing through a tall drive wheel, and punched through the thin armor. The armor liquefied under the energy and sprayed as white-hot droplets through the interior. The slug kept on going, ripping into the massive engine block of the AFV and breaking it into large pieces. It still had enough energy to slice through the AFV's other side and finally embed itself in the far cliff face. By the time it did, the AFV had exploded, its fuel and ammunition erupting so violently the AFV was torn in half.

The result was that the entrance back into the pass was partially blocked, which was Hardin's intention.

"Gunner, target. HUPAX, Long Sword, 10 o'clock, 450."

The turret swung to the left as the tank leapt off a small rise. Now doing close to 40 KPH, the stabilized gun leveled on the dark shape of the HUPAX. Hardin saw the tall war machine fire several emerald-green lasers at a target to his left. A spray of sparks on its center marked a hit from a Bob Cat using an older cannon. The old guns did not have the velocity of the newer weapons half the company carried. But the gun aiming system was the same and the accuracy was almost absolute.

"On the way!"

His tank jerked with the blinding blast.

"Stay on it. Driver, do a one eighty right."

While the turret continued to face the Long Sword's left side, the tank turned to its right and headed back in the direction from which it had come. As Hardin came out of the turn he saw an explosion in the darkness, a thrust of flame shooting a hundred meters into the night sky as violent as the exhaust of a rocket.

The death signature of a tank.

Again his Bob Cat fired. Hardin saw a spray of flame on the Long Sword as an ammunition container exploded. From the arcing, burning debris, he guessed it was a bin of missiles. The Long Sword turned away, paralleling the course of the convoy. Out of the darkness and low to the ground came individual streaks of missiles from the infantry. Some hit the Long Sword, though he saw little indication that they inflicted major harm. Other missiles found the convoy. A tanker truck was hit, a flash of light followed by nothing as the vehicle slewed to one side and stopped. Another truck, hit by a missile, burst into flame, lighting up the battlefield. Where were their own HUPs?

A violent flash of pure white light on the other side of the convoy answered his question. The other enemy HUP was dead, its fusion-ion power plant erupting in an all-consuming fireball. Even from over half a kilometer away Hardin felt the wave of heat as the HUP died.

The dark Long Sword rushed forward, trying to intercept whatever killed its wingman. Hardin's tank fired again, and he saw another flash, this time on its back. There were other flashes across its armored body and then searing red beams of light lanced from the darkness ahead. The Benderist HUPAX staggered and then tumbled to the ground. It started to rise but there was a massive flash in the darkness ahead – he guessed it was a pair of twin recoilless rifle turrets – and the HUP fell again, flame streaming from it.

"Driver, heading three zero zero. Gunner, target, APC, 300. Cancel. It's gone. Target, APC, 350, now 11 o'clock."

"On the way."

For the last time that night, Hardin's Bob Cat roared. The tracked APC, swinging wide to avoid a burning truck in front of it, presented its side to Hardin's gunner. He saw the flash as the slug ripped into the armored personnel carrier's thin armor. Smoke seemed to suddenly stream from every seam of the vehicle and it rolled to a stop.

"Armor Six, Anvil Lead. I have some enemy personnel on the ground but no organized resistance. All vehicles appear destroyed."

"Roger, Anvil. Did they make the call?"

"Affirmative. I heard it myself. They even got our HUP types right."

"All right, let's gather up our troops and get out of here."

"Yes, sir."

Hardin watched the two Wild Geese HUPs, a Long Sword festooned with a variety of bulbs and stubby antennae and a Long Bow, turn away and head for a small opening in the southern end of the canyon wall. Some of the Militia APCs came up and loaded the infantry. One APC headed for the eastern mouth of the pass to pick up the Recon teams. The Chekinov Scouts, watching the approach of the enemy force to the west, had their own APC hiding up on the plateau.

Hardin led the ten surviving tanks, several of which were damaged, into a semi-circle formation and waited for the APCs to load and clear the canyon. From time to time some ammunition in a burning vehicle would explode, momentarily lighting up the battlefield.

"Armor, Recon Lead. We checked your tank. Sorry, it doesn't look like anyone got out."

"Thank you, Recon."

He had known that would be the case. The explosion was too fast, too violent, for there to have been any survivors. As he watched, the two most distant APCs came back and joined the others. All moved towards the southern exit. He glanced at the dead Bob Cat, its turret a dozen meters from the still burning hull, and crossed himself in the Orthodox fashion. Then Hardin keyed his microphone.

"Company, follow me."

The Second Battalion of the 173rd Brigade regarded itself as the elite of an elite, calling themselves "The Spur of the Red Cocks." It had a good mix of HUPAX, ranging from medium up through heavy weights. Facing the abandoned Alliance position, they remained on guard even though no Alliance forces remained. When the panicked call came from the ambushed convoy, they already had a fast reaction force ready to move. Confused transmissions from the convoy indicated an ambush by armored forces backed up by a small number of HUPs. A Long Bow and a Long Sword were identified specifically before transmissions stopped.

The reaction force numbered seven HUPs, enough to handle the ambushers. As it left the battalion compound, the battalion commander, Major Danson Fuhmal, ordered the rest of the battalion to form up. He would follow in less than fifteen minutes with an additional eighteen HUPAX plus a small assortment of tanks and armored vehicles. The two columns would be enough to deal with any threat they might encounter.

Fuhmal's decision to mobilize the entire battalion was triggered when he tried to relay the convoy's distress call to the brigade headquarters in the hope of getting some air support. He was surprised to discover headquarters was not responding. As he climbed into his HUP, a green and dark blue War Lance, he tried not to worry about why there was no contact and decided that, unless he made contact with brigade, after they cleaned out the ambush, the Second would push on all the way back to headquarters. Better safe than sorry and there was nothing out in the abandoned Alliance position for them to face.

A quick glance at the map showed him that any enemy in the canyon White Snake Pass widened into had only two places to go. He doubted they would head east towards the brigade headquarters and the First Battalion.

That left the southern route, a twisting box canyon with no way out unless they had brought an elevator with them.

Now the important thing was the need for speed. Fuhmal told the reaction force, already deep into White Snake Pass, to pick up its pace. The convoy was no longer transmitting, not even its HUPs, and he was becoming increasingly worried about the silence from brigade. As the remaining HUPs formed around him, he ordered the command HUP, a 130-ton four-legged Broad Sword carrying a communication and electronic warfare module just forward of its vertical launch bay, to keep trying to contact brigade. Then he swung towards the pass. His formation was not as fast as the reaction force but he would move as quickly as he could.

Part of Task Force Pueblo included two companies of combat engineers. Racing in the dark in their Prowlers across the plateau cut by White Snake Pass, they confirmed what they read from the geological survey maps. Here and there along the pass, they installed markers, dully glowing chemical beacons invisible from the pass below. As each marker was laid, a HUPAX closed to within two hundred meters of the marker, carefully sighted in on it, and then shut down. Pilots lay strapped into their ejection seats and waited.

Alisti Mahmud al-Kheyntamenti waited as well. His Rapier also stood on the plateau, powered down except for his communication receivers. Behind him stood most of the other HUPAX of the Combined Arms Battalion (Heavy). They were like still figures in the dark, blacker than the night around them, invisible except for when they blocked starlight.

The engineers were gone, racing across the plateau to the canyon ambush site. They hardly spared a glance into the canyon where most of the fires were out anyway. Instead, they slid their vehicles to a halt at the southern exit to the canyon, through which Captain Hardin had taken most of the ambushers moments before.

The engineers jumped out of their vehicles. They could not see them, but the two Wild Geese HUPs from the ambush stood in the exit from the pass, looking back at the western end of the canyon. Like everyone except the hard-working engineers, they were waiting.

The other two battalions of the Militia regiment lay in the dark of the plateau. Their armored vehicles, powered down like the nearby HUPAX, had their hatches open as their crews enjoyed the cool night air.

The reaction force made good time through the pass, urged on by their commander. Major Fuhmal told them that their Broad Sword's electronic warfare team, crammed into their module, was picking up transmissions from the southern end of the canyon ahead of them. At least two HUPAX were there. He wanted the team to hurry, because the southern exit opened into a box canyon seven kilometers long. According to his maps, unless they were very light HUPs, they would be unable to climb the almost sheer cliffs ringing the canyon. Still not hearing anything from brigade, he wanted the ambushers neutralized so the battalion could keep pushing east. Fuhmal did not want living enemies on his flank as he came through the ambush site and established his link to the brigade.

The Chekinov Scouts operated in triads. Their first team was five kilometers from the western entrance to White Snake Pass and the corporal team leader saw the reaction force coming fast. She keyed her microphone and spoke into a recorder.

"Team Three. Six, no, seven HUPAX. I see a Saber, a Scimitar, a Cutlass, a Short Sword, two Javelins, and a Gladius. No armor. Speed about 65."

Then she rolled away from her overlook position and plugged the recorder into her satcom transmitter. She keyed the transmitter and it sent her recording as a brief burst upward in a tight beam. A satellite received the signal and broadcast it back down to Kodomir.

The transmission was brief and tight enough the EW HUP trailing the Second Battalion CO did not spot it. The electronic warfare specialists continued to monitor the transmissions of the two HUPs in the canyon ahead of the reaction force. They still had not moved. If they just remained in place another fifteen minutes they would get a payback for the ambush.

Kheyntamenti received the transmission from the scout team. He wanted to trap the entire enemy battalion in White Snake Pass, if it came, but he was concerned about the reaction force. It might get through the narrow part of the pass before all of their battalion was in it. If that happened, the two Geese HUPs in the mouth of the box canyon were going to be faced with a desperate chance. He hoped the combat engineers working above them were as good as Colonel Jonivov said.

Lieutenant Stephanie Elinshen, she still found the word "lieutenant" in front of her name sounding strange, looked at her sensor screen but there was still nothing.

"Lead, Dash Two. Anything?"

"No joy, Two," Elinshen said.

Her HUP, a Long Bow, had better sensors than her wing, a Long Sword salvaged from the Storm Cloud Raiders, but the Long Bow had electronic warfare "black boxes" that enabled it to intercept communication transmissions. Sevin was at the controls of the low-slung HUP and she knew he did not want to hang around facing the ambush site any more than she did. But if the enemy got this far, they had to have a target to draw them in deeper.

The rest of the ambush team, Hardin's armored company, was now deep into the box canyon and nearing its southern end. She glanced at the time display in her visual field. Any time now they should get a call from Captain Hardin that the tanks had gotten to their objective.

And unless the Second of the 173rd was totally incompetent, any time now the first blue and green HUPAX ought to sticking its snout around the corner of the pass, looking for them.

The Scouts monitored the progress of the reaction force, each team making its call as the HUPs pounded through the pass below them. Kheyntamenti plotted their progress and waited to see if any other HUPs were coming. If not, he would settle for these seven.

"Team Three. Multiple hostiles coming east. A large number of HUPAX. Still counting. Armored vehicles in the lead, six tanks. Other APCs in trail. No light HUPAX. Most are very large. Speed 50. Some APCs have missile launchers. Make that eighteen HUPAX, largest three War Lances and a Broad Sword."

"Team Four. First group emerging into ambush site. All scouts, fall back to our APC."

Too soon. Elinshen and Sevin had to run for their lives.

Elinshen had seen the enemy HUPs approaching the opening to the ambush canyon while she and Sevin deliberately kept up their chatter, hoping the Benderists were listening to them. She waited for the call from Kheyntamenti that would trap the first seven, the quick reaction force, but it never came.

"Dash Two, looks like we engage and run." Without thinking she pulled her seat straps tighter.

"Roger. I've really enjoyed being bait."

"Lead, Armor Six. We're set."

"Roger, Armor. We are a little busy just now."

Staring through her visual presentation carried by the mindlink into her brain, Elinshen watched for the first Benderist HUPAX. She saw it, a pointed-nosed Saber, as it came out from behind the large boulders framing the pass. It paused, a mistake, and she fired both of her twin GTL5 laser turrets. Another red beam from Sevin's HUP sliced through the air and stabbed into the Saber. A yellow flash announced the launch of a missile from one of the two launchers the Long Sword carried. It streaked across the canyon and exploded in the upper portion of the enemy HUP. Elinshen had a brief glimpse of it spinning and falling to the ground from the impact as she moved and did not stay to study the scene further. She ran into the canyon and fell in behind the Long Sword.

"All right, Dash Two. We have introduced ourselves. Time to leave."

"Catch me if you can, lieutenant. I am out of here."

"Roger. Break. Armor Six. We are inbound."

"Roger. I hope those engineers are awake."

The engineers were awake. With the fighting down below them, it would have been impossible to sleep, if any had been interested. The crack of large lasers superheating the air, causing it to violently expand away from the beams in seven-hundred-meter-long tunnels and then slap back, sounded like lightning claps and the missile scream sounded like some monstrous night bird.

The engineers were just finishing their work in the rock clefts above the Geese HUPs now running south. Their leader, a young Reserve lieutenant, motioned everyone else back. Picking up what they called a "hellbox," he ran towards the ambush canyon overlook. A sergeant wearing night vision goggles was already in place and provided a running commentary as the lieutenant skidded beside him and fastened wires to the box.

"Aye, laddie, sir, I see our boys swatted that first one mighty hard. It is not getting up. Oh, look, it's beginning to burn. Isn't that lovely? Now, L-T, don't you be lookin', that was just a figure of speech. You get your wires together, pardon my saying, sir. Here they come. Four, five, six. I don't see any others. Here they come. They are *very* fast. Are you done with the wires, now, sir? Don't forget your 'press to test' button. Are you getting a green light, sir? They are almost here, laddie. First one is through and into the box canyon, here come the others. Two, three. Oh, they do kick up a great deal of dust, don't they now. Five, six. Lieutenant, they are all in. Any time you please, sir, you may close the door behind them."

The lieutenant looked over his shoulder at the other engineers, dark shapes huddled on the plateau, making sure they were still well away. He took a deep breath.

"Fire in the hole!" He yelled as loudly as he could. He flipped the safety cover from the firing button and punched it.

Six 100-kilogram demolition charges exploded in the cleft of the rocks over the entrance to the box canyon. The flash dazzled anyone looking in that direction, though most of the blast was below the surface of the plateau. The cleft served as a fault in the rock and the explosion was like a giant wedge splitting the rock.

A huge piece of the cliff split away and fell into the mouth of the canyon. As it fell it impacted the wall opposite, jarring loose more tons of rock. Massive boulders slammed into the ground. For a moment it seemed like the roaring avalanche would never stop but it finally did.

The sergeant and lieutenant got up, unconsciously wiping rock dust from their faces as they approached the edge. Peering down, for several moments they could see nothing, even with their goggles. Finally, the dust settled. Huge rocks were wedged into the opening, forming a wall that climbed three quarters of the way up the cliff.

"Aye, lieutenant," the sergeant said after a moment. "I think you are beginning to understand this demolition business."

The lieutenant nodded at the compliment and adjusted his headset. He touched the transmit switch of his communication device.

"Stopper in place."

Kheyntamenti heard the broadcast and keyed his own microphone.

"Victors and Cats, power up, and take them out."

Elinshen saw Doc's Long Sword drawing away from her. That was the good part. The bad part was the enemy was in the box canyon behind her and closing. If it were not for the occasional slight curves to the canyon walls and small hills in it, they would have had a shot at her by now. She heard Kheyntamenti's call to the mercenary detachments but knew they would not be in position to help her for several minutes.

A flash split the night to her right. The reaction force had at least some HUPAX faster than hers and they were closing. She had to get some distance from them.

"Doc has the landing ship in sight."

At the end of the canyon a Militia landing ship, the last of a pair that had brought in the ambush team, waited to pull her and her wing out of the now sealed canyon. But she had to get to it first.

Something struck the back of her Long Bow – from the lurch, Elinshen guessed it to be a rail gun round. Her sensors showed the enemy force closing, their formation stretching out as the faster HUPAX left the slower ones behind. A large laser burned its beam into the Long Bow's right pylon while another sliced through the air further to the right. She turned in that direction, anticipating her opponents would correct their aim.

Elinshen felt the impact as a large laser ate into her Long Bow's back armor, instantly causing rivulets of armor to stream away. Another laser passed her cockpit on the left, close enough to dazzle for a second her visual light sensors on that side of the HUP. Her sensor display showed all six HUPAX were within laser range while the ground in front of her was becoming flatter. She had nothing left to use to hide behind. She saw death coming in the form of six red dots in the bottom of her visual field and decided to see how many of these weak-hearts she could take with her.

"Elinshen, turn left to heading one five zero and hold it."

She did not recognize the tense voice but did not hesitate. Elinshen spun the Long Bow sixty degrees to the left. Something smashed into a rock in front of her throwing sparks and fragments up in a violent fountain. Elinshen swiveled her fuselage to the left as far as possible, trying to protect her back and right arm.

Another laser struck her. Elinshen bit back a curse, started to turn again, but held her course.

"Just a little further, sarge, just a little further."

Now she recognized the voice. It was Major Vermeil. Her mind leapt back to her first encounter with him in the mountain valley south of Coyote Bay.

"Turn right and hold behind the hill."

She turned the Long Bow and swung her fuselage forward. There was the hill, more of a large rock outcropping. As she brought her HUPAX to a shuddering stop, throwing dirt and gravel up in a wave, she caught a flash of light above her.

Elinshen looked upward and saw a sheet of multi-colored flame ripping down from the canyon's edge. A half dozen HUPAX, more, were lined up along the edge and were pouring fire down on her pursuers. Various types of lasers, recoilless rifles, and missiles made a waterfall of fire. She felt a flush and was tempted to turn on the enemy and join the fight.

"If you don't mind, sarge, please continue on. People are waiting."

Of course, it was the correct thing to do. As Elinshen turned away there was a bright flash as one of the enemy HUPAX died. A red dot vanished from her display. She sighed as she ran forward. It would have been so satisfying to turn around and kill one of those black tongues herself.

Running hard, Elinshen's landing ship quickly came into sight. The low shape of the Viper-class landing ship was partially hidden by some large ripples in the ground at the far end of the box canyon. She ran her Long Bow up the ramp and into the main bay. As a HUP captain guided her into position, she felt the ship rise. She backed into her locking bay and saw Sevin climbing from his Long Sword in a neighboring bay. The ship vibrated as its gunners added to the fire put down on her pursuers. She keyed her microphone.

381

"Major Vermeil, Lieutenant Elinshen. I am safely aboard. Thank you for your assistance, sir."

"Oh, that's right; you got promoted for beating up on me. I'd forgotten. Well, sorry about calling you 'sarge' back then. And you are welcome."

"No problem with rank, major. I will buy you a cold one when this is over.

"Looking forward to it. Nice job, lady."

Elinshen leaned back in her seat and finished shutting down her HUPAX. She opened the cockpit hatch and took off her mindlink helmet. As she ran her fingers through her short, damp hair, she looked around the Long Bow's cockpit and then petted the instrument panel.

Nice job, lady.

The Red Cock Second Battalion commander heard the reaction force call for help but there was little more Major Fuhmal could do. The battalion was moving as fast as it could and stay a coherent formation. White Snake Pass was narrow and, judging from the height of the walls on either side of his War Lance, too severe for any of his HUPs to climb out.

Fuhmal understood the danger – if there were HUPs on the plateau engaging the reaction force in the box canyon, then those same HUPs could hit the main body of the battalion. A quick study of the map showed him that he had a terrible choice to make. If he turned the battalion around, he could have it out of the pass fairly quickly, but it would mean abandoning the reaction force and helping out the brigade's headquarters from whom he still had heard nothing. On the other hand, if he proceeded, it would take longer to get to the entrance to the box canyon and he still would not be guaranteed that he would be able to help the reaction force.

When the reaction force leader told him that the entrance to the box canyon was blown closed, Fuhmal decided he had no choice. Even if the battalion continued it could not get into the canyon containing the reaction force with the way blocked. And the blowing of the pass made it clear the enemy was on top of the plateau. He had to turn everyone around and get his battalion out. Maybe, once they were out, they could swing south and pick up one of the slopes of the plateau. The reaction force would just have to hold on until then if it could. And maybe one of the other battalions could help headquarters.

Fuhmal ordered the battalion to halt and turn around. This placed him and the larger HUPs at the rear of the now west bound column. He gave the command to move at each unit's best possible speed. Getting out of this pass and its deadly potential for an ambush was the priority now.

The battalion support vehicles, tanks and a variety of tracked APCs, were now in the lead. They ran through the darkness, their headlights illuminating the white sand and sheer rock walls. Close behind were the medium-weight HUPs, well capable of going faster than the tracked vehicles but unable to pass them in the narrow confines of White Snake Pass.

Fuhmal looked at his map. The battalion did not have that far to go. All they needed was a little more time. Then he saw the long line of red dots appear on the southern side of his sensors.

"This is Kheyntamenti. Hit the marks."

When the engineers placed their glowing markers along the edge of the pass, they selected positions where the rock surface showed fault lines and divisions. They did not have sufficient explosives to mine each position and, even if they had, there was no way of telling which ones would be most useful. So they marked every one they thought might be vulnerable.

That vulnerability was tested by the awakening HUPAX of the Wild Geese. Each marker was covered by an ion pulse weapon-equipped HUP that fired into the spots lit by the dim markers.

An ion pulse weapon accelerates nuclear-sized charged particles, using the power of a HUP's own fusion-ion power plant. As their energy becomes too great to be contained within the electromagnetic "race track" of the accelerator, they are released in a burst. Now accelerated to velocities close to those of the speed of light, the controlled release of the ion pulse is guided by superconducting magnets. Coarse aiming is accomplished by the aiming of the weapon while fine adjustment uses the variable magnetic fields of the superconductors. As the ion pulse moves down the channel, a second pulse enters. Typically, twenty ion pulses will be in the channel at once.

As the ion pulses strike their target, their hypervelocity causes them to have a sequential impact of greater total force than many explosive weapons. Along with the force of their impact, the ion pulses transfer their charge to the target. The net effect of impact and charge transfer is a surge of heat and an electromagnetic pulse. The EMP can disrupt sensors, controls, even the mindlink of a HUP.

The end result of the technology is the production of a superheated blast of almost pure energy.

The HUPAX tagged for the assignment all carried at least two ion pulse weapons. The energy fired into the fault line was greater than the demolition charges used by the engineers on the other side of the plateau. Across the top of the black plateau, lightning appeared to fly almost sideways and bury itself into the rock.

The force of the ion pulse hits was powerful, but what was catastrophic was the imparting of the energy of each hit as heat. Some portions of the tops of the cliffs shattered as the stone violently expanded, throwing sparks and razor-sharp rock fragments into the air. The expansion of the heated stone pushed outward, against the rocks making up the cliff face, as hit followed hit. In several places the faults and crevices broke away and tons of rock peeled away and fell towards the white sand below.

The support and armored vehicles of the battalion were almost caught in an avalanche that slammed into the floor of the pass less than a hundred meters in front of the lead vehicle. They slammed on their brakes and came dangerously close to piling into one another. Behind them, the first group of HUPAX, seeing the pass ahead vanish in a cloud of dust and tumbling boulders, also halted.

Behind the lead element other avalanches fell. Some were relatively minor, serving only to leave a pile of loose rock the oncoming HUPs could climb over, though sometimes with difficulty. But several were extremely large, tearing away portions of the cliff face as they fell and even jarring loose boulders from the other side of the pass.

Several HUPs were damaged in these avalanches and two were crippled by having their leg and hip mechanisms damaged. But what was dangerous, though not immediately recognized as such, was that these larger avalanches dropped walls between portions of the battalion, segmenting it.

Confused and disoriented by the rock falls, most HUP pilots abruptly stopped their HUPs and waited for the dust to settle. It was a mistake but the fatal damage had already been done.

Above them, moving like Apache ambushing a Spanish column in a scene from the Pueblo Uprising of 1200 years before, the Wild Geese HUPAX moved up to the edge of the cliff and selected their targets.

The first to understand what was happening were the tanks and support vehicles. The Militia Mace that had dropped the avalanche stopping their progress walked up to the edge and peered down. The pilot, a young Kodomiri, saw the cluster of vehicles and aimed her twin ion pulse weapons into the mass and fired, throwing her HUP into reverse as she did.

The dust was just clearing as the two ion pulses slammed down from above. For an instant they lit up the pass, partially blinding anyone looking in their direction through light amplification devices. Then the pass was even more brilliantly lit as a tank exploded in a fireball and a missile-equipped APC erupted in a fountain of flame. The half dozen light HUP pilots behind the vehicles looked upward, trying to acquire the already gone Mace.

Above and behind them a Javelin piloted by Chi Lore took aim at the rearmost Benderist HUP, a Rapier. The pilot carefully aimed his two GTL4 lasers at the roof of the cockpit and fired. The combined beams lanced down through the flickering light of the fires and tore open the top of the Rapier, burning alive the pilot inside. The Militia lieutenant took his time and raised his eyes to the next HUP, a frantically turning Ballista. As the HUP swung around, he fired again while throwing his Javelin into reverse and releasing a missile.

The beams caught the Ballista in its left leg. They burned away the armor covering the knee connection in a glowing spray of yellow-glowing metal and destroyed the structures beneath. The momentum of the 95-ton Ballista was sufficient to apply a fatal amount of torque to the now-weakened joint and it failed, toppling the HUPAX to the ground and knocking its pilot unconscious. The missile emphasized the HUP's helplessness by detonating against a laser turret, severing it from the HUP.

The other Benderist HUPs in the lead group managed to get off several frantic laser shots of their own and the retreating Javelin took a hit in the underside of its fuselage as Chi pulled back. As they fired upward, the Mace came back to the cliff edge and fired into the group of HUPs, damaging two.

385

The senior Benderist pilot, realizing the danger they were in, ordered the surviving HUPs to charge forward and climb over the rockslide. To do this without stepping on any of the vehicles pinned in front of them or running into each other meant the pilots had to focus their attention in front of them.

This gave the Wild Geese HUPs above, now joined by a Long Bow, clear shots with no heavy return fire. They targeted the smaller HUPs as they struggled their way forward and up the pile of rock. With the exception of a Javelin whose fusion reactor erupted in an uncontrolled spray of searing white light, the remaining HUPs made it over the rock and ran down the pass and around a curve that sheltered them from fire.

But the pass twisted like the snake it was named after, which meant that their hunters quickly crossed the arc of the curve and were waiting for them as they came around the bend. Two more HUPs died on the white sand and only one succeeded in escaping around another curve to the west as the three Wild Geese HUPAX turned away and headed back towards the rest of their battalion.

Passing the rockslide, the Mace leaned over and destroyed two more vehicles as their crews scattered and then continued on, searching the pass for anything more worthy of its firepower. The three joined with a small group working on another segment of the enemy battalion.

"Black Cat Lead, Kheyntamenti. What's your status?"

"Some minor damage, colonel. They had some climbers but we handled them. Looks like the Victors have put down the rest."

"Aye, colonel. Had a little skeet shoot there for a while but the lead group is finished."

"Very well. Come on back. The enemy is divided into three groups. The one closest to you has their largest HUPs, including two War Lances, what looks to be a Broad Sword, and a Crossbow. Major Vermeil, have your HUPs join the group dealing with them – they could use your firepower. Major Welsh, continue about half a kilometer to the second group. Some mediums and heavies there, so be careful."

"Victor Lead, roger. I haven't seen a Broad Sword before."

"Cat Lead, roger."

Major Fuhmal felt a growing sense of desperation. His calls to his Broad Sword and its attached communication capsule were unanswered, but only it had the range to reach the brigade headquarters for help. And help was needed. Saving the reaction force was no longer the issue. Now his concern was saving his battalion.

The pass east was totally blocked by a pile of rubble none his large HUPs, the lightest of which weighed 120 tons, could climb over. The loose debris offered no purchase and more than once a HUP came sliding back, its legs half buried.

The other direction looked a little easier. When the cliff face had come down, a huge piece had separated from the rest of the plateau. Shattering on impact, it was in very large pieces that looked like they would not shift under the large metal feet of his HUPs, though finding a route up and over would be difficult.

Fire from the plateau above was spotty. The enemy HUPs up there were only four or so and none of them were particularly large. Still, their comparative small size meant they were able to come up to the edge, shoot, and pull back before being tracked and hit by his HUPs. Fuhmal keyed his microphone.

"All right, people. Let's get organized. Crossbow, you are pretty agile. See if you can find a way over that pile of rock. The rest of you back away from the south wall and take aim at the edge above. Anything pokes its nose over, shoot it off. Crossbow, when you find the path, we'll start shuttling over and join the others."

For a while the plan worked. They caught two of the enemy HUPs with solid multiple laser strikes to the front of their fuselages and ripped a pylon off another HUP with a pair of rail gun rounds. The enemy pulled back and for a few precious minutes they were not molested.

Suddenly, from above and to the left, fire in the form of ion pulse and large laser beams swept down on them. Fuhmal turned to see the attacker but his War Lance rocked as a barrage of missiles slammed into it from the right.

The attackers had hit on the solution of simply spreading out and it was very clear they had been reinforced. Fuhmal glimpsed a Scorpion withdrawing its angular body as it unleashed another ion pulse attack.

Through his radio he could hear the pilots of the middle portion of the battalion frantically trying to hit the HUPs firing down on them. More ominously, he heard nothing from the lead group. Not even the tankers were talking any more.

The other War Lance, fire streaming from its left side, suddenly lit up the pass as its missile launchers exploded. The big HUP, piloted by his executive officer, staggered forward a few meters. The cockpit exploded in a flash of light as a rail gun round lanced through it and the blue and green HUP collapsed.

Almost immediately a glare of white light came from the rock pile. The Crossbow vanished, turned into unrecognizable fragments as its fusion power plant lost its containment field and erupted. Fuhmal's HUP rocked with the shock wave. The deaths of the two HUPs seemed to drive the enemy into a killing frenzy. HUPs poured fire down in a rain of fire and metal and energy that the surviving battalion HUPs could not match, though the desperate pilots tried.

It was over, Fuhmal realized with a sickened sensation, and any further resistance would just get the rest of his people killed.

"Second Battalion, this is Major Fuhmal. Cease fire. I say again, cease fire. Point your weapons down; bend your fuselages forward if possible. We are surrendering. Cease-fire."

He reached over to his communication console and changed frequencies with a shaking hand.

"Enemy force, this is Major Danson Fuhmal, Commanding Officer of the Second Battalion, 173rd Brigade, requesting an immediate cease-fire. I say again, this is the commander of the Second Battalion requesting an immediate cease-fire. We are holding our fire. I say again..."

"Major Fuhmal, this is Colonel Alisti Mahmud al-Kheyntamenti, commander, Task Force Pueblo. Stand by; I am passing the order to hold fire."

It took a moment but finally the deadly fire from above ceased. Fuhmal let out a sigh.

"This is Major Fuhmal. I would like to discuss terms."

"There are none, major. Get out of your HUPs and stand clear of them. Have your people walk east. You will find the remains of your supply convoy. One of the tanker trucks still has water. You can wait there for your brigade to come and get you."

"And our HUPAX..?"

"Will be destroyed where they stand."

Fuhmal felt a flush of anger sweep through him.

"You Alliance bastards…"

"Alliance? Who said we were Alliance? Now, get out of your HUPs or fight. You have thirty seconds to decide."

Not Alliance? They couldn't be the militia of this backwater planet. Could they?

"Second Battalion, this is Major Fuhmal. On my orders, you are to leave your HUPAX and vehicles and march east. Ensure that none of our wounded are left behind. Bring any commo gear you can carry. Our people will be here soon and we will arrange for our pick-up."

The "soon" was a bluff and Fuhmal suspected his opponent knew it. The acknowledgements from the surviving HUPs slowly came in. It was disheartening to hear how few of his pilots were still able to transmit. He looked around his cockpit. Fuhmal had fought for the Holdings his entire adult life and took pride in being a good soldier. He also knew that his defeat would be viewed as an unutterable disgrace.

"Colonel al-Kheyntamenti, my people are complying with your orders. As per the Articles of War, I require you to ensure their safety as prisoners of war."

"Major, we are taking no prisoners. They are free to go. They will probably be picked up before noon. We are going to tell your headquarters where to find them."

"Thank you, colonel, for that, at least. Fuhmal, out."

Fuhmal unlocked the lower portion of his harness and pulled his handgun from its holster. For a moment he let it lay in his lap. He shut down his HUP and removed his mindlink helmet. He picked up the pistol and then placed the muzzle in his mouth.

On Kwangdo, the imagery was self-explanatory, though General Thomas Akagi allowed himself the pleasure of explaining, in his most dispassionate voice, what they were seeing.

"I gather this is delayed slightly due to the technical challenge of uplinking imagery from the battlefield and getting it to Kodomir's subspace communication site in Kiroff City. My people tell me it is encoded digitally and is relayed here to our subspace communication system, where it is immediately fed to us." He smiled slightly. "All very complicated and well beyond my grasp of such things." Akagi tapped the small earpiece he was wearing. "There is narration supplied with the imagery, but I understand you are not a military man and it might be useful if I explain what we are seeing."

"Yes," Ambassador Bostan said, his attention fixated on the light amplified imagery.

"This is the better part of a battalion of HUPAX caught in a narrow pass. Classic ambush situation. They are not moving, so those rock slides we saw earlier must have them trapped."

Akagi made himself fall silent and enjoy the spectacle of a Benderist tank exploding in the pass. In his ear a quiet voice of an officer told him what the imagery would show next. He had not bothered to tell the ambassador his people were examining the imagery before transmitting it to his office. With difficulty he kept his face neutral as he heard the tech talking.

"The Kodomiri claim they attacked the brigade's headquarters and inflicted significant damage to it. In the process they liberated a dozen hostages Special Envoy Baer was holding, apparently in an attempt to gain the cooperation of the Kodomir government." Akagi shook his head. "Acts of terrorism, taking hostages, hardly in the tradition of the Baron, would you think?"

On the screen a HUPAX in the pass fell to the ground, fire streaming from its shattered torso. Then it seemed the scene froze. It was a minute before it became clear both sides had stopped firing.

"An apparent ceasefire," Akagi said, leaning forward as the imagery magnified. He and Bostan watched as the soldiers in the pass, some of them dropping from HUPAX that had aimed their turrets at the ground in a position suggesting helplessness, slowly formed small groups and walk down the white trail.

The scene shifted. They watched as a tall HUPAX, Akagi knew it as a Mace, approached the edge of the cliff, its torso swinging back and forth.

Then it stopped and fired. A second HUP joined it and added to the fire. Akagi noticed immediately they were conserving ammunition by only using beam weapons. The voice in his ear spoke and Akagi nodded.

"The Second Battalion of your 173rd Brigade has surrendered. The Kodomiri Militia is destroying the remaining HUPAX and vehicles of the battalion. The survivors have been permitted to move to a sheltered area pending the arrival of the brigade."

Akagi took a sip of tea. He hated tea, but the Benderists expected all Kwang to like the stuff. It did make for a dramatic pause, he thought. He carefully put the cup down as yet another Benderist HUPAX exploded and collapsed.

"Perhaps you might wish to communicate with your embassy, ambassador. This is fairly significant news."

Bostan leaned back in his chair and shook his head. He turned and looked at Akagi and grimaced.

"Do you think, Minister Akagi, that Baron von Bender will cut and run because he has lost a battalion?" He shook his head. "No, he won't. That would be a violation of his sense of honor. Cowardly. What he *will* do is tell the rest of the brigade to take the fight to the enemy, hunt them down, and kill them all." He looked grim. "It will take more than the loss of a couple of dozen HUPAX to give him pause – there is too much to gain by continuing."

"What Baron Karl von Bender will do," Bostan said, "is order Kodomir burned to ash. And Special Envoy Baer is just the man to carry out that order." He looked at the screen. "This war has just begun."

Chapter 27: A problem of time and blood

21 December 2824

The cool, dispassionate facade Esteban Baer maintained was gone as he surveyed the scene. Smoldering columns of smoke still punctuated the brigade headquarters area, though most fires finally were out. Tight-lipped, he walked with General Mannheim. The morning sun was only a little way above the low eastern hills. Fourth Battalion's HUPAX, newly arrived from those hills and the town of Portaka City, rumbled around the base's perimeter.

Baer stopped, looking at a burned-out HUP, smoke still streaming from within it.

"What are our casualties?"

"Latest count," Mannheim said, consulting the datapad he carried, "is five missing, twenty-five wounded, seventeen dead."

"I meant among our HUPs."

"Five destroyed," Mannheim said. "Two severely damaged, eight more light to moderate damage. First Battalion has nineteen HUPs operational, in other words. The brigade's support and command HUPs add another five." He looked off at a prowling perimeter HUP. "With the Fourth back, you can add an additional twenty-five."

"Where are the other three battalions?"

"I don't know," Mannheim said. He had learned a long time ago it was never a good idea to try to answer a Baer question when you did not have the information. "Colonel Halleck will be able to update us." On the other hand, he also had learned a long time ago it was always a good idea to have someone else deliver any potential bad news.

The two turned and headed towards the temporary brigade headquarters, a surviving barracks module that had been cleared of its bunks. They found Halleck leaning over a communications array stacked on a broad table, looking over the shoulders of a pair of techs. He walked over to them as they entered the room, his face grim.

"What do you have for us, colonel?" Mannheim said.

"Our damage assessment is complete," Halleck replied. "You know our personnel losses – two of the missing are now KIA. The HUP repair facility was damaged, so repairs are going to be slow. Supplies and munitions were hit hard. I'm going to ask for a landing ship to land to assist in repairs for our HUPs and to resupply us." He walked while talking and took the other two men over to a map pinned to a wall.

"You saw the Fourth Battalion arrive. Third is moving towards us from the south and will be here within the next two hours. We had no contact with the Fifth until our commo techs raised a tower. It is coming down from the north but slowly." He looked up. "An enemy landing ship landed north of us last night. It may have been one of those that brought in the attack, but we can't be sure. In any case, I've directed the Fifth to do a sweep in those northern hills and see if anything is up there."

"We have had no contact with the Second Battalion. The Third reports that they heard multiple transmissions from their general area, maybe a little further east, shortly after we were hit. Signals were weak but it sounded to them like it was coming from HUPs, not their headquarters or commo unit. We're still trying to raise them but there's a big plateau in the way so it may be a while."

"Major Felden Pierce, First Battalion Commanding Officer, is standing by. He engaged the raiders last night and he has some information you will want to hear." Mannheim glanced at Baer and then nodded to Halleck who left the room.

"Sir," Mannheim said, "I do not think this was done by the Alliance."

"Why do you say that?" Baer looked surprised.

"We are still alive," the general replied. "They have two regiments above us. If they had hit us, they would have done it in force. This area would now be firmly in their hands and they would be rolling up our remaining battalions. It's not the Alliance."

"Who, then? We still have their hostages," Baer began and was interrupted.

"No, sir, you do not," said Colonel Halleck as he entered the room. Beside him was a younger man with bandages covering much of the right side of his face. "Gentlemen, Major Pierce." The officer stepped forward with a slight limp, came to attention, and saluted Mannheim. He nodded towards Baer. Mannheim noticed the nod, though Baer was still looking at Halleck.

Young pup doesn't like our Special Envoy. I wonder why not?

"Go ahead, major, and have a seat," Mannheim said, looking at the officer's wounds. Pierce eased himself onto a folding chair. "Now, what happened last night and what do you have to tell us about the prisoners?"

"Sir, when the attack took place, I moved from my billeting area towards our HUP park. We took heavy indirect fire – artillery and missiles, a lot of it in the form of cluster bombs. By the time I got outside, the first bombardment was over and they were shifting to secondary targets. They had the coordinates cold, sir." Pierce started to reach up to his face but stopped.

"I am guessing they had people on the ground with designators, either during the attack or feeding coordinates before it. Anyway, I took a group of HUPs to establish a southern perimeter. We went by the gymnasium, where the prisoners were, but saw nothing to attract our attention. A little later I spotted a trail of a group leaving our area. I and another HUP followed it. I saw blood in the trail and thought it was from wounded commandos. But when we got up into the hills we found an enemy landing ship, a Viper. It took out my wing and damned near got me." He motioned at his bandages.

"I got a good look just before we were hit. I definitely saw the prisoners and my gun camera has their imagery. It also shows two others, soldiers, lagging behind them." He shrugged and winced at the movement. "Anyway, we called for help but no one got to our area in time to do anything. I barely got my Saber back."

"The prisoners did not escape," Mannheim said. "They were released by the soldiers, it appears."

"The Alliance may have done that to curry favor with the Kodomiri, general," Baer said.

"It wasn't the Alliance, sir," Pierce said. "I saw that landing ship and I got her imagery with my gun camera, though not intentionally. You can see her markings." He stopped and looked at Mannheim, who nodded. The major got to his feet with some effort and stepped over to a display unit. He took a card from his shirt and dropped it in. He bent over the controls.

"I've already keyed it to the shot you want," he said, and touched a panel.

An image sprang to life in front of them. It was a shot under natural light, so there was not much to see. The exhausts of the landing ship backlit it enough that its type was discernable. "Raw imagery," Pierce said. "Here's the same view through the light amplification system."

The exhausts were a pure white flare and obscured some of the underside and rear of the landing ship, but the port side and nose were easy to make out. Pierce touched the controls and the image was magnified, centering on a space beneath the bridge. Two emblems could be seen, darkly drawn on the lighter gray of the hull.

The first was a black circle across which two long-necked birds flew. The second was a simple shield. A bar divided it diagonally. Above the bar was the head of an eagle. Below was a stylized knight on horseback spearing a dragon.

"Kodomiri Militia," Mannheim said. "Eagle and Saint George, classic Russian symbols."

"And the birds in the circle, what is that?" Baer asked.

"The emblem of the Wild Geese," Colonel Halleck said. "Mercenary unit that came to Kodomir and helped drive off the Raiders. They were made citizens. Professional killers." He looked at Baer. "You predicted they would fight, Envoy. Your prediction has proven correct."

"Yes," Baer said, still studying the imagery. If he heard the slight tone of sarcasm in Halleck's voice, he did not respond to it. "They have brought themselves down here for us." He looked at Halleck. "Will your brigade have any difficulty in finishing them off?"

"Sir," Halleck said, "we are at present ignorant as to their location or numbers. They have landing ships and can move quickly. Ours are being held in orbit by the Alliance. As long as that is the situation, they have an advantage if we try to move against them. They can flee, strike, do whatever they want."

"Your recommendation is to do what, then?"

"Hold here until we get our landing ships. Then load the brigade and attack a position, such as their Militia base near Kiroff City. That will force them to come to us."

"Colonel, that is not a bad plan," Baer said. "It's underlying principle of forcing them to defend an asset they cannot ignore is a good one, but the flaw is the need to wait until we get our landing ships. An additional confrontation, especially one with the Alliance, is not desirable. At least," he glanced at Mannheim, "not at this time. Instead, what I recommend is that you gather your brigade and head east, straight at Portaka City."

Baer reached forward and turned off the imagery. He folded his arms and smiled.

"They have revealed a weakness to us, gentlemen. They did all this," he gestured towards the base outside, "to liberate a dozen prisoners. What do you think they will do to save a town?"

Jonivov was washing the camouflage paint off his face when Kheyntamenti was admitted to his landing ship quarters. He groped for a towel and Kheyntamenti handed one to him.

"You weren't supposed to be out there," Kheyntamenti said.

"I know, don't scold me," Jonivov said and grinned. "Polrany ripped me up one side and down the other when I reported in and he saw I was still in camie paint." He looked sheepish. "I forgot I still had the stuff on." He draped the towel over the edge of the small steel sink and motioned Kheyntamenti to take a seat while he dropped onto the edge of his bed.

"You got the Tiger Moths' report?" he asked as he took off his boots.

"Yes, sir," Kheyntamenti said, taking a long drink from the mug he carried. "No movement westward by the 173rd. They're gathering their battalions at their headquarters."

"There goes the plan to ambush them when they came to assist their battalion. I think they haven't figured out yet what happened to it but probably have a good idea. And I don't think we'll get away with another long-range strike," Jonivov said. "At least not with anything other than the Frogfires. They'll have active patrols and sensor teams out." He put his boots together neatly beside his bunk and rolled off his socks. He checked his feet for blisters.

"Our advantage," Kheyntamenti said, "is that we can move faster than they can, but knowing *where* to move is the issue."

"Major Garito says he thinks they are going to hold their position with their forces consolidated. That would present an overwhelming array of firepower."

"They might," Kheyntamenti said. "If we try to assault the whole brigade, even with one battalion eliminated, we will lose. But I do not think they will do that."

"Neither do I," Jonivov said. "What's your reasoning?"

"They need to kill our HUP force. To do that they have to force a confrontation, most likely by sitting on something or threatening something that we value. When we come out to fight, they have us."

Jonivov studied his toes for a moment and then he looked up.

"I figure it will go down the same way. Now, what do you think they will sit on?"

"Well, there aren't a lot of important targets near them. The most important would be Portaka City." Kheyntamenti shrugged. "To force a fight in a town is against the OSW Articles of War but Portaka City is pretty small and if they win there won't be anyone around to file a complaint."

"Yep," Jonivov agreed. "Not that the OSW would do anything about it anyway." He thought for a moment. "Portaka City is only about thirty kilometers east of where they are now. The ground is open. No sneaking up by running through the hills. They will have good fields of fire with the sea at their backs." The landing ship shuddered as it lifted off. Kheyntamenti leaned back in his chair and took another sip.

"I think we have a little time before they ascertain that the 2nd Battalion is out of the picture. We could set up a blocking force between them and Portaka City."

Jonivov began to pull on a clean pair of socks. "I think they will be looking for that. They already know we have landing ships in play and can get ahead of them."

"True enough," Kheyntamenti conceded. "You're not thinking of fighting *in* the city?"

"No. 'Stalingrads' work only if you can feed more people into the attrition meat grinder than your opponent. And we can't."

"Then what do you have in mind?"

"Did I ever tell you I spent a summer in Portaka?" As Kheyntamenti shook his head, Jonivov pulled on his boots. "It was for a biology class. We dove off the coast. Stayed in town. Perfect place for a bunch of kids – nothing else there except school work." He smiled. "No night life, no other kids, even the beach wasn't any fun. Rock and gravel on top of flat, dull shale stretching a couple of kilometers or more out into the shallow bay. It made for a nice little port, but very boring if you were diving looking for fish." He stood up.

"Don't think chess, colonel," Jonivov said. "Think checkers."

A puzzled Kheyntamenti followed him out of the room.

"I had thought we might bring in all eight of our landing ships," Jonivov said to the officers in the briefing room, "and use them as an offensive force. But if we did, I think there's a pretty good chance Baer would order in the Benderist landing ships and the Alliance be damned, especially if we got close to *him*. On top of that, despite the skill of our captains," he nodded towards Captain Cochran, "Intelligence tells us theirs are generally larger. Therefore, we need to keep the landing ships out of the correlation of forces as long as we can. On the other hand, if we haven't gotten the job done by the time the Alliance leaves, they will bring them in anyway."

"Time," Jonivov said. "It is about time. Time for our people to succeed on what Minister Jevon is calling, and rightly, 'the second front.' That's the effort our people are putting in to driving a wedge between Baron von Bender and Envoy Baer and his expansionist faction. But it is also about blood. We need to savage that brigade so badly that the expansionists are discredited. Up to now they've taken over a huge chunk of real estate and paid very little for it."

"They still have close to a hundred HUPs, near as we can calculate. Satellite imagery says all four remaining battalions are now grouped together. A convoy of trucks was seen leaving their area, headed towards the survivors of our ambush, so they know the 2nd Battalion is past history.

So let me show you what I have in mind." He turned and a map of eastern Portaka came onto the screen.

"All right, here they are. Their relief convoy is just about half way to the canyon ambush site. Now, take a look at where we think they are going." He changed the map and satellite imagery replaced it.

"Portaka City is just on the edge here. Nothing much near it. The hills to the west, about twenty klicks away, have the road, this brown line, coming through that connects their current location at the Militia base to the civilian airstrip on the outskirts of town. Now, look here and here. These are HUP patrols. They are already pushing out a reconnaissance towards the town, making sure we're not waiting for them in the hills. It's a nice idea, but a tight fit. Hard to get there from here without letting everyone know."

"To the east is the sea. Nothing out there except these scattered islands used by the fishing boats from Portaka, beginning about five kilometers off the coast. You can see three of them there now. Let me magnify them. There, you can see their small station. A dock, refrigeration storage plant where they can offload their catches and go get more, a few buildings, VTOL pad, nothing else. Usually, a couple of boats are there day or night. Main fishing grounds are further north and east." He shifted the map to the previous view.

"Portaka City is a small place, about 12,000 people in all. Mostly miners and company staff, support personnel, some families, and the fishing folks. Town spreads out from the docks, streets radiating like a fan. If the 173rd moves into town, they'll probably park their fire support HUPs here in this large, central square. The town administration buildings are on the east side of the square and that's where all the town commo gear is located. I'd guess they'll use that for their headquarters." Jonivov turned to the others.

"Now, these people are not stupid. They made a mistake in keeping their battalions so spread out but at the time they thought their enemy was on the ground to their west. If the Alliance had moved overland, they would have had time with their interior lines to reinforce any point of attack. Good thinking on their part for what the threat was then. So don't underestimate them." He touched the controls and the map centered on the town and magnified.

"I, and Colonel Kheyntamenti agrees, think they are going to sit on Portaka City in order to force us to give them battle. Three battalions in the perimeter, one in town in reserve along with their support weapons and headquarters. They probably figure us to land to the west and use the hills for cover and either assault from there or along the coastline. Since they are expecting us to do that, we are going to do that." Jonivov smiled.

"Colonel Kheyntamenti told me earlier about how another outnumbered force handled a situation like this. Colonel, this might be a good time to fill in everyone on that story about Prince Tepes."

Kheyntamenti stood, but was not smiling.

"The story may be apocryphal," he said. "It happened on Earth, a long time ago."

After the briefing, Kheyntamenti was in his quarters when his door chimed. He keyed the door and saw Gwielgi. He paused and then motioned him in.

"I did not get an opportunity," Kheyntamenti said, "to congratulate you on your freeing of the prisoners."

"Well, you know I'd never let Tsunasdi go in alone. That guy couldn't find his butt with both hands and if you gave him a map it would just mean he'd have one less hand." Gwielgi shifted his weight from foot to foot, and then looked up at Kheyntamenti. "Thanks. We were very, very lucky. Those gunners hit everything right and Nguyen handled her landing ship like a fighter pilot. If it weren't for her, we'd all be a free snack for some Hoare Cat."

"Sergeant Tsunasdi tells a slightly different story, though he didn't take anything away from Nguyen or her people. He says you took out the guards by yourself."

"It happened the way we planned it," Gwielgi said. "He had the long-range radio, so we had him cover the entrance. I went in. They were not expecting anyone."

"Possibly not," Kheyntamenti said, "but he says you did good work."

"Thank you." Gwielgi's eyes were level. "I did what was necessary."

"I agree," Kheyntamenti replied. He waited for a moment. "So how are you?"

"I think I'm all right," Gwielgi said. "Being out in the desert helped clear my head a little."

"Tsunasdi told me you were accepting your commission back."

"I don't think we are in the kind of business that you can do half way," Gwielgi said. "I decided if I was going to come back, it would be all the way."

"Good." Kheyntamenti touched a display panel and a map of eastern Portaka appeared on his console. "What do you think of our plan?"

"Even if it does not work, it will disrupt them," Gwielgi said. "But you can't let Coltrane lead the Scouts. He's really beat up. I don't think he could walk a klick in his present condition."

"The decision was made above me."

"Politics, I guess. There's no way the younger brother of the senior Chekinov tribal leader is going to stand down while his warriors take on the hairiest mission of the war." Gwielgi shook his head.

"Well, he's pretty resilient. There will only be a dozen of them."

"And a dozen Recon, and a dozen of our troops. It will be a crowd."

"Too many, you think?"

"One sentry with night goggles and they've had it."

"Well, our job will be to keep their attention fixed."

"The tough part is going to be later, after things quiet down."

"They are all volunteers, well qualified, handpicked. They can do it."

"I didn't mean that. I meant living with it."

"So did I," Kheyntamenti said. He looked up at Gwielgi from the map. "Did you come here to try to get a place on the team?"

"No," Gwielgi said. "You are going to need your sharpest for that and I am not as good as those kids are going to have to be to make this work. No, I've done enough of that ground-pounder business for a while. But what I'd like to do is take the blocking force."

"You've done something like that before?"

"Absolutely not," Gwielgi said and grinned. "I don't think anyone has. I'd like to see what it's like."

"Marjessa Boyington volunteered her group to do it."

"Not enough. We'll need more HUPs to have a prayer if it hits the fan."

"I was thinking Lieutenant Elinshen, Sergeant Tsunasdi, Boyington and her people, and you."

"You'll lead the distracters?"

Kheyntamenti nodded. "And I'll have the supporting fires set."

"One thing – you knew I'd go in when you sent Tsunasdi. That's why you sent him instead of one of our real commandos."

"Is that a question?"

"No. I would have gone no matter who was sent."

"I know. He volunteered, insisted. Something about honor."

"Currahee honor." Gwielgi shook his head. "An oxymoron, but he's a good man to have around in bad times."

"True. There's going to be a detailed briefing of the landing party in twenty minutes. Get together with your pilots before then. We're going to use Zombie for the raiders and we're already shifting HUPs over. All are configured for knife fighting, or will be by the time you start."

"Yes, sir," Gwielgi said.

"*Lo*," he said, using his friend's nickname, "We're going to have thirty-six of our kids trying to get out of there. Bring them home."

"Aye, Khey. Everyone comes home."

Zombie lifted shortly before sunset. The large Crocodile-class landing ship climbed high into the purpling sky until its exhaust was just a glowing dot and then it moved northeast, gathering speed until it was out of sight. The other landing ships, huddled together in a valley well to the south of Portaka City, waited until dark. By that time the lead elements of the enemy brigade were moving into the town. Then they rose on columns of blue-white fire and headed northwest.

Captain Cochran stood on Zombie's bridge, watching the sensor displays. Beside her, Gwielgi watched the imagery unfold. Cochran's people performed their tasks quietly and, as far as he could tell, efficiently. She was regarded as an aggressive captain, always willing to take on the enemy, whoever the enemy was, but always did so intelligently. He glanced over at her. Like all members of the Wild Geese, her regular uniform was gray, but today she was wearing the closest thing the unit had to a dress uniform, a set of tiger-striped camouflaged infantry fatigues.

"You planning on leading the marines?" Gwielgi asked quietly.

"No," Cochran said with a smile, "but whenever I'm putting our jarheads ashore, I put these on to remind my people who it is we are here for. Besides," her smile broadened, "I think I look good in them."

"Aye, captain," Gwielgi said, matching her smile. He pointed at a tactical display. "I think this shows three fishing boats. Is that current?"

"Yes, it is," Cochran said. "We're getting a direct feed from the satellites. This one is usually used for assessing ocean temperatures and the like but they have it pulling double duty. Colonel Jonivov said Kiroff was in touch with the fishing station and they've agreed to cooperate."

"Glad to hear it," he said. "I think I'll go below and check in with the landing party." He drew himself up. "Permission to leave the bridge."

"Granted, major."

Gwielgi made his way through the various passageways and hatches. Requesting permission to leave the bridge reflected the attitude of landing ship captains like Cochran who ran their commands as if they were ocean navy units. In the Wild Geese, it was common to hear landing ship crew refer to their infantry counterparts as "marines," a further reflection of the sea-going attitude. And since a ship can only have one captain, crew usually referred to noncrew officers having that army rank by bumping them upward in rank; hence Cochran's referring to him as a major. Gwielgi smiled to himself and wondered if he could put in for a temporary boost in pay on the grounds of his shipboard "promotion."

The infantry team leaders, Zombie's marines, were entering the briefing room as he arrived. The other HUP pilots were already present. All stood as he entered and he motioned for everyone to take a seat. It was crowded and not everyone could sit but there was not, other than the HUP bay itself, any other place on the ship with enough room to bring everyone together.

"Captain Cochran says cooperation of the fishing company has been gained," Gwielgi said. "While there are three boats at their piers, I recommend just using two to keep the traffic down, but I will leave that up to Captain Ho'nehe to decide. Current word is that several other fishing boats have returned to Portaka City without incident." He touched a wall and a map of Portaka City and its adjoining bay was projected onto it.

"Cochran will put the HUPs down *here*," he said, pointing to an area over the water two kilometers from the city. "Our HUPs will move toward the city and stop just short of showing ourselves, where the depth is about fifteen meters. Joe," he turned to Ho`nehe, "I will be able to hear you at that depth. We should be in position before you get to the fishing company piers. If we are not or you can't raise me, hold off coming ashore." Ho`nehe nodded.

"After the landing party disembarks, the HUPs will move forward. We'll go feet dry south of the fishing company piers, at the ramps used by the coastal hovercrafts. That's when things will get tricky." Gwielgi changed maps and displayed a close view of the city. "You can see we have a pretty straight shot at the central park. If they have sentries at the ramps or fishing docks, they'll see us. That area *must* be clear."

"It will be," Ho`nehe said. "My team will clear the fishing piers and secure them. Then Recon will move through us and swing down to clear the ramps. When that is done, then all three teams will head for their objectives. I will confirm a clear path for you."

"Right," Gwielgi said. "When we come up the ramps, we'll move to the central park area and will be pretty much in trail of Recon. I plan on stopping us about two blocks in from the bay. If things go badly wrong, the teams can pass through us to get back to the boats. Make sure you're talking to us if that's the case – hard for HUP drivers to make out good guys from bad guys." Ho`nehe nodded.

"Now, here's the current situation in Portaka City." Gwielgi touched the wall and satellite imagery overlay the map. "In the central park, we have their support HUPs, several Morning Stars and a Crossbow. All are heavily loaded with missile launchers and, in the case of the Crossbow, artillery. We can also see the HUPs of their brigade command: two Scorpions, a War Lance, and a Broad Sword. There is also a scattering of armored vehicles in the park: some APCs and the like. All this suggests that Colonel Jonivov was right. They are using the municipal buildings at the near end of the park as their headquarters. And their living quarters area is probably the Crown Inn Hotel that borders the south end of the park." Gwielgi smiled and turned towards the group.

"The intelligence people checked that out by a real covert move – they made a call from Kiroff to the hotel. One of the clerks said all the guests were being hustled out. Then commo was cut off to the outside. The guess that they are using it for quarters is probably a good one as well." Gwielgi turned back to the map.

"We have options and will play this one as things develop. Basically, after the teams get back to their boats, the HUPs will move out of the city to one of several landing zones where Zombie will pick us up. Which LZ we go for will depend on how they react to the feint the rest of the Regiment will throw at them from the west. Wherever they shift forces away from we will use as our exit and Jonivov will be watching imagery from the satellites in real time to advise us." He turned back to the group.

"What we do *not* want is a HUPAX fight in the middle of the city. Collateral damage would mean a lot of dead civilians. Three of their battalions are outside of town in a rough arc. The one to the north is about a klick out and using the low hills up there for a defensive position facing the mountains further north. The one to the west is sitting on top of the civilian airstrip, slightly less than a kilometer from the city. The one to the south is about a kilometer and a half. They are using a dry wash and are keeping a watch on the low hills about five klicks from town." He drew an arc around the edge of the city.

"Their remaining battalion is set as an interior perimeter just on the outskirts of the town all the way around. That makes them pretty thin, so we could punch through them when we head out but we would then have to face one or the other of their battalions. The idea is that the regiment's demonstration to the west will capture their attention. If it does not, then we go one of two ways."

"We either run north or south along the coast, whichever way looks least defended. That would be a really tough thing to do because we would be pinned against the sea on our flank and it would be easy to get in front of us. If we slow down, then they can catch up to us. We really want that demonstration to be successful. And we want the fact that there are HUPs in town to come as a surprise. I'd like them to learn that we are there as we leave, not before." He turned back to the group. "Our job is to cover the landing teams, not get kills of our own. Stay focused on that. Questions?" There were none. "Joe?"

Ho'nehe stood up and walked over to the map. He magnified the area between the docks and the park and studied it for a moment.

"As Gwi said, our three teams, Geese, Recon, and Scouts, will move from the docks to the area of the park. My team will clear the fishing piers and Recon will pass through us and clear the ramps. Recon will then head for the hotel. It has two entrances opening onto the main lobby, one facing the park and the other facing the street the south. There are entrances at either end that go directly into the halls. Depending on how they have their sentries set up, Recon will clear their external security and then probably enter by the entrance on the eastern end of the building."

"The Scouts will trail my team as we move west from the fish processing plant area and then south. Both teams will go for the municipal building and first clear the external security. That building has its main entrance facing the park and several others facing the street. We'll have to see which way gives us best access. My team will enter the building while the Scouts set up at this intersection." Ho`nehe touched the map. "If we spot additional buildings being used by the Benderists, I may call them in on them, but otherwise they will be our reserve and may cover our withdrawal or reinforce either team." He looked over at Coltrane. "As we've discussed, you will have to be able to move in a heartbeat." Coltrane nodded.

"If all goes as planned, Recon and my team will meet with the Scouts at the intersection and we all go back to the piers, get back on our boats, and leave. If shooting starts, we go to the same place but the HUPs will cover our withdrawal. Like Captain Gwielgi said, ideally they should not know our HUPs are in town until they leave and go through their perimeter from behind." He nodded to Gwielgi and sat back down.

"All right, folks," Gwielgi said. "This one is a real gamble. A lot of things can go wrong. But if we pull it off, we will take this war to the people who started it and maybe take some very long steps towards ending it. Keep the lines of communication open, stay focused on the mission, and stay cool." He nodded and everyone stood to leave. Only Marjessa Boyington remained behind. As the last person left, she walked over to Gwielgi.

"Captain," Boyington said, "this plan is exceptionally dangerous."

"I *thought* that would appeal to you," Gwielgi said, leaning back against the now blank wall.

"To a certain extent," she replied. Gwielgi could not tell if she was serious or jesting.

The Currahee sense of humor needs to be studied by anthropologists.

She studied his face for a moment, as if trying to understand something.

"I would like," Boyington said, "to discuss the plan further with you but there is something that I need to address first." Gwielgi remained silent; he knew Currahee valued patience.

Besides, I don't know what the hell is on her mind.

"Charles Tsunasdi," she said. "His name is known to me through our records. He was Currahee."

Gwielgi noticed the use of the word "was" but said nothing.

"I talked to your Lieutenant Elinshen about him," she said. "You know he was declared weak-heart. I was concerned with having such a person with us on this mission."

Gwielgi said nothing and waited but he felt his anger stirring.

"She said that he has conducted himself honorably while with the Wild Geese," she said. "And that you and he had formed a bond, almost like a Dideyohvsgi and Dedeloquasgi. That means…"

"I know what it means, major," Gwielgi said, his voice harder than he intended. "It means teacher and student in the simplest translation. Currahee use it to mean a moral guide." He paused. "I'm no one's Dide and Charles is not my damned Dede. He doesn't need one – he's a good man who's proven his courage, moral and physical, more times than you can count. As for the Currahee labeling him a weak-heart, you people got it and him wrong, on all levels, and if there's anyone in the Encampment, or here, who wants to argue that, I'm easy to find."

Boyington looked at Gwielgi and cocked her head slightly to one side as she studied his face.

"Captain," she said slowly, "your words sound almost like a challenge, as if you would throw down a gauntlet before me in defense of Tsunasdi's honor." Before Gwielgi could say anything, she held up her hand and slightly smiled. "It would be inappropriate, I think, to take your words to that point. Therefore, I will not discuss this subject further, at least not for now, except to say two things. Any man who could generate such loyalty from one such as you, might be other than a weak-heart and any man who would defend a friend so accused might be easily mistaken for a Dideyohvsgi." Something that might have been a smile crossed her lips.

"Now," Boyington said, "we need to consider our upcoming mission. I find it hard to believe that eight HUPAX are going to remain unnoticed on a town's streets for very long."

"Well, that's true." Gwielgi paused, gathering his thoughts and wondering what had just happened with Boyington. "It will be around two in the morning and I don't think any Kodomiri who see us will feel obligated to tell the enemy that we've arrived. On the other hand, there's a good chance that the teams will stir things up or a roaming patrol will see us."

"And if we are spotted?"

"If the teams are clear, we head north or south out of town."

"Have you fought in a HUPAX in a city before?"

"No, not really," Gwielgi said.

"I have," she said. "Allow me to make a suggestion..."

Chapter 28: The head of the snake

22 December 2824

Colonel Halleck was beginning to believe that Esteban Baer never slept. Even General Mannheim had retired for the night. But Envoy Baer remained awake, prowling Halleck's headquarters. Halleck loved the idea of curling up for a few hours and getting some sleep – he had been awake for 24 hours, ever since the strike on the brigade – but there was simply too much to do.

With the arrival of the single, damaged Saber and its traumatized pilot, it was clear that the entire Second Battalion was gone. He had hoped against reality, even after the rescue column gathered up the survivors. Their reports had been fragmented and the very nature of their combat gave him the justification for believing that at least some had gotten away after the battalion was divided in the canyons. But only the Saber returned.

About all the Saber pilot reported that they had not known from the survivors was a sighting of an APC on the mesa, racing away. The pilot had not considered trying to engage it – Halleck thought the young man probably had saved his own life by keeping his head down but Baer had cursed him. The brigade intelligence section thought the APC had picked up the spotters who undoubtedly had watched the battalion enter White Snake Pass. The battalion…

Halleck worked to keep himself from thinking about it. He had been, earlier in his career, the commander of the Second, and still regarded it with an affection that he tried to hide from the rest of the brigade. Now it was gone, cut to ribbons by a bunch of militia farmers and mercenaries.

And some ex-mercenaries, too.

And for what? Halleck did not regard himself as anything other than a simple soldier. But it did not take an expertise in foreign affairs to realize that revealing the Alliance secret of sponsoring the mercenary raids on Kodomir had given the Holdings a potential opening in the establishment of a good relationship with this world. That potential was now, of course, gone. He suspected, though he did not wish to, that Baer and Mannheim wanted it that way. They did not want a diplomatic victory but one dictated at the point of a bayonet.

What could he do about it? The question carried with it the same answer. There was nothing he could do about it except try and win the war as rapidly as possible. That was the job of a simple soldier.

As Baer paced in the background, Halleck studied again his map of the area. Any approach to Portaka City was covered, though his eyes kept being drawn towards the northern mountains. A force there could certainly get close enough to use the Kodomiri long-range weapons, but their ability to withdraw quickly in the face of a counter-strike would be hampered by those same mountains. Still, when morning came, he would have scouts get into that area.

On the other hand, to the west the ground was much more open. Any approach from there would be spotted quickly. The south had distant hills, though not as potentially dangerous as the northern mountains.

"Anything to report?" Baer's voice cut into his thoughts.

"No, Special Envoy," Halleck said. "All our perimeters report no contact. It will take them some time to develop a plan of attack on this position. Our sensors reported some landing ship movement to the southwest earlier this evening. They may be moving up towards us but it will take time for them to form for an attack. Maybe at dawn, maybe later."

"As long as they come," Baer said.

His tone irritated Halleck. It was easy for a civilian, someone out of the line of fire, to look forward to battle. He took a breath. There was no sense in antagonizing a man who had the ear of Baron von Bender. Careers had ended for less.

"Indeed, sir," Halleck said. "Perhaps you would care to retire so that you are rested when the battle takes place. I would imagine negotiations with the Kodomir government will rapidly follow and you may wish to be sharp for those."

"Don't like having someone peering over your shoulder, colonel?" Baer asked with a slight smile. "I'll be out of your hair in a little while. I'm just unwinding a bit from the day. How do you expect them to come?"

Halleck shrugged. He had work to do preparing for the expected attack. If Baer wanted to stay up all night, fine. He began to show the envoy what he was anticipating.

"Cochran to Team Red Lead. Be advised Team Blue has finished boarding. We are five minutes from your drop-off point."

"Red Lead copies."

Gwielgi, his response made, checked again the displays his Javelin placed in the visual center of his brain. In the red-lit landing ship HUP bay he could see the other HUPAX, all still held in place as Zombie raced low across the water, heading for their landing zone.

A HUPAX had advantages over most other weapon systems. A hovercraft was faster on flat terrain. A fighter was nimbler in air or space. A self-propelled gun might be able to shoot further. But a HUPAX had tactical mobility and modular firepower. And one other thing.

It could fight anywhere. Being a closed system using a fusion-ion power source, it could operate in the absence of air. Most often this meant invulnerability against chemical or biological weapons on the ground or attack ability against space stations or fighting on airless moons. But it also meant that a HUPAX could go underwater. Usually that ability meant no more than the ability to ford especially deep rivers.

Team Red was going to use that ability in a manner most would not expect. They were going to conduct an amphibious raid without landing craft, depending on their HUPs' ability to move through water.

It should work, Gwielgi kept telling himself. If the bottom was firm enough and if the currents were not too powerful. Some HUPs weighed a lot but underwater that weight would be far less. Further, the sheer size of the HUPs offered the currents in the bay a great deal of what was called "sail area," which simply meant that the HUPs were big and broad enough that a powerful current could greatly slow them down. The strongest currents in the bay would occur near low tide, when the reduced depth of the water would tend to concentrate them. The team would be walking in shortly after low tide and would encounter currents flowing towards shore and circling within the bay.

"One minute, Team Red."

The clamps restraining his HUP snapped back. In front of the Javelin a HUP captain stood, waiting patiently. For a moment he remembered the times he had lay strapped into a HUP and Jackie Peregrine had stood in front, preparing to guide him out and into battle. Then he nodded and focused on the HUP captain.

He was motioned forward as the clamps were released on the other seven HUPs and the bay doors slid back. It was pitch black outside and as he approached the opening, he had no sense of how high he was. It was not supposed to be very far. He heard Cochran's voice.

"Fifteen seconds. Good luck and good hunting. I am with you. Ten seconds."

Zombie slowed its forward momentum and, as it did, spray rose from beneath it. More than spray – steam.

"Team Red, go!"

Gwielgi stepped into space. Like most HUPAX, the Javelin had a high center of gravity. It fell forward and was almost horizontal when its trailing leg cleared the deck edge. Gwielgi saw only the steam raised by Zombie's engines.

Cochran had brought the landing ship down to almost zero altitude, which meant the Javelin had very little distance to fall before hitting the water. To Gwielgi, it seemed like he was plummeting for several minutes. The crash into the water, a 90-ton belly flop, jerked him forward in his straps but bothered the HUPAX not at all. It immediately sank.

Gwielgi fought to get the HUP's feet under it before he touched bottom. The small reaction jets, normally used in space, aided the process as did the Javelin's vaguely humanoid shape. As he touched down, he guided the HUP forward, trying to clear where he landed, knowing another HUP was on its way down.

The Javelin, which he had named Brother Wolf some months before, responded beautifully, aided by the agility inherent in its "backwards" legs.

He turned on his floodlight and switched his communication unit to voice-activation.

"Red Lead is down. Bottom as predicted. Moving to assembly area."

He heard a clang and then another a few minutes later, noise transmitted through the water and loud enough it entered the insulated hull of Brother Wolf's fuselage. Not everyone was able to get away from their touch down point before the next HUP descended. Well, as long as no one had a hull breach, there would not be a major problem other than some nanoskin having to stitch itself up.

Gwielgi waited in his HUP while the others joined him. Through the dark of the water he saw light flare overhead as Zombie departed. On his tactical display blue dots appeared around him.

"Follow me. Lights off."

Gwielgi moved his HUP forward and watched his velocity indicator slowly climb. On land under normal gravity his well-armed Javelin could do 80 KPH with no problem. In the depths of the bay, he was barely making a tenth of that. The smaller HUPs were walking slowly to avoid surging ahead. Inherently faster, they also offered less resistance to movement through water.

It felt like Gwielgi was moving through molasses. The feedback provided by the mindlink made it seem that his body was pushing its way forward and he could feel his legs and arms twitching. He took a breath and focused his awareness on the mindlink while willing his body to relax.

Gwielgi glanced outside through the narrow, armored windows but he could see nothing. He slid the armor covers back into place and stayed with the visual field provided by Brother Wolf. He settled back in his seat and tried to get comfortable as he kept walking forward. This would take a while.

Captain Joseph Ho'nehe remembered that he had never like oceans, the memory triggered by the smell of the fishing boats and the island's processing plant. He sat in a small building near the docks, the cup of surprisingly good coffee in his hands rendered almost undrinkable by the smell drifting in through the open window. The captain of one of the boats, an older woman with white hair done up in a tight encircling braid, poured more coffee into her own cup and then sat down opposite him. The other two captains, one about her age, one much younger, deferred to her.

"The company says we're to render you 'all aid and assistance,'" Captain Svetlana Zaitsev said as she ladled enough sugar into her coffee to send most people into a diabetic coma. "But they didn't say exactly what all that was. Now, all of a sudden, a military landing ship is tearing up the beach and you and a bunch of other very serious looking people carrying a lot of guns appear. And you tell us you want to take all 36 of you into Portaka City, quiet like, so you can raise some kind of hell with those Benderist dog-lickers." Zaitsev blew across her coffee and looked at Ho`nehe with eyes blue and cold.

"So, you say it is going to be dangerous, but you want us to hang around at the dock until you all come back and then bring you back here." She took a sip and put the cup down. "You don't say anything about paying us, about insuring the boats, about anything else. Just want a ride there and back and, oh, yes, don't forget to duck. So do I have it about right, boy?"

"Yes, ma'am," Ho`nehe said. "I'm sure the government will cover any expenses and..." The other two captains laughed out loud and Zaitsev smiled.

"Relax, boy," she said. "We'll take you to your little party. Let us worry about the government. I was just teasing you. We already agreed to it. Besides, I have a niece in the Militia. Always happy to help out. Now, about your plan. As far as it goes, it's fine. But let me suggest a couple of things." She hitched herself forward. "We have a little experience at this sort of thing." She looked at the other two captains who smiled and nodded. "We've been known to take some cargos ashore that wouldn't bear close examination by various people."

"Smugglers?"

"Ah, well, you know how it is," Zaitsev said, tracing designs on the table with a finger, avoiding Ho`nehe's eyes. "Customs duty laws change from time to time and cargos making their way here sometimes discover that the duties are not what they were expecting. We've been known to lend a hand in such circumstances."

"Smugglers," Ho`nehe said. He paused and then he grinned. "I have an uncle working a landing ship at New Singapore who's in the same line of work. What's your plan?"

Less than fifteen minutes later the three fishing boats were casting off. They fell into column formation, their night running lights on full power. They gradually picked up their speed until they were racing over the quiet sea at better than 45 knots. Phosphorescence flared at their bows and in their wakes. Ho`nehe stood on the bridge of Zaitsev's boat, watching the navigation display update their position.

When they passed the HUP landing zone, he turned on his communication unit.

"Grunt Lead, Team Red Leader. Gwi, you up?"

"Affirmative, Grunt. We're holding about 400 meters from the ramps. Everyone except me is powered down."

"Roger, Red. We have the city in sight. Next contact when feet dry."

"Roger, Grunt."

"Well, boy, time for you to join your mates," Zaitsev said. The scattered lights of Portaka City were getting closer. "We'll let you know when you can come up."

"Aye, captain," Ho`nehe said. He left the elevated bridge and proceeded forward to a deck hatch. A crewman waited for him and guided him deeper into the boat. They descended two decks and then moved forward.

The crewman knelt in the passageway and pushed against the side bulkhead. A portion of it no more than a meter tall pivoted inward. The crewman grinned and motioned into the darkness it revealed. Ho`nehe got down on all fours and started crawled in.

About two meters in the narrow corridor turned sharply left. He moved forward until he bumped into someone. The smell of fish was overwhelming.

"Ah, Captain Ho`nehe," Staff Sergeant Tendelli said, invisible in the dark of the smugglers' hold. "So nice of you to join us this evening." Someone laughed and Ho`nehe smiled in the total darkness. It helped to keep your eyes closed, he decided as he brought his legs under him and sat down.

"Wouldn't miss it for the world," Ho`nehe replied. "We're a few minutes out. The HUPs are waiting on us. So far so good. All we have to do now is wait."

"Aye, sir," Tendelli said. "Still have time for a bit of a nap, then."

They sat in silence for a while longer and then Ho'nehe felt the fishing boat gradually slowing down. As it did it picked up a rocking motion. Coupled with the smell of old fish he knew it was a question of time before he would be sick.

One of the other soldiers beat him to it and it seemed to be a trigger for several others. The sound of retching and the sharp smell of vomit were more than he could tolerate. He turned his head to one side but still covered part of someone's leg with his most recent meal. Someone apologized.

The boat seemed to be holding still and felt like it was gyrating in space. More than anything he had ever wanted in his life in a very long time Ho'nehe wanted out of the confined space of the smugglers' hold. He grit his teeth and focused on the fact the same feeling was probably occurring with more than a few of the other eleven soldiers around him.

"Just a little while more," Ho'nehe whispered between dry heaves. He heard Tendelli's deep, regular breathing verging on a snore. "And someone wake up Staff Sergeant Tendelli – I'd hate for him to miss all this fun." His weak joke seemed to help him for a moment and the nausea abated.

Ho'nehe was thrown to one side as the boat thudded against something. There was another thud, not so violent. Then the boat was blessedly still.

"Take some sips of water," Ho'nehe whispered. "It'll help settle your stomachs. It'll be a few more minutes, maybe more." He took a little water, swirled it around, and swallowed, and then took a larger drink. As he put away his canteen he strained his ears, trying to hear.

After several minutes they heard footsteps to one side. They faded away and for ten more minutes there was nothing. Then, very gently, they heard a voice whispering into the hold.

"Captain says to come along," the man said. A low light flickered on and provided weak illumination of the low crawl way. "Best we hurry."

Ho'nehe led the way. As he emerged the crewman turned off his flashlight. The passageway lights were on. The man stepped back.

"A little rough down there, was it, captain?" The man didn't wait for an answer and motioned for the soldiers to follow him. Ho'nehe held up a hand until all the others were out. Then he nodded to the crewman who led them back to the ladders taking them higher. He stopped them just short of the main deck and proceeded by himself. Zaitsev came down and sat on the ladder.

416

"There are two of them on the dock," she said, her voice low. "They checked the boats and called in by radio. They said we'll have to wait for daylight to offload our fish and we're all restricted to our boats. The other two boats are on our pier, one behind us and one across from us. The two sentries are at the end of the pier, maybe fifty meters off our port bow. The pier lights are on – if you go onto the pier, I think they will see you easily."

"What's the lighting to starboard?" Ho`nehe asked.

"There isn't any. We're on Pier One, so there's nothing to starboard except a stone breakwater, maybe seven meters away. No lights on it."

"It connects with the dock?" He tried to remember the map of the area.

"Yes," Zaitsev said, nodding. "Forms a right angle to the end of the dock."

"We'll go that way." Ho`nehe turned to the others. "Tendelli is with me. We go over the side, swim to the breakwater and move to the dock and take out the sentries. Everyone else move up onto the main deck on your bellies. If you hear anything, Corporal Strehl, open fire. It's a bit far for silenced weapons, but that will be our last resort. We'll leave our gear with you. Everyone got it?"

There were nods and murmurs. He and Tendelli shrugged off their packs and combat belts and handed their gear to the others. Ho`nehe nodded to Zaitsev.

"Lead the way, captain." She turned and went back up the ladder.

Once on the main deck Zaitsev casually walked and looked around as if inspecting the boat's tie lines. They lost sight of her as she walked aft. Finally, she stood next to the hatch, her hands in her pockets.

"They're still where I told you," she said. "Talking to one another. Stay low."

Ho`nehe came up the ladder bent over and slid onto the main deck on his stomach. He lay still as Tendelli joined him. Zaitsev turned and faced aft.

"There's a line opposite you to get down into the water, boy," Zaitsev said quietly. "Saint George be with you." Then she walked aft again. Ho`nehe hoped her movement would attract the sentries' attention if they looked towards the boats.

He crawled to the starboard side and found the line secured to a rail cleat. Ho`nehe slowly raised his head and looked around. Just over the port

417

rail he saw the sentries, standing beneath a light. One of them held a datapad and was explaining something on it to the other. Grabbing tight to the line and staying as low as he could, Ho`nehe swung over the side.

He lowered himself hand over hand. The water felt warm at first but as he penetrated the surface it became cold. Once fully in the water, Ho`nehe let go of the line and used a gentle breaststroke, trying not to disturb the surface of the water.

There was enough reflected light that Ho`nehe easily made out the gray stones of the breakwater as he approached it. It was sharply inclined but the gaps between the stones made for narrow handholds.

Climbing the breakwater carefully, he slowly came out of the water. He waited while Tendelli climbed alongside. Ho`nehe checked their position and looked down the breakwater. He nodded to Tendelli and they slowly made their way toward the dock.

Ho`nehe kept them low, their feet just barely out of the water, trying to avoid observation. They were almost to the dock when Tendelli slipped. He slid and started to enter the water. Ho`nehe reached for him but the sergeant was too far away.

Tendelli jammed his left hand into a gap in the rocks. Ho`nehe heard the muffled click of a bone breaking but the big sergeant stopped sliding. Tendelli paused, his lips tight, while his feet and remaining hands sought gaps in the stones. Slowly Tendelli pushed himself up and extracted his hand. He looked over at Ho`nehe and nodded.

Ho`nehe made his way to the intersection of the breakwater and dock and then climbed the stones. He glanced back. Tendelli was following, though with difficulty as he held his left arm tight against his body.

Ho`nehe stopped at the top of the breakwater and lay half on it, half on the dock. Lighting was indirect and this end of the dock was in shadows, but if the sentries looked in their direction they would be seen. Tendelli came up beside him and grimaced when Ho`nehe looked at him. Tendelli brought around his right hand. It held his fighting knife. He nodded to the officer and Ho`nehe nodded back.

Keeping on their stomachs, the two men crawled together across the dock, deeper into the shadows on the other side. Ho`nehe kept waiting for the shout of discovery but there was only silence.

On the other side of the dock various pieces of gear lay in orderly rows. Spare nets, boxes of various sizes, mobile cranes, and other things lay undefined in the dark. Ho'nehe pulled out his own knife and the two men moved towards the sentries, quietly moving from shadow to shadow.

They were close to the sentries, closing on them from behind, when the one with the datapad snapped it shut. Ho'nehe heard the other man laugh and make a comment and the first echoed his laugh. Then one of them walked down the dock towards the pier with the fishing boats. Ho'nehe watched for a moment. Tendelli was somewhere behind him in the shadows, waiting for the walking sentry to get further down the dock before moving.

The remaining sentry was peeing into the bay. Ho'nehe glanced towards the other man. He was still walking away. This was the chance, he decided. Ho'nehe stood and took four quick steps, treading as softly as a cat.

One hand went over the sentry's mouth as the other drove the blade into the man's lower back. He twisted the knife, pulled it free, and then cut the man's throat, all while dragging him back into the shadows.

He was almost back into the darkness when the other sentry stopped and turned. Perhaps he heard the sentry's heels drag on the dock, perhaps he remembered something he forgot to say. He froze for a second and then dropped his datapad and swung his slung automatic rifle off his shoulder. Ho'nehe saw the movement out of the corner of his eye and, even as he dropped the dead man and tried to roll behind cover, had a sudden sense he was a dead man himself.

Out of the shadows sprang Tendelli. The big man clamped the crook of his left arm over the sentry's mouth and Ho'nehe saw his other hand drive into the man's back. The rifle fell onto the dock with a clatter. Tendelli dragged the man into the shadows and then emerged to pick up the rifle. He moved up and crouched beside Ho'nehe.

Ho'nehe looked down the dock, checking for other sentries but there was no one else to see. He stepped onto the dock and into the light. He motioned with his hand and ten dark-clad figures streamed quietly off the fishing boat. Strehl helped him get his gear on and then led the others down the dock, making sure it was clear.

Ho`nehe adjusted his headset and gave his beret a tug. He looked at the far end of the dock. Strehl and the rest of the team were spread out among the pieces of gear and dock equipment. He heard her quiet voice in his ear.

"Blue Lead, it's clear."

"Roger. Break. White and Green, you are cleared to disembark. Red Lead, Grunt Lead. Do you copy?"

"Loud and clear, Grunt. Sitrep."

"Dock secure. Stand by."

"Roger."

Ho`nehe looked back and saw dark figures coming off the two other fishing boats and quickly moving down the pier. The first person to get to him was the Recon team's leader, Imael Garito.

"Dock is secured," Ho`nehe said in a quick whisper. "HUPs are standing by." Garito, his face obscured with black camouflage paint, nodded. He glanced back at his team and made a pumping motion with his hand and Team White double-timed down the dock, their soft-soled boots almost silent on the planks.

William Coltrane and the Chekinov Scouts making up Team Green were close behind. Quickly Ho`nehe motioned them into the shadows beyond the dock and then led them towards the front of his team. As they passed each Blue team member, she or he would join the column. Finally, he arrived at Corporal Strehl's position. She pushed her night goggles up to her forehead, leaned towards him, and spoke quietly in his ear.

"No sentries seen so far but there's some movement on the other side of the ramps. View is blocked. White is checking it out. Garito sent four down the street the ramps connect to. They are out of sight, around the corner of this warehouse."

Ho`nehe nodded. He adjusted his own goggles. The ramp area was poorly lit but he could see details easily. There were two broad ramps emerging from the water, each almost fifty meters wide. Their slope was gentle and they joined with a broad street that intersected with an equally broad street running beside the row of warehouses behind the dock and piers. As Strehl had reported, on the other side of the ramps various pilings and equipment partially blocked the view of the dock but he caught some movement of at least an individual. He could not see any of Team White.

"Grunt Lead, White Lead."

"Go, White."

"I'm on the other side of the ramp. We have people over here, all civilians. Fishing off the dock."

"At three in the morning?" Ho`nehe didn't add they were fishing in the middle of a war zone. Civilians…

"Yeah. Change of tide coming in and its dark. They're after snapishki."

"Roger. Tell them to get under cover. Things might start happening soon."

"Roger, leader."

Ho`nehe had no idea what a snapishki was but this was not a time for an explanation of Kodomir fauna. He glanced back. His own team and the Scouts were gathered close to him.

"All teams, Grunt Lead. Move out. Break. Red Team Lead, you are cleared to go feet dry."

"Red copies. We are moving."

With a wave of his hand, Ho`nehe led the two teams forward. On the other side of the ramp, he saw the crouched figures of Team White coming out from behind cover and pacing his movement. All they needed now was time.

Gwielgi carefully walked Brother Wolf forward as the other HUP pilots acknowledged his command to move. Within a couple of minutes, his cockpit broke through the surface of the water. The sensor feed over the mindlink was swirled and confusing until all of the HUP's sensors cleared the water. Gwielgi saw the streetlights were still on though the ramps themselves were well shadowed. The other HUPs were on line to his right or in a second line behind his Javelin.

When Gwielgi's HUP stepped on the ramp it slipped but then its powerful metal foot found purchase and it climbed rapidly out of the water. As he got to the top of the ramp, water running in small rivers down the flank of the powerful HUP, he glanced to his left. Peeking out from behind dock equipment were the faces of civilians, men and women and even a few children, fishing poles jutting up around them. Their eyes were wide as the HUPAX thudded past. Gwielgi shook his head. Whoever they were, they picked a hell of a night to go fishing.

The street the ramps led to was broad but not wide enough to accommodate eight HUPs in line formation. The first three formed an inverted triangle while the remainder formed a staggered column and followed. As Gwielgi studied his visual field, the first of the three intersections he wanted covered, two blocks from the docks, showed a yellow circle in the middle of the intersection. The overhead map at the bottom of his visual field showed all of them.

"Red Seven and Eight, turn south and take the next intersection. Red Two and Three, remain here with me. Red Four, take your other two north to the next intersection and secure it."

The other pilots acknowledged his call. It was expected. Now the HUP group was divided into smaller fireteams, each mutually supporting. Tsunasdi and Elinshen were with him. Two of the Currahee were moving to the southern intersection while Boyington led two more north. For the first time Gwielgi realized he was the only non-Currahee on the team.

Gwielgi backed the Javelin off the main boulevard and onto the less well-lit street connecting the other fireteams. On the other side of the intersection Elinshen's Scimitar and Tsunasdi's Rapier, with the long barrels of rail guns jutting from turrets at the end of its arm-like side pylons, did the same. Glancing to his right he could see Boyington's fireteam deploying. The southern fireteam was deep into the shadows – there seemed to be few streetlights down there – and would have been invisible if not for Brother Wolf's light amplification devices. He looked at his map. The southern team was near the old ore processing plants that crowded the southern dock area.

Directly to the west of his location was the municipal building, out of sight in the darkness but less than a kilometer away. Somewhere in the shadows the infantry teams were moving forward. All he had to do now was wait.

"As I said," Kheyntamenti had explained to them all before the start of the mission, "the story may be apocryphal. There is much that is unknown about Prince Vlad Tepes and his defense of the passes through the Carpathian Mountains. But we have already seen that there is little that is new in war, for our earlier attack on the Benderist battalion was modeled on the attacks carried out during the Pueblo Uprising organized by a Tewa traditional healer known as Popé. During the uprising, a Spanish column was cut into segments in the mountains and then annihilated, one piece at a time. Now we are going to borrow a page from another warrior…"

Imael Garito's team arrived at its target, the hotel, without incident. While the streets were deserted of civilian traffic, there did not seem to be much Benderist security patrolling. They saw a light military vehicle moving down a side street but its speed suggested it was not looking for anything and may have been a courier. As he radioed the contact to the other teams the small vehicle disappeared, heading south.

Garito saw the main entrance of the hotel had a single sentry standing under the entrance lights. The near eastern end with its service entrance appeared unguarded. Holding his team in place, he moved north a short distance, checking on the hotel entrance facing the park.

Another sentry stood there. Garito could also see Benderist vehicles and HUPAX in the park. A Morning Star, its broad back hiding a vertical launch box and carrying a GTL5 laser turret and a SLAT155 preloaded artillery cannon, was closest. A portable service gantry was alongside it and he could see technicians working on the HUPAX. To his right was the municipal building.

Garito quietly made his way back to his team and whispered in his report to the other teams. Then he turned to the others gathered around him. He touched the chest on one black clad figure and pointed at the position he had just been at. He raised two fingers to his own eyes and then made a horizontal movement with his hand, a slow arc.

You go there and watch this sector.

The Recon soldier nodded and moved down the street. Garito repeated his instructions to another soldier, placing her where she could see the other sentry. As she left, he made a circle motion with his hand and pointed at the eastern end of the hotel.

The rest of the team followed him to the service entrance. It consisted of a large roll-up door about a meter off the ground and a regular door next to it at the top of a short set of stairs. He bounded up the stairs and tried the door. As expected, it was locked. He motioned to one of the soldiers who came up the stairs, a lock-breaking tool already in his hands.

The soldier inserted the tool's thin blade into the lock. Then he pulled off his black cap and wrapped it around the end of the tool. He pushed on the back of the tool and Garito could hear the muffled sound of metal sliding on metal as more blades were wedged into the lock. Finally satisfied that no more blades would go in, the soldier opened the tool's handle and rotated a bar until it was at a right angle to the tool. While Garito held the cap over the lock, the soldier rotated the tool using the bar. There was a snap and the tool suddenly spun. Garito could hear shattered metal grinding.

The soldier pulled the tool free. A piece of metal fell to the steps with a clink that sounded as loud as a HUPAX step. It started to roll down the steps but the soldier stepped on it. Garito looked at the soldiers hiding in the shadows watching the sentries but heard nothing in his headset. The soldier reached into the cavity of what had been the lock and carefully removed pieces of metal with his fingers. Then he tried the door.

It swung outward easily. The team stepped into the hotel and the darkness of a large supply room. Closing the door behind them and following Garito, they passed through the room. A door in the opposite wall opened into a dimly let hallway that ran the length of the hotel. Across from the door was a stairway leading upward.

Garito led them up the stairs, past the first floor, and up to the second. He motioned for half the team to continue upward to the third floor while he and three others carefully stepped into the second-floor corridor.

The hall was lined with doors. One soldier came with him as he checked the first door on the right. The other two checked the door opposite. Their door was locked. His opened. He stepped in softly, the other soldier close behind. He heard the sound of someone snoring.

There were two beds in the room but only one was occupied. Garito raised his submachine gun and held it on the dark figure for a moment, his hands squeezing the short stock and grip. He took a slow breath and fired.

The silenced weapon made a hollow popping sound. The weapon had two barrels, each using a preloaded chamber of ten caseless rounds electronically ignited. There was no internal mechanism of the gun for reloading, no ejected shells bouncing on the floor. The three rounds, programmed by a selector switch, were fired so closely together they sounded like one round and all three were gone before there was much barrel rise. Garito held his position for a second until the other soldier touched his elbow. Then he turned and left. There was no time to lose – there were many rooms in the hall.

"According to the story," Kheyntamenti had continued, "a great Turkish army advanced on the passes, intent on cutting their way through. Tepes quickly understood that a conventional defense of the pass would ultimately fail for his force was so outnumbered that the Turks would not be long held back. The spirit of the Islamic warriors was so great that death in battle was seen as a blessing. No matter how many casualties they took, they would not cease their attack. Even if he had enough soldiers to defeat them in battle, the price would be enormous. So, he decided to defeat them another way…"

Ho'nehe cursed silently to himself. The municipal building was both well lighted and well-guarded. Not only were there sentries at each entrance he could see, an APC was parked on the street beside the building. Motioning for the two remaining teams to hold in position, he made his way north and then cut west on an intersecting street. This brought him to a position a block north of the building with the park to his west.

In the park Ho'nehe saw some lights of what might be maintenance vehicles and equipment. There was no mistaking, even if dimly lit, the shapes of HUPs jutting above the park's trees. Ho'nehe slowly moved to the park's edge. A Morning Star was in plain view with several maintenance vehicles around it, barely 200 meters from the building.

He looked at the municipal building entrance opening onto the park and then increased the magnification of his goggles. Ho'nehe studied the entrance carefully and then examined the ground between the entrance and his current position. There might be a way after all, he decided. He crawled back into the shadows and then back to the teams.

He crouched next to Coltrane and whispered quietly.

"Change in plan. We cannot go in the way we planned. But the front door only has one guard. There's a way we can get to it. I want your team a lot closer to the park in case this doesn't work, so follow closely."

Coltrane nodded. Ho'nehe looked at the Chekinov leader. Coltrane was still not at his full strength following his captivity and looked drained. He suspected Coltrane, born and raised in the mountains, was even less use to being on a boat then he was and probably had a worse trip.

Ho'nehe led the way to his position north of the building. He gestured to Coltrane who nodded and spread his team into a semicircular formation just inside the park, taking advantage of bushes and trees for cover and concealment. Ho'nehe, moving on his stomach, led Team Blue through the shadows.

His earlier study of the ground had revealed a set of ornamental bushes bordering a sidewalk that ran the length of the municipal building front. He thought if the team stayed behind the bushes, they would be invisible to the single guard at the top of the steps leading to the entrance. As he crawled, he paused from time to time. He discovered that there were gaps in the bushes, making it easy to see the sentry as they approached. And easy for him to see them if he cared to look carefully, Ho'nehe thought.

When he was opposite the sentry Ho'nehe glanced towards the park. The Morning Star was still being worked on but nothing else was happening. The hotel seemed silent. He keyed his microphone and talked as quietly as he could.

"Team Blue is entering now."

Then he rose above the bushes with his submachine gun aimed at the guard.

"The other way," Kheyntamenti had told them, "was to make these devoted, dedicated warriors feel afraid. That would not happen in battle for they would die before they knew defeat. Therefore, there could not be a battle. Instead, he would bring them a sense of helplessness and that would lead to despair and fear..."

Colonel Halleck stretched, working the kinks out. The brigade maintenance detachment was using the night to do some scheduled work on several of the support HUPs and continued repairs on those damaged during the attack; their latest summary was on the table in front of him. The battalions surrounding Portaka City on three sides were reporting nothing moved in the night. He had not expected anything but it paid to be cautious.

Like any HUPAX commander, he disliked being in a town. A HUP was happier in the open countryside where it was difficult for anyone to approach it without being seen. He had read the intelligence summary of the Kodomiri overthrow of the Storm Cloud Raiders. These people apparently had had some sort of underground resistance movement and he wanted to be out of Portaka City before anything like that had a chance to form against him.

Halleck decided he would walk over to the hotel for some sleep. Envoy Baer had left, finally, twenty minutes before. He stopped at the duty officer and was checking on the watch schedule when the communications watch sergeant, his hands pressing his headphones to his ears, turned to them both.

"Sirs? I think you want to hear this." He turned on an external speaker and they heard a swirl of voices.

"It's artillery fire, bloody frigging accurate. Hitting positions near the south end of the airfield."

"Roger, we're getting some of the same thing at the north end."

"Get your pilots into their HUPs! They have to move! Two HUPs are already hit."

"By artillery? Can't be. They must have snuck some HUPs in closer."

"What the hell was that!? We just lost a HUP to a direct hit! Something large..."

"Get the HUPs moving!"

"Trying to, but we're getting fire here and we've had a pilot killed, two wounded, trying to get to their HUPs."

Halleck grabbed the microphone.

"Third Battalion, this is Brigade. What is your situation?"

For a moment no one answered among the shouting voices. Finally, he heard someone respond.

"Everyone, off the air! Brigade, this is Captain Sharp. Battalion CP vehicle has been hit and I think our CO is gone. I'm in my HUP. We're getting very precise long-range arty and heavy missile fire from the western hills. We have some positions triangulated but we do not have weapons that can reach them."

"Roger, captain. This is Halleck. As of now, you are acting commander of the Third Battalion. Get your HUPs crewed and moving. Long-range artillery cannot hit moving HUPs. Anything holding still is meat on the table for these people."

"Yes, sir, understood."

"I'm going to detach a company each from the Fifth and Fourth Battalions to reinforce your position. Stay alert. They may try to come in under the barrage. Remember, the Kodomiri Militia loves artillery."

"Got it, sir."

Halleck contacted the northern and southern battalions and ordered the reinforcements. As he keyed the microphone to order the entire brigade to full alert, a figure in black came through the entrance. Instinctively, Halleck fell to the floor as bullets impacted the duty officer and communications tech, throwing them to the ground. He rolled away, trying to get behind his table.

He heard the submachine gun firing again no louder than fists striking each other and chunks of rug and flooring exploded around him while spikes slammed into his legs. He lay as still as he could and heard running footsteps. A very calm voice sounded like it was directing traffic.

"Left, you two, left. You two go right, and you, right. Upstairs, you three upstairs. Go, go."

Halleck heard a man walking around the area they had used as their command center. Papers rustled. The radio was silent and he could smell burning insulation. It must have been hit with the first burst of gunfire.

Suddenly, the walking man was next to him. He held his breath as he heard the papers on his table being examined. A boot brushed his ribs as the man turned and then walked away.

The others were coming back, pounding down the stairs and running up the halls.

"Clear, captain. Nothing upstairs."

"All right. See if you can drag that sentry in here without attracting attention."

"Yes, sir,"

"Found a commo set-up, captain. Spare gear, looks like. We've rigged it."

"Fine. How's the wrist?"

"Nano suit is holding it like a brace. Nothing that a couple of beers wouldn't take care of, sir."

"They're on me. Rig this room as well."

"Aye, sir."

"Sir, the other hall is clear. Some civilian offices, nothing else. Looks like they only occupied this area and the other hall."

"Very well. All right, listen up. That thunder you hear is ours. Time for us to go. Two at a time, stay on this side of the hedge, make your way back to the rally point. Stay cool, we're almost done. Tendelli, you and the medic go first. When you get to the point, get a splint on that wrist to reinforce your suit. Strehl, you and I will bring up the rear."

Halleck heard the sound of feet shuffling on the carpeted floor. Someone was whispering, signaling when to leave the building. Then the man with the quiet voice was speaking.

"All teams, Grunt Lead. We are leaving. Heading to the rally point."

If there was a response Halleck did not hear it. He waited, feigning death, until he could hear nothing else. He slowly raised his head but saw nothing other than his dead duty officer. The pain in his legs was still quite sharp.

Halleck slowly sat up. A bullet had gone through the outer muscle of his right leg, leaving a deep gouge only partially covered by skin. His left leg had been grazed. He felt around his field belt and found the first aid pack. He pulled a dressing out and wrapped it around his right leg. Other than the pain, he did not seem to be badly damaged. He tentatively stood and found he could walk. It hurt, but he could move.

The radio was destroyed. Several spare sets were down the hall and then he remembered the commando's report to his officer. Something about them being "rigged." And this room, it was supposed to be "rigged" as well. Halleck saw the satchel charge out of the corner of his eye. It was propped beside the desk holding the radio. He did not know how much time he had but immediately realized he had to get out of the building. He headed for the front door, hoping the charge did not have a motion sensor.

If he could get into the park, he could go to the hotel or the HUP lager. He decided on the HUPs, an instinctive move but one supported by common sense. There were no communication systems in the hotel but a HUP could talk to everyone. He pushed on the door and lurched outside.

That was it. Get to a HUP and he could mobilize the entire brigade.

As it happened, he did not have to.

"You make a soldier," Kheyntamenti said, "feel helpless by striking in a manner that does not allow the soldier to strike back. So Tepes took a small group of his most dedicated, personal guard and, leaving their armor and long swords behind, infiltrated the enemy camp in the small hours of the night. Then they carefully and deliberately killed as many of the enemy as they could. But not just any of the enemy. They singled out the army's leadership, easily identified by the banners outside their tents. They crept into the tents and cut the throats of the leaders while they slept. Then Tepes and his men slipped away into the darkness. When morning came, the enemy soldiers were horrified to discover what was done to their leaders. Their morale was broken and their surviving officers could do nothing with them but take them home..."

William Coltrane was exhausted. Still weak from his ordeal as a hostage, the trip in the fishing boat had been horrible. Now dehydrated, he tried to ignore his physical weakness, determined to fulfill his obligation as a Chekinov warrior. His honor demanded it.

After Ho'nehe's team left his position, Coltrane watched the park carefully. Over the tops of a small grove of trees to his left front he could see the top of a Morning Star. Here and there he saw armored personnel carriers and other support vehicles. He saw a small group approaching a pair of vehicles, similar to the Militia's light Prowlers. He studied them. They were talking as they walked. When they entered the vehicles, they were still chatting away.

What was going on? They were several hundred meters away, next to the pond. The vehicles rolled forward, moving in the direction of the municipal building. Had they noticed something? His earpiece hissed to life.

"All teams, Grunt Lead. We are leaving. Heading to the rally point."

"Team White copies. Pulling out now."

In the stress of the moment Coltrane saw the vehicles threatening Team Blue as it retreated from the municipal building. Something had to be done. He turned to his team.

"Two vehicles, twelve o'clock. Antiarmor team, hit them."

A Scout stood up, a rocket launcher already on his shoulder. He paused, tracked for a second, and fired. A flash of rocket exhaust flared out the back of the launcher with a noise as loud as a grenade. It streaked into the small vehicle. The rocket, designed to pierce the armor of a fighting vehicle, went almost all the way through the lead vehicle before it detonated and tore the four-wheeled vehicle in half.

The gunner already had the launcher off his shoulder while his assistant thrust another missile into it. He swung it back up to his shoulder and peered through the sight. A stream of tracers from the second vehicle whipped through the air and sent him tumbling backward.

The assistant grabbed the launcher as the team opened fire with their submachine guns, but the short-barreled weapons with their integral silencers had almost no accuracy beyond a hundred meters. The gunner in the vehicle used their muzzle flashes to guide on and only the bouncing of the vehicle kept the whole team from being shot to bloody pieces. Coltrane heard one Scout scream while the head of another vanished as a large caliber bullet obliterated it. The assistant aimed, paused, and fired. Before the missile was half way the assistant was dead, cut down by the gunner.

Coltrane threw himself towards the missile launcher as the second vehicle dissolved in a fireball. From somewhere in the park voices were yelling. The maintenance lights went out. He was loading a third missile when Ho'nehe and Team Blue rolled into their position.

Ho'nehe did not waste time asking questions. He punched on his radio.

"Team White, Grunt Lead. Fall straight back. Head for the docks and the boats. Load up. Move out."

"White, roger. Lead, we think we see HUP movement in the park."

"Roger. Break. Team Red. We have a problem here. We need cover."

"On the way, Grunt. Can you get clear or are you engaged?"

"Clear for the moment. We have people down and are pulling out with them. North end of the muni building."

"Roger. Break. Watch for our people in the streets, folks."

Then Ho'nehe heard the whine of turbines and the creak of tracks. Armored vehicles were coming.

"Red, we got armor on the way."

"Roger. Be there in one. Get out."

Ho'nehe whistled loudly. "Pick up all wounded. Head due east, straight down this street," he yelled, pointing. "You'll hit the docks. Hang a left.

The boats are there. Sergeant Tendelli, you are in charge, lead'em out! I'll bring up the rear with Major Coltrane. Go!"

The group of Wild Geese and Scouts, several carrying wounded, rose from the position and ran across the street. Ho`nehe saw several of the Scouts go to each of the dead and take something from the bodies. He dropped down beside Coltrane.

"How many rounds do you have for that thing?"

"Two, one in the tube," Coltrane said, gasping for breath. "The other is in that bag." Ho`nehe rolled over to it and pulled the stubby missile container free. He quickly crawled back to Coltrane.

The sound of the approaching tracked vehicle got louder but Ho`nehe was not sure where it was. He glanced at his watch. Only a few minutes had passed since he had seen the first explosion while crawling down the line of shrubs.

"No plan of battle survives first contact with the enemy," he muttered, straining to see with his night goggles while he unpacked the last missile.

"Indeed," Coltrane said in a tired voice. At almost the same instant he fired. Ho`nehe shoved the remaining missile into the tube and looked up to see a boxy APC burning at the edge of a grove of trees.

Then he heard a HUPAX powering up. There was no mistaking the sound of the fusion-driven war machine. Compared to the sound of the armored vehicles, it was the difference between the bark of a pet dog and the howl of a wolf.

"Oh, hell," he said.

"Indeed," Coltrane said again. He looked over at Ho`nehe, his eyes hidden behind his goggles. "Captain Ho`nehe, I have always admired your unit. Your Wild Geese remind me of my own Tsalagi."

"That's wonderful, major," Ho`nehe said. "Maybe we could compare notes some time."

"I have been hit, captain," Coltrane said. "Badly. I will not make it. I am about to order you to leave. We do not need two people to fire this weapon's last shot. In addition to my order, I have a request. On my wrist is a bracelet that I ask you take back to my sister. And around my neck is the ID tag of another Militia officer besides my own. Please take them as well."

"Take them your damned self," Ho`nehe said. "Where are you hit?"

"Right side. Liver. I will bleed out if they do not kill me before then." Coltrane pulled a chain from around his neck and passed it to Ho`nehe. "Please take care of this. It belonged to a very honorable soldier." He started to fumble with the woven bracelet on his wrist when they heard the growl of a tank.

It passed the burning APC and swinging its turret back and forth, like a predator looking for the movement of prey.

"You can't hit it in the front and kill it. Armor's too thick. Try to get the turret when it is broadside to us."

"Yes," Coltrane said.

The tank stopped less than a hundred meters away. Its turret seemed to be pointed at them, the long cannon level. It rotated to their left, but not far enough, and then stopped. Then it swung back, slowly. Was it searching for the HUPs? The turret kept moving. Gradually it exposed its thinner side plating. Ho`nehe saw a hatch on top swing open and the tank commander emerged. The figure carried a pair of binoculars with it and swept the area. The turret kept swinging.

Ho`nehe saw a blue and green HUPAX, lit by the flickering light of the fires, coming up behind the tank. It was a bulky Cutlass. If they fired, even if they killed the tank, the HUP would see them.

"Captain, I order you to leave," Coltrane said.

"Shoot the damned tank, major, and then we're both leaving."

The missile launcher fired for the last time. The missile hit the side of the turret. Almost immediately there was a second explosion inside the tank. Then a violent column of fire erupted through the turret hatch, burning like a rocket engine. Even as it roared, Ho`nehe grabbed the launcher and threw it to one side. He rolled Coltrane onto his back and then picked him up onto his shoulders.

"Leave me," Coltrane said, his voice weak.

"Major, shut up." Ho`nehe turned and ran down the street. He was half way across the intersection when a HUPAX emerged from the shadows. He felt a wave of despair before he saw the arrow and feather emblem on the shin of the Javelin. Behind it were a Long Bow and a Ballista.

The Javelin kept walking forward, as if it didn't see him. He ran to one side as it fired at the Benderist Cutlass.

The large lasers of the Javelin dazzled his vision, though he was looking away. The crack of the collapsing vacuum they made in the atmosphere was powerful enough that he staggered. Out of the corner of his eye he saw the Long Bow fire a second later. Twin rail gun slugs moving at hypervelocity speeds produced another sonic crack so loud it set his ears ringing.

Ho'nehe did not look back at the Cutlass. His focus was on keeping his feet moving and he pounded down the street even as it was lit by HUP fire behind him. His nanotechnology suit enabled him to maintain a dead run for a block, the heavy body of Coltrane on his shoulders, and then the huge expenditure of energy caused its augmentation of his strength to quickly lessen.

With the suit's power fading, it quickly became what it was – a suit of armor that tried to drag him to his knees. Ho'nehe, the weight of the suit and Coltrane seeming to increase with every step, started staggering from the effort. He continued to run as fast as he could down the dark street while the sound of fighting echoed around him, pacing him and reminding him of what might be pursuing him.

Ho'nehe forced himself to slow down so he could concentrate on placing his feet. Falling at this point, he realized, might be fatal. But when he crossed the next intersection, he caught his foot on a curb. Stumbling, he didn't have the breath to curse. A bandaged arm caught him around the chest.

"Aye, captain, shall you be needing some help, then?" The tall form of Tendelli was beside him and other hands were easing Coltrane off his shoulders. They all continued down the street.

"Thought I ordered you to the boat," Ho'nehe said, his voice raspy.

"Lots of people disobeying orders tonight," Tendelli said. "With all respect, sir. Major Coltrane's mike was voice activated. We heard what was going on. I whistled up some of these Scouts and we came on back to see if he wanted you court-martialed. Sir. With all respect."

"Red Lead, scratch one."

"Roger. Red Team, come up to the edge of the park. We will go in all together. They are expecting us to retreat. We are attacking."

Garito's team had the furthest to go. By traveling straight east, they met the docks at the hovercraft ramps. All the civilians were gone, if not chased away by the sight of the HUPAX emerging from the bay, then terrified by shattering sounds coming from the park. Garito turned his team north, towards the fishing boats, and heard the sound of battle intensify. Slightly to his surprise the boats were still there, though their lights were off. He heard their powerful engines throbbing as they waited.

The other teams were already there, forming a rough semicircular defense around the piers. As he ran in he looked for Ho`nehe to report to. He started to ask one of the black-clad soldiers where Ho`nehe was when a sudden, large explosion in the direction of the park. A brilliant flash of light, the signature of a dying HUPAX, lit the sky.

Ho`nehe and a small group came running down the street.

"Landing party, back on the boats! Team leaders, report your casualties."

Garito motioned his team towards their boat and paused in front of Ho`nehe.

"We're all right," he said. "One twisted ankle."

"Good," Ho`nehe said as he watched his own team run down the pier. "Get your charges fixed?"

"Affirmative," Garito said. "About three minutes to go."

"All right, Imael, nice work. Get aboard and see you on the island."

Imael slapped Ho`nehe's arm and turned away. Ho`nehe looked toward the west. Over the buildings of the fish processing plant there was a bright, steady glow of fires. He heard a ripple of muffled explosions and the glow suddenly increased in intensity. He jumped up on his boat and heard the roar of the boats' engines as they backed away from the pier.

"Team Red, Grunt Lead. We are pulling out now."

There was no response and the glow became brighter.

He almost forgot to do it, but at the last moment, just before coming into sight of the first Benderist HUPAX, Gwielgi turned on his camera and initiated transmission. Hopefully, somewhere above a communication satellite received the signal and relayed it to Militia Headquarters in Kiroff City. From there it would be compressed and sent on. He also hoped it would do some good and that it would not include the shot of a HUP being destroyed as viewed from the HUP itself.

Gwielgi saw a Cutlass explode just as he started to target it. The flare of its dying fusion power plant lit up the entire area and he saw a Morning Star almost directly ahead. Its back was to him and service cranes were clustered around it. He fired directly into its back with his GTL4 large lasers and a missile while he used his quad 57mm chain gun to cut down running figures. On his right, Elinshen's lighter Scimitar joined in with two more laser turrets but it was the multiple recoilless rifles of Tsunasdi's Rapier, tearing through the weakened back armor, that killed the missile-carrying HUP. There were several internal explosions and fire poured out of its back.

To Gwielgi's left he saw the southern fireteam of HUPs coming up to the corner of the park, close by his own small group. Boyington's fireteam was on the other side of the municipal building, paused and looking for targets. In the park itself he could see glimpses of the tops of HUPs, some moving, above the scattered trees.

"Red Team, on line. Advance. Dress your line on me. Call targets."

He stepped forward. Boyington's earlier suggestion to assault the park was a gamble, but if they could smash things up, especially the brigade's communications, it would make it hard for anyone to pursue them. Gwielgi held his speed back, allowing the other HUPs form up on either side. Then he picked up the pace.

The brigade's support HUPs, mostly equipped with long-range weapons like the already destroyed Morning Star, were encountered first. Of the four remaining, one, a Mace capable of carrying infantry and other modules, was still powered down. Another HUP, an angular Long Sword, did not attempt to engage and veered off to the right and disappeared down a side street even as lasers licked at it.

The other two, another Morning Star and an ion pulse weapon-equipped second Mace, turned to fight, perhaps trying to cover the powered down Mace. The active Mace fired its ion pulse weapon at Gwielgi's Javelin. One shot, a blue-white bolt of lightning, missed to the right but the other hit dead center, spraying glowing droplets of melted armor into the darkness. His sensors were momentarily confused but Gwielgi fired on instinct and saw his large lasers score hits on the enemy's centaur-like torso. The Mace lunged forward into the park pond and raised a faint column of steam around itself as it did.

"Take the Mace."

Gwielgi heard Tsunasdi's call as he turned his HUP to the right, trying to break the other pilot's track on him. The Mace, distracted by fire from another HUP, swung its turrets to face the new threat. Gwielgi hit the bigger HUP before it got a shot off. The Mace's turrets, located at the ends of its stubby arms, swung back towards him. Elinshen's Scimitar plunged into the pond, throwing up a sheet of water as she fired. The right pylon of the Mace was sheared off, taking with it an ion pulse weapon. But the left fired again, this time hitting the Javelin's left leg. Again Gwielgi's visual field swirled as the chaotic energy ran through his HUP.

Even in the pond the smaller Scimitar was still fast and she ripped into the Mace, which outweighed her by sixty tons, with her three laser turrets. Staggering, the Mace snapped a shot into the water just behind her. He corrected and Gwielgi saw the next pulses walk up the Scimitar's left arm and side.

"Team Red, Grunt Lead. We are pulling out now."

Gwielgi was too busy to answer. He launched another missile and it exploded into the upper torso of the enemy HUP. Tsunasdi ended the encounter with his pair of twin recoilless rifles and two large lasers. The Mace physically staggered under the impact and its ion pulse weapon suddenly fell silent. The HUP half turned away and then fell sideways into the pond, sending up a large wave that carried the Scimitar a dozen meters.

"Where's the Morning Star?"

"Dead. And the other Mace is down."

"All right, reform."

"Lead, did you get Grunt's call? They are leaving."

"Good. Get on line. Let's get to the other side of this pond. I have movement on the right and left. Remember, there are some command HUPs in here, big bastards and... Damn!"

Out of the trees and less than a hundred meters away two large HUPs stomped into view. While the trailing Broad Sword turned to one side, the lead War Lance fired virtually point blank into Gwielgi's HUP. He saw a sudden flash of heavy cannon, two yellow-white explosions from the pylons of the 125-ton HUP and Brother Wolf, just coming up the slippery slope of the pond, recoiled under the impact. He heard a variety of warning signals sounding and for a moment had the strangest feeling of drifting.

Then his Javelin slammed into the pond on its side. Gwielgi struggled to right the HUP and get it back on its feet, but the bottom of the pond was soft and it was hard to find a solid grip.

Smoke drifted through the cockpit as Brother Wolf lurched. His damage display told him his missile launcher was history, his cockpit and the left side of the HUP had been hurt. As his HUP started to rise, Gwielgi saw the War Lance. It was paused on the bank of the pond, its torso facing to the right, firing at another HUP.

Brother Wolf slipped again, a powerful leg splaying out behind. But at least he was upright. Even as he fought to get both feet under his HUP, Gwielgi raised his eyes, bring with them the targeting reticle. Impulsively he flipped off his light amplification system and turned on his magnified display. At this range he could not miss but he wanted to hit something in particular. He ran his eyes up the enemy HUP and rested them on the cockpit. Then he fired.

The twin GTL4 lasers were not enough to penetrate the cockpit and kill the pilot but they damaged it and threw off the War Lance's tracking. It fired its 155mm rounds as it jerked from the impact. Now aware that its enemy was down but not dead, it swiveled its heavy turrets back towards Gwielgi.

Still aiming at the cockpit, Gwielgi fired his lasers again and saw the flash of armor evaporating. Its turrets kept turning towards him. He saw the red beams of a pair of large lasers jab into it from the side and melted armor poured down its side like slag. Brother Wolf finally stood erect just as the War Lance's weapons were brought to bear. Gwielgi, his eyes focused on the enemy pilot's cockpit, fired again but the War Lance's turrets were now pointed directly at him.

From the left Tsunasdi's Rapier poured fire into the War Lance but the big HUP was like something out of a nightmare and seemed not to notice. Gwielgi bit his lip, waiting for the blast.

But it did not come. Frozen in surprise, he failed to react for a second. Then he fired and the large lasers tore into the head of the larger HUP. Still it did not move.

"He is dead, Gwi. I think your lasers got into his cockpit."

Gwielgi closed his eyes for a second as he stepped forward. Some days it helped to be lucky more than it helped to be good.

Gwielgi looked to the left, searching for the Broad Sword. What he saw instead were two burning HUPs tangled together.

"The Broad Sword?"

"Dead as well."

"Who did we lose?"

"Charlene Tanner."

One of the Currahee, and a special one in his memory. She had been a slave on Farnham when the Wild Geese raided its mine. Other than during the briefing, he had probably not exchanged more than a couple of sentences with the woman, but he felt a bond to her. It was more than time to leave, Gwielgi decided. He keyed his transmitter.

"All right, we've stirred them up. Their garrison battalion will be here soon. We are pulling back to the docks and then heading south. They will take some time to determine we are no longer in town so we may have an edge. Destroy any vehicles you see. And hose down the hotel and muni building...no, wait."

The two buildings were on fire. Sometime during the fight, stray rounds or beams had hit their roofs and set them on fire. As Gwielgi turned the formation toward the east, an explosion blew open the middle and one wing of the municipal building. Before they had taken ten steps, the HUP pilots saw a series of similar explosions rip through the second and third floors of the hotel, collapsing the burning roof onto the remains of the structure.

"Save your ammo. Let's go."

The seven HUPs, their fuselages rotating back and forth and occasionally emitting long lances of laser fire and tracers as they spotted possible targets, stalked out of the burning park and vanished into the night.

Halleck sat beneath a tree near the southern end of the park pond. He had witnessed the HUP battle, expecting any moment to die in a spray of fire. But he had been spared. He saw other figures moving in the darkness and half-lit by the light of burning HUPs and equipment.

When the timed charges in the municipal building and the hotel went off, Halleck took it as a signal the attack was over. He got up, dusting himself off as he did; it was an instinctive move, reflecting his need to appear as neat as possible in front of his soldiers. His task now was to reform the brigade and determine what was to be done. To begin that, he needed to be able to communicate. He limped through the park.

The damage was extensive. Whether deliberately or accidentally, almost all of the armored security force and the maintenance and support vehicles were destroyed. Even the portable HUPAX repair gantry had taken a hit.

The human damage lay in every direction and in the burning wreckage of the buildings and machines. Halleck watched his medics somehow gather themselves together and respond to the cries of the wounded and the survivors' calls as they found silent injured. He watched as a medic crouched over a soldier, the wounded woman's uniform still smoldering. The medic did not hesitate and even as he worked, he made the opportunity to speak soft, reassuring words to the terribly burned woman. Whether she could hear him Halleck could not tell but her shuddering whimpering eased. As he passed the medic Halleck patted him on the back, suddenly finding he could not speak.

How do they do it?

Forcing his mind back to the catastrophe in front of him, Halleck counted seven destroyed or damaged HUPs. Only one belonged to the enemy. He shook his head. How had they gotten through his double perimeter? And where were they headed now?

The surviving support HUP, a tall Long Sword, slowly came up alongside the burning hotel. The pilot had been quick to save his HUP. Halleck knew from the maintenance report he had read just before the raid – had it only been twenty minutes ago? – that the 'Sword was almost unarmed, waiting to get its pair of missile launchers reloaded. He walked past the burning hotel and the small group of people gathered outside of it and stood next to the Long Sword.

The cockpit hatch opened and the pilot leaned out. Her eyes widened with surprise when she recognized Halleck. Halleck cupped his hands around his mouth, trying to be heard above the burning building and occasional explosion from within the park.

"Call First Battalion. Tell them to send me their commo vehicle and to get a company here for security."

She yelled something back in response but he could not make it out. She ducked back into her cockpit and emerged a moment later.

"On the way, sir," she yelled. He could hear her now. "Also sending a medical detachment and their maintenance team."

Halleck waved in acknowledgement. Good thinking – he should have asked for the other units as well. He looked over at the fire as the distinct odor of burning human flesh came to him. Portaka City fire vehicles were arriving but were holding back, uncertain as to their reception, he supposed. He saw a soldier and told the man to tell the firefighters to proceed. Not that there was a real point to it. The hotel was totally destroyed.

He walked towards a group of people standing in front of the still burning hotel. As they recognized Halleck, they turned towards him. He nodded to them and exchanged quiet greetings with anyone he knew. He came up on the brigade Sergeant Major who was organizing people and sending them off on jobs.

"Sir," the man said as he snapped to attention. "Excuse me, sir. I didn't expect to see you."

"Stand at ease, Sergeant Major." He looked around. "I'm not dead yet," Halleck said, "though it was damned close."

"Yes, sir, good to see you." The soldier glanced at Halleck's leg and motioned to a medic. The medic gently led Halleck to one side and made him sit down and then set to work. Halleck looked at the Sergeant Major.

"What happened here?"

"As near as we can put together, they hit us with a couple of squads. Second and third floors. First floor was ignored, maybe because of the guards in the lobby." He shook his head. "They killed everyone they could get to without waking anyone up. Silenced automatic weapons. They left behind timed charges at the ends of either hallway. That's what brought everything down."

"Casualties?"

"Still calculating but at least 30, maybe 40 dead. Those the assassins missed were mostly out of the building when the charges went off. The firefight woke us up."

"General Mannheim?"

"Unaccounted for," the sergeant major said. "But he had a suite on the third floor."

"Oh, damn," Halleck said. "And Envoy Baer?"

"I'm fine," a voice said from behind him. He turned and found the Special Envoy standing alone, bare foot and wearing a robe. "I was on the first floor. Heard some explosions from the park. I stuck my head out to look." A slight tremor ran through Baer. It remained in his hands, which he clenched and hid inside his bathrobe.

"They came here, in the middle of this town, through the entire brigade," Baer said, his eyes haunted. "Through all of our HUPs. Just to kill me."

Halleck looked at the Special Envoy with barely concealed contempt.

"Envoy Baer, they came here for the *brigade*. You were the one who said they would fight. Once again, you have been proven correct." He looked around the park at the fires still flickering and shook his head. "You pointed out that they risked much to save twelve and asked what they would do to save a town. I think you have your answer, Envoy. What would they do? Kill every one of us they could reach."

"What will you do now?"

"What are your orders, Envoy? Apparently, General Mannheim is dead. The brigade is under your command." In the flickering light Baer did not see Halleck's grimace.

"Call in the landing ships, colonel," Baer finally said. "Load them and then we go to Kiroff City. We will force their surrender by seizing their capital."

"Envoy, the Alliance landing ships outnumber ours two to one. If ours move, they could attack. Even if our ships land successfully, the Alliance has two regiments to field. It will mean war between the Holdings and the Alliance." Halleck stopped for a moment, reigning in his temper. "The Alliance will pick up Kodomir as an ally if they come into this war, the exact opposite outcome of what the Baron has charged us with."

"Colonel," Baer said, his voice flat, "the Alliance can go to hell. These farmers have twice humiliated one of the Baron's finest brigades. Do I need to remind you how this might appear to the worlds controlled by the Holdings?" He shook his head slowly. "This could be the first crack, the first break. Unless we can pursue this to victory, and quickly, our enemies, our internal enemies, may seize on this as encouragement for insurrection." He looked at Halleck. "Do you want to spend the rest of your career putting down uprisings?"

Halleck said nothing for a moment. He heard the arrival of several vehicles and HUPs. One was the First Battalion's communication APC. He nodded to Baer and walked over to it. A junior officer jumped out and came to attention. He ignored the young man and entered the APC's red-lit interior. The junior officer followed. Halleck leaned against the vehicle's hull, his arms folded. He didn't look at the officer as he spoke.

"Contact the landing ship Task Force commander. On the orders of Special Envoy Esteban Baer, he is to leave his current position and bring all landing ships to the airfield west of here and prepare to embark the brigade for tactical operations elsewhere on Kodomir."

The young officer saluted again and took a seat in front of a communication console. Halleck heard the whine of the transceiver antenna being raised and left the APC.

"It is being done," he said to Baer.

"Fine, fine," Bear replied. "Now, as we leave, I want this town destroyed. Burn it down."

"We cannot do that, sir," Halleck said, his voice tired. "Under the Articles of War of the Organization of Settled Worlds, such destruction is not justifiable."

Baer stared at him and Halleck realized his career was over. The envoy was about to speak but Halleck interrupted him.

"Sir, the Baron would not support such action. He would regard it as a stain on his personal honor. Think about it, sir." Baer said nothing for a moment. Then he smiled.

"Of course, colonel," he said, "you are correct. Thank you for preventing me from committing a grave error. I will find a way to personally reward you for your assistance."

Halleck felt a small sense of dread. The real meaning of the "reward" was clear to him.

"But when we attack Kiroff, colonel, tell me," Baer said, still smiling, "now that would be a legitimate target, would it not?"

"Yes, sir, if they do not surrender, it will be."

"Fine." Baer leaned forward, his face close to the colonel's, his voice low. "And they will *not* be permitted to surrender until we destroy that city." He kept his face close for a moment and then leaned back. He looked around and then back at Halleck. "See to your brigade, colonel." Baer turned and walked away.

"Boss, Team Red Lead."

"Go, Red."

"We're pulling out. How does it look?"

"Both the northern and southern battalions have shifted HUPs to the vicinity of the airfield and recon reports they are edging west. All are on full alert."

"Roger. We are not being pursued yet. We jogged south but I think we can retrograde back into the bay."

"Understood. Which landing zone?"

"North. If anyone saw us heading south, I'd rather not go there. Besides, the current will be behind us once we leave the bay."

"Yes, until high tide. I will pass the word. Sitrep?"

"We lost one of the Currahee, colonel. Charlene Tanner. Looks like the grunts hit their objectives but they got in a firefight. We intervened. Took out some support facilities and armor. "

"The imagery has been transmitted."

"I think we destroyed five HUPs, probably one more, and heavily damaged another. Credit Tanner with a Broad Sword. Most of it took place within the park – I don't think there's a lot of collateral damage to the town."

"Roger. Good work."

"Not yet, not until I get the team home."

"Understood."

"Tell Cochran not to be late. Elvis has left the building."

"I do not understand."

"I'll explain later. Red Lead out."

Akagi did not bother with the tea this time. The frantic look edging its way onto Bostan's face was refreshment enough. He showed the subspace imagery from Kodomir to the ambassador with only an occasional comment but he permitted himself the enjoyment of pointing out the destroyed Benderist equipment. After it was over Bostan sat back in the overstuffed chair, a hand covering his mouth.

"We have prepared a copy for your use, Ambassador Bostan. Both sets of imagery, including the long-range views from what was apparently what the military calls a *demonstration* as well as the somewhat more dramatic material from the strike team."

"The Baron," Bostan began and then fell silent. "The Baron will not be pleased," he finally said.

"I deeply regret having to share this with you, sir," Akagi said, bowing his head, which helped him hide his smile. "And I am distraught to provide you with even worse news." He waited a heartbeat as Bostan stared at him.

"I have come into information which I regard as shocking concerning your good friend Special Envoy Esteban Baer. It is not conclusive; I am told corroboration is being sought and may be forthcoming very soon." He reached forward and picked up a thin folder from a table and passed it to Bostan.

"There is reason to believe Envoy Baer has been involved with a group of Frontier Raiders and used them to advance his personal fortunes. The list of charges includes involvement with political assassinations, commercial piracy, and slavery. As I said, corroboration of these charges, all made by his contact with the notorious pirate group called Storm Cloud, is being sought. Again, my personal regret at having to share this disquieting news with you." Again, Akagi bowed his head.

Bostan quickly read through the papers. He got to the end and carefully closed the folder and then placed his hands on it.

"You alluded to these charges earlier," Bostan said. "While there is more detail here, in their present form they carry no legal weight."

"Indeed not, ambassador," Akagi said. "Even so, given their specifics, if they were to get into the hands of Envoy Baer's political rivals, I am concerned they might inflict a great deal of damage on the man's good name. Baron Karl von Bender's emphasis on honor is, of course, legendary."

"True," Bostan said. "But damage is not *destruction*. The envoy has a great deal of influence and many friends in the Baron's court. These charges, these statements of Iriki Tykaw's, would produce a storm, certainly, but one he could ride out over time. And the effect, in any case, would be too late to be of consequence for the fate of Kodomir."

He stood up and walked over to Akagi's tea service and poured two cups. He carried one to Akagi.

"If there is definite corroboration," Bostan said as he passed the cup, "then everything might change. Everything."

As the fishing boats raced beneath the star flung night sky, the teams sat and lay on the upper decks. There was no need to hide.

Imael Garito sat in silence as the cool wind swept across him and his team. He looked around. Most were sitting very still in silence. The slaughter of the sleeping Benderists lay on them like a heavy hand. He finally motioned to them and led the way to the fantail where the bridge structure blocked the wind. He waited until the team was standing and sitting around him.

"We had to do something that was very hard," Garito said, raising his voice slightly over the noise of the boat and ocean. "And it doesn't matter that they were the enemy, that they were the people who hired Storm Cloud when we were invaded. It was hard killing them while they slept." He pulled a canteen off his field belt and took a drink.

"It is a good thing," Garito said, "that this bothers you, for killing should never come easy. It is also a good thing that we did it, for each of them dead is one less who could kill one of ours. They were soldiers, asleep, but still soldiers, and what we did we had to do." He took another sip and then passed the canteen to the Recon soldier to his left.

"We are all responsible for what we choose to do," Garito said. "But I am responsible for putting you in the position of having to make that choice. I believe as completely as I believe anything that we, that you, did the right thing." He watched as the canteen made its way around, each woman or man taking a sip. It came back to him and he hefted it.

"You did what a soldier's honor required," he said. Garito raised the canteen and drained it. The team stood and drifted away, murmured conversations starting. A thin sergeant, shorter than Garito, and wearing the crosshairs patch of a qualified sniper stood next to him and watched as the others left.

"What do you think, Sergeant Tyree?" he asked. "Will they bounce back?"

"Yes, sir," Tyree replied. "They're good people. And you said the right things."

"Lot different than fighting Raiders," Garito said. "They were so bloody evil it made everything easier."

"It was still about killing, sir," Tyree said. "It always is."

"And honor, sergeant. Don't forget it is about honor."

"Yes, sir," Tyree said, nodding his head. "And sometimes it is a dark honor we earn."

Ho`nehe stood by holding a small light as the medics worked on Coltrane, trying to save him. Finally, one of them stood and leaned next to Ho`nehe.

"Captain, we've done what we could, but his wound is massive. We can't stop the bleeding. Maybe the sickbay on the landing ship can do something but…"

Ho`nehe nodded. Coltrane's eyes flickered opened. He looked around and then saw Ho`nehe.

"Captain," Coltrane said, his voice weak and hard to hear over the sound of the engines and the wind. Ho`nehe kneeled down beside him. "You disobeyed a direct order."

"No, sir," Ho`nehe said. "I obeyed an order." Coltrane looked at him with raised eyebrows and Ho`nehe leaned close. "The First Precept: 'We shall leave none of our own behind.'"

Coltrane said nothing for a moment as his eyes closed. He reached for his neck. "Something I want to ask…"

"You already gave it to me," Ho`nehe said. "I have the ID tag."

Coltrane nodded. Then he held up his arm. His sleeve had been cut away for an IV bag resting on his upper arm. Ho`nehe saw the bracelet consisting of threads woven into a cord tied off in a knot. Ho`nehe untied it with some effort and started to put it into his chest pocket.

"I remember. I will give this to your sister."

Coltrane shook his head negatively. He tried to speak. Ho`nehe leaned forward, his ear next to the dying man's mouth.

"Wear it for me," Coltrane said, and then was gone.

For a moment, Ho`nehe said nothing. Two of the soldiers gathered close around assisting the medics were Chekinov Scouts. Ho`nehe looked at the bracelet for a moment and then at the two Scouts who were watching him and the cord.

"He told me," Ho'nehe finally said, "when we were at the park, to give this to his sister." One of them nodded, his face impassive. "Just now he told me to wear it."

"Will you?" the Scout asked.

"What does it mean, his asking me to wear it?"

"It is customary," the Scout said, "for a Tsalagi cord to be passed on after death to the deceased's closest relative, the one with whom the person had the deepest bond. That is why he wanted you to give it to his sister. They are very close." The Scout fell silent.

"But to change his mind and give it to me to wear? Was that just the effect of the wound and his weakness?"

"No, sir," the Scout said. "If a Tsalagi warrior has a close relative who is also a warrior, as his Anastasia is, then he may pass it on to remind the warrior of their relationship. To be asked to wear the bracelet of a warrior is to be asked to preserve his legacy." He looked at the other Scout, an older man, who nodded.

"It is the highest honor that a Tsalagi warrior can bestow, captain," the older Scout said. "He was asking that you carry his heritage, his honor, as a warrior. Once put on, only death may remove it. The bracelet is a record of the Tsalagi's life. To the tribal colors are added threads only warriors wear. Each of those threads, each one of red or gold, of the cord signifies an important event."

"And the honor of a warrior?"

"Is the same for all warriors, of course," the Scout said. "We live to protect our people."

Ho'nehe looked at the bracelet for a moment and then at the Scouts. He placed it on his wrist and tried tying the ends with his free hand. The older Scout crouched beside him and silently tied it off. He stayed beside Ho'nehe for a moment.

"It is just made of woven threads," The Scout said. "It will wear out. When that happens, a new one is made. It will be made of the same colors, the same patterns, but new threads may be added then. The old one is burned." He looked at it for a moment. Then he looked at Ho'nehe.

"Thank you, captain," he said. "You do William Coltrane and his family, his people, our people, a great honor."

Ho'nehe bowed his head. He had nothing to say. He leaned against a bulkhead and looked up at the stars as the sea sped past and thought about honor.

Chapter 29: The snake turns

2 December 2824

Colonel Jonivov watched as the last Team Red HUPAX climbed up the loading ramp of the Crocodile-class landing ship Zombie. The sun was approaching its noon position and he was eager to be moving.

The question was, where?

He walked up the ramp following the Javelin and behind him the other landing ships carrying his regiment began to lift, their engines rivaling the glare of the sun. As Jonivov stepped onto the bay deck, the ramp was raised and the large, sliding doors closed.

The tan-colored Javelin changed color in response to the bay lighting as it was directed into its travel locks. Jonivov, who had been in the infantry his entire military career, was fascinated by HUPs and found it amusing that such powerful machines were apparently so clumsy. The Javelin followed the directions of a technician, what the Wild Geese called a "HUP captain," and backed into the locks. They slammed into place with a clang that echoed. A gantry swung into place as the cockpit hatch opened.

Jonivov waited while the pilot, his face drawn with fatigue, talked with the HUP captain and did a walk-around of the damaged HUP. Jonivov could see raw armor, twisted and melted, where the nanoskin had been blown or burned away. The streamlined box of the missile launcher over the cockpit was gone. Only a few torn pieces of metal showed that anything had been there at all. He shook his head.

To be strapped down in something that stood a dozen or more meters tall, that attracted the eye of everyone on a battlefield, riding a machine whose power plant captured the energy of the sun, energy that could come ripping out to kill the machine it powered. For the second time, he shook his head. He used to think the Militia fighter pilots in their obsolescent Swallows were crazy until he met the HUP pilots of the Wild Geese. He would have to come up with a new word.

Captain Gwielgi said a few last words over his shoulder to his HUP captain and walked over to Jonivov. He was dangling his mindlink helmet by its strap and had his fire-retardant coverall opened. But what Jonivov noticed were his eyes. Tired, yes, but there was more than that. An almost haunted look. He held out his hand.

"Well done," Jonivov said. Gwielgi took his hand automatically.

"Thank you, sir," Gwielgi said. "Are the grunts all right?"

"We picked them up before dawn," Jonivov said. The two men walked across the bay. "They had seven wounded, five dead. From what our intercepts can tell, they tore up the command and support personnel of the brigade pretty badly. It sounds like the Benderists are still assessing their damage. Your people did a fine job covering them and the imagery came through perfectly. Unexpected bonus, killing those HUPs and vehicles. Their ability to maintain themselves has been greatly degraded."

"Glad to hear it, sir." Gwielgi saw several of the other HUP pilots standing to one side. "Sir, I have to debrief my team and take a shower. May I make a formal report to you and Colonel Kheyntamenti later?"

"Of course," Jonivov said, coming to a halt. "See to your people and get something to eat. There's no rush."

"Thank you, sir." Gwielgi turned and walked over to the other six pilots. Jonivov watched them disappear through a hatchway.

Jonivov looked around the bay. Every HUP in it showed battle damage. Armor was dented, shattered, sometimes missing, and sometimes frozen in streams. He knew the answer but still found himself asking what could cause the armor of a HUP to melt? He shook his head.

Yes, he needed to find a new word.

"Red Cock Lead, Task Force Command."

"This is Red Cock. Reading you loud and clear."

"Roger, Red Cock. We are inbound at this time. I am surprised to report the Alliance ships are making no move to intercept us. I repeat, no move to intercept us."

"None? You mean those bastards were bluffing all this time?"

"Maybe. They may be waiting for us to land to pick you up, but I would expect them to start moving soon if they are going to do that and they do not appear to be getting ready for it."

"I'll be damned. All right, continue on in. We'll have our new perimeter set up around the airfield west of the city."

"Understood, Red Cock. The earlier call we received said you were only moving four battalions. Is one staying in the city?"

"Negative. We lost a battalion. The Second."

"Roger, Red Cock. Sorry to hear that. Well, we'll pay them back for that."

"Roger. Red Cock out."

Jonivov sat with his battalion commanders, a paper in his hand, frowning.

"Well, our bluff has been called. The Benderist landing ships are on their way. They now know the Alliance is not going to fight." He put the paper down. "So, what do they intend to do with those landing ships?"

Imael Garito spoke first. "They won't stay there," he said. "While they have interior lines, they know we can snipe at them from the hills on two sides, especially with the long-range weapons. Long battle of attrition, one we might win."

"Agreed," Jonivov said. "So where are they going?"

Joseph Abrande, commanding officer of the regiment's infantry battalion, motioned at the map as he stood up.

"They had the right idea, just the wrong location. Pick a place that we have to defend so they can destroy us," Abrande said. "Next time they will go somewhere that we will not be able to sneak up on, where they can force an open fight so their superior numbers will have the edge. I'm guessing they won't head to Coyote Bay. Those mountains to the north and south could be used by us to get close."

"I think Joe is right," Kheyntamenti said. "They are headed to Kiroff City. It is wide open in almost all directions except to the southeast. They

452

will likely drop down in the farmland to the west and then form up and move on the city. Nothing fancy; straight ahead. If we defend from within the city, they will destroy it. If we don't, they will seize it and we will have to destroy it trying to get rid of them."

"Playing to their strength," Jonivov said. "The landing ships will provide supporting fire for their assault."

"More than that," Kheyntamenti said. "Typically, a HUP unit that has its own landing ships will use them for supply and support. Our destruction of much of their repair capability may not mean much when the landing ships arrive. They may even be able to replace their lost HUPs. The other card they will bring is fighters. Those four we destroyed at the Militia facility cannot be all they have. Remember, when they supported Storm Cloud, they split their squadron and we saw the same number of fighters. I think they have at least four, and maybe more, still onboard their ships."

The four men fell silent. Finally, Garito looked at the others.

"Any recommendations?"

For a moment, no one said anything. Then Jonivov raised his head, looking at the map of Kodomir.

"Those landing ships can never lift once they land," he said. His voice was quiet. "If they get the brigade on board, we will not be able to stop them. We have to attack."

"They have somewhere around 95 HUPAX," Garito said. "We have less than 30. They will outnumber us in landing ships and the ones they have are Vipers or larger. They are and will be on full alert. We will not take them by surprise. The airfield they will use is in the middle of open country. We can fire on them from the western hills but that will not keep them from loading and departing."

"The Frogfire and artillery batteries have all received full ammo resupply," Jonivov said. "If there was a way to keep them on the ground, we could chew them up here on Portaka. That would be ideal."

"Any word from the diplomatic front?"

"Nothing, other than they are spoon feeding the imagery and information we have so far on Baer to the Benderist ambassador on Kwangdo. We have no idea if it is swaying the Baron's mind at all."

"Killing off his brigade might give him second thoughts," Abrande said.

"Which takes us back to our central question," Jonivov said. "What do we do?"

"Well, there is one thing we might try," Kheyntamenti said. "The odds are very much against it and the timing would have to be perfect."

"What is it, colonel?" Jonivov smiled slightly. "Another lesson from history?"

"Possibly, sir," Kheyntamenti said. He looked at the small group. "Consider this point, gentlemen – what operation by a military unit is more difficult than a landing on an opposed shore?"

Militia intelligence officer Captain Peter Arkady was beginning to really dislike university professors. Going to college had left him with the usual negative impression of most academics and graduate school had not helped that view, but the past week had set a new level of loathing.

Did none of these people keep records? Did none of them bother to tell anyone what they were doing? Tracking down the missing documents from Storm Cloud's archives led from one dead-end alley to another. Everything was supposed to be stored at the University of Kiroff library. It was not. At least two other colleges had some of the material. Everything was supposed to be indexed. It was not. Either because of other priorities, laziness, or an effort to hide material from rival researchers, the contents of the various archives were incomplete.

Where contents were listed, the descriptive information was virtually meaningless. What the hell did "Bed/j/61b/47-53, 55" mean, anyway? It had taken him most of a morning to find that it stood for "Bedoreh journal from 2861, the datapad version, entries 47 through and including 53 and entry 55 because we don't know where we put entry 54 but it might turn up later." These people acted like spies.

Getting out into the field and tracking down the documentation was only slightly less frustrating. Every professor they encountered had some of the material, though often not what the library they took it from thought they had, but little of the material was useful.

He rang the doorbell of the two-story dwelling in the suburbs of eastern Kiroff for the second time and shook his head waiting for someone to come to the door. According to his datapad, this was the residence of Vladimir Suryeivitch Godonov, Ph.D., Chair of the Department of Political Science of the University of Kiroff. Apparently, the good doctor was either slow to respond to doorbells or he was partially deaf. Arkady shook his head. They told him he should have stayed in Recon.

The door opened and a middle-aged man appeared, smiling happily.

"Professor Godonov?"

"Yes, I am," he said, leaning forward and studying Arkady's uniform. "Captain, is it?"

"Yes, sir, Captain Peter Arkady. May I ask you a few questions?"

"Oh, concerning the Storm Cloud material. They called me." He opened the door wider. "Of course, come on in. You're *that* Peter Arkady. Delighted to meet you." Arkady followed him into a neat living room and sat in a chair as the professor gestured. "You're quite a hero. My delight. Pleasure of the house. Would you like some tea?"

Before Arkady could reply, the professor had disappeared into another room. He returned a moment later carrying two glasses of tea in silver holders.

"Forgot to ask you if you like it sweetened," he said as he set a glass down on a table next to Arkady, "but it wouldn't have mattered inasmuch as I forgot to buy sugar." He sat down on the couch opposite Arkady and took a sip, studying the younger man over the rim of his glass. "Now, captain, how may I help you?"

"Sir," Arkady said as he put his own glass down, "the university library told me you checked out some of the records formerly belonging to Storm Cloud officers. Specifically, the papers of Tokovan Bedoreh and Liban Kidowsky."

"Yes, I did," the professor said. He leaned back and began lecturing. "Bedoreh was a long-time companion to Iriki Tykaw, the self-titled 'Duke' of Storm Cloud. And 'companion' is the proper word, can't say 'friend' when talking about Tykaw. Had him shot, killed him in the same quarry where he killed First Minister Brevar Toland and his military staff. Very ironic, don't you think? Kidowsky, who was Storm Cloud*'s* intelligence officer and head of that awful Public Security Section that killed so many people, betrayed him. And you want some additional irony? Blaine Toland, the First Minister's son, during the attack on Coyote Bay, killed *him*. And Blaine didn't even know he killed him. Thought he was just another Stormie soldier." Godonov shook his head and chuckled. "I love history."

"Ah, yes, professor, I know about all that," Arkady said.

Sweet Jesu, I'm back in a classroom again? Can't any of these people just say yes or no?

"The records, do you have them?"

"Oh, yes, certainly." Godonov rose. "Haven't done much with them. Other projects, you know." He wandered from the room. "Did a quick review of them. Nothing in them terribly interesting. Quite dull, really."

Arkady heard Godonov opening and closing doors. There was a pause and then the professor came back into the room. In his arms he had a small box.

"Yes, quite dull. Old things, mostly," Godonov said. "Contracts, copies of communications, banking and payment records. Things someone in economics might find interesting" His tone made it clear he did not. He handed the box to a disappointed Arkady. "Nothing about the occupation of Kodomir at all. Old stuff, all before that time."

"I see. Well, thank you, sir. We will return this once our people have gone through it." Arkady rose and turned towards the door. Godonov accompanied him.

"You remember me mentioning the role of irony in Storm Cloud's history on Kodomir, captain. Well, here's another example." Godonov chuckled softly. "Did you know that Benderist Special Envoy Esteban Baer, the fellow who's been giving us such difficulty recently, had worked with Iriki Tykaw and Storm Cloud in the past? Fascinating how paths cross. Reminds me…"

"Sir?" Arkady said as he stopped. "Where did you get that information?"

"Oh, it's in those records I gave you. Anyway, as I was saying, it reminds me…"

Arkady ran from the house, leaving a mystified professor behind him. As the young officer leapt into a groundcar that sped away like the driver considered local speed limits to be the minimum, Godonov shook his head. Just because a man was a war hero did not excuse him from being polite.

Pietr Jonivov and the others were tired but the plan was laid out in front of them. He leaned back in his chair.

"Timing, timing, timing," he said.

"Absolutely," said Kheyntamenti. "Too soon and we lose. Too late and they will simply leave."

"Leave? No, colonel. Too late and their landing ships will eat us for lunch. We have to mix it up with enough of their people present so their landing ships cannot intervene." Garito shook his head. "Our artillery better be having a very good day."

"The first part will be the easiest," said Abrande, "not to be confused with 'easy.'"

"We only have to be within a kilometer," Garito said. "We've had teams operating closer than that already. We can send them in tonight."

"What if they deploy their Firerays to cover their movement?" Jonivov frowned at the thought. "Other than the four Tiger Moth helicopters attached to Kheyntamenti's battalion and the four supporting Abrande, we have no air power. And Tiger Moths are not going to make much of a dent against fighters."

"If Garito's people spot them on the airfield," Kheyntamenti said, "then we will have to take them out first. I hate diverting long-range fire onto them. I think our armor will have to get it done."

"Getting our force in there is the main challenge," Abrande said. "My infantry battalion is 'air mobile' only in name with all of our lift VTOLs back at Coyote Bay. Our landing ships can get us there, but..."

"Yes, 'but.'" Jonivov said. "A landing ship is a very large object to be pushing around. Tends to capture the attention. They will be seen coming in."

"It may not matter that they are seen," Kheyntamenti said, "if no one can do anything about it."

"Your boys and girls are good, colonel," Garito said, "but I think every time I go over this plan, we are asking for too much from them."

Jonivov sighed. "Maybe we need to transplant this plan from Portaka to Kiroff. At least there we would have air support and the rest of the Militia."

"If we do," Kheyntamenti said, "then they can drop anywhere, and remember – they can drop virtually their entire brigade, 90-some HUPs, almost all together. This will be our only opportunity to have a last chance at taking them on piecemeal."

"Air support," Garito said. He paused for a moment. "Sir, is the Tiger Moth division leader available? I have a question I want to ask about our Swallows."

Colonel Halleck leaned over the map table in the First Battalion command APC and frowned. His observers reported no contact with the Kodomir Militia. Fast moving pairs of HUPs had swept through the hills to the west and north and found nothing, though they had found an apparent landing site to the north, probably where the earlier raiding party was picked up. He had figured out that the most recent attack had come by sea and now had a skirmish line of HUPs facing the bay.

Not that it would do any good. The one thing the Kodomiri could be counted on to do would be something different. The lack of contact meant they had pulled back. Why? Were they anticipating his move and positioning themselves near Kiroff City? That would be fine, if true. Halleck wanted them to do that.

But what a military commander wanted was not always what happened, and sometimes the wanting could blind you. Halleck sighed and stood up, his arms folded, and studied the map. What were they up to?

Thus far the Kodomiri had made all the right moves. A smaller force facing a larger has to rely on tactics that avoid a confrontation with the enemy's main firepower. Catching the brigade's Second Battalion in a preemptive strike was a good move and trying to decapitate the brigade leadership verged, in his opinion, on brilliant. That was the kind of thinking they *had* to use or they would be without any chance at all.

All right, so look at the map from their point of view. What brilliant gamble would he perform in their shoes? It was a bit of a stretch for him, since most of his combat experience involved being in the larger force, not the smaller, but Halleck was not a stupid man.

Take it from the beginning. The brigade's landing ships begin to arrive. The nearest cover for a threat is the hills to the west. They used them before for their distraction force during the raid; they know them. If they are still in the area, they might push some people into them and snipe as the brigade loads up.

What if they put a major force in those hills? How would that work? He ran through it in his mind. No, most of their force, including their HUPAX, would have to come down out of the hills to get within accurate range. And if they did, he would have them. Trying to run from the hills to the airfield would expose them to fire from the brigade and his landing ships. End of story. These people were not suicidal. Halleck shook his head. They won't assault from the hills.

Any other way they might try to get at the brigade? Embarking with an enemy nearby was always dangerous and it would be a good time to attack, but the distance from the hills was simply too great, the fields of fire too clear. No, some long-range fire is the worst they would be able to do.

Halleck started to turn away from the table and paused. Something he had read. That book, the one about the Kodomiri war with Storm Cloud. It was written by one of those former mercenaries. He let his memory wander, not trying to force anything. Then he had it.

The attack on Kiroff. The Raiders had a fortified position around the airfield. That was what was jogging his memory. They attacked from inside the base by using the airport subway. He turned back to the map.

No subways to the airfield outside of Portaka City. Still... If they wanted to attack, the brigade would be most vulnerable when loading onto the landing ships. How could they do that, and do it in a manner that would place them in a position like that of the subway strike – right in his lap with little or no warning, so close to him that his landing ships would not dare fire? How would *he* do it if the situation were reversed?

Of course. Halleck saw it and suddenly knew with certainty what would happen. The Kodomiri would make a high-speed attack using their landing ships. Drop the HUPs right into the middle of the brigade maybe, or very close by, so close his own landing ships would have trouble providing supporting fire without hitting brigade HUPs. In the middle of the attack the Kodomiri would move their supporting artillery and missiles into range and start pounding the landing ships themselves.

Hit him when most of the brigade's HUPs were in their landing ships and locked down. His Firerays would already be onboard, they would have to be loaded first because of the structure of landing ship bays, so his advantage in air power would be meaningless. Smash his HUPs that had not embarked and then, as the others tried to get back on the ground, kill the remainder as they fed themselves into the fight. In the meantime, their artillery and missiles would be pounding the landing ships, maybe damaging or destroying some before they could get their HUPs back out.

The most difficult military maneuver was withdrawing from contact with the enemy. It could turn into a disaster if the enemy chose the right moment to strike. That is what they were planning to do to him. He nodded.

A desperate plan. The odds would be very much against them. But it was their best chance. And these people had shown a willingness to run risks. The still present smell of the fires reminded Halleck of that.

If they did it use an airborne assault, what would be his counter? He bent back over the map. Their scouts would be watching the embarkation process. Halleck nodded his head. He could use that. Maybe it was time he presented them with a surprise or two of his own.

Chapter 30: Blood in the sand

23 December 2824

Out of necessity, the Kodomir Militia Second Regiment moved quickly. Its HUPAX force pulled back to the now destroyed Militia facility west of Portaka City and embarked as Militia landing ships arrived.

One of the landing ships had done double-duty, racing back to Kiroff, loading ammunition supplies and the remaining Militia Frogfire battery, and the equipment and supplies needed for two squadrons of Swallow aerospace fighters. The two squadrons represented all those stationed on Kiroff Airfield. The Swallows themselves, led by Major Blaine Toland, came in low from the northwest and landed on the quickly cleared runway. With insufficient range to intervene on Portaka and then return to Kiroff, repositioning them on Portaka was the only way to get them into the fight. The first order of business was to replenish their fuel from their accompanying landing ship. Jonivov hoped they would be a violent surprise for the Benderists.

The Tiger Moth detachment aided in the fighters' refueling, though Leba Chinaren found herself pushing an irrational resentment at the arrival of the Swallows. Flying near landing ships in helicopters was suicidal, something she knew from her own experience, and getting the faster Swallows into the fight, hopefully secretly, was a very good thing.

Still, it meant the Tiger Moths would have little to do. The eight rotary-winged attack aircraft would sit in the hills while other people decided the outcome of the battle. That, in fact, had been the theme of the whole expedition to Portaka.

But there was nothing to be done for it except what Chinaren was doing. She clamped the hose-lock into place and waved to the soldier at the fuel bag pumps. Then she stepped back, her hands on her hips, and waited.

Chinaren thought that's what she would be doing all the next day: waiting.

As darkness fell, the rest of the regiment already was moving. Calculations from the trajectories of the approaching Benderist landing ships showed them arriving shortly after dawn. Jonivov planned to attack when his reconnaissance troops saw at least two thirds of the Benderist HUPs stored onboard their landing ships.

Garito's First Reconnaissance Battalion was the natural choice for monitoring the Benderist brigade. While the accompanying Chekinov Scouts were excellent, especially in the mountains, they were not well trained in desert warfare. Shortly after midnight, First Recon came down out of the western hills and slipped into positions where they could see clearly the Portaka City airfield. Other teams of observers took up positions to watch the northern and southern Benderist battalions' flanks.

Captain Hardin's armored company escorted the long-range support weapons into position in the hills west of the airfield. The first to drop off as they moved forward were the Frogfire launchers. Hardin, standing in the turret of his Bob Cat tank, wished they had ten times as many, though it was good to see two more launchers deploying into covered positions.

The next units to be dropped off were the self-propelled artillery vehicles. The gunners ran up their guns as the tracked vehicles settled into position beneath the stars. For the moment, they used satellite imagery for their coordinates, but would refine their targeting once the recon teams sent back data.

Hardin's company was the last to deploy, setting up a screen with the Second Battalion's infantry and light vehicles on the reverse slopes of the last hills before the plain leading down to the airfield. He knew they were little more than a speed bump if the Benderist brigade came towards the hills, but it would give time to the supporting vehicles to get away.

While this was happening, the regiment's close to three dozen HUPAX completed loading. Each HUP was backed into position in the bays of the landing ships and locked down. It was not a process that could be done quickly, something Jonivov was counting on to be true for the Benderist HUPs as well. Even as the Militia HUPs were seized by the bay locks, HUP technicians swarmed over the damaged ones, trying to finish repairs. Damaged or not, every HUPAX that could move would be going into battle.

Gunnery Sergeant Steve Tashan oversaw the attachment of rocket-assisted descent packs to each HUP and double-checked the firing circuitry. The packs provided minimal steering ability, so the HUPs would depend on their landing ships to drop them in the right place. He knew that a skilled pilot could crudely steer a descending HUP by using neural inputs to the HUPs steering jets to pitch it one way or the other, but it was not a process of fine precision.

He would be very happy, Tashan decided as he helped close an access panel, if he never had to try it. Tashan would be piloting one of the Wild Geese HUPs simply because they were in desperate need of pilots. When the call for volunteers went out to the HUP technicians and the Militia students, the only people besides the regular pilots who had any familiarity with the war machines, Tashan had placed his name on the top of the list. He and a handful of Kodomiri students would be used as the regiment's reserve.

Like most people, Tashan had minimal mindlink abilities and could tolerate the stress of joining with a HUPAX S-computer only for the brief periods needed when working on the war machines. Even then he tended to rely more on the back-up manual controls to move a HUP around and saved getting onto the 'link only for checking that system. That made for clumsy control, to be sure, but it was enough for maintenance.

It was not enough for combat. Whatever happened, Tashan would have to be on the 'link. With it would come a blinding headache, dizziness, and even nausea. All he could do was hope that he and the others never had to be used.

He gathered the four students together for an informal briefing. They were nervous but all were trying to act calm, as if they faced war in a

HUPAX on a daily basis. He closed the hatch to the small conference room off the HUP bay.

"Here's the deal," Tashan said as they settled into their chairs. "We're the regiment's HUP reserve, which means we will be in the most screwed-up HUPs we have. They're going to hold us back to be used as and if needed. If we go, I want all four of you to stay with me." Tashan looked at the four students, three men, one woman.

"You got that? *You stay with me.* If they send us in it is because the situation is very, very bad. That means, if we go, we have to go together to make a difference." He saw them nod, the reality of what he was saying soaking it. "I will call targets. You may hear me shift us to a different target before the first is dead. Don't worry about it. A helpless HUP may be enough and the more of them we can hurt the better."

"You people," Tashan said as he sat down, "are all officers. I'm just a sergeant. I know you don't have a problem with that since the Militia and the Wild Geese don't sweat rank in tactical situations." He looked at the four. "If I go down, Beria has lead. If he goes down, Murphy takes command. If she is down, Kelly has it. If Kelly is down, Brown, well, you'll be talking to yourself but it will be your first combat command." There were a few forced chuckles.

"Beria and Murphy, you were with me when we blocked the Victors. You've been in it before. Stay cool, focus on the job, and get hits." The other pilots nodded. "All right, go check your HUPs. Pay particular attention to what is *not* working. As I said, we've got the dregs." That brought a couple of more smiles. Tashan stood, as did the students. He began gathering some papers and then looked up. The students looked young and he felt old. Tashan needed to say something else but could not think of what it might be. "And just one other thing. Stay together. We bring everyone home. Understood?" The others nodded and started to file out. Murphy, closest to the door, stopped and looked back.

"Gunny Tashan, something I want to say." Everyone paused. "I read the history of Kodomir's War of Liberation that Captain Gwielgi wrote. In it I saw you were one of the people who voted against the Wild Geese joining the Kodomiri to fight Storm Cloud for free, just to save us." She held up a hand, cutting off his response. "Hold on, sergeant, let me finish. I also read that when the Geese made the decision to go in, Colonel Kheyntamenti offered to leave you and all the others voting against the decision back on the landing ships. You argued with the colonel, refused to accept that offer, and you went in with the infantry." Tashan nodded.

"The book," Murphy said slowly, "and I remember this, says that the Wild Geese have a saying, a motto, something their people say to one another before going into combat. I'm not in the regiment, much less the battalion we still call the Wild Geese, just a HUP student pilot. But if it would not be offensive," she said as she drew herself up, "I'd just like to say, I am with you."

The other students looked at Murphy, who remained at attention. They looked back at Tashan. He paused, papers in his hand. Then he carefully placed them on the table and came to attention.

"I am with *you*," he said.

Jonivov stood on the red-lit bridge of Zombie as the reports came in from his various units. The deployment was going smoothly enough, not that it was particularly complicated. The regiments' Tiger Moth attack helicopters were parked near the landing ships. Technicians were busy doing final checks, making sure fuel was topped off, and loading the last rocket launchers, though there would be little for them to do. Jonivov counted far more on the Swallows.

The Swallows, the new card in the game, were ready to launch from what would be a bumpy airstrip. Right now, their young pilots were trying to get some sleep after their long flight from Kiroff. Some were in their cockpits while the others were curled up on their fighters' wings, flight jackets acting as blankets.

"We have everyone loaded," Captain Peggy Cochran said. "A bit of a tight fit, but having the armored and support vehicles deployed freed up some space."

"Very well," Jonivov said. "All the landing ship captains up to speed?"

"Yes, sir," Cochran said as she examined a sensor screen. "We've never done anything like a formation HUP airborne drop of this size but it is pretty straight forward." She adjusted the screen and a map overlay appeared.

"We have a good visual guide here to the south of the airfield. There's a dry wash that runs east out of the hills. At its closest it's about a klick and a half from the airfield. We'll run in well north of it."

"Should be easy to see," Jonivov agreed. "It widens out south of Portaka City and disappears but you are right, it's easy enough to see." He smiled. "I hate those desert washes. Got caught in one when it flooded years ago. Barely got my lieutenant-tail out of there in time."

"Floods in a desert?"

"Yes," Jonivov said. "Washes like this go up into the hills. You get any rain up there, it collects and gets funneled and makes these washes. They can be pretty deep. Of course, we're in Portaka's high summer now, so I won't bother to take my water wings."

"Well, even if were filled with water, as I said, our people won't drop in it. It's not very deep, anyway." She looked at the contour overlay. "Maybe ten to twelve meters at most in the area south of the airfield. Banks are pretty steep."

"That's typical of a dry wash," Jonivov said nodding. "Like a cliff edge, carved by the water. But the banks are typically soft. Problem for tracked vehicles but I would think a HUPAX could climb out of one."

"Easier getting in than out," Cochran said, "though the further east you go, the shallower the wash."

"Good thing to make sure our HUPs don't fall into. What's the forecast for winds? Any chance of our drop getting blown into it?

"Weather people are expecting the usual Portaka morning. Cool, stable air, rapidly heating up and producing a west wind by late morning, early afternoon." She shook her head. "Shouldn't be a factor."

"Good," Jonivov said. "Now, you'll take the column of landing ships back to the western hills. We've got a thin screen in front of you with some armored vehicles but it's not much."

"Not a problem, colonel. Each of our captains knows where to land once their HUPs are away and I bring the column back to the hills. Hopefully, only Zombie will be shooting once we all land."

Jonivov nodded. Zombie carried an impressive MS150 cannon, capable of scoring hits from well out of range of any other indirect-firing weapons expected to be in the fight other than the Frogfires. If the landing ships had to use any other weapons – ion pulse weapons, missile launchers, and so on – from their positions in the western hills, it would be because the enemy was closing on them, and that would mean they had lost the battle.

"Their order of battle shows mostly Viper landing ships," Jonivov said. "And a few Alligators."

"Yes, sir," Cochran said. "Standardization of maintenance is their goal, plus lower cost for the ships." She smiled. "They are not nearly as rag-tag as our own fleet, though we have a lot of Vipers courtesy of Storm Cloud and those mercs in the last raid."

"I wish we had a dozen of the Crocodile-class, like Zombie. Stand back about thirty klicks and let the MS150s and missiles settle their hash for them."

"That would be easier," Cochran said. "But inevitably it still would take people on the ground occupying their position to finally end it. Always has."

"True enough," Jonivov said.

Garito's people were in place before 0400. The two-person teams, most equipped with laser designators and shrouded in camouflage gear, began scanning the airfield and its approaches while it was still dark. Almost immediately they spotted the movement of HUPAX and support vehicles. No one had ever seen so many HUPs in one place at one time and Jonivov, listening in, heard a level of tension in their voices not present before.

The Benderist HUP battalions formed a screen around the airfield and faced outward. Using their light amplification function on their designators, the team spotters looked at what seemed to be an almost solid wall of HUPAX, like a mountain range suddenly forming around the airfield.

Sergeant Tyree was paired with a young corporal, Shannon Felawasi. She was handling the designator from their position beneath a cluster of desert scrub bushes. A Reservist, like most of the Kodomiri Militia, she was combat experienced, also like most of the Kodomiri Militia. Though she had been a high school student during the Storm Cloud occupation, she had fought against the mercenary attacks of the past year. Nonetheless, like almost everyone else lying under the stars of the Portaka desert within rifle shot of the Benderist brigade and its ninety HUPAX, she appeared to be afraid.

Tyree could see it in her breathing and the slight tremor in her hand as she adjusted the laser designator. She avoided his eye, another sign. Everyone afraid in combat always thought they were the only one, he knew. Tyree spoke into his headset microphone, his voice barely more than a whisper.

"Team Nine is set."

"Roger, Niner. Good luck and good hunting."

Tyree double clicked his mike and lowered his eye to the telescopic sight of his rifle. He knew the best way to help someone get past their fear was to go about your job in a calm fashion. All right, he told himself, it might not be the best way, but it was his way. Hell, it had worked for all the other people he had teamed with in combat.

For her part, Felawasi was not afraid, which is not to say she did not experience fear. She did feel some, but her fear was not about being killed or wounded; like most soldiers, her greatest concern was about doing her job right. The deepest fear was doing something that got someone else killed. Her experiences to this point put those fears largely at rest, but not totally.

What Felawasi felt now was mostly not fear. Like many, she had found her own defense against fear. For her, it was an eagerness to get at the enemy, to fight. Perhaps there was something in her genes, a warrior strip of DNA that responded to the drums as it had in Africa back when humans thought the Earth flat. Or maybe it was the awful fury that it seemed that only a woman in war could experience, the rage at having her home invaded by outsiders, her people endangered.

As they prepared, Tyree glanced over and caught a look in her eye, and saw a flicker of flame. He was a professional soldier and he recognized what he saw. From somewhere in his memory a scrap of something he had read came into his awareness. Centuries before, British army officers had offered toasts before battle with her people, toasts for queen and country. But the author noted that, for all the toasts for success and glory, none said aloud the wish all held in the deepest part of their hearts.

Lord, let us not fall alive into the hands of their women.

Tyree saw Felawasi was not trembling with fear but with eagerness.

"Brigade, sentry Alpha."

"Go ahead Alpha."

"I've gotten a couple of intermittent infrared readings to the west, all within a kilometer or so."

"Anything now?"

"Negative. I think we are seeing some troops getting close."

"Understood. We are expecting that."

"I can put some long-range fire on them if you want."

"Negative. We want them out there. We'll take care of them this morning."

"Roger. Alpha out."

Alisti Mahmud al-Kheyntamenti stood before the HUP pilots, finishing his briefing. The men and women followed his words. Some occasionally made notes on kneepads but most simply watched. The plan was very simple. Land, attack, and kill them. And try not to die. He finished and stepped in front of the map.

"The sequence is, then, the Victors and Black Cats drop first, then the Currahee, and then the Geese. Gunny Tashan and the students will be held on board and in reserve. Remember, first to drop will be furthest away. Avoid getting close to their landing ships – they'll be towards the center of the airfield. Stay close to their HUPs on the perimeter. Our support fire will be targeting the landing ships and their close-in weapons will be very dangerous. It will be hard for them to use their longer ranged weapons if we keep the fight a big fur ball."

"We have 35 operational HUPs – they have over 90. Look for their battalion and brigade commanders," Kheyntamenti said. "Look for four-legged HUPs and kill them. These people are not nimble and are used to being under tight control. Kill the head and the body will become confused. We saw some of that in the raid on Portaka City. With the brigade commander out of communication, the battalion commanders were slow to react. Look for their markings. According to our intelligence people, they put their commanders in the biggest HUPs they have in order to protect them. Their Second Battalion commander was in a War Lance. Try to kill the big ones first and then work your way down."

"Anyone have any questions?" He looked around the room. There were none. Kheyntamenti nodded and for a moment was silent.

"We have customs, traditions, begun in the Wild Geese and carried over when the people of Kodomir gave us a home. We are pressed for time and cannot do everything we would ordinarily do before a battle and it would probably seem strange to many of you in any case. But allow me a colonel's privilege to summarize all of it in just a few words." He looked slowly around the room, making eye contact with each pilot.

Marjessa Boyington drew herself up to attention when he looked at her. Vermeil smiled sardonically and made a "thumbs-up" gesture. Walsh nodded calmly. The Wild Geese, Gwielgi, Tsunasdi, Elinshen, Sevin, Tashan, and all the rest, stood. Kheyntamenti smiled slightly. "We bring everyone home," he said, echoing an ancient slogan of mercenaries. He paused for a moment and then spoke again in a voice not much more than a whisper but was heard by everyone in the room.

"I am with you."

Tsunasdi and Gwielgi walked across the HUP bay towards their HUPAX. Technicians and HUP captains were scurrying around them while the clank of metal and shouted commands echoed in the well-lit open space. Tsunasdi looked at his friend out of the corner of his eye.

"You seem in good humor," he said.

"Nothing as liberating as knowing you are going to die," Gwielgi said, grinning sardonically.

"It is knowledge that brings with it a certain freedom," Tsunasdi said. "But do not get used to it."

"Why not?"

"Think how disappointed you are going to feel if you live through all this."

"Something I want to say," Gwielgi said. He stopped in the middle of the bay. He held up his hand and Lieutenant Stephanie Elinshen walked over. She stood without speaking.

"I asked Elinshen to be present and be here for this. She tells me this should be witnessed." He slowly and carefully reached down and took Tsunasdi's arm in his hand and raised it. A white bracelet encircled Tsunasdi's wrist. Gwielgi looked at it a moment.

"When I saved your life, I told you I would not accept you as a Dedeloquasgi."

"That is true."

"I refused you the opportunity to die."

"That is also true."

"You placed this bracelet on your wrist yourself, true-word?"

"Aye."

"A warrior's bracelet would be made of his family colors and those used to note his honors. A white bracelet is for someone who is Dede to a Dideyohvsgi, someone who has stepped forward to be the Dede's moral teacher, among other things." He looked at Tsunasdi. "Don't look so surprised. You Currahee have been slipping into the Settled Worlds for years, in spite of the isolation edict of the Encampment. Several are here in the Wild Geese, like Stephanie. Did you think I would never talk to them about you? And just because I'm older than you doesn't mean I'm blind. I saw this damned thing a couple of years ago." He rolled the bracelet, exposing a thin line of colors forming a plaid.

"Since a Dedeloquasgi has not earned the right to wear colors on her or his bracelet, the only color to be found has to be hidden. Usually, the colors are those of the Dideyohvsgi." He looked at the bracelet. "Gray, purple, and green. I get the first two, colors of the Wild Geese. The green...?"

"For you. Celtic."

Gwielgi nodded. "And it does not come off until the Dide says so. It is supposed to happen when the Dede has demonstrated the virtues of a warrior, whatever the Dedeloquasgi's vocation. Interesting that none of the virtues have to do with skill with weapons. Courage, yes, and integrity and morality." He shook his head. "I knew of your people's past and I thought, until I learned better, the Dede lived as no better than a slave trying to earn his freedom on the battlefield. Killing to prove a right to freedom was an idea that grated on me." Again, Gwielgi shook his head. "I was wrong."

Gwielgi held Tsunasdi's wrist, still lightly, with his left hand. His right reached down and pulled a thin bladed knife from his boot. He gently placed the blade under the bracelet. "Your courage has been proven beside me on too many battlefields for this bracelet to remain. Your integrity to your beliefs can never be questioned. And your morality is something I have always envied." The knife moved and the bracelet split.

For a moment longer Gwielgi held Tsunasdi's wrist. Then he released it. He put away his knife.

"I pass on to you something that was given to me a very long time ago," he said, straightening up. "You are free, Charles Tsunasdi. Your honor is more than restored for it could never be taken away, only added to, unless you gave it up, and you never did. Some day you will be commemorated as an example of how a warrior's honor, a true warrior, cannot be expunged." Gwielgi hesitated and then reached into his pocket. He glanced at Elinshen and then looked back at Tsunasdi.

"It is customary for the Dide to give the Dede his new bracelet. It should be made of the Dede's, the *former* Dede's, family colors." He brought his hand out of his pocket and opened it. A woven bracelet lay in the palm of his hand. "Stephanie and the other Currahee in the Geese did not know what your family colors were, so they used the colors of your family here, the Geese and the Kodomiri. Then they added a warrior's colors, the gold and red. I hope it is acceptable, even if only as a gift." He handed it to Tsunasdi who took it slowly and studied it.

Gwielgi looked around the HUP bay at the other pilots approaching their HUPs. "No slaves and no Dedeloquasgi will fight beside me this morning. Only free people." He looked back at Tsunasdi. "True word?"

Tsunasdi stood silently, staring at the bracelet that had fallen to the deck and the one in his hand. All these years he had hidden it from his friend, his master, bringing it out to be worn only in combat, and then quickly hidden away. The white bracelet, though not given by Gwielgi, had given him a focus, a purpose. He thought release from the white bracelet would never come. And yet here it was. This was not a Currahee Dide talking to him but a freeborn mercenary. If he was no longer his Dede, then what was he?

He was free. And, for now, that was enough.

"Aye." Tsunasdi looped the bracelet around his wrist and fastened it. The colors seemed to glow. He looked at Elinshen.

"You and the others have done me honor."

"The honor," Elinshen said, "was ours. We knew you were no weak-heart and understood your silence. When your friend came to us, we formed a Warriors' Council." She smiled. "It was good to go back to some of the old ways. And when all this is settled, if you wish, we would, as a Council, represent you before our people to have your name and honor cleared and be restored to your home."

"Again," Tsunasdi said, "you honor me, and I look forward to having my name cleared. But I am already restored to my home." He held up his bracelet. "I wear its colors."

Elinshen nodded and smiled. She touched Gwielgi's elbow silently and turned and walked off towards her HUP. Tsunasdi looked at his bracelet for a moment longer.

"Well," Gwielgi said, "this is very touching. It will make a great second book. Maybe I can finally retire on its proceeds. But let's try not to get killed. It'll make for a really unhappy ending."

"Everyone comes home," Tsunasdi said almost automatically.

"Aye."

Elinshen glanced over her shoulder at the two men and turned back to find Marjessa Boyington standing in the shadow of her HUP calmly watching.

"Interesting," Boyington said. "I am impressed."

"Tsunasdi *is* impressive," Elinshen said.

"I referred," the Currahee Boyington said, nodding towards the other side of the hangar, "to his Dideyohvsgi."

"Is that it?" Arkady stood over the four people going through the recordings and files from Professor Godonov.

The senior of the four, an intelligence major, was nodding his head slowly. His hand groped towards the communication console while his eyes remained on the documents in his hand. Arkady reached over and picked up the handset.

"Who do you want to call, sir?"

"General Polrany," the major said, his eyes still on the documents. "And right now." Arkady punched the buttons

Polrany appeared almost immediately on the screen.

"You have something for me?"

"Sir, we have it, we have it *all*."

"Slow down. What do we have?"

"All of Storm Cloud*'s* records of dealings with Esteban Baer, sir." The major ignored the figure on the screen and kept going through the transcripts. "Everything Tykaw said is true. Going back a decade. Tykaw was one paranoid son of a bitch. He not only kept records of every deal,

473

including bank transfers, but he recorded almost every discussion with Baer – a snake not trusting a snake. And Bedoreh was even more thorough. We have the contract, the original contract, for the invasion of Kodomir. We have Baer's name on the ownership papers for the combine that operated the slave mine on Farnham. We have political opponents that the Stormies murdered for him. My God…" His voice trailed off.

"Major," Polrany said. "What the hell?"

"Sir," the major replied. "Two of the people Baer paid to have murdered. Relatives of von Bender himself."

"Take all of this information to the subspace communication site right now," Polrany said. "Send it, all of it, raw, transcripts, imagery, everything. Understand?"

The major nodded absently, still leafing through the printouts from the transcription computer. Arkady leaned forward and spoke.

"Yes, sir. We are leaving now." He turned the communication unit off and grabbed his superior officer under an arm and got him to his feet. "We have to go, major. We are long since out of time."

The major nodded silently and gathered up the papers and data cubes. There would be a time for reading later, if there was a later.

"Task Force, Red Cock Command."

"Read you loud and clear, Red Cock."

"Say your position."

"Just about to enter atmosphere. Expecting communication blackout momentarily."

"Roger. Brigade is formed around the airfield and ready."

"Roger. You think they still intend to come?"

"Hope so. It will simplify our job."

"Understood."

"Second Regiment, Militia Command."

"Roger, Command."

"Pietr, we have multiple landing ships entering the atmosphere now. Trajectories are all inbound to Portaka."

"Roger, general."

"We need time, Pietr. The check is in the mail."

"Really? Well, I hope it works. This is going to be a little rough."

"Understood. Saint George be with you."

"Thanks, Stevar. Right now, I'd settle for the dragon as an ally. Second, out."

Tyree and Felawasi watched the long landing ships roar out of the morning sky. Three spherical 6000-ton Alligator-class landing ships led the parade, followed by eight 2100-ton Vipers, completing the first wave. The second wave, fifteen minutes later, had three more Alligators, each capable of carrying a dozen or more HUPAX. Close behind them came six more aerodynamic Vipers. Each Viper could carry four to six HUPs and a pair of fighters. Tyree did the math as they watched. Twenty damned landing ships. The task force could lift at least 128 HUPs, more if some of the Vipers had kicked out their fighter slots and converted them to HUP stations, which was common. More space than they needed, but, of course, they were now a battalion and some short. Lots of space for the trip home.

Tyree saw that they placed the Alligators on the taxiways while the Vipers were arranged in neat rows along either side of the north-south runway. It was a little tight but well within the HUP perimeter. The HUPs immediately began the process of boarding, forming into columns and marching up the loading ramps of the landing ships. He keyed his commo unit.

"Team Nine has targets."

"

"Roger. We're getting imagery now. Stay low. Things are going to get interesting in a little bit."

"Cochran to all ships. Rise and form. Time to go downtown. Watch your spacing. You have your parking assignments. Let's keep it tight and get our HUPs where it will do some good."

The eight Militia landing ships slowly rose and moved east toward Portaka City. Captain Cochran watched as each ship took its proper position. She knew the long-range fire support would try to distract the enemy ship gunners from hitting her formation on its way in but she did not intend to be passive during their approach. Every weapon the formation carried was armed and ready to engage.

The plan called for crossing south of the airfield. Moving in staggered column, the HUPs would be dropped close to the field, within easy sprinting distance. The landing ships would concentrate their fire on the Benderist ships at the southern end of the field as they passed. It was not quite the classic "crossing the T" maneuver Horatio Nelson had used, but it was close enough. Chewing up the southern Benderist ships might deprive the enemy of some of their fire support.

And maybe she could kill a couple of the bastards.

Envoy Baer seemed unable to leave Halleck's side until the colonel left the communication APC and climbed into his 145-ton War Axe. As the HUP groundcrew helped him strap into the dark blue and green HUP, Halleck decided it was worth getting shot at to get away from Baer.

Virtually all night long Baer had stayed close, watching everything. Fortunately, he kept his mouth shut and had no questions as Halleck prepared the trap. Still, Baer's eyes seemed to be everywhere and Halleck was under no illusions who would take the credit if the tactic worked.

And who would take the blame if it failed.

Halleck stood by as Third and Fourth Battalions walked their HUPs into their assigned landing ships. He kept expecting to hear the call spotting the attacking Kodomiri but there was nothing. Were they still in the area? His people thought during the night they had seen movement in the dry desert plain to the west of the airfield, perhaps more of those damned commandos that had attacked earlier. But now there was nothing.

He ordered the Fifth Battalion to act as if they were loading and watched as the screen of HUPs around the airfield contracted still further. Maybe the Kodomiri were not going to come. Or maybe they would wait for the landing near Kiroff.

"Colonel, we have eight landing ships approaching from the southwest."

"Roger."

Halleck felt a wave of relief – they had taken the bait. He took a few steps forward and spotted them against the clear blue sky of morning. They were less than a kilometer in altitude and already slowing down. He admired the way they maintained formation. Those landing ship captains were good.

"Shall we commence fire?"

476

"Negative. We want them to come in."

Halleck knew he was snapping his response, but how many times did he have to tell people the idea was to get them close so their HUPs could not escape? He shook his head.

"All battalion commanders, stand by. It looks like they are coming in by landing ship and will air-drop south of the airfield. Hold for my signal. Let them all come down. Don't move prematurely."

They would run, of course. After they charged his position and discovered it was the trap they would try to run, however many of them were left. He would hold his brigade back a little as they did, clearing the fields of fire for his landing ships. Depending on how many were left, he might actually load a battalion and leapfrog ahead of them and trap them. If there were only a few, he would let them run. A handful of HUPAX might not be worth pursuing. Maybe he would shift his attack to their support weapons and landing ships. It would be very satisfying to kill off that long-range support fire that had plagued his brigade since the first raid.

Very satisfying indeed.

Tyree tapped Felawasi gently on the shoulder. Without removing her eye from her designator, she started talking.

"Fire mission. Landing ship, Alligator-class." Her voice was calm.

"FDC copies. Your shooter, Frogfire. Warhead, penetrating."

"Roger. Standing by."

"Roger, this will be a TOT. Lining up other shots. Stand by. Stand by. Team Nine. Flashlight, flashlight, flashlight."

Tyree saw Felawasi's finger lightly press on the laser designator. An invisible beam of coherent ultraviolet light lanced out and caressed the upper structure of a landing ship slightly more than a kilometer away. Tyree heard the Fire Direction Center soldier talking softly.

"Five seconds. Three. One. Splash."

The distance to the target made the impact of the warhead seem relatively minor. A small column of smoke shot up along with a little debris. It seemed inconsequential, especially compared to the more dramatic things happening up and down the row of landing ships.

Other spotters had illuminated targets and large-caliber artillery rounds were slamming into landing ship armor with explosions that were much more satisfying in appearance.

But the Frogfire warhead Felawasi guided was 1200 kilograms of shaped charge. It ripped through the upper armor of its target and the force of the blast went downward, a jet of white-hot gas as big around as a man's leg. It went through four decks and buckled a fifth before it dissipated. Fires flashed into existence on all five decks, triggering the automatic fire suppression system. The system succeeded in halting the fire but not before every member of the crew in the compartments penetrated was dead.

It was one of four such warheads arcing down out of the sky. The second hit one of the massive landing struts of another Alligator, almost severing it from the landing ship and so mangling it that it would be impossible to retract. The other two landed on top of the same Viper. One ripped open the hull over its HUP bay and did relatively little damage since the bay was empty. The other punched through armor on the port side, destroying the loading ramp and bay doors.

The Benderist landing ships had unleashed their defensive lasers. Small weapons, they were designed to strike incoming missile and artillery fire. But to hit anything they had to see it and the Frogfires carried their own jammers as did some of the artillery rounds. Coupled with the jamming coming from the approaching Kodomiri landing ships, the Benderist fire control officers ground their teeth in frustration. Their computers automatically pressed into service the ships' main batteries, trying to fill the sky with wild energies even when they couldn't see the descending missiles and artillery rounds.

Sudden bursts of black smoke above the ships showed where they scored successes and explosions on and in the ships showed where they failed. The fire control officers' computers studied the fall of the rounds and quickly calculated the probable locations of the artillery but the guns were self-propelled and quickly moved, sometimes firing as they shifted from one position to another. Only the landing ships were stationary and they continued to take hits.

As the first rounds struck, the response from the brigade was instantaneous. With artillery falling on and around the landing ships, the dark blue and green HUPAX guarding the perimeter opened fire, sweeping the area around the airfield. At the same time two of the Vipers opened their bays forward of those used to receive HUPAX. Ramps were extended and Firerays eased out onto them, their VTOL engines already coming to life.

"FDC, Team Nine. We have their attention. Firerays disembarking." Felawasi was still calm but her voice was quick.

"Roger."

The landing ships joined in, sweeping with fire any positions that might have recon teams. Though only one team had been pinpointed, they put fire down across the broad plain, burning out likely positions with ion pulse weapons, lasers, and even the occasional missile.

While several teams were eliminated, killed or wounded, the net effect of the lavish display of firepower was to force many of the other teams to duck while the ground around them was fused into glass by searing energy weapons or churned by missile warheads. Coupled with their intercepting fire at the falling rounds, this tactic brought the ships some respite, though fire on registered coordinates continued and landing ship captains winced with every impact.

"Sundance, scramble. We have four bandits inbound."

"Sundance Lead, roger. Fighters on the roll." Blaine Toland worked hard to sound laconic.

"Roger. Your vector zero nine zero."

"Copy zero nine zero. Sensor contact zero eight five, overtake 1200."

"Roger, that is your target."

"Roger, Judy, out."

After taking command of the intercept from the ground controller in a mobile van, Blaine Toland spread his division of four Swallows in a "finger-four" formation. He targeted the lead Fireray and watched as the telemetry showed each fighter in his formation had acquired and targeted an opponent.

Looking through his canopy, he saw a red box appear inside his visor, though he could not make out the Fireray within it.

"Lead, Dash Four. Two are dropping down, going for the Frogfires."

"Roger, take them. Dash Two, stay with me and take the top two."

"Four, roger."

"Roger, leader."

A high tone sounded in his helmet and he squeezed the trigger. A warning indicator almost immediately began flashing. The Fireray pilot had launched at almost the same moment.

He jerked the Swallow to one side and let it drop towards the ground. Falling almost weightless, he slammed the throttle forward. The nimble little fighter accelerated like a meteor. He held it nose down while the warning tone became more frantic. Then he pulled the stick back. The fighter threw its wings forward as its speed bled off, which enabled it to pull an even tighter turn back towards the sky. The warning tone stopped.

"Four's down, three's in."

"Lead, Dash Two. You got one. The other is at your four, high. Pull starboard, now!"

Toland whipped the fighter to the right. His vision went red but he kept the stick back. Something whipped past his high wing. He could make out only that it was shiny and swept-backed. Almost immediately the red lance of a large laser passed the same wingtip.

"Got him, lead."

"Where's Three?"

"Two o'clock, low. Engaging both 'Rays."

"Follow me."

"Lead, I'm on fire!"

"Eject, Three, eject!"

"I don't see a 'chute, lead."

"Take the one on the right, Two."

"Roger. Fox away."

"Roger. Fox."

"Fireball. Make that two."

"Roger. Stand by. GCI, Sundance lead, scratch four bandits. We have two down over the Frogfire area. I think one launcher was hit. Any chance of getting a SAR sweep in here?"

"Not just now, Sundance Lead. Take CAP at your current location, angels ten. We have two to join you in three."

"Lead, Two. What's happening?"

"It's hitting the fan, Two."

Tyree wiped the dust off his face. That last barrage had dumped dirt and debris all over them. Felawasi was very still, the designator pressed against her face. Tyree had a sudden feeling of dread and he reached to her shoulder.

"Something weird, sarge," Felawasi said, slightly startling him. "They've been loading their landing ships, more than half of the HUPs now. But they are not locked down. They're just in the bays."

Tyree looked through his sniper sight. The Vipers closest to them were facing him head-on and he could not make out their bays. He shifted his crosshairs to the Alligators beyond. It was hard to see through the dust and smoke of the Militia artillery bombardment, which seemed to be falling randomly with most of the teams dead or ducking at the moment, as well as the fire the Benderists were putting out into the desert. Then he saw one of the Alligators clearly and, as he did, he heard the sound of the approaching Militia landing ships.

"FDC, Team Nine. Wave off our landing ships! It's a trap! Their HUPs are not locked down; they are at the top of their ramps, ready to go. Wave them off!"

"Copy, Nine. Trying…"

It was too late. Tyree looked up and saw the first Militia HUPAX appear below their landing ships, descent rocket packs flaring. He swung his sights back to the enemy landing ships. Their HUPs were moving, stomping down their ramps.

The trap was sprung.

Kheyntamenti heard the command to drop and stepped his HUPAX, his favorite Rapier, out and away from the landing ship. He fell for two seconds, clearing the ship and the next HUP, before his descent pack fired. The G force kicked in, pressing him into his semi-reclined ejection seat.

"Kheyntamenti, Jonivov. They are not locked down. It's a trap!"

The call froze him for a heartbeat. A glance downward revealed the first Benderist HUPs moving south through the swirl of dust kicked by the Militia artillery fire. A dropping HUPAX using a descent pack has very few options for changing its trajectory though a skilled pilot can, with effort, alter the eventual point of landing.

It was time for everyone to be very skillful.

"All HUPs, Kheyntamenti. Shift your drop point south as far as you can. On landing, head one eight zero. Vermeil and Walsh, set up a perimeter in the dry wash one point three klicks south of their nearest landing ship. Boyington, fall back and reinforce the perimeter. All others, proceed toward the friendly HUPs to the south. Their landing ship fire will be partially blocked by their own people. Don't stand and fight. Multiple HUPs are inbound."

As Kheyntamenti looked around, his visual field was filled with blue boxes of dropping Militia HUPs in a line running from west to east. Looking at the ground was like looking down into an angry anthill. The northern portion of the field was filled with small red boxes, the indicators of dozens of Benderist HUPs, and all were coming south.

Halleck saw the descending HUPs start to veer away. It was hard maneuvering a HUPAX like that but most of the enemy HUPs were doing it. They had spotted the trap, but too late to do themselves much good.

"Landing ships, open fire on any enemy HUPs you can reach. Watch your line of fire and cease when our HUPs close with the enemy. All battalions, forward. Go for them now!"

Captain Piotrowski, strapped tightly into the ejection seat of a Militia Gladius, was not sure what was happening but a rising volley of fire from the Benderist landing ships made it clear things were going wrong. He saw numerous dark HUPs running from the airfield towards his intended landing zone.

He wrestled with his Gladius, trying to follow most of the other Kodomir HUPs shifting further to the south. It took a cool hand and a lot of input through his mindlink helmet to cause the HUP to lean enough to change its trajectory. Piotrowski was just beginning to get it to respond when the first ion pulse tore into his HUP.

It scrambled his mental inputs to the HUP's computer and for a moment it felt like the Gladius was out of control. Sweat was dripping down his face as he struggled to keep the HUP upright. He had just succeeded when two missiles and more ion pulses blew apart his descent rocket.

The blast knocked him unconscious and the 60-ton HUP fell the last two hundred meters like a rock, slamming into the desert and destroying one of its legs and heavily damaging the other.

The fallen and stationary HUP was too tempting. Every Benderist HUP and almost every landing ship gunner in range opened fire on the Gladius. Its armor evaporated under the onslaught and its fusion-ion engine, its containment field shot away in less than a second, died in a flash of light, sending a dust-raising shock wave across the desert floor.

Piotrowski's death saved others, at least for a few seconds, as they tried to get their HUPs to land away from the original landing zone. The long-range fire from the Benderist landing ships took a moment to reacquire the other HUPs still dropping. By then their own HUPs were leaving the airfield perimeter, blocking their lines of fire, and the gunners had to hold their fire.

Still, half a dozen Militia HUPs were hit during their drops. Jammers and antimissile lasers held most of the missiles at bay so most of the damage was done by ion pulse weapons. Only the fact that the Benderists had aligned their ships close together along the length of the north-south airfield saved some of these HUPs from destruction, for many of the landing ships had their fire blocked by adjacent ships.

Captain Peggy Cochran, leading the column of eight Militia landing ships, steered Zombie in a wide turn to the south when she heard Jonivov's call and Kheyntamenti's commands. The original plan called for her and the other landing ships to join the support weapons in the western hills. That plan, she realized, was dead and so were the Kodomir HUPAX unless she did something, and quickly.

"All ships, Cochran. Follow me down. Tighten the turn and descend. We are going to land about half a klick behind the dry wash our HUPs are headed for and form a line in support of them. Their ships are blocking each other and cannot easily reach us but we can support our people as the enemy comes into range."

Cochran heard the acknowledgements. Putting the landing ships on the ground so close to the Benderists was very dangerous and she knew it. But hiding in the hills would cancel all of the landing ships' direct fire weapons and their firepower was now desperately needed as the plan fell apart. The danger was clear: the Benderist HUPs, and her screen showed nearly a hundred of them, could overrun her own HUPs and get within range of the ships. As tough as they were, landing ships could be destroyed, something the Wild Geese had demonstrated in the past. They would have to fight like hell.

"Guns, Captain. Direct fire weapons on the HUPs. Let fly the missiles. Put the MS150 on the nearest Benderist landing ship."

"Aye, Captain. Targets acquired. We're joining the party."

Zombie vibrated as its light missile launchers fired against the horde of dark Benderist HUPs closing with the Militia HUPs just touching down. A second later the ion pulse weapon and laser turrets fired, sending searing lines of lightning towards the ground.

The missiles initially dropped towards the ground, leveling off within the chaotic formation of retreating Militia HUPs. Close to the ground, they were more difficult to detect and destroy than their Benderist cousins had been when they climbed into the sky after the Militia HUPs. Racing no more than two or three meters above the ground and accelerating, they wove their way through the friendly HUPs and then sprinted into the faces of the Benderists.

As Zombie settled, Cochran saw she faced the same problem as the Benderist landing ships – her own HUPs were in the way of much of her firepower. The situation would be worse for the formation's Vipers that were lower to the ground than Zombie.

"Damn!" She permitted herself an angry outburst and then keyed her microphone.

"Kheyntamenti, Cochran. Get your people out of there now, colonel. Fall all the way back to me and unmask my weapons."

"Captain, we cannot. If they get close to your ships and damage them, we lose, because they can then leave and take Kiroff and we will be unable to pursue. We're headed for the dry wash between you and us. We are going to form on line there. Have your gunners open fire. I say again, open fire."

"Damn!" Cochran glanced at the formation of Militia landing ships. They were in a staggered line with four up and four slightly back. The last one was just touching down but there was little fire coming from them. Everyone was hesitating, fearful of hitting their own HUPs.

"All ships, this is Cochran. Line up your shots and open fire. We have no choice. Our folks are dead unless we can help them. Open fire. Repeat. Open fire."

Only Zombie carried the MS150 that lofted its rounds in a shallow arc over the onrushing enemy and friendly HUPs. Its multiple chambers were rotated as fast as the barrel cooling system would permit. The electronically ignited rounds cleared their chambers in less than a second and a half while the computer-assisted control system kept the rounds on whatever target Zombie's MS150 gunner looked at. Her eyes fixed on her viewing screen, the older woman mechanically chewed on a piece of gum while she fired. Next to her the assistant gunner spoke quietly into his headset and ensured each sheath of 150mm rounds was fed smoothly into an empty chamber.

The missile turret gunners had a somewhat more difficult task. Two of the turrets could not bring their weapons directly to bear due to their placement on Zombie's egg-shaped fuselage. Still, once the enemy HUPs came close they could fire their anti-armor missiles "around the corner" and score hits. The other two turrets used their sensors to select targets. Rather than stay with a Benderist HUP until it was destroyed, they deliberately allotted three missiles per target and then would move on, hoping that the missiles would cause enough damage to take the HUPs out of the fight even if they were not killed.

The anti-HUP missiles were bright enough to steer for vulnerable areas on HUPs – cockpits, legs, and back armor. As they scanned their targets, they sometimes identified areas of the oncoming war machines already damaged. Complicated algorithms were consulted and more than one missile decided to strike at the damaged area.

Fireballs and halting HUPs marked the first rank of Benderist HUPs and gave the retreating Militia some respite from their fire.

"Vermeil, this is Kheyntamenti – call when your people are in the dry wash. Walsh, hurry your people there and help the Victors form a perimeter. Everyone, fall back to the wash. It's not much but if we go any further they'll be among our landing ships and we cannot let that happen."

"Victor Lead copies. Move quick, people. Looks like you got a ton of trouble coming after you."

"Colonel, Boyington. We are forming among the Victors."

Halleck saw the Kodomiri landing ships landing in the distance and smiled at the unexpected move. If he could keep his brigade close to the enemy HUPs, he would get among their landing ships as well and tear them up. A plan began to form in his mind, one that would envelope the entire Militia force.

He glanced at his map display. Halleck's battalion commanders were pushing their HUPs forward. Formations were abandoned in favor of speed. But the Red Cocks First Battalion was coming from the northernmost landing ships. There was still time for it to be formed properly so it brought its power to bear coherently.

"First, Red Cock Lead. Stop at the southern perimeter and reform your battalion. I want you to hit them like a fist, so close up. Let the other battalions maintain the pursuit."

"Roger, leader."

"Task Force Commander, prepare to shift the northern half your force to the other side of those landing ships."

"Roger, Red Cock. Glad to get back into the fight."

Halleck had them cornered. All he had to do was keep the pressure on. He ran his big HUP towards the First Battalion commander's War Lance. He wanted to be a part of the kill.

Gwielgi had walked his HUP, the barely patched-up Javelin he called Brother Wolf, forward out of Revenant and felt the descent rockets kick in with reassuring power. He glanced around and tried to see Kheyntamenti's Rapier but the HUP was too far below him so all he saw was a small, blue box in his visual field.

Gwielgi heard Kheyntamenti's call and slid his HUP to the south. His sensors showed Militia HUPs scattering, their neat formation falling apart as they tried to move south. As he worked with Brother Wolf, he saw the lightning bolts of ion pulse fire slashing across the sky, cutting through the dropping HUPs.

Five meters above the ground he separated from the still burning descent pack. The 90-ton HUP slammed into the ground as he lunged forward. He twisted his fuselage towards the airfield to unmask all his turrets and immediately had a target lock indication. The newly installed missile launcher had not been fully checked out when they replaced the one lost during the raid on Portaka City. As the missile tone came on he fired, unsure of what Brother Wolf had seen other than it wasn't friendly. The missile roared out of its launcher over his head and he turned south.

The north end of Gwielgi's map display showed a wave of red dots coming south at a high rate of speed. There was no real formation to them and the faster HUPs were beginning to distance themselves from the slower. Ahead a thin line of blue dots marked the perimeter formed by the Victors and Black Cats. Looking across the ground showed them as a series of blue boxes in a row well in the distance with the Currahee HUPs just merging with the others. It was not, he understood immediately, going to be enough. Close to a hundred HUPs were charging towards less than thirty.

Gwielgi thought about his remark to Tsunasdi, about how knowing you were going to die was a liberating experience and decided he was wrong. All in all, it sucked.

Chapter 31: Revenge of the Swallows

23 December 2824

Jonivov saw what was happening on the tactical display of his command APC. There was no question but that the Benderist HUPs would overrun the Militia HUPs. He wondered what the politicians and diplomats would think of that imagery. He shook his head and focused himself to think. He had to get supporting fire into the game. But without spotters, there was little the artillery or the Frogfires could do except fire on old coordinates; hitting the charging HUPAX was impossible.

He looked at the display for a second and then reached for the microphone. There was something that could be done but it would cost others their blood.

Vermeil assembled his five heavy HUPs in the shallow dry wash and spread them out about 200 meters apart. The Currahee arrived as his people got into position and joined his line. He was in one of the mercenary unit's Scorpions, the one that seemed to be a magnet for enemy fire in previous battles.

This may not have been the best day to get into a HUP called Bull's Eye…

The smaller Black Cat HUPs ran over the edge of the wash and quickly dispersed themselves among the larger HUPs. For the moment they were out of the line of fire. Vermeil studied his sensor display. His line was beyond the range of some of the weapons on the Benderist landing ships but the swarm of red dots crawling down his screen promised someone would be shooting at him soon.

"Victors, Cats, Currahee, this is Vermeil. On my command, climb up and shoot and then back down. Ready, go."

Some of the Currahee and Cats' HUPs were quick and bounced up from their positions. The rest ran up with the slower moving Victors. He crested the low lip of the wash and had no trouble acquiring a target – every HUP in the Benderist Holdings seemed to be running straight at him.

Vermeil locked onto a Cutlass directly ahead at slightly less than 800 meters. The ion pulse weapons of his HUP, though not nearly as powerful as those carried by a landing ship, could reach well beyond that. While he carried four of the powerful weapons, he did not salvo them. Instead, he fired them in pairs, pausing a second or two between firing, concentrating on keeping his eyes on the target.

A rail gun slug ripped passed his cockpit as Vermeil stepped the tall HUP backwards. He had time to fire a pair of ion pulse weapons again into the now staggering Cutlass before he dropped back into the wash. Bull's Eye's 120 tons raised a small sand storm as he stopped. He checked his displays and was surprised to see they said he was still alive.

"Don't worry about kills. Cripple them. We'll kill them later."

Kheyntamenti saw the battle line formed by the Currahee and mercenaries and headed for the western end of it. To his surprise, he saw he was being paced by two blue and green light Benderist HUPs, both less than 300 meters away. The pursuing Benderists had lost their formation and the fastest HUPs were actually getting among the Wild Geese.

Kheyntamenti swiveled his fuselage, revealing all his weapon turrets, and placed his sights onto the closest one, a Saber. The mindlink told the fire control system where he was looking and it automatically computed lead for the two twin recoilless rifle turrets. He fired and the smaller HUP vanished for a moment in a cloud of dust and its right arm went bouncing end over end across the desert. His large lasers burned into the damaged fuselage and the HUP turned away, streaming smoke. The other HUP, a

Short Sword, suddenly realized the danger of getting too far in front of the main formation and it, too, turned away.

Kheyntamenti lashed its back with the lasers and fired his rifles into it and had the satisfaction of seeing the 75-ton HUP go sprawling face down in the dirt. It wasn't dead but he suspected the pilot would be slow to bring his damaged HUP back into the fight.

In the distance he saw a Wild Geese HUP explode, its ammunition stores erupting in a fireball throwing tendrils of burning debris in all directions. There was no time to see who it was. Closer, other Militia HUPs were running, taking hits as they fled to the perimeter.

As he entered the wash, he saw the Militia landing ships firing. They were being careful, trying to avoid their own HUPs, but his sensors showed the Benderists were not slowing down. Kheyntamenti saw what they were trying to do.

He studied the screen. Without supporting fire, and a lot of it, the thin line of Militia HUPs would not last long. As it was, some of the HUPs staggering into the wash had already been mauled.

Lieutenant Elinshen saw Piotrowski's Gladius explode out of the corner of her eye as she steered her own Gladius over a slight rise and down the other side. Her screens showed her the trailing mass of Benderist HUPs coming on strong. Ahead, the Militia formed a line in a shallow dry wash. Her HUP was the furthest back of any of the surviving Wild Geese HUPs.

Something slammed into her HUP from behind. She twisted the body of her HUP, trying to shield the damaged rear armor and angled her HUP to the right. Again, her HUP was hit and her damage display showed a weapons pylon was damaged. She twisted her fuselage in the other direction.

A rail gun round ripped through a stunted desert tree in front of her while her cockpit was filled with the warning tones of a missile launch. Elinshen held her course, letting the missiles get a good lock on whatever portion of the Gladius they saw. Trusting to her instincts, she twisted her fuselage in the other direction and reversed her turn.

It partially worked. The pair of missiles tried to get to their aimed point, her damaged pylon. Having to circle sent one slamming into the desert floor when it caught a slight rise. The other, two seconds in trail, kept coming. The antimissile system fired, exploding it less than 50 meters away, splattering shrapnel across her HUP. She turned her HUP back towards the dry wash, her lips tight with fear and anger.

"Sundance Lead, GCI. We are scrambling the rest of Sundance and Ajax. Hold at your current position to take tactical command."

"Roger. Where are we going?"

"Sundance Leader, this is Jonivov."

"Roger, sir."

"I want you to head one two zero and then take an attack heading zero three zero. Targets are multiple HUPAX in the open. Take a right hand pull to avoid their landing ships."

"Roger, sir."

"Blaine, our spotters are out of action so arty is blind. We're working to reestablish contact with them but right now your fighters are almost all we have to support our HUPs. I can't send in the Tiger Moths – the landing ships will blow them away."

"Roger, sir."

Captain Hardin's tank was crouched behind the crest of a hill well to the west of the airfield. His armored company and the missile launching APCs assigned to it were supposed to protect the Militia landing ships, but it looked like the plan had changed. Now the ships were down to the south and he and his force had nothing to do.

His commo unit buzzed and he pressed his hands against his helmet as he listened. After a moment, his face suddenly still, he acknowledged the order.

"Armor group, this is Hardin. Form on me. Tanks, arrowhead. Missileers, center. We're going for the flank of the Benderist attack. Once you are in range, hang onto them but do not get close to them. Missileers, no closer than 800 meters. Follow me."

Hardin dropped into his turret and ordered his driver to take up a heading to the southeast. Time, he remembered from a military tactics class, was the most precious commodity on the battlefield. He was about to buy some.

Tyree and Felawasi crawled a hundred meters to their right as fire swept through their old position. How they had been spotted didn't matter. Apparently the Benderists were having pretty good luck at shutting down the other spotter teams as well because a quick glance towards the airfield showed that the Militia artillery fire was slacking off and what fire was coming in was not scoring many hits.

Almost all the enemy HUPs were streaming south, though a final group was forming near the southern edge of the airfield. Tyree led the way and found a shallow depression. He rolled into it and raised his head to call to Felawasi. He heard the high, rushing hiss of incoming rockets and dropped back down.

A ripple of explosions threw dirt and rocks into the air and he felt his back being slapped as he hugged the earth. Then Tyree scrambled to the edge of the depression and looked for Felawasi.

He saw her ten meters away, laying still. Tyree climbed out of the hole and ran towards her, half expecting to encounter more missiles on his way but there was no further fire. He slid beside her.

Felawasi was unconscious and bleeding from her upper shoulders and the side of her head. He picked up the laser designator by its strap and the corporal by the back of her equipment harness and dragged her into the hole.

Quickly he freed her harness and ripped open her shirt. Rolling her on to her stomach, he uncovered her back and slapped field dressings into place. The wound to her head had stopped bleeding, though dried blood had sealed her right eye closed. He picked up the designator and flopped down on the edge of the hole.

A quick look showed him why the landing ships were not firing in his direction. Their turrets were turned towards the fleeing Kodomiri HUPAX. Near the southern end of the line two dozen Benderist HUPAX were forming up, smaller HUPs in front, heavier ones in the rear. This was their breakthrough punch getting ready to be thrown, Tyree realized.

He looked further south. It was almost impossible to make out what was happening. In the far distance he could just see the shapes of the Militia landing ships. Closer the smoke and dust of a HUP battle obscured everything. He swung back to the Benderist Landing ships.

"FDC, this is Team Nine. What Frogfires are ready?"

"Nine, FDC. Good to hear from you. We have three launchers left. Each has one each solid penetrating or cluster, you call."

"Roger. Give me all the clusters. I have HUPs standing in the open among their landing ships at the south end of the airfield."

"Roger. Stand by. Stand by. Flashlight, flashlight, flashlight."

The three Frogfire missiles, all lofting cluster bomb warheads, dropped their loads in overlapping patterns onto the southern edge of the Benderist landing ships. Twenty-seven HUPAX had just gotten into formation when the small bombs struck.

Tyree heard what sounded like a giant piece of canvas ripping, the explosions were so close together. Three hundred, more, flashes of light raced back and forth across the HUPs and landing ships, shrouding them in dust and smoke. It seemed to go on for minutes.

"That's impressive," Felawasi said as she crawled alongside him, pulling on the remains of her ripped shirt. She rolled onto her back and poured her canteen onto her face and wiped the dried blood from her eye. Her torn shirt only covered one of her breasts but Felawasi did not seem to notice or care. She rolled back and reached for the designator. "Let me get back to work."

The low Bob Cat tanks moved in an arrowhead formation. In the center of the arrowhead infantry platoon APCs traveled while behind came the missile carriers. They had barely traveled half a kilometer when missiles flew from the formation.

Hardin realized the missileers weren't waiting to get in range of the enemy HUPs and were firing their first salvoes at the few landing ships they could reach. He understood they were taking the shots as they presented themselves and using their ammunition while they had the chance. Still, their targets were the enemy HUPs and tangling with landing ships was a very bad idea. Of course, tangling with 90 HUPAX wasn't exactly a good idea. Nonetheless, Hardin gave the command to cease-fire and steered the formation away from the landing ships and then angled back to the southeast.

Hardin happened to be looking to the east when the Frogfires slammed into the battalion staging among the southern landing ships. He raised his binoculars and saw a great deal of smoke and several fires, though among the HUPs or landing ships was unclear. As he scanned further south, he saw HUPAX turning out of the main formation.

They were turning towards him.

Did the Benderist landing ships think his small formation had been responsible for the Frogfires? He glanced back at the HUPs in the impact area. They, too, were turning towards him. Worse, they were starting to move.

"Command, armor. It looks like we have HUPs closing from the airfield as well as from their main group."

"Roger. Head west and see if you can draw them towards the hills. We have some support coming."

"Roger."

He turned his formation and slowed the tanks down to allow the less heavily armored APCs get ahead. Now the four missileer APCs were firing as fast as they could. Each APC lofted one of its ten missiles every few seconds. Hardin couldn't tell how much damage they were inflicting but they seemed to making some people very angry. Hardin counted a dozen or more HUPs coming from the landing ships and maybe twice that number peeled off from the main body and running at him.

Hardin blessed the ability of all his vehicles to swing their turrets all the way around and cleared his gunner to fire on the closest enemy HUP, a Mace that looked off balance for some reason. Buying time was what the colonel wanted, and that is what he would get, but it was going to be a very expensive purchase.

In wiping the blood out of her eye, Felawasi had opened her wound and blood oozed down her face. Tyree tied a bandage around her forehead even as she shifted the designator.

"What is loaded for me, FDC?"

"Niner, we have three penetrating Frogfires in the rack plus Diamondback one-two-two and two-tens in the tube waiting for Flashlight. Reloading three cluster Frogfires."

"Roger, FDC, I copy. Niner has multiple targets. Landing ships. Requesting one penetrating Frogfire per target, plus whatever arty can fire. Stand by. Target: Landing ship. Tracking. Fire for effect."

"Roger, on the way. Stand by. Stand by. Flashlight, Flashlight, Flashlight."

Eight hundred meters away a Viper took a waterfall of artillery rounds. The 122mm shells were like a series of jackhammer blows as the self-propelled guns rapidly rotated their breeches and fired their load, lofting the last one before the first struck. The 210mm guns were not nearly as fast as their smaller counterparts but their impact was noticeably larger. Shattered hull armor, antennae arrays, and a weapon turret were flung about by yellow and black explosions. Into the middle of the carnage, the 1200-kilogram Frogfire warhead punched into the upper hall, its entry almost unnoticed. But a secondary explosion ripped through the side of the landing ship, blowing flame and debris out a loading hatch. Felawasi was already sliding the designator to the next landing ship.

"FDC, Team Nine." Her voice was still calm but there was harshness in it. "Next target. Requesting one penetrating Froggie and arty fire for effect. Stand by. Target: Landing ship. Tracking. Fire for effect."

It had taken a few moments to assemble the First Battalion, but they were well-disciplined troops and they responded quickly to command. Halleck watched to one side as their commander, Major Feldon Pierce, formed them into two ranks of a dozen each. The lighter HUPs were in the first rank. The last rank had a few medium weights but was mostly heavy four-legged HUPs.

As Pierce organized his battalion, Halleck studied the battle and saw the enemy HUPs were forming a line under the shelter of their landing ships, a maneuver which could buy them some time if the added firepower of the ships blunted the three battalions racing towards them.

A line is always vulnerable on its flanks and that is where he decided to send the First Battalion, against the eastern end of the Militia line. And he would leapfrog half of his landing ships forward in support once the battalion was engaged, forcing the Militia ships the terrible choice of staying and being annihilated or pulling out and leaving their HUPs behind.

The first three Frogfires cluster bomb warheads arrived as Halleck started to explain his plan to Pierce. It was like being in a tornado, a swirl of fire and dust and a terrible sound of hundreds of explosions coming so close together it was a continuous roar.

Two of the bomblets struck his War Axe, inflicting minor damage to one pylon shoulder's armor. Other HUPs were not so lucky. Through the drifting smoke and dust he saw three smaller HUPs burning while others showed various levels of damage. One Short Sword standing nearby had a pylon gone so cleanly it was as if taken during a maintenance check. From the commo calls other HUPs had been hurt as well. Landing ships near the battalion were hit and several had lost some of their external armament. And any personnel in the open were dead.

Halleck heard someone on one of the landing ships yell that they were being fired on by armor coming out of the western hills. While the low, fast vehicles were difficult to see individually, there was no mistaking the dust cloud they raised. He glanced at his tactical display map. The Third and Fourth Battalions were closest to the enemy HUP line and were fanning out in the face of return fire. The Fifth Battalion was closest to him and, given the direction of the enemy armor, in a good position to intercept it.

"Fifth, this is Halleck."

"Fifth Lead here. Go, sir."

"Major, we have an armored group with heavy missiles at your four or five o'clock. Detach a company of fast movers to intercept them before they can do any more damage."

"Roger, sir."

"I see them!"

Halleck did not know who it was who yelled but the voice was a trigger. Suddenly First Battalion HUPs were running past him, chasing the armor.

"First, resume your formation. First Lead, this is Halleck."

Then Pierce appeared out of the smoke. His War Lance appeared undamaged until Halleck saw the flashing spotlight carried on the big HUP, the signal of a HUP that its communication system was knocked out. He cursed and shifted from his command frequency to the one used by the First Battalion.

"First Battalion, this is Colonel Halleck. Return to your formation. We have HUPs on the way to deal with those people. Return to formation."

He breathed a sigh of relief as he saw the HUPs slowing down. A few, apparently exchanging fire with the armor, now turning away to the west, stopped. He was about to call them again when they started to die.

Benderist HUPs were not the only ones dying that morning. Gwielgi saw one of the Victor's Scorpions, anchoring one end of the line in the wash, turn to face three flanking enemy HUPs. He ran forward to support it.

The Scorpion's heavy firepower almost shredded one HUP, a Ballista, heavily damaging it and throwing it off balance so its fire went wide. But the next two, a Javelin and a Rapier, obliterated the Scorpion. With its back to him Gwielgi could not tell what killed it but the sudden explosion rocked Brother Wolf as he approached.

His own lasers tore off an arm of the Rapier but all three turned away in perfect unison, clearly a well-drilled team. Gwielgi locked a missile on the badly damaged Ballista and saw it evaporate in a fusion flare as the missile caught it on the rise of a dune. The Scorpion was little more than burning fragments at his feet.

Gwielgi swung his HUP to the west and started to go into a crouch when the remaining pair of enemy HUPs came racing back over the rise their wingman died on. Gwielgi turned his fuselage while raising his HUP but knew he was going to be hit before he could move.

A HUP darted past him, another of the Militia's low Gladius. Its twin GTL3 lasers hit the one-armed Rapier just below the cockpit, shattering its armor plates. For a split second Gwielgi could see inside the HUP as pieces of armor bounced across the desert. Then he fired his own large lasers into the gaping wound and the Rapier fusion power plant blew up.

Brother Wolf was knocked down by the blast from the Rapier, a fall that saved it from two rail gun rounds from the enemy Javelin. The Gladius, staggered by the blast but still on its talons, fired into the front of the blunt-nosed cockpit. Then Brother Wolf was on its feet, firing into the enemy HUP. The Gladius killed it with a final stab of its lasers.

This is really getting to be interesting.

Gwielgi heard Sevin's comment and grinned as both pilots backed their HUPs further into the dry wash.

Major Blaine Toland was on leave when the Storm Cloud Raiders invaded Kodomir. But like every other Kodomir Militia Air Force pilot, he knew of the attack of the Swallows based at Kiroff against the Raider HUPs and how they were cut to ribbons by the Benderist Fireray combat air patrol flying cover for Storm Cloud.

Killing the four Firerays earlier meant far more than he would have said. Now they were going against the Benderist main force. Fighter pilots have to be unusually aggressive to be effective but Toland took his pilots' fire and made it incandescent. As he led the two squadrons into the broad plain, Toland keyed his transmitter.

"Dancers, take it low. Go burner on. Get hits."

The well-known words, the last transmitted by the squadron commander of the Swallows who opposed the Storm Cloud invasion in the Depford Valley, were like lightning to the other pilots – the Red Cocks' First Battalion would be the first to feel its heat.

The HUPs pursuing Hardin's force were taking hits from missiles and the fire of the Bob Cats, but a burning APC missileer showed it was not all one way. The HUPs, hearing Halleck's order, were just beginning to turn back when the Swallows came howling across the desert.

Each of the fifteen Swallows carried a missile launcher and a long-range laser. As they came in range of the HUPs their missile bay doors snapped open. The missiles carved gray smoke trails above the desert, though the savage red beams of the lasers arrived first.

Many of the HUPs were damaged from the Frogfire strike or the fire from Hardin's group. Pausing to turn made them easy targets. Perhaps a handful of missiles missed or a laser fused sand into glass instead of melting HUP armor. But watching from the open hatch of his tank Hardin could only think of a sideways hurricane of fire that swept away two HUPs as he watched, sending them tumbling and burning, while a third blew up in a spray of white light.

As a fourth Benderist HUP had a leg torn off, he slowed his formation and fired on the retreating enemy. And still the Swallows' missiles and laser beams slashed across the desert. More HUPs were savaged and Hardin found himself smiling. Maybe the cost of time would not be as expensive as he thought it was going to be.

The Swallows were not done. Pulling to the right, they found themselves facing the fast-moving company detached from the Fifth Battalion. Toland snapped a quick shot with his laser – there was no time to get a missile lock – and yelled a warning to the other pilots.

They did better than he did. Alerted to the additional targets, they put their missiles and lasers into the faces of the onrushing HUPs. The speed of many of the smallest HUPs helped some of them avoid heavy damage but the firing of the Swallows drew Hardin's attention to the approaching danger. Dropping back into his turret, he ordered the infantry to deploy from their APCs and then sent all the lightly-armored APCs further west. He led his tanks beside the infantry, getting everyone behind low hillocks and dunes with only their turrets exposed.

As the last Swallow finished its run and burning columns rising into the sky showed that several of the oncoming HUPs were dead, Hardin took a quick look at his tactical display. Twenty HUPs were still coming. For the APCs to get away, they would have to be slowed down. Buying time was still the plan. He wondered what the purchase price would finally be.

"Gunner, target, HUP. Eight hundred, twelve o'clock."

As he flew over the Benderist company, Toland pulled another right-hand turn.

"One more time, right-hand pull. Let's hit them again."

He took the two squadrons in a tight circle and brought them in again on the enemy HUPs. This time he was looking for them.

The HUPs ran into a wall of mixed fire from the Bob Cats, some of which were using older model cannon while others fired high velocity rail guns.

A wave of light missiles rose from the infantry platoon. Their wire-guided missiles had little punch compared to the defensive armor of a HUPAX, but the missile crews were not aiming at armor. Peering through their guidance sights and trying to ignore the flash of fire around them, the gunners steered their wire-guided missiles towards the cockpits of the oncoming HUPs. All they had to do was keep their crosshairs on target while the simple computer in the sight did the actual steering of the missile.

The first missile struck the pylon shoulder of a Saber, causing little damage other than momentarily distracting its pilot. The second caught front of a Scimitar's cockpit. Its shaped charge warhead punched through and instantly killed the pilot while the HUP ran on for another twenty meters before sprawling on its face. The third slammed into the cockpit of a Short Sword. The blast seriously wounded the pilot who barely maintained control of her 50-ton HUP as she turned away, trying to get to safety and aid.

While the HUPs had difficulty seeing the infantry and their missile launchers, they could see the muzzle blasts of the Bob Cats. A multi-colored spray of lasers of various kinds swept the ground. Two tanks died immediately and a third was immobilized as a laser melted a track in half. Then the Swallows came in for their second run.

Once more, missiles swept in low, leaving gray streaks as they hunted their targets. The red beams of large lasers shot across the battlefield and HUPs burned and exploded. The Benderist company commander, seeing three of his HUPs in front of him die almost simultaneously, ordered a hasty retreat. It was a major mistake, for the HUPs had to turn away, essentially holding still for a brief moment as the Bob Cats and missiles from the APCs sought them out. Toland saw them running as he turned the formation. It was a long time since the fight at the mouth of Depford Valley, but the Dancers were avenged.

Of the original twenty-five HUPs of the Fifth Battalion company, less than ten made it back to the shelter of their landing ships.

Chapter 32: Fire under the sun

23 December 2824

But the Benderist landing ships had problems of their own. In addition to Tyree and Felawasi, two more spotter teams, one consisting of a sole survivor, came back on line. The Fire Direction Center quickly shifted battery assignments so that each team had a mix of firepower to bring to bear.

Felawasi acquired an Alligator-class landing ship and pounded it with 122mm and 210mm howitzers. The guns shifted over, once the coordinates were solid, to shells not fitted with Diamondback guidance systems, saving them for new targets.

As she watched, the explosions on the landing ship were suddenly joined by an extremely large one, very nearly on the top of its hull. Felawasi saw smoke and fire pour from the hit.

"FDC, Niner. Did you just send a Frogfire? I thought they were reloading their launchers."

"Negative, Niner. That's Cochran's MS150. They're using burst-fires of five. She's in the fight."

"Roger. Tell her to get her own damned targets."

"Roger, Niner."

Peggy Cochran's maneuver had saved, at least for the moment, the thin line of Militia HUPAX. Her staggered column put down a searing fire that accounted for a dozen Benderist HUPs in less than a minute. With the

Militia HUPs crouched in the dry wash, the landing ships were able to keep up a steady volume of fire, breaking up the frontal assault of the three battalions.

Her flagship, Zombie, had the only MS150 cannon in the fight, but trying to hit moving HUPs was a waste of rounds, especially compared to the rows of fat landing ships sitting in tight formation on the airfield. After a hurried apologetic call from the FDC, she had her gunners link up with the FDC and soon massive rounds were screaming towards as yet undamaged Benderist ships.

Cochran smiled. At least this way anything Zombie killed would be entirely credited to her ship and not those grunts, bless their mud-slogging hearts.

For Halleck, the problem suddenly was clear. His brigade outnumbered the enemy HUPs, but to get at them they had to get close to the Militia landing ships, a task rapidly becoming suicidal. It was time to use his own ships. Quickly he ordered his battalions to flank to either side of the Militia line of landing ships while staying at far range. This had the effect of taking the Militia landing ships in the middle of their column out of the fight since the ships to the left and right blocked their fire. Then he gave the task force the order to leap frog.

That was when he heard the horrified transmission of Admiral Canaris, the task force commander.

"Colonel, five of our twenty landing ships cannot raise due to damage. Several that can are seriously damaged. If we land on the other side of their ship's column, we will be at a severe disadvantage, since that will put us even closer to their ground-based long-range artillery and missiles plus they will still be able to reach us along with their landing ships' fire. They now have air supremacy as well. Colonel, call your brigade back."

To pull back would be to admit defeat. Halleck had one chance and he would have to steal the enemy's plan.

"Red Cocks, this is Halleck. Rush their HUPs! Get in among them so their landing ships cannot fire on us. It is our only chance."

As he sent his War Axe running forward Halleck took a quick glance to the rear. His landing ships were being pounded with renewed fury, no question of that. They had to move, and quickly.

"Admiral Canaris, lift all available ships and take up a new position southeast of the city. Repeat, south of the city and east of their column. That will put you out of accurate range of most of their supporting fire. Concentrate your fire on the end of their landing ship line closest to you. Your fire from there will not be blocked by our HUPs. Do to them what they've been doing to you. We can still win this."

"Roger, colonel. Good luck."

Halleck thought he would need it. He could see, amidst all the swirling dust and smoke, his brigade was doing what he asked of it and was turning toward the Militia HUPAX. He knew they would take casualties on the way in but once among the Militia HUPs their superior numbers would restore their advantage.

Felawasi saw the first flare of landing ship engines and then almost all were lifting from the ground.

"FDC, their landing ships are launching!"

"Roger. Checking fire until we see where they come down."

Cochran saw the brigade begin its charge and looked up when her MS150 gunner shouted a warning. Seeing the Benderist ships lifting and moving southeast, she suddenly realized what they were going to do. There was time only for a desperate countermove.

"Aft line, form a line at a right angle to the front line, anchored on our east-most ship. Just like a swinging gate. Do it now, we are about to have company!"

Then Cochran turned her attention to the charging brigade. She had just removed almost half of the supporting fire for the Militia HUPs in the wash – there was nothing more she could but trust her gunners and wait.

"Black Dog, Jonivov."

"Black Dog Lead, roger."

"Their landing ships are lifting. It's a gamble, but this may be your best chance to hit their HUPs. See if you can't cut some of them down before they overrun our people in the wash."

"Yes, sir. Dogs are lifting now."

The eight single-seat Tiger Moth helicopters climbed upward as Leba Chinaren looked around. She had followed the battle on her datalink displays, watching as red and blue symbols appeared and disappeared. She found it impossible to tell who was winning but the fact that the most fragile machines near the battlefield were being thrown into the fight made it clear that the situation was desperate. She shook her head, remembering her earlier disappointment at being out of the fight. Well, you asked for it.

The lifting Benderist ship captains were relieved to be moving. Sitting still and being hit by artillery and those awful long-range missiles had been frustrating and a little terrifying. Though five landing ships were still on the ground and several in the air were streaming smoke, at least they were moving and relatively safe. When they came down, they would have overwhelming firepower to bring against the end of the enemy landing ship column. The roles would be reversed and they were looking forward to it.

But they were not safe. Toland's Swallows completed their run on the Fifth Battalion's shattered company and made a wide circle as he contemplated what target to take on next. He had decided to try to run against the HUPs attacking the Militia perimeter when he saw the landing ships climbing into the sky on pillars of yellow-white fire.

"Sundance and Ajax, we're going after their landing ships. Roll in, launch your missiles, and pull away. Do not close with these bastards. Follow me."

The closest landing ship, an already damaged Viper, took the brunt of the attack. Each Swallow launched a missile before rolling away. Probably at least one missile, in the stream of 15, malfunctioned but it made little difference. The ion pulse turret on the starboard side of the Viper exploded as missiles slammed almost the entire length of the ship's side even as its lasers ripped a wing from a Swallow. Fighting desperately to control the stricken, burning landing ship, the bridge crew succeeded in crash landing it less than 500 meters from their take off point.

"That's one. Let's get another."

Kheyntamenti saw the charge coming and pulled his HUP back down into the ravine. He only had seconds.

"Stay in the wash. Work in pairs and hit them as they come over the top."

As he spoke, fire from the Militia landing ships slashed over his head. Ion pulse weapons laid down a sheet of lightning and missiles covered the blue sky with their exhaust trails. As the enemy HUPs came closer, the landing ships used their lasers and ion pulse cannon with increasing accuracy.

It was not enough but it was something. Benderist HUPAX fell, tumbling, cockpits destroyed or legs shot away, as others exploded, their ammunition or their fusion power plants ripping them apart from within.

Halleck saw the front ranks disappearing as if melting away, candles under a blowtorch, but he saw the rest of the brigade was going to make it into the wash. Even as he watched, the first HUPs disappeared over the lip of the wash.

Now. Now we have them.

Chinaren did not bother to look behind her. She knew her Tiger Moth was low enough that she was raising dust from the ground as she raced over the low, rolling terrain. The rest of the Black Dogs were on line with her, irregularly spaced on either side.

The rising enemy landing ships had not bothered to fire in their direction, probably because of the harassment from the Swallows and because they were blocking each other's line of fire. She saw small explosions on the landing ships and her resentment at the Swallows vanished.

The Benderist Task Force Commander, Vice Admiral Thomas Canaris, watched a second Viper fall out of formation, its damaged hull unable to protect it from those damned Militia Swallows. His ships' own missiles were not doing much good, for the fighters were peeling away as they fired and the landing ship missiles were encountering intense jamming plus the problem of running out of fuel trying to keep up with the fleeing fighters. His fist beat against his leg. He had told them he wanted more Firerays. But the early experience of the Benderist fighter pilots more than two years before had led the Air Marshal, safely back at the Baron's court, to disparage the effectiveness of the Kodomir Militia Air Force. Canaris wished for a second that the arrogant bastard was here now.

Canaris wrenched his thoughts to the problem at hand. If there was any good news, the landing ships the Swallows could reach were the ones already most seriously damaged, the ones closest to the western hills and the Militia supporting fire. Their sacrifice was costing him little in terms of firepower, for several had already lost their fire control systems or many of their weapons. In the meantime, they were distracting the Swallows from the other landing ships. It was a bitter thing, but it might just be the key to victory.

Canaris grunted – sensors showed a flight of helicopters running across the battlefield below. They were not of any consequence for the landing ships but the brigade's HUPs might be hit, especially that last battalion Halleck was forming unless he got them moving quickly.

"If any fire can be spared," Canaris said to the ship's captain standing beside him, "especially from our ships to the north of the formation, see if they can knock down some of those helicopters."

The captain glanced at the screen and then spoke briefly into his headset. He looked back at Canaris and nodded. Canaris returned to the management of his maneuver.

As his formation moved across the sky Canaris designated landing points for each of his ships. They would bring an overwhelming amount of fire against the eastern end of the Militia column. Four quick kills would do it, he thought. That would be a major catastrophe for the enemy. They would have to withdraw or surrender.

There was a small cheer on his bridge. He looked up to see a smear of flame on a viewing screen; another of the Swallows had been swatted.

He hoped it was a harbinger of things to come.

"Ready now."

"Niner copies. Launch all."

"Roger, launching. Stand by, stand by. Flashlight, flashlight, flashlight."

Before the word was spoken a second time Felawasi had her finger tight on the laser designator button. Tyree, half standing up, his eye close to his telescopic sight, watched the running mass of Benderist HUPs. The reloading of the Frogfire launchers had taken a large piece of eternity and he had felt a growing sense of helplessness as the enemy ships climbed into the sky.

Felawasi knew that conventional artillery, even artillery using Diamondback laser guidance, had little chance of scoring a hit on a fast-moving HUPAX. But both the 210mm howitzers and the Frogfires could cover an area with cluster munitions. Precision was not as great an issue but she was illuminating the enemy brigade anyway, keeping the electronic dot on the highest point she could see, the upper portion of a War Lance. Tyree kept his own rifle crosshairs on it. It seemed to be in the center of the brigade, no more than 300 meters from the Militia HUPs.

He was still watching when he and Felawasi heard the crack of the supersonic Frogfires overhead. They did not see the cluster bomb warheads open.

Then there was little to see. The dust raised by the charging HUPs already partially obscured the scene and the quick wave of explosions from the bomblets completely covered everything in smoke and dust. Even the arrival of the 210mm cluster munitions, two seconds behind the Frogfires, was invisible.

The Frogfires had their patterns adjusted conservatively out of fear the bomblets would fall among the Militia HUPs. They came down in three large ovals, each slightly more than 200 meters long and parallel to the Militia line, but only 100 meters wide.

Each of the three Frogfire antiarmor cluster bombs delivered 110 shaped charge warheads and all three guided on the same laser-designated spot. Still traveling at supersonic speeds, the 330 bomblets arrived essentially simultaneously across the middle of the main portion of the attacking brigade.

Halleck saw it from the inside. If there was a hell, he was in it for the second time that morning. The ground around him, already being churned by the Militia landing ship covering fire, suddenly erupted, as if a large number of small volcanoes had sprung into existence. He saw the heavily armed War Axe in front of him take two direct hits, one striking the vertical missile launcher, the other exploding on the GTL5 turret on the HUP's right pylon. The damage to the pylon was minor but the missile launcher vanished in a fireball as the remaining missiles within it detonated.

Striking from above, the bomblets were prone to hitting cockpits whose overhead protection were typically thin ejection hatches. He saw a Morning

Star to his right, smoke streaming from its cockpit, suddenly sink to its front knees and pitch forward as the legs collapsed completely, a signal its pilot was unconscious or worse. The cries of wounded pilots filled communications.

One of the bomblets struck his War Axe a glancing blow. Ignoring the minor damage to his back armor, Halleck steered around a burning Cutlass, intent on gaining the dry wash and coming to grips with the enemy. He saw other brigade HUPs still moving forward. The fire from the enemy landing ships had decreased noticeably. Just a few more minutes.

Three of the Black Dogs were gone, vanished. Chinaren thought she saw a dazzling beam of light out of the corner of her eye but wasn't sure. What had been a formation of eight was now one of five.

Looking ahead, the Benderist HUPs were in a full sprint, running towards the wash. She looked through her helmet's tactical display and watched the red symbols imposed on the rolling tan ground ahead slowly expand. She engaged the datalink and assigned targets to the surviving Dogs. A yellow circle appeared around a red symbol. That one was hers. Her eyes narrowed as she flipped the arming safeties off.

You asked for this.

This time she was talking to the enemy.

"Second rack ready."

"Roger, launch. Reload solids. We'll try for those landing ships south of town."

"Roger, launching. Stand by, stand by. Flashlight, flashlight, flashlight."

For Kheyntamenti, it was a knife fight, savage and quick in the dry wash as the Benderist HUPs came spilling over the edge. Almost immediately his Rapier collided with an enemy HUP while he was firing on another one. The damaged Short Sword he fired on exploded, its entire right side erupting in a fireball that threw chunks of armor plating into the confined quarters of the wash and inflicting damage on half a dozen HUPs from both sides.

The HUP plowing into him was a Morning Star. Its torso was swung away from him and its pilot must have been concentrating on another target. Kheyntamenti's HUP pushed against the heavier missile-carrying HUP. In turn, it kept trying to grind forward. At least being this close dissuaded other Benderist HUPs from snapping shots in Kheyntamenti's direction. His rail guns reloaded and he stepped backward. The Morning Star staggered forward, almost falling, as Kheyntamenti fired everything his HUP carried into the round body of the enemy HUP.

It was suddenly gone, out of his field of view, and he saw his HUP's right arm go flying into space as the Rapier rocked from a hit from behind. Kheyntamenti swerved and twisted his fuselage, trying to find his attacker. Less than ten meters away, a Long Bow came running by, its fuselage swiveled to track him. He fired and saw his large lasers melt armor off of its legs.

Then the Long Bow was gone in a swirl of dust and smoke. Kheyntamenti pushed forward and turned, looking for something to shoot.

For Elinshen, it was a dance of death. Her Gladius's low profile gave her an immediate advantage and her skill compounded that advantage. She fired her weapons into the back hip of a Trebuchet and kept moving. The Trebuchet foolishly stopped and tried to swing after her. He invited his own destruction as fire from two other Militia HUPs was drawn to the tall, almost stationary target. A leg was ripped from the damaged hip and the 135-ton HUP fell in an accelerating arc, bounced off the side of a Saber and sending it tumbling against the wash wall, and finally impacted the ground face down.

Poor dancer to be in this ballet.

For Gwielgi and Sevin, it was a blur of dust, smoke, and swirling HUPAX. Both pilots tried to work together, attacking the same target. For a few seconds they would see the length of the wash – a solid mass of fighting metal – then, like a curtain dropping, the dust and smoke would obscure everything and they did not have a target until they walked into one.

From the right a large War Lance appeared and bored straight in towards them. Sevin wondered, in the part of his brain not trying to stay alive, why the big HUP had its spotlight on while fighting in the bright sunlight but then things became too busy for any kind of question.

He was backing up while Gwielgi tried to flank the enemy HUP. The pilot briefly swiveled in Gwielgi's direction and fired, enveloping the Javelin in dust. As it emerged, Sevin could see Gwielgi's 80-ton HUP limping, one leg badly damaged. He fired his lasers into the 'Lance; it seemed to ignore the damage but he gained its attention. The massive HUP turned towards him. From one side he saw Gwielgi's Brother Wolf fire, sending a stream of four missiles on a flight of less than fifteen meters. They smacked the big HUP in the side, momentarily throwing off its pilot's aim and sparing Sevin the impact of twin rail guns.

Sevin had his HUP in full reverse and felt his Gladius lurch as it climbed backwards out of the wash. The War Lance pilot kept coming, ignoring Gwielgi's limping HUP. Doc took two more backward steps and was out of the dry wash and leveling the weapons on his pylons. As the War Lance climbed up the embankment, an ion pulse sliced into him from the side, and then a blur of them. One hit Doc and his mindlink blinked off for several seconds and the Gladius continued to step backwards on its own. Static electricity crackled around the Benderist HUP. Just as it began to dissipate, large laser beams lanced into it from two different directions. Fire erupted from its torso as armor splashed in molten streams. The HUP started to turn away as its pilot tried to protect the damaged area but it was too late. A pack of missiles slammed into it, some of which went through the gaps in its armor and deep inside. The HUP exploded as the pilot ejected.

As Doc regained control of the Gladius and stepped back into the wash, he glanced over his shoulder and promised himself someday he would buy a landing ship gunner, any gunner, all she or he could drink.

For Tsunasdi it was easy for the first few minutes. Crouched in the wash, his Rapier killed the first HUP that raced over the edge. The Scimitar, its cockpit suddenly obliterated, crashed beside the bigger HUP. Tsunasdi never paused to look. The next HUP, a Mace, stepped up onto the edge and fired twin ion pulse weapons into the mass of HUPs in the dry wash. It did not seem to be aware of Tsunasdi's Rapier and was fixated on scoring easy hits on the struggling HUPs below. It was a mistake, for as the Mace paused he gave Tsunasdi the chance to place his reticle carefully on the cockpit before firing.

The combined rail guns and lasers, an "alpha strike," heavily damaged the armor of the cockpit and the area around it. Aware of his danger, the pilot instinctively turned his HUP trying to see who was firing at him rather than rely on the mindlink to his sensors that gave him a 360-degree field of view. This was his second and final mistake. By not immediately moving forward, he gave Tsunasdi precious seconds in which his weapons recycled.

Badly played, Tsunasdi thought, and fired. The Mace stood still for a second, collecting an unnecessary laser hit from a landing ship gunner, and then fell to the ground.

For Vermeil it was an introduction to horror. The first few Benderist HUPs that came into the wash near him were apparently intent on gaining position, for none stopped to shoot at him. On the other hand, his quick snap shots scored no hits.

Focus, you dumb son of a bitch!

His words to himself worked and the next HUP, a fast-moving Short Sword, took an ion pulse hit as it got to the edge. Never pausing, it leapt from the dry wash edge. Vermeil hit it in midair and, as it landed, once more. The 'Sword tried to get away, but Vermeil was now almost on top of the smaller HUP and he used all three ion pulse weapons at once. It was like turning on a fire hose and the jabbing beams burned their way up the side of the smaller HUP and tore into the head.

The control systems were shot away and the HUP staggered out of control and fell, fire streaming from the its fuselage. Vermeil saw the cockpit hatch start to open and then stop as smoke poured out of the opening. The enemy pilot pushed and the hatch, showing signs of battle damage, opened only a little further. The pilot tried to crawl through the narrow opening but could only get an arm out.

Vermeil watched as the enemy pilot's face contort in a scream he could not hear as raw flame licked around him. Vermeil hesitated a second and then aimed his weapons at the hatch opening, the sight reticle on the pilot's face, and fired.

Then he turned the Scorpion away and stalked down the wash.

For Leba Chinaren it was routine. Suddenly routine. In the dash of Black Dog flight across the battlefield she had glimpsed repeated scenes of destruction and signs of bloody and desperate struggle, an impression increased by the obliteration of three of her flight.

Then, suddenly, she saw the shallow ridge ahead. She rapidly decelerated, as did the other four Tiger Moths. The ridge was barely higher than a Moth and when she raised her bird high enough to clear the sensors on top of the rotor mast, she could see the Benderist HUPs streaming towards the wash.

It was just like a training exercise.

The formation fired without exposing itself, launching missiles that popped over the ridge and, using the guidance from the mast sensors, flew towards their targets. Chinaren kept firing missiles, switching to a new target as the old one fell, watching the symbols in her helmet display just like in training.

No one fired back and, in a moment, the five helicopters' missiles were gone. While only a handful of HUPs were killed outright, she doubted that a single missile had missed and many more HUPs were damaged or crippled. She paused. Was that all there was to it?

They still had their guns, the long barreled 37-millimeter cannon slung under the Tiger Moths' noses. Tactical doctrine was, situation permitting, after using missiles the attack helicopters would go after their targets with their guns. She eased her Moth upward and the others followed.

"Let's go."

Just like in training.

For Peggy Cochran it was what she lived for. Freeing the MS150 crew to engage the descending enemy landing ships, she had the rest of her gunners concentrate on the Red Cock HUPs. Each fireball or fusion flash was a victory.

As the Benderists dropped into the wash the number of targets decreased but the slowest HUPs were the largest HUPs and her gunners were lighting them up as fast as they could. She thought no enemy HUP made it to the wash without damage, and many did not make it at all.

The second wave of Frogfires, she would later concede, broke the enemy's back, since it caught most of their largest HUPs in the open, along with the remains of a battalion hurrying to catch up to the others. The Benderist pilots, many of whose HUPs had crippling leg damage, nonetheless kept coming forward. If they could not fire accurately into the dogfight in the wash, they fired at the landing ships. These acts of defiance did little damage but attracted attention.

Cochran saw HUPs dead and dying in the broad plain from the airfield to the dry wash. In the wash there was a violent mix of HUPs, slamming into one another, firing at point black range, exploding and falling. Occasionally one would come out of the wash and then dive back in.

The landing ship gunners had ceased using missiles – more than one friendly HUP had taken a strike from a missile meant for an enemy. Even the ion pulse gunners were hesitant. The laser turrets still fired, but they were operating more like snipers, carefully placing each shot. Nonetheless, in the swirl of combat, friendlies were still hit. When a HUP came out of the wash that was enemy, it seemed like every gunner in every landing ship in range tried to kill it. The mass fire was deadly but the opportunities were few and fleeting.

The Swallows looked to be out of missile ammunition. Firing into the wash was too dangerous, as was trying to take their large lasers against the enemy landing ships. She saw them switch to making runs on damaged HUPs on the plain. Then she heard Kheyntamenti.

"Tashan, Kheyntamenti. Disembark and form your team near the west end of the gully. Hit them from behind."

Her closed-circuit screen showed the lower HUP bay. Crew personnel scattered and the bay doors slid back as the disembarkation ramp extended. She shook her head. Those youngsters were in no way ready for the devil's den they were about to enter. She silently wished them good luck and, because she was Peggy Cochran, good hunting.

Chapter 33: Retreat under fire

23 December 2824

For Steve Tashan, it was so confusing as to be beyond terrifying. Pressed into service to fill the seat of a Long Bow, the maintenance gunnery sergeant led his team of four students away from Zombie and towards the west end of the Wild Geese position. They took no fire from the savage battle raging in the wash, probably because the further west they went the deeper the wash and the greater the difficulty in seeing out of it. Once he brought the team to a position beyond with the end of the perimeter and the fighting, he swung them facing north in an arrowhead, with his HUP in the lead. Already he was getting the beginning of a headache from the mindlink but he ignored it as he looked ahead.

A mass of Benderist HUPs filled that end of the wash, pressing east. No reason to let them know they were coming.

"Check sensors off. Follow me."

Tashan kept his speed down, though speed control was about all that worked on his shot-up Long Bow. One rail gun and a couple of small laser turrets were the only weapons that could be jammed into it in the time they had had to prepare. Its damage display showed damage already existing on every part except his left arm weapons pylon.

It was missing.

The student HUPs were not in much better shape: a Trebuchet that limped as it struggled to stay up with the others, barely able to do 50 KPH; a Long Sword whose damaged fire control system meant that its battery of

514

lasers could barely be fired one at a time; a Ballista whose missile launcher's reloading system was still not functional; and a Short Sword whose recoilless rifle turret's damaged ammunition bin precluded a full load of ammo. It was a very ragtag group.

Tashan led the arrowhead into the wash and pivoted to the right. Through the dust and smoke he could see the backs of eight or more Benderist HUPs. He keyed his microphone and glanced at his chronometer

"Start with the Ballista."

Five HUPs concentrating their fire on the back of another HUPAX will kill their target quickly, even if they are cripples themselves. The Ballista's back armor evaporated under the assault of multiple lasers of various kinds and the following rail gun and recoilless rifle slugs met little resistance as they tore into the interior structure of the HUP. It blew apart, its engine and ammunition cooking off together, before the pilot realized that he was being fired on. The explosion damaged the HUPs on either side of the Ballista. Tashan felt the headache suddenly surge and a wave of nausea swept over him as he keyed his microphone again.

"Now the Broad Sword."

The big, two-man four-legged command HUP started turning, trying to get its weapons into play, as the first rounds hit. The volume of fire was not as sudden or large as it had been against the Ballista for the students were blocking each other's lines of fire as they concentrated on their target and neglected their formation.

"Aim for the cockpit. Keep formation. Stay on target." Tashan tried to keep his voice calm, coaching the students.

The Broad Sword turned in place, its four legs pumping up and down as it turned. Tashan imagined its pilot was yelling for everyone else to join him but there was nothing to be done for it. He kept his targeting reticle on the cockpit of the big HUP and finally heard the signal that the rail gun was ready. He fired and saw the slug rip into the cockpit. The students' fire increased as well as they regained their formation. The wash was filled with streaks of red and other colors.

The Broad Sword lurched, fired a pair of large lasers towards the right-hand student, the Trebuchet, and then the pilot ejected. The HUP, smoke and, suddenly, fire streaming from the cockpit, froze in place.

"Take the Rapier."

But the Rapier was not the only HUP turning around. It looked like all of the remaining HUPs in the group, and maybe some of the ones further down the wash, were aware of the five. They turned and accelerated towards Tashan's team.

It was like an avalanche of iron. HUPs came running and slammed into him even as he tried to fire. Tashan did not know if he scored any hits with his rail gun or lasers but fired as soon as he laid his eye on anything. He watched in amazement as a Benderist HUP salvoed four large lasers into the leg of another Benderist HUP and then shut down as its pilot was rendered senseless when another HUP slammed into it at full speed from the side. Tashan tried to target it but was slammed sideways himself by yet another HUPAX. He barely held his fire against the ramming HUP before he realized that it was a friendly, the Short Sword. It vanished behind him. A laser burned into the side of his cockpit and he saw the bulkhead turn a cherry-red from the heat.

Tashan heard warning tones sounding continuously as he tried to move but the Long Bow was immobile. He saw a Rapier suddenly step in front of him, its fuselage swiveled to one side as it tracked a student. As he fired into it, he heard an explosion from deep within his HUP. His damage indicators were all at maximum and suddenly his cockpit was flooded with a new wave of heat. The Long Bow pitched backwards as he initiated the ejection system.

Part of him monitored the sequence and noted with a maintenance technician's approval that everything functioned as it should. The overhead hatch blew clear even as he and his seat were enveloped in a cocoon of metal. A rocket fired, slamming him into the seat.

Then Tashan was on the ground, the wind knocked out of him, and daylight was pouring into his face. He clawed his buckles and freed himself, rolling out of the cocoon and sprawling on the ground. His headache was gone.

The first thing he was aware of was the roar of the battle. The hypersonic rail gun rounds, the lightning crack of ion pulse weapons, the sonic boom of lasers, the jackhammers of cannon, the explosions of missiles, and the death sounds of dying HUPs were so loud it was almost paralyzing. He supported himself with the side of the cocoon and got to his feet. Thanks to the ejection system, he was out of the dry wash by a hundred meters.

Behind him were the Militia landing ships. He looked back and saw the upper torsos and heads of fighting HUPs. A blue and green Scorpion suddenly disappeared, its head vanishing downward like a swimmer taken by a shark. He could not tell what had happened to the students.

There was nothing more for him to do here. Tashan started to jog towards the ships, wiping his bloody nose with the back of his hand. He saw his watch and stared at it as he ran. From firing on the first Benderist HUP to this instant was 31 seconds. He spat blood to one side and kept running.

The move of the Benderist landing ships meant that there was little fire from the area of the airfield. Still, Chinaren kept the Black Dogs low. The five remaining landing ships, though damaged, might still be capable of taking out a helicopter.

The Dogs pounced on individual HUPs as they came across them – a large number appeared damaged, with some limping towards the wash. But Chinaren did not delay getting to the wash. She had a glimpse of a HUP ejection capsule fire out of the swirling mass in and around the wash; a blue bracket around it said that it was friendly.

The five helicopters swung over the ravine and Chinaren and the other pilots found that their tactical displays were almost worthless. The HUPs below were too close together. Blue and red symbols from transponders and IFF systems overlapped so completely as to make targeting through the datalink close to impossible.

Chinaren did not hesitate. She cut off the tactical display and used her own eyes. The 37mm cannon followed where she looked while the helicopter's computer adjusted the aim. She keyed her microphone.

"Theirs are green and blue. Kill them."

It was no longer like training.

Cochran looked to the east through her bridge's view ports, though the best view of the battlefield was on her screens. The enemy landing ships had counted on only having to face the few Militia ships at the end of the column, not an entire line. Instead of four they were dueling with six. Seven, if you counted Zombie's MS150 cannon. The odds were in the

Benderists' favor for the moment, but the transmissions she heard in her headset promised that would change soon.

"Niner, can you see their far landing ships?"

"Just barely, FDC. Wait one."

Felawasi stood up, throwing off the camouflage netting Tyree had spread over her a few moments before. Placing an elbow on her hip, she brought her eye to the designator sight. She squinted as it stabilized.

"FDC, I can't see all of them but I can paint several. I've got four I can make out, no problem."

"Roger, stand by. All right, we're set. We're giving you pairs of Frogfires, all penetrators. The other teams will put the one-twenty-twos on the ships on the airfield. After the Frogs, I'll give you the two-tens. Got it?"

"Roger, FDC. Transmitting coordinates for set-up."

"Roger, Niner. We have them and passing them on to the launchers. Stand by."

"Niner, FDC. First pair, Frogfire, penetrator. Launching. Stand by, stand by. Flashlight, flashlight, flashlight."

Tyree was not watching the targets but the landing ships at the airfield. There were five of them. One had a fire onboard but the other four still looked lethal as hell, though their lack of flight suggested they were badly hurt. Felawasi standing seemed to him to be like a major announcement of their presence and he waited for them to open fire.

Small explosions worked over the five airfield landing ships. Tyree was glad to see it. Maybe it would keep some of those gunners down. He glanced in the direction Felawasi was aiming. He couldn't make out much from his prone position and looked back at the airfield.

From two of the landing ships, he could see what looked like a bunch of dots of light hovering in the air in front of a small, gray curtain. Suddenly he realized he was looking at missiles being launched directly towards him. He heard Felawasi say something about, "Nice work," and then he pulled her down and rolled her back into their shallow hole. He covered her with his body as the missiles impacted.

The ground shook so hard they bounced. The crack of the explosions was like a continuous scream that suddenly was muffled. He felt something burning his back and as dirt clods and stones spattered across the hole and the explosions died away, he rolled to one side. Felawasi slowly got up, her eyes wide.

She checked her designator first and then looked at him. He heard her talking but her voice sounded very strange. It was a few seconds before he realized he was deaf in one ear.

"Sarge, are you all right?"

"I don't know," he said. "My back."

Felawasi rolled Tyree on his face and he heard her suck in her breath. For a moment, he could not tell what she was doing but when he tried to raise himself, he felt her hand on his shoulder firmly push him back down. Then she was reaching under his chest and he realized she was wrapping him in a bandage. Things were going a little out of focus but he grabbed her leg.

"Listen, I'm fine." His voice seemed to come from very far from himself. "Just need a drink of water."

"Hold still," she said. He felt the prick of a needle in his arm. "This will help. Don't move around, you'll mess up my bandage. I've got to get back to work." A canteen appeared in front of his face and she was gone.

Tyree wondered where the canteen had come from and was thinking he should know as he lost consciousness.

The first two Frogfire warheads slammed into an Alligator-class landing ship. Taller than the Benderist Vipers, it had caught Felawasi's eye first and paid the price. The pair struck almost simultaneously. One penetrated the central core of the oval ship and ripped down the central elevator shafts with its blast while the other landed more precisely on the hull directly over the bridge. The superheated gas, technically referred to as a plasma, burned its way through the hull and two decks before emerging into the closed space of the bridge, instantly incinerating every person there and destroying the ship's fire control system.

It was almost two minutes before the next pair arrived. Felawasi had waited until the last second before popping up and acquiring a target, hoping the incoming Frogfires would be close to the previous coordinates. She placed the electronic dot of her sight on a second Alligator just as the FDC coordinator gave her the "Flashlight" call.

One Frogfire struck the upper hull of the Alligator, penetrating through an ion pulse turret and starting fires in the spaces around it. The second struck the landing ship below the curve of the bridge and when it detonated it blew out hull plating in a jagged line down the ship for several decks.

As they hit Felawasi dove for cover and waited for missiles to impact around her but nothing happened. She stuck her head up and saw that the 122mm artillery was now concentrated on the two landing ships that had fired on her. She decided that she was going to have to do something nice for the teams guiding those rounds and wondered if they liked ginger snap cookies – her mom made some killer snaps. Then she hefted her designator and stood back up.

Tyree awoke and looked around. His back hurt and he was still thirsty. The canteen was still there and he reached for it. As he did, he looked up and saw Felawasi standing above him. She was looking in the distance, her designator cradled in her arms, her shirt hanging in tatters from her body, exposing one of her breasts. Her lips were pulled back in a snarl, a white slash across her dirty, camouflaged face; her entire focus was on killing.

Lord, let us not fall alive into the hands of their women.

It was insane. To sit here, trading fire with other landing ships, while the Kodomiri supporting fires found their range again was insane. Killing a landing ship was not easy, but a damaged landing ship could not go easily into the vacuum of space. The Kodomiri were insane as well, but their landing ships had no intention, no need, of going into space – they were home. They had no star ships to make their way back to. Of course they were willing to slug it out on this miserable desert floor; the bastards lived here.

Admiral Canaris cursed under his breath. His ships were inflicting as much damage as they were receiving from the Militia landing ships, perhaps more, but he had no force to balance out the effects of the incoming artillery and missiles from the ground forces – he didn't even know where they were.

Every ship in his command was now reporting damage. Antimissile systems were saturated. He regretted not pushing the issue of retreating with Halleck sooner. The admiral looked around his bridge. Esteban Baer was nowhere to be seen and had not been on the bridge since the first

Militia weapon struck a landing ship. He was down in his quarters, deep inside the ship.

Well, the insanity had to end. Canaris reached for a microphone.

It was insane. Halleck's War Axe seemed to be hit almost continuously. It was like being a ping-pong ball in a bucket, though this bucket had serious teeth. It was the kind of fight he had never been in before. There was no tracking of an enemy HUP, no clever maneuvering, just shoot at whatever came into your sights, though several times he had to check himself when the HUP in his sights was one of his.

The dry wash was too confining; there were fewer Militia HUPs than Benderist, but his brigade, what was left of it, was getting in its own way. And taking the fight out of the wash invited the damned landing ship gunners to join the party. He heard someone screaming on the commo net that they were being flanked at the west end but from his position he could see nothing.

A searing line of tracers stabbed down into the wash, tearing into a blue and green Cutlass, ripping a turret off its shoulder. Stabbing down? Where the hell did that come from? A shadow pass over him and another line of tracers, so solid it looked like a garden hose, caught the Cutlass again and it fell, dark brown smoke suddenly coming from its cockpit.

Sensors were useless and even the visual light imagery to his brain was little more than a blur with the fog-like smoke and dust in the confined space of the ravine. Halleck had the thought that it was combat by touch, war by the blind.

He turned his HUP, his view momentarily blocked by a Trebuchet. Halleck fired his GTL5 lasers, ignoring how his cockpit suddenly felt like an oven from answering fire, and saw the lower portion of the right pylon of the tall HUP explode into fragments. Almost immediately something hit Halleck in the right side and one of his large laser turrets was history.

Halleck saw a Militia HUP just before it slammed into him. He wasn't sure what type of HUP it was, though it might be a Rapier, but there was no mistaking that desert camouflage pattern. The damned HUP was firing directly into his side and another of his large lasers went dead.

Then the Rapier exploded in the flare of white light that signified its fusion power plant had been split open. Halleck staggered under the impact and he heard warnings sounding. He stepped forward and turned to face the other side, looking for the Trebuchet but it was gone. He glanced down at his tactical display and then looked again.

When the brigade swept into the dry wash, even after its pounding by the enemy landing ships, they had outnumbered the Militia HUPs by better than two to one. But the numbers of red and blue dots on his tactical screen were now almost equal. And with the reduced numbers, the Militia landing ships were finding it easier to snipe shots into the battle.

Halleck was a dedicated, competent soldier. But he had never faced a situation like this. Fighting for the Baron had meant striking with overwhelming force against planetary defenses that usually surrendered quickly. This was different. He saw another dark-colored HUP fall to the ground, flame coming from the cockpit. This was going to turn into a slaughter. The odds had shifted. Now his concern became saving the brigade and task force.

"Red Cocks, this is Halleck. Move east. Get to the eastern end of this gully. Break. Admiral Canaris, get ready to provide us with cover fire. Extend the boarding ramps of any landing ship that can still lift."

"Roger, Red Cock. Make it quick."

"As fast as I can."

Kheyntamenti spotted the Benderist movement first. His Rapier, now missing both arm pylons and with smoke pouring from its right side, was on the edge of the wash where he had just gotten a Benderist Javelin to follow him. The Militia landing ships had crippled it and it now lay on the ground, one leg twenty meters away.

His tactical display showed the surge of the enemy to the east. As their HUPs moved, they became concentrated. He saw another blue symbol vanish.

"All hands, pull out of the wash. Do it now! Cochran, they are moving east and we are getting out of their way."

"Roger, colonel. I see it. I don't know what it means but we will try to cover you."

"I don't think there are enough of them now to be a major threat to the landing ships, captain. All hands, disengage and fall back to the landing ships."

Gwielgi at the eastern end of the wash thought his commander's call was a good one; it just wasn't one he was going to be able to obey. Brother Wolf was by now a walking scrap heap. All armament was gone except a single laser turret. One leg was barely responding and causing a jerking limp as the HUP struggled along. The other leg was the only part of the HUPAX the damage display was not alarmed about. He was ignoring the display.

Gwielgi had lost track of Sevin and didn't know if the other pilot was even alive. The enemy indicators in his tactical display were all coming his way, though exact interpretation was difficult as some of his HUP's sensors were dead and others were confused from the jamming. He moved as fast as he could as Brother Wolf dragged itself around the funeral pyre of two intertwined HUPs and headed for the embankment. If anything, the smoke and dust was getting worse, probably because of all the burning HUPs.

A shadow flashed over him but was gone before he could see what it was. His tactical display was offering electronic gibberish in the bottom of his visual field and only his visual-light and infrared sensors were working.

Gwielgi swiveled his fuselage so it faced up the wash. His visual field immediately showed the red box of an enemy HUP imposed on the smoke and dust and he fired. A pair of rail gun rounds ripped back in reply and Brother Wolf's left pylon and his last weapon fell into the wash. Smoke was seeping from deep within the HUP and his cockpit felt very hot.

The HUP took a step onto the edge of the wash but the ground flowed away beneath its foot. The heat in the cockpit was becoming worse. Through the smoke and dust, he could now make out shapes, hulking forms of HUPAX, coming closer. But he had no choice.

He sent the Javelin into a crouch and then shut it down. As the straining power plant whined down the HUP all but collapsed. Gwielgi felt for the cockpit hatch handle and waited to see what would happen.

Chinaren and the rest of the Black Dogs ran down the wash, firing at anything moving wearing green and blue until they ran out of ammunition. She banked over a smoking Javelin – it looked like one of hers – and took the flight on a heading back to the helicopter landing zone.

523

She looked around as they flew across the desert. Incredibly, all four survivors were still with her. She shook her head. The run down the wash had been incredibly easy. The Benderist HUPs were too busy dealing with the Militia HUPs and the enemy landing ships were trying to handle Cochran's ships. Everyone ignored the helicopters. She took a deep breath and slowly let it out as they flew. Then she saw the wreckage of the three Black Dogs.

Chinaren slowed down and took the flight in a slow circle around them. They still smoldered and it was clear no one had gotten out. Then she turned the flight away.

It was not at all like training.

Admiral Canaris saw fire leaping up from a Militia landing ship. His people were scoring hits, but it was clear to him the impetus of battle had shifted. The brigade was decimated and he thought less than thirty of its HUPAX were moving towards the eastern end of the wash and the safety of his ships' covering fire.

He looked at the status board for his landing ships. All but two of his ships of his present formation could lift, but two others that could fly were no longer space-worthy. That meant seven ships would be left behind out of the original twenty. Nine if they withdrew to space. And these insane Kodomiri might chase them up there. He could not continue dueling with their landing ships, not with the fire support they received from their ground forces.

Canaris bent over his tactical display, trying to shut out the shouts coming over the communication system. An aide stepped up to him, her face flushed.

"Sir, we just received this from Kiroff."

"The Kodomir government?" His face was grim. It was probably a demand for surrender.

"Negative, admiral," she replied. "Broadcast message relayed by the people at the subspace communication site there. Our encryption." She held out the single page. Canaris took it and read it. Then he looked at the tactical display. The brigade was coming out of the wash, headed to the safety of its landing ships.

"Interesting," Admiral Canaris said. The grim look on his face did not change.

Gwielgi, his cockpit overheating, opened the hatch as he triggered the fire suppression devices manually. For a moment nothing happened. Finally, the system fired, if the quickly vanishing white mist around his feet meant anything. The heat from below slowly faded, though the desert air wasn't much cooler. He started to close the hatch when he realized that the environmental system was shut down. Rather than suffocate, he left the hatch open.

He looked up and saw dark blue and green HUPs, all showing some battle damage, rally in the broad open end of the dry wash. They were ignoring his shut down HUP as they formed themselves for the dash to safety. Fire was still coming in on them and he could see some HUPs edging backward, creeping toward their landing ships. They were close to cracking.

A heavily damaged War Axe walked among them and its presence seemed to have a calming effect. The Benderists formed two lines, a small one of cripples, HUPs that had suffered damage to their legs and hips and who were struggling to move. The other line formed between them and the Wild Geese, trying to protect them.

But the opening to the wash was very broad and the some of the Militia landing ships could fire into it without difficulty. Missiles began arriving and ion pulse blasts probed their ranks.

The Benderists did not break. The first line moved, though slowly, while the second followed, backing up, and returning fire. Apparently Kheyntamenti was holding the Geese back for the Benderists were not sending out the volume of fire that Gwielgi would have expected if they were being closely pursued by HUPs.

As the second line drew abreast of Brother Wolf, Gwielgi saw the War Axe. It was moving back and forth behind the line, supplementing its covering fire. The husky looking HUP came up alongside Gwielgi and started to fall back with the line. Then it paused.

Gwielgi saw the War Axe's viewing ports were open, probably because the HUP's sensors were damaged, and the cockpit hatch was partially slid back allowing light inside. He looked up at the pilot in the other cockpit, barely visible behind his viewing ports. Gwielgi saw a head in a mindlink-helmet looking back at him through the narrow port. The War Axe's surviving twin GTL5 laser turrets were pointed into the Javelin's cockpit, following the eyes of the enemy pilot. If the Benderist fired, Gwielgi knew he would never have time to eject. For a second the enemy pilot looked at him. His face was too shrouded in shadow for Gwielgi to make out any expression.

Then the enemy pilot raised his hand to his helmet in a salute. Startled and almost responding by reflex, Gwielgi did the same. Then the big HUP spun away and was gone.

Gwielgi slowly shook his head and reached below his seat for his canteen. He propped his feet up on the instrument panel and took a long drink. He decided that, for a morning, it had been a hell of a long day.

Kheyntamenti definitely was holding the Wild Geese back, not that they were in good shape to mount a pursuit. He did not want them getting in range of the Benderist landing ships. A few HUPs probed with long-range fire as the enemy brigade retreated. A glance at his screen told him more than he wanted to know. They had come to Portaka with 35 HUPs – less than twenty were still moving.

The Militia landing ships were in decent shape, though it looked like Gladiator had a nasty fire amidships. Its captain raised it and took it out of the battle line facing the Benderist ships. A relatively fresh ship took its place from the western end of the line. He thought it might be Revenant. Kheyntamenti saw that Cochran was shifting the landing ships that had been covering the Geese into the line facing the enemy ships. Most of their fire was aimed at the opposing ships and only a little still harassed the enemy brigade. "A little" was, of course, relative. As he watched, two more Benderist HUPs died.

Kheyntamenti glanced at his chronometer. It seemed impossible, but only 27 minutes had passed since he had dropped with his Rapier.

"All HUPs, form on me."

He climbed out of the wash and headed to a position behind the Militia ships. Now they had to wait and see what the Benderists decided to do. This fight was not over.

Felawasi and Tyree got the call that the Frogfires were out of missiles. Another team was in a better position to guide the 210mm rounds, though the Diamondback guidance rounds were becoming short. A lot of the fire was being visually adjusted. While accurate, it was the difference between hitting a landing ship in the bridge and just slamming a round into it somewhere.

They stayed low in their position and checked each other's wounds and bandages. Tyree felt light headed but was no longer having difficulty remaining conscious. Felawasi checked the seal on a bandage on his back and then looked across the battlefield. Her voice was tired.

"What's going to happen next, sarge?"

Tyree shrugged, though it hurt his back to do so.

"I think it is going to depend on who thinks they lost and who thinks they won."

Chapter 34: The other side of the hill

23 December 2824

Halleck had been the last of the brigade to walk his HUP up the ramp of a landing ship. Quickly getting out of his War Axe, he dashed across the HUP bay of Galahad. In a minute he was on the bridge of the landing ship, a towel draped over his sweat-soaked coveralls. Admiral Canaris was standing at a viewport, looking across the desert towards the Kodomir landing ships.

"They've stopped shooting," Halleck said as he looked out the port. "Are they surrendering?"

"No, colonel," Canaris said. "I have asked for and they have granted a cease-fire. One of my officers is currently negotiating permission to sweep the battlefield to recover your wounded." He turned to the brigade commander. "We have not gotten to the issue of my damaged landing ships here and at the airfield that cannot lift." He reached to one side and picked up a piece of paper. "We have a problem to discuss."

"What is there to discuss?" Special Envoy Esteban Baer asked as he walked onto the bridge. "We need to destroy them, to finish the battle with a victory."

"Sir," Halleck said, turning away from the viewport, "a victory is not possible. Our landing ships are damaged or crippled and the brigade..." His voice stopped. "My brigade has less than a battalion of HUPs still able to move, and few of those are battle worthy. Our fighter squadron is eliminated. If we try to lift the brigade it will mean abandoning seven landing ships," he said, gesturing at the status board. "And those people will follow us and they will finish what they started." He turned to the Envoy.

"Sir, there is no military option. Admiral Canaris has managed to extract a cease-fire from them, but you know what they are like." Halleck shook his head. "As we speak, they are undoubtedly preparing to attack and annihilate us. They've regrouped their HUPs. With fighter cover and their landing ships, I say again they will annihilate us if this battle goes on."

"Colonel," Baer said, his eyes hard. "You are a defeatist and the expression of those sentiments under combat conditions is a treasonable offense." He glanced at Canaris. "The admiral has given us an opportunity. Your HUPs are loaded. We can use our former plan." Baer turned back to Halleck and held him by the arm. "We move back into Portaka City, perhaps even spring all the way to Kiroff. If they attack, they will destroy their own population. If they do not, then we will simply demand they surrender or burn it down." He stared at Halleck. "We can still win this."

Halleck shook his arm loose. "Baer, you may be a close aide to the Baron, but the taking of an entire city hostage again would bring dishonor to him and the Holdings." He turned and walked towards the communication console. "This war ends now," he said over his shoulder.

The sound of Baer's gun firing was magnified by the enclosed space of the bridge. Halleck took a step and then collapsed, a red stain spreading across his back. Baer turned to the admiral, the gun still in his hand waved vaguely in his direction.

"Admiral, you have command of the expeditionary force. You can do as I order or you will be relieved."

"Special Envoy, I assure you I will obey all lawful orders I am given." He bowed his head slightly.

"Good. I believe you will find that you have made the right choice." Baer looked at Halleck. "First thing, get that trash off the bridge." He turned back to Canaris. "Then I want..." He stopped and stared at Canaris, who was pointing a small pistol at his head.

"Mister Baer, I would advise you to make no sudden moves; I hold a silver medal in pistol shooting from the most recent fleet competitions." Baer stood still, an expression of shock on his face. Canaris, his eyes never leaving Baer, motioned to a junior officer.

"Lieutenant, summon a medical team to the bridge to tend to Colonel Halleck and ask the Officer of the Guard to bring some marines up here to tend to this person. And take that gun away from him before he hurts someone else."

As the lieutenant took away his gun, Baer staggered as if struck. He dropped into a chair, the expression of shock on his face unchanged. Canaris kept his pistol pointed at his head as the medical team arrived and worked on Halleck. A moment later the Officer of the Guard and two marines walked onto the bridge.

"Baer, I would have done you a favor by letting you keep your gun," Canaris said. "I think you are going to wish you had used it on yourself." He looked at the marines. "Take him to the brig and secure him there on the direct orders of Baron Karl von Bender. Mister Baer is no longer a Special Envoy of the Baron and no longer holds any rank within the Holdings. He is under arrest for crimes against the Holdings, to which will be added the murder, or attempted murder, of Colonel Halleck." The marine officer clicked his heels, motioned to the other two, and they dragged Baer from the bridge.

Canaris sighed and walked over to the medical team. He watched in silence. One of them looked up after a moment.

"Good pulse, sir. Bullet hit a lung. He'll be in surgery." The medic looked back at an electronic monitor. "He'll make it." Canaris said nothing as he nodded. A few minutes later they were moving Halleck's unconscious form off the bridge. Canaris turned back to the viewport, the lieutenant beside him.

"Now, let's find out how badly those people want us dead."

Halleck awoke to a world of fuzzy pain. It seemed fuzzy because he could not clearly define it either in terms of where it was or how bad it was. With surprising clarity, he realized he was under the influence of pain medications and was in a landing ship's dispensary. What was not clear was how he had gotten there.

Then Halleck remembered. His eyes, which had begun to open, clenched shut. But he was still alive. He slowly opened them.

Admiral Canaris stood beside his bead, his arms folded, a slight smile on his face.

"Colonel," he said, "you are almost resilient enough to serve in the navy. Have you ever considered a transfer?"

"Sir," Halleck said. His throat was raw and Canaris handed him a small cup of water. He took several sips and nodded his thanks. "What happened?"

"A great deal," Canaris said, pulling up a chair. "Former Special Envoy Baer shot you approximately an hour ago. Do you remember that?" Halleck nodded. "In summary, our Kodomiri friends were broadcasting their battles with us to our ambassador on Kwangdo in an attempt to persuade the Baron to withdraw. They misjudged him. His honor required that he avenge every defeat or setback we underwent. But then they found apparently substantial information linking Baer to a variety of high crimes, including deaths in the Baron's own family. They sent that information to the Baron along with a statement that they placed all blame for the current hostilities on the envoy, not the Baron, and requested an opportunity to find an honorable settlement."

"Right word to use with the Baron," Halleck whispered. He took another sip.

"Indeed. It appears the Baron is disavowing all knowledge of Baer's actions and is taking the position we were sent here merely to balance the aggression of the Alliance. I suspect it will be discovered that Baer is a covert agent of the Alliance or something similar."

"But the Baron was involved," Halleck said, half rising from bed. "I was there when Baer received permission, the communication..."

"There is and was no such communication," Canaris said. "You were not there. Baer was never given permission to use force against Kodomir. Our logs are clear on that point." He held up a finger. "Because if there was, the Holdings has suffered its first military defeat in twenty years and by what is considered by most to be a backwater world defended by a farmers' part-time militia. In these days, that might be seen as a sign of fatal weakness." He held up a second finger. "And if there was, the Alliance has a golden opportunity to intervene and, if war comes now, we will lose, for we are weak. Our forces are too thinly spread to fight a major war." A third finger went up. "And if there was, then the Baron was a conspirator to attack a peaceful world that offered no threat to the Holdings, a conspirator with an individual who was involved in political assassinations, slavery, and the murder of two of the Baron's own family. That would make the Baron a most dishonorable monster."

Halleck sank back onto his bed, thinking. He looked at Canaris.

"What happens to the brigade?"

"Colonel, it does you honor that your first concern is with your troops." Canaris scratched his chin. "I have sent a report to the Baron in response to his command to arrest Baer. In it, I described your gallant actions in refusing Baer's order to destroy Portaka City and your near fatal wounding complying with von Bender's orders." He smiled.

"Yes, I know you think you did not know of the Baron's order before being shot. Your memory is incorrect, undoubtedly from the shock of being wounded." Canaris leaned back in his chair. "I think you will find that the Baron is going to be very happy to find someone he can point to as having behaved honorably in this whole affair. Your brigade will probably be reconstituted and you will likely find some fancy piece of ribbon and gold dangling from your neck." His smile broadened. "I suspect I may as well."

"That is not true, admiral," Halleck said. "That is not how it all happened."

"This is not about truth, colonel," Canaris said. "It is about honor."

Halleck shook his head and stared at the ceiling for a moment. He looked at Canaris. He took a deep breath and let out a slow sigh.

"Then, if it is for honor," Halleck said, "it is as you said."

Chapter 35: Closing the day

23 December 2824

The late afternoon produced a steady, western wind, and from time to time dust devils ran across the battlefield. Almost all the fires from the destroyed HUPAX were out, though here and there some smoldering ruins put up thin columns that the wind quickly took away.

Jonivov stepped up beside Cochran and surveyed the scene. She looked at him out of the corner of her eye.

"What is the word, colonel?"

"The word is we stand in place," Jonivov said. "The fighting is over. It's in the hands of the diplomats."

She let out a sigh and shook her head. "It is tempting to say we were lucky," she said. "But I think all this had very little to do with luck."

"It had everything to do with skill and firepower."

"Yes," she said. "And going 'into harm's way.'"

"Polrany says Jevon has received a long communication from von Bender. The short of it is, we won. The long of it is, those people are going to leave." He nodded towards the Benderist landing ships. "Within one day. Anything that cannot lift under its own power is ours, including any landing ships." He looked at her. "That will give us a hell of a fleet. Do we have the rank of 'admiral' in the Militia?"

"They'll get most of those landing ships flyable by then," she said, "but it's a nice thought. What about the rest of this mess?"

"Apparently the Baron wants to compensate us for any damages. That means the battlefield is ours and there will be some kind of reparations. Details."

"And now?"

"Now we pick up the pieces."

Kheyntamenti was at the foot of Zombie's ramp. From above he could hear the clatter of the HUP technicians, working hard to repair the Wild Geese HUPAX. He glanced at his datapad. Every surviving HUP was damaged except the Scorpion called Bull's Eye. Ironic name.

He heard footsteps and turned. Major Vermeil walked down and stopped beside him. His eyes looked haunted.

"You brought the Scorpion back without even a scratch to its armor," Kheyntamenti said. "You had no damage at all?"

"No," Vermeil said, looking toward the dry wash. "No damage."

Captain Walsh joined them, limping slightly as he came down the ramp.

"Awfully damned noisy up there," Walsh said. "Do we have a final accounting of everyone?"

Kheyntamenti shook his head and handed over his pad. Walsh studied it for a moment.

"This many people still listed as missing? Is there any hope, really?" There was something in his voice but Kheyntamenti held up his hand and leaned forward, trying to hear something in his headset.

"Acknowledged," Kheyntamenti said into his microphone and turned to Walsh. "We still have sweeps out. We are picking up people all over the place, though most we are finding are wounded. Ejection beacons are so many they are interfering with one another. They are trying to do a systematic, physical check of downed HUPs. The Militia and Victors have some APCs, hovercrafts, and Prowlers out." He turned to Vermeil. "One of your vehicles is coming in. They found three more." Vermeil nodded absently, his eyes on the wash.

They heard the squeal of an APC's tracks before they turned and saw it. It raced up to them and turned sharply and ran up the ramp. Medics met it at the top and were boarding it before its rear ramp was completely lowered. By the time the three officers walked up to it, the medical teams had carried the stretchers away. A sweaty noncom walked over to the tracked vehicle with a hose.

As they watched he washed downed the interior floor and they could see blood flowing out onto the deck. The sergeant suddenly looked up. He tried to come to attention.

"Sirs, it's all right," he stammered. "Captain Cochran gave us permission to wash out our vehicles after bringing in wounded if we needed to. Easier to clean them when they're wet then after they dry, she said."

"At ease, sergeant," Kheyntamenti said. "We've seen them doing this all afternoon. You are...?"

"Squad Sergeant Jake Ellington, sir," the tired man said. "I'm one of Major Vermeil's." Vermeil nodded but remained silent.

"Who did you bring back this time, sergeant?"

"Three, sir." He turned off the hose and put it down and pulled a slip from his pocket. "We got a 'Bent' HUP driver, head wound when he ejected, was just stumbling around, name of Colin Lipke, and two of ours. Militia corporal, Jennie Dema Nimeroff, one of the spotter team people. Bad burns, ion pulse worked over her position, killed her partner. The other is one of our HUP pilots, Anna Parr. Black Cat. Bad wounds to both legs." He nodded at the wet floor of the APC. "Artery let go while the medic was working on her. He thinks she's going to lose one; tourniquet was on too long." Walsh turned and quickly left.

"Thank you, sergeant," Kheyntamenti said. "Carry on."

"Yes, sir," Ellington said. He paused. "Colonel, your guy, Gunny Doc-Sevin. He all right? I haven't seen him."

"He's fine, sergeant. He's over on Revenant."

"Thanks, sir," the sergeant said. He grinned. "Glad to get some good news." He turned back to washing out the APC.

It was odd, but the sound of splashing water from the sergeant's hose seemed to carry over all the noise of the repair crews as Kheyntamenti and Vermeil walked away. They paused as Sergeant Tashan came up.

"Colonel," Tashan said, "I talked with Doc on Revenant and we'd like to get some salvage vehicles into the wash now that the search teams have finished there."

"They've finished recovering everyone out of there?" Vermeil asked.

"Yes, sir. I was down there myself." Tashan paused for a moment and then his voice went very quiet and they had to lean forward to hear him. "I was looking for some people." He paused again and then continued, his voice normal. "It's like a giant junk yard but I think some of those HUPs can be repaired."

"Have they taken away the dead or just the wounded?"

Tashan looked at Vermeil. "Sir, we took out all the wounded we could find. We'll remove the dead before we do any salvage work." His voice became softer as he read Vermeil's eyes. "We won't let any harm come to them."

Vermeil nodded and said nothing.

"Sergeant, how many of the students made it?"

"We lost Brown and Murphy," he said. "Beria is fine, a little shook up. Kelly is in surgery."

"Our vehicles are out running grid searches for missing and wounded," Kheyntamenti said. "The Benderists don't have much rolling stock left and its over at the airfield. So mostly it's our job to find everyone. We'll work on salvage after the grids are clear and the wounded are accounted for." He looked down the ramp. "I don't want anyone laying out there in the dark."

"Aye, sir," Tashan said. "Understood." He turned and walked away.

Toland and three pilots were back in the air, flying a slow figure eight over the battlefield. They did not expect trouble but refueling and rearming the remaining Swallows was being rushed.

The Benderist fire control sensors were all off. He saw no warning strobes on his screens. And the only things moving on the battlefield were Militia vehicles.

Maybe it was true; maybe the war was over. It seemed very strange. Someone had turned it on and now it was turned off. Just like that. Was that how it was done?

Toland shook his head and watched the late afternoon sun slowly make its way down towards the western horizon.

Just like that.

Tsunasdi found Gwielgi in the messhall of Zombie. He sat near the hatchway, a datapad on the table beside him, and as other Wild Geese came in, he would rise and shake hands. Tsunasdi stepped in and Gwielgi took him by the hand.

"Good to see you again."

"And you," Tsunasdi replied. "Are you checking everyone in?"

Gwielgi nodded. "We have people scattered in a couple of the landing ships and we've been putting together a list, but it's like…"

"You have to see them to believe it."

"Yes." Gwielgi sat down and picked up a large mug of tea. He looked around. The room had a scattering of HUP pilots and other personnel. "I think I'm mostly checking to see if I'm alive."

"The rumor is you are," Tsunasdi said as he poured himself a cup of coffee from a large urn. He sat down opposite Gwielgi.

"Yeah," Gwielgi said. "But you know rumors."

Tsunasdi slid his hand across the table and revealed the severed pieces of his white Dedeloquasgi bracelet. He put them in front of Gwielgi.

"You are supposed to take these," Tsunasdi said. "Throw them away, burn them, whatever. They are yours." Gwielgi looked at the cords and then at Tsunasdi. He nodded and swept them up. He walked over to a trash receptacle and dropped them in. Then he came back and sat down.

The two men, the two free men, clinked their cups.

The last survivors were found the following morning, despite Kheyntamenti's hope that none would be left out overnight. One was a Benderist major named Pierce. His shattered War Lance had rolled, pinning him inside. His communications had been out since early in the battle, he explained, and he had been unable to call for help. After taking a very long drink from Sergeant Jake Ellington's canteen, he asked who had won. Ellington looked around the battlefield with tired eyes – he had been searching all night – and shook his head before speaking.

"No one, major," he said. "No one won." Then he grinned. "But you guys lost."

Chapter 36: Aftermath

3 January 2825

First Minister Alexis Jevon walked down the ranks of the Second Regiment. The sky was overcast with dark lumps that threatened rain at any moment. An aide had suggested that Jevon forego the formal inspection. Most of the regiment could fit inside one of the large aircraft hangars and the First Minister could deliver a little speech, pin a medal on a couple of senior officers, and then leave without being exposed to any weather coming through. That aide was now at a desk in Volgagorsk, stamping permits for the Directory for Fisheries.

As Jevon walked down the ranks, pausing for a few brief words when he recognized a face, he knew he was doing more than the usual politician song and dance for the cameras. On a very deep level, one he had difficulty expressing, he was responding to a sense of honor.

It was not about his honor – as with courage, he did not see himself as a man of honor. It was a word that he would never apply to himself, especially not here and now, in front of these serious faces, some carrying bandages and burns of recent combat. The honor was theirs. He was here simply to acknowledge that fact as the spokesperson of their people. They had done what had been asked and some of them had died in the attempt and some of them were in hospitals from trying. No, Jevon would have said, had he spoken of it, he was just a politician, a mouthpiece, little more, and certainly not someone to be honored.

He followed General Polrany and Colonel Jonivov down the line of HUPAX. He knew many of the machines were in the maintenance area. That these were the "healthiest" had him shaking his head. As he passed each HUP it crouched and pointed its weapons downward. A salute from machines. No, from the soldiers controlling those machines. It was too easy to anthropomorphize a HUPAX. It was always, always, about the man or woman at its controls.

Each war machine's salute was an acknowledgement of authority, an acknowledgement that this man who regarded himself as neither courageous nor particularly honorable controlled them. He paused in front of a grim-looking Trebuchet and walked up to the shin. Across the symbol of the Wild Geese frozen rivulets of melted armor ran in streams. What kind of power could do that?

Jevon looked up but the pilot was invisible in her armored cockpit. And what kind of person could face that? He turned and continued walking down the line.

He had visited the hospitals that held the regiment's wounded and stopped by each soldier's bed, Kodomiri or mercenary. That last had produced a muted murmur from some quarters but he ignored it. They had fought alongside his people. That was enough. Besides, he remembered with a slight smile, some of his people had been mercenaries not so long ago. And he was politician enough to remember, though he damned himself for thinking of it, they voted. He followed Polrany as Jonivov saluted and returned to his position in front of the regiment.

Jevon was expected to give awards at this point. The now fired aide had suggested for the sake of brevity to give out the handful of highest awards and then allow all the rest to be bestowed by General Polrany. Jevon had rejected this immediately. He would personally hand them all out and had spent the night before reading the official citations. And he had seen to it that the families of all award winners were present. These pieces of metal and ribbon were all anyone took with them, save what was in their hearts and minds. He was determined to ensure everyone remembered.

As he stood waiting for the line of Militia soldiers to form up and march to him, he kept remembering the phrases he read in the cool, unemotional commendations.

In keeping with highest tradition of honor…

The Militia custom was to bestow the highest awards first, and, if there was more than one recipient of a particular award, to bestow them in reverse order of rank. Thus, the first person in front of him was a young woman. She was clad in the field green uniform of the Militia and wore the black beret of a Reconnaissance soldier, a distinction confirmed by the gold arrow on her breast. She walked directly in front of him and snapped him a salute. He saw her wince slightly as she did. She looked a little nervous, which surprised him. This woman had stood in the open directing fire against the Benderists after being wounded while landing ships shot at her and she was nervous about meeting him?

"Corporal Shannon Felawasi," General Polrany said softly.

"I know," said Jevon. He reached and removed the Kodomir Cross with Stars from its presentation case. As he placed it around her neck he added, "I know Corporal Felawasi. I saw your Sergeant Tyree in the hospital yesterday afternoon." He fixed the clasp and adjusted the ribbon. "He said to say that he was proud to have served with you, and then he said something about having to return your canteen." Jevon smiled and she did.

"Yes, sir," she said. She stepped back and snapped a salute. Again, the wince, but she did not drop her smile. She turned and walked back into the ranks.

The rain held off until Jevon finished with the last award. He shook hands with General Polrany and walked away. He was to meet with several members of the Assembly from Coyote Bay and its surrounding districts to brief them on the state of negotiations with the Alliance and the Holdings and try to line up some votes on several appropriations bills. As he stood by the open door of his staff car, Jevon looked back at the regiment, his gaze intense as he seemed to try to unravel a puzzle. Whether he did or not, he finally nodded and, a small smile on his lips, entered the car.

After Jevon left, Polrany stepped forward and gave the command to Jonivov to dismiss the regiment. In turn, he passed the command to the battalion commanders. In a matter of minutes, the troops were marching to their barracks with the exception of those receiving awards. They dispersed to their watching families. Polrany saw young Felawasi run into the arms of a short, heavy-set black woman and a tall, very serious looking black man. Their other children stood around, staring at their sister for a moment, and then they were hugging her as well.

Hug her as tight as you can and maybe she will remember the hugs more than what happened.

Polrany nodded and turned to watch the armored vehicles and HUPAX of the Combined Arms Battalion head towards their area on the base.

It had been so close. The plan had been a desperate gamble, one that had appeared to go wrong almost immediately. But they had not panicked. They had continued to fight, and they fought well. Then the enemy had made mistakes. Waiting to use his landing ships, letting them be pounded while he threw his HUPs into the battle, that was the fatal mistake.

The rain came first as a drifting mist and an aide handed Polrany the raincoat he had insisted the general bring. He threw up the collar as he walked across what had been the parade ground, his polished boots throwing drops of water has he strode.

But maybe there was a larger, more fundamental mistake. Maybe it had something to do with the Benderists asking their soldiers to do something dishonorable. The taking of hostages, had that begun a crack in their worth as soldiers? And the killing of the wounded, had that widened that crack? And using the civilian population of Portaka City to hide behind, what had been the consequences of that to morale and effectiveness?

Polrany shrugged. He knew none of the answers for the questions of what had happened "on the other side of the hill," the phrase used for the enemy's perspective. The historians would undoubtedly explain it all in as many ways as there were historians. He stopped at his car while the aide patiently held open the door. The rain was coming down quite emphatically now.

Polrany turned and looked through the rain and mist towards the backs of the distant, marching HUPAX. No, he did not know what might have happened to the enemy's sense of honor and what role it might have played. But what he did know was that honor and much else had been maintained by those people disappearing into the mist.

He stepped into the car and it drove him away.

Sevin found Tashan in one of the HUPAX maintenance hangars alone, leaning against a hangar door and watching the rain come down. He had a cup of coffee in his hand that was lightly steaming into the cool mist.

"Hey, Steve," Sevin said as he came up, "we're on 'stand down.' We get the rest of the night off. You can get back to work on these piles of tin tomorrow."

Tashan said nothing and took a sip from his cup. Doc saw something flicker on his friend's face and the tight set of his jaw and said nothing, waiting.

"I tried to bring them all back," Tashan finally said. "But we never had a prayer."

"No, you didn't," Sevin agreed.

"What in all that hell was the point?" Tashan's eyes burned like lasers as he stared into the gathering gloom.

"You threw them into confusion, delayed them. You bought the rest of us time. Maybe it was the final straw. I don't know how you calculate those things."

"Trading us, those kids I led, for time? Was it worth it? Was it really?"

"I don't know. I don't know how we'll ever know unless one of these days someone from the 173rd comes by and says, 'Oh, yeah, meant to tell you. That charge by Tashan and those four students? Made all the difference.' Short of that, I don't know, but maybe you're taking the wrong approach to understanding this."

"What do you mean?" Tashan turned to look at him.

"Listen, I'm no philosopher. You know me. But the thing, the one thing I've learned in all these years, is that the worth of people is found in what they do." Sevin reached over and took Tashan's cup and took a sip. He handed it back. "Not what they say, not the rank on their collars, their education, their money, or their fame. What they do."

"Those students," Sevin said, "they were asked to, what was that phrase Captain Cochran used the other day when she was giving us that debrief? Yeah, they were asked to 'go into harm's way,' and they sucked it up and did it." Sevin nodded. "And they did it pretty up and walking good." He looked at Tashan.

"That's courage. Being afraid and doing the right thing anyway. Kind of the basis for everything else, like purpose and honor and all of that."

"Yeah, I get that," Tashan said. "But what was the purpose?"

"Well, that's a good one," Sevin said, nodding. "Historians will wrestle with that question if you mean it one way, but if you mean it the most important way, then it's already answered. The purpose was to take care of their own."

Tashan fell silent again and watched the rain coming down in the darkening day. He took a sip and offered the cup to his friend who shook his head negatively.

"I suppose," Tashan said, "that's the value for everyone. I mean, every soldier, all through time, wherever. Whatever the flags and uniforms, ultimately it's about fighting for the people around you."

"Yes, that's what I think, too," Sevin said. "Currahee, Wild Geese, even Benderist. When you get down to it, most of us fought for the people next to us. Just like those students. Just like Steve Tashan." He smiled. "Probably how it's always been, going back to Troy, to Thermopylae."

"Hell," Tashan said, smiling, "let's ask Gwielgi. I think that old bastard was there."

Sevin laughed. He looked outside. The rain was slacking off but it was almost completely dark. He tugged his purple beret.

"What do you think, jog on over to the messhall and get something better to drink than that vile stuff you brew in your office?"

"Sounds good to me," Tashan said. He pulled on his own purple beret and glanced at the sky. He threw the remains of his coffee outside. He looked at his friend. "They were good kids, Doc."

"They always are," Sevin said, and then they ran out into the darkness.

Kheyntamenti looked up at the short rap on his door's frame. Marjessa Boyington stood, waiting quietly.

"Please come in, Captain," Kheyntamenti said, rising.

"Our landing ship is lifting in a few hours and..." Her voice trailed off. It was uncharacteristic for a Currahee to lose their train of thought, Kheyntamenti realized. He rushed to fill in the silence.

"I have composed a letter," Kheyntamenti said. He picked up an envelope. "It concerns the service of your platoon and your two who gave their lives, Tanner and Kyle, on our behalf. There is also a short note about

Charles Tsunasdi. Might I request that you deliver it to your Elders' Council? I know it is an unusual request."

"I will deliver it personally," she said. Boyington picked up the envelope and turned it in her hands for several seconds. "Colonel, did you see Kyle's death?"

"No," Kheyntamenti said. "He was well to my west."

"Nor did I, but Gunnery Sergeant Steven Tashan showed me gun camera footage that contained it. He died well, with many of his enemies dead before him. You will want to see the imagery yourself."

"What is on it?"

"When Kyle's HUP lost a leg and fell, he continued to fight, of course. But being stationary and unable to protect his back he was very vulnerable. No Aniwaya was near him to protect him that far to the western side of the perimeter. The only people there were Tashan and some students, and Tashan's HUPAX was already destroyed." She looked down at the envelope. "Two of your students covered Kyle, stood over him, covering him. Perhaps they thought he would eject. They did not know he would never leave his Short Sword while a weapon was left. It is not our way. It would not be," Boyington paused, "honorable." She looked up.

"So they stood above him, only knowing that he was one of theirs, with their crude skills and damaged HUPAX and faced seven, eight, it is hard to be sure from the imagery. One of them died, I am told. The other is in the hospital, blinded, awaiting ocular transplants and reconstructive surgery for her face. I visited her before coming here. What I told her is what I would like you to convey to your people."

"I told her it was an honor to serve with you." Boyington took a step back and brought her hand up in a salute. Kheyntamenti did the same. She said nothing else and turned and walked away.

Walsh and Vermeil walked into the Wild Geese messhall. Captain Gwielgi waved and they waved back and grabbed a couple of cups of coffee. They found an empty table.

"What's the word on Parr? What do the docs say?"

"She'll live," Walsh said. "They saved the leg but it's pretty badly torn up. Lots of rehab in front of her and it's not at all sure she'll get everything back. Might be better to just go ahead and grow her a new one and graft it on. Her decision."

"The lady has been through a lot," Vermeil said. "Thank the stars the Kodomiri have some of the best medical stuff going."

"Yes." Walsh took a sip. He looked at the mercenary major and slowly smiled. "Did I look as shocked as you did when they read off our names and told us to come forward to be decorated?"

"I almost dropped a log," Vermeil said. "No one told me about that. Hell, I haven't walked on a parade ground in years."

"I thought you were going to put your own eye out when you threw Jevon a salute." Both men chuckled.

"Yeah, I wasn't expecting it," Vermeil said. He paused, studying the contents of his cup. "What are you going to do?"

"Well, our contract has some time to go."

"Yeah, so does ours. What I mean is," he leaned forward, "Polrany hinted that they might offer extensions. What are you going to do if they do?"

"I'll take it, if they do. It's good duty," Walsh said while Vermeil nodded. "Combat bonuses are coming through and with the reparations the Holdings and the Alliance are offering, each trying to outbid the other, and all the military salvage they got, these farmers are going to be an even tougher nut for anyone to crack. Nice to be with winners." He paused and took a sip. He looked over the rim of his cup at Vermeil.

"Besides, they have treated us honorably."

Vermeil raised his cup in silent toast and both men drank.

"What are you going to do, write another book?" Tsunasdi put the cup of hot tea down in front of Gwielgi.

"Oh, lord, you may shoot me if I try," Gwielgi said, a smile on his face. "No more books."

"That," Tsunasdi said, "remains to be seen." He sat down and took a sip of coffee. Then he loosened his collar. Militia dress uniforms for enlisted ranks had high, uncomfortable collars. This was the first time he had had to wear his, just to get a medal. Well, two, actually. One dangled on his chest, under his gold HUPAX pilot badge and newly bestowed silver crossed rifles emblem of an infantry soldier. The other hung around his neck and glowed softly.

Gwielgi was more comfortably attired in an officer's uniform. He wore the same medals as Tsunasdi and the same badges glinted above them. He waved to several people coming into the Wild Geese messhall. Considering the fighting that had taken place at Coyote Bay at the start of all this, they had done a good job in fixing this place up, he decided.

"So, what are you going to do?" Gwielgi asked. He played with the rim of his cup, avoiding Tsunasdi's eyes.

"I am giving some thought," Tsunasdi said, "of entering a monastery."

"I didn't know you had converted to Reform Orthodox," Gwielgi said as he took a sip.

"I have not. More precisely, I am thinking of starting a monastery, a cloister, a retreat house. Something of that nature. Open to all. Bring in teachers, philosophers, priests, elders, imams, whomever on Kodomir or elsewhere I can find. Let them speak. Study what they say. Maybe teach myself."

"What subject?"

"Finding peace," Tsunasdi said with a Currahee's directness.

"You are going to turn down the commission Kheyntamenti mentioned?"

"Aye, at least for now. I need to take the time to think, to study, and I believe such a place might appeal to others who are trying to understand who they are in the aftermath of all this." Tsunasdi grimaced. "I am no priest and it is probably arrogant of me to think that I could assist anyone else in their searches."

"If you do it, I would like to come and spend some time," Gwielgi said, his voice low, still avoiding Tsunasdi's eyes.

"Studying with me?" Tsunasdi asked.

"Yes," Gwielgi said. He looked up. "I need to understand some things and there are few others whose words carry as much weight for me as yours." He shrugged.

"It would be my honor."

"There's that word," Gwielgi said. "I've never understood it, but I have seen it perverted in a hundred different ways."

"As have I," Tsunasdi said. He looked around the messhall. While they had been talking it had slowly filled. People were working the coffee and tea urns and having conversations.

"I have always thought, my friend," Tsunasdi said, "that you were driven by honor. Not by glory. Glory is not honor. Glory is simply recognition by others, fame." He flipped the medal on his chest with his finger. "These reflect honor, at their best, for they are, they should be, representations of honorable behavior. People often confuse honor with glory. It is a mistake that often costs the one at the gaining of the other."

"The honor of a warrior…" Gwielgi said.

"As you told me – the honor of a warrior is found in the gift that is given to others." Tsunasdi looked around the room. "My friend, we are among people of very bright honor."

Excerpt: Mercenary's Code by Steven M. Silver

Prelude

Black Flower Mountains, New Sudan
3 April 2804

The mercenary made his way carefully through the dark. Riding a horse was not his usual practice but it was available; its owner was probably dead among the ashes of a couple of dozen destroyed farms a hundred kilometers or so to the north. The mercenary had watched the farms burn with disinterest – the battles fought on that ground over the past month represented a paycheck and little more. That the battles were fought between equally despicable rivals, provincial governors struggling for control of New Sudan, and over the farms and towns of relatively innocent people was a reality he made himself ignore.

His unit's employer, with victory in her grasp, had elected not to pay her mercenaries and ordered her regular soldiers to kill them. The mercenary had been expecting betrayal – he *always* expected betrayal – and his pack was loaded and near at hand when the employer's soldiers began their encirclement of his barracks. He grabbed what weapons he could and fled into the darkness. Several soldiers had tried to block his way but a knife with a blackened blade wielded by a hand that was ghost-like in the night cut them down.

He had moved on foot quickly through the remains of a battleground, one of those that had seen the mercenaries bring their employer victory. That was where he found the stray horse, one of the descendants the original colonists of this backwater planet brought with them centuries before. It was tame enough to allow him to mount it and followed willingly his urging south into the mountains.

Now he was very tired, his thighs aching from unaccustomed riding. As the rock-strewn path climbed over a ridge, the moonlight revealed a scene he had not seen in many years. He pulled lightly on the horse's mane and it stopped, perhaps grateful for the rest.

Ahead of them a cross stood in the night, jammed into the earth, and on it was a man, crucified. In the pale light of the moon, the blood from his hands looked black. The mercenary studied the scene for a moment, no longer feeling tired as he slipped a short, automatic weapon into his hands from its position on his pack. He paused and looked around him, listening to the night noises and smelling the air. Partially satisfied, he slipped off the horse and dropped the pack beside the animal's hooves. He slowly walked forward. The weapon remained in his hands as he kept looking around.

The crucified man was a little over average height, though it was hard to judge. His hands had been impaled by broad-headed nails and ropes were tied around his wrists to hold him to the crossbar. He wore the remains of a shirt and trousers and even by moonlight the marks of lash and burning were easy to see. His legs were tied to the upright post and the mercenary saw the flesh of the man's feet, a meter above the ground, was rubbed raw from the effort of relieving the terrible, inexorable pull of gravity on his arms.

But it was his face that attracted attention. It was gaunt with high cheekbones and an almost Oriental slant to the eyes. His nose was large and hooked and his lips were thin. His hair was a sharp widow's peak, black, and long, with loose tendrils hanging in his face.

Death by crucifixion is caused most ordinarily by slow suffocation, aided by exposure, dehydration, and blood loss. Supported primarily by the arms, the weight of the body puts pressure on the lungs, slowly squeezing

Steven M. Silver

them and exhausting the muscles used for breathing until they can no longer bring in enough air. It is a way of dying that can take a long, painful time. The mercenary, who had seen many people die in his years, guessed the man had been on the cross for a long time, perhaps several days.

The man's eyes, though, glittered with alertness, almost as if lit from behind. The mercenary stood beneath him for a moment.

"And I thought I was having a bad day," the mercenary finally said. He looked around and then back up at the man.

The man tried to speak but failed. He paused, and finally swallowed enough saliva that he could talk with a hoarse voice.

"That is a good horse you have," the man said.

"You like it?" The mercenary said, looking over his shoulder at the animal. "It's been years since I've been on one. Frankly, I've always thought anything that big with teeth should be avoided." He looked back at the man. "And who did you piss off so thoroughly as to end up here?"

"Not just one person," the man said. "I managed to antagonize the better part of a whole town."

"Congratulations," the mercenary said. "How did you accomplish that?"

"I tried to take away something of theirs," he said. He started to shrug and winced in pain.

"And that would be...?"

"Their slaves."

"Well, yes," the mercenary said with a shrug, "I can see where they would be unhappy with you. Everybody on this world owns slaves or is a slave or is going to be a slave or is fighting over who gets to own slaves. One, big, happy pile of slavery, that's what New Sudan is. You get into the slave business, you're going to have some tough times. Competition can be fierce." He turned and walk towards his horse. "Crucifixion is part of the overhead, slaver," he said over his shoulder as he walked away.

"Not a..." The man's voice trailed away.

The mercenary kept walking. He got back to his horse and knelt down beside his pack. He stood and came back to the crucified man. Something in his hand glinted in the moonlight.

"'Not a' what?" he asked.

"I am not a slaver," the man said, his harsh, dry voice emphatic. "Pale Rider."

550

The mercenary said nothing as he approached. The thing in his hand was a long bayonet, the former property of one of his ex-employer's soldiers, and he raised it to the man's chest. The man felt the tip of the blade on his flesh. It was cold and hot at the same time. Then it slid to one side, pushing the remains of his shirt away.

"Damn," the mercenary said. "You really are."

On the man's chest was a small tattoo of a hooded rider on a white horse over the Cross of Lorraine, the mark of the mercenary unit called the Pale Riders. The long knife descended.

"I haven't seen one of those in a long time," the mercenary said. "We heard there was a raid around here three or four days ago. I take it you were here on a John Brown Society contract."

"Yes," the man said. He licked his dry lips. "They financed our raid. We liberated maybe eighty slaves when the local militia counterattacked. I was part of the blocking force. We got split up and I did not make it back in time for the evacuation. They took me prisoner."

"I guess they thought it appropriate," the mercenary said, squatting down and studying the bottom of the heavy crucifix, "to take care of your butt this way, Pale Rider cross and all."

"That is somewhat how they phrased it," the man said.

"Kind of a mediocre and obvious sense of irony on their part." He moved around to the back of the cross. "Slave holders always tend to overreact to the subject of slavery. I guess you've noticed that. And they didn't stay around to watch you die?"

"For the first day," the man said, "there was a pretty large crowd. Then people got bored. Yesterday, I think it was yesterday, there was some kind of excitement. A battle or something had happened north of here."

"That would have been my people," the mercenary said. "Day before yesterday. We overran some warlord for another warlord. Our employer decided not to pay us. Killing us was cheaper, she thought. A bunch of us scattered, though I don't know where the others got off to." He pushed against the cross and it moved a little.

"No sense of humor," the mercenary said. He crouched at the base of the cross again. "That's one of the big problems with slaveholders. No sense of humor." He walked away for a moment and returned with a large rock in his hands. He looked up at the man.

"They've jammed your cross into the ground with a couple of wedges. I'm going to knock them lose. This thing will fall and it's going to hurt. I'll try to get under it. But I don't have a ladder and I don't think that horse is steady enough to sit on while I pry those nails out. Besides, the sun will be up soon and I suspect someone will look up here while having breakfast and then things will really get interesting. I'd like to be gone by then."

The man closed his eyes. He felt the cross shudder each time the wedges were struck. The cross lurched and he cried out as it tilted and jerked him by his hands. For a moment it hung, held by the hole in the earth. He realized the mercenary was under the tilting cross, trying to support it. Then it swayed and fell.

It hurt with a pain that took away his vision but this time he did not cry out. The pain was so great he did not notice the first nail being levered out. The mercenary, knocked flat in his effort to break the fall of the cross, had rolled to the nail, the bayonet in hand. He jumped across the man and slipped the blade under the broad head of the second nail. Digging the tip into the crosspiece, he pried it upward. This one the man felt but it was pain that he embraced for it meant he was free.

"Hold still," the mercenary said. The bayonet was cast aside and a shorter knife appeared in his hand. He sliced through the ropes holding the man's legs and arms and stood back.

The man lay in place for a moment, his eyes closed. He slowly rolled off the cross. He tried to rise to his hands and knees and failed. He took a deep breath and tried again and made it.

"Relax for a moment," the mercenary said. "Get off your hands." He had his pack with him and assisted the man in getting to a sitting position. He opened a small kit. He pulled out bandages and pressed one on either side of the man's hand.

"Nanos," he said. "They'll ease the pain, clean the wounds, and repair almost everything except nerve damage." He wrapped the small pads with their flat tabs that adhered to the bandages, securing them in place. "You'll want to have a real medic take a look at them to see what damage was done to the nerves and fix them." He sat back and handed the man a military-style canteen.

The man took it and nodded his thanks. He was having trouble controlling his fingers but he got the cap off and took a long drink. He started to hand it back but the mercenary waved it off. "Finish it. You need it." Then the mercenary bandaged his feet. The nanotechnology pads itched for a moment until the anesthetic took effect.

The east was much lighter, though banks of clouds suggested the sun would be hidden when it finally rose above the hills. The mercenary opened his pack and pulled out a small loaf of bread and gave half of it to the man.

"You Pale Riders need to remember that the mercenary business is not personal. It's business." He shook his head. "Taking contracts at cost from those Brownies kind of makes a mockery of the whole mercenary ideal."

"You don't object to slavery?"

The mercenary said nothing for a moment while his jaw worked on a piece of bread and his eyes studied the eastern horizon. "It's a business, that's all. I'm just in it for the money," he said finally. He looked at the man. "You been doing this long?"

"Not really," the man said. He took another sip of water. "I joined the Riders six months ago. Before that I was a professional soldier and then worked security for some new colonies." He took a bite of bread. "You?"

"Always been a mercenary," he said. He looked at the sky. "We're going to have to get a move on. Rain coming." He looked at the man. "A hundred kilometers south of here is the town of Dayport. They have a landing field there. Word is, they are looking for mercenaries to supplement their home guard. Getting some security is a good idea, what with New Sudan broken into a dozen or more warring factions. If you can make your way there, you may be able to hire on with them and get enough for a ticket off this rock. Maybe even get back to your Riders."

"Is that what you are going to do?"

"No," the mercenary said. "I've got enough cash. When I leave it will be first class all the way back to the Security Forces Agency on Swordpoint. No, I'm going to give this horse to you. I'm going to wait for a while longer and, when I'm sure no one is pursuing me, I'm going to turn around and go north, see if I can find any of my mercs, and then kill my former employer. Then I'm going to go to Dayport." His voice was calm, as if describing something ordinary.

"Sounds like you're taking all this very personally," the man said. He drained the canteen.

"No," the mercenary said. "It's just business. I just want to remind her that a contract is a contract and it is not appropriate to renege on a signed contract."

"Remind me," the man said, "to be very careful about making contracts with you in the future."

The mercenary smiled and went through his pack. He pulled some articles out.

"Here're a couple of shirts. You're thinner than me, so they'll fit. On this planet, you'll want to keep that tattoo covered. I don't have any spare footgear but if you keep your eyes open you may find some farmer who'll part with his boots. You can have these other nanobandages – they're pretty tough but they're not shoes. As for weapons," he said, "you can have this."

He handed the man a pistol and then picked up the bayonet from the dirt and passed it over.

"Don't go north with those," he said. "Used to belong to my former employer's soldiers and someone might recognize the types."

As he pulled on one of the shirts, the man saw the mercenary had a short-barreled sub machinegun lashed to the side of his pack.

"Keep your eyes open when you get to Dayport," the man said. "I will be there."

"All right," the mercenary said. He stood and shrugged his shoulders into the pack. He reached up and pulled the submachine gun free. As he did the man saw his sleeve slide back, revealing a short knife in a forearm sheath. The man stood up and held out his hand.

"I am Alisti Mahmud al-Kheyntamenti," he said. "Thank you."

"No thanks needed," the mercenary said as he briefly shook the man's hand with a very gentle grip. "Mercs should trust no one except other mercs. Keep your head down, Alisti. Stay out of sight until you are well away from here. Someone's going to notice your cross is down and they will come looking for you."

"That would be fine," the man said, and his smile revealed sharp, white teeth.

The mercenary shook his head. "Wait until you get your strength back," he said, smiling. He started to walk away, still shaking his head. He paused and pulled something out of his pocket. He walked back and stuffed it into the man's shirt pocket.

"For the medics in Dayport," the mercenary said. "And a place to stay until you can find work."

"I will pay you back," Kheyntamenti said.

"That would be lovely," the mercenary said, grinning sardonically in the slowly growing light. He turned and walked towards his horse.

"What is your name?" Kheyntamenti asked.

"Oh," the mercenary said, glancing over his shoulder as his well-practiced hands freed the magazine from the weapon for his inspection and smoothly slipped it back into place, "I'm Gwielgi."

Additional Information

Mercenary's Honor cover by Eric Strehl
Blackheart Studios
www.ejstrehl.com

Also by Steven M. Silver

With Susan Rogers, Ph.D. *Light in the heart of darkness: EMDR and the treatment of war and terrorism survivors.*

Poetry
American Travelers
Hot Chrome, Smooth Leather, and a Red Bandanna
Victor Echo Zero Five

The Wild Geese Saga
Mercenary's Heart
Mercenary's Honor
Mercenary's Code
Mercenary's Logic
Mercenary's Destiny
Mercenary's Soldiers
Mercenary's Redemption
Mercenary's Courage
Mercenary's Peace

Mercenary's Justice
Mercenary's Humanity
Mercenary's Promise

The Ellen Parker Series
A Dangerous Man
Killers
Woman on the Wire
Hidden Things
Child in the Dark